PUSS & BOOTS
IN THE 23RD CENTURY

BY
JACK McCLURE

COVER ILLUSTRATION
BY IAN CHRISTY

PUBLISHED BY
IRON THUMB PRESS
WINCHESTER, VA

Printed in the United States of America

Cover illustration by Ian Chisty
www.ianchristy.com

PRINTING HISTORY

First Printing / January 2008

Published by Iron Thumb Press through Lulu Printing Services.

www.ironthumbpress.com

Library of Congress Cataloging-in-Publication Data:

McClure Jack, 1937—

Puss & Boots in the 23rd century / by Jack McClure; 1st printing; Winchester, VA;

Iron Thumb Press through Lulu Printing Services, 2008

ISBN: 978-0-6151-9460-8

ix, 668 p.,: map; 23 cm

Main Entry: McClure, Jack

1. Culture war / military science fiction — Fiction

2. Female soldiers — Fiction

PZ4 .P87 2008

PRINTED IN THE UNITED STATES OF AMERICA

10 9 8 7 6 5 4 3 2 1

I dedicate this book, such as it is to my father, John Edwin McClure. He was born in 1897 and died in 1990, and so was able to influence many people during his long life. He went to high school in a horse and buggy, and watched all of the wars, riots, moon shots and changes in society as they happened during his century, while he went about his job of helping people in his own quiet way.

My father graduated from the University of Kentucky in 1918, missed the Great War by one month and after a few years back on the family farm, became the County Extension Agent for Daviess County, Kentucky. He really was the essence of Norman Rockwell's painting, "The County Agent", and served his rural community for 45 years.

The County gave "Colonel Jack" as they called him, a retirement banquet and more than two thousand people attended, because he had helped their grand parents, their parents and themselves to farm their land better...

I am glad I knew my father.

Jack McClure, Jr.
(A very Junior one)

ACKNOWLEDGEMENTS

This book was long in its making, and I am honored by the many people who gave me help along the way. They were generous with their talents and support as Puss & Boots came to life while I learned the English language, sort of...

My first honorees in this award ceremony are my son, Jed and his friend Ian. These two concepted the story over a couple of beers, then gave it to me. I turned into Puss and Boots in The 23rd Century with their permission, and cautious trust...

My next honorees must be three stalwart friends who stayed with me through the thick and thin times of P&B (mostly thin). I am privileged to know Marian Powell who had an ancestor in Jamestown in 1607, Keith McCormick who is a woman proud of having a man's name, and Olivia Fowler whose talents go far beyond portraying Arvin very well. We all met at a Sci-Fi writer's workshop given by Orson Scott Card in 2001 and these three unique talents have taken time away from writing their own extraordinary novels ever since then, to slap me into shape and teach me how to write reading, sort of...

Many other friends helped me with their criticisms and comments as they read the sample chapters I inflicted upon them. They are, in no order of preference:
• Dick Griffiths, for being my major resource on weapons and kill skills, as well as on how to live life;

- Jackie Vance, for her enthusiasm and encouragement in a difficult time;
- Carol Whitlock, for her meticulous reading of early versions and her comments on them;
- Barbie Knebelkamp, for commenting on my work in friendly detail, despite having no interest in Sci-Fi;
- Teresa Perez, who read and commented on my sample chapters while volunteering in the New York City command centers during the immediate aftermath of 9-11;
- Bob Maranville, an old friend who was my first and most enthusiastic critical reader of Puss & Boots, but who did not live to read its ending;
- Perry Caudill, a fellow Kentuckian who took time from his own writing to give me the benefit of his wisdom and talent; and
- Piotr Mierzejewski in New Zealand, whose enthusiasm for life as well as for Puss & Boots has inspired me to model a main character in Book 2 on him (and his brigade of Flying Monkeys...).
- ...and a big thank you to Katee Sackhoff who wished me luck with my novel.

I finally wish to thank John Ringo who, during the course of a snowy weekend one February while we scouted for novel settings in the Shenandoah, not only convinced me that present tense would never work for P&B, but also gave me good advice on its structure and format, as well as some very good cigars.

These friends all supported me to the max as I brought my book to life so I am very grateful to them, and to you who read "Puss & Boots in The 23rd Century".

Jack McClure

Contents

Map of Molly's Valley near Kitimat, Former British Columbia

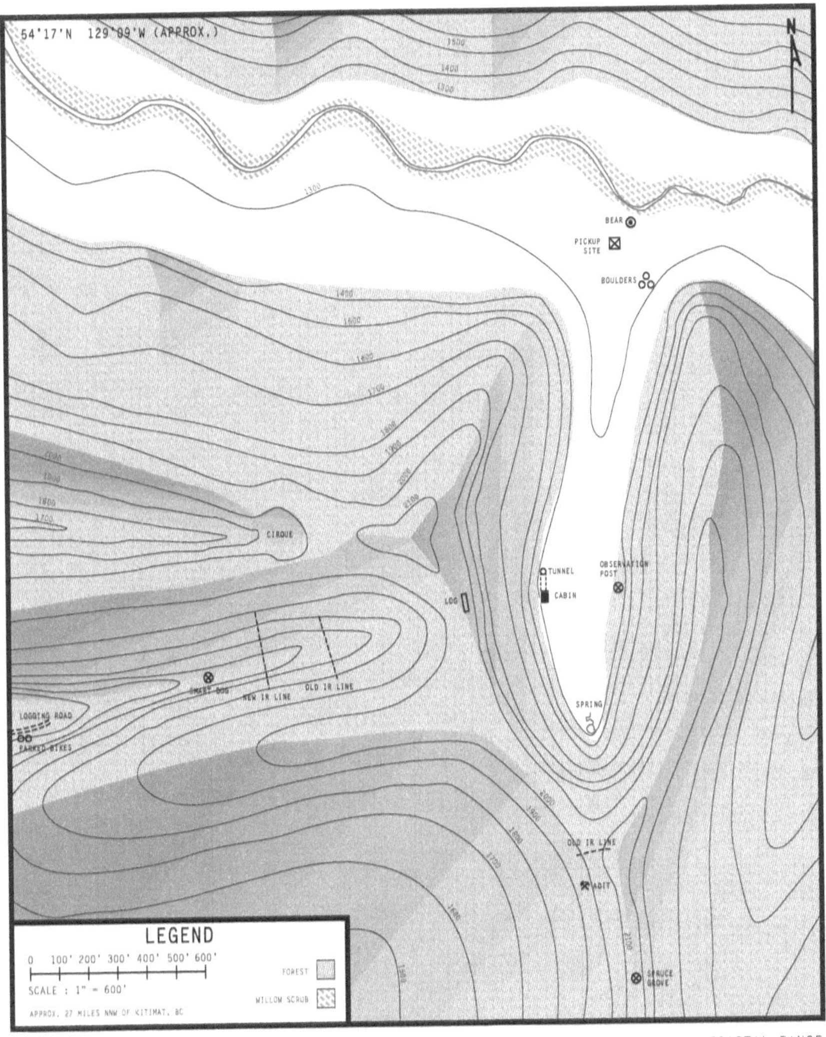

COASTAL RANGE
FORMER BRITISH COLUMBIA, CANADA
MAY 1, 2276 AD
(DETAIL)

Chapter 1
The Bounty Hunters

May 1, 2276 AD
Coastal Mountains of British Columbia

The two women were near the crest of the ridge when Puss grabbed Boots' wrist.

She signaled with finger taps, *"Smart dog. 3 o'clock."*

"It starts now," Boots whispered as she turned slowly to their right, "Get hard girl!" The only other sound was the wind sighing in the treetops of the forest.

Boots inched a tranquilizer dart from her belt pouch and peered around through the gloom of the forest until she spotted the smart dog under a laurel bush twenty meters away. She loaded her gas gun and fired all in one smooth motion.

"Looks like I still can still hit the easy ones anyway," she whispered, as the dog slumped with a rustle of the dried leaves on the ground.

The two women walked with silent steps across the pine needles to the laurel bush. Boots pushed its branches aside and looked down at the mongrel dog sprawled on the ground. It wore a thick plastic collar that sprouted a stub antenna, and several control dials.

Puss dropped to her knees and peered at the collar for a moment then nodded to Boots. Her eyes grew bleak as she bent her face close to the dog's head again and grimaced, then she mimicked the dying squeal of a chipmunk and the growls of a dog eating.

"You've looked like that every time we've met one of these damm things. I don't think you like dogs much," Boots mouthed as she squatted next to

Puss and drew her belt knife. She then cut the sedated dog's head off with three precise strokes.

Puss ignored her friend's comment as she grabbed the collar when the dog's head flopped free and shook away the spatters of blood on it. She slipped her arm through its loop and clamped its body-heat and pulse sensors in the warmth of her armpit. The two women stood and faced each other.

"Pay dirt!" Boots signed to her friend, *"Mark is near here! His bounty will lift our mortgage big!"*

"Another dog is dead anyway," Puss signed with a shrug. *"But I will not count my sheep before they hatch! We collect this mark, sell him and get our credits before I lift the skirt on my mortgage!"*

Puss grinned then and gave Boots a play punch on her arm, *"Good shot for an old girl though!"* she signed, *"But must we dump this collar quick."*

"Yes," Boots signed back with a smile, *"If no vitals or sound are transmitted from it soon, mark will know something happened to his smart dog."*

"Yes," Puss signed still grinning, *"Also, we are at much risk if we keep this thing. You maybe stumble and make a big noise that mark will hear from his dog's collar!"*

Boots made a face and stuck her tongue out at Puss, *"Little girl make big joke,"* she signed playfully then she smiled in a different way, until Puss froze her with a look like a gust of Arctic air.

"Dammit! I told you!" Puss signed with a scowl, *"We go to work now. I will find a way to get rid of this thing."*

Boots dropped her eyes before Puss' glare for a moment then raised her chin and closing her face as if pulling down a helmet visor, signed, *"Yes! What do you think? A bambi?"*

"Yes. I will scope for one now," Puss signed back with a perfunctory nod, then she signed with eyes that were still cold, *"We will talk about you and last night later."*

Puss set her infrared heat sensor on high sensitivity and began to scan the forest as she stalked silently up the ridge.

Boots looked at her friend's retreating back, and sighed after Puss carried the collar out of range, "I think I really did ferk up biggers that night. I just wish I could remember what I did, dammit."

Then she knelt and pulled her dart from the dog's chest and placed its severed head so the nose was under its tail, "OK doggy, you can lick um' for all eternity now," Boots muttered as she piled leaves and pine needles over the carcass.

"Shat though, my doghouse is way cold too, just like yours," she whispered as she got to her feet. Then she shrugged and loading her tranquilizer gun with a dart set at minimum dose, paced silently after her friend.

*

"*Go some!*" Puss signed with a smile, "*300 meters north,*" as she pointed to the left of the route they were following.

"*Good Girl!*" Boots signed, "*And you win.*"

Puss motioned with her shoulder and gave an even wider smile as she signed, "*We'll talk after we lose this thing and collect the mark.*"

Boots nodded and the two women stalked silently up the ridge through the old growth trees to its crest. When they reached the top, they followed it around to the head of the next valley north of the one they had just climbed.

The landform here was a cirque, a small semicircular depression gouged by an ancient glacier, and found at the heads of many valleys in the mountains of the West. This cirque had an almost level floor and it was less heavily wooded than the ridges around it.

The two women circled to approach from down-wind and crawled to the edge overlooking the glade. Boots sighted on a small doe among the six deer bedded down in the lush grass, dozing and basking in the morning sun. The other deer stirred at the hiss of the dart gun, then bounded away when Puss leaped into the glade. She ran to the doe still on the ground and kneeling, lifted its head and slipped the dog's collar from around her arm and over its muzzle. She then worked the device over the doe's flaring ears and settled it around the animal's neck.

"Go with Manitou," Puss mouthed as she bent and kissed the helpless but aware animal between its wide eyes. She laid the doe's head back in the grass and pulling Boots' dart from its flank, began creeping away from the animal on all fours as its leg muscles began to quiver. Puss continued to back on her hands and knees toward where Boots waited.

The tall woman considered her friend's form for a moment, then became all business again when Puss bounded to her feet out of the collar microphone's range and trotted to Boots with a grin of triumph. The two women turned and trotted back a hundred meters from the cirque, then they stopped and did a happy double hand slap.

"OK, Big'un, we've cut through his first defense line! Now let's collect that som'bitch real quick before he wonders why his smart dog is acting sort of different-like!" Puss whispered with a grin as she handed her friend the expended dart.

"You got that right!" Boots murmured with a brilliant smile, "Let's just go Do It! First one to catch him gets to unzip his pants!"

"What-the-hell-fer?" Puss snorted.

"So we can put our leash on him, why else?" Boots replied as she reached out to ruffle Puss' short hair, her deep blue eyes wide in innocence.

"Jeseu Buda, gal!" Puss exploded in laughter, "You're one way weird dudette!"

"Yeah, but you have to admit it takes great Strinth of Carachter for me to be that way, let alone do it all the time," Boots sniffed as she lifted her head with an exaggerated look of noble purpose.

"Da' words is Strength and Character you furkin' Heathen," Puss teased as she reached up and gently griped Boots by the chin, as the Alpha wolf does to the others in its pack.

"Ja Boss," Boots replied, remaining passive.

"OK Buddy," Puss whispered, "Now let's just go do it!"

"Yep Kiddo," Boots murmured, "But we know he's near here now so it's war paint time," as she pulled a camouflage makeup kit from a belt pouch and began to streak her face.

"Right," Puss said as she flipped her own kit open and started daubing on various colors of dark greasepaint.

Boots watched Puss as she began by making three vertical black streaks on her forehead before partially covering them and the rest of her face with splotches of green and gray.

"She always does it that way. Wonder why?" Boots thought as she pulled the hood of her cat suit up to cover her long black hair and her head except for her face. She stepped back under the shade of a hemlock and to the casual eye, disappeared.

"How's this for a party dress?"

Puss finished painting her face and hands and after jamming her wide-brimmed field hat down over her auburn hair, she backed into a laurel thicket also disappeared.

"Pretty good. How about me?"

"You be good, Squaw Woman," Boots answered with a grunt, "So now let's just go do it!"

*

Boots was tall and had wide shoulders and strong legs. She was dressed

4

in a cat suit colored with splotches of gray-green that matched the spring foliage. She wore light field boots, a small back pack and a field belt carrying a pistol, equipment pouches and a field knife. She was also armed with three knives in a sheath at her right hip. The woman had high cheekbones and a generous mouth, over a stubborn jaw and moved with the grace and precision of an athlete. Her blue eyes had the intensity of a hunter and looked as dangerous as a dagger blade.

Puss wore a camouflaged Army jumpsuit with many pockets. She had on light field boots as well and had a combat belt on with a pistol, gear pouches and a large knife. She also wore a small backpack.

Her dark auburn hair was cut short and her emerald green eyes always seemed to smile because of small folds in her lower lids. Her father called them "Rifleman's eyes."

She was a head shorter than Boots and very erect, and her jumpsuit did not hide her firm body. Her skin, under the camouflaging paint on her face and hands was the color of new copper. She looked capable, and strong.

Puss nodded to Boots and they began moving through the forest, as silently as two hunting cats.

Kristina Hamier known in their gritty profession as "Boots" and Marybell Bolling, called "Puss" in the same circle had ridden to the base of the ridge on their fuel cell trail bikes early that morning. They had hidden them in an old burn area covered with scrub at the edge of the forest after driving in along an overgrown logging road in the Coastal Range of the one-time Province of British Columbia.

When Puss was satisfied that their bikes were well concealed, she then began methotically looking around the clearing, and into the forest beyond. She let her senses expand to feel anything she sensed to not be natural. After a few moments, she turned and nodded to Boots indicating that it was safe.

"The intel from the Network shows him somewhere in this ten klick-wide area," Boots said in a low voice. "And the IR survel sat cams picked up the heat signature of a cabin over this ridge," she added with a gesture toward the tree line, "Ready for a walk in the woods?"

"Always," Puss answered with a grin.

"Attagirl," Boots murmured as she made a final adjustment to her pack straps and looped the sling of the thick-barreled tranquilizer gun over her shoulder. Then she entered the tree line in a silent trot.

Puss followed her friend an easy and even quieter pace, and opened her senses when they entered the shadows of the forest. She let her conscious expand as she always did in the wild, listening to it and feeling its nuances...

The two had climbed halfway up the ridge when Puss sensed something was not right. "The under story birds have stopped calling," she thought.

She had paused then and gripped her friend's arm. Boots had halted in mid-stride, and the two froze except for their eyes. Puss slowly slipped a small tube from a thigh pocket. Without raising her arm, she slowly swept the area with the small infrared heat detector.

As it swung past the laural thicket on their right, her instrument had vibrated a "hot" signal, indicating it had picked up a heat signature in the shadows.

***

Chapter 2
The Mark

May 1, 2276 AD
Coastal Mountains of British Columbia

Boots and Puss crouched behind the trunk of a fallen spruce on the ridge crest. They raised their heads and peered down into the little valley beneath them, and at a small cabin built against the base of the ridge. The little valley widened out to their left into a natural meadow before opening into a larger valley. They could see a line of low-lying scrub willows and alder bushes meandering through the larger valley and knew that a stream probably flowed there.

"Boss Rat of the Network said this mark is real crafty-like," Boots whispered, "So if this is his place, he probably has foot poppers out there as well as trip wires and more IR beams like the one you sniffed on our way up."

Puss whispered, "If it's him down there, you think he'd fall for our "jangle the other side" trick or is he too much smart?"

"Only one way to find out. You or me?"

"Hey Buddy, you shoot better. I sneak better."

"Is that a "tall" joke?" Boots whispered with mock indignation.

Puss smirked as she rose to her feet, "You'll be safe up here Big'un, if you just remember to use your bomb snuffer before you stomp off into the bushes to squat OK?"

Boots snorted, and made a rude gesture as Puss turned and walked silently away toward the head of the little valley.

"Jesu Dulce, if my buddy's not the Ghost of all the Indians that ever were fer' Buda's sake!" Boots whispered as she watched her friend disappear into the forest gloom.

*

Puss finished her circling stalk around the head of the little valley and began moving down the slope facing the cabin. She held a small black instrument in her left hand with a long telescoping probe. The probe had a clamp near its tip that held her infrared sensor. She paused at each step and waved the probe over the ground to her front, and moved forward again when she was sure that her next footfall was clear.

Puss got a silent warning vibration from her instrument halfway down the ridge. She halted, and using the tip of her probe gently brushed the leaf mold on the forest floor aside, and uncovered the trigger of a foot-popper land mine. It was made in the shape of a flower and colored a bright yellow that would capture a child's attention.

"You scum-sack! Using these damm Chin kid-killers!" Puss hissed, "I'll toss you into Rat's nest myself if they don't do it fast enough after we collect you!"

She knelt then, and pulled a device like a giant corkscrew from her back-pack. She positioned it next to the mine and screwing its spiral shank down into the sandy soil, positioned one of its arms over the trigger. She cocked this spring-loaded arm and set its timed-release catch, checked her watch and started its timer.

Puss walked away from the mine that was now her decoy, and on down through the forest, still sweeping the ground before her with the sniffer. She got a magnetic signal less than a hundred meters beyond the foot-popper and found a dull brown trip-wire at ankle height stretching through the sparse underbrush.

Puss screwed another of her devices into the soil beside the trip wire and grinned slightly, as she set it for a later release when she cocked its arm and started its timer.

She made her way on down to the base of the ridge without finding any other alarms, and crawled into a thicket where the forest bordered the open meadow. She pushed to a place where she was hidden but could see both the cabin to her left and Boots' position at the top of the slope to her front.

Puss pulled a monocular from a pouch with her left hand and set it to wide-view as she settled into her blind. She trained it on the cabin as she opened the flap on her holster. Then she dropped the glass and glanced at the complex field watch on her wrist.

"I'll bet it is him in there," she whispered, "About two more minutes until his damm foot popper goes, then the wire will slam and we'll see if the som'bitch flushes."

She sent a signal to Boots by rapidly patting her hands over her mouth while making a whirring sound deep in her throat to mimic the drumming noise of a ruffled grouse's mating signal. She turned back to the cabin again and watched it through her scope, and waited in the bright stillness of the morning, its quiet emphasized by the sound of insects humming in the sun's warmth.

*

Boots heard Puss' signal where she crouched behind the log on the ridge above the cabin, and whispered, "Damm if she didn't do it again! That gal sure gives good sneak!" She willed herself to be motionless and as alert as a jungle cat beside a game trail, but then grinned as she whispered, "If this is him, I'll bet he doesn't know that those birds do their looove drumming way earlier in the year than now."

*

Puss checked her watch and the timing of her decoys then zoomed up her scope to focus in on a loophole-sized window in the wall of the cabin. A muffled "crack" sounded from the ridge behind her as the mine detonated and she saw a shadow appear behind the window. When it disappeared a moment later she whispered, "That's the trip wire going. Now we'll see what we've got here."

Puss zoomed her scope out to wide-field and tensed for action, but stayed hidden. She caught a flicker of movement at the edge of her field of view a second later and turned to see a figure emerge from the ground 50 meters away from the cabin. Puss shrilled the whistle of a diving kestrel hawk then whispered, "You sneaky ferker, you dug yourself a cute little bug-out tunnel."

The figure began a scrambling run slanting up the slope of the ridge behind the cabin and Puss muttered, "Thanks for showin' me the safe way through your ferkin minefield you poor sucko. And Kris makes crossing shots like you aint gonna' believe."

*

Boots was alerted by Puss' whistle and clicked her mind into a focus on only her weapon, and her target. She saw the figure come up the slope in a panting run and pass her 20 meters out. Boots rose to her knees and with precision of a missile system tracking an incoming target, fired her dart. The

9

figure took several more running steps on its momentum before it fell, and buried its face in the leaves on the forest floor.

*

Puss saw the figure go down and pushed out through the brush of her hiding place. She crossed the meadow with the aid of her sniffer probe, then bounded up the slope on the same route as the running figure had used. She found Boots kneeling over a man on the ground when she reached the top.

Boots was turning his head out of the leaf mold to let him breathe. He had an aware but helpless look in his wide-staring eyes, and his mouth and limbs were slack. He was young with lank greasy hair, was slightly built and had pimples on the white skin of his face. He wore a faded windbreaker jacket, tattered `clave workpants and old Chin combat boots.

"He sure looks like the ID pic Rat gave us, but something funny's going on here Buddy! Two good shots in one day! You been sneaking in lessons on me?"

"Ha, ha," Boots replied without humor as she reloaded her dart gun.

"What's wrong?" Puss asked, suddenly serious.

"It's him alright, but the sucko's wearing an armor vest. I don't know how much dope he got when the dart went through it before sticking him."

"Buda's butt!" Puss muttered. "And we can't give him another dose without risking making a permanent doper out of him."

"And Boss Rat don't pay for bait that aint awake," Boots finished.

"OK now what, move fast?" Puss asked, dropping her pack and groping in it for fetter-straps.

"Yep, and hope to Jesu-Buda that the Rat-catcher will move in as fast as we do," Boots replied as she flipped out a Network com-set from her belt pouch.

"Here Ratty, Ratty, Ratty! Mummy has goodies for you little rodents!" she intoned as she keyed the send switch. Boots released it and the two women heard a squawk.

"All right - cut tha' comedy you brass-assed bimbo. When and where?"

"Shat!" Boots exploded to Puss, "That's Wart Face! He don't like me ever since I broke his nose."

"Oh, how petty of him!" Puss replied with exaggerated concern, then she snapped, "It's our money dammit, so be charming, dammit!"

Boots keyed her mike again and replied in a voice that dripped cool professionalism, "The coordinates are 45.90.357.002 by 89.47.239.220. Pickup

10

must be 400 meters due west of this centroid in zero hours, thirty minutes, zero seconds."

"I hear ya' Big Buns. Ya' better be right!" crackled from the com-set before the unit went silent.

"I'll boil his balls for breakfast!" Boots screamed to the sky, wild-eyed with clinched fists and veins bulging in her neck.

"Hush, that's for later," Puss snapped as she squatted and began binding the mark's ankles.

Boots' responded with an animal snarl as she knelt and roughly secured the mark's wrists with fetter straps from her own pack. Finishing that, she jumped to her feet and hacked down a sturdy sapling with her belt knife. She stripped its branches away to make a carry pole then slid the sapling between the mark's bound wrists and ankles.

The two women shouldered the pole with the mark hanging from it like a game trophy and Boots lead the way down the slope. She used her sniffer to sweep their path as they made their way toward the flat beyond the mouth of the little valley.

*

The Seeker strode through the shadows under the canopy of the unfamiliar forest around him. He moved along the game trail as silently as a wraith on his journey through what was to him an alien place.

He had avoided any contact with the few humans he had sensed during his long trek southward, because he felt they were different from the ones he sought...

His brown hair was roughly cropped above his shoulders and he had a broad, light-skinned face with high cheekbones and a strong chin. His beard and moustache were the same color as his hair and were also hacked short. His eyes were a clear light brown and gold-flecked as in amber - bright eyes that were intelligent and alert.

He was two meters tall with broad shoulders and powerful arms and legs. He wore a leather shirt that hung to mid-thigh. It was decorated with subtle patterns of stitching and sewn-on small white beads. A leather pouch, an intricately woven fiber sheath holding an antler-hafted knife and two curiously carved sticks all hung from the braided belt tied around his waist. He wore leather leggings and thick leather foot coverings that came to mid-calf.

He had a small leather packsack on his back and carried two light spears that were fletched, and one that was much heavier.

Bila, or "Seeker" in his language, had an aura of primal force and was a natural part of the wilderness he walked through.

*

He had awakened on the graveled shore of the cold sea twelve moons ago then he had made his way to the south as he searched for his people, except during the most severe cold of the past winter. He was worried because while he had encountered many more small animals than he thought normal, he had seen none of the large ones that he knew.

He had hunted and killed quickly as he traveled and taken only enough game for his needs while he had searched the strange forests and mountain valleys, and sought the cool broad grasslands where his people surely awaited him.

He now thought about all of this as he paced through the dappled gloom under the leafy canopy, fretting that these trees were so much taller than those he knew and seemed to never end. Then he saw that the light was becoming brighter through their foliage. He sensed that the slope he was walking down would end in an open meadow.

Bila quickened his pace, as he decided to drink from the stream he knew would be flowing there.

*

He pushed through the underbrush at the edge of the tree line and stepped out into a meadow. He paused for a moment while he waited for any feeling of danger. He sensed none so he trotted across its grassy flat toward the low line of scrub willows that defined the course of the stream that did indeed flowed there. He pushed through the scrub to its edge and squatted on a gravely bank where the water gurgled past, and drank from his cupped hands until his thrust was satisfied.

Bila sat back on his heels and facing the sky, closed his eyes and inhaled deeply with pleasure - until he caught the scent of one of his enemies. It was a faint whiff, but enough. He bounded to his feet and crouched in a tense on-guard position with his heavy spear at the ready. His jaw was clenched, and his eyes were wide and blazing.

*

Boots and Puss strode into the larger meadow near the little stream and dumped the trussed mark on the ground. When Boots flipped out her com-set, Puss hissed, "Remember dammit, be nice!"

Boots growled in the back of her throat, then keyed the mike and switched its locator beacon on, "Here Ratty, Ratty, Ratty, come get your goodie now!" she announced with a saccharine voice.

"About time," the receiver crackled, "You two bimbas are always late!"

Boots gripped the com-set with white knuckles, "Ground Collection Group 01 has completed the designated pickup and is in place," she hissed.

"We are 400 meters due west of the site centroid we gave you - at zero hours, twenty nine minutes, zero seconds from last contact. Where are you?"

"Don't be cutesy with me, Poopsie, I call's the shots around here, so you better be nice - to Wart Face!"

Boots' eyes blinked wide and she hastily signed to Puss, *"How does he know that name?"*

"Do not know" Puss signed in reply - then she frowned at the com-set in her friend's hand.

Boots scowled, then signed, *"They have bugged this thing,"* before keying her mike and responding in a light tone, "Gee, you must have lost my signal. What I said was War Ace, `cos you remind me of an instructor I had back in the Academy who was mucho studo."

"Good try, Big Buns," crackled from her com-set, "But I know all about you. If you really did have that poor sucko, there aint too much left of him that's useable now anyway."

"Whatever," Boots answered in a cool tone, "I repeat, do you want this hunk of Rat Bait or not, because he just might trade us some good techy-stuff to let him go free instead."

"Get the Bait ready, here come me and my hook!" her receiver crackled.

The two women waited for five minutes until they heard the sound of a helicopter in the distance, then Boots stepped to a clear area in the meadow and pulled a small smoke flare from a belt pouch. She popped its cap and dropped the canister on the ground as it began emitting a red plume to show the direction and speed of the slight breeze.

She walked back to where Puss stood and the two women lifted their limp captive and carried him to the center of the landing zone. They dropped him on the ground beside the flare then slipped out of their backpacks. Boots laid the tranquilizer gun aside as Puss pulled the carry pole from between the mark's trussed wrists and ankles and rolled him over to a face-down position and turned his head to one side to keep him from choking on his drug-relaxed tongue.

Boots flipped out her com-set and keyed its homing signal again to confirm their location when they heard the wap-wap-wap sound of rotor blades.

A helicopter flew down the main valley from the east a moment later and banked toward where they waited. It was dull black and its only marking was a small symbol on its side, three white circles touching tangentially on each point of an inverted white triangle.

"Come on in Rat Catcher," Boots spoke into her com-set. The noise from the beating blades of the approaching 'copter changed to wop-wop-wop as the craft slowed, then steadied and descended to hover 25 meters above the two women.

"OK Power Chickies," Boot's com-set crackled, "We aint got all day! Hook tha' mark on the line and let me get outta' here!"

"Sure will, friend. Just drop us down a little old irrevocable credit chip with your hook, an' then you can haul up some real good Rat Bait," Boots replied as the down-blast from the rotor buffeted her hair.

"Alright, Poopsie," crackled from Boots' receiver; "Value for value, sez Wart Face, just don' try ta' break my nose ever again. Get it? And look out you dumb twits, tha' hook comes down now!"

Suddenly, there was a rattle of background chatter in the 'copter from Wart Face's open mike.

"What's that? Holly-sheet, waddy-ell's down there?" He screamed.

"We get three IR blips showin' in tha' bushes!"

"Waddy-ferk sneaky thing you bimbas trying to pull!"

The rotor beat suddenly increased in frequency and the nose of the craft began to lift and turn as he shouted, "We're out'a here!"

"What'n hell you talking about?" Boots yelled. "Give me the ferkin credit an' you got your damm mark!"

"Hey, Big Buns, You're tryin' to pull something on me! You got some kinda' force in them bushes! Get rid of it before I come back tomorrow! And I gonna' back-charge you for this abort, ya' hear!" he finished with a snarl.

"G'dammit, there's nothing in the bushes!! It's just me 'n Puss and the mark here! What tha' hell you flippin' about?" Boots screamed into her com-set.

"IR scanners don' lie!" the speaker crackled. "Straighten up you act bimbas, or I gonna' haul both you into Rat's Nest one day - and me 'n the boys will have some major fun with your sweet bods on the way!"

The helicopter angled upward, and noise of its rotor beat diminished as it sped back eastward along the main valley.

"G'dammit! You come back here!" Boots screamed into the com-set again as she and Puss stared after the disappearing 'copter. "We got everything togath..." she started to continue when she felt a sharp sting in her right buttock. She spun around, then sank to the ground on failing legs as numbness began to engulf her.

Boots saw the mark grinning at her as she started falling. He was sitting up and holding her dart gun in his now-freed hands and as her limbs went limp and her strength faded, she saw him cut away the fetters on his ankles with a small knife. She got the full effect of the drug then and collapsed as she became totally relaxed. She watched through helpless eyes as he scrambled to his feet and started running toward the brush lining the little stream.

"Hold it right there Buster or I shot your foot off!" Puss shouted as she spun about when she sensed movement behind her. She drew her pistol and held it in a two-handed combat grip covering the man.

He paused and faced Puss as she motioned him back with its muzzle, until a high-pitched animal squeal sounded from the brush to her left, followed in seconds by a deep grumbling growl from her right.

"Hey Mama Bear," the mark shouted, "I figgered you'd be here!" He said with a shrill giggle, "Come an' get your dinner!"

Puss glanced over her left shoulder and saw a small bear cub at the edge of the scrub lining the stream bank. Then half turning to her right while she still held her pistol steady on the mark, she was dismayed to see a large sow grizzly crash out of the thicket and begin a lumbering run toward them.

"Shat!" Puss hissed - then she glanced down at Boots' limp body at her feet and gritted, "Shat, shat, SHAT!" She snapped her gaze back toward the mark in time to see him turn and trot the remaining few meters to the bushes.

"Serves ya' right, you saddo' bitches!" he yelled with another shrill giggle as he forced his way into the scrub and disappeared.

Puss dropped him from her thoughts and turned to place herself in front of Boots' body. She settled into a gun-fighter's crouch and sighted on the charging sow. She waited serenely for it to get within effective range.

"Sure wish I had brought my .44 with some big bullets, instead of this damm 5.7 with its lotsa' little ones," Puss muttered as the snarling sow charged toward her and her friend.

When the bear neared the 20-meter point where Puss had decided to begin firing, she realized in dismay that its lumbering and seemingly awkward run was covering the space between them with amazing speed. But worse, the sow's low-to-the-ground and head-down stance also kept her from targeting its vital areas.

"Sweet Jesu," she whispered as she tried to sight on the bear's muzzle and rage- reddened eyes while its head whipped up and down with each leaping stride, "We sure could use some help here..."

She was totally focused on the charging beast and she was about to give the final gram of pressure to her trigger and begin firing when she sensed rather than saw a movement to her left, and a long shaft suddenly sprouted from the bear's flank. It was followed by another within seconds that slammed in next to the first even as the bear faltered in its stride and swung its head to face the new assault.

The sow's forelegs stiffened and it wrenched itself from its path toward the two women in a shower of torn turf. It roared in rage and lunged around to snap at the shafts in its side.

The bear stopped its charge less than 10 meters from where she stood and Puss saw it now presented her with a full broadside target. She did not fire however, instead she muttered, "What the ferk?" She then caught a sudden movement in the willow thicket from the corner of her eye, and a human figure jumped into the meadow from the spot she knew the flying shafts had been launched.

It was clad in brown and gripped a heavy spear in both hands as it ran in leaping strides at the roaring beast. Puss noted abstractly that the figure was large, male and dressed in leather, then a wave of mild shock swept over her and she became a detached observer of the scene. She slackened her trigger finger and watched with wide eyes.

The man in leather braced at a halt three meters from the bear, stopped and stood erect with his feet planted wide and arms outspread. He brandished his spear in one hand and roared a grizzly's attack challenge. The maddened sow turned from her frantic attempts to escape the pain in her flank and with a screaming snarl, reared up on her haunches into the same attack position as the man.

He leaped to the sow in three long strides and landed before it was at its full height. He dropped in to a crouch inside the reach of its waiving forelegs with his spear at the ready, then without pausing and before the bear could begin a first swipe with her massive paws, he thrust his spear into her chest below her sternum and into her heart. He reversed his hands on the shaft as soon as he planted his weapon and with amazing strength, used the imbedded spear to fend off the struggling bear and keep out of the range of her claws.

The sow's roar suddenly changed to a gurgle after she began only a third smashing swing of her forelegs. Bright arterial blood gushed from her jaws as she stopped clawing, and her hind legs began to collapse. The man savagely churned his spear in the bear's breast then, and used it to push her off balance and down to the ground where she landed on her left flank. He withdrew his weapon with a practiced jerk as the sow fell and stepped back to avoid the blood spraying from the gaping wound. Then he knelt and while keeping a wary eye on the dying bear, cleaned his spear by wiping its bloody point and shaft on the soft grass of the meadow.

Puss noted the deft grace and strength of the man's attack as she numbly watched the primal scene before her and smelled the blood and reek of the dying bear.

"Damm if he don't look like he sure knows what the ferk he's doing," she whispered, "And Sweet Jesu,You sure know how to come through in a pinch! Thanks, I think."

The man rose to his feet when the bear gave a final wheezing spasm and turned toward Puss for the first time since he had leaped from the willows. He showed a crooked smile as he looked directly into her eyes and took a slow step toward her and another, then he bent and placed his spear on the ground.

She saw that it was tipped with a finely worked flint point bound to its shaft with rawhide. She gasped.

He rose again and now standing only two meters before her, tapped himself on his chest, "Bila," he said in a pleasant baritone as he opened his hands wide in the universal gesture of peace and stood before her, and waited.

Puss was still holding her pistol in a double combat grip but she had let its muzzle fall while she watched the astonishing scene take place. Now she forced herself to snap out of her shock.

"G'dammit Girl, Get Real!" she gritted as she tensed and tightened her hands on her pistol. Then the reality of the events finally broke the last of her trance, and her mind flooded with a cascade of impressions. She sorted them and sought coherence and while she stood looking at the man, who continued to hold his hands out and gaze at her with a slight smile.

"Gawd, he's big!" she whispered.

"And he's not Indian.

"What's that language he's using?

"And that's elk skin he is wearing.

"I've never seen a flint point like that before.

"And I've never seen a bear killed that quick, let alone with a furkin' STICK!

"And shat, he's not even breathing hard!

"And where'n Buda's back yard did he come from anyway?

"Gawd damm - he is furkin BIG!" she finally whispered again.

Puss moved her eyes slowly and deliberately over him as she was sorting out her impressions. She took in the white beads, subtle stitching and decorative seam-work of his leather hunting shirt; the stag horn hilt of a knife in a woven fiber sheath hanging from a sash of plaited animal hair around his waist, his height and the breadth of his shoulders and finally his face. She looked up at him, still smiling and towering a full head and a half over her.

Marybell met his peaceful gaze directly and saw something in the depths of his eyes that touched her inner core of self, the core that she had learned to trust ever since she was a child. She dropped out of her combat grip and holstered her pistol, but without snapping its flap and stood erect from her gun-fighter's crouch.

She tapped her breast and said, "Marybell," then she added quietly, "Thank you."

His smile widened and he stepped forward, he held out his right hand to her - open with his palm up. Puss refused to allow her reactions to his size or nearness show in her face as she calmly raised her gaze from his chest, which seemed to fill her horizon as he stood close to her. She looked into his eyes and smiled and again acting on her instinct, slapped her palm on his.

He nodded and said, "Marybell. Thank you," in a perfect copy of her pronunciation. He added, "On!" as he made a gesture with his left hand, then his smile faded as he pointed to Boots' form lying in the grass with the dart sticking out of her hip. The man asked "Burtzi?" then more softly, "Hil?" as he looked Puss with a question in his eyes.

Puss blinked and snapped, "Oh-shat!" as she whirled and dropped to her knees by Boots' side and checked under her friend's jaw for a pulse. She found it was strong but slightly uneven, so she moved Boots' head to get her slack tongue out of the tuft of grass then bent low to look into the woman's staring eyes. She saw awareness in them and straightening back up, removed the dart with a brisk yank and tossed it on the grass. She became aware of the man again while she was groping in one of her belt pouches for a field dressing. He had stepped around the prostrate woman and now squatted at her other side.

Puss saw him peer at the dart lying in the grass without touching it, then look up as she deftly stripped the wrap from a bandage. He pointed to Boots and asked, "Bizi hura? On!" while he made a complex gesture with his right hand.

Puss glanced up from preparing the bandage and shook her head with a frown at his unrecognizable words. But when she saw his gestures she fumblingly responded with several of her own in the Amerindian sign language that her grandfather had patiently taught her when she was young.

"She lives. She sleeps," Puss signed as she turned her attention back to her friend. The man grunted and nodded.

She pushed her friend's thighs apart and reaching between them from the rear, grasped the tab of the bottom zipper of Boots' jump suit at its waist in the front. She pulled it down along the crotch seam and up to its end at the base of the woman's spine.

Then under the man's openly interested eyes, she pushed back the elastic fabric and exposed Boot's firm buttock and the small red wound from the dart. She removed the dressing's inner wrapper, folded it to pop its bubble of antiseptic and with a great deal of unnecessary force, slapped its adhesive surface over the needle mark.

"Serves you right for letting yourself get unfocused, dammit!" Puss growled as she contemplated the bright red mark in the shape of her hand that now decorated her friend's white bottom.

Puss heard a slight snort and looked up at the watching man in time to see him hide a fleeting grin, but when she started re-zipping her friend's suit, his look changed to one of puzzlement as the open seam of the woman's clothing grew back together under Puss' guiding hand.

Puss was still intent on tending to her friend and only vaguely noted his reaction to the zipper, but she sensed him tense when she turned Boots over onto her back and her head rolled over to show her staring blue eyes.

She looked up to see him staring down at Boots' face with a look of profound sadness and loss which then changed into one of infinite tenderness.

The man raised his eyes and gazed at Puss with the most searching expression she had ever experienced, then just as suddenly his expression changed again, to careful neutrality. He signed, *"Good"* and whispered, *"On!"*

Puss nodded her head but she continued to suppress her thoughts about the last twenty minutes as she concentrated all of her attention on Boots. She bent and lifted her friend's shoulders upright with her left arm and tugged at the woman's legs with her right.

"I got to get her away from this stinking dead bear and in to a safe place 'till she comes out from under the dope," Puss grunted.

The man looked at her with a silent question from where he squatted. Then without waiting for a response, he slid his arms under Boots' shoulders and knees and stood without effort, easily holding Boots' limp body. He motioned with his chin towards several large glacial erratic boulders setting in a triangle near the mouth of the mark's little valley and began walking toward them. When he strode away toward the haven he had chosen, Puss shook her head and blew a deep breath. Then she collected herself and grabbing their two packs and the dart gun, dashed ahead to make a resting place for her friend.

The man had no difficulty in carrying Boots' relaxed body but he took care to pace smoothly in order to not strain her neck as her head lolled back over his arm. He also watched the slow rise and fall of her breast as she breathed and noted the chiseled beauty of her neck with its milky skin and faint tracery of fine blue veins where it was exposed below the streaked paint on her face.

He knelt when he reached the ring of stones and carefully settled Boots as Puss indicated, with the woman's body reclining against the sloping face of one of the boulders. He held Boots' head away from its rough surface while Puss cushioned it with her folded field hat then settled herself beside Boots and slid her left arm behind her friend's neck for support.

The man placed the two women's field packs at Puss' side then he stood and looked down at her with an expression which now was different.

He spoke, and made graceful hand signs at the same time, "Nahi," and then to Puss' shock, uttering an exact mimic of the mark's shrill giggle as he fled. The man finished, "Hilzki?" as he made a final sign.

Puss listened to his words without comprension but read his signs at a subconscious level, *"You want dead?"* She vigorously shook her head in the negative.

The man looked at her for a second then he showed a crooked smile as he asked with both his voice and his hands, "Nahi bizirik?"

Puss understood his signs again, *"You want alive?"*

Puss signaled her assent with a very positive nod and as she watched, his smile changed to grimness and his eyes suddenly sparkled - but now with a light that had no humor.

The man turned and ran in an easy lope to the spot where he entered the meadow and her life less than thirty minutes ago. He pushed into the willow scrub and disappeared.

Puss considered his expression and the powerful grace of his movements for a moment.

"Oooo shat, I'll bet that a tiger in tha' jungle gets that same look," She whispered in awe, "When it goes out to get a goat for supper."

*

The man emerged from the willows within moments and trotted back to where the two women sat, pausing only to wrest his light shafts from the bear's flank and collect the heavy one from the grass Puss had made her determined stand.

He now carried a leather packsack and two curiously carved wooden sticks, all of which he dropped on the ground beside their packs. Then stepping away, he cleaned the bear's blood from his two light points by wiping them in the grass before propping them against one of the boulders.

Puss just sat and watched him, her thoughts still slightly scattered by the shock of events as the man untied his woven belt and dropped it with the pouch and knife sheath it carried. Then he grasped the bottom edge of his hunting shirt and stripped it off over his head and dropped it next to his pack. He unlaced the bindings of his heavy foot coverings and kicked them off, then untied a strap around his waist and released his leggings. He balanced easily on first one foot then the other and stripped them from his legs. Now clad in only a soft leather breechclout, he rummaged in his pack he retrieved and tied on a pair of strangely patterned leather moccasins.

He groped in his pack again and pulled out a small coil of thin line that was woven from the same animal hair as his belt. He shook it out and inspected a small pouch formed into its center. Then he re-coiled it and held it in his teeth while he re-tied the belt with his pouch and knife around his waist. Finally, he tucked the coil of line under the belt beside his pouch and turned without a glance at the two women, grasped his heavy spear and jogged at an easy gait across the meadow. When he reached the line of scrub he thrust his way in to it at the same spot as the mark had and disappeared.

Puss cradled Boots' head and slowly allowed her fighting tension to drain away while she mulled over all that she had just witnessed within the last half hour, a very large and obviously very strong man who killed a bear with amazing ease as it was attacking her, and who now had gone off on a mission at her request, without question.

She sighed and raising her right hand, gently caressed Boots' forehead as she whispered, "Thank you Sweet Jesu, and for real this time." Then she dropped her hand to her side and drew her pistol. She laid it ready on the grass near her thigh and finally allowed herself to relax. After a moment and with another little sigh she announced in a dreamy whisper, "Buddha's Butt! That's the most major ferkin' alpha male I've ever seen!"

Then after a long pause she added, "And the pheromones pumpin' out of him are enough to make a gal's head get real giddy, and that loin-cloth," She chuckled, "Looks pretty loaded too."

Puss blinked after another moment then gently moved Boots' head to where she could look into her friend's staring eyes.

"I know you can hear me under this dope," Puss said. "And I know you're gonna' be pretty much out of it for another hour. So Sweetie now we'll talk, except all you can do is just lie here an' listen," she finished with a wicked little smirk.

She cradled her friend's head and helplessly relaxed neck as she continued, "First though, I think I'll clean us up some," and pulled out her camouflage kit. She used its treated tissue wipes to remove the grease paint from Boots' face then she balanced the kit on her friend's breast and used the mirror in its lid as she cleaned her own face and neck. Finally after cleaning the backs of both their hands, she closed the kit and said, "Now that we're all pretty again I think I'll see how you kiss when you're under like this..."

"You know, it's sorta' fun when you're helpless Sweetie," Puss gasped a minute later. "I think I could get to like you having lie here and just take it," she murmured. Puss gazed into Boots' eyes for a moment longer then she dropped all playfulness.

"I love you Kris," she whispered, "We are a team according to my tribe and you know we don't get bent about teamed folks sharing their goodies around."

"But kid, what you did with those crazy bitches at your regimental party the other night was way too self-destructive. They'll kill you someday and dammit, I just can't let my heart watch you die."

"So," she growled as she grabbed the woman's chin and whispered with a glare, "If you ever let those freaks do that to you again, I've got to split forever - because I love you too much."

Boots' eyes flooded with slow tears then she forced a groan through her drug-slackened throat, "Nnnoooo...!"

Puss looked down at her friend's struggling face and welling eyes, then kissed Boots' forehead, "It's OK buddy, I think you got my message." She cradled her friend's head on her breast and gently stroked it until the woman's was calm again.

Puss continued after a moment, "We didn't have time to talk much before we jumped out on this mission so I didn't get to tell you about my own visit to your officer party after they sent you home, all stuck full of their crazy-candy needles."

"Anyway, when I had found all the damm things and pulled them out of you and calmed you down, then I had time to think about those sickos and what they had done to you while I waited for you to stabilize. When I was sure you'd make it, I tucked you in and took a little walk back to their party."

"Short story is that I went on the war path and called Code Duello on your Colonel. I snapped her spine big-time and also smushed up some of her other officer furts on my way in and then back out of the place that night."

"So Big Buns things could be kinda' tricky when we get back to the `clave."

Boots' head stirred and Puss felt the woman's fingers twitch.

"Hey kid, you're pretty good to be coming out from under the dope this quick!" Puss raised Boots' head and looked into her friend's eyes, and saw them sparkle.

"Gooo gurrl," Boots slurred.

"OK buddy, if you're gonna' be this tough let's see if we can help you along!" Puss said with a grin as she got to her knees and began vigorously massaging Boots' arms and legs to increase their blood circulation and speed the metabolization of the drug in her system.

*

Boots was sitting up with Puss' help, and starting to flex her limbs. She slurred as she said, "Gadammit, I'll get that l'ill som'bitch if it's the last hit I pull!"

"Quit spinnin' your spurs Sweetie!" Puss grunted without looking up from rubbing her friend's thighs and calves, "There's time for that later."

"Ja, Boss," Boots grunted, "And I will wait but I will get him, and when I do it's better you don't watch."

Then she added in a clear voice, "I would have loved to seen you take Colonel Creep though. That's what we called that whacked-out bitch in our outfit. I took her a couple of times in practice sessions, until she was always too `busy' to come out and play with me anymore."

"But," Boots added in a voice like a grindstone, "You must have made her body fluids squirt biggers when you gave your war-whoop and vaulted over her head, and busted her from the back!" Then Boots grinned with evil delight as she asked, "Did you take her scalp?"

"OK Buddy," Puss asked in mock severity as she sat up on her heels, "How `n hell do you know that's what I did?"

"Simple," Boots voice softened and she answered with a crooked smile, "That's how you took me the first time, but you were nice enough to pull your punch then!"

"Shat, I'm getting too damm predictable in me old age!" Puss giggled. Then she said with steel suddenly in her voice, "I didn't take her scalp though, I left her a present instead. I took that nasty thing she had stuck in you and rammed it through her tongue."

"Humph" Boots grunted, then after a moment she whispered, "Kiddo, you're getting to be one sort of scary injun. That sounds like something I would do."

She changed her tone to one of command and ordered, "Enough of this idle yakey! Help me up!"

Puss squatted by her side and draped Boots' right arm over her shoulder while the woman placed her other hand on the rough surface of the boulder. As Puss rose Boots braced against the granite and used her friend's steady strength to struggle to her feet. Then she stiffened her knees and stood upright leaning back against the rock, and looked around in confusion.

"Alright," she snapped at Puss with her brow wrinkled, "I just remembered floating or something. How'd you get me here from the landing spot after that damm mark stuck me? And what in hell was all that roaring I heard while I was down looking at bugs in the grass? And who'n hell was that crazy guy I think I saw dancing around taking his clothes off?"

"Well Kiddo," Puss answered with a grin, "It's about time you asked but it's sort of hard to explain..."

"What tha' ferk's hard to explain about it?" Boots snapped, again.

"I can tell you what I saw and what I heard and what I felt, but I'm not too sure I know what it was and I don't really believe it yet myself."

Then Puss stood before her friend and in a calm voice, related to an increasingly incredulous and skeptical Boots all the events that occurred during the time since Wart Face's helicopter departed.

***

Chapter 3
Bila

May 1, 2276 AD
Coastal Mountains of British Columbia

"OK, C'mon here, and I'll show you G'dammit!" Puss snapped over her shoulder as she marched out into the meadow from the ring of boulders. Boots shrugged off her weakness and followed, at first haltingly then with more sureness in her stride as she regained her strength.

"What tha' hell you think that is, a furkin' rug?" Puss asked as she pointed to the body of the sow. She smiled then, as Boot's scowl of skepticism changed to wide-eyed wonder when the woman realized the size of the dead bear and the amount of blood on the torn turf around it.

"Shee-it! And you say he did it with a furkin' spear?"

"Three actually," Puss answered. "Come on back, and I'll show you something else that'll really snap your straps," But as she started to turn and lead the way back to their rock shelter, a whimper sounded from the other side of the dead sow's bulk.

"Shat," Puss hissed, "The cub!"

"What are you talkin' about?" Boots asked with irritation.

"We were between the sow and her cub, and the `copter scared it. Mama bear didn't like that and that ferkin' mark knew they lived around here."

"So?" Boots asked.

"So the cub won't make it with no mama, and the wolves will tear it apart soon as we leave," Puss replied in a soft voice, "So, dammit, we got to put it down."

"You or me?"

"Well, I took out the smart dog when he was just doing his doggy thing," Boots answered in the same soft tone, "So maybe it's your turn, Kid."

"Yeah, I reckon so," Puss whispered as she stepped around the sow's body and drew her pistol. She held it muzzle-up in a precision grip with both hands, closed her eyes and raised her face to the sky for a second. Then she looked down at the tiny creature vainly nuzzling its mother's cold flank and into its distressed little eyes.

She triggered her pistol twice and killed the cub instantly, as two tears trickled down her cheeks.

Puss turned, and holstering her pistol started marching in cold furry back toward the boulders. Boots caught up with her friend and matched Puss' step, only slightly faltering. She slapped Puss lightly on the shoulder.

"Your real, buddy. That's what I like about you."

When Puss gave her a small strained smile, Boots muttered, "And you tell me he carried me all this way, and wasn't breathing hard when he put me down?"

"Yep, just after killing momma bear with these, and he didn't even pop a sweat," Puss answered, recovering her grin as she stopped and pointed to the light spears the man had left leaning against one of the boulders.

"These are two of them that he used to kill it. The flint points are shrink-bound with rawhide thongs to straightened shafts. The points aren't like any I have ever seen before, and the shafts are fletched. And I know about Indian points and projectiles because my grandfather was a curator at the old Smithsonian, before the Chin blew it away."

Boots reached out to grasp one of the shafts, until Puss said, "Don't think I'd do that, until you ask him first."

"Why in hell not?" Boots snapped, displaying more of the irritation that had been building in her since she had been confronted with a situation which she neither fully understood, nor controlled.

"Because he's bigger than us and he's being nice right now, and I like it that way."

"Shat, he aint coming back," Boots growled, "If he's off chasing that crafty little rat of a mark, we won't see him again, because that little bastard will get him totally lost in these woods!"

"We'll see. Anyway, I got more to show you," Puss said as she stepped into the space among the boulders, and led her friend away from committing the ancient insult of touching another's weapons without permission.

Puss squatted besides the man's piled clothing and pack, "Alright buddy, look at this shirt."

"So?" Boots asked, kneeling beside her. "It's just an Injun's deerskin hunting shirt. Some of them that are still alive around here have gone back to their old ways, now that the Chin have cut and run. What of it?"

"It's not deerskin. It's elk skin and heavy and it's new and from a big stag, and the Chin killed and ate all the elk while they were here. And it isn't Indian," Puss replied with increasing precision, as she enumerated her points on her fingers. Then she dropped the informal slang the two used between themselves when they were relaxed.

"The decorative stitching is not Amerindian, since we never used this particular chevron pattern, and there's no fringe of any kind on the seams, which are sewn with fresh sinew by the way. And I suggest you also examine the beads."

Boots, now more curious than skeptical, responded with equal precision, "They seem to be either of bone or something similar, and they are very well made."

"Yes, they are well made, but by hand. You can see some faint abrasion marks in spite of polishing, and their size and the holes drilled through them vary slightly also.

"But most importantly," Puss added, placing her hand on Boots' knee as she looked solemnly into her friends eyes, now alight with curiosity.

"They are not bone. They are ivory. And it's fresh ivory, not fossil."

"It can't be fresh; there are no walruses left over here, and the African and Indian elephants were all eaten a hundred years ago!" Boots exclaimed with authority.

"Yes, I know," Puss responded in the same tone, her eyes locked on those of her friend. "But I also know beads and beadwork, and fresh ivory as well since I helped dissect the last walrus carcass that washed up on the shore out here."

"But there's more," she continued in a quiet voice, "Look at his mukluks, and tell me what kind of leather they are."

Boots touched one of the heavy boots, and squeezed the edge of its top between two fingers to gauge their thickness and texture. Then she bent low and examined them without touching them again.

"I don't know," she said. "The leather is very thick, yet it is well tanned to be soft and pliable, and it seems to have a large cell structure which would provide good insulation. The uppers have been de-haired, and have a wide-spaced pore pattern on the skin side and the soles are covered with an additional sewn-on layer of thick hide that is not de-haired."

"This layer is also oriented so that the coarse hair is toward the heel, to give better traction I suppose."

"But I have never seen anything like them before," she finished quietly as she straightened up again.

"I can't identify the leather or the style of the mukluks either," Puss said softly. Then she pointed to the wooden wands with bird's heads carved at one end that lay beside his pack, their small hooked beaks polished and chipped with use.

"And these are atlatls," she whispered.

Boots' eyes widened as she looked at the simple objects - then she gasped, "Gadammit, you're right! What the ferk is going here anyway?"

"And there is something else I just remembered about him," Puss replied as she tapped her friend's thigh, "I don't think he's ever seen a zipper before..."

Puss' eyes suddenly gleamed and she finished with a grin, "Anyway Big'un, I don't know who or what we got here, but he do sure look way different!"

"Yeah, Squaw Woman," Boots started to respond with a grin of her own, "And we just might have us some funs with..." Then she stopped in mid-sentence with a sharp intake of breath.

Puss spun around into a defensive position when she felt her friend's leg tense and dropped her hand to her pistol on the grass. She saw the man standing three meters beyond their sheltering boulders. He was breathing easily and his body glistening with light perspiration in the rays of the afternoon sun, and now carried a burden over his shoulder slung on the butt-end of his heavy spear.

He gave Puss the same crooked grin as when he left her, but now his eyes gleamed in triumph.

"Tori!" he said, and raised the point of his spear to let the burden he carried slide off and drop on the ground behind him. He stepped aside to reveal the body of their mark. The man's hands and ankles trussed with the cord of braided hair and he was gagged with a wad of meadow grass tied in his mouth by a length of vine.

"Shat!" Boots shouted and leaped to her feet. She lurched slightly, then recovered her balance only to pause again when she realized just how large the man really was who stood before them. She paced out of their shelter on stiff legs and confronted him as she took a stance with her fists planted on her hips.

"Alright, Buster," she snapped, "Just who-in-hell are you?"

Boots was irritated that she had to look up because of his height, and the light brown hair sprouting on his chest irritated her even more.

"Bera bizirika, On!" the man said as he looked past Boots to Puss with a smile, and a nod. Then he turned his gaze down to Boots and said with a word she recognized, "Here," as he pointed to the bound figure lying at his feet.

Boots glanced down at the mark at his gesture, and was forced to smile at the bound man whose eyes burned with impotent rage above the crude but very efficient gag in his mouth. Then she looked up to the big man again.

"Thanks. But I still ask, who are you?" as she glared into his amber eyes.

"Well, for one thing," Puss snapped as she got to her feet, "He's the guy that saved your big butt from being the main course at a grizzly's picnic, as well as mine. And two, he's the guy that also saved our mission for us, which as I recall," she added in a cool tone, "You said he couldn't do."

"So kiddo maybe you ought to be more polite."

"His name is Bila by the way," Puss finished with a smug grin.

*

"Are we going to camp here tonight and call in Wart Face tomorrow?" Puss asked her friend as they sat leaning against "their" boulder. "And you want a rash bar? I'm sorta' starving."

"Yeah, and yeah." Boots replied. "But what are we gonna' do with little nasty here for the night? We'll have to pull his gag and feed him soon to keep him plump for Boss Rat, and he's getting sort of twitchy so we probably got to squat him pretty quickie as well."

"But I really don't want to listen to his whines, or let him listen in on us at all."

"Don't worry," Puss said with a grin. "I've got sodium oxybate and sco-polamine in my med kit that will put him away 'till morning. It'll also make him tell us some stories before his nap time and not remember a thing after, if we want to listen to what this scummo babbles."

"Ah, a shot of the old sing sauce," Boots said with a little smile. "You know, Kiddo, you're really starting to think sneaky-like! It makes my old heart glad to watch you develop such a good set of baads," she added with a straight face and innocent look.

"Shat, I got damm good sets of everything, as you ferkin well ought'a know!" Puss giggled. Then she became serious as she asked, "When do you want me to shoot him up?"

"Lets squeeze and then feed the scum-sack first, then we can see about getting him to warble us some tunes before we put him out." Boots said as she rose, pulled a coil of light line from her pack and expertly tied a sliding noose in one end, then knelt next to the mark. She snugged the loop around his neck then jumped to her feet and to one side as Puss drew her pistol and fired a single shot. The bullet nicked the man's uppermost ear as he lay on his side before them.

Boots waited until the mark's muffled squeals died away then she removed his gag and stared into in his frantic eyes. "We are going to untie you and let you relieve yourself," she said matter-of-factly, "Then we will feed you."

Puss raised her pistol again and her eyes were green ice as she looked over her gun sights into his, "But if you do not do immediately and exactly as we command, I will shoot you again, in your left foot - first. Do you under-stand me?"

"I would also like to impress upon you," Boots added in the matter-of-fact tone of an executioner adjusting a condemned man's head on the chopping block, as she un-snapped the flap of her own holster, "That my friend is a much kinder person than I ..."

The mark ceased to struggle, and Boots knelt beside him again and care-fully untied the cord of braided hair binding his wrists and ankles.

"On your feet! Move!" she commanded as she bounded back up and jerked on her line around his neck. Boots turned and strode away from their camp, dragging the mark stumbling toward the edge of the scrub willows as blood dripped from his ear.

Puss followed behind at a calculated distance with her pistol held ready at her side, until Boots stopped and growled, "This is far enough. Now do it!"

"I can't with you looking," the mark whimpered.

"Learn quick," Puss said as she pointed her pistol at his left foot.

Abashed and now totally cowed, the sullen and red-faced man fumblingly complied under the stony gaze of the two women.

*

They forced the mark to sit cross-legged with his back against one if the boulders after they returned, and strapped his ankles into a position that made it impossible for him to stand. Then Puss dressed his ear and tossed him two ration bars. As he was tearing the foil of one open and starting to wolf it down, she got to her feet and after groping in her pack, retrieved several more of the bars.

She handed one to Boots and the two sat on the ground near the mark. They chatted idly until the mark finished eating, and had emitted the belch and flatulence that always came with the rations provided by the `Clave government.

The two leaped on him then, and as Boots jerked his shirt and flack jacket up over his head Puss plunged a hypodermic syringe into the pale skin of his belly and injected him with the drugs.

Boots released the mark, and the two squatted next to him like carrion crows waiting beside a dying dog while the drugs took affect. When the mark began to hallucinate, they interrogated him quietly and persistently until he finally slept. Then they relaxed his bonds and re-tied him into a fetal position with his fetters.

Puss stepped over to Bila while Boots finished securing the mark. He was sitting on the ground, also cross-legged and quietly sorting through the items in his pack and pouch, and apparently oblivious to all their actions with the mark. He looked up to her with a smile and then with curiosity when she handed him a ration bar. He took it and examined it, then looked up with a question in his eyes.

She showed her own bar to him, and slowly and carefully tore its foil cover open and peeled it back. She took a bite of the brown mass within, and smiled.

The man noted her actions and copied them, except for her smile. He opened his bar, took a tentative bite and chewed. He looked up at Puss again as he obviously considered its flavor, and still showed no emotion when he abruptly dropped the bar and leaped to his feet. He grasped one of his throwing sticks and strode out of the circle of stones. The two women heard a faint sound of "Pi-too!" after he left.

Boots muttered, "Well, that's one way of getting' rid of him. But shat!" she snorted in a sudden burst of laughter, "He's not so dumb, I can barely gag this crappo down myself."

Some minutes later after both women had stepped away to answer their own calls of nature as dictated by the ration bars and were returning to the circle of boulders, they met the man as he strode from the direction of the larger valley.

He was carrying an armful of firewood and the haunch of a young deer hung from his shoulder by his braided cord. He nodded to them as he dropped the bloody trophy and entered the circle.

He knelt and scratched out a small fire pit in the turf with the butt end of a broken branch as the two women stood watching with silent curiosity. The man next laid a fire and started it by striking sparks with a small stone and a piece of pyrite from his belt pouch. He blew gently on the smoldering sparks in the tender under the pile of kindling until it began to blaze up, then he selected several leafy branches from his pile of dry wood. He squatted on his haunches and reaching in his pouch, pulled out a blade and deftly pruned them and peeled away their bark.

He stood again and went to where he laid the venison haunch, and skinned it with the bone-handled knife Puss had seen on his belt. He sliced off three filets, impaled them on his green branches and returned to squat by the fire again. He laid the skewers of meat on the blazing coals and as they began to sizzle and blacken, he carefully repositioned them so that both sides were seared.

Puss and Boots moved to stand by the fire and watch, first in disgust as the flesh charred then with increasing fascination, as the man expertly raised and rotated the grilling venison filets over the hissing flames. When the aroma of roasting meat replaced the stench of it searing, Boots looked at her friend and said with a sudden grin, "Shat, that smells like real food!"

She plopped down to sit across the fire from the man and slapping her thighs, said, "Ta' hell with a bunch of `Clave rash bars! Let's eat good stuff!"

"OK, Big'un, but how do you know he's gonna' share?" Puss asked as she seated herself on the grass next to her friend.

"I don't, but I sure hope he does," Boots murmured as she patted her friend's knee and smiled at Bila. He concentrated in silence on his cooking as he had done ever since he had built the fire. Boots continued to smile and watch the man, and Puss sat quietly watching them both while the twilight deepened and the firelight began to highlight their faces. She glanced at Bila, sitting on his heels as he did his grilling, and noted the slightest flicker of a smile at the corner of his mouth.

Puss immediately saw that he was aware of their interest, and was toying with them and their hunger. She glanced at Boots and saw that her friend's expression of open and friendly anticipation had not changed.

Puss choked back a giggle as she thought, "Shat, she either looks like a 14 year-old waiting for her first date, or a "rent-a-gal" waiting for the night's first customer, or both! But I've never seen her sit like this and just wait for someone else before, so what tha' hell's going on here anyway?"

Bila removed his skewered meat from the fire and planted the sharpened butt of one green branch in the ground beside the coals. He held the other two forked sticks with their sizzling fillets and looked across the fire at the two women for the first time since he had tasted their field ration. Then he rose to his feet and stepping around the fire, gravely presented the grilled venison fillets to them with a crooked grin.

Boots smiled and accepted hers as gracefully as a princess, then looked at the fragrant offering on the forked branch and hesitated.

Puss lifted her own skewer and after taking a healthy mouthful of her meat, started gnawing it free.

The man's eyes sparkled but he kept his grave demeanor as he seated himself and took the third skewered filet with his left hand. He held it before his face and bit at its edge, and with a deft slash of the flint knife severed a mouthful. He began to chew it with a contented smile.

Puss and Boots immediately drew their field knives and began to eat their filets according to his example.

*

"Whoosh! I'm full." Boots declared as she straightened out her long legs and flopped back on the grass. She patted her stomach contentedly as she looked up into the night sky, "Damm. That was good…"

"Yeah buddy you got that right," Puss replied with a happy sigh as she lay back on her side and propped up on her elbow to face her friend.

She continued, "Your chin's greasy."

"So's yours," Boots said, and smiled with smug languor, until Bila stirred on the other side of the fire. They both watched as the man stood and stretched with his arms over his head. He twisted his torso side to side several times then walked out of the circle of firelight without a word.

Puss watched her friend's face as Boots' eyes followed the man when he disappeared into the darkness. She said casually, "Sure is a lot of him, aint there."

Boots, still gazing into the darkness beyond the firelight replied in a chuckle, "Yep, and in that outfit he almost doesn't have on you can see about all of him too." Then she added slowly as she continued gazing into the dark where he had gone, "Ya' know, I don't think I'll kill him just yet."

"Ya' know," Puss mimicked, "He might have just decided the same thing about you Big'un!" Then she continued in a serious tone, "Like I said before, I like him being happy so I wouldn't do anything to make him change his mind if I were you."

"Shat! I could take him out in a minute if I wanted to." Boots growled in reply as she turned to Puss.

"Yeah, sure Kid. I'll bet that's what that ferkin' bear thought too!" Puss snapped. "Anyway, enough of your strutting Buddy, we gotta' talk about him serious, and private."

She placed her hand Boots' arm and continued in their silent language of finger touches, *"This man way different!"* She tapped.

"Tell me!" Boots tapped in answer as she grasped Puss' wrist, and grinned.

"Dammit, I serious" Puss tapped, *"He total primitive I think, and he damm good."*

"He feed us in ritual!"

"They did same thing in old world!"

"My people do that," Puss tapped.

"Leader kill. Cook. Give out first meat of hunt. Feed tribe."

"You say big man he own us?" Boots tapped furiously as she sat bolt upright.

"I say he treat us same way he treat he tribe. Wherever it be. You speak wrong. Dumb not the word for he," Puss tapped.

Then she began, *"I watch him –"*

"I see you look to him. You hot little chicken!" Boots leered as she tapped her friend's wrist.

"Dammit, talk straight!" Puss furiously tapped in reply, then emphasized her message by punching her friend's shoulder. *"He back soon. Us need plan."*

"What to plan? Call `copter. Sell mark. Loot cabin. Get bikes. Go S'attl."

Then Boots signed with her hands rather than with finger-taps while looking at her friend with a suddenly stony face, *"If is he is dumb and gets in our way. We chill him. Simple! So I ask, what is there to plan?"*

Puss started to respond, but Boots, looking over the younger woman's shoulder gave her a warning squeeze as the man strode back into the fire-light. His hair and beard were damp and clean as were his hands and arms. He stepped over to his pile of clothing and dropped his animal hair belt, and pulled on his leggings. Then he pulled his leather shirt on over his head and tying a knot in the braided belt with his pouch and knife, slung its loose circle over his over his shoulder and allowed his shirt to hang free.

He seated himself by the fire across from the two watching women and after adding more wood, picked up a discarded green willow twig. He meditatively chewed on its end and began cleaning his teeth as he stared into the glowing embers.

Puss smiled briefly in his direction then she resumed her position on her side with her back to the fire, and to the man.

Taking her friend's hand, Puss continued in finger taps, *"Me tell you dumb. You know me war medic. Me help head doctor. Test Chin POWs intel."*

"So?" Boots touched back, still sitting up with her chin on her knees and keeping an eye on the man under the guise of watching the fire, *"You say he more smart Chin grunt? Me know that two minutes!"*

"OK," Puss touched back, *"Man primitive. But he see `copters. Zippers. Cloth. Steel knife. Pistol shoots all one day. He see crazy women in war paint. He learn they language. He not do mistake. How smart you think he?"*

"What steel knife?"

"Know you not see!" Puss smiled as she tapped rapidly, very aware of the man sitting on the other side of the fire. *"He cut meat. Eat with flint knife. Use mark knife cut sticks. Me watch he use. He look it. Test it. He see quick it more tough than flint. He use like tough. You tell me he intel."*

Boots, refusing to back down from her skepticism tapped with her hand on Puss' wrist, *"What primitive? He renegade militia. Play wild man"*

"Militia got guns. Wear funny clothes. Not big men. Not can carry you big butt!" Puss then finished as her eyes blazed, *"Militia not have leather shirt of big animal skin. Not wear ivory beads. Not kill grizzly bears!"* she tapped with flying fingers as she shook the tall woman's wrist for emphasis.

Boots looked at her friend for several seconds while she considered Puss' statements, then she cocked an eyebrow and whispered, "OK kid, you've made your point. What do we do next?"

"Talk to him I think, and ask him..." Puss said aloud as she gracefully rose to her feet.

"And just what language we gonna' use, Doctor?" Boots asked with a grin, her blue eyes suddenly sparkling.

"Whatever works, Kiddo." Puss muttered as she stepped around the fire and re-seated herself on the grass facing the man. She waited silently and gazed at the beadwork on his shirt until with a start, he looked up from the glowing embers and smiled to her.

Puss looked directly at him and made the hand motions she remembered from the lessons her grandfather had given her as a child. She signed what she recalled to be the universal opening.

"Greetings and welcome. What is your name and tribe? My name is," then tapping her breast, as she said, "Marybell," again and signed, *"Friend."*

The man smiled broadly and his amber eyes gleamed as with flying hands and interspersed words in his language he responded, "Bila, medico regaled." Then he continued as his expression abruptly changed to one of open pain and anxiety, "Bodacious jade nerve?"

"Shat, I can't follow him," Puss muttered over her shoulder to Boots as she slowly signed, *"I not understand,"* and smiled ruefully to him in apology.

Boots, who had been watching and listening to the two intently, suddenly spoke from the other side of the fire, "I know a language that just might work." She got to her feet and stepped over to her field pack and rummaged in it until she pulled out a flat gray plastic case. She stepped back to the fire and seated herself cross-legged between the man and Puss. Boots put several more branches on the coals and then as the flames started blazing up again, opened her case to reveal a sketch pad and clips holding several pencils.

She said with a grin, "Lets see what the old universal language can do," as she braced the pad on her knee where the man could see it. She considered for a second then selected a soft black pencil and quickly sketched the likeness of a deer up in one corner of the paper.

Bila leaned forward and watched her work with obvious interest as the figure appeared under her hand. Boots finished the sketch and tapped her picture with a finger, then touched one of the greasy venison skewers discarded by the fire. She announced, "Deer!" as she quickly sketched a stick figure in a lifelike pose standing next to the deer and holding a spear She touched to the figure then tapped the man on his chest with the same finger. He smiled and nodded, "Bila."

Boots smiled at his quick understanding and began another sketch as the man watched intently. Puss leaned forward and held her breath, and was absorbed by the movements of her friend's pencil as well. Boots rapidly created the lifelike figure of a rearing bear on the paper, and again added a stick figure. This one was poised facing the bear and holding a spear. She tapped the bear's image, then pointing out into the night toward where the sow's body lay.

"Bear," She said then she touched the stick figure and tapped the man's chest once more, as she smiled.

"Bila," He responded with a wide grin and nodded.

Boots quickly sketched two more stick figures near her image of the bear, one lying down and the other standing in defense. She looked over her shoulder at Puss sitting beside her in rapt attention and asked, "Quick, what's your Injun' sign for thanks?"

Puss started then she made a simple one-handed motion.

Boots turned back to the man and tapped the standing figure in front of the charging bear on the paper and patting Puss' shoulder, said, "Marybell."

She tapped the prone stick figure in her sketch, followed with a slap on her own breast as she said, "Kristina." Finally she signed as Puss had shown her, "*Thank you,*" as she gazed solemnly at the man.

He responded to Boot's words and signs by looking into her eyes for a moment, then he nodded as he turned to Puss, sitting beside the tall woman. He signed slowly and carefully signed to her, *"Friend."*

Puss responded with the same sign as she said in a clear strong voice, "Friend!" and then she held her hand out palm upward.

Boots, taking her friend's cue responded with the same sign again and echoed, "Friend," as she held out her hand as well.

The man's eyes gleamed and he smiled broadly at Boots and Puss. He grasped both their hands in his and responded, "Friend."

Puss whispered, "You're stuck with him now Sweetie. You can't go back on your word after this - ever."

Boots gasped as her fingers were engulfed in the largest hand she had ever seen. Then she recovered her composure, relaxed her fingers in the man's grasp and motioned with the sketchpad in her other hand. He immediately released her hand and looked at the pad with interest.

Boots regained her feet as she muttered in an aside to Puss, "Enough huggy-kissy! Now lets see just what tha' ferk is really going' on with this bucko!" as she stepped over to the man's gear lying on the grass and picked up one of his thick leather boots. Returning to the fire, Boots sat in front of the man and handed him her sketchpad.

She leaned forward and touched the discarded venison skewer again with her right hand as she tapped her sketch of the deer with her left. Next, she pointed in the direction of the dead bear with one hand and touched her sketch of it with the other. Then reaching for his arm, she briefly pinched the sleeve of his leather shirt as she made the same pinching gesture with her other hand over her sketch of the deer, while she looked at him with a question in her eyes. The man glanced down at the sketch then looked up at her, and shook his head.

Boots reached to the pad in the man's hands and flipped to a blank page. She raised an eyebrow at him, then pointed to the page and offered him her pencil.

He accepted it and holding it lightly in his fingers as she had while doing her sketches, made a few tentative strokes on one corner of the paper. He paused as he considered their effect, then he smiled and returned the pencil to her and pulled a charred twig from the fire burning beside them. He gazed blankly at the pad for a moment then began to sketch on it with swift strokes of the twig's blackened tip.

Boots watched him intently as he drew on the pad, using his left hand as easily as his right as he stroked the paper and used the tips of his fingers to blend and shade his work. He reached over to the fire pit after several moments and selected a small lump of clay, dried and reddened by the heat of the campfire. He crushed it the fingers of his left hand and dipping his forefinger in the dust, used it to add touches of color to his drawing.

He inspected his work for several seconds then looked at Boots without expression and handed her the pad.

Boots, and Puss leaning over her shoulder, saw the likeness of a heavy-necked stag with a magnificent rack of antlers. It was expertly drawn and shaded both with the charcoal and the reddish earth. Bila had included a small stick figure holding a spear, it stood next to the animal but it was only was as tall as the animal's shoulder.

"Wow!" Puss said, "He's damm good. Wonder who the kid is tho?" Then she added, "Or is his perspective just a little off?"

"Yeah, maybe," Boots whispered while she stared at the page in her lap. Then looking up, she gazed blankly at Puss for the space of ten heartbeats until her eyes slowly widened and she whispered, "And then maybe not..."

"What!" Puss hissed, "What do you mean?"

Ignoring her friend's question, Boots flipped to a fresh page and handed the pad back to the man. She reached out and touched the woven hair belt slung around his shoulder first then one of the ivory beads on his shirt and finally she lifted his heavy boot on the ground beside her and grasped its thick leather top between her finger and thumb. She looked at him with a question in her eyes, and pointed to the pad.

Bila nodded to her and selected another charred twig from the fire.

Boots placed her hand on Puss' knee then gripped it.

"Hey kid, what's wrong? And what's goin' on?" Puss whispered in her friend's ear as she craned over Boots' shoulder to watch the man begin sketching again.

"I think we'll know pretty quick," Boots whispered as she watched Bila with an intent stare. "Now hush."

Puss felt the tension radiating from her friend, but then she became absorbed in the totality of the scene of which she was a part. The velvet black of the night, the glowing campfire softly popping at her side and releasing orange sparks to swirl upward and the three of them seated in the small circle of its light.

She rested her head on Boots' shoulder as she watched the man making his drawing, then she shivered as she was captured by a strange familiarity with the scene she was seeing, and of which she was a part.

"I've been here before!" she whispered.

Boots' only response was to hiss, "I said, hush." And to further tighten her grip on Puss' knee. The two women sat frozen for the remaining minutes while the man finished his sketch. After a quick final inspection, he handed it to Boots. She released her grip on Puss' knee and accepted the pad with both hands. She looked into his calm eyes then she took a deep breath and looked down at the open pad resting on her lap - and the blood drained from her face.

"Shat!" Puss exploded looking over Boot's shoulder, her face reddening in embarrassment as she shook free from her déjà-vu trance.

"He's pullin' some stuff on us! There's no damm elephants left anymore, and they never were any out here anyway!"

Boots ignored her friend's outburst and raised her eyes from the drawing to stare again at the man, as she searched his face for any hint of guile or hidden humor. She found nothing but open honesty, so she turned back to the page with his sketch of the stag, and tapping the small human figure he had drawn, asked, "Bila?"

She released her long-pent breath at his smiling nod of agreement, and then taking another breath, she turned back to the page with his last drawing. Boots placed her finger on the human stick figure with a spear that he had included, one that stood very small in relation to the precisely executed large animal that dominated the page. She stared again into his eyes as she quietly asked again, "Bila?"

The man smiled and nodded vigorously again in agreement.

Puss exploded, "Alright dammit!" What the hell is goin' on here with you two? Why's he drawing little people? And what do ferkin' elephants have to do with anything anyway?"

Boots relaxed and took several deep breaths then she turned to her friend, and responded calmly and carefully as she looked into Puss' wondering eyes.

"First, I do not know what is going on, but I believe that he is being truthful." Then she added enigmatically, "However if he is being truthful we are facing an impossible situation.

"Secondly, he is not drawing little people. He is drawing very large animals with himself in proper perspective.

"And thirdly, his clothing and gear appear to have been made from parts of those animals.

"Finally, you are right. There are no more elephants, "She continued in a carefully neutral and flat voice. "But he did not draw an elephant, nor did he draw a deer."

Boots looked down at the page again, with Bila's sketch of a pachyderm with a high domed head and massive shoulders sloping abruptly to low hindquarters, a coat of long hair almost sweeping the ground and enormous curving tusks.

"He first drew an Imperial Irish elk," She whispered, "And here he has drawn a very good likeness of a woolly mammoth."

"What are you saying?" Puss demanded, then gasped, "But they are all gone! Where did he get his stuff?"

"Good point." Boots responded, "But there is a larger aspect to this and to him if all of this is true, which you picked up on it this afternoon. For you see, these two animals are of the late Pleistocene glacial period. And you are right, they are all gone - but here's the problem.

"They have been gone, or extinct for about," Boots gritted slowly, as she stared into Puss' widening eyes, "Fifteen thousand years.

"But it appears that he can draw them from life..."

***

Chapter 4, The Cabin

May 2, 2276 AD
Coastal Mountains of British Columbia

Puss opened one sleepy eye and peered out into the mist-shrouded dawn from, where she snuggled on the sleeping pad against Boots as they lay together under its thin heat-conserving cover. She vaguely considered the morning while her back still nestled against the warmth of Boots' chest and thighs. She was only half awake as she began to mull over the previous day, until she remembered its series of strange events.

She gasped then sat bolt upright with her eyes opened wide, and looked at the small pile of gray ash from their campfire of the previous night. And then beyond it to the place where the man Bila had lain down to sleep, after he had caused her and Boots to first consider and then confront the impossible.

His place was empty.

She heard a muffled "Mumfph?" from behind her and she felt Boot's arm slide around her bare waist. She ignored her friend's touch and the chill on her naked shoulders and breasts, as she grabbed her pistol from beneath their cover. She looked rapidly around the camp and the area beyond its three encircling boulders.

The valley was still partially cloaked in an early morning fog, and she saw that their prisoner was still sleeping soundly under the effects of the drug she had given him. She also saw that Bila's heavy footgear was still on the other side of the fire where he had made his bed, but neither he nor his pack was in the camp.

Boots threw off their cover and jumped to her feet with her own pistol at the ready, unconscious of her nudity as she crouched in a wide-legged shooter's stance with her pistol in an action grip. Her blue eyes blazed as she looked about and her long black hair flew around her head.

Puss bounded up from their bed as well and admired the tall woman's pale body and long limbs as she said, "Hey Kiddo, it's not time to kill just yet, at least I don't think so. Anyway, the mark is still out and down, so what-say we get dressed before my nips turn into ice cubes, then we go and find tha' big guy?"

Boots, now satisfied that danger was not immediate relaxed and answered with a grin.

"Yeah, good idea. You are lookin' sorta' perky Puss-cat. Come here and I'll warm 'um up real quick."

"Save that for later dammit. Help me find my underwear instead."

"It's down at the foot of the bedroll where you left it in your fit of lust last night, or don't you remember," Boots leered as she bent and retrieved her own cat suit from the same place.

"I remember telling you to not tear them, you smokin' savage," Puss chuckled as she stepped into her briefs and slipped into her bra. Then she knelt and ordered in her best professional tone, "Anyway, turn around before you put that thing on!"

"Oooo, I must a' been a bad girl last night," Boots cooed in her "innocent" voice. She continued as she bent and clasping her ankles, waved her bottom in exaggerated invitation, "Do I get some candy after?"
"Ooww, that hurt," She gasped then, as Puss jerked away the adhesive bandage on her right buttock where it covered her dart wound.

"I WILL remain professional! And I will NOT make comments about overly full moons or other such un-lady like subjects!" Puss declared with mock severity as she prodded the site of the puncture.

"And I now find your grievous wound healed, and thus pronounce you fit to return to duty. But first," she said as she delivered a skin-reddening slap to Boots' other, unwounded buttock displayed before her.

"Ooww that hurt!" Boots yelped as she sprang erect and wheeled to face her friend, caressing her twice abused behind. "What you do that for?"

"You're repeating yourself!" Puss said primly as she stood and pulled up the pants of her jump suit. "And you had to pay for your crime you know."

"What ferkin crime? Waddy'ell you talking about?" Boots indignantly snorted as she began pulling up her own garment.

"Why what you did just now! Sweetie, you are guilty of flourishing a deadly we · wea · weapon..." Puss started to tell her friend with wide-eyed seriousness, until she sputtered into an uncontrollable fit of giggles.

Boots held her indignation for only a second, then she grabbed her friend's shoulders and the two half-clad women embraced and supported each other as they broke into roars of laughter, and released some of the buildup tensions because of their work for Boss Rat.

*

"That big som-bitch is gone, if he was ever here! And I'll bet we never see him again, if we ever did..." Boots growled in her command voice as the two women buckled on their field belts. Then a trick of the morning breeze brought the faint odor of wood smoke to their nostrils, along with a whiff of something else.

Boots glanced at the mark. He was still asleep and snoring through his slack mouth, so she looked at her friend. "Well, Slug Snott's still out anyway," she shrugged then continued, "And OK, I've been wrong before, at least once I think."

"But enough yakking! Let's see go what the ferk he's up to now," Boots growled as she stalked from their camp and toward the source of the smoke.

Puss made a rude noise, and then grinned as she followed her friend out into the misty meadow.

*

The two spotted a shadowy shape and a flickering gleam of firelight through the fog when they reached the grassy flat in the larger valley, and then Bila's leather-clad figure became clear. He was squatting on his heels by a small campfire with a strange contraption hanging over it. The two women walked to him and saw that it was a tripod of sticks supporting a small, bulging leather bag over the coals. The bag glistened with drops of moisture on its surface and had wisps of steam wafting from its opening.

"Hi Bila! What's cooking?" Puss asked with a grin as she slowly signaled in the Amerindian sign language, "Food?"

The man smiled at the two women and nodded a greeting. Then he pointed at the boil-bag hanging over the fire and shook his head. As Boots looked on from behind her, Puss signed, *"What?"* while she asked, "What's in the pot?"

The man returned her look without expression then turned aside, but as he did so, Puss caught the same fleeting flicker of a grin at the corner of his mouth she had seen the evening before.

She took an exaggerated stance that signaled "show me", by planting her fists on her hips as she frowned at him with a cocked eyebrow.

Boots assumed the same pose as her friend, but she grinned.

The man turned back to his fire and grasped a green willow wand he had whittled at its midpoint so he could fold it and use it as tongs. He fished with in the boil bag, and pulled out a bear claw.

Boots wrinkled her nose in disgust at the steaming thing and asked, "That's breakfast?"

"No, Kiddo - I think not. Just wait and watch," Puss whispered as she recalled her childhood on the Pamunkey reservation.

The man dropped the claw on the grass and removed two pieces of flint from his pouch. Then he picked up the claw from the grass where it lay cooling. He held it as he scraped the softened flesh and gristle from its base with his flint tool, then used the other flint tool to drill a hole through the base of the cleaned claw. When he finished with it and dropped it on the grass again, the two women gazed at its wicked 9-centimeter length with awe.

Bila turned to his pack and pulled out a ring of objects strung on a leather thong. They clattered as he dropped the circlet on the grass beside his new trophy. Boots started and then gasped, as she looked at his string of bear claws.

She recognized what they were, and saw and that the shortest one was longer than the one Bila had just prepared - and the longest ones were impossible...

"Do you know what these are?" Boots hissed to Puss as she knelt and examined what she saw were newly dried claws on the man's string, two of which were at least 15 centimeters long. She turned and shook the string at her friend's face.

"He could have faked the boots and the shirt and the ivory beads and the sketches," Boots snapped through clamped jaws, "But G'dammit he can't fake these!"

Then the woman went rigid and screamed aloud to the sky with glairing eyes, "These are from Ferkin' CAVE BEARS, the biggest bear that ever was! And CAVE BEARS are Ferkin' EXTINCT for the last FIFTEEN THOUSAND Ferkin' YEARS! But G'DAMMIT, these claws are Ferkin' FRESH!!!"

Boots slumped to her knees and looked up at her friend with eyes that stared blankly in wonder. She turned her awed gaze to Bila then, who was still squatting by the fire and calmly watching the two women.

Puss first shuddered, then stirred herself out of another déjà-vu reverie of the scene, like that of the previous evening while Bila was doing his impossible drawings.

She took the circlet of claws from Boots' unresisting hand and stepped over to the man sitting on his heels. She bent gracefully as she retrieved the fresh claw and untied the knot in thong holding the others. She threaded the new one onto one end of the collection, and straightening, held the string of trophies out to him, open at the level of his chin.

At his slight nod, she placed it around his neck and after re-knotting its thong, stepped to one side.

The man then rose to his feet and responding to Boots' declaration as well as Puss' instinctive ritual of acknowledgment, stood before the kneeling woman while the morning mist and while the smoke from his fire wafted around them, he proudly displayed the trophies on his neck.

Puss, standing at the man's side placed her hand lightly on his arm and gazing down at her friend, responded to Boots' last statement with wonder in her eyes, "And I truly believe he killed all of them."

Boots looked up at the two figures standing over her obscured in the mist and smoke and suddenly felt a tingling in the back of her neck.

She leaped to her feet and roared, "Enough of this crazy mystic crappo! We've got work to do!" she turned and shouted and began striding purposefully back toward their camp.

Puss looked up at Bila, and shrugged with a small smile as she turned to follow her friend. Bila collected his gear and doused the fire without showing any expression, then followed the women back to their campsite.

*

In mid-morning after the sun had burned away the mists of dawn, the two women stood in the grassy flat at the helicopter landing site again, with Bila. The trussed mark was now placed some distance away, blindfolded and his ears plugged with wads of meadow grass.

"What's the side-scan range of those heavy IR detectors in a 'copter anyway?" Boots asked puss.

"About 500 meters horizontal at 50 meters elevation, above that the image is foggy, and below that the range closes in real quick. Why you ask?"

"Because I don't like to show everything I got, ever. And I think that it's best we keep a few of our new finds on this mission to ourselves."

"Like him," Puss replied, nodding toward Bila beside them. Then she asked, "Why?"

"I don't like them giving us a bugged com-set or Wart Face's comments yesterday, and because of what Slug Snot babbled last night. They all reminded me too much of what I had already heard before."

"What's that?"

"Folks in our line of work aren't considered to be real permanent help by Boss Rat, but more like `talent' just waiting in the wings, until they give another casting call."

"What are you thinking?" Puss asked quietly.

"I'm not thinking yet, I'm just feeling. But I'm feeling that we might want to be real careful in dealing with Rat, and maybe we want to drop off their screens pretty soon anyway, before they decide to put us on-stage, in starring roles as it were," Boots replied somberly to her friend. Puss considered Boots' words for a moment, and then nodded in grim agreement.

"How much of last night's dope you think that li'l som-bitch's still got in him?" Boots continued.

"It's not all metabolized out of him yet, and if he's not been too big a doper on other stuff, the effect will be recurring for a couple of weeks."

"What happens if we give him another little snort?"

"If it's fairly small the effect comes back more often and he stays pretty flaky, but the reason won't be obvious and he won't black out, and he won't remember it anyway."

"Hmmm," Boots grunted. Then she asked with a grin, "And tell me Doctor, would that be such a bad thing to have happen, considering what he has seen and the answers he might give when Boss Rat starts probing his memory lobes?"

"Actually Professor, in my considered judgment it could be positively therapeutic, for us anyway." Puss answered in mock pomposity then she added, "Five cc's of brain fogger mix coming right up," She said with a grin" as she turned to her kit and prepared an injection for the mark.

Boots turned to the large man standing quietly, beside her. "Bila," She said, and then she raised her forearm straight up and bending her wrist, rotated her hand and open fingers as she made a "wop-wop-wop" sound. She next pointed to the sky where the helicopter had appeared the previous day. At his nod of understanding, she pointed at the morning sun overhead, and moved her pointing finger to indicate its approximate position after another hour, and repeated her helicopter sign and sound.

He immediately nodded again and pointing in the craft's direction of approach from the east yesterday, mimicked her sign and sounds, but waved his hand down to point at a position between them and stamped on the ground. Then he pointed to the mark and making a clutching motion with his hand, raised it in the air and waved it back toward the east as he again intoned "wop-wop-wop."

Boots grinned, then after pointing again toward the craft's approach direction she gripped his arm and shook her head negatively then reached up with both arms and spread her hands protectively over his head as the man glanced toward the sky. Grasping his arm again, Boots gave it a tug as she pointed then motioned walking with her two fingers toward the ridge on the other side of the valley. Then she tapped him on his arm and screened her face behind her hands as she peered through her widespread fingers before mimicking the helicopter's "whop-whop whop" sound again.

Boots motioned away with her hand as she showed its departure direction and after a moment she smiled and tapped his chest again, as she waved from the ridge back to where they stood.

The man looked at Boots and nodded, and he again gestured the air-born pickup of the mark, and continued by copying her signs showing his return from the ridge. But then he gazed at her with anxiety obvious in his amber eyes, and tapping her arm said, "Kristina?" then "Marybell?" as he indicated the young woman just rising from her ministrations to the mark, and finally, "Friends?" as he pointed to the ground.

Boots frowned for a second, then she blurted without thinking, "Why that's sweet!" and with a broad smile said, "Yeah friend, we're staying here," as she held her hand out to him.

"What's sweet?" Puss asked.

Boots blushed slightly as she said, "Well, after I told him to hide while Wart Face is here for the pickup, he was afraid we would go back with them in their 'copter."

"Nah', we don't ever leave friends behind!" Puss said with a grin as she grabbed Bila's other hand and squeezed it.

The large man smiled at the two women as he gently returned both their grips for a moment. Then he nodded and turning, he grasped his spears and his pack and loped away through the scrub willows lining the stream and toward the ridge on the other side of the valley.

"You think he understands about hiding from the `copter? And how'd you get your message across to him anyway?"

"Well, Kid, it looks like your right. Seems like he's smarter than a `clave dweller, so he can understand my Paleface signs," Boots muttered. Then she added quietly, "And it sorta' looks like he wants to be on our team."

"I vote Yes," Puss announced, in a tone that Boots knew through experience meant that her friend had taken an irrevocable decision.

"I kind of lean that way myself, Kid," Boots answered, "Because for one thing, I'll bet you rash-bars to roast beef that he's an Undoc and so won't show up on the `Clave screens anywhere. And that attribute of his might be real useful to us in our old age, if we ever get to have one."

Then her voice changed as she continued, "But my jury's still out on him - so I will not let us be suckered by some big thud, just because he acts nice!"

"Sure-sure, Buddy, but stop spattering yur' spit for right now. Just whistle up Wart Face and let's get Slug Snot sold outta' here so we can root and loot his cabin, OK?" Puss snapped.

"Ja Boss," Boots replied with a crooked grin as she retrieved her com-set from a belt pouch. Boots' grin widened at Puss' suddenly cautious look, and then she reached in another pouch and with a flourish presented its battery.

"I jerked this sucker out yesterday! First time's their fault, second time's mine," Boots growled as she inserted it into the instrument and keyed the send switch.

"Hey Rat-Catcher! Want yur' goodie?"

"Well if it ain't tha' Super Sluts. I figgered you two had quit an' gone native on me," the receiver crackled back with Wart Face's snarling voice.

"Oh no sir," Boots said sweetly, "We have just finished an internal training session in our unit, on why the Network is good to watch while doing one's laundry, and other mindless tasks."

"Watch it! Your gettin' real close to tha' line."

Boots winked Puss as she replied, "Hey, we're the best bait-catchers Boss Rat's got, and don't you forget it, O Minor Functionary!"

The receiver sputtered, "G'dammit, I'm telling ya' - you're gonna be tha' center pieces in a 5X pay-per if you don't change your attitudes ya' dumb twittos! I know a bunch more about what tha' Rat does to bait-catchers than you two ground grunts do!"

"Fact is, I bet you don't know that the families o' Rat baits get to buy vids of what happens to their catchers later, when it's their own turn at bait. So smart thing fer' the two of you is ta' be nice ta' Wart Face. Get it?"

"Yeah, that's good to know," Boots responded in a level voice, "We'll think about that a lot," as she gave her friend a grim nod. "Anyway, you want this hunk of bait `er not? We can't yak around all day, `cos we gotta' get back to our pickup zone pretty quickie."

"Ja Boss," the scratchy voice sneered, "Here we comes, to haul in a hunk o' fun!"

Boots gritted her teeth and violently started to slam her com-set on the ground when Puss grabbed her arm with equal strength, and held it until her friend regained control of her anger.

Then Puss signed, *"OK, we been bugged for a long time! Now we know. Move on."*

"You are right. But I am major mad that I not see this coming from Rat." Boots signed.

"We are staring to know things now. We know their tricks now," Puss signed, then smiling and looking directly into her friend's troubled eyes she signed.

"Don't mope. Just cope!"

Boots took a deep breath, and became her icy-hard self again, as if she were putting on armor.

"Come on in, Catcher One," she intoned into her mike as she popped another red smoke grenade in the center of the landing zone, and pulled up the hood of her suit over her long hair to keep it from the prop-wash from the incoming aircraft.

*

The black helicopter, marked with the white inverted triangle with circles at each of its points, swooped in from the east and the head of the larger valley. It circled the spot marked by Boots' smoke flare twice before slowing its blades and coming to a hover fifty meters above the pick-up zone.

Boots' com-set crackled with Wart Face's sneering voice, "Alright, what's tha' story on that force in tha' bushes yesterday?"

"Hey Big Stud, it was just a Momma Bear and her two cubs, and `cos of your totally unwarranted freak-out, we had to put them down. You want to see the bodies," she continued with cool sarcasm as she waved a hand in direction of the bears.

"I pick up two deaders `bout 50 meters from ya', but there's another fuzzy little blip on tha ridge behind ya."

"Must be the other cub, 'cos I missed it and, it got away while I was re-loading." Boots coolly responded. Then she continued, "Anyway, are you here to buy, or just vent rash-bar gas?"

"Watch yur' lip and yur' head Bimbo! Here comes tha' bait hook!" Rat Face's voice snarled out of the com-set as the 'copter descended to 15 meters above them and a pickup line snaked down from it.

The line carried a shackle holding a modified parachute harness, and a clip with a plastic credit chip. Puss steadied the line and harness over the bound mark and Boots removed the card. She examined it closely then growled into the com-set.

"No deal dammit! Our contract is for Swiss Gold Chips, not 'Clave Prom-issory Notes! So give me real money or get gone!"

"Calm yur' self, Sweet-hips, I musta' made a mistake. Here come the right card," and another light line descended from the hovering craft.

Boots gave this second card a brief glance then flicked it contemptuously away on its supporting line. She motioned to Puss and the two started to reposition the pole they had used to carry the mark.

"Hey, waddy'ell you doin'?' Wart Face squawked, "Gimme that bait!"

"I repeat," Boots gritted into her com-set, "Swiss Gold Chips, not chips on some ferkin off-shore bank on some puny island that's renamed itself Swiz-zerlant! Do you understand me? And do you really want to go back to Rat without one of their best 'puter coders?"

"WHAT! How you know that? Who told ya?" Wart Faces' voice shrieked from the com-set.

"Swiss Gold Chips," Boots repeated in a cool tone, "And no mission abort back-charge either. You want him or not?"

The light line suddenly snaked back up into the hovering craft, and without comment rapidly descended again with another square of plastic. Boots pulled a small scanner from a belt pouch and clipped the card with its embedded microchip to her instrument. After glancing at the amount and authorization indicated on its tiny screen, she re-pouched it along with the card as she nodded to Puss and keyed her mike.

"Pot's right," she said serenely, "We're hooking him up! You want to look at your fish before you reel in?"

"Nah, I gots a positive' ID on 'im when we circled. Now hump yur' bumps dammit, I'm gettin light on fuel!"

The two women knelt and swiftly buckled the limp mark into the harness and then leaped to their feet and away from his probable impact area if the cable failed. As they watched his limp body being winched up into the black helicopter Boots keyed her com-set again. She purred, "Hey Stud Guy, we looove doin' business with you. Got any more marks on your shopping' list?"

Her receiver crackled after a pause, "That's him alright, but how-come he's sleepy? What ya' got in him?"

"Just trank dart juice, but he is sorta' scrawny - the dose might a' been a little heavy, that's all," Boots answered in a cheerful tone.

"Hmmm, he better not go under 'cause that 'ud be fraud, and that's the one reason yur' fancy li'l gold chip could be revoked Sweetie," Wart Face said, but in a surprisingly mild and businesslike tone.

"Anyway, there is another one out here somewhere, a 'puter chick that's young and has white skin an' white hair. They say she's some kind'a alb-somthin'. She ran off same time he did and for some reason her price is pretty good too, most as much as this one. Ya' want a contract?"

Boots looked at Puss and raised an eyebrow, and at her slight nod responded, "The technical word is albino and yeah, we'll take a short one for a couple of days, but then we got some fun spending' to do back in the 'Clave," she finished with a wicked chuckle.

"Hey, ya could buy yur' ole' buddy Wartsy a snort 'er three, and teach me some more of them fancy words too!" his voice giggled from the com-set.

"If your nice - nice things can happen," Boots cooed as Puss struggled to keep a straight face and stifle a belly laugh. Then Boots continued briskly, "If we get lucky and find Boss Rat's little white mouse I'll give you a call, otherwise we'll catch ya' back in town. Ground Collection Unit closing down transmission," Boots finished abruptly as she clicked the com-set off and nodded to Puss.

The two women picked up their gear and started trotting toward the nose of the ridge above the mark's cabin as the black helicopter changed its rotor pitch.

Puss said with a chuckle as they jogged through the grass of the meadow after Boots had once again removed the battery from the com-set.

"You and Wartsy getting together? Hmmm, looks like yur' classic love-hate relationship is developing here."

"Yeah, he wants to looove on some parts of me, and I hates all of him,"

Boots snarled as they neared the tree line.

The helicopter's rotor beat increased behind them then it rose and tilting its nose down, gained forward speed and disappeared back up the valley to the east.

The two women abruptly stopped as soon as the noise of the craft faded away, and began retracing their steps as they discussed what they had just learned, or deduced about the Network from its loose-lipped agent.

"It's worse than I thought," Boots said quietly.

"Yeah, and let me tell you what I picked up on, then we can right brain it together."

"Hey Sergeant, If you can't left-brain and right-brain at the same time, how can you march along in this outfit anyway?" Boots said with as growl as she wrapped her arm around Puss' shoulders and gave her a squeeze.

"Well Sir, if you will back down from your pitifully obvious "Buck Up Tha' Troops In tha' Face of Dire Straits" mode I, the best ferkin' mil-psych-intel specialist ever will give you my assessment, Sir/Ma'am!"

"Buda's Butt, they're puttin' more tofu in the rations again - my troops are starting to think!" Boots said with a grin. Then as they arrived back at the `copter landing site and seated themselves on the grass upwind from the bear's carcasses, she ordered, "Alright G-2, make your report now, and make it snappy!"

"I will slowly and carefully list my findings and there will be a quiz after!" Puss said, "And if you don't understand don't be ashamed to raise your hand, Sir." After the echoes of Boots' exceedingly rude noises died away, Puss continued.

"One - their IR scanners have much more range than I thought."

"Two - their ID scanners have very much more range than we had been told and act as locators as well."

"Three - their survel systems are therefore much more efficient than we knew."

"And Four - we should probably begin to reconsider our career choice because of their functionary's braggadocio statements to you and explore other options - as you have already suggested, Sir/Ma'am."

"Very good Sergeant, I'm glad your left brain picked up the basics." Boots said, "But now let's consider the totality of the situation.

"Boss Rat gets urgent in paying big chips for a mark that ran away that he "forgot" to tell us is one of its top coders, and now we learn that Boss Rat is also looking for a little albino bimba that Wart Face tells us is a cyber chick, and names a price on her that's way too high for normal talent.

"So waddya' figure is really going on at the Rat's Nest - Miss Psycho Intel Right Brain Specialist Puss-cat?"

"Seems to me like that the Network is having difficulties staffing their coder slots, but I'm a just a ground grunt, OK. So you tell me, O' Mighty Strategic Thinker, Sir/Ma'am."

Boots snickered, "Jesu Buda, now I really gotta' bump up yur' protein ration Kid, if you can't see that it's obvious Rat is in major ferkin' trouble."

"Waddya' mean - the Network runs everything, and in all the `claves, not just S'attl! And you know that all the Mil-Govs out here are all just fronts for Boss Rat," Puss hissed between clinched teeth.

"Yeah, but what happens if all of Rat's program transmission control `puters go down, and at the same time all of a sudden?"

Puss considered for several seconds, then her eyes widened as she whispered, "Oh shat! Rat is dead in the water."

"Yep, and outta' control heading' toward one damn big waterfall," Boots chuckled. "Here's Bila," She then announced as the man pushed out of the willow scrub lining the little stream and walked in long steps toward them.

Boots waved him forward with a smile as she continued, "Now go let's go take a look at Slug Snott's nest."

*

"Alright, walk behind me while I sniff the path, and be sure to only step where I step," Puss said as she led the two from the grassy flat into the little valley and toward the mark's cabin. Boots reeled out an orange monofilament line behind them to mark their cleared path as they moved forward.

"Sniff?" Bila asked in as Puss got a signal from her instrument. She paused and stopped the other two with her raised hand.

"This," she said as she used the tip of its extended probe to carefully uncover the bright yellow trigger of a foot popper land mine.

"This?" Bila asked as he signed, *"What is?"* and squatted at her feet to peer at the little device.

"Don't touch it!" Puss exclaimed as she grabbed his shoulder.

"No," the big man grunted in reassurance as he looked up at her. He repeated, "Sniff?"

Puss wrinkled her nose and inhaled noisily through it, then said as she pointed to the tip of her probe, "This does sniff." She pointed at the little yellow trigger and inhaled again and shook her head and frowned, "This sniff bad," and gave the Amerindian sign for evil.

Bila inhaled deeply several times and then looked at the mine trigger, and nodded as he regained his feet.

"Let's us now demonstrate the true nature of this pretty li'l flower," Boots said after watching the man's reactions thoughtfully, "Take him back out of range."

"Yeah," Puss grunted, and grasping Bila by the arm lead him five meters back along their path.

Boots joined them then she turned toward the mine as she drew a throwing knife from the sheath on her belt. She flipped the knife in the air and caught it by the tip.

"This is the way I knocked these things out back in the war. My little baby's all steel so she won't get hurt." Then she hurled the knife at the mine with a practiced snap of her wrist, and hit its trigger exactly.

The mine detonated with a wicked "crack" that blew soil and tufts of grass into the air.

"OK, now lets show him the effect of that nasty li'l ferker," Boots said with a grim smile as she lead the way back to the smoking hole in the ground.

Bila squatted beside the site where the mine had been planted and examined the small crater gouged in the ground by its explosion. He sniffed at the air above it several times, then searched through the grass surrounding the crater until he retrieved Boots' smoke-blackened knife. He cleaned it on the grass, then he got to his feet and presented it to her as he said quietly, "Thank you."

Then he turned and started very slowly pacing through the meadow grass toward the cabin in the mark's valley.

Puss started to leap toward the man as she shouted, "No! Let me sniff the way first! You'll get hurt!"

Boots clamped a restraining hand on her friend's arm, "Cool back and just watch, Kid. I think your gonna see something that'll really flop your sox."

Bila paused in his careful stride after a moment and sniffed the air several times. Then he reached in his belt pouch and in one smooth motion withdrew an egg-sized granite pebble and hurled it at a tuft of grass four meters in front of him.

When the "crack" of another land mine exploding was still echoing, the man turned to the two women and asked, "OK?" as Puss gaped in astonishment.

"Score one more for tha' Big Guy, and one for tha' Boss as well," Boots murmured, "Looks like my left brain still works anyway."

"Waddya' talking about?" Puss yelled, "Stop him right now before he looses a foot, dammit!"

"Wait a bit Kiddo, and reflect upon what you've just witnessed."

"Ferk That! You let him go forward with out a sniffer, and he got a lucky hit on the companion popper to this one. Dammit, that wasn't nice!"

"He knew it was there." Boots stated flatly, as looking at the man she said with a smiling nod, "OK!"

"Look at me dammit! Waddy' ferk are you saying?" Puss hissed through clenched teeth as she gripped her friend's arms.

"I'm saying that this primitive can sniff explosives about as good as your instrument does, because he must have grown up without any chemicals around him and so had none of their odors to numb his nose, unlike us civilized suckos," Boots replied with a lazy grin. "If you don't believe me, cover his eyes and toss a pistol cartridge out in the grass, and watch him find it after sniffing another one."

"Are you really starting to believe that prehistoric crappo?" Puss hissed again, as tears suddenly glistened in her eyes.

"I have to, because of Ockham's Razor," Boots continued in a grave tone as she dropped her playful smugness.

"Who's what?" Puss snapped, "Don't get ferkin' cryptic with me dammit! Bila's our friend and you let him almost get hurt!" she gritted as she shook Boots in cadence with her words with tears now trickling down her cheeks.

Boots calmly accepted her friend's outburst, then placing her hands on Puss' shoulders she gently drew the younger woman to her breast and kissed her forehead, "You know I would cover a grenade for you if you needed it, don't you'?"

"Yes, and you know I'd do it for you," Puss sighed as she calmed herself and relaxed her grip on Boot's arms.

"Well, I'd do it for him now too, if I thought he needed help," she said quietly as she tipped Puss' chin up and looked into the young woman's still troubled eyes.

Puss suddenly smiled like the sun breaking through storm clouds as she said wonderingly, "You would, wouldn't you. Well, I would too, after..."

"Yeah, after he's already covered a ferkin grizzly bear for us," Boots said with a grim chuckle.

"Alright Sergeant," she then announced as she switched to her command voice, "You take the point with tha' big guy and back him up with your mechanical marvel as you sniff our path, but I'll bet you a back rub he finds them all before you."

"Aye Cruel Captain, you're on! But Sir, what's that stuff about razors? I thought you always used wax." Puss said with a giggle over her shoulder as she held her hand out to Bila.

"William of Ockham was a medieval monk who was a scholar and a logician. He also got in hot water a lot because he was usually right, and stubborn," Boots responded in a pedantic tone.

"He became noted for using a principle he called a Logic Razor, which he described as "Plurality Should Not be Posited Without Necessity". I can also give it to you in Latin if you're interested, my sweet."

"Not necessary Professor, I always shave in English," Puss deadpanned, "But pray continue."

"As you wish Doctor," Boots said with a brief smile. "I have found it quite useful, because it means among other things that after you remove or slice away all the unnecessary or overly-elaborate explanations for a question until only the simplest one is left that still fits all of the facts,"

Boots paused and looked gravely at her friend, now standing and holding Bila's hand and suddenly intent on her words.

"Then that one remaining explanation is the only one that is correct - no matter how improbable it may seem..."

*

They had successfully negotiated the length of the little valley, and Bila had found and detonated two more mines both before Puss' sniffer had noted them. Now the three stood before the mark's cabin and its door.

"Bet you he's got threshold poppers like crazy planted in there," Boots growled.

"Yeah, in the door and in all the windows and other places too," Puss grunted, then she said, "But how about his tunnel?"

"You think you can find his exit hole?"

"Hey Buddy, just 'cos I'm a friend, I'll let you rephrase that statement."

"Ha Ha! Fer' Buda's sake, just go on and do it, dammit!"

"Ja Boss," Puss chuckled as Bila looked on with a quizzical expression.

Boots glanced at the big man and was careful to note his reaction but said nothing except to announce in a stern tone.

"I, your Max Leader, will wait here for the two of you to successfully penetrate the objective and open the door for me. But I will also shake you down for unauthorized loot afterwards, you hear!"

"Ja Boss, sure-sure," Puss said over her shoulder as she lead Bila back down the little valley toward the spot where the mark had emerged from his tunnel the previous day.

*

"Dammit, you and your pal Ockham are right," Puss announced as she threw open the cabin door before the waiting Boots. "Your ferkin Primitive saved my cute little butt from being splattered all over Slug Snott's tunnel 'cause he picked up on a sneaky gadget that this damn sniffer box didn't!"

"So waddya' want, a hug?"

"No dammit, we got them all disarmed so it's safe for you to come in now, but I want to get even!"

"Well, you might have come to the right place, M' Dear," Boots said sweetly, then more slowly, "Yeah, we just might really have come to the right place..."

"What do you mean?"

"I don't know," Boots whispered as she stepped through the door, "But I've got a feeling that we'll find out something in here."

*

The three looked around the front room of the small cabin which was essentially bare except for a number of built-in cupboards, and a large rumpled bed made with rough-sawn timbers mounted on casters. The bed was pushed away from the wall to reveal an open trap door in the floor.

"Looks like his "romper room" to me," Boots growled.

"His what?" Puss asked.

"Doesn't his collection sort of give you a clue my darlin' Candide," Boots drawled as she indicated the array of fetters, whips and other X-rated paraphernalia displayed on the wall above the bed.

"Oh I know what they're for dammit, but what's this Candide stuff?"

"Don't worry about it Kid, that's just one of my internalized pet names for you. Anyway, let's see what's in the next room."

But as Boots was speaking, Bila stepped forward to a closed door in the partition wall of unfinished planks. He looked at it for a second, before grasping the end of the latch rod protruding through a slot in its wooden planks.

59

He held it in two fingers and gently tested its movement in several directions. Then as the two women watched in sudden silence, he slid the rod back and pushed the door open.

"I think we've just seen a first," Puss whispered, "If your friend Ockham is right."

"Yeah, maybe..." Boots replied, "But anyway for now, let's just go see what's in the other room, alright?"

"Ja Boss," Puss suddenly chuckled, "But by watchin' him open that door, we also might have seen him lose his maiden, in a manner of speaking."

"Jesu-Buda, you got a dirty mind, which I will discuss in detail with you later," Boots snorted. "But for right now, just quit impeding tha' mission with your savage lusts OK!"

*

The interior door opened into a cluttered workroom that took up most of the other half of the cabin's space. It was lined with workbenches and sets of shelves. With the exception of a small kitchen area in one corner the benches all appeared to be dedicated to various crafts. Electronics and compute parts were on one, leatherwork and clothing were on another and various tools were mounted on the third. The wall shelves above the benches held the supplies for each bench.

Boots happened to glance at Bila after a taking a perfunctory look at the interesting things, and saw that he was staring intently at a door in the end wall of the room. It was cut in a partition that reduced the size of the workroom in relation to the front room of the cabin.

"Bila," she whispered, and then as the man glanced at her, she pointed at the door and cocked her eyebrow. He rapidly pointed to her, and then Puss, then himself and then he made a sign that Puss tried to catch.

Puss signed, *"Everyone?"* He shook his head in frustration, and slowly another gesture.

"Oh," she whispered as she then signed, *"Someone?"* At that, he nodded grimly and stepped in silence to the door, and grasped its latch handle.

When he opened the door outward, light from the workroom flooded in to reveal a large closet, bare except for a pad on the floor and a covered bucket in the corner, and a small woman standing in the middle of the space, blinking in the sudden brightness. She was very young and very thin and her skin was startlingly white as was her short hair. Her eyes were the palest of blue and were staring wide with fear. She was nude except for a dark leather collar around her neck, and she was very pregnant.

She trembled as she cradled her swollen breasts with her hands, opened her mouth into an "O" and assuming a slight squat with her knees wide spread, presented herself in the age-old posture of crude sexual offering. Then her eyes suddenly flooded with tears and with a whimper she cringed and collapsed on the floor of the cramped space, curling into a ball with her hands spread over her bulging little belly. A light chain connecting her collar to a sturdy ringbolt in the wall behind her was now visible, and rattled with her movements.

"Please don't hurt me!" she sobbed.

"Please don't. Please, please..."

"What the shat?" Puss snapped as she pushed past Boots and where Bila stood in the open doorway to kneel on the floor beside the girl.

"Take it easy kid, nobody's gonna' hurt you while we're here," she said as she gave the girl's shoulder a squeeze.

"Yeah," Boots growled, "Where are your clothes? And what's that damn thing around your neck? And how'd you get your self in this fix. And what's your name anyway?"

"I'm Molly. Durwood put it on me because I was supposed to stay here and slow you down to let him get away. That's what he said I had to do."

"Hey kid, you don't have to do nothing you don't want to!" Puss said with iron in her voice. "Where's the keys to this damn thing anyway?" she continued as she slid her fingers under the heavy leather dog collar locked around the girl's neck and examined the second lock fastening it to the chain from the wall.

"Here, just cut it off!" Boots said with a growl as she drew her field knife and offered it to Puss. Then Bila suddenly spoke from behind them in a chillingly flat voice.

"Aritu nor hau?"

Puss, in the act of reaching her hand up for her friend's knife, swiveled in her position when she heard his burst of unintelligible words, and looked up at the man as he repeated his question, signing it to her with graceful hand motions that somehow she understood, "Who do this?"

"Sweet Jesu, I'm sure glad I didn't," Puss thought to herself as she looked into the stony depths of his eyes, then she gave him a slight grin and exactly mimicked the mark's shrill giggle.

The young girl huddled on the floor, cringed at Puss's voice while she moaned through her tears with her eyes squinted shut. Bila's eyes blazed and he tensed his massive shoulders - before relaxing. He returned Puss' grin and motioned with his right hand. First he pointed upward, and then he cupped the hand he held upright with fingers spread and rotated it while precisely intoning the "wop, wop, wop" sound of the helicopter. Then he drew his finger across his throat in an ancient and unmistakable gesture as he cocked an eyebrow at her.

Puss understood his signs and nodded her head as she said, "Yeah, sorta," with a crooked grin.

"He'll wish he was, anyway," Boots added as she turned to the huddled girl.

"On! Eskerrik," the man said as he showed the same grim smile as Boots. He paused and considered for a second, then looking directly into Boots' eyes he repeated in recognizable English, "Good! Bad he."

Boots blinked in amazement, and with a startled squawk of, "What," Puss leapt to her feet and spun to face the man. The chained girl cringed away from the path of the heavy knife in the young woman's hand, which caused Puss to mutter in an aside, "Don't worry kid, I know yur' there."

Boots glared at the man and snapped, "All right Bila! What'd you just say?" as Puss strode over to where he now stood in the middle of the workroom. She threw her head back and grinned up to his face, and slapped his arm with her free hand as she exclaimed, "Wow! Now you're talkin'. Gooders!" and then she added with a giggle, "But how much of what we're saying are you really picking up?"

The man's eyes sparkled with humor as he repeated himself to Boots again recognizably, "Good! Bad he."

Then with a sly grin he looked down at Puss with his eyebrow cocked and asked, "Gooders?" He nodded to her then and affirmed, "Gooders!" as he turned and switching his attention, began to examine the cluttered workbenches.

Both women were still standing with their mouths gaping in astonishment when he stepped over to a table a moment later and picked up a small bundle of doeskin. He shook out to reveal an Amerindian-style woman's outer garment. He handed it to Puss as he said, "Jantzi bera!" and pointed to the nude girl who was now sitting up on the floor with her knees under her chin and her thin arms tightly hugging her slender thighs.

Puss shook her head and muttered, "Shat! Yeah, that looks like her dress, good thinkin' guy!" She took the garment from him with one hand and stepped back to kneel beside the girl. She placed the field knife on the floor and draped the skin dress over the girl's slight shoulders, and then she grasped the knife once more.

"Here, lets get that nasty thing off of ya'," Puss said as she reached for the collar.

"Oh no! Don't cut it! He'll just whip me again!" the young girl whimpered as she tried to pull away from Puss.

"Hey kid, that mean little som'bitch is not going to whip on anyone any-more ever," Boots, snapping out of her own daze said, "Because we sold him to the Rat Catcher this morning. And Rat Bait doesn't do anything. Rat Bait is done to, at least for as long as it lasts."

"Oh," The girl said, then in a flat voice she continued, "Yes, I know," as she calmly lifted her chin and allowed Puss access to her collar. The leather parted easily to the keen blade as Puss cut away the cruel restraint.

"Thank you," the girl said quietly when the collar fell away with a rattle and she began to gently rub the ugly chafe mark from it, startling red on white skin of her neck. "But they won't kill him, you know, he's way too valu-able," she added with matter-of-fact assurance."

"We'll see," Boots said over her shoulder as she joined Bila in looking around the work room and its contents, while at the same time giving her friend a quick warning sign. Then she turned back to her investigation, as well as to keeping a wary eye on Bila.

"Oh no," the girl insisted as she rose to her feet, unconscious of her na-ked body, bulging stomach and swollen breasts. "He's their best `puter guy in `S'attl." Then she added seriously, "As long as they don't get me back."

"Yeah kid, sure. Now just how old are you and how'd you get here, and if that `puter guy is so damn good, why'd he run away from them?" Puss asked with a smile as she took the dress from Molly's shoulders and reached to drop it down over her slight frame. Molly blushed from her brow down to the middle of her chest at the young woman's gesture and her albino skin turned a red so deep that the chafe on her neck almost disappeared.

She closed her pale eyes and like a child standing before its mother, held her arms up for Puss to dress her, which the smiling young woman did. Puss gently asked the girl as the dress fell into place, "Where's your shoes kid?"

"I'm 14, and I've got some mocs over there where he tossed them under the table," the girl replied stepping around Puss and out of the closet. She stood first on one foot and then the other as she slipped on a pair of crude deerskin moccasins and asked in the same tone a child with a new toy would use, "You want to see our 'puter?"

Molly continued in a darker tone without waiting for an answer, "I used to work for him at the Rat's Nest in 'S'attl. He was their chief coder until he decided he could break away and make himself much credits by blackmailing them."

"Na'- that's no good!" Boots growled over her shoulder as she stood before an open cupboard and rummaged through its contents. "Boss Rat don't care what folks think about their stuff, or their methods, and none of those jerkos in the 'claves even bother to think anymore, anyway." Then she asked with studied casualness, "He have any guns?"

Molly ignored Boots' last question as she answered the first. "No, he wasn't going to try that, he was going to mole into their main net and screw up their pay-for-view transmissions," she stated calmly then added with childish pride, "And with me to show him how, he could do it too."

"Bango!" Puss exclaimed, "That gets the Rat where it hurts!" as she returned the field knife to her friend and started poking through the litter on one of the benches as well.

Boots sheathed the blade and looked around at the girl with sudden interest, "Yeah and hey, why don't you show me his 'puter."

"OK. Sure," the girl replied, then she suddenly paused - and froze.

"Wait a minute!" she squealed, "Shat! I remember now!"

"I've heard about you two," then in a rising voice, "You're Puss an' Boots!" Then she shrieked, "You're damn bounty hunters!"

"And you're gonna' sell me back to the Rat!" she sobbed as she turned and blindly rushed toward the door.

She slammed into Bila's leather-covered chest with an "Ooof" of expelled breath. He had spun at the sound of the distress in the girl's voice and was momentarily startled by her impact, but acting on instinct he clasped her in his protecting arms. She clung to him with her thin arms wrapped tightly around his large torso.

"Please don't let them send me back!" she cried, "Rat will cut my feet off! Please Don't! Please…" and moaning, she buried her face in his hunting shirt.

Puss looked at the tableau of the skinny young girl holding desperately on to the large man for several seconds then she spoke from her heart.

"No!" she snapped as she stepped forward and glared at Boots in defiance.

Boots was speechless at Molly's sudden outburst and Puss' equally sudden declaration, so she could only respond to her friend with a confused frown and a scowl.

Then Bila asked in a carefully flat tone, "Bera zara nahi bidaliera Rat?"

Boots turned her gaze to meet his, and his clear eyes bored into her soul as he repeated his question in the same level voice, but now in recognizable English, "You girl Rat give?"

Boots' eyes opened in astonishment, then flared in anger as she glared at him and started to respond to his unexpected question, but then she paused for a second under his compelling stare.

When Boots hesitated, Bila said in a very quiet voice which at the same time filled the room, "No."

Puss looked back and forth between the two, feeling tension that was crackling out of her friend and the calm authority projected by the man.

"Shat, Puss whispered with a shudder, "I just defied her, but that ain't no ferkin vote he's giving. He has taken the command away from her, and baby look out, 'cos nobody's ever done that to her before."

Puss gulped and tensed, as she prepared to leap between the two powerful figures in a desperate attempt to prevent violence and probable bloodshed.

Boots stood quivering and rigid. She drew herself fully erect and returned the man's gaze with a glare of blue lightening from her staring eyes. She shuddered with the effort to control her rage as she took deep breath and opened her mouth to speak...

Then she paused, and glancing around at her friend, saw the concern on Puss' face as the young woman stood with her body taut and poised for action.

Boots turned back to Bila and meet his calm gaze again as he stood caressing the cowering girl's thin shoulder. She looked into his eyes and realized after a moment that there was no challenge in them, but instead something that she could only describe later to Puss inexactly as "truth".

Boots took several slow deep breaths as she looked at Bila while she calmed her anger and gradually relaxed, then she muttered as she showed a crooked grin and stepped over to the man and the huddled girl.

"Well, they say that the sign of a true leader is their ability to lead folks, in which-ever ferkin' way those folks want to go..."

"So," she continued in a quiet tone looking down at the girl, "Don't worry about your feet kid, you are not going back to the Nest. You must be pretty hot tho'," she added as she gently placed a hand on the girl's brow, "Rat's got a big price on your little head!"

As Molly looked up with eyes that still showed some fear, Boots grinned and gently ruffled her thin white hair.

Then Boots raised her gaze to face the man who had relaxed his protective arm around the girl's shoulders. Looking directly into his eyes and still grinning, the tall woman planted her fists on her hips, tilted her head and cocked an eyebrow at him. With the language of her whole body re-enforcing her question, she asked him, "OK?"

He smiled and with the same quiet look still in his eyes, nodded. However, as Boots watched, his look changed to one of subtle mischief as he replied, "Ja, Boss," and reaching out with both hands to the astonished woman, started vigorously ruffling her black hair.

Boots at first went rigid again as his strong fingers tossed her long tresses, then with a scream of mock furry followed by a howl of hysterical laughter, she planted her fingers in his shoulder-length hair and ruffled it with maniacal glee. The man roared in laughter and redoubled his tousling of her locks, as Molly ducked and leapt away from the two very large and apparently insane people.

Puss, stunned at the sight of the two locked in their playful combat exclaimed, "What tha' Ferk? She's never let me do that to her hair!! And she really has a real heavy non-thing about men… Jesu-Buda, what tha' hell's goin' on here anyway?"

The man suddenly became aware of Boots' strong female presence close to him at the same instant she sensed his aura of primal male. They both froze and stood motionless, and looked into each other's eyes for a second without playfulness. Then they each removed their hands from the other's head as if dropping hot coals and turned apart, with brightly flushed faces.

Puss relaxed as she watched these actions and reactions of her friends, and murmured to herself, "Oh, what tha' ferk!"

She strode over to the man and smiled up into his still-confused eyes and said, "Thanks again Bila." Reaching up, she pulled his head down and gave him a long and thorough kiss on his lips. She released his mouth and after catching her breath and blushing, looked up at him again. Reaching higher, she suddenly giggled as she started vigorously ruffling his already-mussed hair.

The bemused man looked down at the young woman gleefully attacking his scalp for a second then with another howl of laughter he responded by rapidly flipping his fingers through her auburn locks.

"OK, enough o' this silly stuff Buster!" Puss growled to the man in playful severity a moment later as she ceased her attack. He instantly stopped his assault on her hair but continued to chuckle as she turned to Boots, muttering, "An' now, for tha' moment of truth!"

Puss stepped over to her friend, gazing into space and oblivious to the wild disarray of her hair and the antics of her friend and the large man. Puss reached up and pulled Boots' head down and also kissed her friend very thoroughly. When she broke away from the Boots' fervid response, Puss gasped, "Thanks, Kid! I want you to know that I really love it when you show your class like you just did."

Puss stood in Boots' embrace, and then she giggled like a schoolgirl a moment later. She reached up as she continued sweetly, "Here, let me help you with your hair," And buried her fingers in the large woman's raven locks and started vigorously tossing them like a restaurant waiter does a salad.

Boots screamed with laughter and returned the attack, flipping Puss' short hair with the fingers of her right hand while clasping the young woman to her breast with her left. She gasped, then playfully snarled, "Alright, Now you'll pay for yur' disrespect to yur' Boss!" and locking her fingers in Puss' hair, pulled her friend's head back to expose her throat and buried her face in its bright copper skin.

Puss squealed as she felt Boots begin vigorously sucking on her neck and panted, "No! No hickeys! No, No!" as she struggled to escape her friend's embrace. Boots only response to Puss' entreaty was to strengthen her hold, and growl in the back of her throat as she attacked her friend's neck even more.

"OK, dammit, that's enough!" Puss said in a stern tone then she continued contritely, "I'm sorry, an' I won't ruffle your feathers any more!"

"Promise?" Boots mumbled without relaxing her hold, or releasing the mouthful of her friend's tender skin.

"Yes, dammit! Now quit, you're makin' a mark!"

"Cross your heart an' hope to kiss a duck?" Boots mumbled again without slacking either her hold with her arms, or her mouth.

"Yes, dammit!" Puss panted as she struggled to escape.

Boots mercilessly continued her playful punishment as she grunted, "Say It! And do it, dammit!"

Puss dutifully chanted the binding oath of childhood, "Cross My Heart and Hope to Kiss a Duck!" and forcing her hand between their two bodies, crossed herself, "Now G'dammit, let-me-go!" she gritted as she tensed her body to enforce her point.

Boots suddenly released her friend and sprang back. She bowed slightly and said with a smirk as she spread her hands wide in mock humility, "But Puss-cat, I thought you wanted to play!"

Bila had watched the two women and suppressed his mirth at their antics, now he burst into a roar of laughter and stepping to them, threw an arm around each and drew them into a friendly bear hug. They were both are startled by this at first, then laughed and returned his hugs with their own.

"You guys are way strange ya' know," Molly suddenly piped. "You want to see his 'puter er' not?"

"Yeah," Boots replied as she broke away from their embrace and combed her fingers through her hair in an attempt to straighten it.

"Yeah," Puss added giving Bila a final squeeze.

He returned it - and felt at ease for the first time since he had gasped awake in the cold sea.

***

Chapter 5
The Computer

May 2, 2276 AD
Coastal Mountains of British Columbia

"What's the power source?" Boots asked where she stood looking over Molly's shoulder. The girl sat at the console of a very modern computer with a large wall mounted display.

"Old Chin fuel cells and storage batteries. There's a big bank of them in the cellar"

"What's the hydrogen source?"

"There's a biogas generator down there too, and I figured out to control it on our local net," Molly giggled. "Want to see?"

"Sure Kid."

The girl powered the computer and brought up a display showing data boxes and two video windows. She clicked one window and it opened to show a large vat with a transparent cover through which fluorescent lights beamed down at a bubbling brown mass. She clicked the second window and after a moment a microscopic view appeared that swarmed with magnified single-celled organisms.

"Hmmm, the cell count looks a little light, I think I'll bump the air and nutrient a bit," Molly muttered seriously in her high voice as she clicked on two of the data boxes.

"What do you use for nutrient?" Boots asked.

"Old rice flour. There's bunches of it around."

"I'll bet. Where did he find all this stuff?"

"He said he was moling around from the Nest one night way back when the Chin were planning' their pull-out and he found where they had listed their secret supply caches on their mil-net, and kept the info to himself."

"Sneaky," Boots grunted.

"Yeah, the Chin were real sneaks alright!" Puss added with a snarl.

"How'd he find this cabin?" Boots continued ignoring Puss' words but then nodding to her friend in reassurance, as a haunted look flashed in the woman's eyes.

"He said he found it by moling into archived survel sat images," Molly answered. Then she continued in a flat voice, "When we got here, he made me hide in some bushes up on the ridge for a day while he went down to the cabin. When he came back to get me, he said that he had made a deal with the owner for this place and for a lot of stuff.

"I never saw the owner," she whispered as she closed her eyes, "But I think I heard a gunshot when I was hiding up on the ridge."

"Durwood sounds like a real nice guy, nice and bad," Puss hissed, "But you're free of him now, OK?"

"OK," Molly sighed as she opened her eyes again, "And thanks."

"Glad to help a gal in need," Boots grinned. "What's his up-link?"

"He set the 'puter up. It's a Chin command unit he found in one of their caches, and it's hooked to six sat dishes in the loft. They beam through ports in the roof and are hooked to the server. And he's got a randomizer program in it switching the feed among a bunch of different telecom satellites so nobody can track it. And I wrote the code for the randomizer!" Molly finished with childish pride.

"So you can dig into the Rat's Network and not get tracked?" Boots asked with studied casualness, again.

"Big time, and the 'clave guv-nets as well," Molly exclaimed.

The two women exchanged careful glances.

"Want me to fire the big gun up and show ya' what I can do?"

"Sure kid," Puss replied, and Boots added in a thoughtful tone, "Yeah, Molly, lets see just what you've got here."

The young girl cleared out of the local net and entered a password, then another, then pressed her fingertip on a box that appeared on the blank screen. As the main operating system came up and the screen lighted she said, "I'll do something that's sorta' cute," as she entered several lines of code and caused the display to split and show two sections.

"The left one is Rat's 2X channel and the right one is my command display."

The left screen came to life to show a studio kitchen where a handsome young couple was presenting a cooking program, prancing around in the nude as they joyfully demonstrated the preparation of various vegetables for culinary, as well as other uses.

"Now watch this. Rat's control-booth jerkoids will think something's gone wrong on their end," Molly giggled as she swiftly typed, and several dozen lines of code appeared on the blank right screen. Then she tapped the activate key, and before the two women's watching eyes and Bila's intent stare, the attractive young couple cavorting in their kitchen began to show signs of aging, slowly at first then at an increasing rate.

Their hair turned gray and started thinning and their faces wrinkled, and they both grew fat bellies. Her breasts sagged and her thighs swelled and dimpled, while his shoulders slumped and his legs suddenly became scrawny and his teeth disappeared. During their whole bizarre metamorphosis however, the couple on the screen continued to act as they had in the beginning which only increased the grotesque of their aging.

The scene suddenly blanked out and was replaced with a message announcing "Network Difficulties". Molly giggled again as she deleted her command screen.

"Cute huh?" she said, "And my program destructs each command as it is executed, so they can never catch me."

"Yeah," Puss chuckled. "Real cute, I'll bet Rat's is just rollin' on the floor right now..."

"Yeah, major cute," Boots echoed. She nodded at Puss' smile, but her tone was thoughtful.

Bila grunted quietly, and reminded the three females of his presence. They looked at him as he leaned forward with a puzzled expression and reaching over the console, gently touched the blank display where the strange couple had pranced a moment before.

"What's the issue with him? He never seen a `puter before?" Molly asked with the bluntness of youth. Then she added in the sarcasm of a cyber snob, "Where's he been all his life, in a cave?"

The two women exchanged glances, then Puss slowly began, "Well, we're not sure..."

And Boots finished, "But yeah maybe not - and yeah, maybe so."

"Jesu, you guys are giga-weird! Anyway, want to see me do something else?"

"Yep!" Boots responded in real interest, as well as to move the conversation away from more uncomfortable questions. "How about going into the `Clave gov-net in S'attl and looking around?"

"With one hand! But why don't you ask for something with real task?" the young girl jeered with a smug grin.

"OK little Miss Geekoid, mole into the Army mil-net and get me a status and position on all the Mark VII armored carriers they have deployed in the west, and where their depots are located. That is, if you think you can handle a simple little task like that," Boots replied, with a carefully straight face, while Puss grinned and Bila watched all three.

"Can a Chin cook rice? Just watch me!" Molly exclaimed as she swiveled her chair back to the console and began rapidly stroking its keys. Under her flying fingers the right screen filled with lines, and then pages of code. She paused, and slowly back-scrolled her entries as she stared at the screen and checked each line. After 10 minutes of intense concentration, she finally straightened her hunched back and briefly flexed her fingers, then tapped the activate key.

"This will find how their net is strung and where their servers sit," she whispered as the left screen started to display lines of data, at first haltingly then with greater speed. The display filled several times, then paused and blinked momentarily until a bright query line blinked on the screen.

"Bango!" Molly squealed, "It's saying, "Hello!""

"You got that right Kid," Boots murmured, with respect in her voice as she recognized the mil-net query as one she had used in her company command three years ago before the Chin War abruptly ended. "And I'll bet ya' a brass Buda they're still using the password I had back in the war."

"Don't tell me! I can find it!" the young girl yelled, as she began keying the console so rapidly that her fingers seemed to blur, and filled the right screen several times over with new code. She typed "Run" and tapped the activate key again.

"This will make it tell us how many passwords there are and what they are, and who has them," she muttered as watched the display. Several seconds later, the right screen responded to her command, and the word "Running" appeared at the bottom and began to blink.

The three women barely breathed as they watched the display, inactive except for the pulsing word. Then the screen filled with a neatly arranged outline showing command levels and names, and their assigned passwords.

"Those lazy bastards!" Boots snapped as Puss gasped in amazement, "I knew they wouldn't change my password after I got out. It's still the same, Redwood3030!" Then she said with a growl, "Here Kid, let me at those damn keys."

Molly rose smiling in triumph and offered her stool to Boots with exaggerated courtesy.

Boots grinned in return and ruffled the girl's hair again as she seated herself at the console. She peered at the list on the right screen. "Hmmm, I think I'll be Col. Kink.," Then she said over her shoulder, "Nah, I can't be her. You just put her in the body shop didn't you Buddy?"

"Sure did," Puss answered with a cheerful grin.

"OK, I'll be Guns then," as she pointed to the name of the Lieutenant Colonel in charge of the ordinance in her regiment, "How do I get to the left screen?"

Molly showed her the commands, and Boots entered a name and a password at the left screen's patiently blinking cursor, and then a string of commands and queries. She waited calmly while she ignored the others watching over her shoulders, and breathing down her neck.

The display blinked after several moments, and then filled with a colored three-dimensional satellite image of an area covering what used to be the states of Oregon and Washington, the Province of British Columbia and the southern part of Alaska. It was sprinkled with clusters of glowing red dots.

"Wow!" Puss whispered in awe as she considered the reality of what they had just done.

"Mega-cools!" Molly squealed, bouncing up and down with childish joy.

"HA!" Bila grunted in triumphant discovery, as he suddenly realized that the objects the girl and Boots had been using were merely another way of dreaming. Intent on the aerial landscape displayed on the left screen, he didn't notice Boot's startled glance at him.

*

"Alright Kid, there's no force close to us right now, so lets talk serious about you," Boots said matter-of-factly as they sat outside the cabin in the warm sun on a patch of grass, which Molly had assured them was not bobby-trapped. "When are you due?"

"In a couple of months, maybe, I think."

Puss said gently, "Molly, I'm a medic. Let me examine you and do a test."

"Good idea Sergeant. Looks like we need some hard intel on this subject," Boots chuckled as the young girl's eyes widened.

"I can do a quick check right now," Puss announced as she removed the tube of a field stethoscope and a small black instrument case from the med kit in her pack. "But I need a specimen," and she offered a tiny glass vial and a disposable funnel to Molly.

The young girl looked in confusion at them for a moment then raised her eyes as her cheeks reddened.

"Hey, it's no biggy, OK! Let's go inside and I'll help you," Puss smiled as she got to her feet and offered her hand to the young girl.

"So, what do you think Bila?" Boots asked idly after the two had stepped into the cabin.

"What?" he replied as he looked at her with a question obvious on his face, and mimicked Molly's typing motions with his fingers.

"Computer," Boots answered with clear enunciation.

"Computer." he repeated accurately then asked, "Computer far see?"

Boots frowned for a moment, then the reality of what the man had just said sunk in, as did her recognition of the quantum intuitive leap he had made in order to ask his question.

Her eyes first widened in disbelief, then collecting herself, she responded in a careful voice, "Yes, computers see far," as she stared at him with mixed wonder and suspicion.

"Good," and looking at her, he first mimicked sleep by tilting his head and resting his cheek on both hands and briefly closing his eyes. Then he moved his hands and arms in expressive gestures over his head for several seconds before bringing them swiftly back to his sleep position, and pretending to waken in fright. Then he shook his head in violent negation, "Bad!"

Boots mimicked his gestures and said, "Dream," then she asked, "Bad?"

The man smiled, and said in clear English, "Computer far see. Good! Dream far see. Bad."

Boots considered Bila's statements for a moment, until she grasped his thought, and what he had just revealed about himself.

"You're a Dreamer, a real flippin' Dreamer..." she whispered as Puss and a beaming Molly stepped out of the cabin door.

"According to what her hormone levels tell my colorimeter, it's coming in two months, and the stethoscope says her little egg is healthy as a horse, and who's dreamin'?" Puss said as she and the girl re-seated themselves beside the two. She glanced at her friend's wide eyes and strange expression, and added, "Hey Buddy, maybe I had better examine you too, huh!"

Molly ignored the three adults as she smiled, and gently stroked her belly, "I heard its little heart beating!" she murmured.

"You told me about the Plains Tribes and their Buffalo Dreamers, remember?" Boots said to Puss while she smiled at the sight of Molly - now aware of the new life growing in her.

"Yeah, and I said that it would be handy sometimes if we could do that now, but I was only kidding."

"I know that," Boots replied as she continued to watch Molly, "But tell me again how they did it."

"They took a mixed dose of natural alkaloids and other substances that were mind expanders and intuition enhancers for the right brain, we think. This caused them to have predictive visions showing where the herds were located, generally as though the dreamer was soaring up in the air.

"But the ones who did the dreaming never passed on the exact mix of botanicals or the amounts, and the knowledge died out anyway when the buffalo were all gone," Puss answered in a dry voice.

"Then Solder Blue put all the buffalo hunters on reservations and turned 'um into drunks," she finished in sudden bitterness.

"Bila just told me that computers are better at far-seeing than dreams, and are safer."

"Oh sure!" Puss said, then as Boots gazed at her without further comment Puss blinked and her eyes widened as she blurted, "What! What did you just say?"

Boots answered, "Why don't you ask him yourself?"

Puss gestured slowly in her fumbling Amerindian sign language, "Do you dream animals?"

"Yes," Bila responded quietly aloud, and continued, "Dream bad. Far see bad!" Then he added firmly, "Computer good. Far see good." Puss shook her head, and her eyes widened in surprise at his statement.

"Congratulations Marybell, you recognized his capabilities long before I." Boots announced with the formal precision she used when discussing such matters with her friend.

"What do you mean?" Puss asked as she turned in her confusion from the man and frowned.

"I now am forced to believe," Boots said, "That not only does he appear to be a highly skilled hunter of extinct animals and has physical attributes that are absent in humans today, but that also he has the ability and knowledge to do a simulated out-of-body predictive trance, and he knows the correct botanicals to use.

"Finally, I believe as well that he has just grasped the overall concept of the uses of computer database outputs and their manipulations and satellite imaging, after watching us for only about thirty minutes when Molly demonstrated her skills. And after doing that, he has compared our computer outputs to his type of dreaming and decided that it is similar but better and safer."

Boots then asked her friends in a quiet voice, "So Doctor, how do you measure an intel like that?"

Puss took a deep breath and glanced at Bila, sitting cross-legged on the grass and watching them. She then looked at her friend and whispered as she slowly shook her head, "You don't Professor. In my experience with cases like this you just admire it."

"And just what other cases like this have you had, Doctor?" Boots asked with mock professionalism and a slight smile.

"Just one actually," Puss answered with grave sincerity as she gazed directly at her friend, "You."

Boots looked at Puss with eyes that suddenly were shining, and shaking her head wordlessly she smiled and squeezed her friend's hand.

"By the way Professor," Puss continued with a twinkle in her eye, "I also note that you have stopped screaming at his revelations and shouting about your findings and deductions as well."

"Yeah, I decided it wasn't real professional – and I was starting to get hoarse anyway," Boots sighed with a crooked grin and a slight catch in her voice as she squeezed her friend's hand again.

Bila spoke suddenly, in a careful and pleasant tone, "Intel what?"

Boots shook her head and grunted, "I think you're gettin' your answer," as Puss started, and ignoring her friend answered the man with a correction.

"What IS intel." She then continued, "Intel is," as she signed, *"Inside"* and tapped her own head then Bila's and Boots', and finally that of Molly sitting on the grass beside her, smilingly absorbed with her belly and ignoring the confusing adult conversation around her.

Bila considered Puss' statement for a moment, then smiled as he announced, "Intel is awake dream."

"Well that ain't bad for a workin' definition I'd say," Puss chuckled," then turning to Boots she continued, "What question - and what answer?"

"The one you asked back inside, about how much he's picking up, an' how much of what we say does he understand," Boots replied.

"I didn't think you heard me. What do you think?"

"Kiddo, I hear everything, and now I'm starting to think that he does to... "So Bila me boy," Boots said with a brilliant smile as she turned to him, "I guess we better start workin' on your `DEF's."

"DEFs?" both Puss and the suddenly aware Molly squawked in confusion, until Puss chuckled, "Oh, I get it..."

"Yeah," Boots said as she reached over and gave Bila a playful slap on his shoulder, "Ya' Big Thud, you've already figgered' out our ferkin' ABCs!"

*

"All right Molly you're due in two months, in July," Boots said to the girl sitting on the grass across from her. "Who lives around here that can help you when it comes?"

"I don't know, not many I guess. There's some militia guys living two valleys over to the east, but they don't do much except grow hemp and run their still for rotgut. Some of them snuck over once, but ran into a couple of Derwood's foot poppers and went back home real quick."

"And there's a bunch over the ridge to the west, with a `puter he could link to without being tracked," Molly continued darkly. "Some of them, the guys anyway, came over once and got out of their heads with him while they watched some 4 and 5X vids he had downloaded..."

"And?" Puss asked gently, sensing distress in the young girl's voice.

"And then they acted them out on me," Molly moaned, as she sobbed and buried her face in Puss's shoulder.

"Why didn't you take an abort pill?" Puss asked.

"I didn't have one, and he wouldn't get me one. He wanted to watch it come - with his friends," she whispered through her tears.

"Then what were they going to do?"

"I don't know - but something bad I think," the girl whimpered as she shuttered and clung to Puss.

Puss wrapped her arms around Molly to comfort her and Boots leaned forward and stroking the young girl's shoulder, asked quietly, "Got any idea who fathered it?"

"Yeess," Molly sniffed. "There was a young one, an' he didn't get out of it, and he didn't do anything bad to me like the rest of 'um did. He tried to stop them, until they hit him a lot and tied him up. But he got loose after the others were all doped out, and then he cleaned me up - and he was gentle..."

"He can live then," Boots said in a flat voice. "If he takes care of you — and if you want him."

"Hu-hunh," the girl nodded with her face still buried in Puss' breast.

"Look Molly," Boots continued in the same tone, "I learned a long time ago when I was about your age, that if your still alive after something like this is over the best thing for you to do is figure how to kill those that did it. So you do as a very wise woman told me a little while ago, don't mope - just cope'."

Puss smiled and nodded at her friend over the young girl's head, but Molly still clinging to Puss and bawled, "I don't know how to kill anybody and I'm not strong like you! I just can't do it," and she broke into deep wracking sobs.

The two women looked at each other in helpless concern until Bila leaned forward and first gently touched the chafe mark on Molly's neck, then brushed his fingers across her back. He asked, "Mark?"

Boots replied perfunctorily, "Yes, it's a mark from her collar, you saw it already."

"Yes, it's from the mark alright," Puss interrupted and pointing to the girl's neck gave a quick giggle like Durwood's.

The man looked at both women for a second, then shook his head as he pointed to the girl's back again and repeated his question, "Mark?"

Puss grasped his thought finally, "Yes, she has whip marks," she said as she stroked the now sobbing girl's back and hips.

Bila nodded and bounding to his feet loped off into the forest across the meadow from the cabin.

"G'dammit, they're foot poppers out there! Stop him!" Puss cried.

"How?" Boots grunted.

The two women exchanged glances of exasperation and shook their heads, and waited. Puss continued to hold and comfort the quietly weeping girl as she said, "Its OK kid, that rat's really gone now," as she patted her shoulder, and glared over Molly's head at Boots.

Bila trotted back into the grassy flat with a large armload of firewood some moments later. He dropped it on the ground and after rapidly scraping a fire pit in the sod with the end of a branch, knelt and started a fire by striking sparks into the tinder again with his pebble and pyrite lump. The man stoked his fire and soon had it to a bright heat as the two women watched with curious eyes. He nodded at the fire in satisfaction after several moments and rising, strode to the cabin.

"G-dammit, what tha' hell is he doing now?" Boots exploded as Bila entered the building.

"I don't know, but I figger' we'll find out pretty quickie.

"He hasn't kept us waiting for long yet," Puss snapped as she continued to hold the young girl to her breast, and to frown at her friend.

They heard a faint crash from inside the cabin, and Bila stepped through its doorway a moment later. His arms were now loaded with the whips and fetters and other devices from the wall of the cabin's front room, and the collar and chain that had held Molly captive in the closet dangled from one fist. The other end of the chain dragging behind him was still attached to the large ringbolt but now was snapped halfway down its shank.

Bila strode to the fire and dropped the collection beside it, then turned to the three women sitting before the cabin. He walked to Molly, and dropping to his knee, grasped one of Molly's hands clutching at Puss' shoulders. He silently urged her to rise, and she did after receiving a reassuring squeeze from Puss.

Bila led her to stand with him above the collection on the ground by the fire. He bent and selecting the cruelest whip in the pile, handed it to her. As she held the instrument of her pain, the big man smiled grimly and hissed through his clenched teeth, "Gaitz!" and clutched his stomach and mimicked illness. Then he gestured for her to throw it in the fire. Molly grimaced also, and then she dropped the whip into the flames.

The man handed her another whip, which she also added to the fire as she began to smile. Then he methodically handed her the rest of the perverse instruments one by one, and gently patted her shoulder as she incinerated each of them.

When the last one was crisping in the blaze and emitting foul odors of burning leather and plastic, Molly suddenly turned to Bila and stretched her arms up around his neck. She hugged him as she whispered into his chest, "Thank you, thank you, thank you..." He remained silent while he held her tenderly in his arms and stroked her head, and looked sadly off into space.

Puss whispered, "Wow, he just dumped her demons big-time. How do you think he knew to do that?"

Boots murmured to her friend, "And if you'll notice Buddy, he never asks before he acts..."

"What you mean?" Puss asked with a puzzled look.

"Remember what you told me last night when he fed us? Which I sure hope does again by the way."

"You mean about it being ritual?"

"Sort of, but you said he was doing it like a leader."

"Oh, yeah I did. So?"

"Kiddo, this guy is a leader," Boots said in a quiet voice. "He is used to taking care of his people when they need, it but he knows to leave them alone when they don't. He's also used to quickly figuring a situation and taking the correct actions, but mainly it's obvious he's used to being the top authority and accepting the full responsibility for his position."

"How do you know all that?" Puss hissed as Bila lead Molly back to where they sat on the grass in the warm sun.

"I look, and listen, and think. Try it sometime," Boots muttered under her breath as she rose and put a friendly arm around Molly's shoulders. "Feelin' better kid?" she smiled.

"Yeah, a lot," the young girl sighed.

"Good," then looking gravely up at the big man and deep into his eyes, Boots took his hand in hers and clasping it in a very strong grip, said, "Thank you."

He returned her handshake with gentle firmness and smiling briefly to her, nodded without a word. Then he stepped back and looked at the sky, and the sun past its peak overhead.

"Food," He said in a stern voice as he pointed to Molly's belly.

Puss leapt to her feet and the two women began a happy chant, "Yeah - food! Real food! Real food! Real food!" and playfully clapped hands and stamped their feet in time with their words, and caused the man snort with laughter.

Molly giggled at their antics, and said, "Hey! We've got a big bunch of rash bars inside; want me to get us some?"

Bila, hearing the words, " rash bar" sternly shook his head, and Boots wagging her finger the girl in mock admonishment growled, "See here young lady, we said real food, not that `Clave crappo!"

"But that's all I've got." Molly whimpered, suddenly crestfallen.

"No it's not!" Puss said as she gave the girl a hug, "You, and we have a great big buddy who knows what tha' ferk real food really is!"

"You got that right Puss-cat" Boots added as she gave Molly's hair another friendly ruffle. Then the two women looked at the man with exaggerated anticipation as they resumed their soft chant, "Real food! Real food!"

Bila laughed aloud and stepping to them, swept all three females to his chest in a brief hug as he chuckled, "Real food!" Then releasing the two grinning women and the startled girl, he asked in a pleasant tone, "Berri suti eraiki?" as he signed *"Make new fire?"* and pointed to a place closer to the cabin where they were sitting.

Puss understood his signs somehow and responded with a happy grin, "Yes Sir! New fire coming right up," as she stepped to the pile of wood by the fire he had started for Molly's therapy, and began loading her arms.

Boots watched her friend's actions for a moment then shouted, "Why does he want another flippin' fire? Just stoke that one up again and don't waste time dammit, I'm hungry!"

"We can't use that one, it's still too full of Durwood's sicko spirit for us to ever cook on," Puss answered with a snap.

Bila nodded to her, and stepped where his weapons leaned against the wall of the cabin. He untied and dropped his belt and pouch, and shedding his leather shirt and leggings, striped to his breach clout. After re-tying his belt around his waist and retrieving the braided line from his pack, he removed the circlet of bear claws and stowed it carefully in his pack.

Then he grasped his two light spears with his throwing stick, and trotted across the meadow and up the ridge across from the cabin.

Boots made a rude noise as she flopped back down the grass and leaned against the wall of the cabin.

"Shat," she grunted, "I'm surrounded by ferkin Stone-age Mystics! `C'm here and talk to me Molly," she added as she patted the grass beside her. "I think you and me are the only two left in the whole damn world that ain't off our tracks total!" she finished with a grin.

Puss had knelt and began laying a proper cooking fire then looked over her shoulder at the now thoroughly confused young girl.

"It's OK Molly," she said, "I promise that I'll always tell you when the Boss gets serious grumps. Like the time she took out a whole Chin patrol column with flame grenades because their advance guard broke in on her field shower one morning. When she concluded that li'l action she finally got around to putting her clothes back on. The folks in her command started calling her Captain Cook after that, sometimes to her face even.”

“How'd you know about that?” Boots snorted with a grin.

”Hell, tha' whole damn Army knew about it almost as soon as you did it!”

“So Molly,” Puss continued, “My Buddy can be real instructional some times, but she's being nice right now. Aren't you?” the young woman suddenly snapped at her friend.

“Ja Boss,” Boots smiled and nodded, then she patted the grass beside her again, and Molly tentatively seated herself next to the black-haired woman with the deep blue eyes.

“It's OK Molly,” Boots gently continued, “Now talk `puter to me.”

The young girl gradually relaxed as she settled in the grass and said innocently, “He really is big, isn't he.”

Both women gurgled as they tried to restrain their laughter, then while Puss sputtered helplessly, Boots gasped, “Uh - yeah. You're right. But for now, just tell me about your randomizer program again, OK.”

*

Bila appeared three quarters of an hour later at the edge of the forest across from the cabin. He paused for a moment and perfunctorily hurled a stone from his belt pouch. Another small land mine detonated and he continued walking toward the cabin.

Puss exclaimed when she saw this, “Jesu Buda, Buddy! What can we do to keep him safe?” Boots replied as she watched the man's progress.

“Nothing kid. Abso-ferkin'-lutley nothing...”

Bila walked to the three women where they still sat in front of the cabin and despite the fact that he has just trotted up and back down a mountain spur, he was breathing easily. He dropped his burdens, the carcass of a small doe and a large bundle of wild greens tied with a length of vine.

He nodded to them as he leaned his spears against the cabin wall again then he lifted the deer back on his shoulder and carried it to a tree across from the cabin. While the three women watched, he tossed his braided line over a low branch and tied it to the deer's forelegs, and after hoisting the carcass up to working height, eviscerated and skinned the animal with practiced hands. Then he separated the liver from the entrails and using the flayed hide as a ground cover, placed the organ on it.

He walked back to where he had laid his pack by the cabin as the three women watched, and rummaged in it with a bloodstained hand for a second, before pulling out his skin cooking bag.

"Molly," Puss hissed, "You got a kettle in there somewhere? Quick!"

"Yeah, but Durwood didn't like to use it on the hot plate 'cos it drained the power cells some."

"Whatever. Tell me where it is an' I'll get it quick-like!"

"In a space under the hot plate, but I'll get it!" the young girl said eagerly as she struggled to rise.

"No," both women exclaimed in unison, then Puss added with a smile, "You sit, I'll get," as she pressed Molly back down on the grass.

Puss bounded to her feet and rushed into the cabin, to return a moment later with an aluminum Chin field kettle. She showed it to Bila as she carefully signed, *"Water?"* He looked at her, and then at the kettle. Then he reached over and touched it, and flipped it with his finger. When he heard its "ping" he nodded and with a grin motioned Puss toward the head of the valley.

"What's he mean?" Puss asked over her shoulder to Boots and Molly.

"Go to the spring and get some water," Molly responded with a giggle.

"What spring?" Puss snapped, suddenly irritated.

"The one up there, where he's pointing, Silly!" Molly piped, "Want me to show ya' where it is?

"There's no foot poppers out that that way, so don't worry."

"How' in hell does he know that there's a spring up there anyway?" Puss snapped again.

"Because he just does, that's his job," Boots said in a quiet tone, "So cool yur' tubes and just do what he says."

"Waddy'ell are you saying? And what's this, do what he says, crappo anyway?"

"I will tell you once again," Boots said in a crisp tone. "Do what he says because I have passed the con to him for now," then she added with a crooked grin, "But only for the short term of course, until he feeds us again."

"What?" Puss sputtered in confusion.

"Dammit, just do it! Go get him the ferkin' water. OK!"

Puss said nothing, just grabbed the kettle and charged headlong up the valley toward its head. When she reached it she found that a clear spring did indeed gurgle gently from a crevasse in a rock outcrop. After it spilled into a natural mossy basin, the little stream overflowed and disappeared again under the soil of the valley floor.

Puss tasted the water from her cupped hands, then she filled the kettle and began striding back to the cabin with her head down and seething in anger, until she glanced up and saw Bila coming to meet her.

He took the pot's handle and lifted its weight from her fingers as looked at her and said, "Thank you." He smiled as he continued, "Amaldeko Kris," while signing, "Kris is mother."

Puss broke into a wide grin as she understood his meaning and slapping his arm as she took the kettle back from him, exclaimed happily, "You got her right, Big Thud! Now let's just go cook!"

Bila led her back to where the deer was hanging, and first held out the liver then the haunch and finally his hands for her to clean by pouring a slow stream of water from her kettle. She did this without thinking and without any communication from him. He bundled the cleaned meat in the hide and trimmed several green branches from the tree before starting back toward the cooking fire.

She followed him, shaking her head and asking, "Now how 'n hell did I know to do that?"

When they reached the fire he took her kettle and handled cautiously at first. Then as he grasped its character, he used some of the water in it to wash his bundle of wild purselane, chickweed and dandelions. He also washed a few wild onions and a handful of fresh morel mushrooms before putting all into the remaining water in the pot. He added a large pinch of ash from the fire and placed the kettle on three cobbles he had arranged at the edge of the glowing embers.

Puss watched him a moment, then picked up the aluminum lid for the pot that she had laid aside. She smiled at Bila and placed it on the kettle as a partial cover. He looked at her and considered what she just did for several seconds then he nodded with a slight grin and with a look in his eyes that showed respect.

Puss suddenly blushed like a schoolgirl receiving a complement from her teacher.

Boots sat watching Bila and her friend from where she still lounged against the wall of the cabin with Molly. She jeered in mock outrage, "Hey, are you two gonna cook 'er just sit around and ferkin look?

"Remember the rest of us, OK? We're hungry G'dammit!"

Puss blushed a deeper red, then turned and she poked at the fire with a stick until she recovered her calm. She snorted after a moment in a theatrical aside.

"Hey Bila, did ya' ever notice how them that can do it just do it, and them that can't always want to boss?"

The man looked around at the three women for a moment then he chuckled and shook his head before kneeling and beginning to prepare the meat. Boots and Puss exchanged quick looks, then grinned and shook their heads in turn about their strange new friend.

Puss moved to kneel at Bila's side and offered him her field knife for slicing. He accepted it with a nod and in turn offered her the mark's boot knife and the green branches with a smile.

When she realized what he wanted, the young woman plopped down cross-legged and started peeling and trimming them into spits for the meat he was slicing from the haunch. They rapidly prepared three filets for grilling between themselves, then as Bila planted the butt ends of the skewers in the ground, Puss asked, "Molly?"

The man smiled and started cutting a portion of the liver into bite-sized cubes that he quickly skewered on one of her peeled branches, interspersing them with thin slivers of wild onion. As he held that loaded branch he said, "Molly Ama," as he signed *"Mother."*

He reached to Puss and gently touched her flat belly as he nodded in the young girl's direction. Then he rose to his feet and retrieved one of the skewered filets, and motioned for her to bring the other two as he stepped back to the fire.

"Oh I get it, mommy food!" Puss exclaimed as she followed his lead but then asked, "Me?" as he motioned for her grill the two fillets she carried. She smiled with pride when he nodded, then watched how he did his cooking and its timing. She also remembered what she had learned in her youth of reservation, and copied his method exactly.

Boots joined the two, as they knelt down side-by-side, intent on their cooking. She squatted behind them and said with a grin as she squeezed each of their shoulders, "Sure hope there's some Krissie food on the menu too!"

Puss kept her eyes on her task but chuckled as she said in a mock aside to Bila, "Don't worry Big Guy, if she's non-lethal when she makes body contact with you she's really just being polite and saying, "Please," in the only way she knows how..."

"Yeah, and the Kid here will squat by the fire with any ole' Big Thud that comes along and saves her life and feeds her real food, right, Sweetie?" Boots grinned as she ruffled her friend's hair.

"Hey, that stuff's starting to smell really good!" Molly suddenly piped in an astonished little voice.

Puss looked over shoulder at the girl and asked, "You got any plates or bowls in there, Kid?"

"Yeah, an' I'll go get them. You're doing the cooking, and I want to help," Molly said eagerly as she struggled to her feet and looked at the three adults with pleading eyes.

Puss was opening her mouth to object when Boots flashed a brilliant smile at the girl.

"Why thank you Molly. That would be a great help to us!"

Puss saw the girl's joy at being included. She added, "Yep, it sure would," as Molly went into the cabin.

Bila smiled. He said to Boots, "Amaldeko Marybell," and motioned to Puss with his head.

Puss blushed, and Boots sensing a story asked, "OK you two, what's going on? What's he saying'?"

Puss snapped, more in irritation at herself than at her friend, "He says that now I'm the one being a mother!"

"And just who did he say was being that way before?" Boots growled ominously as she slowly moved her fingers into the man's thick hair and his shoulders shook in silent laughter.

"Save it for after we eat," Puss said in a stage whisper, "Then when he's fat and sleepy, we can sneak up on him an' take our dread revenge!"

"But what if we're fat and sleepy too?" Boots grunted, as a smiling Molly stepped out of the cabin with four Chin mess kits clattering in her hands.

*

"It tastes good! I can't believe it, it tastes so good!" the young girl sputtered through her full mouth. "And the weeds are good too!"

Puss briefly interrupted her sensuous pleasure with a mouthful of crisply grilled venison to grunt, "Real food."

Boots just growled as she chewed contentedly and Bila ate in silence, with a peaceful expression on his face.

*

"Al'right troops," Boots sighed as she sat upright from leaning against the cabin wall, where she had dozed in the warm noon sun for several minutes after her meal. She paused then emitted an impressive belch. "Time to talk," she continued with a pleased look.

"About what Mommy," Puss asked in wicked innocence from where she lolled on the grass.

"I'll Mommy you with a switch if you don't snap to Trooper One!" Boots grinned. "Now pay attention. We've learned a lot today and we've had a chance to play with our new friends and to eat..." Boots paused and pointing her finger cued Molly.

"Real food," the girl sighed with a dreamy look.

"Correct Trooper Two! And I'm hopeful that our new Trooper Three in charge of G-7 will continue to perform at the level we've now come to expect," as she nodded to Bila.

"G-7? There ain't no G-7 dammit! What's this G-7 stuff?" Puss exploded in a semi-serious voice.

"There is in this outfit, Kiddo. G-7 is the military function of "just doing what needs to be done", and Bila fills it pretty damn good don't you think?" Boots said as she looked at the man sitting, and quietly watching them all.

"He knows what you're saying, I can feel it," Molly suddenly piped from where she laid on her side next to Puss.

Bila looked at the girl and to her delight, winked. Then he turned his gaze to Boots and said, "Ja Boss."

"G'dammit here's another one I can never underestimate again," Boots said with a growl as she turned and gave Puss a quick smile. Then she continued in her command voice, "Alright, enough back talk! You troopers will only answer questions and give information when called upon, get it?"

At their nods, which ranged from fearful to calm according to their body mass, she continued.

"Molly, how long did you work in the Rat Nest and how long ago did you cut out from there with your good friend Durwood whom we just sold to them this morning? You get a cut of his price by the way because of your hospitality."

"I worked for them for two years, and we made our run a year ago. And like I told you, I don't think he was my friend..."

"Smart troops, do I ever like Smart Troops!" Boots said with a smile to the girl. "Anyway, you started with them when you were only eleven so you really are cyber-hot! Did they give you a physical when you started, and did they give you any shots?"

"Yeah, and I remember they gave me one that really hurt. And it still tingles sometimes."

"Where did they stick you kid,"

"In my bottom, right here," the girl responded in a little voice as she pointed to her left hip.

"Alright! Credits to Chin script, they poked a homing implant in you and now we know Durwood had one too. That's how Rat could send us so close to your place here.

"We have to go back to S'attl for a while now that you have the necessary backup to be safe here. But we'll come back for your blessed event or maybe before even and we just might stay for a while then and play a new game.

"But right now to make a real bad pun, Puss has to pull your butt bug, OK? Otherwise Rat will find you before we get back and then you really will be walking on stumps," Boots said with a serious face as she patted Molly's shoulder.

"What!" Puss squawked. What are you saying? What the hell you doing? G'dammit!"

"Did you listen to what I just said, Trooper One?" Boots grinned.

"Yes I did, G'dammit, but how'd you come up with these ideas? We haven't talked yet," Puss sputtered.

"Sorry Kid, but we got to get moving now that we've had our fun and established some new relationships as it were. And you know what I know, so if you have another plan that fits all the parameters, speak out," Boots said as she squeezed Puss' hand.

Puss glared at her friend for a second and considered Bila and Molly for a long moment. Then she sighed and grinned back to Boots, "Your right – again, G'dammit. I'll get my kit."

*

"Alright Molly," Puss said, "Hike your dress up and lay across my buddy's legs, the light's better out here and I will numb you so you won't feel anything, OK?"

Molly tremblingly complied, and lay face down across Boots' thighs as she spread them to accommodate the girl's swollen belly. Boots leaned against the cabin wall and stroked the Molly's head with a gentle hand as she said, "Don't worry, I've let her work on me too, and haven't had to kill her yet."

"If you make me snort I might miss my cut and maybe hit a bystander," Puss murmured as she seated herself at Molly's other side and bent over the girl's small pale bottom, and began by examining the girl's left buttock, and, probing at it gently.

"Ha! Found the scar," Puss muttered after a moment.

"This will sting for a second, and then you will be numb," she continued as she pinched the girl's white skin and inserting a tiny syringe needle, made an injection. She massaged the small mound of the girl's bottom for a minute then pinched it. "Feel anything?"

"Noo," Molly answered in a reluctant little voice.

"So, now kid, you start telling me your life story," Boots commanded.

"We really want to know all about you, and how you got to know what you know. An' don't let yourself be distracted by any small stuff that's going on down there, OK!"

Molly began to talk in a girlish sing-song while Puss swabbed the pale skin of her bottom with an antiseptic pad, and then after using a scalpel to make a narrow incision at the scar, began exploring the girl's flesh with a ceramic-tipped bullet probe.

Puss broke her concentration for a second when she felt a presence and found Bila kneeling beside her, watching what she was doing with silent interest.

She smiled vaguely at him and resumed her careful probing as Molly continued talking to Boots with tearful determination.

Bila watched Puss' delicate operation for a moment, then took an antiseptic pad and began to sponge away the trickle of blood from the incision with a gentle touch. Puss gave him a smile of gratitude, and Boots watched what he was doing, while she listened to Molly's story and stroked the young girl's head.

"Ha! Got it," Puss exclaimed in triumph a moment later. She held the probe in place with her left hand and used projectile forceps in her right to remove a metallic capsule the size of a peppercorn from the incision. Molly flinched, and interrupted her recitation of her short life.

"That hurt didn't it? But you can handle it, can't you Trooper Two," Boots asked as she stroked the girl's head.

"Yeees, if you say so," Bila grasped Molly's hands with his fingers. She turned her head in Boot's cradling arm and saw Bila looking down at her with extreme tenderness.

"Yeah, I can handle it, now that you guys are here." She said with a happy sigh.

*

"Its probably activated by body heat and powered by using cell fluids as its electrolyte," Boots muttered as she held the tiny device in her palm and examined it under a magnifier from her belt pouch. "You got some kind of radiation or wave detector on one of your benches in there, Kid?"

"There are a couple that he used to check the 'puter cable shielding and leads for micro eddy currents and leaks.

"I'll get 'um, because I want to stand up for a while anyway," Molly answered as she awkwardly started to rise from an uncomfortable half-reclining position on her side.

"Yeah, let me help you," Puss said as she hopped to her feet. "I laid a heavy dose of Quickset on your butt, and we can pull your stitch tomorrow, but sorta' take it easy with your little bottom until then, OK?"

Molly accepted her hand to rise, then scampered through the door of the cabin, giggling over her shoulder, "Yes Mommy!" Boots snorted and Bila grinned.

Puss sputtered as she rushed after the girl.

While they waited for the two, Boots opened her hand at the man's gesture and quizzical look. He held her hand in his as he peered at the tiny object glittering in her palm for a moment without touching it. Then he sat back and rotated his hand in the helicopter sign as he said, "Boss Rat. Computer dreamer it," with a grim look.

Boots nodded then considered him for another moment with equal grimness, before she responded with a crooked smile, "Bila Boy, you're gettin' damn good."

"And damn fast too," Puss added as she returned with Molly who carried two little instruments. "He's figgered who owns that sucker, hasn't he?"

"Yeah, and what it does too," Boots nodded as she held out her palm to the girl. "Set them as low as they'll go, and scan this thing to see if you can pick up any signal."

Molly made several adjustments on the dials of the small boxes and placed the tiny loop antenna of the first one near the micro-transmitter, then the other.

She shook her head, "Nothing."

"I didn't think so, my hand's the right temperature but it's dry. Let's check it again, after I sort of alter its environment," Boots grinned as she spat in her palm and covered the tiny transmitter with saliva.

"Hey, I'm gettin' something now."But it's starting to fluctuate."

"Quick Buddy, turn it off!"

Puss plucked the thing with tweezers from her friend's wet hand and dried it with a sterile pad.

"Anything now, Molly?" Boots asked as she watched the girl re-check the device her friend carefully held in the square of gauze.

"Nada! Blank screen!" Molly announced, "You guys are really over-the-top smart, you know."

"About half as much as we need to be, but thanks for the thought anyway," Boots said, then she continued, "Alright troops, what do we know now, and what do we have here? Quick!"

"I'm safe!" Molly sighed, "Thanks..."

"Yeah Kid, you are, but we gotta ice this thing somehow," Puss added with a worried frown.

"Yur' gettin close Troops but," Boots said as she started to give another lecture, until she paused and turn to Bila at her side. Her eyes met his, but now she saw the red sparks of a feral hunter in their amber depths, and no mercy.

He made a sign as he grunted, "Eraka!" with a crooked grin.

"Shat," Puss whispered, "His sign means a lure or a decoy, but I don't understand: what's that got to do with anything."

Boots gazed into the man's eyes for several heartbeats then she returned his crooked grin, and touched her brow with a salute she would give an equal.

He smiled slightly as he nodded in return, but the sparks his eyes did not change.

"What's that all about?" Puss asked with a sputter, "What's he saying?"

"You're repeating yourself, Kid. But anyway it looks like Wart Face was right for once," Boots said in a very quiet voice without taking her eyes from those of the man.

"What are you talking about?"

"It appears that there was a major force out there in the bushes yesterday after all..."

***

Chapter 6
The Breakfast

May 2-3, 2276 AD
Coastal Mountains of British Columbia

The sun was sinking behind the ridge behind the cabin when Molly walked with a slight limp over to where Bila sat beside the dying fire, watching the sunset with a far-away gaze. She knelt at his side with a grunt and touched his leather-clad arm. "Please Sir, could I have some more, Sir?"

The man gave a sudden start and with an obvious contriteness, leapt to his feet. He handed the girl up as he nodded vigorously to her and led her in blushing confusion back to Boots who was struggling to control her laughter at Molly's unknowing classical allusion.

Puss just looked up with a smile, first at Boots then at the man as helped the girl seat herself beside them again, then she shook her head as Bila turned and within minutes had the cook fire blazing again, and within 20 minutes more had grilled another round of venison filets and liver, and was serving the two women and the eager girl.

"Please Sir, could you heat up the weeds again too? They are really good!"

*

"Are you gonna' be OK in your bed tonight, now that Bila changed the scenery so to speak?" Puss asked. "We're gonna' sack out here where we can sniff the breezes."

"Oh sure, and I learned to ignore most stuff like that a long time ago," Molly said with a sleepy yawn.

"Molly girl, I think you're a pretty strong for just being fourteen and I like that," Boots murmured.

The girl blushed in pleasure, and then rose awkwardly to her feet. She said nothing but gave a shy smile to Boots. Puss rose with her and said, "Let's check you again and see how your new battle scar is doing. Then we can all sack, 'cos Kris and I gotta' move on out pretty quickie in the morning."

When Molly and Puss entered the cabin, Bila got to his feet as well. After stretching, he pulled on his leggings and hunting shirt and strolled out to the tree where he had hung the deer. He hoisted carcass out of the reach of predators, then walked toward the main valley and its stream.

Boots watched him walk away as she laid out their bedroll next to the fire.

*

"Well, she's tucked in now and you'll think it's way funny, but when she asked for a goodnight hug I gave her one. That kid's had a full day I'd say," Puss murmured as she knelt to help her friend arrange their bedding.

"I don't think it's funny at all. I'll bet that's the first hug she's had in about five years according to her story anyway. And the rest of us sorta' had that same kind of day as well, agree?" Boots said.

"Yep, sure do. Where's Bila?"

"Taking a walk down to the creek."

"Want to talk?"

"Yep," Boots said, as she sat on their sleep pad and patted the space beside her.

"You may begin then, Professor and give me the result of all this left brain thinking you have been doing recently," Puss said primly as she plopped down on the pad next to her friend.

"Thank you Doctor I shall, although I must admit that it is still pretty much right-brained at present."

"However, we have already assessed the new information about the Network, and its operations and capabilities that we gathered this morning. Based on that information, we have decided that new directions for our activities should be examined in light of the generally negative nature of said information. Correct?"

"Yes, I do recall our taking that decision."

"Well, Doctor since then we have gathered additional information this day subsequent to the departure of the network functionary, I submit that these data also be considered by our committee, and perhaps factored into our

93

decision process as well.

"And this new intel looks pretty ferkin' positive to me anyway, Kiddo!

"So now you tell me what you think, but gimme' a kiss first..." Boots continued as she threw an arm around her friend.

"Well, you sketched it out pretty well after the first time we ate today". Puss responded, after she gasped for air. "Which by the way wasn't no ferkin lunch, since his food is way too good for that word.

"But I shall now expand on my remarks on your remarks, just for the record of course," Puss continued.

"It is very clear to me Professor that Bila can care for Molly like no one has ever done before, and is quite willing to do so.

"It is also obvious that she has bonded with him and with us, and apparently he has done so with her. Additionally is also in the process of doing that with the two of us as well.

"Finally, I am also detecting a strong inclination on our part to accept all of these new connections.

"However, your discussion this morning, when you were assessing his leadership abilities leaves me somewhat puzzled. And I also do not fully understand your reference to our returning here for the birth of Molly's child, although it undoubtedly has sentimental appeal.

"Additionally, I do not see the point in your non-verbal communication with him over the implant I extracted from Molly, when you two referenced "lures or decoys", or in your seemingly lighthearted reference to him as 'G-7', and to the two of them as Troopers Two and Three.

"These statements, and actions of yours are puzzling to me, and deeply so since I have never known you to say or do anything capriciously, or without an ultimate purpose in mind.

"And finally, your extreme interest in Molly's ability to crack into the 'clave nets without detection hits my tripwire way over the ferkin' top!

"So talk to me, dammit!" Puss snapped as she gripped her friend's knee with a glare that demanded a response. "Just what tha' hell are you thinkin' anyway?"

Boots considered Puss with a level gaze for several long minutes in the deepening twilight as the dying cook fire quietly popped beside them. Then she answered in a soft voice.

"You can see the bright thread that runs through the fog too, can't you. I always thought you could. But no, Buddy. Instead, you tell me what you think I'm thinking, or feeling - or just dreaming..."

*

"Whoosh! That's a plan alright," Puss whispered as she climbed stiffly to her feet and realized that night had fallen during the time they were talking, and that the full moon was rising over the ridge.

"I gotta' take a walk, and I gotta' think about this for a while," she said over her shoulder, "But I'll be back Kiddo, so save my place," she murmured as she strolled out of the circle of firelight.

Puss paused for a moment, and let her eyes adjust to the night before she walked along the path she and Bila had cleared toward the larger valley. She stopped and after relieving herself as discretely as a forest cat, continued strolling through the meadow in the growing light of the moon while she mulled over the actions her friend proposed - and their possible consequences.

She was lost in thought until she vaguely sensed a shape in her path. Puss focused back on her surroundings with an impatient shake of her head, then realized that she was standing before the three boulders of yesterday's sanctuary. She stepped closer and saw a form standing quietly within their circle. She knew with calm certainty that it was Bila - waiting for her.

She walked to meet him.

His eyes gleamed, and his teeth flashed white in a broad smile as he held out his hands to her in the same gesture as when he had first greeted her, a time that now seemed long ago.

She took his hands and felt again their strength and gentleness as she stepped close to him and looked up into his face, and returned his smile.

He raised his hands without releasing hers or her eyes, lightly traced the line of her jaw from her ears to the corners of her mouth with his forefingers.

She gasped at the electric impact of his feathery touch and felt its harmonics spread through her body, echoing and amplifying in the core of her being. Her eyes dilated into dark circles and she saw only him as she rose on her toes and with lips that suddenly burned, moaned a wordless invitation from deep in her throat.

He bent to her mouth without releasing her hands and claimed it with his, as lightly as a butterfly landing on a rose petal.

Her pulse pounded in her ears and without releasing the gentle contact of his lips or hands, she leaned against him and felt the powerful beat of his heart through her breasts as she pressed them against his chest. They stood motionless for a minute, connected by only their hands and lips and hearts.

95

But these connections seemed to glow and emit sparks, and have the strength of the fiery welds forged by a master smith as he hammer-welded two pieces of fine steel into one...

Bila released her hands and then her mouth. He stepped back and looked at her with longing, pride and sadness inexplicably mingled in his eyes. He dropped his arms - and waited.

Puss returned his gaze for several heartbeats then she took a deep breath and unbuckled her field belt. She dropped it to the grass with a slight smile and without removing her gaze from his, balanced first on one foot then the other and removed her boots, unzipped her jumpsuit and slipped out of her bra.

She pushed the suit and her briefs down over her hips and stood proudly nude above her fallen clothing - and waited.

Bila marveled at the intricate beauty of Puss' body, glowing in the moon-light, and at the generous offer in her enormous eyes. He slowly removed his hunting shirt and spread it on the grass where they had sat the previous evening, when he had made his precise and impossible drawings and where she had felt strangely at home for a moment.

He turned and looked at Puss again as he shed the rest of his clothing without removing his eyes from her face. He stepped to her and bent his head. She lifted her face, and their lips touched for a moment, then they clasped hands and took the few short steps to their improvised couch.

Puss seated herself on his shirt and reached up to him. He knelt beside her and with hands moving as gentle as a feather, caressed her shoulders, her arms and then her breasts and belly. She gasped as a wave of passion exploded out of her inner self with an unfamiliar strength then she made an animal sound deep in her throat that combined a growl and a purr. She fell back and pulled Bila down on top of her.

As he lowered himself, she opened to him and embraced him with her arms and legs. Then making another throaty sound, she pushed his arms away and pulled his whole weight onto her body. Tightening the grip of her legs around his back even more, she used her amazing strength to urge him into a frenzied attack.

Bila was startled at first by the fierceness of her acceptance and he hesi-tated then he responded to her need with primal grunts, and a savagery that was also gentle.

Writhing and straining, they quickly climbed their mountain together and exploded as one. Then as they slowly floated down its other side, Puss clasped him to her relaxing body and pulled at him, still demanding his full weight be on her.

Panting slightly and top breathing as if she was wearing a tight corset, she purred under him as she stroked his back and hips and thighs with light touches of both her hands and feet, sensuously feeling his soft body hair and the strength of his torso and legs.

She nuzzled into the hollow of his neck then with a tiny sigh began nursing a mouthful of his skin as she breathed deeply and inhaled his scent.

He submitted to Puss' gentle assault on his throat as a chuckle rumbled from him like a minor earthquake. But within moments he began to respond to her touches and caresses in a different way. She felt his response and answered it with sudden urgings of her lips, and hips.

They coupled again, but this time they moved with each other slowly and deeply, and as one entity. Then Bila gently broke her embrace and pushing up with his powerful arms, raised his chest over her. He placed his supporting hands above her shoulders and held his upper body still as he looked down into the calm beauty of her face in the moonlight and into her shining eyes, while he continued to compliment the movements of her hips.

Puss gazed up at the man possessing her as she gripped his arms. She could see his bright eyes in the dark silhouette of his face against the moonlit sky, and felt his gaze entering her soul as she joyfully accepted him into her body. The two locked their eyes together and created the tension of passion between them again, and felt its power throbbing in their veins as they slowly moved toward a climax once more.

As their tender war began to surge, Bila slowly lowered his face and chest back down to hers and she felt the quivering strength in his shoulders and arms. Staring directly into her unblinking eyes, Bila brought his face closer, until his two dilated pupils blurred and merged into one in her vision.

At that moment they reached their peak together and as a wave of bright heat exploded from where they were joined, a light seemed to pass between their eyes and Puss felt an unfamiliar warmth touch at her mind.

She opened her self while the pulses of ecstasy were reverberating in her body, and allowed a rippling of tender strength to enter her being from the man she held in her arms. She welcomed Bila into her mind while her passion continued to rage, without hesitation.

She also let that which she knew as herself pass through the door that had somehow opened between them, and knew the comfort of the lofty space that was his mind and soul.

Then they relaxed and slowly retreated back into themselves - and became two happy lovers again, just lying together in the moonlight.

Bila rose onto his elbows a few moments later and stroked Puss' damp forehead with his hands. He whispered.

"Thank you Marybell," as he smiled down at her.

"Thank you Bila," then she asked in the same whisper, "What did we do just now?"

He slowly shook his head in questioning wonder. He asked, "Good?"

"Good, I think," she murmured. Then she caresses his brow as she corrected herself with a tremulous smile, "Good - I know."

He raised his upper body away from hers again and he smiled in return, then with a sudden boyish grin blew his breath down on her sweat-damp breasts and belly and cooled her heated flesh.

A faint memory stirred in her subconscious, and a strong feeling of familiar suddenly washed over her when she felt his breath on her body.

She gasped, "Bila dammit, we've been together before!" Then she added softly, and in confusion, "Right?" as she looked up at him with searching eyes.

He left her and got to his feet. Then he knelt back at her side with a sigh. He took her hands and holding them between his, returned her gaze with eyes that were wide and open and looked deeply into hers - and said nothing.

He kissed the tips of her fingers where they protruded from the warm haven of his hands with a crooked grin. And released her after this gesture. Regaining his feet, he offered her his hand. She accepted it and rose to stand with him.

Puss looked up at the tall man, his form blocking much of the moonlight and still gleaming with perspiration from their lovemaking. She suddenly felt a mischievous urge, and blew her breath up and down the broad expanse of his chest.

Bila started and stared rigidly at Puss for a second then he dropped to his knees and burying his face in his hands, groaned with the sound of a dying soul.

Puss dropped to her knees beside him and tenderly stroked his tense shoulders - and pulled his head next to hers.

"You loved her," she whispered in sudden understanding, "Is she dead?" Then remembering his words from yesterday she added softly, "Hil?"

He shuddered for a second, then with an action that somehow seemed familiar to her, shrugged and closed his agony within himself as he shook his head and answered very softly, "Maitatu hura. Ezhil hura. Galdua hura!" While he looked at Puss with eyes of stone- almost.

Not understanding what he said, the young woman only squeezed him tighter and swayed slightly as she crooned a wordless moan of sympathy.

He allowed her to do this for a moment, then he patted her shoulder as if she were his child and rising, he handed Puss again to her feet. He retrieved her clothes from the grass and offered them to her as he said, "Thank you."

Then he put on his leggings and the shirt that had been their couch and offered Puss his hand. She pulled on her boots and bundled her clothing, then clasped his hand and walked in outward serenity with him back to their camp.

Puss enjoyed the night breezes that caressed and cooled her naked body while she considered what had just happened between them - and her feelings about it.

*

When they reached the cabin, and their camp in front of its door, Bila smiled to Puss and released her hand with a squeeze. He took a place on the other side of the dying campfire from where Boots lay with her back to it, quivering with silent anger like the ground tremors from a wakening volcano.

Puss went to her friend's side and kneeling next to her, sat erect on her heels and waited, in silence.

Boots muttered icily over her shoulder after several moments "Oh. You're back. I saved your place like you asked."

"But it doesn't look like you'll need it tho. Are you satisfied now, Slut One?"

Puss remained silent, gazing at her friend's back as the woman remained buried in their bedroll.

Boots growled after another moment, "Well, you smell pretty musky. Was it good?"

"Yes."

"Why'd you go with him?"

"'Cos he needed me."

Then Boots snapped with a whispered snarl, "Then what-in-hell are you disturbing' my ferkin' rest for? Why don't you just go and jump back in the bounce sack with him again G'dammit?"

"'Cos I need you."

Boots body remained rigid for several long moments, then in a carefully neutral tone that Puss had never heard her use in all their time together, she rolled to face her friend.

"You've never said that to me before."

Puss sighed as she gazed down at her hands on her knees, "You're right. And it never hit me 'till now - but I just have been shown what it really means to have someone that you need, and to then loose them. Bila has lost someone, and I felt his need. But I don't want to loose you either."

Boots stared without expression at her friend sitting patiently beside her with downcast eyes. Then after a long minute she said in the same flat voice, "Come to bed before you catch cold. I'll think about this tomorrow," as she held their cover open.

*

Later in the night when the moon was setting and their fire had died to ashes, Puss looked over at Bila, taking care to not disturb Boots who slept nestled against her back. She saw that he lay with his hands clasped on his chest, and that his eyes glistened in the remaining moonlight as he stared somberly up into the night sky.

Puss thought about him and how they had contacted each other, and of the pain he hid. Then she thought of Boots and of the woman's brilliance - and the demons her friend carried within her. A tear rolled slowly down her cheek.

As it did, Bila turned toward her and signed with slow motions with a sad smile that she could plainly see.

Thank you. I am good. You are good. She is good. Sleep now." Then he rolled over and turned his back to her.

Puss understood his message at a subconscious level and stared at his form for a moment. Then carefully turning her head and looking up at the stars, she mouthed in silent wonder, "Sweet Jesu, please, please tell me who he is. And what he is..."

*

Boots wakened in the pearly light of the pre-dawn, and carefully disentangling herself from Puss sleeping form, got to her feet without a sound. She looked across the ashes of their fire to where the man had slept. He was gone as she had expected, but she saw that Molly's kettle was absent as well.

Boots slipped on her boots and pulling on a singlet that barely reached her hips, and glowered. She grasped her pistol, and strode off through the misty meadow toward the spring at the head of the valley.

She was halfway there when she met Bila, returning with the kettle full of water and carrying a handful of dried brown branches. She stood across his path with her legs spread in a fighter's stance and her pistol at her side. She released its safety as she gritted, "That's far enough! Now we talk - if yur' lucky."

Bila stepped slowly toward Boots until he halted close enough to be almost but not quite threatening. He said in a quiet voice as he gazed down at her, "Thank you. For Marybell."

Boots clinched her jaw and tensed – but then as on the previous day, she paused and looked into his eyes and saw no challenge. Rather they displayed a sure strength that was vaguely comforting, as it was at the same time disconcerting – which again irritated her.

Boots kept her glaring eyes on his as she thought over all she had observed about Bila. All that she has surmised as to who he was, and all of the strong and conflicting emotions this man has raised in her - a man who was so totally different from any other she had ever known. And who caused feelings in her that she had never experienced before...

Then as she stared into Bila's calm eyes, a vision of Marybell, sitting on her heels beside their bedroll the previous evening with her head down and patiently waiting, entered her mind.

She considered Bila for several brief seconds longer, then her eyes widened as she realized that Puss had acted from her heart. And had been right.

And she herself had been wrong - both with her friend the evening before, and about the man she confronted now.

As this thought formed in her mind, Boots felt a wave of comfort and peace roll through her self so strongly that she gasped - then she slowly relaxed.

"Thank you Bila - for bringing her back to me..." Boots finally whispered after several moments as she snapped her pistol back to safe.

She blinked several times, then added with a sudden grin.

"Here, let me give ya' a hand so you don't spill it, ya' Big Thud," as she reached out to help carry the kettle.

Bila happily shared the light load with the woman, but supported most of its weight as they walked back, ensuring that it would still be mostly full when they reached the cabin.

*

Puss awakened just after Boots stalked out of the camp toward the spring and immediately realized that her friend had gone to confront Bila. She pulled on her coverall and boots and started to run after her to try and stop an eruption of the serious violence that Boots held in herself. Then she halted abruptly after only her third step. Turning, she had shrugged and thrown up her hands.

"Shat!" she snapped aloud, "What in Hell do I think I'm doin'? Buda himself couldn't ferkin' stop those two from killing each other if their minds are set on it!"

She slowly walked back and knelt by the fire pit, and somberly began rekindling a blaze from the glowing embers in the ashes.

"Where is everybody?" Molly piped, as she yawned and stretched from where she stood in the cabin door in her cotton sleep shirt.

"They're out huntin'. I'm building the fire to heat some water." Puss growled.

"What are they hunting?"

"Trouble, each other, oblivion, who tha' ferk knows?" Puss snapped over her shoulder with a choked sob.

"What's wrong?" Molly asked with sudden concern as she ran to Puss and awkwardly knelt by her side with apprehensive eyes...

"Oh, nothing that a bunch more common sense and a heap less pride around here couldn't fix," Puss gritted as she fanned the rising flames, quivering with rigid control of her anger.

Molly and Puss sat silently sat by the fire for several minutes until the two tall people came into view, strolling through the mist on the meadow and carrying the kettle between them while they laughed easily at some shared non-verbal joke.

"There they are; they just went to get water!" Molly squealed, as Puss glowered and struggled to control her temper.

Boots and Bila stepped up to the fire which was now blazing up briskly again, and moving almost as one, placed their kettle on the three blackened hearthstones.

"Well Buda be gonged! Jack and Jill finally made it to the bottom of tha' damn hill with a full pail of water! A ferkin first as far as I can figger'." Puss snarled with her eyes glowing like two coals from the fire at her side.

Boots looked at her friend for a second, then glanced at Bila and said,

"Uh-oh. She's on the warpath - biggers!"

"Marybell happy, not," he nodded.

"Alright G'dammit, why'd you go after him with heat! Huh? Answer me that G'dammit!!" Puss snarled, springing to her feet.

"I thought he might need some help," Boots blushed, and mumbled as she looked away from her friend, and stepped over to toss her pistol on their bedroll.

"Look at me dammit, and DON'T cow-flop me! Again I ask, why'd you carry force when you went after him?"

Boots stood looking at her friend with eyes that now showed her true self, and answered,

"Because I was wrong - again. "That's twice about him in one day and now I've been wrong twice about you too. So let's just say I am tryin' to learn as quick as I can, but I'm real slow, OK."

Puss stepped to her friend and grabbed her by the chin. She whispered in a very flat and chilling tone, "If you ever - ever go after Bila with force again and you don't take him out, I will! And if he hasn't already, I will then take you out also," she hissed.

"And then I will take my self out! Do you understand me G'dammit?"

Bila watched the two intently, and then said in a quiet voice, "Ja Boss."

Boots smiled tenderly down at her friend and echoed the man, "Ja Boss. I understand you real good. But we've worked it all out between us this morning already, and Bila has damn-well set me straight on a bunch of things.

"So you don't have to worry about my doing something dumb like this again, ever. Now come here an' gimme a hug. Please..."

Puss hesitated for a second, then choking back a sob embraced Boots and felt the big man's arms wrap around her as well. She experienced a wave of comfort flow in to her from both of them such that she had not felt for years.

But after a moment, she looked up to them with a friendly sigh, and saw the same expression of wicked glee appear on both their faces. They murmured almost as one, and with identical grins.

"Poor Puss-cat's not happy."

"Marybell big happy need."

Before Puss realized what the two intended and while she was still relaxed in their arms, they struck with glee. Each threw an arm around the other and they clamped her between their bodies as they took turns ruffling her hair and exploring body for tickle spots.

Puss squawked in indignation and struggled in vain, then as the two continued administering their cure she broke into shrieks of helpless laughter.

Boots and Bila stopped their teasing and relaxed their hold, and Boots gently smoothed her friend's hair as she whispered, "All better now?"

Bila stroked Puss' shoulder, then bent and kissed her forehead, "Marybell good?"

"Ya' know, I thought I had seen weird before, but you people really wrote the whole darn manual!" Molly piped, "What's for breakfast? I'm starving'! And who are these Jack 'n Jill people anyway?"

Puss ignored the girl for a moment as she fiercely hugged both of her friends and then gasped, "Jesu Buda! Living with Kris has really been way on the edge, but now with both of you together - my life is so far out on tha' end of the flippin' curve I can't see its middle anymore."

Then she smiled up at the two people she held in her arms and murmured, "Funny though, I'm getting to like it out here."

As Bila smiled down at them both, Boots gently kissed her friend's lips as she whispered, "It's all better now Buddy, and forever, OK..."

*

Puss followed Molly back in to the cabin to rummage for breakfast supplies while Bila seated himself by the fire and began pulling the wrinkled red berries from the thorny branches he had collected near the spring. He crushed each one in his fingers before dropping them into the pot of water now beginning to steam over the fire.

Boots finished dressing herself and returned to stand over the man. "What's that?" she asked.

Bila looked up at her for a moment as he considered, then he sat erect and flexed both arms over his shoulders in an unconsciously graceful pose as he said, "Good feel make. Friends all for," and relaxing, he tapped his own chest, then nodded to her and toward the cabin, before turning and continuing to prepare the red berries for the pot.

Boots looked at the man for a long moment as she considered his strength and grace, and his apparent total ignorance of the affect he had on others.

Then she whispered, "Ya' know, I really do want you on our side..." as she moved to kneel by the fire. She dipped her finger into the water in the pot, which was now turning a reddish tint as the crushed berries steeped in the steaming water. She tasted it.

"Humph! That's pretty good, could use a pinch of sugar but not bad," then her voice suddenly changed as she said, "Alright Thud-guy, just who'n hell are you anyway?" as she leapt at him with a throwing knife suddenly in her hand and forced him back onto the ground.

He relaxed as she lay across his chest pressing her blade against his throat – and laughed. Boots looked into his eyes then, just as suddenly as she had sprung at him she relaxed with a laugh of her own and gave him a quick sisterly kiss on his lips.

Bounding to her feet and re-sheathing the knife she exclaimed "Buda's Butt Bila! Damn if you ain't major cool under fire! So now, do you want to join our crew?"

He looked up at Boots with the slightest hint of a smile then he slowly regained his feet with the lazy rippling strength of a tiger awakening from a nap. He gently clasped her by the waist as she gazed up at him - then her eyes widened when she felt his fingers turn in to a circlet of iron.

Bila easily lifted her straight above his head and looked calmly up into her stunned eyes. He said very quietly, "Ja Boss" before she could think to struggle, then he gently lowered her back to the ground and releasing her, stood waiting.

Boots breathed deeply for a minute as she glowered at him, then she laughed aloud and held out her hand as she said, "Ja Bila! Welcome aboard."

He gave a crooked smile as he took her hand in both of his and said, "Thank you, I think."

"It takes her a while, but she generally gets tha' picture, if you keep your message real simple." Puss said, stepping out of the cabin door holding several canisters and followed by Molly carrying their mess kits. "Put it there, Bila!" she continued with a smile, holding out her hand after dropping her load by the fire. When he clasped it Puss said softly, "I'm real glad you've joined us."

"Thank you, I know," he answered with a firm nod to the young woman, and then he nodded to Boots as well.

"Interesting sign-up ceremony I must say though," Puss grinned to Boots. "First time you've ever seen him in action isn't it? And how does it feel to be man-handled for real, Sweetie?"

"Your perception is pretty perfect once again Trouper One," Boots said with a slight smile.

"Oh, and to which of my many such do you refer, O Mighty Leader?"

"The one about us keeping the relationship that links our personal well-being to Bila's happiness strongly positive at all times," Boots chuckled as she ruffled her friend's hair, "But now, what's fer' breakfast?"

"Crew big?" Bila suddenly asked.

"First two," Boots answered holding up two fingers and putting her arm around Puss. "Now four," she indicated with four fingers and gestured at him and toward Molly.

"First two, now four," he replied pointing to the women then to the girl and himself. The look of a hunting wolf flashed briefly in his eyes as he finished, "Four start be."

"Aside from learning to count pretty quickie, what tha' hell's he talking about?" Puss asked.

"Are we ever gonna' eat?" Molly piped plaintively.

"What did you find in there, Buddy?" Boots asked, without taking her eyes from the man's face.

"Oat meal and dried soy milk and some sugar. What's already in the pot?"

"Those dried red things he brought back from the spring. Why don't you two cook up something while I try to find out what's on his mind this time?"

"OK Buddy," Puss responded and stepping to the fire with Molly, stirred the colored water steaming in the pot then tasted it. "Hey, rose hips! Great!"

"What's rose hips," the girl asked peering down at the pot with suspicion.

"Some berry things that have a bunch of vitamins in them to make you really healthy, ya' little rash bar rat," Puss grinned as she squeezed Molly around her shoulders. "Here, let me teach you how to make a decent breakfast."

While the two knelt by the fire and chatted happily, Boots retrieved the sketchpad from her pack and motioned Bila to the cabin wall. Seating herself and leaning back against it, she patted the grass next to her and offered him the pad as he dropped down to sit cross-legged at her side.

"Four start be?" she asked in his words.

He took the pad and flipped to the page of his last drawing - the impossibly accurate rendering of an extinct woolly mammoth. Pointing to the one small stick figure holding a stylized spear he had sketched beside it he said, "Good more is."

Boots corrected him, "More is good," then looked at him questioningly as she opened the pad in his hands to a blank page and offered him a pencil.

He looked at her for a second without expression before dropping his eyes to the paper and considering it for several more. Then taking the pencil from her fingers without removing his eyes from the page, he began drawing. Boots contented herself with watching him as he worked and restrained from intruding on his thoughts by looking over his shoulder. She was again fascinated by the delicacy with which he used his large hands.

After several minutes of rapid sketching he paused and inspected his work, then handed the pad back to Boots, with the feral look again in his eyes.

She examined the page, then absorbed its content and growled, "Alright Bila, Dammit! I ask again. Just who'n hell are you anyway?"

"I've asked that myself a lot lately and got no answer at all - yet. What's he done now?" Puss said as she stepped over with a stirring spoon in her hand to where the two sat.

"Ferkin' declared war for us it looks like!" Boots chuckled as she handed the pad up to her friend.

Puss took in the page and realized that it showed a sequence of three events, all drawn with stick figures around a large animal. In the first event the beast held two limp humans in its mouth, while in the second four humans with spears held it at bay. But in the last picture, the beast was down and surrounded by numerous humans who all were stabbing spears into its body and throwing darts at it launched with short sticks.

In all three sketches the human stick figures were very lifelike in their forms and indicating both males and females were involved, but it was the beast that grabbed her eye.

In each case it had the realistic body of a gigantic bear but its head was a simple one-dimensional device. It was the outline of an inverted triangle with spheres at its three points, as was painted on the side of the helicopter that had taken Durwood away.

"Yeah, I've been noticing that he catches on real fast, and real deep too," Puss said slowly as she looked at the sketch. "And these are?" she asked him, as she tapped the short sticks he had sketched.

"Eskumakila botaldi," he grinned as he signed, *throw sticks.*

Puss nodded, as she again somehow understood the meaning of his hand motions, then she shook her head as she announced, "That's not the sign for an atlatl, which is our Amerind name for those things.

"Buda's Ferkin' Bongos Mister Ockham, I'm startin' to think you really are right!"

Puss handed the pad back to the man as she turned to Boots, "Anyway and whatever, lets eat now, and then talk whilst I figure out how to raise an army for you two big-picture bozos, since I don't do either mystic crappo or major policy early in the morning - let along on an empty stomach dammit."

*

The four sat around the fire waiting for the morning mist to finally clear and the women were eating the porridge Molly had concocted under Puss' guidance. They smiled contentedly at each other, but Boots also watched Bila's reaction to what she realized could be a new food to the man.

She saw that he at first cautiously observed them begin eating with their spoons, then after a moment's hesitation the man nodded and grabbing a spoon, plowed into his oatmeal with the happy absorption of a hungry teenager.

As she watched him eating Boots felt a tingle in her spine again, which she again suppressed.

Puss ignored the interplay between the two and smilingly lectured Molly between mouthfuls.

"Old but true story kid. About 500 years ago some Englishman was in Scotland and looked down his nose at oats cooked like this which tha' natives were having for breakfast. "In England, we feed oats to our horses!" he sneered.

"Then a Scot remarked, "I hear ye raise strong horses back in England, right?"

"Of course, we're famous for that!" the Englishman sneered again.

"Well, Scotland is famous fer' raising strong men, the man replied and then, according to my Dad anyway, the Scotsman drew his broadsword and lopped off some of the Englishman's body parts," Puss finished with a grin.

"No, I don't believe you. Nothing like that would ever happen 'caus everybody knows that Talking Back is Not Nice!" the young girl responded seriously. "But this oat stuff is real good though."

The two women looked at each other and shook their heads, then Boots said quietly, "They told you that stuff in school right? With posters all over the walls, right?"

"Yeees," Molly responded tentatively, as her pale eyes widened on hearing a tone in her new friend's voice that was not playful.

"Well Kid, now I'm going to tell you the truth now," Boots said as her eyes bored into those of the young girl, "And I'm only going to say this once, so you listen to me real good. Do you hear?"

At her wordless nod, Boots continued with deadly precision, "Molly, you are going to give birth to a child in two months but a baby is not a toy, it is a full time job for you from the moment it comes out of your body. Even if you have help from its father, which sounds somewhat possible, the command responsibility is ultimately yours. So it is now time for you to grow up.

"Therefore by the time I finish speaking to you will have become an adult, if you want you and your child to survive in this world. Do you under-stand me?"

The young girl's eyes grew even wider as she hesitated for a moment. Then straightening her thin shoulders, she said softly but with a sudden determination, "Yes Ma'am."

"Good. I thought you would. Now for starters, everything your teachers taught you in school that was not about math or reading or communication was wrong. And they told you and all of your classmates that they were there to help you, correct?"

"Yeees..."

"Wrong! Your teachers are part of the government, right?"

"Yeees..."

"So why should the government want to help you?"

"Because they're supposed to, and they say they will."

"Wrong! They only do things for you, or to you that will help them selves. You have to realize that now Kid. I learned this way damn fast in one night when I was 16, and it was pretty heavy and much painful to me at first, but then I made it real bad for those who made me hurt. So I am trying to save you a small amount of pain by telling you this now - as my gift to you. You're going to have enough hurt coming to you anyway, but I would not be talking to you if I didn't think you could take it.

"Right so far?"

The young girl nodded wordlessly, but Boots just stared at her until Molly answered quietly with her head held high, "Yes Ma'am."

"Good," Boots nodded with an approving smile. "Now here is your situa-tion. We must go back to S'attl for a while to attend to our affairs and to as-sess the situation there, with respect to both the Governors and the Network.

"You must stay here and not be found by Boss Rat or any others who would sell you to them. Bila will stay here with you and among other things see that you are well fed," then Boots grinned.

"By the way, you are looking much healthier after only a few meals of," she interrupted herself with a slight smile as she cued Molly with her pointed finger. The girl blinked then responded with a happy sigh, "Real Food!"

"Right. How are you feeling now?"

Molly said with a puzzled look, "I didn't feel tired this morning. Why?"

"Because you are now eating enough food that's real and makes you healthy, not the stuff that the Governors want people like you to eat. Bad nutrition is a trick the Governors learned from a bunch of thugs about three hundred and forty years ago in Europe, who starved their labor slaves in order to control them.

"Don't bother about that in the short run though, but you really should read up about that bunch when you have some free time. For now, just eat what Bila cooks, OK!"

"Yes Ma'am," Molly whispered.

"Good. Now to continue. Molly, you have a bunch of things to do. One is to mole in and bring up the sat-maps for this area and locate both of those bunches of so-called neighbors of yours, and show Bila where they live. You have the access passwords and I will give you names that are safe to use, but be very careful and do not - I repeat not be cute when you are in there, understand?"

"Yes Ma'am!" Molly, but now said with a firm note in her little voice.

"Attagirl, you are starting to sound like the real Trooper Two! You're important to the mission of this outfit and we need you to be safe here when we come back."

The girl's eyes opened wide as Boots continued, "Your second job is to teach Bila to communicate in our language and to show him about our culture as well, what little there is of it left anyway.

"You may have a couple of months but I don't think it will take that long somehow," Boots finished with a grin as she nodded toward the man.

"A coupla' days is more like it," Puss drawled.

"Right again Trooper One. Now Two, the final thing you have to attend to is security for this site and that of Trooper Three as well as of yourself. So, how many trip-wires and IR beams do you have out there?

"How many guns do you have and do you know how to shoot them? What do you have for bolt-holes and hiding places?

"Where is your net server 'puter located, and is it safe where it is? And what about your antenna dishes, are they really as undetectable as you think?

"And Durwood is going to be operational again pretty soon, after Boss Rat adjusts his altitude and he comes out of the joy trip my Buddy sent him on. So you have to major security and mole-proofing stuff to do on what is now your system, to protect it from him when he gets back on line."

Then with a slight smile, Boots relaxed as she finished, "So ya' see Kid there's a lot of things for you to attend to really quickie."

"Especially since two Rat 'copter flights in and out of here in two days might have got the attention of some of your neighbor folks, who just might decide visit and see about lootin' your cabin if they thought that you and Durwood had been collected, so either those friendly Art-lovers you told us about from over the ridge to the west, or even some of those dimwitted cammy-wearin' militia mongoloids could be dropping by any minute."

As Molly's eyes opened even wider and she gasped in astonishment. Boots turned her attention to Bila for the first time and asked as she looked at him.

"You understand?"

"Yes Ma'am" he replied with the same look of calm strength that she had already seen when she confronted him at their first meeting, and again in the dawn this morning. Without taking her eyes from his, Boots nodded - and again felt a faint tingle in her spine.

"Shat, I think you really do," she whispered. Then in an aside to Puss, she added quietly, "You know Buddy, your over the-top ideas might just work out after all."

"Mine? I just came along to make field observations on tha' behavior of a bunch of real crazies! You're the one that's far away and out on some unknown mind expander!" Puss snorted. Then she grinned, "Fun trip so far tho."

Boots growled, "Enough yakey! Molly, you got a gun in there? We got fifteen minutes to teach Bila how to shoot and then we gotta be out of here."

"How'n hell you going to do that in a quarter of an hour? You know damn well It takes a week to teach a recruit basic marksmanship!" Puss exploded.

"You saw him throwing rocks and spears, right?"

"Yes. So?"

"So you know what I know. Bet ya' another back rub, OK!

Puss looked at Boots, and then at Bila. She muttered, "Shat, you're probably right again, dammit! But you're on!"

*

The weapon Molly brought out from the cabin was a light rifle with a curiously thick barrel and a curved box magazine protruding from its receiver. Handing it and a small carton to Boots she said proudly, "We lucked up and found a real good cache that somebody sealed up a long time ago."

"You sure did," Boots murmured as she examined the weapon. "I've found some of those old arms stashes myself. They were done more than 200 years ago, but the stuff was so well sealed that it was still like new."

"I've read about this piece too, it's a Ruger semi-automatic Model 1022 in .22 caliber rim-fire, with a special silencer they put on at the factory. You guys find much ammo with it, and have you ever shot it?"

"Yeah, a whole bunch. The old ammo stored with it wasn't too good, but there were a lot of new Chin bullets in one of the caches Durwood found, and he said this one was mine so I taught myself to shoot it real good too."

"Show me," Boots said as she groped in her pack and retrieve a ration bar. Pacing off 15 meters, she hung it on a stick that she stuck in the ground. As Boots strode back, the girl laid the rifle on the grass and removing the magazine, began clicking tiny brass cartridges into it.

Bila watched with unblinking attention while Puss looked on, and observed both Molly and the man.

"It holds 25 but I'm only loading 5. No sense in being wasteful," Molly said. After closing the little box of ammunition, the girl placed it aside and retrieving the rifle, locked its bolt open and inserted the magazine. Then she stood stiffly at attention facing the target and holding her rifle at port arms across her chest.

She piped, "Ready Ma'am!"

Boots responded with a grin, "Commence firing Trooper Two." But then as the girl raised the rifle to her shoulder, released the bolt to chamber a round and stepped into a classic target shooters position all in one motion, Boots' grin faded and Puss' eyes opened wide. Bila continued to watch the girl's every movement.

Molly's first shot hit the middle of the ration bar and the impact of the small slug spattered brown goo several feet around, and the sound of the rifle's report was no louder than that of a large twig snapping. Molly rapidly fired three more times and blasted away the remaining pieces of the bar and its wrapper. Then with a final shot, she nicked the supporting stick and caused it to lean.

"Poot, I gotta practice my trigger squeeze more!" Molly growled, unconsciously copying Boots' battlefield voice in her own high-pitched tones as she clicked her rifle to safe and brought it back to the ready position.

"Good shootin' Molly! Real good. I was major glad you are on our side before but this is one more real damn good reason," Puss said as she patted the suddenly blushing girl's shoulder. Bila knelt and examined one of the ejected cartridge cases, now blackened and empty.

"Yeah and congratulations Molly girl, you've just made it three for three for me. And rubbed my nose in it max too," Boots said with a rueful little grin.

"Did I do something wrong Ma'am?" the girl squeaked as her blush of pleasure faded.

"No Two, you are doing everything exactly right, and very well too" Then as the girl's blush returned in even greater strength, Boots continued, "And by doing so you are showing me that I am continuing to underestimate you as well as your two very competent fellow troopers."

"So, if I am wrong about the outcome of my next prediction I will step down and let you elect another leader for our crew, if you wish," Boots said. Then she ordered crisply, "Trooper Two! Demonstrate the drill for your piece to Trooper Three!"

"Yes Ma'am!" Molly squealed. Turning around, began carefully showing her rifle's operation to Bila, now intent and focused on what the girl was saying and doing."

As the improbable pair worked with their heads together in total absorption and mostly silent communication, Boots led her friend several steps away and murmured, "Still want to bet Buddy?"

"You're not backing me down Big-un! But even money only, you don't get odds on them from me again, ever again." Then Puss added quietly, "But ya' know, it looks like those two working together is really going to be something pretty special..."

Boots laid her arm around her friend's shoulder and whispered in her ear, "Yep, your Mystic Injun Right-brain seems to be calibrated pretty good today Squaw Gal. But now I'm going to give you odds. I'll do back rubs on you for a whole ferkin' year if we don't see a major forward leap of about a hundred an' fifty centuries in the next few minutes..."

*

"Please, Ma'am, may I use your sketch pad for a minute?"

"Sure Kid, what for?"

"I want to draw the correct sight picture for him Ma'am," Molly replied in a serious little voice.

"Good idea," Boots responded with equal seriousness. Then in another aside to Puss she grinned, "Bet still on?" Puss stuck her tongue out at her friend, in a marked manner...

After briefly showing Bila her diagram of the proper alignment of its front and rear sights, Molly handed him the rifle with the empty magazine and the small box of ammunition, then awkwardly trotted back into the cabin.

The two women watched with feigned casualness as the man squatted with the rifle across his lap, and placing the opened box on the ground used his large hands with delicate precision to load ten of the tiny cartridges into its magazine. Then he closed the box and stood, waiting until the young girl emerged from the cabin with her slim arms filled with hardware.

"This is a target frame we found and a bunch of rash bars to shoot at too," Molly panted with pride as she started walking down range toward the remains of her own target.

Puss leaped to join Molly and helped her in erecting the metal support and arraying it with ten of the insipid rations. Then the two raced each other back to where Bila stood with Boots. As they shuffled playfully to a stop beside their friends, the girl's cheeks glowed with healthy exertion and Puss smiled at Molly's new enthusiasm.

"Ready Ma'am," the man said, and using the same movements as Molly, inserted the magazine, charged the rifle and stood in the ready position.

"Commence firing, Trooper Three." Boots said, in a quiet voice.

Bila snapped the bolt shut, raised the rifle to his shoulder and faced the target exactly as Molly had done, and after aiming for several seconds carefully touched of his first shot. It splattered the leftmost ration bar hanging from the frame. Then after a pause he did the same to the other nine in measured sequences, and caused Boots' smile to widen at each successful hit.

Puss remained grave, but her eyes grew bigger as each bar disintegrated, and Molly's eyes danced happily as she held her breath.

When the sound of the last muffled report had died away the man clicked the safety on and returned to the ready position, and looked at Boots with an honest question in his eyes, "OK?"

"OK! Shat, Very OK," Boots said with a wide grin as she stepped to him and pulling his head down, gave him a quick kiss and ruffled his hair. But the two suddenly tensed again and abruptly stepped apart - he still holding the little rifle but now staring over her head, and she turning aside to the others with a noticeable blush on her cheeks.

"WOW!" squealed Molly as she bounced with glee, "You're really good Sir!"

"OK? Is all you can say, just OK?" Puss sputtered as she pushed past Boots. "Bila, you are a really good shooter. But how did you do that?" she asked as she gazed at him with questioning intensity as she signed, *"How?"*

He looked in her eyes for an instant, to the same depth as he had at the previous evening when they had become as one, then he smiled and raised his head as he announced to all three women, "Habaila berri era - Ondro berdin!" and signed, *"Same!"*

He placed the rifle carefully down on the grass and stepped to his pack-sack beside the cabin wall. He removed the coil of braided animal hair and grasping its ends, drew a stone from his pouch and positioned it in the pocket of the sling. Then with one swift swing around his head, he hurled the stone down the range - where it whizzed straight through the target frame and knocked away the hanging remains of the center rash bar.

Bila turned and holding the sling in one hand and picking the rifle up in his other, smiled to them all and asked, "OK?"

Puss shook her head in an effort to deal with the fact that while she did not recognize the words he spoke she somehow knew exactly what he meant - and had demonstrated with his sling. "He's telling us they are the same," she said quietly as she stared at the smiling man.

Boots read the language of his demonstration without waiting for her friend's translation, and laughed, "Ha! Score one more for the Big Guy, and a real big one for yur' Boss! I figgered he had an instinct for ballistics about as good as a Chin fire control `puter anyway, but by Buda's Bathtub now I think he's even better!"

*

Boots handed Molly a page torn from her sketchpad. "Here are the coor-dinates for a net address in S'attl. You can mole into it easy then you follow this addy to a bulletin board that the Govs have set up for their employees and families to place want-ads for stuff. Then you can post any of the coded

115

messages I have listed here as ads if you need to. We will see them, and I will post back using these coded replies - if it is necessary for us to respond."

"Our communication will be sort of limited, because I can't monitor the board except occasionally, but it's better than nothing, and it's safe - if you're as good a `puter mole as you look,"

"They won't catch me, Ma'am!" the girl said in a determined squeak. "Don't worry- I won't let you guys down! But who's addy is it anyway? And what kind of stuff?"

"My mother's. And it's best you don't know about the stuff folks put on it,"

"Oh, that kind of stuff," Molly shrugged indifferently. "Durwood used to mole in and read those boards all the time. You want a Chin `salt rifle to take back with you?"

"Sure, if you got a spare,"

"We got ten, and bunches of ammo sticks too!" the girl said proudly over her shoulder as she trotted into the cabin.

Puss smiled as she watched Molly's new vigor.

"A little real food is makin' a real girl out of her real quick." Then she turned to the man as she whispered "Thank you Bila" and pulling his head down, kissed him gently with her eyes wide open - as they had done the previous evening.

Boots stood quietly watching the two and a strange feeling slowly grew within her, of contentment mixed with something else she didn't recognize, but which was also pleasant. Then the spell was broken as Puss and Bila parted and Molly charged out the door of the cabin proudly carrying a Chin assault rifle with a full bandoleer slung over her arm.

"Is this OK, Ma'am?" the girl panted to Boots as she presented the crudely finished weapon noted for its effectiveness.

"It sure is Kid," the woman growled as she accepted the rifle and checked its action. "Thanks, it might come in handy if we meet another grizzly out there, while you've got Bila in your school back here," she added with a grin as she slung the weapon over shoulder and buckled the bandoleer with its ten sticks of its caseless ammunition around her hips.

Then she shouted abruptly, "G'dammit! Let's Move it!" and turning to Bila and glaring at him while gripping his arms, she said, "You take care of her, and of yourself, OK!"

He looked at Boots for a long moment. Then he said distinctly as his eyes bored into hers, "Yes. You care of Marybell. You care of You!" then he continued with calm certainty, "We wait come you. You come no. We go you at."

Boots was speechless for a moment after she grasped what the man had said, and what his speaking these words signified.

Puss looked at them both and shook her head as she muttered to Molly, also suddenly dumb-struck, "Well kid, looks like yur' teaching task is gonna be a fluff, but our Buddy's got a real hill to climb if she wants to be his Boss."

"I heard that, and no I don't," Boots said in an even voice over her shoulder. Then she turned and stared again at Bila, "Because nobody bosses the wind. You just spread your wings and fly with it - to wherever it takes you."

She smiled at the man and squeezed his arms again, and said very quietly, with slightly glistening eyes "Thank you - I know! And I am happy you are with us."

Boots turned before he could respond and gritted in her command voice, "Al'right Sergeant, you gonna' yak all day, or are we gonna' move this damn outfit on out of here?"

*

The two women trotted up the safe lane in on the slope behind the cabin and Boots muttered to her friend, "You got Molly's butt bug safe?"

"Yep, nice and dry, along with some other field samples."

"Good. Now, we will not, repeat not discuss or think about these last three days until we are outta here and safe, wherever that is. We stay focused, Right?"

"Right Buddy! But I really don't want to loose what we just found, because I think both of us have been sort of looking for this, and waiting for a long time, whatever this is."

"Yep. Now tighten it up kid, and let's just go do it."

*

Bila and Molly stood together watching the two run up the ridge. As they neared its crest, the girl shyly reached for the man's hand for reassurance and comfort. He engulfed it in his as they continued to watch their new friend's leaving.

Then the two figures paused and turned at the top of the slope. The taller one snapped a military salute while the smaller one blew a kiss and signed with enough exaggeration for Bila to read, *"Friend!"* Then they turned and vanished into the forest.

"They're gone," Molly sighed, "Do you think we will ever see them again,

Sir?" as she looked up with sad eyes to the man.

"Yes," he said firmly as he continued to gaze up the slope at where the two women had last stood. Then he abruptly shook his head and smiled down at her, "Now Molly Bila teach, OK?"

"OK!" she squealed, "Come on, and let's just do it!" as she turned and started to trot back into the cabin.

"Go slow. For baby," the man admonished with a grin as he followed.

She smiled over her shoulder, "Yes Sir!" as she slowed her pace.

*

Bila stood beside her at the computer bench in the back room and held the chair out for her. She paused before seating herself, and looked at a small control panel on the wall.

"I think I'll check the Infra Red alarm net first," she said in a serious little voice as she clicked several switches. A small display screen lit up.

"I need to look at the history. I haven't done that since Durwood went away." Suddenly a tone sounded and a red light began to blink, and several messages appeared on the screen.

"Omygod! Somebody was up on the back ridge yesterday morning!"

***

Chapter 7
The Bunker

May 3, 2276 AD
Coastal Mountains of British Columbia
And The `Clave of S'attl

Puss and Boots halted their ground-covering trot at the foot of the western ridge inside the tree line at the clearing where they hid their trail bikes three days before. Boots un-slung the Chin assault rifle from her shoulder and charged a round from the stick of ammunition clipped on its barrel. The two were perspiring but breathing easily as they examined the area with their eyes and with Puss' I.R. scanner.

When they were satisfied, Boots gripped her weapon in one hand at the long trail and nodded. Puss drew her pistol led the way in silence through the brush at the edge of the clearing and onto the old logging road.

Puss examined the bushes hiding the bikes when they neared the place they had left them. She peered at the placement of the branches she had arranged to cover them, and froze. Boots saw her friend tense and stopped between strides. She lifted her rifle, slipped its safety off and waited in still readiness.

Puss turned and signed to her friend.

"Someone has been here. Markers on your bike have been moved."

"Be careful, Kid," Boots signed back.

Puss nodded and backtracked along the verge of the logging road to a place ten meters behind Boots without making a sound, then dropped to the ground and slid into the brush. She inched along on her stomach under its low leafy canopy until she neared Boots' bike. She examined it intently then spied a slack loop of thin monofilament around its front wheel fork. Without moving except her head and eyes, Puss followed the strand back to where one end was tied to the branch of a laurel bush a meter to the front of the bike. Its other end disappeared through the foliage.

Puss slid around the base of the shrub using only her elbows to pull herself over the leaf mold and sandy soil, and saw where it ended. The strand was tied to a ring protruding from the side of a small orange box lashed with plastic strapping to the trunk of a sapling three meters beyond the laurel.

Puss eyed the device for a moment then recognized it, and with a suppressed snort inched back to her original position next to Boots' bike. Once there, she removed a little pocket knife from a breast pocket and with a slight smile, used its blade to scrape and fray the monofilament line close to its anchor point on the laurel bush until it parted, much as would have been done because of a field mouse's nibbling.

Puss inched back out from under the thicket then, and erased the signs of her passage as she returned to the trail where Boots waited. Rising to her feet on the side of the logging road, she brushed away the dry granitic soil and leaf mold from her jumpsuit and nodded to her friend.

"What you find?" Boots signed to the young woman with one hand as she held the assault rifle's butt braced against her hip with her other.

"Some cute dudes want to know when we were leaving the area." Puss said with a smirk, "So they looped a pull string around your bike that would jerk the send switch of an old Chin downed pilot locator. And if they left a monitor receiver turned on to catch its signal; they would then know when we were pulling out."

"So, what now?"

"So, we can go now, because I, the best sneak you've ever known have saved our cute little gadgets once again."

"OK Injun' Gal, I gratefully acknowledge that action, but just whom do you think wants to know when we are going to haul our butts back out of this ferkin' forest wonderland?"

"Well Max Leader now that you ask it, occurs to me that since our good friend over the hill probably had amassed himself a hefty bunch of abandoned Chin mil stuff, maybe his so-called buddies over to the west might have collected some of that same hardware for themselves too."

"Hmmm... looks like I really do have to think about adjustin' the rations in this outfit. Your thought processes are getting way too sophisticated for a mere grunt." Boots grinned. "And what did you actually do to secure the situation, whilst down in the bushes crawlin' on your belly like a reptile?"

"Taught a passing chipmunk to nibble their trip-line in two, so we are now free to go any time the mood strikes without un-wanted fanfare, and they'll never know when we left - or that we figgered 'um out."

"And by the way Sir/Ma'am, I would also like to point out to you as well, that none of my grunts are ever merely Mere!"

"I stand corrected," Boots grinned. Then becoming serious she asked, "Now, how long do you think they'll wait before they come back over to do a visual recon?"

"I found one clear boot track that showed a worn Chin tread pattern and its edges were still sharp in the soil and not slumping yet from day-night temperature changes, so I'm guessing at yesterday or the day before at the earliest for them to have found our bikes and had time to scamper back home and back with stuff to rig their telltale. I figure it will be at least another day before they start to wonder."

"You think they left any more little surprises lying around as send-off presents, so to speak?"

"I didn't see anything, and it wouldn't make sense anyway. They want us gone so they can grab Durwood's goodies, not for us to be mad at 'um. But I do want to check those bikes real close now, for Rat bugs..." Puss finished grimly.

"Me too, so let's do it," Boots growled as she slung her rifle and strode to their hidden machines.

"Ja Boss!"

*

"Well, I don't see anything, and the signal detector Molly gave us didn't ding either, so maybe Boss Rat hasn't had a chance to get to our trusty rusty steeds yet," Boots muttered.

"We have never taken them into S'attl, and they are Chin anyway, so maybe they're clean," Puss shrugged.

"Don't forget Kiddo, the Chin command liked to keep tabs on their own troops just as much as the 'Gon did us. So if Rat felt any need to find, or buy or steal the transceivers for their type of locator bugs, it would have 'um in a nanosecond,"

"Is that faster than a rash bar furt?" Puss asked innocently, with wide eyes.

"Damn close, but not quite. Nothin' is that fast!" Boots grinned. "Now let's head for the shed double time."

"Think we ought to warn Molly and Bila?" Puss asked with sudden seriousness.

"We already have, this morning. What we have here is confirmation that our warning was correct," Boots answered, looking directly at her friend.

"We have to do our mission in the `Clave and can get back here as soon as we can. If we stay here and fight their battles for them, Boss Rat and the Governors will catch on real quick and come down with major force. And Buddy, we aren't set up to handle that, not just yet."

"Do you think they're ready?" Puss asked in a very quiet tone.

"Yes, I do. Don't you?" Boots responded, reaching out to her friend.

"I suppose, but we're risking their lives with our judgment without giving them a vote. It doesn't seem right." the young woman sighed as she gripped Boots' hand.

"We will be risking all our lives and all of our judgments, all the time from now on - and they're no voting booths in the Governor's world," Boots replied. "Do you want to go back to our friends?"

"No. Yes, I want to, but I have a feeling that they're ready too. I just hope I can trust it. Anyway, enough o' my yakey. Let's saddle these critters up and head on out!"

"Ja Boss," Boots grunted. Then she whispered, "But Buddy, please remember one thing. I have learned to always trust what you feel as much, or even more than I what I think."

"I know," Puss responded with a smile as she gave her friend's hand a last squeeze, and mounted her bike.

*

The two regained the Chin military highway after leaving the old logging road and made good time as they traveled southward along the coast. They covered over three hundred kilometers in four hours before they stopped to rest. They were able to travel from their area of activity between the ruins of the old town of Prince Rupert and the site of the village of Kitimat, because of this road that the Chin had built during their long occupation.

The Chin road system was very direct in its design and so the two women were able to travel in a route that would not have been possible before the war. A trip to Seattle from Kitimat then required a major divergence eastward for an additional 900 kilometers, before travelers could turn back west and south to reach the city. However before the invasion, the former government of British Columbia did not have the conscript labor for road building...

The Chin did, thus transportation was now vastly improved because of the efforts of the pool of workers used by the Chin. This pool was made up of locals who had stubbornly refused to flee when the Canadian government had acquiesced to the Chin territorial demand, and of the numerous US soldiers who had surrendered when were overwhelmed by the Chin during the early phases of the war – and trusted them to observe the ancient Geneva Convention on war prisoners.

The many that died during the road building process were honored though by being included in the great work though, when their stripped bodies were punctured and flattened under the spiked wheels of motorized compaction rollers before being covered under the next load of soil. This was done so that the subsequent decomposition after their burial in the roadway fill would not create voids and slumps, and so cause dips in the pavement.

Over the years of the Chin occupation, their road engineers had perfected this efficient disposal method to deal with the erosion of the conscript workforce, and so their two-lane military roads were very direct and had even surfaces.

*

The two women sat beside their parked bikes just inside the tree line on the side of the road. They were resting at one of the rare stretches where it ran in flat terrain and did not go over fills or through cuts, so they had an easy place to turn aside into the cover of the forest.

"Damn if I don't wish Bila was here and doin' his G-7 thing with some more venison steaks so I could just use this chunk of `clave crappo as a target!" Boots sighed wistfully as she gestured with the half-eaten ration bar she held.

"My sediments exactly Sweetie! And just how much dirt you figger' they mix with their soybeans when they make these damn things now anyway?" Puss gasped after emitting a sudden belch, followed seconds later by a muffled flatulence as she rolled over on one hip. "I think they're gettin worse every batch!"

"As much as they think they can get away with," Boots muttered, and then she bounded to her feet and hurling the remainder of her rash bar off through the trees with disgust, growled, "I can't finish it. Let's roll, and I'll buy us steaks at Rick's tonight."

"Yur'on Buddy! Want a swig to wash it on down?" Puss asked as she held a water bottle up to her friend, her green eyes smiling.

"Yeah, thanks," Boots grinned as she accepted it and took several swallows. Then wiping her mouth with the back of her hand, she continued as her own eyes turned playful, "And now I want a kiss for tha' road."

"Only if ya' promise to give it back," Puss giggled as she rose and stepped into her friend's strong embrace.

Several moments later they relaxed and parted, each breathing deeply. Then Boots commanded, "You watch how you straddle that bike when we're back on the road Missy, I've got some ideas about what we can do later - after we leave the club," as her voice became a husky whisper.

"Don't fret yourself none Honey Chile'. Bikes are fun at first, but like everything else that's mechanical, they get boring after a while," Puss smiled sweetly as she bent and retrieved her helmet. Strapping it on, she then mounted her machine and settled into its saddle with several markedly suggestive wiggles, and sensuously licking her lips murmured, "You aren't gonna' be 'mechanical' tonight, are you?"

"Dammit ya' little mink, you know you can make me get real animal anytime you want to," Boots smiled as she buckled on her own helmet. Then switching on its intercom mike she kissed it loudly as she leered at her friend.

"Yep" Puss replied with a smug smile, "And don't you ever forget it, Big'un!" as she kissed her own mike in return.

"Don't worry Baby Doll, I can't," Boots whispered. Then becoming all business again she growled as she mounted and her bike, "OK, let's beat it on to that damn bunker. Buda's Butt, I want to shower for an hour!"

*

They sped southward on the nearly straight road and crossed several large rivers and fjords, which the Chin engineers had spanned in fashion uniquely secure from aerial attack. They had built their bridges on strings of pontoons that could be opened in the center, and the two parts swung into hardened shelters in each bank when not in use. In order to not waste energy or time in deploying the large floating span for small numbers of vehicles however, the builders had also equipped each crossing with several ferry craft guided by tethering cables strung across the bodies of water, and propelled solely by the force of its currents. The two women used these boats, and so lost little time at the river crossings.

*

They reduced their speed when they reached the overgrown side trail that was their destination and turned into the forest at a point where the main road rounded the nose of a ridge in a sweeping curve. Boots throttled down and raised her hand after they had rolled along the faint track along the grassy center between its two ruts.

Puss slowed her machine to a gentle stop as well and both women dismounted and propped their bikes. Boots knelt and reaching into the rotted cavity at the base of a dead spruce, and pressed a hidden signal switch.

A patch of the forest floor silently hinged upward ten meters from the tree and the two walked their bikes down the ramp under the camouflaged portal into an abandoned Chin vehicle bunker, and racked them beside a number of other bikes.

They removed their gear from the carrier bars and connected their machines to the bunker's hydrogen generator for recharging. Then Puss checked the temperature and the levels of nutrients and dissolved oxygen in its large microbe-breeding vat and cleaned the screens of the sun lamps shining down into the thick soup of cyanobacteria slowly bubbling within. Making slight adjustments to the nutrient and air feed controls, she grinned as she looked through the view port of the tank and crooned, "Nice little buggies... Now go poot out lots of hydrogen for Mommy, OK."

Boots took a small haversack from a hook beside the entry and the two women shrugged in to their packs and walked up and out of the bunker. Boots also slung the assault rifle over her shoulder and was preparing to add the trank gun as well, when Puss took it from her friend's hand and slipped its sling over her own shoulder.

"No no, Young Lady! Teacher is going to keep this until Little Krissie learns to not leave it lying around loaded, where any bad old mark can play with it. Why goshey-gee, someone might get hurt!"

Boots grunted, then pouted theatrically for a moment before she sneered as she twirled an imaginary moustache, "Hah, Me Proud Beauty, you'll pay dearly for yur' disrespect to Tha' Boss later tonight!"

"Oooo, I can hardly wait!" Puss giggled over her shoulder as she knelt and pressed the hidden switch to close the door to the bunker. After it sank back in to place, the two women adjusted the vegetation growing on and around it and hid its outline in the forest floor.

Boots stood and was all business again as she muttered, "Based on recent intel, I think I'll dress a little more carefully before we head up to our bunker," and pulling the hood of her cat-suit up over her hair, she brought out her camo kit and began streaking her face.

"Good thinkin'. And you get a merit point, if you can color inside the lines like I taught you," Puss grunted as she applied the paint to her own face, again beginning with three vertical black lines on her forehead.

"Thanks, Sneaker One," Boots growled.

"You're welcome, Kiddo," Puss grinned sweetly.

They both turned and paced in silence up the slope above the bunker. When they neared the crest of the ridge, they slowed their pace through the dappled gloom of the forest and slipped among the boles of the towering trees until they stopped beside an ancient fir. It had been struck by lightening in a previous century and had lost its crown.

Its trunk was badly scarred by the discharge and a hollow had rotted into its exposed heartwood gaped at its base. Boots knelt and reached in the hollow. She pulled out a small brown plastic box that had three thin cables attached to it which trailed off under the needles and leaf mold on the forest floor.

She opened its watertight lid to expose a panel with a single computer port. She reached in the haversack on her shoulder and brought out a small interface unit and plugged it into the port, and activated its screen.

"Entry looks clear," Boots whispered after the tiny display lighted with an image. Then she keyed in another signal and watched as the view changed to picture a stark room, glowing in the strange colors of infrared light. "Looks the same you think?" she asked as she showed the screen to Puss.

"Maybe. Check the bug scanner."

Boots keyed in another entry and stared at a graphic readout that replaced the image. "Hmmm, flat lines," she whispered. Then she set the timer on her field watch. The two waited in silence as they gazed at the screen until Boots looked at her watch again.

"Hmmm, still flat lines, and no activity spikes - not even from the room-radar's scan every minute. This must be caused by a power loss, don't ya' think?" she whispered in exaggerated innocence.

"Sure Buddy, or by our radar's program putting itself in undercover mode because it picked up someone walking into our bunker."

"Bouncin' Budas Gal, you think someone would really try a sneak into to our humble home?"

"Yes. Actually such an entity does come to mind, like the ferkin' Boss

Rat's bunch," Puss hissed. "Present company excepted of course."

"Thanks Buddy, I appreciate your complement, of finally excluding me from that gang," Boots whispered with a crooked grin as she shut down and unplugged the display. Stowing the viewer in her haversack, she closed and replaced brown box in the cavity. Then she groped in it for a moment, and withdrew a smaller black plastic box trailing a single slender cable. She unclamped the lid and hinged it open, and pressed the button marked "Test" the tiny panel within. After a green light momentarily flashed, Boots pressed the tip of her right index finger on the tiny recognition pad next to the test button.

She nodded grimly to Puss when an amber light began blinking, then she offered the box to her friend.

"Think we'll need it?"

Boots shrugged without comment - and after considering for a moment, Puss firmly pressed her finger to the pad as well, and watched without expression as the small light changed to a steady red glow.

Boots closed the box and replaced it in the hollow of the tree then she and Puss stood and moved with extreme caution for another hundred meters until they reached a level area where a bench had been excavated into the side of the ridge. It was overgrown with a dense thicket of mountain shrubs and saplings in contrast to the sparse under story growth in the surrounding forest.

They worked their way through the brush to the vine covered concrete arch of the entry to the command bunker built in to the steeply sloping face behind the bench. They stepped over the forest litter in the short tunnel and stopped before a rust-streaked steel blast door.

Boots faced a corroded panel set in the concrete wall beside the door and keyed in a code sequence on its faded number pad. The panel swung open to reveal a control board behind it, also corroded and rust streaked. She noted that the pressure gage set in the board showed a reading of 6.2 bars. Then she pulled a small flashlight from a belt pouch and brought her face close to the board. She shined its light through one of the rust holes in its surface as she peered through another to one side.

*

When the two had first discovered this abandoned Chin command bunker, Boots had designed several additional security precautions that the two then installed. One allowed them to monitor for intrusions in their absence by means of a hidden second air compressor and pressure tank which was the real air supply to the cylinder operating the blast door. Upon leaving, any intruder knowledgeable of typical Chin bunker design could be expected to start the compressor originally installed as a part of the door's machinery, and thus rebuild the air in the pressure tank connected to it. This would replace the air expended to operate the door, and thus hide the fact of a covert entry.

*

Boots abruptly sprung upright and un-slung her rifle as she signaled to Puss, "Pressure 3.2 bars on real gage. Need 3 bars one door cycle. They run old compressor when they leave. Old compressor vent outside. Not hook to system we add, or real gage."

"What do?"

"Go in – max alert!"

Puss drew her pistol and signed, *"Careful. We got date tonight, remember?"* as she smiled and gave Boots a brief squeeze on her bottom. Then her eyes changed to green ice as she clicked her safety off and stood ready at one side of the door.

"I not forget important stuff," Boots signed with a slight smile, then she slapped the control button on the corroded panel and sprang back to stand ready at the other side of the portal, as the rusty steel door slid back with a hiss.

The two waited for a second after the door opened and the room inside flooded with light as the glow strips switched on automatically. Then they sprang through the opening to land in action stances – each covering half of the space in the room with their weapons at the ready.

The room was empty, and after the two saw that there was no overt threat, they relaxed, slightly.

Boots cradled her rifle and groping again in the haversack, she pulled out another instrument. She signed to Puss after clicking it on and extending its short antenna, *"See if new bugs be in our rug."*

"Well Kiddo," Boots continued in a normal voice after peering at the instrument's dial, "Looks like we knocked off another one," then she cued Puss with a nod.

"Yep, Buddy, and I'm ready for a little relax therapy."

"You got that right. Why don't you turn on the water heater and soon as it gets hot let's hop in the shower an' get all slick and steamy?"

Puss scuffed her boot soles on the concrete floor several times without leaving Boots' side, then stood and watched the instrument in her friend's hand as the needle on its indicator dial flicked off zero for a second.

"Burst transmission from new bug!" Puss signed as Boots nodded with grim eyes.

"Who did? What want?"

"Rat tracks I think. Want us..."

Puss nodded, *"Major agree. Think they put cams in here?"*

"Bursts too short for cams. Only audio."

"OK. What next?"

"Check things. Grab what we need. Get." Then Boots continued aloud, "You hungry like me?" as she drew her pistol and turned to the door.

"Yep. I'll see what I can find," Puss announced in a cheerful voice as she stepped over to one of the bunks and bending, retrieved a duffel bag from under it. She spread it open on the bunk and unsung the tranquilizer gun and placed it in the bag, then in swift silence added several Chin and U.S. assault rifles with folding stocks from a rack on the wall.

After loading another rifle and slinging it over her shoulder, she continued filling the bag with ammunition, a carton marked "Grenades, Gas, Mk. 8", several propellant cylinders and a box of darts for the tranquilizer gun, and finally two archaic large-caliber revolvers with their ammunition.

Puss then strode to a locker, and grabbing jumpsuits, underwear and socks for the two of them, stuffed the clothing into the bag it where it would pad the weapons and ammunition. Then she paused, and after considering for a second grabbed several handfuls of sealed plastic envelopes from an interior shelf and added them to the bag as well.

She zipped it closed and waved to Boots as she swung the whole locker out into the room on its silent hinges. Puss spun the dial of the small safe in the wall behind it, and after opening its door, removed a little red plastic box. She tucked the box in a breast pocket.

"Well, here's some cheese and crackers that ain't too stale, and I think there's some bubbly an' caviar in the reefer," Puss announced as she pushed the locker back against the wall and clomped noisily to the refrigerator in the cooking area of the stark room. She opened its door, and leaned to peer intently at the single bottle of champagne and tin of caviar on its shelf.

Puss straightened and moved silently back to where Boots stood facing the door and watching the almost imperceptible flicks on the dial of her meter as the listening device transmitted its brief bursts.

"Bottle is moved. Looks different." Puss signed.

"You think the water tank is hot yet? My poor old pelt has a real bad case of tha' creep-crawls," Boots announced as she stepped to the open refrigerator.

"I'll check on it Sweetie,"

"Good," Boots mumbled after a moment, faking the sound of talking through a full mouth as she grasped the bottle and lifted it from the refrigerator rack while Puss watched with wide eyes.

Boots held it before her and inspected it closely as Puss signed, *"It in different position. Label same, but crooked. Not our bottle!"*

Boots placed her cocked pistol on the table then retrieved her small flashlight. Shining its beam through the dark green glass, she held the bottle and quickly examined its lighted interior from the neck down. She noted its base was curiously thick even for a champagne bottle. Then she changed the angle of her light and caught the telltale gleam of a tiny microcircuit board imbedded in the base.

She pointed it out to Puss and signed, *"Someone know we like champagne. This is pressure activated signal box or I be a Chin grunt!"*

"What for?"

"So they know time we open bottle and drink stuff inside. I bet the stuff inside is not good wine. And not good for us."

"What now?"

"We open it! But in my way!" Then Boots called, "Is that damn shower water hot yet?"

Puss ran with silent steps to the other side of the room and responded in a muffled yell, "Yep! Come on in!" as she turned on the shower taps and created a hissing noise that partially covered the sound of their movements.

Boots holstered her pistol and grabbing a note pad lying on the table, hastily penned a message. After doing that, she stripped the seal from the neck of the bottle and removed its cork, creating a loud "Pop" as she squealed, "Here I come, an' I got goodies!"

Then with a look of distain on her face that could have stop a rutting bull moose in its tracks, Boots placed the bottle on the table next to her note and waved her friend toward the door.

The two women grabbed the heavy duffel and silently ran from the bunker into the scrub growth on the flat beyond its opening. They moved through the brush away from the line of the entry tunnel and dropping to the ground, backed under the foliage at a spot where they could see the portal, and waited.

A burly figure in black coveralls appeared at the top of the top of the cut-bank above the entry five minuets later. He stared down for a moment, then he and three others, also in black, clumsily slid down to the bench. They gathered themselves before the entry and rushed as a body into the bunker.

Boots' eyes gleamed with a look of innocent joy as she counted slowly in a whisper, "One. Two. Three. Four. Five. Six. Seven…" then she paused and smiling like an angel, murmured to Puss, "OK. You or me?" as she opened her hand for the red box Puss held.

"It's my turn dammit," Puss purred as she flicked the power switch in the box to "On", then thumbed open the cover protecting the only other button on the box - and calmly pressed it.

There was the muffled rumble of a massive explosion seconds later and a dust cloud gushed from the bunker doorway as the six claymore mines the women had planted in the walls of the room detonated and blasted shrapnel throughout the space, immediately shredding all of its contents, and occupants.

The two women felt the shockwave in their bellies as they hugged the ground and instinctively opened their mouths to protect their eardrums. A second explosion erupted after a moment which sent a gigantic fireball out through the bunker's opening scorching the bushes and small trees in its path, when the hydrogen tank from the bunker's fuel cell ignited.

"Hmmm, I'll bet all that Rat-burger in there is now fried well done, or perhaps crispy even," Boots whispered.

"Yep." Puss replied in a level tone. "Now let's go see where the scum came from, OK?"

"Ja Boss. But let's see if the door still works first," Boots replied as she sprang to her feet and leapt toward the smoking entry. Puss followed, and watched as Boots palmed the still hot control on the scorched control board. After the door closed with a hiss of compressed air, Boots then turned a valve handle beside the control, and with another prolonged hiss, the real air tank discharged while she stood and licked her burning fingers.

"Well, now they're gone fer' good fer' sure," Puss grunted as she turned and started trotting toward the end of the bench.

"Yep, with no fuel cell, no compressor and no air pressure, it'd take a howitzer to get through that door when it's closed," Boots said with a grim smile as she followed her friend up the ridge to backtrack the men who had worn the Rat's coveralls.

*

"Pretty sloppy campers if you ask me," Boots grunted as they stood looking down at the crumpled bedrolls and ration bar wrappers left behind by their would-be attackers.

"How'd they know where to camp, and where to plant their little surprise, is all I'm asking Buddy."

"And I'm thinking, OK!" Boots muttered. "So turn on your famous right brain and give me some help Kid. We know a damn-sight more now than when we came out on this op. And I know that almost all of these command bunkers are located and mapped. But I don't know how they found the one we use..."

Then she paused as her eyes narrowed, "Unless they trailed us on our way out somehow, sometime." Boots paused again, and her eyes suddenly glared as she hissed, "Like maybe with a locator in that damn bugged com-set they make me use to call in their copters!"

"Good start, although it could also be with the ones we sit on" Puss gritted as she began moving about the campsite collecting the discarded ration bar wrappers.

"Yep, and we're gonna have to do something about those soonest. Anyway, to change this depressing subject - I know you like to keep the woods clean Squaw Gal, but is it time right now?"

"I also like knowing how long those Rats squatted here waitin' for us, O Mighty Thinker. And it looks like about a day, `cos there are twelve wrappers, and there were four goons and nobody can eat more than three chunks of that crappo in 24 hours," Puss said.

"Then that means that they were launched yesterday, like a little while after we sold Durwood them," Boots snapped. "I think I smell something mighty musty around this op, like a little sneak with a big Wart Face," Then she squatted and opened an abandoned field pack. "Anyway, let's see what they left for us."

Puss did the same with another and gritted, "Sleepy drug syringes and gas canisters, they were going to collect us, Dammit!"

"Yeah, I've got some here too, and some fetters. And something else, that might actually be helpful".

"What?"

"This," Boots replied, holding up a small field computer. "Though we can use the sleepy stuff too."

"Think it's bugged?"

"Probably. But I've got an idea," she said as she placed the computer on the ground and removed its battery pack. She used the tip of a throwing knife to snap open its back, then after inspecting its interior for a moment, gently removed the computer's operating and memory unit. She carefully placed the unit in a belt pouch and restored the back cover and its battery. However as she closed the computer, she blocked the battery's terminal contacts with a small piece of ration wrapper.

"What are we going to do with the memory?"

"Give it to Molly, and see what she can pull out of it."

"Good thinkin', but what are we goin' to do with the 'puter? If we leave it, whoever comes looking for their goons will figure pretty quickie that it has lost its brain. But if we take it with us, it still might have a bug in it."

"Yep, so we'll just take it half way."

"What?"

"Later. Now let's stow our stuff and head for the 'Clave."

"Ja Boss." Puss muttered.

They collected their items into Boots' haversack then as they were leaving, Puss asked with a grin, "Oh, and just what did yur' little love note to those goons say?"

Boots chuckled with cold eyes, "Waiter! This wine tastes funny! I think it's going off!"

Puss snorted then they returned to the top of the bench and glissaded down its steep slope. The two collected their heavy duffel from the brush and began an easy ground-covering trot back down to the vehicle bunker.

*

They unpacked the duffel in the narrow space next to their bikes and after inspecting their weapons, placed them in a rack on one wall.

Boots growled as she stripped, "I really wanted that shower and those skunk-butts took it away from me, blast their hides!"

"I think we already sorta' did just that," Puss chuckled as she slipped out of her own jump suit and underwear. They both cleaned the paint from their faces, then removing a small canister from her field pack and handing it to her friend, Puss added, "Put a couple of squirts of this in all the right places, and you'll be able to live with yur' self 'till we get back to hot water."

"I dunno', I'm pretty ripe."

"Well, go on and use it - so at least I can live with ya'," Puss giggled.

"Is that so!" Boots snorted. "Well Little Buddy, maybe you need it more than me," and leaping at her friend, she began squirting the deodorant at various parts of the young woman's body.

Puss spun and twisted to escape for a minute, but after pausing in an action crouch, she grabbed Boots' hand with eye-blinking speed and wrested away the canister. Smiling sweetly all the while, she then began dancing around her friend and firing accurate bursts of the spray at the tall woman's pale form as she chanted, "Right place number one - right place number two - right place number three..."

Boots stopped trying to evade her friend after a moment and Puss stopped her attack. The two stood and stared at each other for several seconds, then broke into howls of laughter and fell into each other's arms, as they let the tension of their combat intensity drain away, mostly...

When they were able to talk again Boots gasped, "OK Buddy, lets get hiking, we gotta go and talk to a whole bunch of men about a whole bunch of horses."

"You're getting cryptic Big'un! You've been reading them damn books again?"

"Actually Doctor, I've already read 'um all!" Boots grinned.

"Well then Professor, you must have learned in your studies," Puss responded pedantically as she stepped into a pair of fresh snuggs, "That while in the long run the pen is mightier than the sword - in the near term bayonets can be damn persuasive, right?"

"Yes. And I think I will have to use both," Boots replied with a face that suddenly was made of stone. She clothed herself in clean garments without further comment.

Puss considered her friend for a moment then she finished dressing in silence.

The two, now clad in the baggy gray coveralls issued to the civilians in the 'Claves, selected other items of gear they would take with them and stowed the rest in wall cabinets. They walked up the ramp and closing its camouflaged door, again removed all traces of their presence in the area. Then the two shrugged on their newly loaded civilian backpacks and began trotting in silence back along the faint track toward the military highway.

*

"Transport net, come in. Transport net, come in," Boots called into her personal comset. "I execute prearranged non-scheduled passenger pickup, authorization number 3XZZ239R3006. Repeat authorization number 3XZZ239R3006. Do you get?"

"We get 3XZZ. Next opportunity in one hour at supplied coordinates. Do you get?"

"We get. We be there,"

"Is good. Out."

"Out.

"OK Buddy, looks like we have some time to sit and think, and talk while we wait. If ya' want to," Puss said quietly as she slipped out of her pack's straps and plopped down on a grassy spot in the right-of-way beside the military road.

"Yep Kiddo we do, and you have the floor," Boots said as she shed her own pack and dropped to sit in the grass across from her friend.

"Thanks. Now first, just what tha' ferk is our Mission back in S'attl?"

"Well, two days ago it was going to be celebration and frolic, but as of yesterday it changed to doing a cautious recon – and after an hour ago I think it will now be to plan a whole new strategy."

"OK, I agree. Number two, do these men and horses we are going to see have anything to do with what Bila sketched this morning?"

"Damn, you're good! Yes. A lot, still want to come along?"

"'Course Buddy, you know you always need somebody to cover your butt while you do policy stuff. However, I have one major question for you."

"And?"

"Why have you decided to do this now?" Puss asked in quiet earnestness as she stared at her friend.

"Two reasons," Boots finally answered in a whisper after looking off at the few clouds in the clear sky for several pensive moments. She brought her eyes back to earth and returned her friend's gaze with naked honesty.

"Partially because of what we found out yesterday and the day before from Wartsy and his bunch. But mainly because of something you and Bila said to me after we found Molly - and she tried to run away from us."

"What did we say?" Puss asked.

"No."

"What? What do you mean?" Puss asked with a puzzled frown.

"When you and Bila took the command away from me because you wanted to save Molly from Wart Face, I realized that I actually had, although only briefly and way in the back of my mind, thought about collecting her.

"But when you two stopped me, you made me remember what one of my favorite professors in my academy told me on the day I first began to learn the truth about the Governors and Boss Rat."

"What was that?"

"He said that the Governors always screen for people with talents like mine," then she added with a soft smile, "And yours. And if they couldn't recruit us, they would try to kill us."

"So?"

"So, yesterday the two of you made me see how close I had come to letting them get their hook into me. And I didn't like what I saw. So Kiddo, since I know now I can never join them – well, it looks like I'll have to just go take them down..."

"No Buddy. The operative word here is We," Puss whispered with a catch in her voice as she clasped Boots' hands and squeezed them with a grip of iron as her eyes glistened.

Boots stared at her friend. She tried to speak several times, then bowed her head and brought Puss' fingers to her lips. She gently kissed them as slow tears welled from her closed eyes and coursed down her cheeks, and dropped onto her friend's hands.

Boots finally raised her head and took a deep shuddering breath. She opened her eyes and blinked until she could see her friend's face again. She smiled like the first ray of sunlight at dawn.

"Thanks. I needed that. And I need you."

Puss just nodded and the two sat in silence for many long minutes, holding hands and occasionally glancing at each other with quiet smiles. Then Puss stirred and shifted her position. "What do you think about Bila?" she asked.

Boots uncrossed her legs and pulling them up, rested her chin on her knees and hugged her thighs as she stared into space.

"What do I think of him?" she finally said, "I don't know for sure, but I think that he is honest, which is most important.

"I know he's over-the-top smart, and learns really fast, and I'm seeing more signs of that every minute we're around him.

"I can tell he's used to being a leader, and a good one I think. But there are two things I really - really don't understand about him."

"What?"

"Well the obvious one is who is he and where does he come from. I think I have figured it out in my mind but I can't really accept what I feel to be true, in spite of Ockham dammit - because it's impossible!"

"OK, I agree. What's the other one?"

"Him. Why did he save our butts? Why did he hunt down the mark for us? Why does he feed us? Why did he save Molly, and he did by tha' way – I could have maybe talked you out of it."

"Could not!"

"OK Buddy, I'll grant you that one. Satisfied?"

"I'll think about it. Keep on talkin'," Puss said with a dry sniff.

Boots took a deep breath and continued, "He's damn big and damn strong and damn fast, and face to face without our "tools of the trade", he could make girl-butter out of both of us in two minutes flat, or do anything else he wanted to with us. And we're the best there are.

"But he doesn't, he just leaves us alone until we need something. And I don't feel any authority grabs or control attempts, or any other ego crappo like that coming out of him - unlike the male jerkoids I've had to deal with before. And finally, I don't think he ever thinks about himself at all."

Then Boots sighed, "And dammit, those are the all things I like about him the most. So now Buddy, how about you?"

"I agree total with everything you say," Puss whispered as she touched her friend's head and turned it to capture her gaze. "But there's something more I haven't told you, about last night. He touched me."

Boots smiled, "Well, I would hope so! You looked, and smelled like you had been "touched" pretty damn ferkin' good when you came back to bed Kiddo."

"No Buddy, listen to me. When we got "there", you know what I mean, all of a sudden I felt him... I don't know how else to describe it, but he opened me up and I felt him enter my mind. And then he opened his mind, and let me go into him. And then it was over. And I didn't know what really happened. And he didn't either.

"But I also know that he has lost someone whom he really loved," she whispered while gazing at her friend with confused eyes. "And there's something else. It first happened when we were sitting by the fire the other night and he was drawing the animals."

"What was that?"

"I got this funny feeling - and I've had it again when I'm doing something with him sometimes," she paused, then blushing slightly, continued in a rush, "Well, that I have done it with him before." She looked gravely at her friend, "And I think you've been getting some of those kinds of flashes too."

"Alright, Dammit! I'm shutting' this line of inquiry down now!" Boots announced, "We don't have enough data to analyze and we don't have enough time to be mystic!" She jumped to her feet and offered Puss a hand up. Then she embraced her as she murmured, "It must have been real good tho - to have you still seeing stars a whole day later!"

Puss returned her friend's embrace but then ignored her comment as she stepped back with a smile.

"I know what you're doing. You don't know what's going on, so you're rationalizing that it's not, but, Buddy something is. I can feel it."

"I know he's a damn good man and I know I am damn glad he's with us. That's enough for now. We can talk touchy-feely stuff later. Anyway, I hear the transport," Boots answered with a wooden face.

*

The noise of the approaching aircraft grew louder and when it came into sight Boots stepped to the center of the roadway and popped her last smoke grenade. Retreating as it began emitting a dense red plume, she grabbed her pack by the straps and stood waiting with Puss as the hybrid plane slowed and began its decent. Tilting its movable wings, the craft hung on its propellers as they repositioned to the vertical. Then the gray-painted government transport descended slowly to the surface of the roadway in a swirl of dust raised by its prop wash and the downward-directed exhaust of its turbojet-engines.

As soon as the craft touched its extended landing wheels to the pavement, a door opened in its side and a red light in the hull above it began blinking, slowly at first, then with increasing rapidity as the propellers continued to spin.

"Hump it Buddy!" Boots shouted as she sprinted for the doorway.

"See ya' inside Slowmo!" Puss yelled as she sped past her friend and leapt up the boarding ladder.

Scrambling into the craft a second later, Boots slammed and secured the entry hatch, before the pasty-faced attendant crouching by it could move.

"Don't worry son, I've been in and out of these crates more times than you got years, so go sit down until you can bring me some coffee!" she growled over her shoulder. Then she walked down the narrow isle between the two rows of canvass seats slung on pipe racks, as the aircraft lurched into its ascent. Maintaining her footing with practiced ease, Boots swung into the seat beside Puss as she exclaimed over the engine noise, "Why in hell do they say that "travel is broadening" when I get these damn narrow-minded seats every time I do it?"

"Because maybe they're makin' the seats normal sized these days?" Puss suggested with a snicker.

"I'll attend to your personal sitter later, Miss Priss, if you don't watch out," Boots growled with a grin.

"Oh, Horrors, Gasp, an' Eeek! even" the younger woman lazily replied as she slumped down and closed her eyes. "Just tell me when we're there, OK?"

"Ja Boss," Boots murmured in a voice barely audible above the noise filling the passenger compartment.

Later, when she saw that the transport was over Puget Sound Boots rose and after groping in her pack in the overhead rack, walked down the aisle and entered the comfort station in the rear of the aircraft.

She returned to sit beside her friend after a short interval.

"Feel better now?" Puss asked sleepily as she stirred and twisted in her seat.

"Yep," Boots answered in a low voice under the cover of the engine whine, "But I remembered too late that these birds don't have holding tanks. Their pots just dump out into the great outdoors. And because of this interesting design feature, stuff can be lost down the tube and go overboard, as it were."

"Like small electronics thingies?" Puss murmured.

"Unfortunately yes," Boots sighed.

"Alas, so sad," Puss whispered with a smile, as she closed her eyes again.

*

The transport throttled back in its decent to the single remaining civilian runway at `S'attl and opened its flaps as it approached the cracked slab in its airplane configuration. Its extended landing wheels met the pavement with a jarring thump, then after several smaller bounces the craft stabilized on the ground and the pilot began taxiing toward the terminal. The two women stirred themselves and carefully rose to stand in the aisle of the transport, along with the other six passengers in the twenty-seat craft.

"I've always heard that any landing you walk away from is a good one, but dammit, I don't walk so good with a busted spine," Boots muttered to her friend as they both balanced themselves while the plane lurched over the poorly maintained pavement. Puss only made an affirmative grunt as she shrugged into her pack. Then the plane stopped and the attendant began struggling to operate the hatch mechanism.

Passing through it after the dull-eyed young man finally got the door to open, Boots flashed a bright smile at him, whom she now decided had been protein-deprived since birth. "Thank you so much for our coffee, it was wonderful."

"Hey Sweetie," Puss chuckled as the two strolled across the apron toward the terminal, "He didn't bring us any coffee."

"I know that! But now he's going to wonder if he really did and he'll worry about it for the rest of his attention span, all five seconds of it," Boots grinned.

"You is Baaad!"

"Yeah but I do it so damn Goood, don't I?"

*

The rusting sheet metal temporary building that had been serving as the civilian terminal for the last 32 years was sited next to the shattered ruins of what had been the main building of Seattle International, its rubble heaps now covered with brush and small trees.

A faded sign over the small door into the present facility proclaimed:

WELCOME TO THE SAFETY OF THIS ENCLAVE.
YOUR GOVERNORS WILL PROTECT YOU.
BE PREPARED TO PROVE YOUR IDENTITY.
SURRENDER YOUR WEAPONS.
OBEY.

Boots and Puss dropped all playfulness and stepped through the door with blank expressions on their faces. They paused just inside until they selected an examination station that was vacant and moved toward it. The two presented their packs for inspection as their fellow passengers slouched toward the other stations in the echoing and dusty building.

"Alright, you two dump all your weapons – now!" the surly guard dressed in the black coverall uniform of the military Governor's security force growled as he rested his hand on his holstered automatic. His female partner behind the metal table also wore the black uniform, stained under her double chin, and strained by her large stomach.

She pointedly drew on latex examination gloves and ordered, "Open 'um up and then stand back. Move it!"

Puss reached into a breast pocket and presented her tiny folding knife while Boots removed a pair of nail scissors from an outside pouch on her pack before placing it on the table. Then the two women un-zipped and laid their bags open and stepped back. They watched stoically as the fat female rummaged through the extremely feminine clothing, undergarments and makeup kits their packs contained.

The male guard closely and ponderously examined their cutlery and with squinted eyes, compared the tiny objects to a tattered chart taped on the splintered plywood wall. Suddenly the female pounced on a plastic envelope in Puss' pack, and then after rummaging in that of Boots momentarily, she slapped another packet on the dented table in triumph. "Where did you get these?" she hissed as she jabbed her finger at the two packages containing sheer black stockings. "They are real silk!"

"We found them in an old Chin bunker where they kept some Comfort Girls for their senior officers," Boots responded in a grudging tone with lowered eyes.

"Ha! This is contraband stuff! I could charge you with trading with the enemy," the fat woman snarled in a low voice, while at the same time keeping the packages discretely out of the view of the guards at the other stations.

"We didn't mean any harm," Puss whimpered. "It's just that they are so pretty, and we like pretty things..."

"You two won't look so pretty in prison smocks Dearie," the male guard growled. Then he continued pompously, "We're confiscating this illegal material for the Good of the 'Clave. But because of your youth I am letting you both off with just a warning this time. Also we won't make a record of your crimes if you cooperate and remain silent about our clemency, and we have ways of knowing if you don't." he finished in an ominous tone.

"Oh thank you Sir and Ma'am," Boots responded in a broken whisper. "We promise we won't do this ever again."

"Yes, thank you very much! We sure have learned a lesson today," Puss added, her eyes wide and solemn.

"Good! Now get your stuff off my table and get your precious butts on through the scan-door. Make your selves scarce before we change our minds!"

the female snapped.

With identical timid smiles, the two women rapidly repacked their bags in silence and hurried to the security archway. Boots stepped into it first and backed up to the scanning screen set in one side, and then went on through as it signaled "Pass" in a green light to her, and the guards. Puss immediately followed, and almost leapt out as she also received clearance. Then the two walked rapidly with their heads down out of the building and on toward the ground transportation area.

The other arriving passengers began forming themselves into a line at the bus stop, standing patiently as the usual afternoon rain cloud passes over and showered them with its large slow drops. They watched with dull-eyed envy as the two women entered the single taxi on duty at the stand and were driven away.

*

"Some things not change. Like greed. How many silks you save before wine go bad?" Boots tapped on Puss' wrist with a crooked grin as they sat on the worn upholstery in the rear seat of the fuel-cell powered sedan, its wipers slapping and its aging springs creaking as it rolled along the rough roadway toward what remained of the city.

Puss glanced toward the supposedly soundproof screen that separated the driver from the passenger's compartment, and then with a slight smile she tapped back *"Ten. Enough do five more trips. If us need strip-search insurance more."*

Boots responded, *"Us might. Us know soon. Glad it work this time. Us not need show us dimples. Or other stuff under us clothes."*

Puss nodded, and then glancing again at the back of the driver's scrawny neck, casually asked aloud, "What are we doin' for supper?"

"Hey, glad ya' reminded me. I'll see if I can round us up some dates," Boots answered with a chuckle as she flipped out her personal com-set and punched in a number from memory. After the connection was made, she said, "Hello Bobby, it's your ole' school buddy, back in town. Want to round up some of tha' guys and get together tonight?"

"Oh you know, the usual gang and at the usual place. We can toss around some words over drinks and swap some lies, and maybe we can even do some dancin' like we did the last time."

Boots listened silently for a moment. Then she finished with a laugh, "OK big boy, we'll see you at 19:00 hours. Bring an appetite!"

Puss glanced again at the back of the driver's head and while noting that he seemed indifferent to his passengers, silently signal her friend, *"That most cryptic data burst I hear long time! You talk this Bobby about horses while you him dance?"*

"Maybe," Boots responded as she leaned back in the seat.

The two sat in silence for the remaining thirty minutes of the ride through the mostly empty streets into the old residential-commercial part of town, until Boots rapped on the partition. After the driver slid its port open, she commanded, "Let us off here," as she handed him a credit chip.

The man pulled over to the curb and stopped the vehicle. Inserting the chip in his scanner, he entered the fare and passed it back to her for approval. The tall woman doubled the amount and authorized payment, and watched the driver blinked at the size of her tip, then frowned as the identity readout for the chip's owner remained blank on the instrument's screen.

"Don't worry, son. It'll go through – unless you try to back-track me. Then it will only give you the meter, get it?"

"Got it!" he smirked, as he jumped out and opened their door with an exaggerated flourish. The two stepped to the sidewalk, and stood on its cracked pavement until the driver re-entered his taxi and drove down the street. They waited until he had turned a corner and disappeared before they turned and walked toward the seedy six-story building behind them.

They entered the little market on its ground floor and Boots nodded to the old woman sitting behind the counter, "Hi Mrs. Kostanis, how've you been?" she smiled as she inhaled the wonderful mix of smells in the shop.

The woman's wrinkled face lighted with a wide smile and her dark eyes twinkled as she greeted the two, "Well hello my babies! I'm so glad to see you again. Are you still being nice little girls?"

Puss replied with an almost straight face, "Well, everybody says we're pretty damn good anyway."

The old woman hopped to her feet chuckling, "You two kids still got a long way to go if you want to be as good as they said I was when I was your age. But enough of the truth about my beauty, what can I get for you today?"

"We want to celebrate. You got any bubbly and caviar tucked away in this dump?" Boots grinned.

"Dump? Don't you dare call my hovel a dump, you Big Barbarian!" Mrs. Kostanis squawked in mock indignation over her shoulder as she scuttled into a storeroom at the rear of the shop. She returned moments later with a dusty bottle, a small tin and a cloth-wrapped bundle all of which she placed on the counter. Stooping, she retrieved a feather duster from under the counter and cleaned the bottle.

"This is some Servuga that we found," she said, motioning to the still-cold tin. "All the Beluga and Ostera we have located and ordered don't seem to get past our US Customs agents back East somehow.

"It doesn't matter anyway. My people called all of it "Woock" and I love any of it I can get," Puss exclaimed with a happy smile.

"Good for you, and me," the old lady chuckled. Then gesturing to the bottle, "This is some old French we finally went out and found, after we tasted that stuff the S'mento 'clave down in Cali is starting to bottle from the vines their Governor ordered re-planted in Napa."

"How is their stuff?" Boots asked.

"Think of a liquid rash bar with bubbles, in a dirty glass," the old woman grimaced.

Both Puss and Boots shuddered. Then Boots asked, "What's in the cloth?"

"Some things I make for my friends. Try one," Mrs. Kostanis smiled as she opened the bundle and revealed a stack of delicate white wafers. "They are what my mother always made to serve with caviar and champagne."

The two each took one, and closed their eyes in pleasure as the light flaky crusts dissolved in their mouths. "Mmmm," Boots sighed in pleasure as Puss nodded silently, "This is Real. Thank you, very, very much! What do we owe you?"

"Let me figure the bill. I am getting so damn forgetful anymore that I have to do everything on paper these days," the little woman sighed as she seated herself behind the counter and reached for an old-style order book.

Opening it to a fresh page, she quickly entered two figures and totaled them, and then tore the top sheet from the book. She made another quick notation on the customer copy however, before casually sliding it across the counter.

Boots smiled as she saw the fair price Mrs. Kostanis was charging for the wine and the caviar then her eyes grew cold as she read the woman's added note.

"Many Rats around your building last two days."

"This seems reasonable, what do you think, Buddy?" Boots replied as she showed the ticket to Puss and offered Mrs. Kostanis a credit chip.

"Yep," her friend said in a sweet tone while her expression turned grim, "That's a real friendly price. Thank you again Mrs. Kostanis." Puss added as she pocketed the slip, placed the bottle and tin in her pack and cradled the package of wafers protectively in the crook of her arm.

"Oh, its nothing, all us pretty young girls have to stick together you know," the woman answered with a smile.

"We sure do friend," Boots whispered as she authorized her payment on the little instrument the woman placed the counter. Then she quietly asked, "May I also use your off-shore credit access to check on an account I have?"

"Certainly dear" and she reached under the counter and brought up another reader which was similar to the first, but which had a slender cable trailing from it.

Boots inserted the Swiss Gold chip from Wart Face, and then keyed in a number of entries at the machine's screen prompts. Then she waited for a moment as her instructions to the anonymous bank in Switzerland issuing the chip were carried out. At the blink of its action complete signal, Boots clicked it back to stand-by and slid it back across the counter to the smiling old woman.

"Thank you for letting me save some time," she said with a quick wink. "So what's Mr. Kostanis doing to keep out of trouble these days?"

"Well, right now he's in the back room putting together a big order for a big client," the woman responded in a neutral voice, with a hooded look suddenly in her eyes.

"Congratulations. May I ask who the lucky person is, who's smart enough to get their goodies from you?" Boots asked with equal caution.

"The Executive Office of the Network. They are having a fancy Gala in their studios day-after tomorrow for our Military Governor, General Butler."

"That's very thoughtful of them," Puss sniffed.

"Yes, isn't it," Boots murmured, then added, "Well, we gotta' run, and wash away a bunch of trail dust from our outsides and insides as well. Thanks again Mrs. Kostanis and say Hi to the Mister for us."

"And you both take care of your selves, OK!" Puss added as the two left the shop and began the short walk to their building while the old woman waved goodbye to them through the dusty front window.

*

"We need be careful," Puss tapped on her friend's hand as they walked down the dusty and dimly lit hallway toward Boots' apartment in one of the

buildings reserved for people at her level on the `Clave nomenclatura.

"We always need be careful! This morning and nice old lady intel say we need be double careful. Anyway Rat money safe now," Boots replied as she halted two meters from her door. She removed a cheap decorator print hanging on the corridor's rough-plastered wall and uncovered the fiber-optic peephole she had clandestinely installed soon after being granted the space. She looked through its eyepiece and viewed her studio apartment through its fisheye lens.

"Look clear." she signed. *"But sure Rat put more cams and mikes. Us now act - not react. Right?"* Then bending, she pulled up her pants leg and removed one of their captured sleepy gas spray canisters from a pouch beside the small holster strapped above her ankle.

"Yes. Anything. Just get me bath and drink!" Puss grinned as she retrieved her own spray canister.

Boots hung the print back on the wall, then with a grim face walked to her door and keyed in a combination. When the latch clicked, she pushed it open and entered quickly with Puss close behind. The two halted just inside the door with their canisters held at the ready in the folds of their baggy coverall pant-legs.

"Well, we're back home, now how about a bath and a drink?" Boots announced while her eyes swept the single room as she closed the door behind them. She leaned against it for a second and screening the action with her body, used her free hand to secure it with the tamper-proof mechanical bolt she had added.

"Can we do `um together?" Puss replied as she stepped to the other door in the small room and peered into the oversized bathroom beyond.

"Hey, we do everything together, don't we?" Boots laughed as she stepped to the tiny kitchen alcove. She opened the small refrigerator and inspected the wine bottles racked in its main compartment. While Puss watched intently from the bath doorway, Boots held one up to the light for a second.

"Same funny wine like bunker!" she signed rapidly to her friend as her eyes blazed.

"I mean the bath and the drink at the same time, Silly" Puss responded with a gaiety that was only in her voice.

"If ya' take champagne into the shower, it gets soggy real quick."

"So I'll just have to drink it quicker, won't I?" Puss replied with a laugh as she joined her friend in the kitchenette and retrieving their new bottle from her pack, inserted it in the refrigerator's chiller well and turned the control to fast. Then she took two stemmed glasses from the cupboard above and after thoroughly rinsing them at the small sink, upended them on the counter while Boots carefully opened Mrs. Kostanis' tin of caviar. As the glasses drained, Puss rummaged in a drawer and finally brought out a small gold handled spoon with a mother-of-pearl bowl while Boots retrieved their now-cold bottle from the chiller.

Boots arranged the champagne bottle and the cleaned flutes along with Mrs. Kostanis' wafers and the caviar tin on an engraved brass tray she had captured from a Chin command post, and balanced the whole on one hand with a flourish. But then she looked at her friend in mock confusion. "It's been so long I forget, what comes next?"

Puss lifted the little spoon aloft with a solemn face as she intoned, "Guide us O Divine Spoon! What Us Do Now?" She mimed listening as she held its bowl to her ear, with intense concentration for a second, before she nodded. "Spoon say Get Wet!" she announced to Boots as she marched into the bathroom, holding the little implement high before her and flourishing it like a drum major's staff.

"Ha! Now I remember," Boots chuckled as she followed Puss. "All thanks be to Thee, O Noble Spoon."

Boots carefully opened the bottle and filled their glasses, and they both served themselves generous heaps of the pale gray delicacy with the graceful little implement, piling it on Mrs. Konstains' wafers. They sighed with the pleasure of true sybarites and took healthy bites of the caviar and follow them with lusty swallows of the wine. They set their glasses aside without a word and kicking off their boots, unzipped their coveralls. As they pushed them down their legs, they covertly released their ankle holsters and left them hidden in their crumpled clothing on the floor.

Boots turned on the shower and dialed it to hot while Puss opened the valve on the double-sized tub and started it filling. As they waited for the stall to fill with steam, the two raised and drained their glasses in a toast, then stepped under the tingling spray with identical expressions of bliss.

They maintained tight control over their instincts as their bodies brushed and touched, while they soaped themselves in the narrow stall and each washed the other's back and hair. Then Boots cracked the stall door and peering out, announced, "Tub's up! We're clean enough, let's go soak 'um."

Pausing only to turban their wet hair with towels and to place more towels and the brass tray by the tub, they both sunk slowly into its steaming water and settled back with sensuous moans of pleasure. After an interval of silent ecstasy Puss murmured, "Want goodies?"

"Mmmm Hmm..."

The young woman stirred herself languidly and after drying her hands, prepared two more heaping wafers of caviar. Then refilling their glasses, she served her friend and settled back with a sigh in the tub beside her.

"Think us show good?" Puss tapped as she gripped Boots' hand under the water a moment later after finishing her wafer and taking a dainty sip of wine.

"I like - anyway," Boots tapped in reply as she showed a lazy smile. *"But I spot one new cam over mirror. We sleep out tonight. Yes?"*

"Good plan. Where?"

"Think two places maybe. Check later."

Puss closed her eyes while holding her own smile, and then after a moment tapped, *"This last tub time we do here long time, right?"*

"Right. Water this place too hot now."

"Much deep too. But will miss this place," Puss tapped, as she remembered the first time the tall, brilliant and complex woman had brought her into this stark white and chrome bathroom. She thought, "I was a pretty messy chickie when the patrol found me and took me back to base, and I really didn't care what kind of hi-jinks she wanted after she finished my verification interview. All I wanted was a bath, and I was willing to put up with anything to get it. But then she saw my hide after the Chin had used me for a month as a Jinying Li De Shibeig, a 'Company Recreational Device' she changed her focus and nursed me like a mommy cat does her sick kitten."

Opening her eyes, she smiled tenderly at Boots as she tapped beneath the water, *"I never forget first time I here."*

"I never forget either. What I learn of you." Boots tapped in reply, gazing at her friend in solemn sincerity.

Boots also thought back to that first day, and how the casual lust she had felt for the newly rescued young trooper had suddenly been replaced with concern, and then anger after she had disrobed the unresisting woman and had seen the marks of abuse on her body. Boots also remembered how calmly Puss lain on the exercise bench in the bathroom while she had used the resources of her extensive med kit to clean and dress each wound and bruise.

The young woman had remained quiet and unflinching even as Boots reopened and probed the many inflamed sores on her body in order to drain and clean their pockets of infection.

She had started with the whip marks on Puss' upper back and chest. Then when she began attending to Puss' hips and loins, Boots had puzzled at the numerous festering parallel scratches on each side of Puss pelvis, until the young woman had tersely told her about them.

Gazing at Puss soaking in the tub beside her, Boots recalled being so shaken with furry at the young woman's brief explanation that she had been forced stop caring for her until she could control her trembling hands again. Then, after tending to those wounds as well as bruises and lash marks on Puss' hips and the backs of her thighs, Boots had finally looked at young woman's feet - and gagged.

Puss had been beaten unmercifully in a bastinado, and the freshly healed scars on the soles of her feet were crisscrossed with wounds that were still open. Boots finally had realized at that moment just how tough this woman really was, to have walked uncomplainingly and without flinching on feet in this condition for the two long days after she had had been found by the patrol from Boots' unit.

Boots smiled and shook her head for emphasis to Puss as she tapped under the water in the tub, *"No. I never forget what I learn of you, Friend."*

Boots then recalled that it had taken her an hour to carefully clean and bandage each of Puss' feet, only to find when she had finished that Puss had drifted off to sleep with a smile on her lips. Boots had gathered her strength and carried the still sleeping woman to her large bed in the other room, gently tucked her in - and had sat in a chair by her side throughout the night.

The next morning she had briefly returned to her command headquarters, took a week's leave, and arranged for Puss to be assigned to her care for convalescence, while she ignored the not-quite hidden snickers of her subordinates...

*

Boots replayed the scene in her mind as she soaked in the tub. She had nursed the young woman for four days without allowing her on her feet until Puss gently but firmly rebelled and had taken charge of her self again, with a smile and a quiet, "Thank you."

Boots squeezed her friend's hand again, as she thought back to the emotions she began to feel toward Puss from that first time they were in this bathroom, extreme respect for her courage along with humility, and other emotions that she had not had felt about anyone for many years before meeting this extraordinary person who was now her friend.

*

The two luxuriated in relaxed silence for ten more minutes then Boots raised her toes out of the water and announced, "I'm starting to wrinkle, time to finish this job."

Climbing out of the tub with a splash, she began briskly toweling her body to a pink glow. Puss joined her and after they were dry they began grooming themselves and each other, silently exchanging manicures and pedicures while finishing their champagne and caviar.

"Want to stretch out for a bit 'fore we start dressing? I might even pay off my debt." Puss grinned as they completed their toilet.

"Sounds good, but what debt?"

"Well sweetie, I seem to remember you winning some backrub bets on Bila out there in tha' bushes, but if you don't..."

"Bouncin' Budas! I've found one honest Injun anyway, you're on Buddy!" Boots laughed as she trotted into the larger room and happily flopped face-down on the bed that occupied much of its floor-space. Puss followed carrying a lotion bottle and settling herself astride her friend's hips, anointed Boots' back and proceeded to apply a thorough and very professional therapeutic massage while Boots grunted and gasped in pleasure.

Fifteen minutes later Puss finished her careful kneading and dropped down to lie on the bed beside her friend. She asked, "Good?"

"Good? Gawd girl, you just turned me into a puddle..." Boots sighed with her eyes closed and her face half buried in the bedding.

"My, my – I'm so sorry," Puss whispered in a husky voice as she drew a fingertip lightly down the length of Boots spine, "We got a half hour before we have to dress. Want a front-rub now?"

"Mmmm Hmmm..."

*

Boots finished drying her hair, and combing the bangs away from her forehead, did it all up with pins into a twist on the back of her head. Then only stopping to apply a faint touch of color to her lips, she walked from the vanity in the bath back to the main room and quickly dressed in a suit of dull black silk. The pants were straight legged and the long jacket was loosely fitting with a high tunic collar. It closed down the front with plain jet buttons and had slightly padded shoulders to emphasize her size. The black leather pumps she stepped in to did also, their heels adding seven centimeters to her height.

Puss paused from where she stood nude before the mirror in the bathroom drying her hair, and looked out from its door. "Hey Kiddo, damn if you don't dress power way good!"

"Thanks Buddy. I've found that there are times when you gotta' make your body speak real loud as well as your voice, so you really get folk's attention," she said with a crooked grin as she emptied her backpack onto the now-rumpled bed.

"You got a plan for tonight for when you're gonna' talk to all your men about horses?"

"Sort of – but..."

"Well, when you're a gal talking business to men I've found that a countervailing distraction can be an asset, so maybe I can be one for you tonight Kiddo," Puss grinned as she ducked back into the bathroom.

Boots smiled then stepped first to her built-in bureau, and to her large bookcase. She selected the few items that she valued most and placed them in her pack before going back into the bathroom as Puss worked on her face and hair. Boots retrieved both of their `clave jumpsuits from the floor along with the weapons hidden in their folds. She paused in the kitchen area when she returned to the main room and casually shielding her actions with her body, opened the cutlery drawer and retrieved her spare set of throwing knives.

She hid them all in the bundled jumpsuits and was placing the bundle in her pack on the bed when the message center on the wall beeped and its screen lit up. Puss poked her head through the door of the bath as Boots stepped to the unit with a frown to read the message on its screen. Her frown deepened as she considered what she read. Then she announced in a light tone over her shoulder, "Hey, we're invited to a party!"

"Oh?"

"Yeah, at the Network headquarters even. It's a gala for General Butler two nights hence..."

"Why us? They havin' trouble raising a crowd?"

"I prefer to think that they only want the best people at their fancy affair, my skeptical little sweetie. The Alpha List as it were," Boots said in the same light tone, as she subtly signed, *"Careful! Rat watch us much now. Max alert!"*

"Well, you know how I like Affairs, and like you said just this morning, we Are the best! So why don't you RSVP them while I get on with my get-up for tonight?" Puss replied with a lilt in her voce, and ice in her eyes, as she ran to grab an outfit from the closet and skipped back into the bathroom.

Boots punched in an acknowledgement of the message, and an affirmative reply. After finding no other messages in its archive, she switched the unit off. She sighed then and glanced somberly around her space - the first in her life she ever had been able to claim with any feeling of ownership. Three of its walls and built-in cabinetry were white and its single small window was curtained to the floor with a rough-textured white fabric. The fourth wall was covered with mirrored panels.

The only colors in the room other than the deep blue of the bedding were the faded covers of the old paper books filling a large floor-to-ceiling shelf, and the intricate rainbow of hues woven in to the very old Persian scarf displayed on the wall above the bed. In spite of its small size, the total effect of the room was one of cool spaciousness.

Boots looked longingly for a moment at her books and the scarf then closing her face, she turned and was zipping her bag shut when Puss stepped into the room.

"Well Kid, I thought I would mess up their brains biggers with my power dress," Boots muttered with a wry grin after she had inspected her friend. "But it's damn sure you're out to twist their heads a full one-eight-oh at the very least."

Puss stood erect in the doorway with her legs demurely together and clasping one hand in the other at her waist with her eyes slightly downcast, in the traditional pose of a private girl's school pupil summoned before the headmistress. However, she was wearing a version of the `clave coverall that would never be seen in a girl's school, let alone on the racks of the `clave commissariat. While being the standard color of gray used by all, it was made of very thin satin cut on the bias and it fit her body snugly, where it didn't cling in soft folds.

The neckline plunged to a belt of copper links around her small waist and she wore dainty high-heeled sandals colored the same copper as her belt. It is also quite obvious that she wore nothing under the thin garment.

Her hair was set and fluffed to softly frame her face and she had made up her eyes to appear wide and appealing. Her pouting mouth was a bright pink that matched the color of her long artificial nails, and she had perfumed herself with a scent that combined magnolia with musk in a disturbing way.

She projected an innocent sensuality that was palatable in the room.

"Like it?" Puss asked with a slight smile.

"Like It? Jesu Bouncin' Budas gal! You're a ferkin danger to us all, dammit, especially to my sanity! How-in-hell do you know how to do stuff like this?"

Puss grinned, "We used to do theatricals a lot when I was growing up, and our drama coach had been on Broadway before he came back to the reservation. He taught us a big bunch of illusion stuff."

Then stepping out of her pose, Puss dumped most of the things in her pack on the bed with Boots' discards and walked to their bureau with a suddenly solemn face, to begin removing favorite items from her drawer and placing them in her pack. Forcing gaiety in to her voice, she continued, "Can't tell what might come in handy if get lucky, and are asked to sleep out, can ya'?"

The last item she chose was a small framed holograph of a young man in uniform. Then she glanced over at Boots who was standing by the door, her face grimly impenetrable. Puss sensed her friend's silent pain at abandoning their home, and considered for a moment. Then she stepped up onto the rumpled bed and removed the Persian scarf from the wall. She gently flapped it free of dust and folded it into a triangle. She draped it around her shoulders and secured it with a loose-flowing knot.

"Hey, we girl-type gals always need to accessorize, don't we Poopsie?" she announced with a girlish giggle.

Boots' expression changed to a smile of gratitude as she realized the deftness with which Puss had created a plausible explanation to their covert watchers, one that allowed them to remove the precious antique without creating a suspicion of flight...

Boots then closed her face again as she draped a voluminous military raincoat over her shoulders and announced, "Move-out time!" She grabbed her pack from the bed, opened the door and stepped out into the hallway. Puss donned a similar coat and grabbing her own pack, strode out to join her friend after closing the door, with a cold click of finality.

*

The two joined the queue waiting on the cracked pavement at a stop for the circulating bus close to their building as evening rain cloud passed over and began to release its big, slow drops again. Their coated and hooded forms blended in with the others waiting for the free government transport service, and not just because of their outer garments. They also assumed the slumping head-down posture of the others in the line as they all stood and waited in numb silence for the next bus, which was late as usual.

The aged vehicle rolled down the street ten minutes later and ground to a halt without pulling over to the curb. It was open-sided, and the waiting line broke and flowed to fill the available seats under its roof.

Puss and Boots hung back until they only had spaces to stand on the outboard steps of the vehicle for overflow passengers and hold on to the rails, and so avoid the I.D. units in the seat cushions inside...

The bus creaked to a stop at the S'attl municipal building twenty minutes later. A bare and rusting flagpole stood before it, armored guard booths were installed beside its doors, and all of its grimy windows were closely curtained.

Puss and Boots stepped down from their perches on the vehicle and again assuming the `clave slouch, walked to the most decrepit of the three taxis that waited at the curb for possible fares. They settled back on its torn and stained rear seat and Boots gave the approximate address of Rick's club without mentioning its name. Their driver powered the vehicle and set it into creaking motion.

While they jolted over the crudely patched pavement toward the old waterfront area, Boots opened her pack on the floor of the cab below the driver's line of sight, and retrieved their ankle holsters and canister pouches.

The two women strapped them on and ensured that they were hidden under their full-cut pant legs then Puss opened her rain coat, and carefully removing the Persian shawl from around her shoulders, gently folded its delicate fabric and stowed it in Boots' pack.

"Thank you. Is much to me. You think fast," Boots signed.

"It is nothing. My brain works sometimes. Not work sometimes."

"You brain always works when we need it. I need you brain real big tonight."

"It is yours."

"Thank you. It is ours!"

Puss just smiled, and squeezed her friend's hand, and the two sat in silence for the remainder of the ride down to the lower end of Madison Street.

Boots tapped on the screen and halted the driver in the middle of the block that contained both the blackened shell of the old bookstore where she had been arrested eleven years ago because of her innocence about the world in which she lived - and their present destination.

Its door was under a marquee with a glowing sign lighted by the archaic method of shaped glass tubes filled with an inert gas excited by an electric current.

The driver slid the screen back and processed Boots' anonymous credit chip. Noting the lack of a name on the I.D. screen without comment, he passes the transaction unit back over his shoulder to her, while flicking his fingers the universal gesture for baksheesh. Boots added a very generous amount to the meter total and then authorized payment, with a fingertip swathed in the fabric of her coat.

As she expected, the payment was accepted without fingerprint verification, and the driver turned and flashed a knowing leer.

Boots looked at the sallow-faced youth for a second, then nudged her friend. Puss opened their door herself and the two climbed from the cab to stand on the sidewalk. They pointedly stared at the driver until his eyes wavered, and he drove down the street and out of sight, as the clouds drifted away and the slow rain finally ceased.

The two turned and as they walked toward the glowing sign that read "Rick's Club Ancienne", Boots somberly reflected on the circular nature of fate - and particularly on this street, the street where her life's direction had been altered forever by the 'clave government - changing it to lead her inexorably from where they had attacked her and made it all began, to where she now stood....

She paused for a moment longer in pensive thought, then she grinned at Puss she squared her shoulders and threw back the hood of her coat, "What tha' hell, why not?"

"Iela jacta ferkin est!" Boots then shouted in a ringing voice.

"It sure is Buddy," Puss replied with a grunt, "But let's always take some stress days in the middle of March, OK?"

"Ja Boss!" Boots said as she closed her face and strode toward the door of the club.

***

Chapter 8
The Word

May 3, 2276 AD
`Clave of S'attl

"We would like to check our bags with our coats, if you could please," Boots asked of the young woman wearing a retro-style short black dress with an exaggerated frilly white apron who stood behind the checkroom counter in the paneled foyer.

"Of course ladies," she smiled with brightly painted lips, and was taking their things when the proprietor strolled up.

"I am glad to see you again Captain," the large black man wearing a white mess jacket cut in the fashion of the 20th Century rumbled around the lit cigarette in his lips.

"Nice to be here again, Rick. You remember my friend Marybell don't you?"

"Yes I do, welcome to the club again, Sergeant."

"Why thank you Suh, I'm very proud to be here," Puss replied in a soft voice as she assumed the same modest pose as in Boots' apartment.

Rick gazed at her for a moment and then he inspected Boots for another.

"Your friends are already here and waiting for you in Room 3 on the second floor. And if I may say so, it looks like this will be an interesting evening."

"Would you care to join us for dinner?" Boots asked as she dominated the foyer with her presence, "And I hope your screening decoys are working very well tonight."

"Do not worry, Ma'am. The diversionary shielding on my establishment is still the best there is."

"Perhaps it would be more appropriate for me to join you over the port though, since I feel that this would be the most informative time to visit with your friends, and you."

"You have always been perceptive Rick. I will wait for you," Boots murmured, then she nodded to Puss, "Shall we join our guests?" and led their way across the main floor of the club toward the private dining rooms on the second floor.

She strode with open confidence while Puss followed demurely behind and when the two passed through the large room, the buzz of conversation from the patrons at their tables first diminished, but then picked up again, in a different tone...

Boots And Puss mounted the stairs then halted in a hallway before a dark paneled door with an ornate brass numeral 3 affixed to it. Boots gave her friend a fleeting smile which Puss returned with a wink then she closed her face and opened the door without knocking, and stepped into the room.

"Hello Bobby, I am glad you could come. It is nice to see you again, and you too, Waldo. And you, General McAuliffe," Boots said as she greeted the three men in army green seated at the round dining table. Then Boots nodded to the compact older woman who was the fourth person with them. Her salt-and-pepper hair was cut en-brose and she was also in uniform, and wore a brigadier general's star.

"I am glad that you could come as well, General, but I am afraid we haven't met."

The four people stared in stunned silence at the woman in black who had taken command of the room without effort then; they pushed their chairs back and scrambled to their feet.

"Hello Kris," the tall colonel she called Bobby sputtered as he stared at Boots. "Please excuse my manners, but you've sure changed since you were at the academy," Then he said in a rush, "And may I introduce you to General Barbara Shaw."

"General, please meet Captain Kristina Hamier."

"Call me Barbara, and can I call you Kris?" the woman announced in a pleasant voice as she moved around the table and offered a hand to Boots.

"I've heard quite a bit about you over the years," she continued with a look of approval in her eyes, "And it is a pleasure to finally meet you."

"I have heard much of you also Barbara," Boots said, "And it is my pleasure to take your hand. I believe you are also a graduate of Bobby's academy, correct?"

"She is, but before it was mine," Bobby interjected, still gazing at his former pupil in awe. Then shaking his head, he held out his hand and smiled broadly, "And thanks again, Kris."

"For?" She asked with a slight smile as she returned his grip.

"For proving me right, one more time."

"She's done that for me too Bobby! And you call me Mack, dammit," The grizzled man Boots had addressed as General, but who wore no insignia, announced as he inspected her. Then moving from his place next to Barbara, he took Boots hand and his expression softened, as he remembered the time he had helplessly watched her struggle against her assailants throughout that long night in the dank cell eleven years ago, and ultimately prevail by refusing to submit. He smiled and nodded to her in approval - as the vision of her trial flashed once more through his memory...

*

Mack had watched the entry of the broad shouldered guard as she led the girl into the dank holding cell. The guard wore leather wrist bands on her muscular bare arms, and her black hair was cropped short. She had a very large bust that strained her leather vest - and a prominent Adam's apple. The girl wore only her underwear...

The guard person had stood in a hulking pose on the entry steps to the large cell, filled with drunken sailors of all nations, either males or indeterminately sexed growls like herself.

"My name is Lacy Jones, and I'll be back for her tomorra'!" the guard person had shouted with a roar that rang through the space. "If she can't walk out with me, you all die. Get that, you bunch of ferkin' losers?"

Then releasing her grip on Kris' arm, Lacy had looked into the girl's frightened eyes for a second without expression. Mack had heard Lacy hiss, "Remember what I told you and you'll make it!" Then she stalked out of the cell and slammed the door with a clang.

He recalled that there was first a moment of silence. It was soon broken with a whistle and a catcall however, followed by a welling roar of shouted curses and obscenities, and mocking invitations. Finally as he watched the mob of drunken sailors had surged forward, he had heard Kris shout, "No! Quit it! Don't you touch me!"

There had been the sound of a vigorous slap, and the girl repeated her words louder and in a higher voice against a background of leering laughter. Then as he watched from the other side of the cell, the group huddled around her and he heard sounds of more slaps and blows.

The taunts from the crowd around the girl had become more vicious, and included cries of, "We got'cha ya' li'l Sweetie!" and, "Hold her legs, Dammit!" and "Pull `er head back!" Their words were interspersed with the girl's screams of rage – and masculine yells of pain.

Throughout her entire ordeal, the girl had not once whimpered in fright or cried for mercy. Instead, whenever it was obvious to Mack, who forced himself to watch helplessly, when she had been overpowered, the girl had never submitted to the mob, but rather continued to struggle until she had was able to break away and fight them off again.

After an hour of resisting the attackers, there was an interval of quiet, until Mack had heard her shout, "Dammit I said, Quit!" then grunt as she delivered a heavy blow. There was another masculine howl of pain – then silence in the cell.

Mack had stayed awake the whole night watching for any further attackers, but Kris' resistance had broken the mob's spirit, so nothing more had happened when the guard person opened the door in the morning.

Lacy had stood with a billy club dangling from her wrist and scowled around the holding cell. She looked first at the corner where Kris squatted, grimly alert in an on-guard position. Then she glared around at the other prisoners. They were either snoring in sleep or sitting on the floor, beyond the reach of the tense young girl.

"Mornin' folks"' Lacy had growled as she closed the door and stalked over to stand above the naked girl. Kris' hair was wildly matted and filthy. She glared up from a badly bruised face with a swollen eye and a split lip.

"Mornin' Kris," the growl repeated in a softer tone, as she held out her hand to help the girl up.

While Mack watched, Kris had ignored the offered hand, and bounded to her feet unaided with a hiss of repressed pain. Then she had braced erect as if she were on parade.

"OK. What's next?" the girl had asked in a hoarse voice.

He had watched while Lacy looked at the battered young girl, her skin covered with bloody scrapes, bite marks and bruises, her face disfigured from blows, with streaks of dried blood on her thighs and an obviously dislocated finger sticking out from one hand.

He also saw that she stood proudly ignoring her nudity, and had stared at the guard with eyes of blue ice.

Lacy nodded, then grinned like a skull as she had gritted, "Payback time. Which ones were the worst?"

Mack remembered thinking, "Maybe there is some justice here after all..."

Kris had stood like a goddess of vengeance above the alter in her temple and raising her hand slowly, pointed to a narrow faced male with a large hooked nose and single bushy eyebrow across his close-set black eyes.

Lacy strode to where the man stood, and without warning slammed the tip of her club into his solar plexus. His eyes bulged and his breath whooshed from his lungs, and he bent forward. The big growl stepped to one side and kicking his legs out from under him dropped him to the floor at her feet. She flipped him onto his face then knelt on his back and pinned him with her knees on his shoulders.

Then Lacy had pushed her club under his chin, and gripping its end with her other hand, viciously jerked the stick back toward her knees. She crushed the man's larynx and throat, and maintained her pressure until his limbs stopped thrashing...

The growl bounded to her feet and looked at Kris. The girl was standing in the same position, and wearing the same stony expression. "Who helped him?" Lacy asked.

Mack thought to himself, "This girl is major tough!"

"It," the girl snapped as she pointed with her hand with the dislocated finger toward a brown-skinned growl with vaguely oriental features.

"Bitch!" Lacy had hissed as she leaped in front of the person whom she would ordinarily recognize as a sister and started to swing with the club in her right hand. When the growl snarled defiance and jerked her hands up to catch the blow Lacy stunned her with a flashing left uppercut to the jaw.

Lacy caught the growl's arms as she started to sway, and raised one foot to the growl's chest and fell backward. She flipped the woman above her and kicked the growl's body straight up into the air with both feet then as the person pivoted helplessly over her, Lacy switched her grip. She clamped the growl's head under her right armpit and held it there as the woman swung over on over to the floor.

The sound of the growl's neck snapping was heard above the thud of her body landing. Its snap was loud in the silent room.

Lacy leaped to her feet again and looked at Kris standing as before. She snarled with a feral smile, "Anyone else?"

"Yes," the girl replied as she stepped forward and confronted a brutish blond sailor who eyed her with a leer. Lacy stepped forward also, until Kris held up her hand without taking her eyes from the man's face.

"I told you to stop it!" she said with a cold stare as she looked at the man.

"What's da' Sweetie want? Som' more lovin'?" He had taunted in reply.

The girl clasped her hands together and Mack watched her draw her arms back in a seemingly awkward double-fisted start of a roundhouse swing.

The sailor had raised his own arms in a practiced guard position before his face, and opened his mouth with its stained and broken teeth in a sneer.

Kris shifted her weight with lightening speed and landed a powerful boxing kick directly in his groin. The sailor's eyes went blank and he clutched himself, as she regained her balance and braced on her feet again.

She paused for a second as he bent double in agony, then with her eyes blazing like welding torches, she screamed in rage and completed a two-fisted blow with all of her young strength behind it.

She hit the man accurately on the side of his head at his temple - and smashed his skull in where the bone was thinnest. His eyes glazed, and blood spurted from his ear as he sank on the floor, and died while the sodden "smack" of her blow still echoed from the cement walls of the cell.

"I told him to stop it," Kris said as she stood over the man's still quivering body with her head held high, glaring at Lacy and rubbing the edges of her hands.

"Losers never listen," the big woman rumbled as she gazed at the proud young girl with respect, and something else showing on her rugged face. "Any more? Looks like we're on' a roll..."

"Yes, one," Kris replied as she turned and walked toward the crowd of her former attackers, who now scuttled out of her path and avoided her eyes.

Mack remembered how she had halted before him where he stood leaning against the back wall of the windowless room.

"You didn't touch me, and you tried to stop them, and you did get some of them to stop later," Kris said with an attempt at a smile despite the pain from her lip. Then she added quietly, "Thank you," and she offered him her hand.

Mack remembered the surge of emotion he had felt then as he took her hand, and held it tenderly.

"Not necessary Ma'am. Rather it is I who must thank you. You see, Dear girl, the courage and strength you showed this last night have reminded me of some things I lost a long time ago. So it really is I who am in debt to you."

Then, with a courtly bow he raised her hand and kissed it, and she had instinctively accepted his homage with quiet grace.

Mack had felt Lacy staring at both of them, a naked and badly battered young girl with dusty matted hair who stood like royalty in a receiving line. He knew that he appeared to be an old wino, but one who was acting with the dignity of an ambassador.

Lacy had sighed then and shook her head in wonder, and stepped to them and rumbled, "Al'right folks, its time to see about going home - for both of you."

Mack remembered that he had looked at Lacy and seen a tenderness in the growl's eyes that he did not expect, considering what she was and whom she worked for.

"Both?" he had asked.

At Lacey's nod of assent, Kris had said, "Thank you," and smiled for the first time to the person whose advice had helped her through the night. She had given Mack's hand a reassuring squeeze as Lacy had lead them through the cowering inmates and out of the cell.

*

"Kris, I saw what you had in you the first time we met, and I am glad you have found it now for yourself," Mack said as he snapped out of his reverie. Then as he had at the end of that terrible night when she had triumphed by her strength of will, he raised her hand and kissed it in a gesture of extreme respect. Boots accepted his honor again, as if she were a duchess.

"Thank you Mack, I am very glad you could come again."

"Ma'am, a Chin division couldn't have kept me away tonight!" he responded with a wry grin as he stepped back to his seat.

Boots turned to the stocky sergeant who was standing near her side, and staring at her with an openly stunned expression.

"You are looking well, Waldo I am happy to say."

"You look ... great, Kris. Ma'am!" he whispered in awe as he instinctively hit a brace, and remembered the first time he had become aware of her...

*

Kris had marched through the doors of the empty gym in the S'attl academy eleven years before. He was waiting for her as Bobby had requested. She

162

handed him a note with a determined look on her face.

"This was given to me this morning, Sir."

He had opened it and read, "Report to Sgt. Waldo in the gym after your last class." The Professor of Military Science and Tactics of the S'attl Academy had signed the note, "Bobby."

Waldo remembered smiling at her as he had said, "You're Kris. I'm Waldo, and my job is to break you. Nice to make your acquaintance."

"Thank you Sir - I think."

"You're welcome. Now try to kill me," he had replied with an impassive face as he stood lounging against one of the vaulting horses in the gym.

The girl had stared at him for several moments, before asking, "Why should I try to kill you?"

"Because I am going to kill you if you don't."

"I don't think you can," she had replied with sudden defiance as she struck a pose with her hands planted on her hips, and stared at him with a cold sneer.

"Bitch!" he remembered gritting as he had launched himself toward her in a blind rage, his hands outstretched.

Kris had waited for the split second before he would have grabbed her throat, then spun aside and kicked his feet out from under him as he rushed past her. When he landed heavily on the hardwood of the gym floor the girl had leapt on his back and slamming her knees on to his shoulders, wrapped her hands around his face and pulled his head back, as Lacy had done to her attacker in the cell two days before.

Waldo remembered his utter surprise at her speed as he went suddenly limp under her hands, and signaled his surrender. She had bounded to her feet without a word and poised herself to one side.

He recalled slowly standing, and glowering at the young girl giving him a smug smile.

"Congratulations, this is the first time I have been suckered in five years. Now die!" he remembered whispering as he leapt to her and sunk his fist into her abdomen.

Kris had blanched as she lost all of her breath from his blow. She fell to the floor, gasping for air and curled into a ball at Waldo's feet. He squatted beside her.

"You're better than I thought you would be, so maybe I'll let you live," he had said in a matter-of-fact voice. "But in the meanwhile, do 100 sit-ups and

100 leg-ups a day, until you get your gut tough enough to take a little hit like that, OK?"

Then he remembered how the girl had screamed in furry when he had started to stand, and viciously kicking her curled legs out into his belly, knocked him onto his back on the floor with a resounding thud.

She then had bounded to her feet, and obviously ignoring a deep ache in her abdomen, gritted out, "Yes, Sir, right away Sir. And there's number one, Sir."

Waldo had slowly regained his feet and stood before the tense young girl. He recalled how he had looked at her without expression for a long moment as he regained his breath.

"If I don't kill you first," he had whispered, "Or you don't kill me, I am going to make you the best killer in the regiment, if that is what you want to be."

As if it were yesterday, Waldo could still hear Kris' reply. She had looked directly at him with a dead stare, and said simply, "Yes."

Waldo had gazed back at the young woman, and looked deep into her eyes. Then he remembered that he shook his head suddenly and had replied, "Sorry Ma'am, my mistake. You're already a killer. All I can do is teach you some more tricks..."

"Thank you, I would like that," Boots had said.

*

"Ease-up friend," Boots smiled to Waldo in the dining room, "This isn't a parade ground you know."

"Technically you are right my dear, but we actually are all somewhat on parade tonight, aren't we?" Mack interjected with a dry smile while the tough sergeant continued to gape at Boots.

Puss had remained standing demurely behind Boots, overlooked by all as they were being dazzled with the power of Boots' persona, except for General McAuliffe.

He had watched the young woman with a keen appraisal when she followed her friend into the room, and continued to glance at her while the first greetings and introductions took place. Puss was vaguely aware of his attention, but ignored it as she watched Boots' deft control of the others in the room.

"My gal's got a ferkin' thousand watt personality bulb in her head, and she can switch it on whenever she wants," Puss whispered, "These poor suckers got nada chanceo…"

Then the grizzled general stepped over to Puss and offered his hand as he said, "I'm Mack, and you are?"

"Marybell. I'm a friend of Kris," she whispered to the man who wore no insignia.

"Your friend has good taste in her friends, I am happy to see," he murmured as he gracefully lifted her hand and kissed it with a diplomat's chaste formality.

"Thank you, Sir," Puss whispered with downcast eyes.

"I have been remiss, Boots exclaimed with a smile. "Let me introduce my friend Marybell to you all," Boots said as she gestured to the tall colonel, "This is Bobby, my Professor of Military Science and the Commandant of my academy. I know he is a kind and patient man, because he didn't pinch my head off when I was a bad student,"

"Only because she was the best student I ever had," Bobby replied as he stepped to Puss and offered her his hand.

"I'm pleased to meet you too Sir," she whispered shyly. As he took the limp hand Puss held out to him the man's smile became forced, and he glanced at Boots.

Boots ignored Bobby's look and continued, "And this is Waldo, who taught me how to be a killer."

The compact sergeant replied, "You already knew how Kris, I just gave you a few pointers on style." Then he turned to Puss and sputtered, "Pleased to meet you," as he took her limp hand, and then looked down at it in confusion, at a loss on what to do next.

"It's real nice to meet you too," Puss sighed, as her bosom swelled against the thin fabric of her garment and she gently clasped his hand with both her hands. She squeezed his slightly, then as his gaze returned to her face the tough sergeant received the full effect of her soft smile and her deep green eyes looking directly into his.

He reddened and gulped, then after several seconds he responded hoarsely, "Yeah, me too." Looking down at her hands again, he released them with a guilty start and stepped awkwardly back to his chair.

Boots maintained her grave demeanor, but enjoyed a surge of wicked glee at her friend's deft wrecking of this competent man's composure with only a few words and a smile.

Then Puss turned to Barbara at Mack's side and whispered, "Ma'am, I'm told that you were the first person to leave the S'attl academy with perfect marks in everything. And when you graduated, you were accepted into the Army with the rank of Private First Class, and you have raised considerably more ever since," She sighed with eyes.

"Yes, but your friend was the next to do so, and perhaps the last, now that the war has stopped. Anyway, I am happy to meet you," Barbara said as she took Puss' limp hand, and inspected the young woman with a critical eye.

"Thank you Ma'am. It's nice to talk with you too," Puss whispered, her own eyes wide and innocent.

"Yes, I'm quite sure," Barbara said her face expressionless as she stepped back to her place at the table.

"Shall we sit down and pleasure ourselves with Rick's menu?" Boots announced with a slight smile as she took an empty seat on Waldo's left at the round table, before the now doubly bemused man could shake himself to into awareness and assist her.

"Allow me young lady," Mack murmured, as he offered the other empty chair on his right to Puss, placing her at Boots' left.

Gracefully seating herself with the general's assistance, the young woman whispered "Thank you Sir, you are very kind."

"My pleasure," he replied with a twinkle suddenly in his eyes as he turned and seated Barbara to his left with equal ceremony, while Bobby blushed as he realized his lapse in courtesy, due to his frowning concentration on the young woman who accompanied Kris.

A waiter glided in from the butler's pantry as soon as they were all seated and after presenting them with leather-bound menus, stood waiting for their selections.

Boots considered hers for a moment then slapped it closed.

"I'll have a double straight iced vodka and the grilled venison with morels, and one of Rick's special salads," she announced with a grin. "I acquired a taste for venison during our last trip to the hills."

The others took Boots' subtle lead to the best and most expensive item on the list and ordered the same, except for Puss. She only ordered the salad in a meek whisper, and caused Boots stifle a chuckle at her friend's act.

"Kris, would you do me the favor of allowing me provide the wine?" Mack asked as the waiter offered the cellar list to Boots.

"That is very kind of you, but not necessary Mack."

"I know that," he smiled, "But it would give me a great deal of pleasure to support you, in any way I can."

Boots gazed at the wiry veteran for several seconds then passed him the red Morocco-bound wine list. "Offer accepted, Sir," she said with a slight smile.

*

The four and Boots discussed current Army matters, including their bitterness at the continuing freeze of promotions for those who had stayed in the combat zones while they enjoyed their food. The other things they talked about were the more humorous incidents when they were all in on active duty, and so they entertained themselves while they ate the excellent meal.

The three men and Barbara appeared relaxed, but Boots felt their unspoken tension as she sliced small bites of her filet and savored them slowly. She chatted with her guests while observing what they did, and didn't do. Puss remained silent and picked at her salad and sipped mineral water instead of the excellent burgundy Mack chose, its bouquet perfuming the room.

Mack attended to his meal with smiling pleasure, and also watched the others around the table with swift glances while taking part in the conversation.

Bobby and Waldo attacked their food with gusto but Boots felt a strong unease radiating from the two men. And as she glanced at the tough sergeant she smiled inwardly again, at the look of a love-struck puppy that appeared on his face whenever he glanced toward Puss.

They finished their main courses meal in this fashion then at Boot's signal, the waiter cleared the table. After he removed the dishes to the pantry he asked, "Shall I serve the port, Madam?"

"If you would. Also, please give my complements to Rick and ask if he can join us now," she said with a smile.

"Yes Ma'am," the waiter replied and was turning toward the pantry when there was a tap on the door. The waiter rushed to open it and the club's major domo entered carrying two crystal decanters by their necks with great dignity. A senior waiter followed bearing a tray loaded with cheese and fruit and, stemmed glasses. Rick then stepped through the door with a wooden case tucked under his arm.

"Your timing is excellent Rick, as always," Boots said with a chuckle.

"Thank you Captain, I try to anticipate my guest's needs and wishes."

"And you do it well. But since I am not a captain any more, just call me Kris if you would please, also, allow me to present General Barbara Shaw,"

Boots said as she gestured toward the woman with a general's star on her collar. "I think you already know Mack and Marybell, and of course Bobby and Waldo are unforgettable don't you agree?" she smiled to the large black man, and then at her two old friends.

Turning to their first waiter she continued as she pointed to her left, "Would you please bring a chair for Rick." He did so promptly and after the large man had greeted Barbara, he seated himself between Boots and Puss. The major domo then placed the two decanters before Boots and so identified the head of the table as the senior waiter placed plates decorated in gold leaf, pearl-handled fruit knives and forks, and crystal wine glasses before them all.

The senior waiter then placed the large tray of cheese and fruit in the center of the table and the major domo displayed a crystal ashtray to Boots "Your wish, Madam?"

Boots glanced around the table, and seeing no dissent nodded her permission. Placing several ashtrays on the table within reach of all, the grave man dismissed the other waiters. Before he left the room, the major domo bowed and handed Boots a small paging transmitter, "I will attend to any of your further needs personally, Madam."

*

Boots felt the vibrations she felt resonating in the room for a moment as they all except for Puss, looked at her with varying expressions on their faces - or none at all. She enjoyed them for a moment, then grasped a decanter by its neck and poured a splash of port in her glass. She sipped the ruby wine.

"Rick, you shouldn't have wasted this good stuff on a bunch of ground grunts like us," she exclaimed after considering its flavor for a moment, "But I am very glad you did!"

Rick only chuckled as Boots slid the decanter to Waldo on her right. He half filled his glass, then suddenly broke out of his bemused state and remembered to slide, rather than pass the decanter to Bobby.

Boots examined the tray of cheeses and fruit and the thin white wafers on it while the others passed the port. She took several wafers and served herself small slivers of each of the three cheeses and used the ornate scissors on the tray to snip off a small stem of grapes.

"I see that you are a friend of Mrs. Kostanis too." She murmured to Rick and lifted one of the wafers in salute.

"I can tell that you are as well," he chuckled. "We are lucky, aren't we?"

"Very!" Boots replied as she thought of the little woman's warning earlier in the day. "She is a person I am glad to know."

Then Boots announced to the table, "Now that we have served ourselves as they said our Navy four hundred years ago, The Smoking Lamp is Lit. And we also know that it's an old American custom to take political decisions in a smoke-filled room, don't we…"

Rick chuckled again and opened the case on the cloth before him to reveal a selection of cigars and extra-long cigarettes.

"These are from my own stock. The cigars are Cuban, and the cigarettes are Egyptian. Please help yourselves," He rumbled, as he selected and lit a cigarette, and then passed the box.

Both Mack and Barbara selected large ring maduro cigars, and after preparing them appropriately, lit up with the ornate silver lighter the major domo had left on the table.

Boots passed on smoking, as did Bobby and Waldo - and Puss. This caused Boots to suppress another chuckle as she remembered Puss' enjoying cheroots with her army-issue whiskey many other times. Then Boots cleared her throat and the others at the table became still.

"Bobby, the morning after I graduated from the academy you told me some things. You said that there was a group who were not at ease with the present state of the country, and that this group had organized itself into a loose confederation and it was waiting, for something to cause a change."

"Yes, and we still are," Bobby replied, cautiously.

"You also said that you were waiting for a word."

"Yes again, and we still are. But do we want to talk about this right now?" Bobby asked, as he nodded toward Puss sitting with her eyes downcast, and the fruit and wine she had ordered untouched.

"Yes. I do," Boots said, as she leaned forward and gazed at the tall colonel with all of her strength and authority suddenly in her eyes and her pose.

Bobby's cheeks reddened as he stared back at this woman, once his pupil but now showing that she was his master.

"I'll be blunt." He said, "This is too dangerous for her, and she may be a danger to us all when we begin."

"Marybell is valuable to me, and you will see that she will also be valuable to us all as well. Do you have any other items to bring up before we proceed?"

Bobby's face reddened even more for a moment, then he relaxed and his expression changed. He replied with an impassive face and in a quiet voice with the military expression of respect to a superior female officer.

"No other items, Ma'am."

Boots' reply to her former teacher was a nod, and a crooked smile.

Mack watched the interplay between the two, and also nodded.

"You said you were all waiting for a word, and you also said that you felt that it might come from me perhaps," Boots continued.

"Yes, I did. And we still are."

"I thank you for your confidence Bobby and of you others as well, but I have to ask, why did you think your word would come from me - and how did you think I would know it anyway, whatever it is supposed to be?"

"Because you are the best, and it had to come from someone who is the best,"

"So you, and I, have waited all these years for one person to make to her mind?" Boots snapped with fire in her eyes.

"Yes."

"Then you all are stupid! And so am I!"

"No!" Mack announced with equal passion, "We want to win, and you had to go out and learn how to be a winner. Simple as that!"

Boots sighed and bowed her head for a moment, then she sat erect and her eyes flashed.

"Dear friends, I finally have realized that I must do what is necessary after all these years. I had my epiphany only this morning, but now I am ready to give my word to you." She gazed at those around the table sitting in anticipation, and apprehension. Then she lifted her glass.

"I give you, The Walrus," she declared as she took a sip of port.

Waldo and Barbara stared at the woman, as did Puss who suddenly looked up. But Bobby released his breath in a gusty sigh of happiness and the General's face beamed in a skull-like grin.

Boots continued in a measured tone, "The time has come, the Walrus said, to speak of many things..."

"Of shoes and ships, and sealing wax," Bobby and Mack chanted in unison.

"And stopping would-be Kings," Boots finished in a grim tone.

"Thank you Kris. We have waited a very long time for you to decide to accept this honor – and burden," Mack whispered as he looked at Boots.

"Then tell me, why do you really think I can do this, and why you want me," she demanded as she glared back at Mack and then at Bobby.

"As I said earlier, I saw what you have in yourself a long time ago, that time when your courage jerked me back straight again, and Bobby who is one of my best officers ever, confirmed it.

"We have watched you ever since and you have a formidable reputation, Captain Cook, you not only always accomplished your missions but you also brought most of your people back home every time. Folks like us remember leaders who can do that."

"Kris, I watched how you controlled yourself in the academy," Bobby added in a solemn voice, "And how you thirsted to learn everything there was available, and how you related with your fellow cadets - could excite them. You are the natural leader we need and must have, to make this revolution really happen."

"NO! I will NOT do a revolution!" Boots snapped with ice in her voice as she slammed her fist on the table and rattled the plates.

"Revolutions are messy and unpredictable - and dangerous! I will only work to restore the Constitution. If you want something else, I will not be a party to it!"

The people in the room sat in stunned silence for a moment, and then Mack's chair thudded to the carpeted floor as he leapt to his feet and saluted.

"Thank you, Ma'am," he said, "I will be proud to serve under you, because you have just shown me that we Will win!"

Barbara and Rick, then Bobby and Waldo also stood and acknowledged Boots as the leader of their fledging movement with brisk salutes. Puss remained seated but gazed so adoringly upon her friend that Boots almost snorted with laughter.

Boots stood instead and perfunctorily returned their salutes. Then she sat again. "Alright, pick up your damn chairs," She ordered in a tone that demanded immediate response, "And let's get to work.

"How many of us are there, and where are they and what assets do we control?"

The others sat back around the table again as Boots took command, and the Restoration began.

*

"That is very good. Our situation is better than I had hoped. Mack, would you consider being my Adjutant? Bobby, would you be my field commander? And Waldo, would you head up Special Ops for me?"

171

"And Barbara, would you do logistics and cover our butts on anything we forget?"

The three men and the compact woman all shouted, "YO!" almost simultaneously as they slapped the table and rattled the china.

Rick cleared his throat, "Perhaps I might be able to add some value to this enterprise as well," he said quietly, "In the area of communications.

"But what do you plan to do now?"

"Interesting that you should be the first to ask about that Rick, and you have both my congratulations, and condolences Sir. You have just been added to our headquarters staff." Boots said with another crooked grin.

Boots continued when Rick smiled, "Boss Rat is suddenly after Marybell and me in a significant way. Probably because of what we learned about the technical situation inside the Network, and the code writing capabilities of the last mark we captured for them, as well as those of one we chose to not bring in.

"In any event, Rat and the Governors are very interested in the two of us now. So, if they could be convinced to try an all-out attack on us with Rat's security force goons, we could create an "incident", and use it as a reason for taking counteractions"

"How would anyone know, and why should any of the `clave dwellers care anyway?" Mack asked with a dry sniff.

"Our last mission was quite revealing about a number of things concerning the Governors and the Rat that I did not know before. We also found a communications capability that will allow us to go directly to the people, and let them know what is taking place without interference from the Network.

"Perhaps doing this, we can make them become unhappy with Rat and by association, their Governors out here in the suspended states as well," Boots said, as in her mind she pictured Molly at her computer, breaking in to the Network's transmissions and the Gov-net.

Mack chuckled then said as Barbara smiled, "Direct information delivery to your target audience along with created incidents! I believe that's the SOP for what's-his-name, the old Chin who wrote "On War", as well as Machiavelli, Che Gueriva and I don't know how many others who were in the overthrow business."

"It was Sun Tzu." Puss whispered, "And don't forget Thomas Paine either," causing Bobby, Waldo and Barbara to all suddenly blink. But Mack only nodded while his eyes sparkled, again.

"How could we take the counteractions you mention?" Mack asked then, as he gazed at Boots without expression.

"How many of the members of our group are, or were in Washington State National Guard?"

"Quite a few," Mack said with a sudden smile. "And the last Washington State Lieutenant Governor elected before martial law was declared is still alive. She is under confinement and continuous surveillance "for her own safety" in a house in Olympia, but although she is 80 she's quite spry and competent. She putters in her garden to have something to do and she knows me slightly."

"Mack, I really am glad you are on my side," Boots said, looking at the man with respect while Bobby and Waldo frowned, and Barbara glanced at her with a quizzical eye. Puss looked down at her plate however and smiled, as she took a first sip of her port.

Boots had noted Mack's reaction to Puss' sudden statement about Sun Tzu and Thomas Paine, so she changed the subject. She wanted more information on their group, but she also wanted to know more about Mack's thoughts as well.

"You mentioned East Coast assets," Boots said, "Where are they? How do you communicate with them? And are you secure?"

"It would probably be a good idea to demonstrate that now," Rick said with a rumble as he stepped into the small pantry adjoining the room. He returned after a moment carrying the wooden box of a telephone made in the European style of the early 20th Century. A twisted cable covered with silk brocade trailed from it back to the room's serving space.

"Please indulge my mild obsession with the cosmetics of this period in the world's history, but surface aspects can be deceiving," Rick continued dryly. "For instance, this instrument connects by hard-wired fiber optic lines to twelve computers, which are in turn programmed to send bits of the transmission randomly out over 300 up-links, along the unused band-width that the network abandoned."

"Our eastern group has the same system, and effectively places our communication network into address-free cyber space, and makes it about as secure as my faithful techno-patrons can provide, and they are the best in all the `Claves."

"Bobby," Mack said quietly, "I think it is time to call your friend and gave him our news,"

"Who is your friend?" Boots asked.

"Only the best Special Forces leader I have ever known, that's all," the tall colonel grinned, "He is even better than me! Before Mack chained us to desks, we used to head up an assault team he called the Chin Gang and we were damn good."

"He's an American Indian and I always call him by the initials of his tribal name. He wouldn't tell me what it was, but he gave me the initials for recognition one time when we were pinned down in a shell crater near Tacoma."

"Where is he now and what are his capabilities?" Boots asked.

"He's a colonel and like me, he heads up an academy, except it is on an Indian reservation in Virginia, close to Washington."

"What do you call him?"

"E.B."

Only Boots and Mack noted Puss' start at Bobby's words. Boots returned her attention to Bobby and his story, but Mack continued to observe Puss.

"Funniest thing about him too, whenever we were putting on our camo paint before a mission, he began every time with three streaks of black on his forehead. He joked that it was his war paint," Bobby chuckled. Absorbed in telling his story, Bobby did not notice Boots' eyes widening, nor her quick glance at Puss.

Mack did however, and glanced at the young woman in time to hear her sudden intake of breath, and to note that she clinched her hands into fists for a moment.

Bobby lifted the handset from its cradle on the instrument's varnished walnut case and entered in two digits into its archaic rotary dial. He listened for several seconds before hanging it up again.

"This will page him for our call."

They all waited in silence, and nibbled and sipped at their refreshments for five long minutes. Mack and Barbara also puffed their cigars and Rick smoked his cigarette, until a small bulb in the base of the instrument blinked green. Everyone sighed then, and released their half-held breaths as Bobby picked up the handset. He listened for several seconds, and then dialed in a string of 15 digits, and waited a minute longer.

"Hey there E.B, how's things over yonder in the flat lands?" Bobby asked.

"Oh well, what the hell. They're trying to do the same thing to my school to. Just drag your feet like I have been doing and mumble. That slows those educator `crats down a lot."

"Anyway, to change the subject, I'm sitting here with some old friends and we have been talking about words in general, and I thought you would like to know that a specific word has finally been spoken."

"Si, Mi Compadre! Damn right, and it as been a way long time. But it looks like the wait is over now. Anyway, we thought you would like to hear it for yourself, so say hello to Kristina Hamier," Bobby finished as he passed the handset to Boots.

"Hello E.B., its nice to talk to you - about the Walrus, and the time that has now come for us to begin speaking of many things..."

"Thank you, I will do my best. And I do think we have a good chance to succeed, due in part to some new assets I have located in only the last few days. Anyway, stand by and I will get a draft of our thinking to you very soon by appropriate secure channels.

"Oh, and E.B. From what everyone here has told me about you, I am glad you're on the team.

"Thank you, it is nice of you to say that. I will be back in touch," Boots said then returned the handset to Bobby.

He passed it on to the grizzled general.

"Hello, Bird Nose, Mack here. Looks to me that we're really green for go finally after a long damn time. More later but tighten security up real good starting right now, you hear!

"And how's Possum Sprout by the way? Is she still pretty as ever, and keepin' you honest and happy?

"Good! Now hold on, there's another person here I think you would like to talk to," he said with a dry chuckle as he passed the handset to Puss.

Puss had hissed between her teeth when Mack used the first nickname, then on hearing the second, she had straightened her shoulders, and her mien had changed to one of alert strength, and the others at the table finally became aware of the interplay between Mack and Puss.

They watched with confused or questioning expressions as Puss accepted the handset from Mack. She covered its mouthpiece with her hand momentarily as she murmured to Mack, her eyes now gleaming with mischief.

"You are very, very good, you know."

He smiled and leaning back in his chair, puffed on his cigar while he watched the others at the table, as Puss detonated the verbal stun-grenade he had constructed from his deductions about her.

"Hello, Daddy! It's me." Puss announced in a happy voice. Then she repeated her greeting in the ancient Pamunkey dialect, "Kencuttemaum, Kowse! Netapewh," and chatted with him for several minutes while Mack smiled, and observed the reactions of the others at the table.

"What tha' flamin' ferk is going on here anyway?" Bobby exploded as Puss finished and gave the handset back to Mack, who replaced it in its cradle.

"Well, it looks to me like we all have much more in common than any of us had thought," Boots smiled. "Mack, how do you know Marybell?"

"Her father was the other most outstanding officer I ever had in my command and he and Bobby led my best penetration teams. Those two killed Chin so damn good!" he crooned, with a grim smile.

"Anyway, I got to know more about EB when the jerkos at the 'Gon got their straps in a twist and hauled me back to Washington for a stint, and then were sorry because I told them how to win the damn war. Fell on ears that didn't want to hear as it turned out."

"But while I was there I was able to help EB get his Pamunkey academy off the ground. So EB leads our resources back east now. Marybell being out here is now one more reason why our crazy attempt to restore the Constitution might actually work.

"You are with us, aren't you," Mack then turned to her and asked.

Puss slowly pushed her chair back and rose to her feet. Boots smiled as her friend assumed her normal persona of competent strength, and looked down to the grizzled general.

"Of course I am. What else would you expect, Running Bear?"

Mack started, then sputtered, "How'n hell do you know that name? The last time I was called that was at my adoption ceremony into your tribe. You were there but you were only twelve."

"Us pesky red-skins do be sneaky devils," Puss, laughed while the others at the table considered these revelations. Both the nature of the suddenly changed Puss, and the fact that a high-ranking army officer had sought to join an Amerindian tribe, and had been accepted into it..."

"You are very, very, very good young lady. Ma'am!"

"Why thank you, Suh'. I appreciate your kind words, and as I said before, you are too," Puss murmured with a smile.

Mack looked at her in open respect, and wry amusement as he recalled her father's proud descriptions in the past of his daughter's capabilities, and attitude.

"Alright, enough side chat you two, let's get back to business," Boots ordered. She nodded to Rick, who had gestured with the hand that held his cigarette.

"I see that we have also acquired a major upgrade to our communications security this evening," Rick rumbled.

"How so?" Bobby asked.

"Remember your military history son, back around 1917 in our first war with Europe and then again in our second one in 1944," Mack said, now all business again.

Bobby thought for a second, and then grinned at Puss, "Hot Damn! Indian code talkers! You and your dad can chat on an open line and the Governor still won't have a clue, just like the Germans and Japanese didn't back then."

Puss smiled sweetly, "You betcha' Big Chief. Us Injuns got lotsa' words for fighting."

Bobby, now relaxing and becoming comfortable with Puss' true self as well as with that of his Boots, former pupil, grunted in mock severity, "Hope your guys also got words for winning too."

Boots chuckled, "Good point Commander," she said. "I like the way you keep us all focused."

The others at the table all nodded or muttered their agreement, but Mack caught Boots' eye as well, he gave her a quick wink of approval at the subtle way she had restored Bobby's confidence, so essential to their cause.

Barbara nodded this also as she muttered, "she is a natural dammit! No wonder they kept her out here and wouldn't promote her past Captain."

Mack glanced at Waldo then, who had been sitting silently while watching everyone with cautious eyes. The grizzled general decided that it was time to release his final bombshell about the daughter of his oldest and most respected friend.

"Marybell, didn't your parents give you a nickname while you were a child like the ones they gave each other? And didn't you also use it sometimes when you were still in the army?"

Puss blushed and looked down at her plate as she replied in a low voice, "Yes Sir."

"And it was?"

"Baby Bird," Puss whispered after a long moment, and as her blush deepened.

"Baby Bird? Wait a minute!" Waldo exploded, "The Baby Bird!"

Puss' cheeks turned a bright crimson that rivaled the port in her glass as she whispered, "Yes," in an obvious agony of embarrassment.

"Sacred Sheet!" Waldo gasped in awe, "You are the greatest there ever was..."

"Greatest what?" Barbara snapped with an exasperated glance first at Waldo then at Mack. The general with no insignia merely smiled.

"The best unarmed combat fighter ever," Waldo continued reverently as he stared wide-eyed at Puss.

"You were champion of your Division five years in a row, and champion of the Army for the last three. They finally had to bar you from competition because the troops stopped entering the contests when they knew that they would have to fight you in the end."

Then, pausing for a moment, and regaining his normal self-control, the tough sergeant continued matter-of-factly, "Baby Bird is the only person in the Army who is authorized to wear two of these," He said, touching the slender black silk aiguillette looped around his left arm at his shoulder.

*

Mack, Barbara and Bobby all wore them as well, as did Boots whenever she was in uniform. The little black cord signified to all the honor of those who had earned, while at the same time it also served a warning about the killing skills of those who wore it...

The unarmed combat methods used by the U.S. forces was a mixture of styles that evolved over the long years of the war, and included elements of judo, karate, English boxing, Thai kickboxing, and raw street fighting. It was very brutal and quite effective since those who learned it were trained to kill their target as quickly as they could and by any means possible. Sportsmanship was out of the question and an attack to merely disable was never performed.

The only times instructors and their pupils pulled their blows even slightly were in training matches. Then the probable looser signaled submission in whatever position he or she was in by suddenly going limp as wolves do before the leader of their pack. Failure by the losers to promptly signal their submission in training and competition matches was a cause of numerous accidental deaths in the advanced combat schools, but this fact was not generally known outside of the service...

*

"Well Buddy, what else is in your past that you haven't thought to mention? No wonder you took me most of the time when we sparred," Boots grinned.

Waldo looked at Boots with respect as he sputtered, "Kris, you took me half the time when you were just a cadet. And now you say you took Baby Bird?"

"To be bluntly truthful, in only in our first two matches, My Little Buddy has taken me every time since," Boots smiled crookedly. "I keep trying tho' just to see how big her bag of tricks really is, but she has never repeated herself yet dammit!"

"Can we Please talk about something besides me?" Puss burst out, her cheeks now a deeper red than the wine in her glass. "It's not polite!"

"Right friend, so let's finish this session and make a plan. Then we head downstairs." Boots flashed Bobby a brilliant smile, "And I'll buy us some bubbly. Then I'll try to remember the dance you taught me a long time ago."

"Kris, if I may call you that?" Rick began.

"You better!"

The large black man chuckled, "Yes Ma'am! If you will allow me, this meal and the champagne to come are on the house."

"How are you going to stay in business if you always treat your guests?"

"You may rest assured that I have received vastly more than I ever expected tonight, so anything that I contribute is miniscule in comparison."

At Rick's statement and the general murmur of agreement from the others, Boots' eyes glistened and she was silent for moment. Then she blinked and squared her shoulders.

"Thank you all. I will do my best."

"That will be more than sufficient for the work at hand," the grizzled general said. "What are your orders for us Ma'am?"

"Thank you Mack, for your re-focus!"

"Bobby, would you alert all of those with us who were in WNG units and who are inactive now to sew their unit patches back on? But they are to wait for your word before they suit up again.

"Waldo, would you see how many small arms caches you can locate that are outside of the 'claves and the active military posts and bases, and work with Barbara on a plan to collect and distribute them when we are ready to go full scale?"

"And Barbara, would you locate the weapons parks and motor pools with assets that used to be owned by the units that Bobby will be manning?"

"That part will be easy Ma'am. I'm WNG myself."

"Good. Would you also work with Waldo on a plan to acquire those assets we need them?"

"And by the way with your rank, you could be the lead candidate for the state's Adjutant General if all of this works out," Boots finished with a slight smile.

"Don't worry Kris, Bobby and I decided back on that night we wetted down your first stripe that we would make it work out for you," Waldo said with a flinty grimness.

"Then I'm in damn good hands, Sir," she nodded to him, before continuing, "Bobby, how many field surgeons and medics do we have that are equipped, and that you can trust to really keep secrets?"

"Not as many as I would like, but at least 30 or so. Why?"

"Because of one of the bits of intel we picked up on our last mission for Rat.

"Remember about five years back when every one on active duty as well as many others were given what Washington said was a new and improved I.D. implant? Well, it was improved all right. These are locator bugs and the Governors can turn them on any time they want.

"So we need some medics we can trust to keep their mouths shut after they de-bug our troops, or to make a really bad pun," she grinned, "We will all have double-crossed buns.

"Marybell can brief them on a procedure that she worked out and which she will also perform on me later tonight."

Puss stifled an instinctive urge to give her usual joking retort and only nodded, to Boots' silent relief.

"Finally but most importantly Mack, could we visit the lady in Olympia tomorrow?"

"That's why you are getting de-bugged tonight, isn't it? Anyway, to give you an answer Ma'am, yes in all probability. Rather than calling first and alerting her so-called security force, I think we will just drop by for a visit as I have occasionally done in the past."

"This should work, with us only showing on their local I.D. screen since due to my retirement, I missed out on being blessed with the one of long range locator gadget you describe. I also assume that your old I.D. implant will be sufficient for the on-site detectors in Olympia as well. I say this because on my previous visits I found the security to be typical of all of the Governors' operatives. About as bright as a snuffed candle," he finished with a dry sniff.

"Good thinking and a good plan Mack. You and Barbara design our communications tree as soon as you can, and I have a final request before we go dance!"

"Your request, Ma'am?" Bobby asked as he smiled at the tall woman whom he now recognized to be the best leader he could ever have hoped for.

"Marybell and I need a reliable car and driver tomorrow night. We have been invited to a party."

"The gala for General Butler at the Network headquarters?" Rick asked quietly.

"Yes," Boots answered with a grim face and Puss nodded with eyes that were suddenly green ice, again.

"They have "special" entertainments at those things which only a beast like Butler or the most advanced 5X addicts could enjoy. I think would be very dangerous for you to go," Rick said.

"It is also very dangerous for the two of us to not go. Until we are all ready to make our move. We have been very careful to behave within profile for the last few days, ever since we started smelling a rat as it were," Boots said with a crooked smile, "So their alarm would trigger quickers if we were to suddenly change our pattern.

"And we have some accessories to our party outfits that aren't real obvious," Puss added with an evil grin.

"Well Ma'am, sounds like you two know what you are doing, so while you do the thinking I'll do the driving," Waldo drawled.

"We also have a car for you that's sorta' developed multiple personalities and has other features that can make your ride home from the Gala more comfortable," Bobby added. "The identification/location transmitters permanently installed in all vehicles by order of the Governor were tamper-proof - supposedly," he said with a grin.

"Thanks Bobby, sounds like we have good backup here as well. Mack and I will figure our next communiqué tomorrow after we see how it goes in Olympia. Then we will use your communication tree to deliver our first message."

"Assuming we are successful in Olympia and your exit strategy tomorrow night is also, what's next?" Mack asked.

"Two things, Sir. First Rick's people need to figure out how to bring our new communications asset into our equation, and then Marybell and I will go back out to make sure the asset wants to party with us."

"And if it does?"

"We start the Restoration."

"And if it doesn't?"

Boots pictured Molly in her mind's eye both as she was when they had found her chained in the closet of the cabin, when she and Puss had left the 14 year-old girl standing by Bila's side with her young face set in adult determination.

"It will," Boots said with quiet certainty. Then breaking the tension she announced, "That's all I have. If there's nothing else you want Troops, let's adjourn to fun!"

***

Chapter 9
The Toast

May 3, 2276 AD
`Clave of S'attl

Rick led them to a table beside the dance floor in the main room and at his nod a waiter opened the magnum already in the icer beside their table. They chose seats and the men seated the women with courtesy. The waiter then filled their glasses and they all took several sips of the champaign, and murmured their appreciation to Rick. He nodded, then excused himself to mingle with the rest of his patrons.

"Bobby, what did you call that dance you taught me the first time you and Waldo lured my sweet young self into this sin den?" Boots asked with a grin, and signified that she had dropped out of her role as their leader.

Bobby answered with a smile, "The Jitter Ma'am, but you probably have forgotten everything I taught you long ago back when you were young, and still innocent."

"Them's Dancing words, Sir, put your feet where your mouth is!" Boots answered with a laugh as she bounded to her feet. She reached to her hair, pulled the pins from it and with a shake of her head, freed it to fall to her shoulders and frame her face. Then she unbuttoned her suit jacket, and tossed it over the back of her chair to reveal the sleeveless top of sheer white silk that was all she wore beneath it. Without her jacket it was also obvious that while the legs of her trousers were loose, its black silk was very snuggly fitted to her waist and hips.

She looked at Bobby for a second then held out her hand and said, "Come on old friend, let's dance."

Bobby stood and took her hand without a word, but his pride was obvious as he lead the beautiful woman across the floor to the sound tender.

Puss grinned at Waldo, "Hey killer, want to help me show those two how the "Jitter" thing is really done?" She asked.

Waldo blushed, "'Fraid I don't know this one."

"I, as a Southern gal know all there is to know about dancing. I'll teach you how then we'll show 'um something special!"

Waldo suddenly grinned. He stood and took Puss' hand and as the woman in the black tuxedo at her control panel changed the music, let her lead him on to the dance floor.

Mack smiled at Barbara when Puss and Waldo left the table, and squeezed her knee beneath it. "That is one of the slickest assumptions of command I have ever seen in all my experience," he said quietly. "Right, Dolly Dear?"

She placed her hand atop his, "Yep, you sneaky old goat, those two are one hell of a team, and they know it but don't show it."

"Kris took control of us and of Bobby totally. She let him know she was doing it and that she could do it, then she convinced him to accept her lead.

"And finally she picked his ego up from the floor just now, dusted it off and handed it back to him with a smile. Did you see the way he walked out on the floor with her?"

"Friend, you're way right about Kris two hundred percent. It's hard as hell to take command over someone who has been your superior let alone your teacher, but she did and with max grace as well.

"And talk about Bobby walking tall, I've never heard quiet pride stomp so loud before," Mack finished with a chuckle.

"Do you think they knew about E.B.s connection with us before tonight?" Barbara asked.

"No, they couldn't have and I could tell from their eyes that they had not. Kris didn't know about Marybell being Baby Bird either, but she handled all this new intel as cool as a veteran three star. Which she would be by now if those bastards at the 'Gon hadn't kept her out here to be shot at all these years," Mack added.

"How did you figure out Marybell?"

"Slowly, my first impression was the one she wanted to project, but then I looked at her again and saw a little too much, I don't know – depth maybe. So I did what you say I do best," he said with a boyish grin, "I played the sneaky old goat.

"I looked at her hand when I kissed it, and then watched her when she sat in the chair when I held it for her."

"And, Billy Goat Boy?" Barbara chuckled, her dark eyes gleaming as she squeezed his hand on her thigh.

"And, my Dominant Little Dolly, sweet young bits of fluff might wear long pink artificial nails, but they don't usually have the callused and scarred knuckles of a fighter. She also tried to keep her hand limp, but I could still feel its muscle density, which is pretty significant by the way."

"So what did you see when she sat down, aside from her exquisitely cute little bottom, my goat guy?"

"Just that."

"Just what?" Barbara snapped, half playfully.

"I saw that, and that her thighs only flattened out slightly when she sat down. Not nearly as much as yours and mine do, and every one else's who is normal.

"When I saw that I knew she really was as hard as a brass Buda and she was trying to hide the fact behind her pink fuzzy act."

"I also had a feeling that I had seen this kind of extreme muscle tone before so I started watching her, until I finally remembered someone else who had her same kind of body mass, my old friend E.B. Then I remembered his daughter whom I met once, as you now know. Even at the age of twelve she was beautiful, with glowing green eyes.

"It was dead easy after that and it was obvious that Marybell was his daughter when she recognized the pet names that E.B. and his wife use for each other."

"I'll bet it was also a nice duty, looking at her and what she had on, almost," Barbara snorted. Then she added with a dry sniff, "And since you can quote Sun Tzu chapter and verse, what's this vague stuff about 'The Old Chin?"

"Hey, we goat guys have to keep our intel current, both so we can figure out just who knows what around the table, and so we also can advise our best friend on the condition of her body tone don't we?" he said with a playful leer as he slid his hand from her knee up the inside of her thigh.

"Thanks little man, but my drumsticks are strong enough to hold you where I want you for as long as I want to until I let you up for air, Goat Boy," Barbara murmured, her eyes suddenly smoky with desire. She stroked the back of his neck while she trapped his hand by clamping her legs together.

"That's no great feat of strength Ma'am, if I'm where I want to be anyway," he whispered, undressing her with his gaze.

Barbara smiled, "We'll see about that later tonight, if you don't get too tired from dancing with me now, Running Bear."

Mack chuckled, "You're on Twinkle-toes! Let's go see if you remember the moves I taught you, if your porridge can stay hot that long," he grinned as he stood and held out his hand to her, after removing it from her between thighs with an exaggerated sigh.

"I love it when you act as a gentleman," she murmured, "It's so deviant..."

"Leaned everything I know from you, M'Dear. But now let's go dance."

*

Sam, the sound tender in her black tuxedo nodded to Bobby and Boots as they stepped away from her console, then she changed her music to a beat that was twice the tempo of the group fast-dances she usually played for the club's patrons.

The two moved to the center of the floor as the other dancers paused at this new unfamiliar beat and left the floor.

Bobby and Boots began responding to the music. They first shuffled, and stamped their feet in time to the driving beat with seemingly awkward movements. Then when the music's rapid pulse captured them they began to dance. They spun and whirled around the floor as they matched their movements with each other and held hands. Boots moved cautiously at first, until she remembered the steps he had taught her on this same floor years ago, the evening after she had graduated from the academy in a very tense way. She regained her confidence and exploded into a welcoming anticipation of his lead.

The clear joy of motion shining on her face as she complemented Bobby's movements to the driving beat of the music brought the whole club to their feet, and the crowd began to clap in time.

Puss began dancing slowly with Waldo at the side of the floor while she showed him the steps and moves. Then when he caught the rhythm of the Jitter, she urged him to join with her and Boots and Bobby in the center of the floor. Puss signaled Waldo to hold her hands as she began leading him in spins and gyrations in time to the music.

Waldo was competent in the group dances of the time, so he caught Puss' signals, and became a partner to her spectacular moves without ever releasing her hand – the essence of the Jitter.

Sam brought the music to a crashing peak that urged the four dancers into a spectacular series of steps and spins, and then she cut the sound. The two couples froze in their last pose - and the patrons burst into applause.

The four were acknowledging the applause as they caught their breath, then Mack stepped on to the floor leading Barbara by the hand.

Sam grinned, and started another set of the fast-driving music when she saw the two general officers join their friends, and laughed when the grizzled man and the compact woman exploded into a frenzy of dance equaling that of the two young couples, who began dancing again.

Several more couples stepped on to the floor as Sam started the music and cautiously begin trying the dance as well. They had watched Puss tutoring Waldo, and his pleasure when he caught the steps and moves, so they dared to join in. The patrons began to clap with a good-natured chant of, "Go, Go, Go," clapped in time with the music.

The brave couples then began to step to the beat, and after learning its flow, danced with Boots and her friends until Sam brought the set to a final crescendo.

The dancers all embraced their partners as they panted to catch their breath while the crowd applauded with loud whistles and cheers.

"All right gang, lets line up and give `um a bow," Boots called as she held Bobby's hand and reached out to Waldo. Puss reached out to Mack while Barbara gestured the other couples to her, and they all formed themselves into a line. Then at Boots' nod, they all bowed to the room while holding hands in a classic theater curtain call. The crowd roared its approval.

Rick walked onto the floor while they all still stood there, panting and enjoying their release from Sam's driving music. He congratulated the other dancers on their bravery and their skill at learning the Jitter, and then he told them that drinks on the house would be served back at their tables.

The flushed couples thanked him, and as they were returning to their seats and their admiring friends, Rick turned to Kris.

"Most of my patrons have also been waiting for the Word for a very long time as well. Shall we give it to them now?" he asked.

"The people here are some of our most important core group, and as you know the screening methods and devices they have installed in my club are vastly superior to the Governor's surveillance systems."

"Yes. We will," Boots said with a quiet nod. She glanced around at her friends, and they became her staff again as they nodded their agreement.

"Thank you Ma'am. If you would also, please allow me to make the announcement in my own way."

"Of course Rick. Your way always seems to be the best somehow."

"Thank you again Ma'am," he said, then he turned and walked over to Sam at her console and spoke with her for a moment.

The woman in the tuxedo listened to him intently - then she nodded as her eyes widened and she straightened from her normal slouch.

Rick walked back to the center of the dance floor as Sam dialed the lighting in the main room up to a normal level, then she turned to her rarely used keyboard on her console.

She put it into piano mode and played the first four crashing notes of an ancient symphony, a tonal phrase that was used to signify "Victory" in a war between America and Europe over four hundred years ago. The room suddenly stilled and all eyes, no matter how unfocused by the club's wine list and well-stocked bar, turned to the large black man in the white dinner jacket who stepped into the middle of the dance floor.

"Ladies and gentlemen, and friends. You know why you come here and why you have helped to make this a place of sanity in an insane world.

"You and I have also been waiting for something, an action signal that we have called for a better label, "The Word."

"Tonight with great joy, profound gratitude and an unshakable resolve, I finally bring the bearer of that word to you."

Then Rick snapped his fingers and the club staff rushed to all of the tables with bottles of champagne and fresh glasses, and began pouring for all of the patrons.

Rick stood silently while the room was served, then he signaled his staff to serve his friends on the dance floor, and himself. As his major domo presented him with a flute and filled it, Rick said, "Please serve your selves and bring the kitchen in also, and all of you stay here with us."

"Dear friends," he addressed room after his staff had filed in to stand at the edge of the dance floor.

"I am sure that most of you know Kristina Hamier, and that some of you also attended the S'attl academy with her as well as fought under her command."

"It is my honor tonight to present Kristina to you tonight, after all our years of waiting," he said as he held his arm out to Boots with a half-bow.

Boots stepped to the center of the floor and Rick moved back to stand beside Sam. Boots stood with the light shining down on her bowed head until the room became silent, and all felt her presence.

"Dear friends and companion," Boots began in a conversational tone, "You have waited for a word for many years. Somehow I have been chosen to bring it to you, and tonight is the time, finally."

Boots bowed her head again as she stood before her hushed audience. She clinched her hand around the stem of her flute then she raised her head and called in a voice that rang through the room, "I now bring you this Word!"

"To The Constitution!" Boots shouted as she raised her glass and took a sip.

"And its Restoration!" she shouted again and draining her glass, smashed it on the floor.

"The Constitution! The Restoration!" her friends behind her shouted, as did Sam and the major domo. The stunned crowd finally awoke to what was taking place and with a straggling chorus of shouts, returned Boots' toast as they also crashed their glassed on the floor.

When the room had quieted somewhat, Rick announced, "We are closing early this evening so that you may return to your homes to reflect on the coming changes, and what your personal contribution can be.

"The overt reason for my early closing is a grease fire in the kitchen, a faked vid of which is now being fed into the Governors' monitors. However before we leave, I would like to express to you my own feelings about what has just happened, and what will soon begin."

Rick turned and nodded to Sam. The woman in the tuxedo played an attention-getting riff on her keyboard then she paused and closing her eyes, faced upward for a moment. She opened them again with a glare, took a deep breath and began hammering out the ponderous notes of the "Battle Hymn of the Republic".

Rick waited for Sam's second repeat of the melody line then he began to sing in a compelling baritone.

"My eyes have seen the glory of the coming of the Lord,"

Boots and Puss joined in with a clear alto and a soaring soprano.

"He is trampling out the vintage where the grapes of wrath are stored,"

Bobby and Waldo, with Mack and Barbara then joined in with strong voices.

"He has loosed the fateful lightening of His terrible swift sword..."

Then, as tears trickled unashamedly down Rick's cheeks, most of those in the room joined in singing the hymns' final chorus, all thundering, "Glory! Glory! Hallelujah! His truth is marching on..."

*

Boots and her friends stood quietly on the dance floor as the rest of the patrons begin leaving the club. There was little conversation but many who knew her from their academy days, or during the war came up to quietly pledge their support.

After the last patron had left and Rick's staff and was busy bussing the tables and sweeping the room, Boots turned to Mack and asked, "How long to Olympia and what time shall we start tomorrow?"

Mack blinked and shook his head, then answered, "At least three hours now considering the state of the roads under non-improvement road plan of the present administration." He added dryly, "It used to take less than an hour."

"Waldo, will you be with Mack and me tomorrow?"

"Hey, Ma'am, you two do the thinking, I do the driving OK?"

"I feel pretty damn well safe then, friend."

"Good. You should. But we go at zero six hundred in the morning, so where do we pick you up, Ma'am?"

"The same place you dropped me off eleven years ago after the first time you and Bobby dragged me in this Sin Den," she answered with a grin, "And we need to beg a ride back there tonight if you have the time."

"Hey, us Sergeants just live to serve, them we choose to anyway..."

*

"Zero six hundred hours tomorrow?" Boots said with a chuckle as she and Puss climbed from the military sedan after Waldo stopped it before an upscale row house. "Sounds like the dawn patrol at oh-dark-thirty to me."

"Yes Ma'am it is. But General Mack is pretty picky about punctuality."

"Good. So am I."

She waved to him as he drove away, then led Puss toward the door.

"OK, so what's this place, one of your safe houses in the 'clave?"

"Sort of," Boots grinned as she keyed the door open and strode through, it and announced in a happy voice, "Mother, I'm home!"

***

Chapter 10
The Lesson Plan

May 3, 2276 AD
Coastal Mountains of British Columbia

Bila heard the unease in Molly's voice as she stared at the instrument on the wall above her computer, with glowing symbols on it that he did not understand. He looked at the girl and tensed for action.

"I wish that darn smart dog hadn't run off, darn it!" she piped in a serious little voice. "Now we'll just have to go up there and set up some more IR beams further out."

"IR beams what?" Bila asked as he relaxed, slightly.

Molly looked up at the large man for a moment while she considered her reply. Then she remembered the simple questions he had asked Boots about computers the previous day, in a conversation she had tried to ignore at the time.

"IR beams are Infra-Red alarm beams. They are like eyes," pointing to her own. She pointed to Bila's as she repeated herself, "Eyes."

She touched the small wall screen of the alarm system as she continued, "An Infra Red alarm beam array is the eyes for our cabin. It tells us when someone comes," She added as she watched the big man, hopefully.

Bila frowned for a moment, then smiled and nodded, "Cabin Infra Red alarm beam array eyes see with," he said as he shaded his eyes with a hand and mimicked a person watching. When she grinned her approval, he paused and considered for a moment, then touched the main console before her, and the large display screen on the wall behind it.

"Dreamer computer more far see, Infra Red alarm beam eyes near see with?" he asked, as he held his arms out and moved them like the wings of a soaring bird, while peering down at the floor.

Molly's eyes widened in surprise, then she giggled and nodded her head, "Pretty close, but they're not beams like the cabin array, they are from the spy sats, and real good IR cams up there."

The big man considered her reply for a moment, and then he said in a very grim tone, "Cabin Infra Red alarm beam Boss Rat see come near? Dreamer computer Boss Rat come see far, Infra Red with?"

Molly remembered the task Boots had given to her before leaving less than an hour ago, the woman she now adored.

"Yes, and other bad people too," She responded with equal grimness.

"People? People what?"

Molly was startled at his question, and thought for a long moment. Finally, she took a deep breath and announced in a determined little voice, "OK! It's time for me to start teaching you like Kris told me to."

Then pointing to herself she said, "I am people." Pointing to him, "Bila, you are people. Kris and Marybell are people." Then stroking her bulging stomach, she said gently, "And you will be people too.

Spreading her arms wide the girl continued, "We all are people. We are good people. You know Rats are bad people, but other bad people live over the ridge," she finished as she pointed upward toward the back wall of the cabin.

"Dream computer over ridge bad people see?"

"Wow! You catch on quick!" she squeaked as she dropped into her seat before the main console and powered it up, "And I'll show you where they live."

When the large screen lit, the girl split it as she had done in her demonstration the previous day and began typing rapidly on the keypad, again filling the right display with lines of code.

"I'm using the names and passes that Kris gave me, and I'll pull down a sat scan that's been archived for five minutes so's I don't spook 'um by jangling their real-time download."

Bila smiled down at the top of the earnest young girl's head as she lost herself in her task, and silently shook his own in bemused respect at her determined, but to him unintelligible words and barely comprehensible actions.

She scrolled back through her entries to review them, then tapped the activate key and leaned back in her seat and waited, as did Bila standing behind her.

The left screen came to life several minutes later and displayed a blinking cursor.

Molly typed the series of the passwords Boots had left with her, and after waiting for a moment, entered a line of code to download satellite images from the Gov-net. The left display blinked, and then opened into a natural-color aerial photograph of the region around their valley as seen from an altitude of 10,000 meters.

The girl entered several more commands that increased the scale of the image as Bila stared at the screen that gave the effect of an airborne viewer dropping closer to the earth in jumps, until they were hovering 200 meters above the cabin.

"The computer can see two ways. This is like a bird sees," then she entered another command that changed the image to the strange hues of false-color Infra-Red. "And this is how the computer sees with IR."

Bila stared at the strangely reversed colors for a moment, then he asked, "Bird like see make?"

Molly switched the image back to normal, and their cabin and its immediate area were again displayed in their true colors.

Bila leaned forward over her shoulder and lightly traced the outline on the screen of their cabin's roof, and then the open valley and the wooded slope behind it. Then he asked, "IR make see?"

After the girl switched the image back, the forest was colored a red with dark and light streaks, and the grassy meadow now appeared in a uniform light red. The cabin, being a non-heat emitter was now a dark blue, except for a faint pink spot pulsating close to its rear wall.

The man carefully touched the pink spot, and looked down at the girl, "Molly? Bila?"

"Yes."

"Cabin IR eye in see?"

"Sometimes," she answered in a serious little voice. "There are very powerful IR cams in all of the survel sats, and when they pick up 'nomalies they automatically focus 'um on the place where an image was downloaded."

Bila smiled, and shook his head at her technical explanation, then asked,"IR see people cabin in why?"

Molly thought for a moment, both about what she knew of the technology, and how to explain it to the man who had such mysterious gaps in his knowledge.

"Infra-red sees what is alive. It shows it as red, because it is warm. Trees and grass are alive, we are alive," then pointing up, she finishes, "And the roof is thin."

"Roof?"

"The top of the cabin, Silly," she giggled.

"Thin what?"

"Wow, you really have been living in a cave," then gesturing with her hands, she first held her palms close together as she squeaked, "Thin." Then holding them far apart and using her deepest voice, she intoned, "Thick."

Bila chuckled at her antics, and nodded his understanding, then asked, "Cave what?"

Molly looked at the man in exasperation for a moment, before she exclaimed, "Ha, I've got it! Come on and I'll show you one," and she got to her feet and scampered awkwardly in to the front room.

Bila chuckled again as he obediently followed her.

She opened one of the built-in cupboards on the room's far wall and revealed a large vid screen. "Most of the stuff that Durwood copied from the Network is pretty harsh, but this one is funny and only 2X. It's about some silly cave people doin' it."

The girl selected a vid chip from a neatly cataloged case of more than three hundred and slipped it in a slot in the machine, then powered it. The screen came to life and a show began that depicted animal skin-wearing hairy brutes of men capturing barely clad and overly coy nubile maidens, and having their way with them accompanied by a chorus of grunts in counterpoint with girlish shrieks. The action took place before a stage-set mockup of a cave.

"Ha! Koba!" Bila exclaimed, his eyes suddenly gleaming. Then turning to Molly, and ignoring the activities on the screen between the captors and their curvy captives, he earnestly asked, "Koba-cave here?"

She clicked off the vid as she muttered in a girlish echo of Boots' growl, "Buda's Butt! Can this guy stay major ferkin focused, 'er I'm a Chin grunt!"

"Yes, there's an old mine tunnel over the ridge, and I'll show ya' it when we go up to set some more beams."

"Thank you Molly. Bila more teach now you me."

*

"OK, now I've shown you the lay of the land, and the places where all our fiends live. So now I'm gonna' show you some more stuff like Kris said," the girl said in a firm little voice as she turned to her computer's printer.

"The Governor is real tight about who gets to archive stuff on paper, but Durwood rigged up this one that the Chin left and we found a whole bunch of sheets with it too," Molly explained proudly as she removed several pages from the machine.

Then she went to the tool bench and retrieved the small box of bullets remaining from their morning shoot. She took her seat again and made a space on the computer bench next to the keypad and laid out the paper and ammunition. She rummaged in a drawer until she found an ink stylus.

"Now I'm gonna' teach you how to count," she said with a nod of determination.

"Friends they not!" Bila announced quietly, as he pointed to the computer display that still showed an aerial view of both the neighboring groups' locations.

Molly looked at the man in expiration for a moment, "'Course they're not! I was making a joke, Silly!"

"Joke what?"

She looked at the big man, and saw the honest question in his eyes. She sighed and answered, "OK, a joke is something that's funny. This kind of joke is when I say something that is not right, that both you and I know is not right, but I say it anyway. That's what's funny about it."

Bila looked into the earnest young girl's pale blue eyes for a moment, then with a chuckle he said, "Bila like Molly not. Not right. Joke that?"

Her eyes widened as she nodded, and smiled tremulously, "Molly not like Bila either. That's a big joke!" Then impulsively she stood and stretched her thin arms around him in a tight hug and whispered to his chest, "A major big joke..."

Bila gently folded his arms around her small frame and kissed the top of her head as he said quietly, "Joke this like." Then after a moment he patted her shoulder as he said, "More Molly Bila teach, OK?"

She gave him a final squeeze, then stepping back she again unconsciously mimicked Boots again as she growled in a squeak, "Alright Trooper Three! You gonna' yak all day, 'er we gonna' get on with the mission? Grab that other stool and sit down here!"

"Yes Ma'am!" the man said with twinkling eyes as he obeyed her order.

"These are numbers, they're ten of them. Now watch me." She took up the stylus and wrote a numeral one at the top of a sheet of the paper as she said emphatically, "One," then she held up her index finger for a moment, before tapping his index with it.

"One," he repeated.

Then she opened the box of .22 caliber bullets and repeated, "One," as she withdrew a single tiny cartridge and stood it on its base above her paper.

She repeated these steps through the number nine, and was pleased when Bila quickly began anticipating the quantity represented by the number as soon as she named it.

"OK, that's all the regular numbers. Now pay attention because this is a special number," she frowned as she wrote another numeral one at the bottom of her column of figures, then added a zero next to it.

"One and zero makes ten," she finished as she held up all ten fingers, and Bila held up all of his momentarily also, before removing a tenth cartridge from the box and placing it at the end of the precise row of nine on the bench, and repeated, "Ten. Zero one ten say make!"

"Wow!" Molly squealed as she clapped her hands, "You are way-out quick Bila! Now see if you get this. Zero is special, because it tells how many tens you have. One zero and a one means you have a ten. Now what does two zeros with a one say?"

His brow wrinkled as he looked at the figure 2 she had written in the column for several seconds, and then he answered tentatively, "Two tens?"

She shook her head, "Ten tens. That's a hundred."

He frowned for a moment, and then he smiled as flicked the fingers of his left hand open twice in a practiced gesture, and then held both hands open with his fingers up. "Ten tens ehun!"

"What? What kind of word is ehun?" Molly squeaked.

"Ehun Bila people hundred word," he exclaimed happily. Then his brow wrinkled and his eyes become sad, as he gazed off into the distance beyond the confines of the little room.

Molly asked gently, "Where are your people, Bila?"

"Know not..." the man whispered, then closing his face and hiding his anguish he smiled again at the girl, "More Bila teach, OK?"

"OK." Acting on a sudden instinct, Molly handed him the stylus. "Now you make the numbers just like I did." He examined it and making a few practice marks at the top of the paper, touched the blackness of its fast-drying ink. Then he began to copy each of the letters, aligning them into a neat column as she had done.

Molly watched him as he submerged himself in his task. She thought, "Wow, he hurts big inside but he doesn't let it show just like I did before they came. I sure hope I can help him like he's helping me now."

After he finished copying her numbers exactly, even down to the extra curl she had given to the bottom of the 3 and the cross-bar on the 7, she said, "That's real good Bila, but now let me show you how zero is a special number in another way too.

"You don't have to see it to know it's there. I'll show you what I mean," as she wrote a ten, and then a one.

"How many is that?"

"Ten and one," as he held up all fingers, followed by his index.

"Right, but this is the way to write it," she said seriously as she made the numeral 11 on the paper.

"What write?"

"Write is the same as draw OK," she snapped, "'Cept you draw pictures of things like animals and trees, and you write numbers and words. Now pay attention and quit interruptin' until I finish!"

Bila nodded, in spite of not comprehending all of the words in her command. He watched the girl as she continued.

"You write, or draw the number eleven, that's its name, this way because zero lets you cover it with another number. That's the second special thing about it. Now you write the next number. It's called twelve by the way."

Bila considered her examples for a moment then he motioned a precise 1, followed by a zero without touching the stylus to the paper, and finally drew a 2 next to the 1. "Zero two let on top sit say twelve she, OK?"

The girl clapped her hands and squealed, "You got it Bila! You're learning real good." Then she timidly patted his hand, "And I'm sorry I talked mean to you just now, it's just that I want to teach you quick like Kris told me to."

The man covered her small hand with his massive one as he smiled into her earnest eyes. Considering his words carefully, he replied, "Molly teaching is Bila write numbers to good very. Kris happy at Molly very be."

Her eyes widened and she gasped, then with a sudden blush on her face, she whispered, "WOW! Bila you're really are getting' it. I'm so glad."

Then she paused and growled in imitation of Boots, "OK, enough mush stuff! On with the mission!" And she continued in her own way to teach the man numbers and their names until she found that he had no comprehension of the need to indicate a quantity larger than a thousand except as "Many".

She turned her efforts to language at this point, and began showing him the alphabet and its basic phonetics. It took longer this time but he finally grasped the concept of coupling combinations of letters into words that could give a message on paper to others.

He had some difficulty and made several false starts because of the vagaries of the English language however, such as the first time he tried to write Molly's name. She had drilled him on the basic sounds of letters and he had written "Bila" correctly, but when he put the sounds together for "Molly", "Mole" is what he came up with...

"OK Buddy, that's pretty good considerin' where you're starting from," She relaxed and sighed, and again unconsciously mimicked Boots, "But now you're in big trouble!" and turning to her computer, she captured an elementary reading instruction program on the Gov-net while Bila looked on with worried eyes.

She brought it up and giggled as she punched his arm, "Now Mister Smarto, you gotta' really go to work, Sir!"

Bila relaxed, and then grinned after she started showing him how to interact with the learning program using the computer's keyboard, screen pointer and sound system.

Molly moved her seat to the side and placed him at the console when she saw that he understood, and she watched him as he immersed himself in learning.

Bila made several false starts, then grasped the techniques of the program and began interacting with its directions. She watched as he mastered its use, and began to realize that Bila understood each element of the teaching program the first time he saw it, and retained him the new knowledge without effort.

Molly sat beside with for several hours, and only helped him when he occasionally needed help to make his way through more illogical quirks of the English language. She remained silent except to answer his questions and she became increasingly impressed at how well he was doing, even as she puzzled at his lack of basic knowledge about the world...

This was evident when he showed confusion at the meaning of the word "Father" in a lesson of beginning vocabulary. She blushed and tried to explain the biology and mechanics of the concept for several minutes, but without success in the face of his gentle disbelief.

"OK, we'll save this one for later dammit! Now back to work, Sir!"

"Yes Ma'am!" he said with the ghost of a grin and turned back to the screen.

Molly watched as he lost himself in learning again, and was again struck at his intensity and focus. She also considered the unfamiliar sense of home and comfort she was beginning to feel in his presence, and realized that she was very happy carrying out her tutoring this strangely ignorant but very intelligent man.

*

The two sat for another hour as Bila learned and Molly watched while silently urging him on, until her stomach gave a little rumble. The man jerked upright and broke away from the lessons on the display.

"Molly food need," he said. Then he corrected himself, "You hungry. Baby eat," As he looked at the girl with obvious concern.

"Don't worry about me; I'll grab a rash bar. You keep on going 'cause you're doing great!" she piped in a happy voice.

"No. Eat at two now you for. Teach me stop. Eat you," he responded in a very gentle tone that at the same time allowed for no argument.

"Bila teach - no," He corrected himself. "I teach real food you," he said with a slight smile as he got up from the computer and held his hand out to her.

Molly tensed in rebellion for a second then relaxed and took his hand and so accepted his fathering, a support that she had never experienced before.

*

Bila led her to the tree in the meadow where the deer carcass hung and showed her how to untie the line and lower it to a working height, then the correct way to slice off a filet from the haunch. He handed her his flint knife and smiled in encouragement, but Molly hesitated at touching the bloody meat.

He watched her reaction for a moment then he touched her belly, "You baby food make. Baby it strong help."

Molly took a deep breath and squaring her shoulders said, "You're right. Like Kris said, it's my job now." Then in an unconscious imitation of the tall woman that made Bila's mouth twitch, she gritted in her little voice, "So just do it dammit," As she attacked the haunch and sawed away a second filet.

Bila showed her how to trim green branches for skewers and impale the steaks securely on them, and to plant their sharpened butts in the ground beside the fire pit. He then showed her the way to lay a cooking fire, and how to take advantage of the slight breeze when lighting the tender under it.

But when he pulled a lump of pyrite and a granite pebble from his pouch and started to show Molly how to strike a spark, she asked, "Can't we use a blazer?"

"Blazer what, No. What blazer is?"

"Wow, that must be some pretty way-back cave you come from, Sir!" she giggled and clambering to her feet, said over her shoulder as she trotted into the cabin, "I'll get us some."

She came back a moment later and grunting as she dropped to kneel beside him and offered the small metal cylinder of a Chin combat match case.

Bila took it from her and tentatively examined it, then tried a gentle pull on its top.

"Here, let me show you how before you break it, ya' Big Thud, Sir," she giggled as she took the case from his large hand.

"You unscrew the top like this, silly. And then you take out a blazer and hold it by this end, and pull the top like this and drop it before it burns your fingers. Get it?" she asked as she shook out a match with a wax shaft and a bulbous head from which a loop of strong thread extending from its top.

When she jerked the loop its orange head erupted into a bright little flame and she dropped the blazing match into the tender where it immediately lit the pile of twigs and dried bark under the firewood.

"Now, you light one," she said handing him another match.

Bila examined it then lit it as Molly had done. He held its wax shaft and grunted in approval as the match head flared up. He drooped it into the already burning tender, and then he took the match case from the girl's fingers as the larger branches began to flame up and peered at the threads of its screw top.

He looked at the case for several moments while Molly watched him with a frown. Then he fitted the cap back on the case and rotated it first one way then the other until he felt its threads engage. He continued slowly turning the cap in that direction as he watched he two pieces join and become one.

He reversed the direction he had just explored and unscrewed the cap again, and did this several more times while the girl's eyes grew wide in astonishment.

"You really never have seen a screw cap before have you?" she whispered in awe.

"Thing this name screw cap?"

"Yes," Taking the little case from his fingers, Molly patiently continued, "But this part is called threads, and if you turn it this way, it is called "unscrew", or if you turn it this way it is called "screw". Screw caps let you close things real tight. OK?"

"Threads," he whispered as he held out his hand for the match case again. When the wide-eyed girl placed it in his hand he unscrewed the cap and let it dangle by its retaining chain.

Then he dropped down to seat himself cross-legged beside the fire pit and plucked a long blade of grass from the turf. Holding one end of it with his thumb against the body of the case, he carefully wound its length into the screw threads around the mouth of the case, and then unwound the grass blade again. He looked closely at its length held between his fingers then put the case on the ground and slowly wound the blade of grass around his index finger and contemplated the helix he formed.

He looked up at Molly in triumph, "Ha! Thread screw smart thing is," then correcting himself he announced, "No, screw thread smart be thing."

Molly stared at the man, then shook her head and again echoed Boots as she whispered, "Buda's balls, Bila! Just who tha' ferk are you anyway?"

Bila smiled, then shaking his head at her question, handed her a skewer as he said, "Bila now - no! I teach Molly now real food make. Molly me teach at, now Bila teach you at."

*

"That really was good Sir," Molly said as she licked the fork from her mess kit and sighed happily.

"Molly good food real – no! You food real make good. You real food like? It good mommies for," the man smiled as he leaned against the cabin wall.

"Now little time wait for food good inside feel we. Tell Bila you - no, you tell me set new IR beams how now."

"Yes, Sir. Well, there are these boxes, OK,

"And you screw them on to trees, OK,

"Then ya' line them up with the built-in laser, OK.

"And then you check the signal to see if it is workin' OK.

"Then you test their alignment... "

*

"Strong foot things got you?" Bila asked Molly twenty minutes later then he corrected himself, "You got things put foots in?"

201

"Sure do!" she exclaimed, as she started to rise, and then lurched slightly. Bila leaped to his feet and steadied the girl.

"Thanks Sir, I guess I'm not used to having this much belly," she giggled as she stepped into the cabin. She returned after a few moments, wearing small Chin combat boots. She also carried a Chin army haversack and her rifle.

"I've never worn these much, `cause Durwood didn't like going out in the woods," she piped. Then her tone changed and she finished as she involuntarily touched the fading chafe mark on her neck, "And he didn't like me getting too far away from him either."

Bila patted the hand she held to her neck. "Gone he, here you. You boss you now."

"Yeah, thanks to you, and Kris and Marybell. I'm pretty lucky I guess," she whispered.

"Lucky what, no. What lucky is?"

"Lucky is when good things happen to you, like you guys finding me."

"Lucky too us. Good us nice Molly find," he said with a smile as he looked down into her pale blue eyes.

They shone at his words...

"Go we now beams set?"

Molly blinked back a tear as she whispered, "Thank you, Bila. You're nice too." Then she straightened her slender shoulders and growled with a squeak, "OK dammit! Now let's go do it!"

Bila collected his two light spears, and grasping her haversack, led Molly around the side of the cabin and up the ridge. He climbed at a slow pace along the path he had cleared of mines while he gauging the girl's stamina by listening to her breathing as she followed him. Halfway up the ridge he paused and turned to face her. He noted that she was breath easily and while her cheeks were flushed, it was with the healthy color of exercise rather than heat distress.

"OK?" he asked.

"Sure, but it's gonna' take us all day and half the night if you can't move any faster, ya' Big Thud, Sir!" she said with a grin.

His eyes sparkled and he smiled at the girl, then he turned and bounded up the slope to its crest in a leaping run that was as fast as a wolf chasing its quarry. He paused at the top, and waited while Molly stormed up the slope after him.

She panted as she reached where he stood, "I'm Sorry, Sir. I didn't mean to be a smarto…"

"Molly is, no! Are very smart! But in you, no! You in Bila's now place," he said as he ruffled the girl's thin white hair. Then with an evil grin that the girl had not seen him use before, he repeated her order from earlier in the day in an exact mimic of her voice, "Now pay attention and quit interruptin' 'till I finish!"

"Yes Sir!" she gulped, as she looked up at the very large man whom now she realized was not only her new protector, but also the first real friend she had ever had…

*

Bila sniffed, then held out his hand to Molly when they were halfway down the slope of the ridge behind the cabin. The girl paused with him while he peered ahead to their left, in the shadowed stillness of the forest.

"We go there not," he whispered to Molly, "Bad sniff there."

She looked around her, unable to see or smell anything, then shrugged and followed him as he circled widely to the right. Then led her on down the slope under the towering trees for another two hundred meters, until she tugged at his arm.

"Here's is a good place for another perimeter line," she whispered as she squatted with a grunt by the base of a large spruce and motioned Bila down beside her.

"This is a monitor unit," Molly said as she groped in the haversack slung over his shoulder and pulled out a small plastic box. It was shaped irregularly on its curved outer surface with a good imitation of tree bark. Its inner surface was smooth and also curved slightly to conform to a tree's bole, and two black screws with fast threads and socket heads stuck five centimeters out from the rough surface.

"You use this tool to screw it to the tree trunk, but only do the screws in half-way 'till I set another one over there to start the line," she said in her little voice as she handed him a tool that fitted the screw heads.

"Then I'll shine the laser to line up the IR beam on this one here. You watch for the red spot and hand signal me when it's on to this target, OK?" she said, pointing to a small polished the rough lens side of the box.

"Then when I give you a signal, you crank the screws in real tight while you hold it real still, OK?" she finished as she took another unit from the haversack.

"And this is what the laser looks like, OK?" Molly said as she pressed a tiny button on the box she held and pointed a glowing ruby laser spot on his the back of his hand, then on a tree trunk fifty meters away.

Bila considered the tiny red spot on the distant tree for a moment then he lifted his palm to interrupt the laser beam, and contemplated the same sized red spot glowing on his hand for a moment longer.

"Laser see Bila like – no, like see I."

"What are you talking about now," Molly hissed. "Come on! We gotta' get the perimeter secured like Kris said!"

He replied in a calm voice, "You here see?" as he held his hand twenty centimeters before her face.

"Of course, Silly. So?"

"You gauhontza see in tree there?" And he pointed toward a distant hemlock.

"What tha ferk is a gah-what-za? An' where is it? And how do you know it's there anyway?"

"Is night bird. Eats things little – No, Little things..."

"An owl!"

"Owl bird. Spots has. Tree in. There."

"What tree? I can't see it, how far away is it?"

Bila considered for a moment, then held his right arm straight out from his side as he replied, "Ehun this. No, hundred be this."

Molly gaped at the man for a moment then gasped, "You can see a little bird at 100 meters?"

A puzzled expression appeared on his broad face as he whispered in all seriousness, "Yes. Not owl bird see you?"

Molly stared at the man for several long seconds, and then she shook her head and once again mimicked Boots as she whispered, "Jesu Baby Buda! I don't know just who tha' ferk you are, but I'm sure glad you're on our side...

"But now darn it, quit yakking and let's go on and do it!" she then hissed with determination.

Bila nodded, and smiled at the girl's earnestness. He took the sensor and held it against the tree trunk as Molly directed. He examined the wrench, then with a nod of understanding fitted it into a screw-head's socket.

Molly watched the big man with her eyes narrowed in caution until she saw his comprehension of the mechanics of the task, then she clambered to her feet and paced fifty meters back north to a large spruce growing next to a granite outcrop. The rugged ledge formed a natural boundary that would channel anyone climbing the ridge toward the easier footing the slope.

Bila screwed the box to the tree and when the glowing red spot appeared on the trunk above his unit, he motioned directions to Molly until the two units were aligned, and then he tightened its screws.

Molly activated this first segment of the alarm and walked back to where Bila waited, and he shook his head at the noise she made.

She knelt beside him and whispered, "You did good. Now let's set the rest of these suckos."

He smiled at her earnestness then whispered in response, "OK. Now walk you me like. Scare not everybody my place in, OK?"

Her face clouded and her lip trembled, until Bila squeezed her shoulder as he looked into her troubled eyes, "Me you teach very well place you live about. Me you help very good. I you teach about place live I. Help you I, OK?"

"OK," Molly sighed, then her face brightened, "Thank you, Sir. I would like that."

"You girl smart very, learn quick more not me." Then he got to his feet and helped her up, "Tree where another?"

"I think that one," she whispered as she pointed to a spruce fifty meters across the slope that was in a line with the first section of their alarm beam.

"Good," he said as he groped in the haversack and pulled out another of the black sensors. "Box this? Same time last?"

"Yes, an' yes," Molly whispered with a firm little nod.

"Good. Watch you. I walk tree at. Us set box. Walk you way me do. Place see put foot me do you. You foot feel. Got eye foot bottom in, OK?"

"Yes Sir."

They set the next segment of the line, then Bila watched Molly as she cautiously paced toward the tree where he waited. He nodded in approval at her careful placement of each step and the silence of her passage.

When she reached his side she looked up at him with anxious eyes. He nodded again and whispered, "You quiet walk my place very good Molly." Then when her face lit up, he grinned and mimicked her, "But Buddy now you're in big trouble! You do quiet walk this all times now Marybell like."

"Thank you Bila," she whispered, "But I will never be as good as she is or you are, Sir."

"You soon do. Know I," he said with confidence. "Now but do it we just! OK?"

*

They set eight more I.R. lines across the most likely approach route up the ridge then Molly tested the whole array. She nodded when a tiny LED blinked once in one of the little boxes.

"They are all talking to each other, so we can go back now," she whispered. Bila nodded and they began walking back up the slope. When they were close to the crest however, Molly paused at the side of a tree in Durwood's original I.R. line.

"Hey, wait a minute!" she said with a frown," How did Kris an' Marybell get through this beam without tripping it? They went back this way too, so they must've come in from the same direction."

"Beam sniff they come up – go back they?"

"But how did they get past the smart dog?"

"Smart dog what is?"

"Durwood had a smart dog to monitor out here. He said it was better than IR beams, but I don't like it much 'cause it's real mean. He used to make it jump at me too.

"Anyway it has a special collar, and is trained to look for people trying to sneak in. If it growls, the collar picks up the signal and lets us know someone is around."

"What dog is?"

Molly paused and thought, then grunted in a high-pitched imitation of Boots, "A dog is a wolf that's a friend, OK!"

Bila nodded, then after a moment he responded innocently, "Maybe dog not smart much so. Maybe Kris and Marybell smart more."

She thought for a moment, then her eyes widened, "So that's what you smelled, they killed that darn dog!"

"Molly smart be..."

"Wow! Those two gals are really damn good aren't they, Sir?" she whispered in admiration.

"Yes," he replied as his eyes sought an unseen horizon again for a moment. Then closing his face, he continued with a chuckle, "We go not back yet. Bila teach you food good get more now."

*

Bila led Molly to the south along the crest of the ridge, and away from the head of the valley with her cabin. The nature of the forest changed as they climbed to one with more spruce and pines, and it became thicker. They walked on the soft needles under the trees for a half hour until he froze, and motioned her to be silent. Molly halted and he beckoned her to his side, he pointed to an understory shrub 20 meters before them.

Two plump spruce grouse were busily feeding as they scratched in the litter beneath it. He touched her rifle, then tapped his forehead and then pointed to the birds.

She raised the gun and after aiming for a moment, shot one of the birds through its head. When the grouse fell and was flopping about on the ground its mate flushed up into the lower branches of a nearby pine, where it perched and peered about in plain view.

Bila gave Molly an appreciative pat on her shoulder then pointed to the bird in the tree. She smiled up to him, and taking careful aim once more, brought the second bird down with another headshot.

"You very good shooter Molly," he said as he ruffled her hair, then he grinned, "I sure glad side you on our."

"Thank you, Sir. I'm glad I am too," she whispered, her eyes shinning with pride.

"Now I you teach make birds to cook," Bila said. "You after show koba-cave me, OK? Go we at then where get real food you call weeds we," he smiled.

"OK!" she piped aloud happily then suddenly covered her mouth with her hand. "Oops!" she whispered as her cheeks crimsoned, "I was too loud. I'm sorry Sir."

"Thank you Molly. I say quick you learn. Now make you Bila say true you," he murmured.

They collected the grouse and Bila dropped to sit on his heels. "We birds fix now," and motioned the girl down beside him. She seated herself cross-legged next to him, bracing on his uplifted arm and shoulder for support.

Bila used his flint knife to take the head off of one of the birds, then to delicately open it and draw its trail. Finishing with it, he handed the blood-streaked tool to Molly and silently indicated the second bird.

She hesitated as she lifted the limp form of the grouse with its lolling wreck of a head, and wrinkled her nose in disgust. Bila watched her for a moment then he gently touched her rounded belly, again...

Molly sighed, then gritted, "You're right, I gotta' do it for my baby, dammit," and so acknowledged the reality of her motherhood. again.

Molly beheaded the bird with a determined slice, then followed Bila's method as she opened and eviscerated it. She finished her task with a sigh and was wiping her hands on the pine needles on the ground as he placed both of the cleaned birds in her haversack.

"This kind bird be always at place here like," as he murmured, "They like this tree kind. Other kind food birds live open place creek by. But this kind easy kill most."

"I see what ya' mean, Sir. They're not real smart are they? What do they taste like?"

"Real good! Now I you teach weeds get, real food be," he smiled as he stood and helped Molly to her feet.

*

Bila was leading the way back down the crest of the main ridge toward the head of the cabin's valley when Molly murmured, "The cave thing is just over there, Sir."

He halted and asked, "Now see it we?"

"Sure, I'll show ya' where it is." She turned from their path and led him fifty meters westward down slope from the ridge crest they had been following to a room-sized pit excavated into the side of the ridge. Molly pointed to the dark opening of a tunnel in the bedrock, exposed by where the pit's back wall had been cut in to the rock.

"Durwood said that this is a real old prospector's test shaft that someone dug back when they were lookin' for silver mines a long time ago. He went in it once when he thought it might be a good place to hide from Rat. But then he got scared in there and never went back in. I stayed out here, and never have been in it at all."

Bila took a deep breath, then with a calm smile stepped carefully across the moss-covered screed and fallen tree branches that littered the floor of the excavation and entered the dark opening with out hesitation. Several moments later he came back out and beckoned to Molly. "This good koba-cave. You come here in me with."

He unsheathed his flint knife as the girl carefully stepped across the rubble toward him, and nicked the tip of the little finger on his left hand. After the blood droplet had swelled he used it to draw a smear across his forehead. He squeezed his finger again and drew a similar smear on Molly's forehead when she reached his side.

"What's that for?" she asked in a startled whisper.

"Dress must right koba go at we, Not She listen not or," he replied as he licked his finger.

"You mean It don't ya'? A cave is a thing, not a person, Silly."

"Silly no. Stay here you want? Wait me for?"

She looked up into his eyes, which now showed solemn purpose and no humor.

"Yes Sir, I mean no Sir. I really want to go in with you, and I'm sorry I made you mad," she whispered.

"I mad Molly not, but go we at koba-cave right way here in," and he tapped the side of his head, then pointing to the smear of blood on his forehead and smiling down at the girl, "Like here out."

"Yes Sir," she sighed and gripped the hand he held out to her.

Bila led Molly over the rest of the stony rubble in front of the entry and into the gloom of the adit tunnel that had been cut into bedrock. As they moved deeper in the horizontal shaft, Molly's eyes adjusted to the dim light and Bila led the way until they reached an open space at its end.

Molly watched the man in the dim light that shone in from the shift. He seated himself cross-legged on the floor of the chamber then motioned for her to sit, pointing to a place at his side and holding up his arm to support her.

Bila began intoning a wordless chant when she was settled. He sang its tune and strange meter echoed in the chamber.

Molly was surprised to find that the sound comforted her and calmed the agitation she was feeling because of the man's inexplicable words and actions, and his insistence on entering what to her was just a hole in the ground in this strange manner.

He chanted quietly for several more moments, then paused and remained silent with his head down and his eyes closed. He stirred finally and looking up, gathered a handful of soil from the floor of the chamber. He moistened it with water seeping out of a crevice in one wall and kneaded the wet dirt into a ball of plastic clay.

Then as Molly watched, Bila pinched off a portion and skillfully modeled a small human figure that she recognized in the dim light as female.

He placed the figure on a small ledge in the chamber wall then made another slightly smaller figure that was also female, and pregnant. After placing it beside the first one, he modeled a third which was obviously a small child.

Bila placed it on the ledge with the others, and gazed at the three of them in silence for a moment. Then he began to chant the wordless tune again while his eyes remained intent on the three figures.

Molly found herself caught up in his music, and after a moment she softly joined her little voice to his, finding that somehow she could follow his lead without thinking.

He did not take his eyes from the figures or interrupt his song, but he reached for her hand and squeezed it in gentle approval.

A few moments later he brought the chant to a quiet close. Molly also anticipated that, and they sat in silence while its echoes died away in the chamber.

"We go now," Bila said as he stood and helped the girl to her feet.

"That was pretty," she whispered, as she followed him out into the light shining through the shaft.

They paused for a moment and blinked as their eyes adjusted, then he looked down at her, "Thank you Molly. You me help." She blushed, and nodded without speaking.

"And IR sats see you not in She," He said."

"That's good to know," she said as her brow wrinkled in confusion, "But I can't figger' why you keep calling that hole in the ground "She". A cave isn't people – it's an It!"

"Koba cave what say you – sometime. Sometimes more..."He said in a quiet voice. Then as Molly opened her mouth in a further question, he held up his hand to stop her.

"Enough yakey!" he announced with a chuckle, "Time finish mission now we. Real food weeds comin' up right!" and he motioned in the direction of her cabin.

*

"This place things Marybell name rose hips be," he explained as he pointed to a clump of dark green shrubbery growing at the edge of forest near the spring at the head of her valley. The tangled vines bore thorns, and small five-pedaled pink and white blossoms.

"I didn't know what these were, but I always thought the flowers were pretty. I never picked any tho, because Durwood said they made him sneeze. But I don't see any rose hips like you brought back this morning."

Bila pointed to several dry branches in the clump where some shriveled brown berries still clung. "This before from last coldtime you winter call.

"More where these now before new coldtime-winter come," he continued as he plucked a blossom and pointed out the small green swelling below its petals. As she nodded in comprehension, he grinned and tucked it in the girl's white hair, "Molly now pretty more!"

She giggled, then asked shyly after a moment, "May I use your knife Sir?"

He groped in the pouch at his belt and brought out the mark's boot knife and a length of leather thong. He slipped the thong in a loop through the clip on its scabbard, and knotting it in a circlet, draped it around Molly's neck so the sheathed blade hung at her breast.

"You knife got all times now," he said with a smile.

"Wow! Thanks Sir! Then she grinned as she drew it, and turned to the rose bush. She clipped off another bloom and turned back to Bila and she stepped close and reaching up, entwined the stem of the flower into the hairs on his chest.

"Now Bila is more pretty too!" she piped sweetly then giggled, as he roared with laughter.

*

They walked down the grassy valley toward the cabin and Bila showed her where wild greens, like purselane and dandelion grew in the late spring, and how they should be collected. The two filled her haversack with them, and then he showed her where to find the tiny bulbs of wild onions and garlic that would add flavor to her cooking.

The sun was low in the west when they approached the little cabin. Molly waved for him to halt as they neared it, and Bila looked on with a frown as the girl knelt by a small boulder. She groped in a hollow at its base then pulled out a small black case.

"I gotta' check the intruder alarms for the cabin before we go back in," she whispered, "And make sure all the traps are safe," as she pressed several buttons on the box.

"OK, we're clear. Now let's go do supper," Molly squeaked as she replaced the little box back in the hollow under the boulder and stood with Bila's help.

"Ja Boss!" Real food right up come," he said with a grin.

Molly smiled to him and went in to the cabin. She grabbed the kettle where Puss had left it in the middle of the floor and walked back out to Bila waiting by the fire. He helped her to sit beside him and then showed her how to pluck one of the birds.

She was amazed at his swiftness and skill and his thoroughness in removing all of its feathers, but was daunted by the work involved.

"You gotta' do this every time, Sir?" she asked with wide eyes.

"You like eat they?" he grinned as he waved a tail feather before her face.

"No, but there must be an easier way…"

"Is. Cut skin bird off. Cook meat, but not fat in skin eat cook that way. Need eat fat, weeds, rose hips. Or not good feel. Baby come out not strong."

The girl gulped. Then she squeaked in a little tone that was now determined, "OK, Sir, do you want me to do the other one?"

He smiled, "No, save next day," and rising to his feet, he asked, "You big knife got?"

"Yes Sir!" she piped as she struggled to get up. Bila helped her and Molly snapped, "I'll sure be damn glad when I can move fast again," as she stomped into the cabin. She returned after a moment and said, "I'm sorry I was grumpy just now Sir," as she held out a long-bladed field knife and a short-hafted field axe, both Chin army issue.

"All mommies same say. You more fast be soon," Bila smiled as he took the implements from her. He drew the knife and tried its balance and swing, then re-sheathed it and tucked it in his belt. He hefted the Chin field axe and tested its edge with his thumb, then he grinned, "Make fire, I soon come."

"Want me to get some water from the spring too?"

"Yes, that good help. Take rifle. Carry rifle all time you me with not, OK?" he with authority.

Her eyes widened then she nodded and responded in a high-pitched copy of Boots voice, "Good idea Trooper Three. Thanks for reminding me!"

Bila's mouth twitched, but he kept his face straight face as he answered, "Glad help I, Trooper Two." Then he turned and began jogging toward the tree line as Molly retrieved her rifle and a scouring rag from the cabin. She grabbed the kettle and started toward the spring, shaking out the remains of the morning's oatmeal as she walked.

*

When Molly returned from the spring with her rifle slung over her shoulder and straining to carry the kettle without spilling too much water, Bila was bending over a contraption of fresh-cut branches. He had constructed it over and to one side of the pit where a newly lit fire was beginning to blaze. He had also brought the remains of the deer carcass from where it had hung and laid it nearby on its spread hide.

"I teach you now cook later for," he said over his shoulder as he heard her step, then when he looked around and saw her exertion, he leaped to her side and reached to take the kettle.

"No! Please Sir, I want to do it myself!" she panted as she lowered her burden shakily, but with ultimate success onto the three stones in the fire pit.

"Phew! I gotta' start eating more real food if I am ever going to get stronger, darn it," she panted as she flexed her arm and fingers. "And I am sorry I didn't get the fire built for you quick enough."

"You do thing best first. You that way right. You strong be always Molly. Now you now learn much strong how be you," he said in a quiet voice as he looked at her with approval.

Molly dropped her gaze. Her only response was to blush a bright crimson and look at the ground, and scuff at a tuft of grass with the toe of her boot.

"Cook now OK, Buddy?" he said, as he smiled down at the embarrassed young girl.

"Yeah! Let's cook!" she piped, and raised eyes that brimmed with unspoken emotion at his words - and his first use of the term of affection Puss and Boots had for each other.

He smiled then continued as if nothing had happened.

"This how bird cook we now. This how make stay meat good later."

"Use hauts, we but better gatz if," he muttered as he picked up a large pinch of the ashes from the fire pit.

"Why do you put ashes on our food Sir? That's sort of messy, isn't it?"

"You ashes word say hauts? OK, ashes food better taste make, not so good like gatz."

"Well, what's gatz stuff then?" she frowned.

"White. Put on food. Make better. Make feel good."

"Ya' mean salt? Jesu Buda, Sir! We've got plenty of that stuff!" Molly squealed and grunted as she got to her feet, then trotted into the cabin. She came out moments later carrying a large plastic canister.

"You want salt, Sir? Here's a whole bunch of salt!" she grinned as she opened it.

He dipped a finger in to the canister and with extreme caution tasted the grains that adhered to its tip.

"Gatz!" he sighed then, and smiled, "We now good." Then he squatted and after helping the girl to sit, began showing her how to wash the grouse and insert slivers of wild garlic under its skin and into the body cavity. Next he showed how to salt the bird and impale it on the forked end of a green stick.

Finally he balanced the spit across another forked stick he planted in the ground and counter-balancing its other end under a stone, positioned the bird above the fire.

"That's a pretty smart way to do it, Sir" Molly piped. "And you can turn it easy to make it cook right too."

"You see good. Now wash weeds and start cook like I do day come before this day?"

"I'll sure try, Sir! And the word is "yesterday" for the day before this one."

"What you word for day come?"

"It's "tomorrow", Silly!"

"You people many funny words. Make Bila's head hurt all them there keep," he said with a grin.

"Now that's a really, really big joke, Buddy! `Cause that's for sure not true," she said in a quiet voice, with a suddenly mature smile.

"Enough yakey! Now we zezin fix for some you tomorrows!" Bila abruptly announced as he blushed at her words.

"Well, I think you got lotsa' funny words yourself, Sir! Just what tha' ferk does zezin mean?"

"Molly sound Kris like,"

"Good, I want to, so quit evadin' the ferkin issue, ya' Big Thud, Sir!"

"Make zezin this haragi orkazki from. What name you this haragi?" he asked as he indicated the deer carcass with a thrust of his chin and his eyes sparkling at Molly's newfound spirit and confidence.

"It's a deer, and the meat is venison. Everybody out here knows that, Silly!"

"Good. I know now orkazki-deer, haragi-venison. Now you learn my place more of. Place now you and baby live," he said with a dry chuckle. "Knife get you I give. Learn."

Then Bila carefully showed the girl how to slice away thin strips of venison, salt them and array them on the rack he had constructed over the fire to dry in its heat and cure in its smoke. Molly sighed, then joined in the work after a moment. The two stripped the carcass of usable meat within thirty minutes under Bila's tutelage and he declared a halt.

"We put this place others eat. Feed them so they not us eat," he said with a grin.

"Where's that Sir," Molly asked as she turned the roasting bird again on its spit and stirred the now-simmering pot of greens at the edge of the fire under it. She saw that Bila had placed the bird so it was partially above the pot, and thus not all of its dripping fat was being lost. She tasted the broth with a long handled Chin cook spoon and exclaimed, "WOW! These weeds are really gonna' be good!"

Bila smiled and nodded to her. Then he wrapped the deer's hide around its raw remains and hoisted it to his shoulder. "Bring gun you. I take you place other eaters be."

She followed him out into the larger valley to where the bodies of the bear and its cub lay. She looked at them with wide eyes, and saw that the cub had been partially devoured and the sow's belly had been chewed open. Then she gasped and clamped her nose shut with her fingers, "Eeueeew! That's grosso!"

"This way my place in be," Bila said in a low voice as he tossed the remains of the deer carcass on top of the bear. "Eat you they or you eat they..."

"That's the way it mostly is in the `Clave too," Molly muttered. "If we're done here now Sir, let's get on back. I still gotta' teach you some more about that place, like Kris told me to."

"What happened to the big bear anyway?" she asked as they turned and as they walked back to the cabin.

"Try it eat Kris and Marybell two yesterdays. Kill it I."

"Wow! That was the day when we heard the alarms and Durwood put me in the closet. But I don't remember any shooting. How did you kill it Sir?"

"I show you get cabin we."

*

"This how kill bear, with burtzi," he responded to her question by pointing to his heavy spear leaning against the wall next to the cabin door.

Her eyes widened as she examined its thick shaft and wickedly sharp flint point, "I saw this before but I didn't think too much about it `cos I thought it was your walking staff. And it's called a spear Silly, not a what-zi! Anyway, how far can you throw it?"

"Burtzi-spear for throw not. Stick for." Bila replied as he grasped it and acted out the last few steps of his leaping run at the bear, and pantomimed stabbing it in the breast.

"You did that," Molly gasped, wide-eyed in astonishment. "You just ran up to that big bear and stabbed it with this spear thing?"

Bila shrugged, "Not big bear. Here big bear," he smiled as he turned to

215

his leather packsack beside the door and pulled out his string of trophy claws. "This bear that," he told the wide-eyed girl as he showed her the shortest claw on the string, and then the longest. "Bear this big be..."

She gaped at them, as she saw that the big one was twice the size of the other. Then she slowly raised her stunned eyes to Bila's, "Oh – My - God! You must be the bravest man in the world," she whispered in awe.

"Bravest what mean?"

"It's what you did when you killed the bear to save Kris and Marybell. And brave is what they are too - when they take on Boss Rat like I figure they're getting' ready to, 'cept they're women."

"Maybe bravest girl in world you be. Join crew you, Trooper Two," he said as he looked down at Molly - and reflected again on how much she had changed since he opened the door to her closet.

*

"Well, the bird is half done, and the weeds are starting to taste real good, so let me real quickie show you some more stuff about my world now, OK Sir?"

"Teach Bila more, Ma'am," he said as he followed her into the cabin and to her computer.

She powered the machine and brought the same satellite image up that showed the area of the cabin from an apparent altitude of 10,000 meters. "I made this view on a tight angle of coverage so that I could show you where we are at first.

"Now I am going to open the angle out to forty-five degrees, and the view will be twenty klicks wide, and you can see us, and where all our "friends" live, she said in a little voice which at the same time had the confidence of a professional.

"What click is?"

Molly paused at her keyboard and considered momentarily, then she grabbed his wrist and with a grunt, held his arm out from his side as he had done on the ridge earlier.

"Ten ehuns of this! Now you know why ya' have to go on and learn about big numbers, dammit!" she growled in her high-pitched copy of Boots' voice.

Bila wrinkled his brow and looked at his outstretched arm then he rapidly repeated his hand sign for one hundred. After a moment of frowning concentration, he slowly held up all ten fingers again and stared at them until he turned to Molly and asked quietly, "That much one click? We look twenty clicks on dreamer computer?"

"Yep! And now I'm gonna' take us up to twenty thousand meters, and open the out angle wider. Then we will see seventy klicks wide, and "klick" has a "K" that always sounds that way. "C's" can sometimes sound like "K's" too, but sometimes not," she piped over her shoulder as she entered several more commands.

Bila forgot her confusing explanation as he watched the image of the land change on the display. The terrain features and the rivers to the sea now spread out before him as if he were two kilometers in the air above them. He became totally focused on the screen while Molly began to move the satellite view toward the south in fifty-kilometer increments, at a pace she intuitively felt would let him absorb all the details of the landscape between where they were, and S'attl.

*

"Hold up here, I gotta' check on supper!"

Bila grunted an affirmative as he peered intently at the image of the southern Puget Sound and the area of what remained of the cities of Victoria and Seattle on the screen while Molly went out to the cook fire.

She said happily when she stepped back in, "I think it's ready whenever we want it. I set everything off the fire, so we can eat whenever. But I can show you more now if you want me to, Sir."

"Yes," he responded very quietly, as his eyes drank in all parts of the land image on the screen before him.

"OK, here we go down in to S'attl. Now buckle yur' seat belt," she giggled as she increased the magnification factor to bring the view up to an apparent 1,000 meters above the center of the `Clave.

Bila stared at the vast open spaces where suburban houses once stood but now which were under cultivation except where overgrown piles of build-ing rubble interrupted their sweep. He also peered at the thousands of small figures, frozen as they stooped in the fields of soybeans that surrounded the remaining buildings that were the `clave.

Then as Molly again manipulated the view to lower their apparent elevation further, he looked down on a desolate cityscape of rundown blocks of boxy buildings surrounded by paved streets or alleys. Some of the build-ings had collapsed roofs and that there were large potholes in many of the roadways.

He began to frown in bewilderment as he looked at the S'attl `clave, a scene totally foreign to him, then he slowly shook his head.

Molly did not notice his reaction as she used the screen cursor to indicate various places while she moved it around the image, and gave a running commentary.

"These are the 'partment buildings and row houses where people that work for the Governors like the 'Crats and officers live, and people like Kris and Marybell more than likely.

"And this is the Governors office building. And you don't ever- repeat - ever want to go down in the basement there," she muttered.

"And all these places are the soy factories where they make the rash bars and the dorms where the soy workers live and that one right there is where I used to live with my mom until I passed the test and they took me in to the Rat's Nest.

"This is the Army airfield here, with the attack and transport 'copters, and these are the barracks where the soldiers live, and here are the tanks and armored cars and cannons. Right here next to the Army is the Air Force base, and these are the hangers and bunkers where the warplanes are.

"Over here is the harbor and the Navy base, and the sea walls that they built a long time ago 'cause the ocean is getting higher, and behind them are the old part of town.

"I used to like going here and walking around with my mom, till she got sick. Then I couldn't go there any more, and then Boss Rat wouldn't let me ever go out of the Rat Nest anyhow," Molly finished wistfully.

Her voice grew cold then as she pointed out a large, square building in good condition, which had the target spot of a heliport on its roof, along with an extensive array of satellite dishes oriented in many different directions.

"That's the Rat's Nest."

Bila whispered, "So people many," as he pointed to the images of crowds at the bus stops on the streets and the figures in the fields. "How people much?"

"Well, most of them aren't my people, 'least not like you and Kris and Marybell are anyway. But I saw the survel records in the Rat's databank one time sorta by mistake, and sorta not," she giggled.

"Anyway, there's 'bout oh dot two five mil here and maybe five mil in Cali, just oh dot one mil in 'Laska and not many at all in Allgone – that's what everyone calls it now, 'stead of Oregon."

"Oh dot two five mil what?"

"Sorry Sir, I was doing `puter talk. That's two hundred and fifty thousand people in S'attl now, but they say there used to be a big bunch more, back before the war."

"Kris and Marybell S'attl now at? Two hundred and fifty thousand people in?"

"Yes Sir."

A look of concern replaced the sadness in his eyes, "Find them, need us help if - how?"

Molly squared her shoulders and set her jaw, "I can find them Sir," she answered, with determination in her little voice. "I can mole in to the `clave survel-net and find them from their ID implants if we need to. But I just know they will be OK and they will come back soon, just like Kris said they would.

"Don't worry Sir," she stated as she patted his hand.

"Thank you Buddy. That good me hear. You know place you very well. But now eat you," he responded gently as he covered her small hand with his, and hid his growing sense of anguish...

***

Chapter 11
The Demonstration

Bila broke away the breast and both thighs from the cooked grouse and placing them in the girl's mess kit, fed himself by gnawing on its back and wings.

"Wow! This bird is really good!" Molly exclaimed in a voice muffled by a mouthful of meat with juices dripping down her chin as she waved a drumstick in the air. "Thanks for showing me about these dumb birds! They're sure are better than rash bars any day!"

"You weeds cook very good Molly. You real food eat make very well you," Bila responded gently, "Tomorrow other bird cook you in pot thing water with weeds. Lapikoko make. Mommy food good very that."

"I really wish you would talk in English, like I am supposed to be teaching you," Molly giggled. "Now, lapa-whatever sounds just like what my mother used to call chicken soup, that she told me my grandmother made back before the war started, and we all had to go into the 'claves and eat rash bars."

"Chicken what?"

"It's a bird like this, sorta' I think, and they grow them in some special farms for the 'Crats and the Governors to eat. I never had any, but if chicken is as good as this, those 'Crats are real lucky!"

"'Crats what?"

"They're people who work for the Governors. They get to tell everybody what to do. And if you don't do what they say, they take you down into the basement of the Governor's building I told you about," Molly responded as her face clouded, "Can't we talk about something else? Please."

"Why let `crats say what do you?" Bila asked with gentle insistence.

"`Caus they know more than us, and it's their job," she answered plaintively.

"Teachers `Crats be?"

"Yeess," Molly responded, slowly.

"Kris say teachers what do they yesterday?"

"Darn It! I could tell you knew what she was saying. You're right, again Sir! They're not our friends dammit! And I see what you are getting' at now."

"`Crats chicken eat. They chicken you not give. Good that?"

"OK, you just made your point, and biggers for sure! I've never been in a fight before, but if Kris and Marybell and you are gonna' take on the Govies and Boss Rat, I want to help," she said as she set her mess kit aside and started to stand.

"First eat. Strong get. Fight then," Bila smiled, as he motioned her back to her seat, and to her supper.

"Thanks Sir, but I really want to help!" she said in a very serious little voice.

"Help you. Do you dreamer `puter buru well very. Buru dreamer `puter you Kris be buru us like, what boss you say well very," he said with equal seriousness.

Molly said nothing for a moment as her face reddened and her eyes went wide, then dropping her gaze to the mess kit in her lap, she whispered, "Thank you Sir, but I'm not anything like Kris."

Bila took a last bite, rose from his seat on the grass the fading light of the day and continued softly, "You that now dreamer `puter with. You Kris like inside soon."

"You pot thing other - more get water in?"

"We got a Chin water can. It's forty liters. Want me to get it?"

"Water keep cave in good thing be, "Molly eat, say Bila Chin water can where."

"In the cupboard - a place in the back room," she giggled, "And you're real Baaad Sir!"

"Baaad be good?"

Molly sighed and started to respond, until she caught the humor in his eyes and the crooked smile at the corner of his mouth.

"Yep, you're real, real Baaad!" she snickered.

He winked at her and went into the cabin, located the storage compartment and grabbed a large green plastic can. He ignored the other interesting things in the space and closed the cupboard, and was examining the can as he came back.

"Here, let me show ya' how to open it before you break it, ya' Big Thud, Sir!" she piped in mock impatience.

Bila looked at her, then grinned as he unlatched a clamp and flipped the cap open, and chuckled as he walked toward the spring.

Her astonished squeak of, "What tha!" sounded behind him and caused him to smile and his mood brightened, slightly.

*

"You want water can other place, No, other room?" Bila asked from the doorway where he stood with a full water can, causing Molly to gasp.

"Oh Shat! I didn't hear you coming. Buda's Butt, but you're real damn quiet when you move, Sir!"

"You learn quiet way more. Where go water Chin can?"

"Yes, I will learn how to be quiet when you teach me. Anyway, I'll show you where the can goes, OK?"

"But then I have to show you something else too 'cause Kris said you need to know it, but it's going to real be rough," she added with a grim whisper.

Bila followed her into the second room and sat the water can on the shelf in the cooking area as she directed, then Molly led him back into the front room and powered the large vid.

She selected a chip from Durwood's collection, inserted it and then rolled the bed around to face the machine. She sat on the edge and patted the space beside her. Bila sat next to her and they watched as the screen came alive.

It opened to show two people leading a blindfolded girl onto a stage with a prominent black-painted timber frame in the center of its floor. The stage was brightly lit and had mirror-paneled walls. The only other object in the space was an operating room instrument cart. The girl was smiling, slightly staggering under their guidance and was naked. She was young but nubile, and appeared to be Central American. She was also very pretty.

The two leading her were an ill-assorted pair; the man was elderly and was dressed in surgeon's scrubs that were stiff with spots of old blood. He had a cadaverous face with a shock of wiry gray hair, and blank gray eyes.

The woman's face was painted stark white and her head was bald. Her scalp was painted black with an exaggerated widow's peak and her eyes were done in the diamond-shaped black shadowing of a classic harlequin. But instead of the flowing garment harlequins wore for that costume, she was nude. Her hairless androgenic body was also painted stark white and all she wore were ballet slippers, short silk gloves and a stiff ruff around her neck. All were in the crimson color of blood. Her lips were heavily glossed the same red as her gloves.

The only thing about her that appeared to be alive as she posed in an exaggerated dancer's stance before the cam were her eyes. They were a glittering black and totally insane.

"Welcome the Freddy and Heidi Show, faithful viewers! Let us see once again, Just How Far We Can Go!" the man announced gruffly as he stared into the camera in a feral smirk that exposed his stained teeth. He then turned and lifted the young girl's arm and shackled her wrist to the frame. Heidi momentarily posed for the camera in a caricature of a comic ballet dancer's stance with her finger under her chin. Then after an exaggerated courtesy, she lifted the unresisting girl's other arm and shackled it to the frame as well.

She knelt and swiftly forcing her legs apart, cuffed the girl's ankles, and strapped her to the frame in an extended "X" position.

The girl still had a dreamy and lascivious smile on her lips under her blindfold as the two stood at each side of her, and began caressing her skin with ostrich plumes. She responded with voluptuous movements of her body for a moment then pouted, and said in a husky tone, "More..."

Heidi selected a steel-bristled hairbrush from the instrument cart and began slapping its sharp wires against the girl's breasts and belly. The girl responded with some writhings of her hips and gasps of pleasure for several moments. Then she pouted again, "Don't stop now, you were doing it soo good she moaned."

When she said that the man leered at the camera as he held up a long needle, then slowly thrust it deep into the girl's lower abdomen.

Bila tensed, and then he grunted, "Why he girl hurt?"

"Hang on Buddy, this is what Rat does for fun," Molly responded in a sad voice.

The girl's reaction to the penetrating needle was a gasp of, "YESS!" and a corresponding pelvic thrust to meet it, and then Heidi turned to the camera and crooned with an insane smile, "Looks she's ready for Freddy!"

"And Heidi," the man added with a toneless chuckle as he selected a scalpel from the instrument tray and made a swift shallow cut through the girl's skin from the base of her neck down between her breasts and along the center of her belly to her vulva. Heidi grasped another scalpel at the same time began making cuts around the girl's neck and wrists, and then in a graceful dancer's bend, cut the skin around her ankles.

The two gave an exaggerated bow and curtsey to each other, then began slicing through the skin along the girl's extended arms and legs and loosening it from her flesh with narrow long-bladed spatulas. Throughout all of this procedure, the girl moaned and writhed in pleasure, and gave gasps of approval.

"Why she let they hurt her bad?" Bila whispered with anguish.

"They gave her a crazy drug first," Molly answered woodenly.

Heidi knelt before the girl and delicately finished freeing the skin of her groin while Freddy whistled tunelessly as he freed the skin from her arms and back, and then from her hips and her legs. Heidi finished her cutting and gracefully rose to pose à pointe facing the camera. She announced as she gestured with a flourish to the girl's quivering form, "And now, for the Big Unveiling - Ta da, Boom!"

The girl shrieked in pleasure and obviously experienced a powerful orgasm as the two jerked her skin totally free from her body and revealed her raw glistening muscles and flesh beneath. There was little blood from their flaying of the girl due to the speed and expertise with which they had carried it out.

"They hurt her much bad. Why?" Bila asked in a hoarse whisper as he turned his shocked eyes to Molly.

"This is what Boss Rat does. A lot of people in our world like watchin' other people get hurt. This is what I had to show you, like Kris said," Molly responded, again woodenly. "It gets worse..."

"Why she still act that way?" he whispered as his eyes filled with tears of pity.

"Like I said, she's been drugged, but now it's wearing off... And ya' gotta' watch so you'll know how bad Boss Rat really is," Molly whispered as she squeezed his hand in sympathy.

Bila looked back at the screen just as the girl's red raw flesh and muscles began to spasm and quiver involuntarily, and she began to frown. Freddy and

Heidi stood together, fondling each other and watching the girl intently, as her reactions began showing the first signs of changing from pleasure.

The girl began to twitch, and move her limbs and torso and moan again, but now in pain. She whimpered, "It hurts. Why do I hurt?" Then she sucked air between her teeth and gasped, "It hurts Real Bad! Make it stop – Please!" Then she suddenly shrieked, "Please - MAKE IT STOP!!" as she began to shudder and pull at her restraints and thrash about in agony.

Freddy and Heidi continued to stare at the writhing ruin of what been a beautiful young girl only moments before, as they fondled themselves as well as each other.

The girl shrieked, "NO, NO - PLEASE MAKE IT STOP!"

Heidi immediately disengaged herself from Freddy' groping hand and turning to the cam, posed for a moment on her toes with her arms stretched in triumph above her head while the girl continued to scream. Then she pirouetted and curtseyed again as she leered at the cam and announced.

"It's Show Time!" She turned, and prancing with exaggerated hip action, stepped to the crying and struggling girl's side, and abruptly ripped away her blindfold with an exaggerated flourish as she smiled again into the into the cam, her mad eyes gleaming.

The girl's eyes blinked rapidly for a moment as they adjusted to the bright light, then she abruptly focused toward the cam, as she saw her own image in the mirror through which the scene was being recorded.

She gaped at the cam for the long moment it took her to realize that it was her own image she was seeing, and then her eyes went wild as she hyperventilated, and after a long second began to shriek - and scream for her mother...

Bila groaned and covered his ears as he looked at Molly with strickened eyes, "Why people want see bad hurt? What people they? Why? Why..."

Molly stepped to the vid and clicked it off, then after a moment she broke the sudden silence in the room, "Because some people in my place like to watch other people be hurt, a lot," she responded in a toneless voice, her face still frozen. "And Boss Rat does it for them."

"Why this people bad hurt girl sick way this?" Bila whispered as a tear trickled down his cheek.

"To see how long she would live after Freddy and Heidi finished with her. This girl only lived fifteen minutes before she died of shock. She screamed and called for her mother almost to the end," Molly responded in the same flat tone.

"This vid was Durwood's favorite", Molly continued with a shudder.

"He watched it a lot, and every time he did he made me take my dress off and he tied me up to those hooks in the ceiling. He would draw lines on me with a red stylus where they made the cuts on her, and when my tummy started getting big, he would make some extra marks on it too.

"Then last week he got doped up before he remembered to put me in the closet, and I had a chance to look in his cache that he always kept locked."

"I found this."

Opening a drawer under the vid, Molly held up a small medical injector vial.

"That what?" Bila asked grimly, his eyes now blazing in anger.

"It's the same drug they gave that girl in the vid, and I found this too," she said in the same flat tone as she held out a gleaming surgeon's scalpel.

"I think you guys kept me from getting hurt real bad," she finished in a whisper. Then she shuddered and dropped the vial and the knife, and her unnatural calm shattered as she broke into uncontrollable heart wrenching sobs.

Bila looked at the girl for a second, standing rigid with her eyes tight shut and her hands clinched into little fists as she bawled like a lost child.

He went to her and lifting her in his arms, sat on the bed and cradled her on his lap and slowly rocked her while she sobbed. She clutched his neck and buried her face on his chest as she cried hear heart out, and released the unspeakable tensions she had held within herself for years.

Bila began softly humming while he stroked the back of Molly's head. She stopped sobbing after a moment, and relaxed to rest in his arms as she listened to his quiet lullaby.

"Thank you Bila, you saved me," she finally whispered into his chest, "From Durwood."

"That friend does," he said, as he kissed the top of her head.

"I didn't know - I never had a friend before." Then she asked in a little voice as she looked up at him, "But we weren't friends when you saved me, why did you do it?"

He reached for the corner of the coarse sheet on the bed and gently dried her eyes and cheeks, and wiped her nose as he answered, "We that time friends. Not only know two yesterdays back."

She sighed happily and patted his chest, then said quietly after a moment, "I got you all wet, I'm sorry."

"Is good do you that. Make clean me. Thank you Buddy," he chuckled.

She giggled, then he laughed, and she sat up and laughed with him as she hugged him tightly.

"Thank you, Buddy."

Then, suddenly animated again, Molly hopped to her feet. "You know, I think I'll take a bath, and with hot water too. I own the fuel cells now dammit!" She faced away from Bila and hiking up her deerskin dress nonchalantly, presented her slender bottom to the amused man.

"Alright Trooper Three," she growled with a squeak, "How's my war wound doing?"

He took a minute to carefully examine the small incision on her buttock where Puss had extracted the Governor's implant and saw that it had now closed.

"You of big trouble Trooper Two now. You bottom butt return duty is!" he responded in a gruff imitation of Boots' command voice. Then he continued with an almost straight face, when she flounced around and faced him with another giggle, "Bath what?"

"It's when you clean yourself, ya' big Silly!"

"Creek I go at, that why. You clean you. Hot water you cook bottom butt maybe. You "thin", he continued in a high voice that mimicked her description of the cabin roof. "So Bila still hungry be yet..."

"Get outta' here and go jump in your darn creek Sir! I'm going to take a bath and get real clean," she announced with joy. Then her voice changed, "Durwood always liked me dirty." After another second however, she looked up proudly in to Bila's eyes, "But you're right," she snapped, "I'm the boss of me now!"

He gazed at the young girl without expression for a moment, then he said, "I say you before learn fast. Now you say I say right?"

"Yes I do, Sir. Buddy..."

"Good. I go jump creek in now. You cook bottom butt you here, OK, Buddy," he said with a grin as he went out the door and grasping his stabbing spear, walked out into the dusk.

*

Bila paced silently through the grass toward the larger valley, angling eastward and away from where the dead bears lay and where he heard the sounds of scavengers busy at nature's work. He reached the stream higher up its course and pushing through the willow scrub lining its banks, relieved himself in a gravely shallow. Then he waded farther upstream until he found a deeper pool in its channel.

He dropped his belt and stripped out of his shirt and leggings, then dropped his breach clout by the pool's edge and placed his spear close by. He kicked his moccasins off and stood in the deepening dusk, until he was suddenly overcome by anxiety.

He felt the loss that had been building at the back of his mind all during Molly's teaching about her world. He thought about the vast number of people in it and their condition, and the casual cruelty it contained.

His eyes filled, and tears flowed down his cheeks, then as he thought of his people again, and his search for them he went rigid and howled his anguish at the night sky.

Bila fell to his knees, and silently pounded the sand with his fists and forehead until his tears finally stopped.

He remained kneeling and still for many moments, then he got to his feet and waded into the pool. He threw himself face down in the cold water and floated there for a while, until he rolled over to gaze at the night sky from his watery bed.

He didn't stir until his body began to chill, then he got to his feet in the waist-deep water and waded to the shallows where he scooped up handfuls of wet sand, and briskly scrubbed his body from head to toe. He dove back into the pool to wash away the clinging grains, and then he stood and walked out of the water.

Bila slipped on his moccasins and carried his other gear as he made his way back to the cabin his body drying in the night air, and his face closed once again.

*

The door of the cabin was outlined with a faint rim of light as Bila approached it, and after pausing to re-fit his breach clout, he leaned his spear against the wall and announced his presence with a low grunt as he opened the door.

"There you are! I was startin' to worry about you Buddy!" Molly piped as he stood in the doorway. "Come on here and get dried off."

Molly was sitting on the edge of the bed that she had rolled away from the vid cabinet and she wore a clean Chin army singlet as a nightgown. The room was lighted with the golden glow from low-energy light strips on the walls and the bed was freshly made.

Bila stepped into the room and closed the door, then looked at the girl for several moments before silently accepting the coarse towel she offered.

He briskly dried his body and his hair and beard then he gave the cloth to the girl. "Thank you, Buddy," he said with a smile as he turned toward the door.

"Where are you going now, Buddy?"

"At sleep."

"Outside?"

He shrugged, and nodded.

"There's room in here, and this bed is real big, Sir. Buddy," she said in a little voice, "And I get cold."

Bila paused and looked at the earnest young girl, and then he smiled again and turned back into the room.

"OK, now that you got tha' picture right sit down here and let me straighten out your messy hair," she piped as she brandished a comb, and patted the bed beside her.

Bila obeyed and Molly got up on her knees behind him with a grunt, and started combing his damp hair. She pulled out all of its tangles without a word of protest from the man, who instead submitted to her grooming with an unfathomable expression on his face. But when Molly began to comb his beard, Bila started at her touch then a tear trickled down his face.

"I heard you cry out there," Molly whispered. "Someone used to do this for you before, right, one of your people, right?"

He nodded slightly, and tightly.

"Don't worry Buddy, we'll find them. And I'm gonna' help you like you've helped me, OK?"

"OK. But sleep now we?"

"Yep," Molly said in a happy tone as she dropped her comb and flopped over to lie on her side. She announced over her shoulder, "Come here and cuddle me. I get cold. Please."

"Cuddle what?" Bila asked as he stretched out next to the young girl.

"This!" Molly exclaimed and reaching behind her, grasped his right hand and pulled his arm around her as she snuggled her back against his chest.

Bila remembered many things for a long moment, and then he replied in a choked voice, "Cuddle good."

"Good, I thought ya' would like it. And you cuddle real warm, Sir.

Thanks Buddy," Molly murmured as she pulled the cover up over them.

"Glurk!" she suddenly hiccupped, then giggled, "It's kicking!"

"Kick what?"

"My baby, See?" she said with pride as she pulled her shirt up and placed his hand on her bare stomach, where he felt tiny feet fluttering inside her.

"Strong it," He chuckled. Then he gently began stroking her belly, and the agitation in her womb ceased after a moment.

"That felt real good, Buddy. And I can tell that the baby feels good now too. I think it likes you," she whispered.

"Good. Baby you like I," then he sighed, "All babies like I..."

She pulled her shirt back down and clutched his hand to her breast as she would a favorite stuffed animal, if she had ever had one.

"Good night Bila. I love you," she whispered.

"Love what?" he asked.

"Love is what you feel inside when you think about your very best friend."

"Then - I you Molly love."

She sighed, "I just knew that. You're my best Buddy!" she murmured as she wriggled her little back against his body and kissed his hand.

"'Corse, I love Kris and Marybell too, she continued in her small voice. "You love them too, right?"

"Yes," Bila responded hoarsely, after a very long pause.

"That's good. Now we all love everybody, right?" she murmured sleepily.

"Right, Buddy, but sleep now, OK?"

"OK," she sighed, and then began to breath softly as she allowed herself to feel safe, and protected for the first time in a very long while.

Bila also let himself relax as he lay with to the drowsing young girl pressed against his chest. He listened to her gentle breathing while she drifted off and a familiar calmness flowed over him. He released himself into a deep restful sleep for the first time in the long months since he had crawled weakly ashore onto the pebble beach at the edge of the cold sea.

***

Chapter 12
The Visitors

May 4, 2276 AD
Coastal Mountains of British Columbia

Bila awakened just before dawn as he and his people always did and lay still, but alert until he remembered where he was. Then he relaxed and taking a deep breath, enjoyed the warm scent of the young woman sleeping next to him and was happy, until he heard a tone begin to chime in the other room.

He slid his arm from Molly's cradling hands without waking her and rising from the bed, stepped to the doorway of the back room. He saw a red light blinking on the small panel of the IR intruder monitor. Its screen was lit and displaying data as the quiet tone continued to sound.

He went back to the bed and knelt beside it. He placed his hand on the sleeping girl's forehead, the safest way he knew to waken a person and bring them back from their dreams without loosing their wandering souls. Molly smiled and opened her eyes then she blinked as she heard the sounding alarm.

"Shat! We got intruders! Battle stations!" she squealed as she hopped out of the bed and clambering over Bila, ran into the other room.

"There's three of 'um, no. Now four, no, five! They just crossed the line we put out yesterday."

"People?"

"More'n likely. These things have a delay factor built in that checks the interrupt times against profiles, and I set them high enough so that coyotes an' other things like that wouldn't trigger them. We gotta get ready!"

"People what? They west from?" he asked as he ignored her incomprehensible explanation for the moment.

"Yep, more'n likely," she answered, then she pleaded, "But we gotta' get moving, Please Bila, Sir."

"They, no. Them people this, are people you hurt, like you say Kris and Marybell two yesterdays?" he asked in a calm voice.

"Yes! And dammit, I just knew that you understood what we were talking about then. But now we really gotta' get moving! Please Buddy!"

"Where move? What do?" he asked in the same calm tone.

Her eyes suddenly showed confusion then she responded, "Something! We gotta' do something, but I don't know..."

Bila went to Molly and grasped her shoulders, "Do we now. Learn you learn kill bears me like," he said in a grim voice as he led her back into the front room.

"OK, but we gotta' hurry!" she gritted in a squeak.

Bila smiled at her determination, and the bravery she was unconsciously showing.

"Put on dress. Have leg things?"

"I've got some leggings that go with this dress, but they're sorta' hot in the summer. Durwood liked to pretend I was his squaw."

"Hunt bears much ready must be. Hunt change maybe, ready be good is. Foot things wear. Bullets bring."

"They're called boots, and you want a Chin `salt rifle? It's like mine sorta', but it's noisy," she asked as she opened a cupboard next to the front door and pointed to one in a rack of six.

"You that gun me teach later. You do ready go now."

She nodded and stripped off her sleep shirt. Bila turned away with a smile at her innocent earnestness as she rooted in another cupboard for her deerskin leggings. She pulled them on and after fitting their bindings around her waist above her swollen belly, slid in to her doeskin dress and slipped on her Chin boots.

"Ready pretty quickie, Sir," she piped as she grabbed several more loaded clips for her rifle from the gun cupboard and dropped them into her haversack. Then she remembered, and hung the boot knife Bila had given her around her neck as well. She slung the sack over her shoulder and grasping her rifle, asked with trust shining in her eyes, "OK, what's tha' plan, Buddy?"

"Hunt them we. We go them at good is. Wait them hunt we good not," he answered with quiet firmness as he tucked the sheathed Chin field knife under his belt and motioned her to follow. He strode out of the cabin, and pausing by the rack of dried venison strips, gathered a handful. He offered them to Molly with a grin, "When hunt we, food take you for, and baby." She nodded and put them in her haversack.

He grabbed his two light spears and throwing stick and then led her at a steady pace up the ridge behind the cabin and then around the head of her valley toward the old mine adit.

*

"You stay koba-cave in, OK? Go I see they who."

"What are you talkin' about, dammit? You said we were going to go kill bears, Sir!" Molly panted as they walked through the mine tunnel again and entered the chamber.

"We do. Keep baby you safe this place. I they find. We they think best way kill," he said with in the dim light with a cold and feral look on his face, one that was a totally new aspect of Bila. She now realized that this man who had been her pupil, and whom she had also started to consider as her big fuzzy pet was different.

He was a hunter, and a killer of men as well as of animals… Molly's eyes grew wide and she whispered with a gulp, "Yes Sir!"

"Good. In here, you see they more better they see you. Kill they if in come. I outside kill person be. You inside kill person be, OK?"

"Yes Sir, but do you think these little bullets will do it?"

"See do they do rash bars at?"

"Yes."

"Bad people here shoot, like not-smart birds shoot yesterday" he said with a grim little smile as he tapped his forehead, "Do same inside here like rash bar. You good shooter, you me help very well."

"Wow, you think I can really do it?"

"Yes. Why I say what I say!"

"You really do trust me, don't you?" she suddenly exclaimed with pride.

"Yes. Molly, strong you. Smart you. Good you. You friend me."

"And you are my friend, and friends help friends, right?" she whispered with shinning eyes.

"Right," he nodded, as he held out his right hand to her with its palm uppermost. She placed her small hand on his and silently returned his nod. After a moment he smiled, and left the rock chamber.

"Good luck, Sir!"

Bila smiled again as her words echoed from the adit, but sadly now, as he inspected the rock floor of the pit outside of it for any telltale signs of their passage. He found none and his eyes hardened as he paced down the ridge, stalking the stalkers.

*

"Gadammit Jimmy ya' lazy bastard, keep up!" the stocky man with the full gray beard and shaved head hissed from where sat on the saddle of the dispirited cow pony he was spurring up the ridge.

The gangling youth with a shock of painfully red hair, white freckled skin and honest blue eyes struggled along on foot with a large packsack on his back.

"Yes Captain," he responded dully.

The three other men in the group snickered but didn't offer to share Jimmy's burden. One was tall and thin with long greasy blond hair and a wispy beard. He was slouching along behind the man on horseback holding a leash that dragged a mangy hound with protruding ribs behind. The second man was short and wiry with dark hair and moustache, and bounded up the ridge with nervous energy. The third was a compact oriental with an impassive expression and glittering black eyes.

All the men carried Chin military pistols on their belts along with the small green cases of Chin field comsets. The short wiry one with the moustache also carried another pistol tucked in his belt which had a thick bulky barrel.

The men were dressed in +-tattered Chin military clothing, and the un-armed youth wore a threadbare U.S. military coverall several sizes too large for him.

"I want us at that cabin while that white-haired little spook is still sleepin' dammit! She's gonna' wake up real quick when I blow my bugle!" the man with the shaved head growled, "So hump yur' lazy bones Boy!"

"Yes Captain," Jimmy panted as he picked up his pace.

"Ken we have a little fun with her a'fore we sell her to Boss Rat?" the man leading the hound simpered.

"Not yur' idea of fun, Lukey. Rat'll only pay us fer' her if she's in one piece and can go back to work fer' them. After some of your kind of "fun" she wouldn't be much use any more."

"What about some of my kind of fun?" the wiry man hissed. "Es gone now and can't stop me anymore."

"Who? Who this one with white hair? She be old woman? They no fun," the Oriental hissed.

"Carlos, ya' crazy beanbag, I'll stop you sure! Now shut up and back off. And Chin, this goes back ta' before you crawled out of that bunker you was hiding in," the Captain growled over his shoulder.

"I mean what I'm saying' dammit! None of you freaks are gonna' touch her, 'cause she's worth too much. You can have his mother all ya' want after we get back, OK?" he snapped as he casually nodded toward Jimmy. The boy tensed and then stumbled – which caused the three to laugh. With a sneer of contempt at Jimmy's carefully blank face, the Captain faced forward and motioned them on up the ridge.

"What tha' sheet?" He snapped moments later, as he reined in the horse.

"What's that?" Carlos hissed.

"I just saw someone run between some trees up there," the Captain said as he pointed to the southeast.

"Was it tha' girl?" Lukey giggled.

"Nah, too big, and too fast."

"Who is it then?"

"Don't know, but he might be some good bait for tha' Rat too," The captain said as he dismounted. "Give me them damn glasses. Quick, dammit!"

Jimmy stumbled forward and shrugging out of the pack, retrieved a pair of Chin army binoculars from its depths. The Captain snatched them from the youth and began glassing the area.

"Ha! There he is again. Damn if he ain't big and naked too! Ten to none he's one o' them Injun reverts. Rat likes them because they last a long time.

"Alright Carlos, you take Lukey 'n Chang and go bag him whilst me an jerko here go get tha' white bitch. Take the Rat comset to call 'um in when you get him, but pull its battery until you do OK? 'Cause I think these Rat sets are bugged.

"Use the Chin set to let me know what's goin' on, so's I can tell you stumbles how to do it right. "And you better take this no-count horse to ride him down, 'cause he looked sorta' fast. Faster'n you three slugs can run anyway.

"Now you get on with it, dammit! We gonna give Boss Rat a real two-bagger, just like we used to!"

Carlos tucked the black-cased comset into his pocket and leapt into the saddle. Then gathering the reins, he expertly kneed the horse in to an easy trot up the slope toward the southwest. He hissed over his shoulder, "Hey Gringo an' you Chin guy, grab my straps an' clump you stumps along side `till we see heem. ¿Entiende usted?"

Lukey tossed the leash to the Captain and rushed to follow Carlos. He and the Chin ran in an ungainly scramble until they caught up, then they each grabbed a stirrup leather and used the assist to help them keep pace as they loped along at the side of the horse.

"Come on Dog. You too Boy, let's us get to that cabin damn quick," the Captain grunted as he started up the slope to the northeast, toward Molly's valley. Jimmy shrugged on the pack again and followed him, leaning forward under its weight to keep his balance.

*

"Gadammit, the li'l white slut ain't here," Captain snarled as he stood in the front room of the cabin while the mixed breed hound sniffed dispiritedly about the floor at the end of its leash. "Look in that other door - mebby she's hidin' in there," He ordered.

Jimmy kept his face blank as he opened the door to the back room and quickly glanced around at the equipment in it. He responded, "Nope. She ain't here."

"Gadammit, she can't be far," the man growled. Whern'-ferk could she go?"

Jimmy returned to the front room, and stood with his eyes cast downward. Then he glanced at the rumpled bed, and saw a green Chin undershirt casually tossed on top of the covers. He hastily turned his eyes away before the Captain could spot his glance - almost.

The man lunged to the bed and grabbing the shirt, held it to the hound's nose, "Hunt, dawg! Hunt!" he commanded. The dog pricked up its ears and came alive. It bayed as it lunged toward the outside door and the Captain whooped in glee as he tossed the garment aside and trotted out behind the straining animal.

Jimmy picked up the discarded shirt from the floor and held it to his nose for a moment, as he remembered the girl and thought of the last time he had seen her. Then he folded the garment neatly and placing it on the bed, followed the man and dog up the slope with his usual blank expression, but now his eyes were hooded.

*

Bila sensed that a hunting group was coming up the ridge, from both the faint sounds they made and their scent, carried on the slight breeze that wafted up the ridge as the morning sun warmed the cool air in the valley below. Bila wrinkled his nose in disgust at their foul smell then smiled as he tensed for action.

He had showed himself to them as they came lumbering up the ridge in order to lure them away from Molly. His instinct told him to lead them to the south, away from Molly's cavern and then across the ridge to the east. There he would lose them in the forest then hunt them silently among the trees until he killed them all...

He trotted up the slope he had just descended, angling away from Molly's cave and showed himself again to his pursuers. Just enough to keep them interested until he could circle them...

*

The Captain pulled the dog to a halt when they were half the way up the ridge. He slapped it until it crouched at his feet then answered his buzzing comset.

"What's that you say?"

"That som-betch es act fooney!" Jimmy overheard. "He run slow in front of us, then he disappear! Then he pop up en different place, an' then he run away again. We don' see heem," Carlos started to continue - when both the Captain and Jimmy heard a shriek sound from its earpiece.

*

Bila stepped out of a laurel thicket and looked at the two panting men trotting up the slope before him, next to the man sitting on the food animal.

"Why does that zaldi stay with them, and not run away?" he wondered to himself even as he noted that the men on foot were dressed in clothes like the mark wore. He cocked one of his light spears on his throwing stick, and heaved...

*

"What tha' hell was that? What tha' hell's goin' on anyway?" the Captain snapped.

"Sheet! he just shoot Chang with a ferkin' spear! An' I still no see heem!"

"What tha' hell you sayin?"

"Is a ferkin' spear man, and Chang `es a deader man, `er gonna' be soon."

*

Bila grinned as he leapt away into the dimness of the forest and circled around his remaining two quarries... The one on the food animal puzzled him

237

still, but he dropped the thought as he dodged from behind a large tree and began trotting up the slope again.

*

"Where'n hell is he? You go find him dammit!"

"I don' know where to look, they bushes all around us. Wait – there he `es. He jus' jump out from behind tree."

"Well go get him dammit! Do I have to tell you every ferkin' thing to do? Get a hump on! Boss Rat ain't gonna wait all day," the Captain snarled into his comset.

"Si Captaine, Let's go Lukey. Sheet, he gone again! We go where he was an' look for he tracks."

*

Bila scrambled on up the ridge in a direction leading away from Molly, and kept the cover of the tree trunks between him and the two men behind him even as he wondered about the other s that had stayed behind when the three began chasing him. He trotted easily for several hundred more meters, taking care to leave no sign of his passage. Then he turned and circled once more…

*

"Now you're startin' to think! `Bout time," the Captain scowled, then he snapped, "Move dog, come on boy" as he kicked the hound into motion. It began following Molly's trail again.

They had only taken a dozen paces however when a shout squawked from the comset, "Sheet! He jus' shoot Lukey wit' spear from behind' us! How he get there?"

"Crappo! Do I gotta' do everything round here? What kind o' shape is Lukey in?"

"He's bad, man. It go all way through he shoulder an' he `es in lotta pain."

"Ferk Lukey's pain! Just get that damn wild man, now dammit," the Captain shouted into the set as his face reddened and veins bulged in his neck.

"Si Captaine. Sheet! There he `es out in front again! He running up over thee ridge! Arriba you damn cayuse! We get heem now!" and Carlos' comset clicked off.

The Captain kicked the hound, and as it started trailing Molly once more he muttered, "Better get him, you ferkin beanbag… Hump it Boy."

238

"Yes Captain,"

*

The skinny man trotting along beside the man sitting on the zaldi had stumbled suddenly just as Bila launched his second spear, so it struck higher up the man's shoulder rather than in the killing spot below his left shoulder blade. Bila grunted in disappointment as he dodged behind a tree and began running again while the man screamed as he spun from the impact of the spear and fell to his knees. Bila ran on up toward the crest of the ridge, and further away from Molly.

He slowed after several moments, and showed himself again just below its crest, then began running at a much faster pace when he saw the zaldi leap forward into a gallop, and the man stay atop its back! He dodged and turned, and kept to thick cover as long as he could but the galloping animal carrying the man kept getting closer...

Bila dodged behind a large tree trunk and halted. He shifted his throwing stick to his left hand and drew the heavy Chin field knife, and tensed himself as he listened to the thudding of the approaching hoof beats. When they sounded near enough, he leapt from behind the tree and raced toward the galloping animal, ready to meet it with a quick slash to its throat as he had done many times before with a flint knife...

The man atop the animal saw him, and pulled on straps tied to its head. The animal stiffened its forelegs and slid to an abrupt halt and the man sitting on its back drew a thing from his belt. Bila noted it was like those that Kris and Marybell carried, but with a much thicker front part even as he raced toward the animal with his knife held ready.

The man pointed the weapon at him and he felt a stinging impact on his chest. He glanced down to see the same thing sticking in him that the mark had stuck in Kris, as his legs suddenly went numb and he stumbled - and he fell to the ground.

Bila fought his dizziness as he watched the man leap from the animal and approach him cautiously. He waited with blurring eyes until the man was within reach, then lunged and began a swing with the knife in a desperate attempt to hamstring him. His arm faltered however and the man was able to leap aside. Bila crawled slowly toward the man, until the numbness engulfed him completely.

After some moments, he felt the man roll him over, and then a sting as the thing in his chest was jerked away. He looked up helplessly as the man stepped into his view with a coil of braided line, and after several tries, suc-ceeded in flipping a loop over a limb above him. The man next stepped out of his field of vision again and he felt his arms pulled roughly over his head and tied together.

Bila heard the rustlings of movement in the leaf mold for several more moments, then the part of the braided line he could see over the limb above him tightened, and he felt his arms begin to rise. When they rose to where he could see them in to his field of view, he saw that his wrists were tied together at the end of the line. Then the line tightened, and he felt himself being pulled slowly upright.

The pull of the line continued until he was hanging by his wrists above the ground. As he spun there, he saw that the other part of the line was tied to a strange leather thing on the zaldi's back, and that the animal was braced against his weight. The man stood beside the animal holding straps from its mouth, and somehow made it step forward more, and pull him still higher in the air. Next, the man looped the end of the line around a low tree branch, and then grunted as he struggled to untie the part from the line on the zaldi's back. When the man finally got the line free, Bila dropped half a meter, and felt the strain in his shoulders from the sudden jerk as the line tightened again.

The man then grabbed the end of the line beyond where he had looped it around the branch, and played it out through one hand as he pulled on the zaldi's mouth-straps and lead it to stand in front of Bila. He man next pushed at the animal's side, and it stepped sideways until it was pressing its side against Bila's belly. The man played put the other end of the line, and slowly lowered Bila to hang limply across the zaldi's back. As he looked at the leather thing on the animal and the short hair on the skin of its flank, he felt his hands being roughly tied to his ankles under the animal's belly. Then he heard the man speaking...

*

"I get heem, but he real fast, and real strong. I ride heem down with the horse, but he steel almost get away," crackled from the Captain's comset fifteen minutes later.

"So you got him. Good. Now call Rat in and take him to the drop spot, like I told ya', and move it out, dammit! We're on the trail of the white witch real good. Tell 'um to wait!"

"Lukey's arm 'es all messed up. I gotta go back to heem first an' pull spear out, but he bleed bad. I gotta' fex bandage for he shoulder."

"Well, ain't you tha ferkin Angle o' Mercy! So Lukey's got another arm, right? So what ya' squealing' about? Fix him quick, and then toss wild man over tha' damn horse and carry him that way - it's quicker."

"I already got thee big ferker loaded on horse dammit! I go to Lukey now," Carlos snapped, then clicked his com set off.

"Poor Lukey's got himself a mama," the Captain sneered as he kicked the hound to move again.

*

"I got Lukey's shoulder fixed an thee bleeding stopped," Carlos' voice sounded from the Captain's com set a quarter of an hour later, "And we ready to go to pickup site, but now Lukey wants to fix hem first for payback..."

"Now wait just a gadamm minute! You two crazy wackos touch him anywhere 'fore Rat picks him up and I'll cut a cento off some part of each of you for every ferkin credit they cut off my price!"

"You hear me, you two ferkin retards?" he shouted into the green comset as his face reddened and his neck veins bulged again, and his spittle spattered the mouthpiece.

When Carlos grunted a grudging affirmative, the captain growled, "And pull out them damn spears an' give 'um to Rat too! They pay good for weird crappo like them! Now do what I say and move it dammit!"

"Dumb sons-a-bitches. Can't do anything right, can they? Right, boy?"

"Yes, Captain," Jimmy muttered as he followed the exulting man and the straining dog along the crest of the ridge behind the cabin.

When they neared the mineshaft, the dog lifted its muzzle and bayed, until the man slapped it on the ear. "Damn dawg you'll make her run harder."

"Yes, Captain." Jimmy said.

"You shaddup too dammit," the man hissed. Then he urged the confused dog forward again. It sniffed around the litter on the forest floor until it picked up the scent again, and started tracking, in silence. The hound suddenly veered to the right and pulling at its leash with urgent scrambling leaps, led them down from the ridge crest toward an overgrown excavation in its flank. It halted before the old mineshaft entry and lifting its muzzle, bayed its treed call, then lunged at the dark opening.

The Captain smiled as he slipped the leash of the straining dog. It leapt forward into the dark tunnel, then yelped as a sound like the snapping of a large twig echoed from inside. The dog howled then, until the snap sounded again and it was silent...

"Gadammit! That' bitch killed my dawg! I'm gonna' kick her butt good," the Captain roared as he started a stumbling run toward the tunnel.

He yelped as a third crack sounded from the depths of the mine and he slapped his hand to his ear and as the bullet that nicked him whizzed past and whacked into a tree trunk.

"Gadammit, she tried to shoot me!" he yelled as he looked at the blood on his hand. "Ya' crazy witch, you're gonna hurt big fer' this"

He stood aside from the tunnel entry and hissed over his shoulder, "Gimme one o' them stunners Boy! Quick, dammit! He continued with a gloating sneer, "I'm gonna slap her real silly with this little popper."

Jimmy shrugged out of his pack and withdrew the green plastic globe of a Chin stun grenade. He paused, then his eyes suddenly blazed and his face flushed. He pulled the pin, then with a practiced jerk.

He held the grenade in his hand as he calmly counted the seconds under his breath.

"Gadammit ya damn pup! Give it to me – now dammit!"

Jimmy whispered, "Four," then said, "Yes Sir!" as he tossed the grenade at the man's feet.

This type of grenade was designed for use against an enemy in confined spaces in urban warfare and was quite effective in those settings. Much of its shockwave of this one was dissipated in the open when it exploded in front of the Captain. The effect on him was still as a swift kick in the groin, however - from a mule...

The captain doubled in agony and fell to the ground. "Wha-?" he gasped.

Jimmy grabbed a small granite boulder with both hands and with a shriek of fury, slammed down on the Captain's head above his ear. Then he slammed it down again, and again, and again...

The Captain's skull shattered under the first blow and collapsed after Jimmy's second, which also crushed the temporal and occipital lobes of his brain. So really, the third and fourth blows were not technically needed, except to relieve the boy's wrath.

Jimmy stood frozen for a moment as he looked down at the man's still quivering body, then he released his breath and dropped the stone. His hands began shaking and his face paled to chalky white.

He stood that way for a minute until breathing deeply again, he turned to face the shaft opening. He held his empty hands out from his sides and called, "It's OK, Molly - it's safe now. You can come out. I killed him…"

There was no immediate response from within the shaft for a moment, then, "Why?" softly echoed out of the opening.

"'Cause he beat my mother every time he got drunk, and that was about every night. And she let him do it, to keep him from hurting my little brother. And he was going to hurt you."

"Why do you care about me, now?"

"Cause it's not right to hurt people. And you're nice…"

There was silence in the shaft, and then Molly walked slowly forward letting her sight adjust to the daylight before stepping out into the open. She carried her rifle at the ready and her eyes were squinted.

"Why should I believe you? And there were five. Where's the others?" she asked in a cold little voice while she held the rifle aimed at his chest.

"I don't blame you for not believing me," Jimmy said as he returned her gaze with honest eyes. "They're over the ridge, calling' up the Rat 'copter."

"What are they going to do to you, when they find out about him?" Molly asked, nodding at the body lying between them.

"Nothing, if I can kill them first. They're just as bad as him.

"He sometimes made my mother do things with them," Jimmy gritted, and suddenly kicked the dead man's face as his freckles stood out on his white face like drops of blood.

Molly relaxed and sighed, "OK, it's gonna' probably be the death of me but I'll believe you."

Jimmy's eyes were solemn as he whispers, "Thanks. But I'll make sure that it's not that, ever." Then he started, as he became aware of her swollen belly.

"What happened to you?" he gasped.

"What do you think happened?" Molly snapped.

"Durwood?" Jimmy asked in a dull voice as his face closed.

"NO!" Molly snapped again. "He never did it the regular way anyway. And if it was his I would have popped a 'bort pill way back, if I'd had one."

"Who then?" Jimmy asked with sudden wonder.

Molly just stared at him.

"Ya' mean, that time?" Jimmy gasped finally.

"None other," Molly gritted.

Jimmy's face slowly lit up with a silly grin, and his eyes suddenly glistened, "Ya' mean I'm gonna' have a baby?" he whispered.

"Well, I think I'll have something to do with it too," Molly growled with a squeak.

"Awwww..." Jimmy sighed as he stepped over the Captain's body and held out his arms.

Molly stood and considered him for a long moment, as she thought back to the first time she had seen him, the afternoon last fall when the Captain had appeared at the cabin, along with the Mexican and the skinny blond man with the strange eyes.

*

Durwood had invited them over in a rare attempt at socializing, and while offering nothing to eat except rash bars, the only food he really enjoyed he had opened his drug cache to his guests along with his extensive collection of 4 and 5X vids.

Molly had noticed Jimmy did not take any of the drugs, and when they started playing the vids he had not watched them. Instead, he sat on the floor with his back to the wall and had looked down in silence, when he wasn't shyly glancing in her direction.

The three and Durwood had not bothered to eat, but had instead begun ingesting or injecting drugs from Durwood's extensive collection, and experimenting with various combinations.

Then they had started watching the vids and as the substances took effect, they began to giggle at the more depraved scenes.

Molly remembered trying to make herself small as she sat on the floor in a corner, and had also ignored the vids and the visitors, except when she occasionally glanced at the redheaded boy. Their eyes met several times, but in each instance they had both looked away from each other after only a moment.

Molly shuddered inside herself while she gazed at Jimmy, quietly standing before her as she recalled that Durwood had lurched to his feet after an hour of watching the vids, and staggered to where she huddled in the corner. He had grabbed her hair and jerked her to her feet.

"Les' all have a contest," He had slurred. "Les' see who can do it better'n than on tha' vids," then he had torn her dress away and shoved her toward the men. They had grabbed her and were starting to paw at her with rough hands while Durwood giggled shrilly when Jimmy had leaped to his feet and started pulling at the one with the moustache as he yelled in a voice that cracked, "You leave her alone!"

Molly shuddered again as she recalled how all three of the men had turned on the boy and had beaten him to his knees. Then the baldheaded one, whose body now lay at her feet, had ordered the others to tie him up.

"Now watch how it's really done you li'l whelp, an' if you ever try anything like that again, I'll break your arms, get me?" he had sneered, then he had punched the boy in the face and bloodied his nose. The man had turned back to her and leered with hard eyes, "And if you don't act like ya' like it Sweetie, I'll break his arms anyway…"

After this, and in front of Jimmy's dazed eyes, the three had taken turns degrading her as Durwood looked on and giggled. When they began using her in multiple ways he had screamed with laughter.

Molly remembered how she had feigned enjoyment, except the few times she had been able to glance at Jimmy, and saw the pain, and shame on his face.

They had tired of her finally and one by one, slumped to the floor as they came down from their manic highs.

Durwood, who had only watched his guests competing in depravity, was the only one still standing, more or less. She recalled how he had jerked her to her feet and dragged her to the closet in the other room.

"Don' wan' my li'l rash ticket goin' by-by," he had slurred as he locked the collar around her neck and closed the door.

She remembered lying on the floor curled in a ball naked, because Durwood had forgotten to give her a blanket, again. She had been sick at her stomach with disgust, and was crying silently when the latch on the closet door softly clicked back.

She had cringed and clinched her eyes shut as she tensed for a blow, until she felt a hand stroking her shoulder. She opened one eye slightly, to see Jimmy kneeling at her side in the dim light from the front room. His nose was bloody and swollen, but he had looked at her with concern and something else plain on his face.

"Are you OK?" he had whispered.

"Sure," she whispered back. "But you better get away from me, or they'll hurt you again."

"Nah, they're way under, those bastards," he had hissed. "What can I do to help you?"

"Nothing. It's like this every time Durwood goes up, 'cept he gets real weird when he's doin' it by himself. I'm cold tho," she remembered sighing.

"Back in a minute," he had grinned, then winched at the pain from his bruised lip.

"Don't..." Molly remembered whispering as he creped back into the front room, to return in a moment with a blanket.

"Not worry, they're really way deep under," he had whispered as he started to drape the blanket over her. Then he stared at her for a moment, and had asked with a blush she remembered seeing in the dim light, "Where's some water and a towel?"

"On the cooking shelf just outside the closet, why?"

He got to his feet again silently and stepped out into the room. She heard a cautious scrape and a quiet gurgle. Then Jimmy had returned to the closet with a pot of water and a cloth, and knelt by her side again.

She recalled the look in his eyes as he had whispered, "Let me help you, OK?" She had nodded, and after dampening a corner of the towel, he began cleaning her.

*

Molly looked at the redheaded youth now, with his eyes searching hers as she remained so long silent - and recalled how she had allowed him to clean her everywhere she had been abused. He had to use a second pot of water before he finished, and get a second towel to dry her.

"You're not disgusted with me?" she had asked at one point as he sponged her face.

"I know you only did that stuff to keep him from hurting me, so it doesn't count, OK?" he had whispered as he nodded his head with confidence. Then he had clumsily but gently kissed her lips which he had just wiped clean...

Molly thought of the feeling that had flooded through her as Jimmy finished cleaning her and was wrapping the blanket around her. He was rising to leave when she had whispered softly, "Don't go." He had paused, then she had pulled at him and he had come down to her, and she had welcomed him...

As he stood before her now with the Captain's body on the ground behind him, she smiled slightly as she remembered his hesitation, and then fumbling acceptance of her guidance – and finally his intense joy as they had joined with each other.

*

Molly lowered her rifle and said as she nodded toward the captain's body, "He beat you up real bad that next morning when he found you'd untied yourself – but you didn't say anything about me, or why you really did it. Why?"

"I didn't want Durwood 'n them to hurt you anymore, and I could take it better than you, that's all. No biggo anyway. Did he ever find out about the blanket?"

"No. He forgets stuff when he's doping, or he used to anyway," Molly' suddenly smiled as she stepped into his arms.

Jimmy embraced her, and sighed, "I've thought about you a lot, ever since," and after a moment, he shyly whispered, "You're so pretty. Can I kiss you again?"

Molly looked up and gravely considered his face for several seconds. "I've thought a lot about you, too." Then closing her eyes, she offered him her lips.

He gently, but clumsily gave her a brief kiss, and backing off with a worried voice asked, "Was that all right? Did I hurt you?"

Molly grinned and reaching for the back of his neck with her free hand, responded in a whisper, "Let me show you a better way to kiss, now that we got some time, and I'm not wearing a damn collar, OK?"

She released him two minutes later with a gasp. He gasped in return, and grinned, "We did sorta' make your chain rattle that time didn't we?"

Then he blushed, because of his obvious arousal. Molly grinned, and wiggled her hips and belly against him as she whispered, "Later Buddy. Let's go do some killing first, OK?"

Jimmy smiled then suddenly in a man's tone, replied, "Yep! We need to go clean out this place, dammit!"

A soft beep sounded behind them and Jimmy muttered, "Shat!"

"What's that?"

"His Chin comset! Lukey 'n Carlos 'n Chang are calling him. I gotta' answer it or they'll know something's wrong."

"Who are they?"

"The other three," he muttered darkly as the beep sounded again. Jimmy turned to the Captain's body, and unceremoniously rolled it on its back and unbuckled the man's field belt, then heaved the body back over again to free it. The unit in its pouch beeped again as he retrieved it and clicked it on.

"Jimmy here," he responded.

"Where ees the Captaine?" Carlos demanded.

The youth glanced around at Molly, her eyes suddenly wide in apprehension and then past her, to the mouth of the mineshaft. He smiled and replied, "He's gone chasin' the white-hared girl but she ran down in this old mine, and he left me out here with the comset, 'cause it don't transmit good underground.”

“Well, tell heem when he comes back out with her that we gave Rat thee beeg man, an’ I didn’t let Lukey cut on heem. Rat say they stand by for half hour, but no more. How long you figure it take Captaine to catch the leettle beech?”

“Damn if I know, but he moves pretty slow sometimes.” Jimmy replied in a sincere voice, as he kicked at the man’s body again. Then he looked at Molly with a question in his eyes.

Her apprehension had relaxed as she listened to Jimmy spin his tale into the comset, so she now grinned back at this gesture of his contempt. He smiled at her grin.

“What’d he say for us do now?”

“Stay close there till he brings her out, he don’t want any help.”

There is a squawk in the background, “Lukey’s hurting reel bad an’ he still bleeds a lot,” Carlos continued.

“Why don’t you plug his shoulder and strap his arm? And give him a pain popper out of the aid pouch?” Jimmy asked. “I put one in the saddle bag last night when you were all out of it.”

“Si. Good idea, Boy. We go.”

Molly waited until Jimmy clicked the set off, then she giggled, “You’re pretty quick on your feet with your brain. And who’s the poor mark they snagged?”

“Awwww,” Jimmy blushed, “I had to tell ‘um something that would keep them away and,” he suddenly paused, then nodded determinedly, “And away from you.”

Molly’s eyes shone, and she hugged the youth to her belly again. “Thanks Buddy. I’m glad you’re on our side,” she whispered into his chest.

“Awwww,” was all that Jimmy could choke out...

“OK! Enough mush stuff, we gotta’ get on with the mission!” she gritted in a high voice. “Where are those three, and who is that poor sucker they just sold to the Rat?”

“They’re only two now. The guy speared Chang, he’s Chin deserter that showed up a coupla’ months ago, and he got Lukey through the shoulder with a spear too.”

“They’re over in the valley beyond your cabin right now. And I don’t know who the big guy is. He just showed up when we were coming up the ridge, and he popped out from behind a tree, and then took off running. I didn't see him, but he," nudging the Captain's body, "Said he was real big, and naked, and he was a revert injun, and that the Rat would pay big for him. Anyway, Carlos and Lukey and Chang took off chasing him while the Captain 'n me came on to your cabin. That's where the dog picked up your scent and we started tracking you. Carlos was on the horse and finally rode him down and got him with a trank gun."

"That's Bila! He's my best friend!" Molly gasped, then she screamed, "You sold Bila you bastards!" as she jumped back and brought her rifle up, and caught her foot on a limb in the litter on the excavation floor.

Jimmy's eyes widened in shock at her rage, but he leapt to her side as she lost her balance and began to fall. He caught her, and steadied her to an easy landing on the ground.

"I'm sorry, I didn't know. And I couldn't do anything anyway until just now. Are you OK?" he asked with concern on his face.

Molly glared up at him for a moment as she lay with his arm around her shoulders. Then she sighed, "He was trying to lead them away from me, I know it now. And I suppose it's not your fault. Anyway, I don't think Bila knows about people riding horses, or about dogs that hunt. So that's the only reason they could catch him, or find me."

"What's that mean, about horses and dogs?"

"Later," she growled in her copy of Boots voice. "Right now we gotta' do something pretty quickie! Help me up, dammit!"

The boy's young strength surprised her as he lifted her to her feet with ease, then he asked simply, "What's next?"

Molly glanced around the excavation, then growled in a firm squeak, "We gotta' drag this lump of dog squat into the shaft so the Rat's 'copter won't spot him if it's flying around."

"How can they spot him here in under the trees?"

"IR scanners. He's not cold yet so he'll glow, and if he's got a butt bug, they can pick that up too."

"How do you know that they can't still spot him in there?"

"Bila told me. Now let's hump, then we gotta get to the cabin real fast!"

Jimmy nodded and retrieving the pistol belt, re-pouched the comset. Without bothering to adjust it to his slim waist, he buckled the belt and slung its loop over his shoulder. Then bending, he grabbed the Captain's wrists and dragged his body into the shaft without ceremony or a great deal of effort. Dashing back, he grabbed the backpack he had carried and dumped it in the shaft as well.

"Let's go," he said as he came back out. Molly gave him a quick smile, and started trotting up the slope.

"Don't go too fast, or you'll wear out before we get there," he exclaimed.

"Right," she panted and slowed to a steady pace on through the forest. Jimmy gave her a hand over the difficult places as they made their way back to the cabin. She accepted his help with a smile.

*

"OK, no intruders inside except you two and that damn dog his morning," Molly muttered as she replaced the query box back under its concealing rock. "Let's go!"

Jimmy followed her to the cabin, through the door and into its back room. She plopped down before the computer and Jimmy said, "Wow!"

"You never saw this when you were here before, 'cause it was dark, and Durwood didn't want anybody to know what we had." Then she continued darkly, "That's why he made me do things to entertain those guys, and keep everybody out of this room, except when you snuck in," she suddenly giggled.

"Awwww," Jimmy whispered as his face reddened and he awkwardly patted her shoulder.

Molly gave his hand an absent-minded squeeze as she focused on the computer and powered it up. The screen blinked to life as she considered the link address and the list of message ciphers Boots had given her. She decided on the one that signaled the highest urgency for a situation here, and then changed its phrasing. After easily moling into the gov-net, she posted her altered message on Boot's mother's place.

Molly exited the site and the net, and her shoulders slumped as she sat before the blank screen. "Well, I did everything we can do for now. But Kris will take care of him, I just know," she whispered plaintively. "Anyway, I'll check back in a couple of hours for her answer."

Jimmy reached for her hand and clasped it, and she looked up at him and smiled – until a little jingle sounded from the intruder monitor on the wall at the same time as the Chin comset beeped.

"Shat!" Molly hissed, "That's the tripwire out front! Someone's coming down the ridge."

"Should I answer this thing? There'll be trouble if I don't."

"If it's them out there, there's already trouble. See what they say," she responded as she stood rose and grabbed her rifle leaning against the wall.

She changed its magazine for a fully loaded one as she strode into the other room and pulled the front door slightly ajar. The comset beeped again as Jimmy followed to stand beside her. He keyed it on, "Jimmy here."

"Where thee hell `es thee Captaine Boy? What `es going on with you?"

"He ain't back out of the mine yet, an' I'm getting worried! Where are you?"

"We wait at thee landing site after thee pickup, like you say he tell us do. You sure you tell thee truth Boy, that he say for us to stay here?"

"He sure did, I promise!"

"Rat `es getting restless een they `copter!"

"I don't know what else to do," Jimmy responded in an affected whine that made Molly grin.

She mouthed, "Lying bastards!" as she pointed to the slope out in front of the cabin.

"Do you want me to go down in the mine and see if I can find him?"

"You do that Boy, but be queek, an' call me when you come back out, ¿Entiende usted?"

"Yep, I understand. I go." He clicked the set off and muttered to Molly, "You think they're out front?"

"That tripwire is more than half way down the slope. They're probably just inside the tree line right now," she hissed as she peered through a small loophole beside the door.

Jimmy stood behind her and looked over her shoulder as he affection-ately stroked it. She leaned back against his chest and sighed, "What are we going to do Buddy?"

He wrapped his arms around her in a gentle hug under her breasts, and stroked her belly as he whispered fiercely, "Kill `um. They need killin' dammit, for what they've done to Mom, and you last year - and what they are tryin' to do to you now."

She turned awkwardly in his arms and looked up at him for a moment then she whispered, "Thanks Jimmy."

He sighed, "Thank you, Molly. I want to keep you safe, for ever." She smiled up at him in silence and they kissed for a moment before they turned back to the loophole.

There was a stirring in the brush at the edge of the forest five minutes later, as the two men emerged into the clearing. Carlos was leading the horse that Lukey rode, hanging on to the saddle horn with his good hand. His other arm dangled limply and his shoulder was bandaged with crude strips torn from his shirt. He swayed in the saddle and his bandage was blood-soaked.

Molly and Jimmy watched the two come closer to the cabin. She clicked her rifle's safety to off, and he drew the Captain's pistol. He checked to see that a round was chambered and held it at his side as they waited.

When the two men reached the spot where Puss had helped her to plant the target frame the previous morning, Molly glanced at Jimmy.

He nodded and opened the door. He stepped out and stood to one side, holding his pistol out of sight along his pants leg.

"What tha' sheet!" Carlos shouted. "What thee hell you doin' here?"

Jimmy remained silent until Molly stepped through the doorway and screamed, "Where's Bila, you bastards?"

"Gadammit that's her! Grab her Boy!" Carlos shouted as he reached for the black comset and fumbled to insert its battery. He succeeded in doing so, and was keying its switch when Molly raised her rifle and fired.

The tiny slug entered Carlos' forehead three centimeters above the bridge of his nose, and its effect on his fontal lobes and cerebral hemispheres was quite similar to that of her shots at the rash bars - except this resulting goo was contained within his skull.

He was slumping and falling when Molly fired at Lukey, as Jimmy's pistol barked. Her shot struck the lanky man above his right eye and had the same effect inside his head just as the slug from the Jimmy's pistol slammed into the man's chest and knocked him out of the saddle.

The horse shied slightly at the pistol report and at the man falling from its back, then it began to graze as its reins slid through Carlos' slack fingers.

The two figures on the ground did not move and after watching them for a moment, Jimmy turned to face Molly and held out his arms. She stepped to him with a sob and clutched for support as she began to tremble.

"It's OK, they're all gone now, Jimmy whispered. "You're safe."

"It's not that," she responded in a little whimper. "I never killed anybody before, and I didn't think I could." Then she shuttered, "But I just did."

"Me neither, 'till the Captain this morning, but I did it when I had to. You had to just now. No, we had to do it. They were bad, and they were going to hurt you," he finished with iron in his voice.

She sighed and raised her head, "You're right. Kris was right. And it was right for me to do it for my baby. No, our baby." she said as she smiled at him. Then she hugged him fiercely with her free arm.

"Awwww..." was his only response, until they heard an indistinct voice from where the two bodies lay in the grass.

"Shat, that's Rat's comset! It's still on and the 'copter is trying to call them, and it's bugged so they can listen even when it's off," Jimmy hissed as he holstered his pistol.

They released each other and ran to where the horse grazed on the grass beside the fallen men. Holding his finger to his lips, Jimmy picked the set up. He carried it back and they listened to the speaker as it squawked, "I repeat dammit! Waddy'ell is goin' on down there with you two? Was that a shot? An' where's the li'l white-haired spook?"

Then the voice continued with words that chilled them, "I'll give ya' five minutes' to check in, or we are commin' over tha' ridge for a recon!"

Then the comset went dead.

Jimmy placed it carefully back on the grass and led Molly ten meters away from it.

"We gotta' get them, and us out of sight, and there's no cave around here," he whispered in her ear.

She frowned for a moment, then her eyes widened, "Yes there is! Come on and I'll show you!" She hissed as she trotted to the hidden mouth of the escape tunnel. She knelt and began tugging at a handle hidden under a flap of sod. Jimmy joined her and grabbing the handle, heaved it up. A counter-balanced turf-covered door opened to reveal a one-meter square opening into a tunnel in the earth. The door had a half-meter thick roof of soil over it.

Molly set the door's prop, then she got up with Jimmy's help and the two ran back to the bodies. They grabbed the one with the moustache's arms and dragged him to the trap door. Jimmy jumped down and pulling the body in after him, turned and dragged it into the darkness.

He leapt up the crude ladder to the surface again and raced back to where the one with the blond hair lay as Molly followed. They dragged his body back to the tunnel; his shoulder bandages making a good grip for her small hands...

Jimmy pulled the man's body into the tunnel then handed Molly down the ladder. He hissed, "Back in a minute," as he bounded up again and raced back to the horse.

He expertly removed its tack and gave it a friendly slap on the rump. The horse ambled away after receiving this familiar time-off signal, and resumed grazing on the lush grass of the meadow. Jimmy grabbed the saddle and bridle and raced to the edge of the tree line. He pushed them out of sight under a bush and snatched up a fallen branch.

He ran back to where the bodies had laid and retrieved the black comset. He glanced around to see if they had overlooked anything, then began backing toward the tunnel. Molly watched anxiously as Jimmy used the branch to brush away the trail they had scuffed in the grass by dragging the bodies.

He tossed the branch aside and dropped into the pit just as they heard the faint sound of rotor blades in the main valley. He helped her swing the thick trapdoor shut, and she took a small flashlight from a hook on the doorframe. She tugged at his arm and gestured back into the tunnel. Then she crawled without hesitation over the two bodies and on toward the cabin. He followed, until she stopped next to the slim tube of a Chin bunker periscope that hung down from of the tunnel's roof. The instrument was quite sophisticated and unique in that it was purely optical and thus emitted no electronic signals that could be traced...

They settled themselves just as the comset crackled again and a voice snarled, "Alright ya' limp sticks, we're gonna find out what the ferk's goin' on down there. An' when we do, you're in trouble if ya' ain't gots tha' white bitch. That's breaking yur' contract and Boss Rat don't like that way big..."

Molly pulled the periscope's eyepiece down and turned it as she viewed the outside. She urgently motioned upward, and scooted awkwardly aside to allow Jimmy get at it. He found that by twisting the handgrips, he could rotate its tiny upper lens in a full circle as well as up to 90 degrees above the horizon. He spotted the 'copter hovering low over the cabin, and grinned as he saw its prop wash flattening the grass where Carlos and Lukey had died, and so erasing all remaining traces of them.

The comset crackled again, "Anything on the scanner?" There was an indistinct mumble in the background, and Molly realized that someone had forgotten to switch off the comset channel. She squeezed Jimmy's arm and her eyes danced with excitement in the dim glow of the flashlight. He patted her hand and grinned again as he understood her silent signal then turned to the eyepiece again as the comset crackled once more.

"Is that their horse? Hell, I dunno'. It ain't got no saddle on, an' all them four-legs looks alike ta' me anyway. You got a fix on the comset locator?"

"No! Waddy ya' mean no? Ya' sayin it's gone?" There was another indistinct mumble in the background. "Look dammit, that thing can't jus' disappear dammit! They work anywhere the sats can pick 'um up! Try again dammit!"

Molly squeezed Jimmy's arm again as she looked thoughtfully at the black instrument lying on the tunnel floor between them. He patted her hand as he continued to watch the helicopter, rotating the periscope's lens as the craft flew back and forth over the ridges and their valley.

Finally the set crackled again, "G'dammit, they can't just drop off tha' ferkin world like that! But you sure you're gettin' nada?" There was an answering mumble in the background.

"Well, ferk it, we got this big un-doc anyway. Give him another shot an' lets head for tha' Roof. Director's gonna' be blasting' everybody on sight tho'. He wanted tha' white bitch back way much!"

Jimmy watched the `copter out of sight then looked at Molly. She clicked the black comset off and carefully examined its back. Then she opened it and removed its battery.

"Think it's dead?" she mouthed. He nodded, and then shrugged. She returned his nod and laying the instrument and its battery back on the dirt floor, grasped her rifle and began crawling on up the tunnel toward the cabin.

Jimmy followed her slender form, silhouetted in the cone of light cast by the torch she held. He squeezed past her when they were under the cabin and climbed up the ladder until he could partially open the trap door. He held it ajar with his head and shoulder and reaching out, rolled the bed away with a grunt. Then he flipped the door back and climbed up into the room. He helped Molly out of the shaft and took her in his arms, and they kissed for a very long time.

After they broke apart, Molly plopped down on the side of the bed. "Whoosh," she growled with a squeak, "That was a lot of ferkin work before breakfast! What's the time anyway, Trooper Four?"

Jimmy looked puzzled for a moment, then following her lead, he snapped to attention and growled back, "Sun's high in tha' sky, Ma'am/Sir, whoever you are!"

Molly giggled, then she responded in mock sternness, "See here Trooper, if you're gonna' join this outfit, you gotta' learn our org chart, so listen real good!"

"First, the proper response in this outfit is always "Ja Boss", get it?"

"Ja Boss," he grinned.

"Good. Now, Kris is Boss of our gang, Marybell is Trooper One, and I am Trooper Two. She paused for a moment as she blinked at a tear, then forced her voice back into a squeaky growl and continued, "And Bila is Trooper Three. Now you're Trooper Four." She finished with grit in her voice, "And there is no damn discharges from this outfit 'till Boss Rat is gone..."

Jimmy looked at her small earnest face for a long time. Then he said in the quiet voice of an adult, "When I sign on to a job, I don't leave. My dad didn't, and I've signed on to yours now." He slowly knelt before her and took her hands "OK?"

"OK," she whispered as she pulled his head to her breast.

*

They sat on the grass outside eating the greens from the previous evening that Molly had reheated on the hotplate, and chewing on dried venison strips from the rack over the dead campfire.

"This is good jerky, did you make it? And the greens are good too. They taste like my mother's"

"Bila taught me how, except he called it zezin. And he showed me how to cook the weeds too."

"Who's this Bila, anyway?"

"He's the strongest man in the world. And the nicest too - except for you," she responded in a serious little voice as she reached for his hand and squeezed it. "And he knows everything 'bout the woods..."

"But, not a lot about our world..."

"I don't want to be pokey, but how do you know him?"

"You're not being pokey Buddy, you can ask me anything," Molly smiled. "Anyway, he was with Kris and Marybell when they turned me loose after Durwood left me behind when they came for him."

"Why'd they come for Durwood?"

"They're bounty hunters for the Network, but nice ones. 'Cept I don't think Bila's one. He's just their friend. And a new one I think."

"They're from the 'S'attl, right? Where's he come from?" Jimmy asked darkly.

"Oh, throttle back yur' thrusters Buddy," she giggled, "Bila's like the best dad in the whole world!" Then she continued quietly, "I never knew mine, he was killed in the war."

"I knew mine. He fought the Chin from around here, until they caught us in an ambush right at the end," he said bitterly. "We should' a known better, because we were good ambushers ourselves. Anyway he stayed to draw their fire while we got away. The last time I saw him he was throwing grenades at

256

an armored car."

Molly placed her hand on Jimmy's thigh. "How old were you then?"

"Thirteen, but I just helped carry ammo and stuff. Dad didn't want me to start killin' 'till I got older.

"I'm older now..."

She pulled his face to hers and solemnly whispered, "And you did it - for me," as she kissed him.

He urgently responded, and they kept their lips locked for a long time, again. Finally he gasped, "I ought to go tell mom that she's safe now, and these skummers are dead."

"Yep!" Molly said with determination then she asked very quietly, "Are you coming back?"

"You're in real deep trouble, Molly. I'm always coming back and you've got no escape hatch from me now, ever!"

"Good! Don't forget your toothbrush," she giggled.

"It'll only take me about three hours. Do you have any grain type stuff I can feed my horse? Actually, it was my dad's and that Captain bastard almost ruined it."

"Oatmeal?"

"That's perfect!"

*

Jimmy whistled to the cow pony and when it responded to his familiar call, he showed Molly how to hold a mess kit filled with the cereal. When the horse began to feed from it to Molly's delight, he ran to the tree line and retrieved its saddle and tack.

"He's sweet!" Molly exclaimed as she stroked its velvet muzzle.

"She's a mare and real good cow pony, and her name is Sugar Plum. Now that those jerkos are gone we can bring her back again pretty quick with the right feed. I'm glad you like her." Jimmy grinned as he placed the saddle on the horse's back and cinched it. Then waiting until the horse had licked the mess container clean, he placed the bit in its mouth and buckled on its bridle.

"I'm gonna' change this damn curb that bastard used to a snaffle as soon as I get back to the barn." he added. "This horse has a real quick mouth and you don't need any more than that, if you know anything about horses."

Molly nodded, as if she understood his words then she asked, "You want to take their pistols back to your mom?"

"Yes, and we better move their meat, before it starts to stink."

"There's a good place for that. Bila showed me."

"He must've showed you a lot."

"Yep. Including' how to kill, and to not be killed."

"Then he's a friend of mine!" Jimmy whispered.

"I'm glad you like him, and I know he'll like you," Molly replied with a grin as she led the way back to the escape tunnel.

Jimmy shook out a length of the lariat coiled on the saddle and dismounting, dropped into the tunnel taking its noose with him.

He climbed back to the surface moments later and mounted the horse in an easy bound, then gently signaled his mount to back toward the open trap door as he took in the slack line.

When the horse obediently stood with its hind hooves only twenty centimeters from the dark opening, Jimmy snugged the free end of the rope around the saddle horn and used his heels to urge the horse slowly forward. Lukey's body was dragged out of the tunnel and up over the exit ladder by the noose looped around his neck as the horse moved forward. When his body was on the surface, Jimmy halted and Molly stripped the gun belt from it and emptied Lukey's pockets, with disgust on her face.

Jimmy asked, "Where to?"

"Out there in the big valley. And don't worry, your nose will tell you where to take it," Molly said with a grim little smile.

Jimmy signaled the horse with his knees and it walked slowly forward, dragging Lukey's body through the grass of the meadow...

He trotted back fifteen minutes later, "I see what you mean, but who killed the big bear?" he asked.

"Bila did, with a spear. I'll show you it back at the cabin."

"Killed A ferkin grizzly with a ferkin spear?" he gasped. "Nada! Nobody can do that!"

"Bila did," Molly stated with a firm little nod. "Now do you see why I'm telling you that he's the strongest man in the world?"

Jimmy looked at Molly, and the sincere expression on her face. Then just shaking his head, he dropped into the tunnel again. He re-emerged moments later with the rope in his hand and remounting, urged the horse forward as it slowly dragged Carlos' body from the tunnel. Molly stripped away Carols' equipment as well, and Jimmy and Sugar Plum dragged pulled it on out to the new bone yard.

*

"I'll get the Captain and the dog and Chang down there tomorrow," Jimmy said as he lashed the two gun belts to the saddle horn. "Let me get back to mom now, and then I'll be back in about three hours. You want me to bring some food?"

"No. I'll make supper."

"What are you going to make?"

"Dumb bird soup," Molly giggled. "Bila told me how." Then her humor faded as she asked in a little voice, with big eyes, "Are you really gonna' bring your toothbrush back with you?"

"'Course, Silly," he answered with a grin. "If I'm not around here all the time now, you'll just get in trouble again!"

"And if you're here?"

"Then we both can get in trouble," he smiled, tentatively.

Molly looked up at him on the horse then whispered shyly, "Come back soon - I think I'm ready for some more trouble," as she squeezed his leg.

Jimmy stared at her small earnest face for a moment, then he shouted, "Move out horse! We got to do a quick trip!"

The cowpony, feeling a familiar seat again as well as Molly's oats snorted at Jimmy's signal and bounded forward as Jimmy waved back to her.

*

The sun was low in the sky when Jimmy walked down the ridge, leading Sugar Plume along the clear path Molly had showed him that morning, and whistled as he approached the cabin. He saw that the jerky had been removed from the drying rack and there was a small pile of feathers beside the cold fire pit. Then Molly stepped into the doorway and smiled at him, and he forgot everything else except her.

"Hi," he whispered. "Mom sent us some stuff," as he gestured to the bulging saddlebags and the other bundles tied to the horse's saddle. "I'm sorry I'm late, but I had to lead Sugar Plum so she could rest some."

Molly grinned, "The horse comes first, then me. I've heard about you cowboys in some of those old songs! It could be worse though, you could be a vid-nut."

Jimmy's reaction was, "Awwww..." with a stricken expression.

Molly chuckled and jumped out of the door to him, and stumbled in the awkwardness of her pregnancy. Jimmy leapt forward and caught her, and she looked up into his concerned eyes.

"You're my new Buddy, so I gotta' explain my sense of humor to you pretty quickly I can tell!" she chuckled. "But just kiss me again for now, OK? And come in and get ready for supper."

He grinned, and followed both of her orders explicitly.

*

Later that night after they had eaten and he had repeatedly complemented her on her meal of the stewed grouse, they talked idly.

"There's no answer from Kris yet, so I know she hasn't seen my post. But she will, I know she will..." Molly sighed.

"I need to make us a table and some chairs," he announced, in an attempt to change her mood, "You need a comfortable place to sit."

"Yes Buddy," she giggled. "But what am I gonna' do while I'm sitting there?"

"Nurse our baby and figger' out what I'm supposed to do next," he grinned.

"Awwww," was the only response she could make, as her eyes glistened again and she looked tenderly at the honest and strong boy.

They finished cleaning up the few utensils, and unpacked the saddlebags and bundles Jimmy's mother sent back with him. Molly exclaimed over the many practical things, and the few artful ones she had included, while he smiled with quiet pride as he stroked her shoulder.

"Mom wants to come over tomorrow to say hello," he said hesitantly. "I hope you don't mind."

"Great. I want to meet her."

"I can call her on the Chin comset and tell her it doesn't suite, if you want..."

"No, I really want to meet her, Buddy. 'Cause I know that she's as nice as you are."

"I think she's real nice anyway," he blushed. "She was a student teacher before the Chin came, and she taught me and my older sister as much as she could. Sharon, that's my sister, has been hiding in the woods ever since the Captain showed up, until now. I would take her food and stuff whenever I could get away, but he always kept either me or mom and my little brother with him, so the other wouldn't run away," he gritted. Then his face changed, "Are you tired?" he asked tenderly.

"Not really, but I think I'm ready for bed now," she whispered with her eyes wide - and gazing directly into his.

Molly was surprised again by Jimmy's gentle tenderness, as was he by her sweet ardor and shyly-offered skills in giving both of them pleasure. Then after a very long and active exploration of each other, they drifted off to sleep nestled together on the bed with their limbs entwined - much like two puppies in a whelping box...

***

Chapter 13
The Homecoming

May 3, 2276 AD
`Clave of S'attl

"Kristina! You're back!" a voice called, "I'm so glad."

A tall woman with gray steaks in her long black hair stepped into the foyer of the row house as she asked, "How long can you stay dear?"

"As long as we need to, I hope Mother," Boots answered. "This is my friend, Marybell. She is with me."

The woman, who bore a striking resemblance to Boots except for a magnificent bosom straining the fabric of her short blue silk robe, said with a smile, "Of course dear, your room is still upstairs. We didn't need it, so we left all of your things there."

"All of them, Mother?" Boots asked.

"Yes dear, all of them..." The woman said, quietly.

Boots took a deep breath and Puss sensed a tension in her friend, different from any mood she had ever noted in her before. Then Boots relaxed.

"Thank you Mother."

The woman who resembled a slightly older more feminine sister to Boots rather than her mother, responded in a soft voice, "I am glad that you let me help you again, Kristina."

Then she continued with a lilt, "Anyway, now I've had a chance to read some of your books while you've been away at war or out and about since it has been over. I didn't think you would mind."

"Do you dear?" the woman then asked with sudden concern.

"Of course not Mother, but- you? reading? Now that's a new side of you

I never would've guessed. And I thought I'd seen 'um all," Boots said with a slight grin.

At this moment a stocky balding man strode into the hallway tying the belt of his black robe and stood beside the tall woman who looked so much like Boots. He placed his arm around her waist affectionately and changed the mood in the small space by announcing, "Hello, I'm Hector. I'm Kristina's dad, and this cutie is her mother Helen."

Then he added with a twinkle in his eye as he looked at Puss with a mock glare, "Please excuse the lack of courtesy in both of my women! You're Kris' friend, right?"

His wife turned and kissed his ear with a shy smile.

Puss took her cue from the man and grinned. "Yes sir, I'm Marybell," as she offered her hand.

Hector and Helen both clasped it, and he announced, "You're very welcome here in our house young lady," while Helen added with a smile that Puss immediately recognized as pure Boots, "I'm glad that you could come."

Puss winked at the couple - then glanced around at her friend with a wicked little grin as she said in a stage whisper, "Why, they aren't at all like what you told me Buddy! They're real nice!"

Hector muttered to Helen, "I like this gal already, she's got brass."

Boots' cheeks reddened as she murmured to her friend, "OK dammit, so I told you before that my folks were into the 'clave culture biggers, ever since I could remember.

"But it sorta' looks like they're doing the main squeeze thing on each other now. Finally."

Her parent's only response was to smile to her, and show a serenity that Boots didn't remember ever seeing in them before.

"Mother used to be a blond," Boots continued with a grin after looking at her parents for a moment, "And the best bed-bouncer in S'attl. Dad acted like he was just her bath mat, but by Buda's bongos, they sorta' look like a pair of hot teeners now, don't they?"

Helen giggled like a young girl and squeezing her arms around Hector and murmured in a husky tone, "He's my tiger guy," as she lifted one long shapely leg and wrapped it around his waist, and licked his cheek. Hector winked to his daughter and Puss, then leered as he squeezed Helen's bottom, "Nice little kitty, Papa's going to tickle your chin real good later on..."

Helen purred in the back of her throat, and flicked the tip of his nose with her tongue.

"Now I know where you get all those hot little tricks of yours Buddy," Puss giggled, "you come by them way natural!"

Boots snorted with laughter, then she opened her arms to her parents and her expression suddenly changed as she threw her arms around them both.

"Thanks guys. You have a nice show going now and I really like it a lot more than the old one. Thanks, for real..."

"I'm glad you're happy with us, dear," Helen whispered to her daughter. "But you showed us what is real and important in life after you lived through that dreadful night when you were sixteen, so we changed some of the things we - No, I was doing after you went off to fight in the war."

"Yes sweets you did," Hector murmured to his wife, "But we both changed from what we used to be. Anyway, I'm very glad that you've come home now Kris, so I can thank you finally."

"For what, Dad?"

"For being who you are, Darlin' Daughter," he said as he looked up at her, "I am very, very proud of you."

Boots gazed first into her mother's deep blue eyes, and saw a new openness and tenderness now in them instead of her old glare of restless and blasé world-weariness. Then she looked in her father's, and in their light brown depths she saw a power and a sureness of self that she had never noticed in him before, in all of her youth in their dysfunctional household.

Her brow wrinkled slightly and she frowned as a wisp of memory flitted though her mind, only to slip away again un-captured. She ignored it as well as a tingling at the back of her neck, but while she considered both of her parents, a vision of her father's eyes lodged in her sub-conscious.

Boots abruptly relaxed all the barriers she erected eleven long years ago, and for the first time since her ordeal she allowed herself to accept and to be comforted by the support and affection of her parents. The smile of the happy and confident young girl she once was lighted her face again as she remembered a more innocent time in her life.

She kissed first her mother then her father softly, "Thanks for letting me come home again."

The three stood silently for a minute with their heads together, embracing each other, and Puss recognized this as a unique, re-defining time for Boots and her parents. Puss remained silent while she waited for them to hide their true feelings again, and cover them once more with the stoic and cynical mask of the `Clave.

"Enough of this mush stuff!" Hector growled finally, "Here, let me get you some refreshments dammit! The hospitality staff is gettin' way too lax around this place!"

"Ooo, I never thought you'd ask! Got any army whiskey?" Puss said happily, as she joined with Hector in lightening the mood in the foyer.

"Sure, I work for the Governor. But we've got amusement alcohol that's way better and safer than that damn rot-belly bore cleaner!"

"Soldier slosh is the only firewater this Injun' really likes," Boots said with a chuckle as she slipped out of her gray overcoat and reached to take Puss'.

"I'm sorry dear, I've been remiss. Here, let me put your things away for you," Helen said.

"Mother Pulease! I think I can still find the hall closet," Boots announced, but then as her mother's smile faded she threw her arm around the woman and kissed her cheek a second time, "Just kiddin', OK?"

Helen smiled again, "You little mink! You always were faster than me! But if you're not respectful to your old gray-haired mother, I'll show your friend the vid we took while we were trying to potty train you!"

"No! Mother, you wouldn't!" Boots said with a theatrical gasp.

"Hell yes, do it! I'd looove to see that!" Puss snickered as she handed over her coat and knapsack.

"We'll see. Just remember to behave, dear," Helen said primly. Then she smiled, "Now, is anyone hungry? I can fix something for you two pretty quickie."

"You mean crack some food packs of something, don't you?" Boots said.

"Actually no daughter," Hector announced. "Your mother is now expert in some new skills, even as she stays in top form in all her old ones as well."

"Humph to you!" Helen snorted, then she bent from the waist and flipped up the back of her robe at him before continuing serenely, "Girls, let's go in the kitchen and see what we've can fix." She turned and led them to the rear of the hallway, and side-swiping Hector with her hip as she brushed past him.

"Egad! I am assaulted with a heavy weapon! Medic! Stretcher!"

Puss giggled, "Hey Buddy, now I'm starting to figger' you out even more! It's your genes that make you waggle the way you do."

Boots responded with a dry sniff and a hip-thrust of her own at Puss as they followed her mother into the kitchen at the back of the house.

*

Boots glanced around at its familiar counters and cabinets when she entered the small room, but then paused before an elaborate cooking range that took up much of one wall.

"Whoa gang! What tha' ever-lovin bug-eyed world is that thing?"

"It's my stove, Dear."

"Mother," Boots growled in mock sternness, "Just what tha' ferk's going on here? First reading books and now this stove are you sure you're you?

"I maybe should run an ID scan to see if you're my real mother, because the one I grew up with thought that Cooking was just another Chin city."

Helen stared indignantly at her daughter for a second while Puss and Hector waited for her lightening to strike. Then Helen laughed.

"Touché Darling! But now you'll pay heavy for that young lady, because I'm cooking for the two of you tonight, and you, little Miss Smarto will have to eat what I make. Then if you really like it, you must lick your platter clean in front of everybody!"

"But Mommy, we ate at Rick's already," Boots moaned in a little girl's voice.

"Maybe you did, Big 'un, but I sure's hell didn't dammit! I'm hungry and I want a drink, and I'm way grumpers because I missed out on a good cigar too, dammit!" Puss growled.

Hector chuckled, "Hell, it's not just brass, this gal's got hard chrome plate where it counts!"

"Just get her a drink sooners Dad! It can ugly-up real fast if she goes on the warpath." Boots said with a grin. "And here Buddy, Rick slipped me these as we were leaving," she continued as she unbuttoned her suit jacket and pulled out a handful of panatelas from an inside pocket.

"Why don't you get us all drinks Sweetheart, and then you three can mingle while I show off what I have learned," Helen asked.

"Yes dear, the usual coming right up. And you Kris?"

"The same as mother," Boots smiled as she gave the woman's shoulder an affectionate squeeze.

"Back in a blink, and don't dare start without me!" Hector ordered as he stepped out of the kitchen.

"What would you like to eat Marybell, since it sounds like Kris didn't feed you very well this evening," Helen asked with tender concern, and a twinkle in here eye that made her daughter snort.

"Ma'am, if you got a horse in that keeper trot it out! Otherwise, anything that you want to fix is fine with me," Puss replied as she held a cigar to her nose and sniffed at it with a sigh of pleasure.

"Well, you look pretty healthy, especially in the lovely outfit you almost have on," Helen smiled as she removed food things from the refrigerator and arrayed them on the wooden-topped table in the center of the room. "So I'll just have to try and keep you that way, won't I?"

Puss stood and struck the schoolgirl's pose and mien, and projected the same innocent sensuality she had shown at Rick's. "Thank you, Ma'am, you are very kind to say that," Puss whispered, causing Helen's eyes widen at her sudden change, and then to shake her head as Boots laughed.

"And I like your skin color too," Hector announced as he walked back into the kitchen with a drink tray in his hands. "Is that a total body tattoo job, or a cosmetic radiation?"

Puss changed again as she hit a military brace. She snapped, "I am American Indian, Sir! My tribe is the Pamunkey of the Southern Algonquin, Sir!"

"And we ferked up biggers when we let you guys get off the boat in 1607 at Jamestown, Sir!"

"And this is the hide I was born with, dammit Sir!"

"I warned you guys about making her go on the warpath!" Boots said in a lazy drawl, "Now give her whiskey and light her cigar - real quick!"

"This is what you want, and straight, right?" Hector asked as he cracked the seal on a flask of the harsh government-issue liquor given to combat troops during the war when they rotated back to their base camps for a brief rest.

"Say when."

Puss watched him pour for a moment, "When is when the damn glass is full, dammit, when else?"

Hector chuckled as he handed her a brimming triple shot of the pungent liquid and then poured two straight vodkas from an ice-frosted decanter for his wife and daughter. Finally he grinned and poured himself a triple of issue whiskey as well, and lifted his glass in a toast.

"Welcome home, to both of you!"

"Hear, hear and more!" smiled Helen.

"Thank you, and big," the two young women said in unison as they lifted their glasses in return.

Boots and Helen took measured sips as they gazed at each other in their re-confirmed friendship, but Puss performed the army ritual of clamping her nose closed with a thumb and forefinger, gulping a third of her drink and then shuddering. When she opened her eyes, she watched as Hector drank in the same fashion.

"Looks like you wore green sometime too, Sir," Puss said with a raspy gasp.

"Sure did, except I wasn't SF like you two. I was just a supply guy, before I went to the civ side," he wheezed.

"I forgot that you were in the service, Dear and anyway, why do you hold your nose like that?" Helen asked.

The three laughed, then Hector began, "If you can choke down the first taste of this stuff..."

Puss added, "Your nose is numb after that, so you think it isn't too bad..."

"Until the next morning, unless you take more than one refill," Boots finished.

"Oh," Helen shrugged, "Well, someone has to drink it, I suppose." Then after sipping her vodka, she announced, "Alright you two, Tiger Guy and I have already eaten so you get it all.

"Tonight's menu is saddlebags, pommes frites François, and asperge maître d'hôtel."

"Hector," she ordered, "You prep the spuds while I pack the saddlebags."

"Yes, Ma'am!" he said as he snapped her a salute, then after tossing off the middle third of his whiskey with a grimace, stepped to the sink and washed and dried the two large potatoes Helen had set out. He turned back the chopping board top of the table and pulled a chef's knife with a gray carbon steel blade from a rack, and after testing its edge with his thumb rapidly cut the potatoes into uniform square strips.

"Wow, your dad is damn good with a blade! Most as good as us Injuns," Puss said as she sipped her whiskey and prepared her cigar. "Anybody got a light?"

"Here Dear," Helen smiled, handing her an igniter and switching on the exhaust fan over the range.

Puss puffed her cheroot alight then asked, "What's a saddle bag?"

"If she's doing what I remember having in a restaurant a long time ago, I think you'll like it, I sure did," Boots murmured.

Helen looked up from her work with a smile and spooning a tiny mollusk from an icy carton on the prep table, held it out to Puss, "Taste?"

Puss happily slurped and chewed, then swallowed. "Omygod! You've got cauwaih! And these are the best I've ever tasted! They're like oyster candy!"

"I'm glad you like them dear, our supplier treats us well, but what are cauwaih?"

"That's the name for oysters in my tribe. Where does your stuff come from? This isn't 'clave commissary for damn sure!"

"They are the local Olympia oysters dear, and Mrs. Kostanis is a very nice person to know…"

*

The two young women took seats at the kitchen table and Hector and Helen served their plates.

"Oh Sweet Jesu, thank You," Puss whispered as she bit into her second slice of the thick filet that Helen had just grilled moments before. She savored the rare beef and tiny, barely-steamed oysters tucked into the slit cut into the middle of the steak.

"I'm in heaven…"

"Mmmm," Boots sighed as she finished her first slice of steak and oysters, then she took a bite of a crisp potato strip.

"Mother, you fried these in olive oil! They're divine!"

"Thank you Dear, your father likes them this way so I thought you might too," Helen said with a smile as Hector uncorked an old burgundy and splashed it into balloon glasses for the two women.

"Here, try this. It should go pretty well with your meat and potatoes and that obligatory green stuff."

Boots smiled at him, and then she lifted a perfectly steamed spear of the asparagus Helen had just drizzled with melted butter and lemon juice. She held her head back and sensuously nibbled at the stalk until she had eaten it all.

"Yummy Mommy," she grinned as a drop of butter ran down her chin.

Helen snorted, "Show-off!" with a smile and Hector chuckled.

Puss ignored them as she continued eating, with dainty urgency and ladylike moans of pleasure with each bite.

*

"Congratulations Mother, I am over the top impressed with your new talent, so you win." Boots said as she stood, and with a straight face saluted the woman. Then she lifted her empty plate and gravely licked it clean as Puss and Hector cheered and clapped while Helen blushed and blinked back a tear.

"Why don't we all go in the vid room now where we can sit on something soft until everything settles and we can talk?" Hector asked.

"Fine idea Dear, I'll be in right after I clean up."

"No, Mother, you sit here and tell us where you want stuff to go," Boots smiled as she slipped out of her jacket.

"Yeah, Ma'am, give us a chance to sing for our suppers," Puss added as she stood and pushed up her sleeves. Then without waiting for Helen's reply, the two cleared the table and Boots loaded the washer with the pots and their plates and utensils while Puss carefully hand-washed the goblets and the carbon steel knife, and dried it thoroughly before replacing it in its rack.

"Looks like you know something about knives young lady, Hector nodded in approval, "Toss me a towel and I'll wipe the table," And the three made the kitchen spotless within minutes.

Helen said, "Thank you dears that was sweet of you, all of you."

"You're welcome kid, but now lets go sit, and catch up on what our darlin' daughter has been doing, and to hear what Marybell has to say about herself as well," Hector said as he clasped his wife around her waist and urged her toward the hall, and the vid room beyond.

Boots gathered her jacket and clasping Puss' hand, asked, "May I escort you into mother's romper room, my dear?"

"Is it safe?"

"Didn't used to be."

"Good! Let's go," Puss grinned as she strode forward.

Boots entered the room across the foyer and looked around its space, the center of her life with her parents for so many years.

"Well, the carpet's new, and nice. And you've re-upholstered. Nice print. And you had them reverse the material, right? I like the look."

"It's kind of you to say that, Dear. The design on the regular side of the cloth was a bit hard-edged, but I liked the bleed effect on the back of the stuff," Helen smiled as she stroked the sofa where she seated herself.

"You've got a good eye, Mother, but where's the vid in this vid room?" Boots asked as she nodded toward the wall where the large-screen unit once had been mounted.

The space was now covered with framed artworks and a shelf of old paper books and an artist's easel with a paint box on a table beside it stood in one corner of the room.

"Well we finally got tired of the Network programs, so we started doing other things. But we have a portable if you want to watch."

"Hell no, Mother! You know what I think about that crappo. But what are these?" Boots asked as she turned to the wall and examined the framed pictures hanging there, all well executed pastels or oils of flowers, except for one.

That one was a charcoal rendering of herself as a teen-aged girl and it was skillfully executed with painstaking accuracy and detail. The life-sized head-and-shoulders view showed her nude shoulders, with one eye bruised and swollen almost shut, her black hair cut very short, and a split lip that was swollen around the stitches holding it together. She held glass of milk in a hand that had one finger in a splint.

The portrait was black and white except for the eyes, which were rendered a deep blue with colored pencil. Since the image was posed looking straight forward, her eyes seemed to follow a viewer around the room. They were stark in their condemnation.

"Where did this come from, dammit? And who took a pic of me that time anyway?" Boots hissed in sudden furry.

"I did it, Dear and no one took a pic. I drew it from my memory of you, when you came home after that terrible night," Helen said quietly as she looked up at Boots.

"Would anyone like another drink? I do for damn sure!" Hector announced.

"Damn sure here too!" Puss said as she relit her cigar. "Anyone else want one of these Cuban ropes?"

Boots looked at her mother for a long moment while Hector attended to the bar tray. Then as she accepted her glass from her father, she said with a nod, "You've taken lessons from Professor Heurtley, haven't you?"

"Of course Dear, I was driven to bring your image in my memory out to where your father could see you as I had, and your nice old professor was kind enough to teach me how.

"Madame, your old dance teacher who is now his friend, has also been teaching me how to cook, and to dance," Helen continued with a slight smile.

"Jesu ferkin Buda's Bouncin' Butt, woman! Just how many new talents do you have anyway?" Boots asked, then grinned.

"She's quite good actually," Hector smiled as he offered the drink tray to his daughter and to Puss. Then he sat on the couch beside Helen, and stroked her knee as she curled her long legs under her, while vainly tugging at the bottom of her robe in an attempt to cover her thighs.

. "She gives me a private recital every once in a while, if I've been a very good boy. And yes, I'll take a smoke. Thanks young lady," he added as he caught the cigar Puss tossed him.

"You're too old for ballet Mother. Hell, I'm almost too old to do it any more!"

"Oh no, Dear, Madame is teaching me Isadora Duncan. It's much easier on my poor feet and I love it!"

"I loved learning her too," Boots smiled in sudden tenderness, as a memory from her youth floated into her mind, of dancing happily in class at the academy under the direction of the Frenchwoman with a care-worn face and the taut body of a young prima ballerina.

"Tell Kris what else Madame is teaching you sweetheart," Hector grinned as he puffed his cigar alight.

Helen blushed, then after a pause she said defiantly, "Belly dance."

"And she is very, very good too, almost more than my old heart can stand," Hector added.

"Mother, you wiggling? I never would have thought it possible, let alone Madam teaching you that kind of dance!"

"Actually she is an expert at it because of the time she spent in Morocco when she was young, before the terrible war, and she is soo sultry when she leads us in our lessons that I won't take Tiger Guy there to watch," Helen leered.

"I just knew it dammit! Puss announced through a cloud of cigar smoke,"It's in your DNA, Sweetie! You're way too good in all your moves to have thought 'um up by yourself! Let's face it, you're pre-programmed to wave it around, Kiddo," she said with a grin as she sipped at her whiskey.

Boots tossed her head theatrically and was opening her mouth to deliver a retort, when a tone chimed from outside the room.

"Who the hell's calling at this hour?" Hector asked as he got to his feet and stepped into the foyer. He returned and strode to one of the pictures on the wall. "I can't stand crooked pictures," he muttered as he gave a slight nudge to the perfectly straight frame.

"Who was it, dear?" Helen asked from the sofa, suddenly cautious.

"A message. About a word," Hector said as he turned from the wall and looked at his daughter.

"Yes Dad?" Boots said, her face suddenly hooded.

"I've just been told that the word has finally been given.

"And that it's the one I've been waiting for with mixed feelings for a very long time,

"I also learned that you're the one who decided it was finally time for the Walrus to speak,"

"You know?" Boots' eyes widened and she gasped.

"Bobby has kept me in the link about you, and how you were developing most all of the time you were out making life real bad for the Chin, so yes I do."

"What did he tell you just now?"

"What I already knew anyway. That tonight you showed you are the best we have, and therefore we will win." Hector said, as Helen rose to stand beside her husband, and smiled with pride to her daughter.

"He also told me that you would only lead a restoration. And that you know the difference between that and a revolution."

"What did you say to that?"

"I agreed, as I always have when he and I have talked about you in the past, first as a possible then as an inevitable force," her father responded with quiet certainty.

"Dad! You knew all along about what Bobby told me when I graduated?"

"Almost. I knew we needed change ever since you were a child, as I watched and learned from the inside what Washington and the Governors were trying to do to all of us in the name of the Chin war's so-called emergency," he gritted.

"But while you were still at the academy I didn't know that you would become the catalyst, I just felt that you would be part of any change that happened. Then after you went into the service, Bobby brought us into the group, when he learned to trust us."

"Us? You knew about this too Mother?"

"Yes, Dear but like your father, I just felt it when you were a cadet, until I finished your portrait and he could see what I saw in you after that day. We both then knew that you could, and probably would change things."

Boots shook her head, then hissed, "Are we screened here?"

"Yes, Daughter, ever since I straightened that picture. This room is totally shielded but the rest of the house is not. We had to leave it that way because of the complexity of decoying so much space, even with the synthesizer that Rick's men set up for us.

"Unfortunately this gap in coverage also extends the bedrooms upstairs," Hector said with a grimace, as Helen wrinkled her nose.

"Well it looks to me like you got yourself a damn strong reserve force at the old home place, Buddy. An asset you didn't know you had," Puss said as she blew a smoke-ring toward the ceiling. "So now, when do you want me to cut your butt?"

Boots slowly bowed her head where she stood before her portrait, and let her arms hang at her side. She sighed after several moments then raised her face. "Please excuse me folks, but I've been processing a hell of a lot of new intel today and the chips in my head are smoking right now." Then she took a deep breath and shaking her head again, smiled at her parents.

"And I'm sorry, but you two are so damn-sure way different from what I remember, or thought you were, that it's taking me a little time to re-route that intel in my brain too."

"Well get focused pretty quickie, Buddy. Time's something we don't have too much left of tonight," Puss said. Then she turned to Hector, "Did Bobby give you any details?"

"No, we didn't have a need to know."

"Good. Kris is going on a critical mission tomorrow morning and the Govs mustn't find out if or where she goes, so I have to get that damn locator bug out of her and keep it safe until she gets back."

"Tell them the rest of it, Doctor," Boots said with a wry grin.

"OK. After she completes this critical mission, I got to re-bug her so we can go to General Butler's gala tomorrow night."

"Well, daughter when you do finally decide to launch, you sure do it with a bang," Hector said with a grim smile.

"Do you really have to go to that horrible affair, dear?" Helen asked. "It's an absolute travesty to call those things "galas" that the Network puts on for that beast Butler and his people."

"Yes, Mother we do. Otherwise Rat, and then the Governors will know that we have picked up some intel about them that they don't want us to know."

"And they'll figure that you're on to something if you act different and break profile," Hector said. "But this operation that you talk about, just what are you trying to do?"

"Cut that ID/locator implant out of her for the time she needs to set her plan up. You don't need to know any more," Puss said.

"Do you want me to tell you about those implants," Hector asked.

"I think we've already got a good idea and I have already removed one from another person. What do you know about them?"

"And how do you know it Dad?" Boots asked.

"Kris, I wrote the performance specification for their acquisition by the government, so I know everything about them, including features that are not obvious.

Boots started then whispered, "Just what is it that you do in the `clave Dad? You never told me."

"You never asked. I am the deputy director of procurement for the whole S'attl `clave military government, and the director is a sot so I am his support and run things, and he knows it.

"Anyway, that's where these implants came from. They were a White House idea five years ago and not the Pentagon's, even though you mil-types were the ones to get most of them. I thought the way it was done was funny at the time and your top field officers volcanoed about it, but then the White House signaled they wanted it, so it happened.

"But now," he said in the same flat tone that Boots used before she began killing, "I see their real purpose damn clear, in spite of them hiding it under the pile of crappo reasons they gave the mil-types to justify their project."

Hector ignored his daughter's gasp and asked with a grave expression, "Marybell, what exactly did you do when you extracted that implant?"

Puss, and then Boots after she recovered her breath, spoke in turn and explained in detail how they removed the bug from Molly and the conclusions they had drawn from their examination of it.

"You say the signal fluctuated when you re-wet it with your saliva?"

"Yes, I figured that it operated using body fluid as an electrolyte. We dried it off when we removed it from the person, and then again after I spit on it and it started transmitting. It stopped each time it was dry" Boots answered.

"Was I wrong?"

"You couldn't have known," Hector said with a shrug. "When this type of implant is first inserted into a person, it programs itself to that subject's mitochondrial DNA. An unfortunately prophetic choice of words earlier, young lady," he said with a dry smile to Puss who was now sitting on the edge of her seat with her eyes wide, her drink forgotten and her cigar smoldering unnoticed in an ashtray.

"Anyway that's how the host's identity is broadcast after it's been implanted, for recognition and matching to their ID in the BuPop database. The broadcast is not short range continuous like the old ones however.

"Those were transmitted for a distance of less than a meter so that is why we all had to bump butts at every check-point, but this model only transmits when it is triggered by a signal from a locator/receiver, but its signal can be picked up at a pretty good distance, depending on several factors.

"The exceptions to this reactive transmission mode are when either the host's temperature drops way below normal, or the unit becomes dry - or it senses a different DNA. In these three cases it automatically sends a continuous alarm signal for as long as it can generate power from its host. We in the nomenclatura call this signal its dying squeal," He added dryly.

"However, the signal may or may not be picked up, depending on if locator/receiver is somewhere within range of the disturbed implant."

"What's the range of the locator/receivers?" Boots asked.

"About three klicks for each of the most powerful stationary units of the blanket grid in all the 'claves, but reception must be line-of-sight for two of them in order to get a good position fix. Otherwise only the presence of the host in the area, or the squeal of the dying implant is noted. The portable units have a range of two klicks and unless two of them are used in conjunction, the only info they can pick up is a vector and an approximate range."

"Why are you telling us this now Dad? I think you're taking a very big risk," Boots asked.

"I've been waiting for five long years to tell what I know about these damn things to someone who needed to know and who could, and would use my info to stop the Governors and the White House.

"You're that person Kris, and I've thought that it would be you for a long time. I just am glad I can be of some help to you now," he said with a brief smile.

"How long did the unit you removed transmit the second time when you spit on it?" he then asked.

"About a second. Do they do burst transmissions?"

"Shat!" Puss exclaimed. "Ferkin' buccal cells! I should have remembered dammit! I'm sorry Buddy!"

"What're you talking about?" Boots asked with a frown.

"The cells that are always sloughing off the lining inside your mouth.

"They carry your DNA too, and the bug could read you when you spit on it - and I forgot," Puss said as she slapped her forehead in disgust.

"Right. Sort of," Hector said.

Boots glanced from Puss back to her father. "Alright you two, its straight story time now dammit! How bad is it?"

"Not bad at all for you, darlin' daughter. The nano-computer in the bug can do a lot of things, but even with atom-sized transistors it doesn't have enough memory for a database that can find a new person's DNA out of the millions in the country.

"It only recognizes that the new one is different from the one it programmed to first. Obviously a design flaw," he added dryly.

"So it didn't squeal on you, just about the fact that it was being pulled and disturbed. Therefore the Governors will just think that your host is dead, but only if the signal was picked up. Where were you when you pulled it?"

"Up in British Colombia, near what used to be the town of Kitimat."

"Well, daughter," Hector said with a smile, "Unless they were circling overhead like vultures, no one heard it when Marybell pulled that person's bug.

"But the risks you two have already started taking now are heavy, and they are only going to get denser damn soon, so be good girls and share with your old dad from now on, OK?"

"And with me as well," Helen added quietly.

"Thanks Mother, but I don't think there's much you can do."

"Hector, how will we keep that nasty little thing from squealing as you call it, when Marybell removes it from Kris?"

"I don't know yet," he responded with a frown. "There are some ways, but since removals are rare I only have a general idea what they are. We don't have the facilities here but the damn thing has to think it's not been disturbed for you trick to work."

"Mitochondrial DNA is female-hereditary, isn't it?" Helen asked.

"Yes Mother," Boots murmured in an absent aside. Then she turned to Hector with a look of command, "So how do we stabilize this little sucker?"

He shrugged in frustration until Helen murmured, "I thought so. Would you like me to help you again Kristina?"

"Yes Mother, but I really don't know what you can do this time," Boots said with a note of impatience.

"Why don't you let me baby sit it for you tomorrow Dear?" Helen smiled as she turned and bared a smooth white hip.

"Mother! Please be serious!" Boots snapped.

"I am, Dear."

"Bango! You got it Ma'am and that's a great idea! Butt bad joke though," Puss grinned.

Hector turned to his wife with a smile of relief, "Thanks, kid. I'm glad I know you." Then he turned to Puss as Boots stared wide-eyed at her mother. "It'll work too, because neither of us was given these new implants, because the Governors figured that they have all of us upper level org-chart hogs totally hooked with the privs they give us. So they don't worry about where Hector and Helen are, since they know we'll never wander too far from their feed trough."

Boots took a deep breath and finally spoke, "Mother, please forgive my blindness. You've just shown me that you can see the bright thread running through the fog too. I'm sorry for being so stupid for so long."

"Kristina, you're not blind dear, nor stupid. You never have been, you have just always had a lot of things on your mind," Helen said with a smile. "But thank you for letting your father and I join your back-up force, so to speak."

"And bad puns aside, you're her daughter so your DNA won't let you be blind or stupid either," Puss announced briskly. "Now, where are we going to do this switcheroo?"

"What do you need?" Helen asked.

"A place big enough for you two to lay side by side, with room for me in between."

"The floor in here is the only safe place where three people can get together now anyway, since our bedrooms aren't screened." Hector said as he turned to the wall and hinged out one of the oil paintings. Boots blushed while Puss raised an eyebrow.

"Be nice, dear. Our bed used to get crowed too, if you will remember," Helen admonished.

"Yes dear. Sorry daughter," Hector replied absently as he examined the small control panel set in the wall behind the picture frame. Micro-dials, switches, a tiny vid display and a keypad were crowed on its surface.

"The screen on this room should be OK, if the synthesizer has been doing its job. The decoy feed program has been cataloging you two with motion capture ever since you came in the front door and I heard you call that you were home, just like you used to," Hector continued with a slight catch in his voice.

"I started it then and it's been compiling all of our interactions, until we came in here just now and I secured the room."

"Just what tha' hell kind of program do you have?" Boots hissed.

"It's one of Rick's. His friends write the best evasion codes we have."

"Why haven't you taken on Rat and the Govs already, if they're so good?"

"We don't have anyone who is good enough to mole into their net. We can fake survel feeds like these to cover ourselves, but we don't have anyone who can manipulate their major systems. We haven't tried to because we didn't want to trip their signal wires with a clumsy probe.

"They have very good, or anyway quite competent code people on their side. Also we didn't have a plan, until now."

"So you have stayed covert and passive," Boots said as she straightened her shoulders and took command of the room. "Good. Now, just what does this decoy program do with all of the peep shots it has been taking of us?"

"We stayed that way Kris, because we've also been waiting for someone with a word and a plan," Hector said. Then he continued, "This program synthesizes a plausible activity scene from our images and voices according to a general scenario it's given. In the case of us in this room now, it has been sending an image ever since we came in that shows us saying hello again after a long time."

He set a dial and snapped several of the tiny switches, and as Puss and Boots peered over his shoulder at the tiny screen they saw avatars of their four selves displayed in a relaxed group sitting and sipping their drinks while Hector and Puss puffed cigars.

"There is a built-in delay while the program integrates any of our movements beyond a pre-set passive behavior threshold, so if we do something that appears to include an exit into the unscreened area it creates a transition continuity.

"Go up to Kris' room please sweetheart, and act normal until we're sure that it is working."

"Which normal do you want, dear my new or my old?" Helen leered with a twinkle in her eye, as she strolled toward the foyer, swaying her hips in exaggerated invitation.

The two women turned their eyes back to the vid display and Boots sighed in admiration, "She's some off the scale isn't she Dad. What's it like to live with her?"

The three watched her image on the tiny screen that displayed alternating views of the decoy feed from the vid room, the stairway, the upper hall and two bedrooms. They saw an image of Helen rising and walking into the foyer as she had just done, but the screen showed the rest of them still sitting around and chatting.

As they watched, the image switched to the stairway again and showed Helen mounting the stairs and entering a small bedroom that contained a large bookcase, and Hector finally whispered his answer.

"It's like parachuting, except you never land, or rock climbing except you never reach the top. You're always up and you're never, ever bored or complacent.

"I love it and her. Always have, always will. And whatever she does, or has done or will do has been, is now and always will be with style and grace. Just like you, Kris.

"Does that explain my feelings to you about your mother, and about you?"

Boots stared at her father and was shaking her head in wide-eyed wonder when Puss placed an arm around Boots' waist. She laid her head against her friend's shoulder and sighed, "I couldn't have said it better my self about Kris. We're pretty lucky aren't we, Sir?"

"Damn right Kid. But call me Hector or Daddo, or whatever you want since you're part of the family now, you poor soul," he said as he squeezed her shoulder.

Helen called from the head of the stairway, "Darling, I've looked all over Kris' room, but your handcuffs aren't here either."

"Looks like the decoy shields are working real good, and we have a comedienne here big-time too." Hector chuckled.

"Bango on both counts, Daddo. Now I'll go get my kit," Puss grinned as she gave Boots a quick hug and after a pause to toss off the rest of her whiskey, strode from the room.

"That's a pretty good code set," Boots muttered as the tiny vid screen showed Puss rising from a soft chair and leave the room, then switched to show her enter the hall, go to the coat closet and retrieve their packs while Helen regally descended the stairs clutching her robe to her bosom.

"It is Darlin' but let's move things along now, because it's getting late, or early even," Hector whispered as they watched the vid screen.

Boots glanced at her father, so different from her memory of him and a fact that she was being forced to confront it willy-nilly tonight, along with the reality of the woman who was her mother.

"Whoosh!" she whispered, "It's been a damn long day with a lot of changes coming at me all at once. Sorry Dad, but my up-taker is sort of hanging limp right now."

"I know that. But I know you can handle the load too, so lets just go on and do it," he murmured, as he wrapped his arm around her shoulders.

"Ferk! I'm getting lots of hugs all of a sudden. This makes visions of a goat being led to an alter pop up in my mind biggers!" Boots snapped.

"Good. This shows you're learning to trust nobody completely, because a leader can't. Check out Machiavelli if you don't know him by heart already."

"Thanks Dad. I do, but I'll look at him again anyway. As for now you're right dammit, let's just let's go do it!" Boots paused then, as her mother and Puss entered the room, and she saw what Helen brought out from the bosom of her robe.

"Here dear, we kept it safe for you but I did take the liberty of reading it many times," Helen said with shining eyes as she held out a clear plastic envelope containing a small booklet with a drab cover.

"Mother, you know that it's banned everywhere in all the `Claves," Boots snapped.

"Of course, dear. That's why I read it and have almost memorized it. Anyway, I thought you might want to have it now and it would be safer for me to bring it down."

"We can have a meeting of tha' damn book club later, dammit, it's time for us to get to the important stuff now! Please," Puss pleaded.

Boots nodded solemnly to Helen then she held out the envelope to her friend.

"This is the most important stuff there is in all the world, Buddy," she whispered. "This is what we swore to support and defend."

Puss took the envelope and read the title on the brown cover of the booklet through the protecting plastic envelope:

THE CONSTITUTION

OF

THE UNITED STATES OF AMERICA

Puss gasped and carefully handed it back to Boots.

"You're right. I'm sorry Ma'am."

"Accepted," Boots nodded as she carefully placed the booklet in her pack. "Butt Doctor you're in charge now, to make a really bad pun," Boots said with a smirk.

"Face down on the floor buddy and you too, please Ma'am."

"Call me Helen, or mother if you wish, and welcome to our family," Helen smiled as she knelt, then lay on the floor and pulled the skirt of her robe over her waist.

"Alright butcher gal, enough yakey! Just get on with your bloody work OK?" Boots said as she dropped the trousers of her suit and flopped down on the carpet beside her mother.

"Thanks for your vote of confidence which we will discuss later. But for now just relax while I get on with numbing your bottoms." Puss murmured as she knelt between them and examined Boots left hip intently.

"Ha, found it! Get set to be stuck, Sweetie."

"Mother, tell me about your art classes and please ignore any rude comments from those behind, and beneath us as it were. Oomph," she grunted as Puss' needle stuck into her flesh.

"Yes, dear" Helen said brightly, then grunted, "Oooch!" as she got her own injection. "Your professor is very good and very patient with people who are as artless as I."

"Mother please, I always known that you're very artful in lots of ways. Now that you've shown me your real art skills, don't be humble."

"And no, I didn't feel that," Boots responded to Puss' vigorous pinch.

"I didn't either Dear. But Kris, I have to be humble beCAUSE!" Helen gasped as Puss' scalpel plunged into her right hip, "I want to learn," she finished in a serene tone.

"OK, Daddo, use these retractors to hold my new Mommy's incision open while I go fishing in your daughter's bottom, if you think you can handle it," Puss ordered.

"Ja Boss."

"Dad! How do you know about thaTTT!?" Boots grunted as Puss made her second incision and began probing.

"Darlin', I told you that Bobby kept us in the net," Hector replied as he inserted the slender blades of the two instruments into the incision in his wife's hip. "Ready here!"

"Although, while I do think that oil is an interesting medium, don't youUU" Helen gasped.

"Yes, I think so toOO!" Boots grunted.

"Got it! Here we come," Puss exclaimed, as she extracted a glittering and blood-wet pellet from Boots' hip and turned to Helen.

Hector carefully spread the incision in his wife's hip while Puss quickly inserted the little transmitter.

"I-ah-FIND pastels are beautiful in their possibilities. DoOOn't you?" Helen gasped again, when she felt the thrust as Puss implanted the module.

"Yes. And you are too," Boots smiled as she clasped her mother's hand. "Thanks again"

"Transfer complete, now let's see if our right brains have really worked," Puss muttered as she held Molly's sensor over Helen's hip.

The other three remained silent until Puss, exclaimed, "Nada! Flat lines gang! We're good to gallop!" she said as she swiftly dabbed an antiseptic cream on the women's incisions and closed them with adhesive patches.

"I've got to keep you both sterile until tomorrow night. Then I can start you healing, but for now you two gotta' stay raw. Kris can handle that, but can you, mommy-new, or do you want another pain shot?"

Helen strained her head over her shoulder and glared at Puss with iron suddenly in her voice, "I can damn well take anything she can, and what you can too, my daughter-new."

"Shat, I think you really can," Boots muttered, as she looked around at this person who was so different from the mother of her memories. Hector merely smiled.

Puss got her feet and looked at the two women on the floor for several seconds then she nodded with a sudden grin.

"Well, we can tell 'um apart now from the rear anyway, as long as they have their bandages on and you'll do, Mother-two. It's nice to know you and I would really like for you to meet my mother-one someday."

"Alright, enough mush stuff!" Hector declared. "It's bedtime if you're going to do your both your missions tomorrow. Helen, you will sleep down here with Marybell because she still has the new bug, and Kris and I now just have the old ones. I also suspect that those bastards have ID sensors for both of you and us planted in our house outside this room, which they activated when they heard that you had come back to town."

"Therefore you, my temporarily de-bugged daughter, will sleep with me tonight. But Kris, you will have to sleep on your stomach because while you look so much like your mother from the back that we can fool their cams, we're in trouble if they get a scan of your chest. The Network has a profile as it were of Helen's front view and you definitely will trip their auto filter screen biggers if you sleep on your back, because you sorta' don't fit it," he finished with a dry smile.

"Any more than a champagne glass-full is a waste anyway I've always heard," Puss snickered.

Boots turned on the floor and rose to her knees then using the muscles of her right leg, bounded erect, "I think I'll ignore that last for the moment, Daddy Dearest."

Hector knelt at his wife's side and helped her to her feet, then tenderly caressed her breasts as she stood before him. "But what if I like lots of champagne?" he asked Puss with a blank look.

Helen stroked his hand as he caressed her, "Now be nice, dear."

Then she continued, "I think you are beautiful Kristina, however you are or want to be, but sweetheart I really do worry because you have used those hormone things for an awfully long time. It can't be good for you to not allow yourself to go on and develop naturally."

"Yeah, and if you did, you could give me a shady place to stand under to get out of the sun, or the rain even," Puss said with a giggle.

"You are very beautiful as you are, Mother but if I let mine grow like yours, I wouldn't be able to swim through the water nearly so fast as I can now," Boots responded with a carefully straight face, as she gave Puss a vigorous pinch in a very private place...

"Oweee," Puss squealed as she leaped away from harm while Helen clicked her tongue in disapproval. Then she smiled at them, and shook her head as she sighed, "You two..."

Hector chuckled into Helen's neck while nuzzling it, "I said, it's bedtime. I'll be at your side, and tend your wound tomorrow night dear, but for now give your robe to Kris, and you two swap personas then let's all slap the pads, OK?"

"Yes, Father," Boots smiled as she shrugged off her silk blouse and accepted Helen's robe.

"Well, you can sure tell 'um apart from the front. But that really doesn't matter much does it, Daddo since they're both damn good looking, aren't they?"

"Sure are, Daughter-two." he sighed.

"Thank you for the complement, dears," Helen smiled as she also removed her bra, "But Kristina is the best looking by far."

"No Mother, I am the one who's been complemented. You're the beautiful one, and tonight I've been learning just how much," Boots whispered with a catch in her voice.

Boots paused while she collected herself, then pulled a sleep shirt from her pack and continued brightly, "This is sorta' baggy on me, so it should fit you real good," as she handed it to Helen.

"Thank you dear, and will be a good fit on me but it might help your profile too, if we can find something to fill it," Helen dead panned as she offered her bra to Boots.

"Good thinking, but how can we flesh it out, so to speak?" Hector asked, as his daughter blushed.

"Real good thinkin' Mommy-two and I got augmentation coming right up," Puss grinned as she rooted in her pack and pulled out a handful of silk underwear, and then the Persian scarf from Boots' pack.

"Put this on Kiddo, so we can change your landscape for the Governors cams."

Boots sighed, then slipped the bra on and stood passively as Puss filled its cups with the soft material. After shaping them, Puss stood back and admired her handiwork.

"Wow!" she said with a grin, "What a rack!"

"Humph!" Boots snorted as she pulled on Helen's robe. Tying its sash she ignored Puss' grin and turned to her mother, "I'm going to visit a little old lady tomorrow who putters about in her garden. What do you think I should wear?"

"Is she in Olympia?" Hector asked, "If the one you're going to see is Regina Drake, she is a genuine lady and her mind is not old, not at all."

"Yes Dad," Boots sighed with exasperation, "She's the one I'm going to see. Is there anything that you don't know something about, dammit, Sir?"

"Around here, not much unfortunately," Hector answered with a dry sniff. "And by the way, you have to go out the door tomorrow or more accurately, this morning, looking like your mother. Otherwise the cam shots of you in our hall without a matching ID scan from your absent butt bug, which you had last night when you came in, will seriously trip their chips."

"Well then, dear," Helen announced, "I think something springy and femmey would be nice. I have a peasant outfit in white native-woven stuff that might do. My mother brought it to me from Mexico back before the war and I think it would suit your occasion quite well, along with some red sandals I have.

"And since I'm the electronic Kris for the time being, you can be the visual me," Helen said with a nod to Hector as she stepped into the small bath adjoining the vid room and returned with a small case.

"This is my make-up for dance class, but I think we can do something with it that will be appropriate for now as well."

"Sit here on the arm of the couch so I can get to your hair."

Kris said with a grin, "This is what I used to hear every morning before school when I was a kid," as she sat with her feet on the cushion and her back to her mother, and her weight on her good hip.

Hector and Puss watched as Helen used a comb to separate strands of Boots' hair and then lighten them with a white cream pencil. "Yep," Puss muttered in admiration, "You got one hell of a back-up team here, Kiddo."

"A team is only as good as its leader. Lucky for me I've got a good one," Hector whispered.

"Don't be silly Dear and don't put me up on a pedestal, it gets lonely."

"Now what do you think?" Helen asked as she gestured Boots to stand beside her.

Hector and Puss gazed at the two women who now were almost identical.

"You do good work, Dear," he smiled. "And besides, having you up on a pedestal is a lot of fun, particularly if you're wearing a short skirt..."

Boots and Puss snorted as Helen blushed, then moaned with affected anguish, "You see what I have to endure? It's like this all the time."

"I think you're pretty lucky, Ma'am," Puss grinned.

"Me too," Helen smiled. Then she took a black cream pencil from the case and handed it to Boots. "Now dear, you make me younger."

"Do you also have a parasol for tomorrow?" Boots asked when she finished darkening the gray strands in her mother's hair.

"Don't over do it Sweetie, or you'll stand out like a load of snow at a landfill," Puss said with a sniff.

"I mean it, dammit!"

"Actually I do, dear. It's in the top of my closet and it would go well with the outfit, but why?"

"For protection, what else?" Boots said with a cryptic grin. "And now let's go slap tha' pad, Dad."

"Yes, Daughter but we must set the stage before we do," Hector said as he turned to the little panel of shield controls in the wall, and began to punch in a string of numbers on its key pad.

"I'm changing the program parameters for the feed. It will start with your mother dropping off to happy sleep on the couch, and me nodding while you two drink it up and start doing things."

"Isn't that out of character for you two? Now, I mean." Boots asked.

"Not really, because we fake our old ways for them pretty often so we can keep the bastards confused. Anyway, I have taken her up to bed with a back-carry several times so that's the way we'll go up now."

"But we're both pretty big gals Dad, are you sure you can do that?"

"Tiger Guy can really be surprising at times dear," Helen said with a purr.

"Hey, it ain't nothin', she's my daughter,"

"I think I've heard that line before somewhere," Boots said, "But anyway what's next?"

"I've set the syncro to live feed the hall cams just after it sees me picking you up in here. So we two step into the hall when it cues us and go up to bed, simple."

"But first, how much decorum should I program for you two gals for the rest of the night down here?"

"None, if you want them to think it's really Kris 'n me," Puss giggled, causing Helen to blush again.

"Hmmm," Hector muttered as he made a final entry on the panel. "OK, it will now show you two frolicking way big for an hour before you flop."

"I'm leaving for the office early tomorrow, which is actually today and I'll try to get more intel on safe parking the implants," he said to Boots. Then he leered to Helen, "And the program will archive a copy of the action it thinks up down here so we can watch it later, together..."

She stuck her tongue out at Hector, Boots blushed and Puss laughed. "You got brass where it counts too, Buster!"

"Thanks. Now you two watch us on the display, and daughter you mount up for the ride of your young life, and be sure to giggle a lot and hug me close," he finished as he leaned forward and braced his hands on his knees.

She grasped his shoulders and giggled, "Look out Horsy, here I come," as she leaped astride his hips and clung to his back - and was surprised at the firmness of his body and the strength of his arms under her knees.

"It's been a long time since you called me that, little Krissie, much too..." Then they were interrupted by a soft beep from the panel.

"Show time," he whispered as he stepped to the door. "Three – two – one, Go!" and he strode into the hall carrying Boots' weight with ease as Helen and Puss looked on in admiration.

The two women moved to the tiny screen and they saw Boots giggle and press against Hector's back as she kissed his neck.

"Yumm," Boots squealed as Hector climbed the stairs with steady steps.

"Hey Sleepin' Beauty me be the kissor, you be the kissee!"

"But Sleepy Booty like nice Horsy man, so she do kissy–kiss," Boots mumbled, and then let her head loll onto his shoulder. She emitted several snores as Hector reached the open hallway at the top of the stairwell and carried her into the master bedroom.

Puss and Helen grinned at each other then watched while Boots remained limp on Hector's back as he entered the room. He walked to a large bed under a mirrored ceiling, knelt at the foot and let himself fall face forward.

"Ooof," he grunted under Boots' weight as she sprawled limply atop him.

He slid out from under his daughter and getting to his knees, pulled her fully on to the bed. Then as he tenderly positioned her head on the pillow she emitted several unladylike snores.

Hector kept a straight face, but Helen and Puss laughed aloud as they watched on the screen in the room below. Then he lay down beside Boots and pulling up the cover, lowered the room lights.

"Let's leave them alone now," Helen said as she hinged the painting back over the panel.

"Yep," Puss nodded.

*

"You gonna' give Li'l Helen a goo' nighty kissy Horsy Man?" Boots giggled.

"Well, yes - Dear. If you've been good," Hector responded, with caution.

288

"I be real goo'," Boots slurred. Then with a mischievous twinkle in her eye that was obvious to her father in the dim light of the room, she threw her arm around his neck and pulled his head to hers.

She raised her face over his and kissed Hector very thoroughly and for a very long time, before releasing him and plopping her head back down onto the pillow.

"Good night Hector, I love you very much," Boots whispered.

He took a deep breath then relaxed as his shock faded. Finally he caressed his daughter's head with a gentle hand.

"Good night "Helen". I love you too, more than you will ever know..."

*

"What are you going to do tomorrow while Kris is away?" Boots' mother asked as she folded the couch out into a bed and turned down its cover.

"Go see a friend of Kris' with a lab, an' then get some things to wear to tha' party," Puss mumbled as she brushed her teeth in the small bath next to the room.

She continued when she came back into the bedroom, toweling her face with the top of her jumpsuit dangling at her waist, "Are you sure you're alright, or do you want some pain pops for tomorrow?"

"No dear. Thank you but a little pain is good. It will remind me of the real world. One can get all caught up in art and forget other things that are important sometimes, can't one?"

"I suppose, but I haven't had much time for art, ever since the real world kicked me in the butt a couple of years ago," Puss muttered as she unclasped the copper link belt and stepped out of her garment.

"I don't suppose you have and I'm sorry. You're quite beautiful you know, and I suspect that art and beauty are a part of you, or were once."

"Mother-two, I grew up in the school my tribe had on our reservation and from what Kris has told me, it was better than hers in all the humanities, and I know it was better than hers in mil-sci because my dad bossed it. Also, my Mother-one is a writer and a PhD and she taught me about all the arts and beauty, and a lot of other things as well."

"Oh dear, now I've upset you! I'm so thoughtless, please forgive me."

"No you haven't," Puss replied, her voice again muffled as she pulled on a sleep shirt from her pack. When her head emerged and the hem of the loose garment had fallen to her thighs she smiled, "Mother-one also taught me to be a lady, but an honest one. So you can believe me when I tell you you're very beautiful too and you ring true with a clear sweet note, just like your daughter.

"But are you really sure you'll be OK? That's a pretty deep dig I did on you," Puss asked with concern as she plopped down on one side of the bed.

"Thank you again but I'll be fine. I'll just sleep on my good side since I don't sleep on my stomach very well anyway," Helen chuckled, "And Hector doesn't like for me to do that either."

"Mother-two, I can see why, for both reasons as it were. Anyway, night-o," Puss murmured as she curled under the cover.

Helen signaled the light level down to a low glow from the wall panels, then lying with her face toward Puss she asked, "One more question, please. How did you and Kristina meet, since it's obvious that you two have teamed."

Puss sighed then turned to lie on her back and was quiet for several minutes. Helen waited, and sensed a tension rising in the young woman. She whispered, "Don't worry, dear. You don't have to tell me anything. You're welcome here just as you are, and however you want to be."

Puss cleared her throat, then softly answered, "Thank you, that is a nice thing to say and you sound exactly like Kris, when she picked me up like a sick kitten after the Chin pulled out, and brought me back from the edge..."

Then Puss continued in a monotone, "My Special Forces squad was on patrol when we ran into a reinforced company of Chin combat engineers. We got into a big firefight with them and my friend Billy took some hits in his leg. When our guys pulled back, I stayed with him to dress it, because he couldn't keep up. Then the Chin found us."

"They were going to kill us at first, but after they stripped me, they decided to keep me as a "company recreational device" and to keep Billy as my behavior insurance. They cut off one of his fingers right there to get my attention, and to show me what would happen if I didn't keep the troops happy."

"Does Kris know this?" Helen whispered.

"No. Not very much of it anyway, and not anything about Billy. No one does - until now."

"Are you sure you want to tell me this?"

"Are you sure you want to hear it?"

"Yes dear."

"OK," Puss continued in the same flat monotone, "They let me dress his hand then they put him in one of their cargo transporters and me in another one, and chained me by the ankle to a tie-down ring in the floor.

"They moved on until the unit bivouacked for the night, and after the troops had eaten their rice, the captain gave me to them for dessert. It was pretty bad then it got worse. Finally, I couldn't take them any more and started to fight back and I broke a couple of them real bad. Then the captain blew on a whistle and all the ones on me stopped and stood back, except for two. They grabbed a field hatchet and ran to the truck where Billy was.

"I heard him yell, then scream. They came back and gave me his big toe.

"They let me go to him and bandage him…"

Then Puss' iron control fractured and she sobbed, "He was so strong! They had cut the toe from his good foot so now he was major crippled, but he just smiled and thanked me, and loved me with his eyes as they led me back to the troops."

She continued in the same flat voice while Helen listened in frozen silence, "After that night, they always gave the whistle to who ever wanted some "recreation" from me and I obeyed them, because every day I saw them taking mess rations into the transporter where Billy was.

"After being real bad, it got over the top really bad. I will never forget the tinkly sound of that whistle when they dangled it in front of my face, before they told me what they wanted me to do next."

"A couple of weeks later some of them decided to laser my feet off because they said I really didn't need them for my current mission. But then a lieutenant stopped them from doing that, because he had a toe-suck fetish.

"Another lieutenant used to make me do all sorts of things until I would finally rebel. Then he would whip me until he splashed. I finally figured out that he only wanted me to resist so he could do his smack thing, so I started refusing to do the weird stuff he demanded, and just let him start whipping me right off. It was a lot easier that way.

"The worst thing was the war dogs they had with them for sniffers. They used to turn them on to me when they got bored."

"You mean that they made the dogs attack you?" Helen gasped.

"Well, in a manner of speakin' – yes…"

Helen considered Puss' words for a moment, and then her eyes blazed. "You mean…?"

"Yes," Puss replied in a careful and very fragile voice.

Helen gazed at the young woman on the bed next to her, so tense and rigid in the grip of her emotion. "You are very strong Marybell. Have you ever told anyone about this before?"

"No, never this much."

"Why do you tell me, now?"

"I don't know. Maybe it's time, and maybe you are the one who is strong enough to listen. But I really don't know... And I don't know why I am telling anyone about this anyway, because no one should know it dammit - not even me," Puss suddenly sobbed as her iron control finally cracked.

"Do you want me to hold you? Would that help?" Helen asked softly as she reached toward the young woman but then hesitated...

"I want to finish first," Puss gritted. "Things were like that for almost a month, except the company kept moving around. I didn't have a map obviously and they chained me in the transporter when they were traveling, but I looked out through a crack in the cover sometimes and from the sun I could tell they were mostly traveling in a circle. I think they were also dodging our patrols, because there was no more action.

"The company captain started acting funny too. He had his own comfort girl so he didn't bother with me at first, until she sneaked out one night and hanged herself from a hemlock tree. Then he used me for comfort and I figured out pretty quickie why she killed herself.

"Anyway, he started acting real nervous when he was around me after a couple of days and I felt that things were going to change somehow, from real bad to major bad. Then we bivouacked in the woods by one of their military roads one night, and at first light the next morning some of their heavy lifter transports roared in and landed on the highway.

"As soon as their doors opened, the Chin troops started tossing all of their equipment and weapons and scrambling to get into the planes.

"The back of the truck they kept me in happened to be open so I could see what was going on. After all of the scrambling confusion and lift-offs, I saw that the captain was standing by the door of the last air transport on the ground, and I saw him grab a grunt in the climb-on line that still carried his assault rifle.

"I watched the captain tell him something as he pointed to my truck. Then the trooper ran toward me and scrambled up into the back where I was.

"I was huddled back into a corner and when I looked at him, I remembered that whenever he came to me he had been clumsy and needed my help. I knew what he was coming to do now though, so I took a deep breath and jumped up and shouted "Ferk All You Chin Bastards!

"He aimed his `salt rifle at my chest and stared at me with a blank face for what felt like for ever. Then he moved the muzzle and fired two bursts to one side of me through the wall of the transporter. After he fired the captain started shouting and he dropped his `salt rifle on the floor and turned around to leave, then paused for a second. He shrugged and snatched the key to my shackle from where it hung on its hook where everyone could reach it except me.

"He didn't look at me when he tossed it at my feet as he jumped out of the transporter and ran for the plane."

Puss paused in her monotone recital then and covered her eyes with her hands for a moment, as she took a deep shuddering breath before she continued in the same monotonic whisper, "I unlocked my chain and grabbed his rifle, and peeked out of the transporter to see if they were really all gone. When I saw that they were, I jumped down and ran to Billy's truck..."

Then she sat up and turned to face Helen, "He wasn't there," she said in a very flat tone. "There was a pile of unopened ration packs – and a big stain of old dried blood on the floor in the corner where Billy had laid when I bandaged his toe.

"There were some hairs still stuck in the dried blood.

"They were blond hairs, and Billy was blond.

"They must have cut his throat for there to have been so much blood and they probably did it after the first couple of days, after they saw that I was going to be obedient.

"They must have dumped his body at night when the company was moving.

She paused then, and looked at Helen with dry eyes that at the same time showed all of the tragedy of the world. "We were on our last mission before we were due to rotate back out of the battle zone. Billy and I were going to take leave and get married..."

Helen said nothing but her face mirrored Puss' anguish as she held her arms out to the tense young woman. Puss hesitated, frozen in her agony for many heartbeats, then with a little sob she fell into Helen's embrace.

"You can cry now. Please let yourself cry. You must cry, it's the time to do it now... Please."

Puss nodded, and suddenly broke in to deep racking sobs that were almost silent and were muffled even more as she buried her face in Helen's bosom. Helen gently held her and stroked her head as Puss cried with powerful intensity for five long minutes.

Then she abruptly stopped sobbing and sighed, "Thank you Helen - for this and for being you. I will never forget what you have done for me tonight. Ever.

"But enough of this drippo crappo, where was I?" Puss asked with a hiss as she abruptly sat up and dried her eyes and nose on the hem of her sleep shirt.

"Oh yeah, I vented the hydrogen tank on Billy's truck and then used a bunch of incendiaries to burn it as the best funeral I could do for him. While I was watching it burn, two of the sniffer dogs the Chin had left behind showed up and sniffed me. I empted the rest of the clip into them and heaved their carcasses into Billy's fire as a final offering...

"After that, I grabbed some rations and ammo and boots and some clothes along with a med kit, which I really needed, and started heading east looking for our guys.

"I got hints of a unit in front of me two days later and I figured it was ours, I stripped because the Chin didn't use girls, to fight.

"It was our guys, and they collected me when I stepped out into their path with my hands up and took me back to their command post. Then they gave me some clothes and evacted me back to our home post at S'attl.

"Kris had the duty the day I got there so she was the officer who grilled me.

"After I was verified, we talked for a while and then she took me home with her. She treated me nice, so I stayed. That's all."

"Marybell, I'm going to echo you," Helen said in a soft voice. "Thank you for being you, I am glad that I know you..."

***

Chapter 14
The Garden

Boots woke at five in the morning as she had willed herself to do before allowing herself to relax into sleep the evening before. She lay with her face buried in the pillow until she became fully alert and remembered that she was Helen for the spy cams. She rolled onto her back and reshaped the breast padding in her mother's bra while still under the cover. Then she rose with a yawn and stretched, as she remembered Helen always did upon wakening.

There was light and the sound of the shower in the adjoining bath so she knew Hector was already up and preparing for the day. She reflected for a moment about all of her new feelings about her parents, and her new knowledge about their real natures. Then she thought about the act she and her father had put on for the survel cams the evening before.

"I'm sure glad they're on my side," she thought as she walked to her mother's wardrobe closet and spotted the Mexican costume after a moment's search.

Boots dropped the blue robe and dressed in the peasant blouse and skirt, and stepped into a pair of red woven leather sandals from her mother's shoe rack. She rummaged on the shelves over the garment racks until she pulled down a lace-trimmed white parasol then located the colorful native tote bag Helen had mentioned and slung it over her shoulder.

Boots inspected her image in the closet's mirror as she combed her hair with her fingers, taking care to protect Helen's artful streaking. She frowned at her reflection for a moment, before selecting an intricately woven red sash from another rack. She tied it around her waist and left the closet, and walked to the bathroom door. She called in to the steam filled space in a perfect imitation of Helen's voice,

"Good morning Dear, how did you sleep?"

"Real good, for what there was left of the night, dammit. But how do you feel this morning?" Hector responded over the sound of the shower. "Want to join me Poopsie?"

"Thank you, Darling, but I'll do mine later," Boots said, copying her mother's light voice. "I'm meeting some friends early this morning and we are going on a field trip so I can get some new ideas for landscapes. Did the girls stay downstairs last night? I want to see Kris before I go."

Hector chuckled, "Probably. They were pretty much in a mood to frolic when we left them, if you remember."

"I don't Dear, but don't you forget to give me a kiss before you leave,"

"Darlin' Helen, I'll never forget to do that, you kiss way too good..."

"You're sweet to say that dear," Boots replied with her mother's light laugh. "I'll be back early, so be sure and hurry home tonight," she called over her shoulder as she walked from the room into the hall and went down the stairway.

Boots found her mother standing in the vid room, with her sleep shirt pulled up and gently probing at her hip around the incision. "Good morning dear, how did you sleep?" Helen whispered, as she made a shush gesture and nodded toward the couch-bed where Puss was still curled under the cover.

"Like a baby rocked in her daddy's arms. How's your grievous wound?" Boots murmured as she retrieved the sketch case from her pack and slid it into the tote.

"A little sore, but there is no inflammation that I can feel so it's nothing. And by the way, I am very impressed with your friend Marybell."

"You talked with her?"

"Yes, but just a little girly talk about nothing much, you know how it is or then maybe you don't.

"Anyway "Mommy", let me go fix you some breakfast," Helen smiled as she shook her head, and caused her un-streaked black hair to fly about her face.

Boots glanced at the dress chrono on her wrist. "No time, I want to be ready when they come for me at oh-six-hundred."

Helen smiled, "All right, then you'll make yourself a quick road box if you'll hurry and come in the kitchen with me and give me a quick cooking lesson, "mother dearest"."

"I don't know where the stuff is, and we don't have much time," Boots hissed.

"Just watch where I tap my finger and then do what you already know how to do sweetheart," Helen whispered and she led her daughter into the kitchen.

Boots hesitated for a moment as they entered the room, then smiled, "Why don't you let me give you a quick cooking lesson Dear?"

"Thanks, Mom," Helen answered in Boots' voice as she rubbed her eyes and yawned, taking care to not raise her arms over her head.

"Of course Darling," Boots replied with Helen's lilting tones. "Now, you just stand beside me and watch what I do.

*

Boots was snapping the food box shut when Hector walked into the kitchen. He wore a jumpsuit that, while the uniformly gray color of the `Clave was precisely tailored of finely woven worsted with touches of crisp white linen showing at his neck and wrists. "I have to leave now sweetheart, I just wanted to say goodbye to you two."

"That's nice dear," Boots said in her mother's voice, "See you tonight."

"Yeah Dad," Helen growled in a good imitation of her daughter, "I'll see you after we get home from tha' party. You want to say by-de-by to Marybell before you go?"

"Sure, Daughter," Hector said with a twitch of a smile as he followed the two into the vid room.

Once they were in there, he first checked the decoy feed screen, then kissed Helen, and gently stroked her hip with the incision, "Take care of yourself, Partner, I'll come home early." He turned to his daughter. "Be very careful today Kris. Remember that what you are doing is important, but so are you!"

"I will, and thanks Dad, for everything," she whispered, with her heart suddenly showing in her eyes.

"Nada," he muttered gruffly as he took her by the shoulders and kissed her on the forehead. "See you tonight, OK? And by the way, "Helen", you look great in that girly outfit," he added with a grin as strode from the room.

Puss had wakened at their conversation, and now sat up with a yawn and a stretch. Then she looked at Boots and blinked, "Hey Mother Two, when you say you're puttin' her in something femmey you really mean it don't you!"

"Ah So! Little girl make big joke maybe" Boots frowned theatrically. "Anyway Buddy, just what tha ferk are you doing today while I'm off saving the damn world?"

"Getting stuff for us tonight, from Sergeant Bill as well as some other places, and calling in a favor from one of your old friends."

"Which one of my many?" Boots grinned.

"The one you told me about. You called her "Lulu the Lab Rat", remember?"

"OK, what favor?"

"Just a simple time check."

"You're getting' cryptic on me - I might have to punish you," Boots chuckled. Then she paused and her face changed, "Some times Lulu could be funny when I knew her before, but she might be not too much funny now, so Trooper Alert."

"Ja Boss, but to continue answering your main question, O Cruel Captain - as soon as you get gone I'm grabbing more pad time, OK?"

"Well, say hi to Sergeant Bill for me, but remember like Dad just said, the mission is important, but you are too, So be careful today Buddy. Please."

Puss yawned then snuggled back under the cover, "Sure-sure, but now let your smarter part put her final touches on you so you can get tha' ferk out of my sleep space, OK?"

"Hold still dear and let me fix your middle," Helen smiled as she re-tucked and straightened Boots' blouse and skirt. Then she tied the red sash around her daughter's waist in a more graceful fashion as Boots glowered, and kicked at the bed, where Puss smothered a giggle under the cover, almost.

"Take a look now Dear, and try to remember to act like you look when you go out and about..."

Boots stepped into the bathroom and glared at her image in the mirror. Then she nodded to Helen as she returned and collected her things, "Thanks Mother, you do good work. I'll be sure and give your name to the next perverted rebel I run into who wants to look like a girl."

"Please, Dear. Only one of you at a time," Helen called after her as Boots stalked out of the room into the hall.

*

The green military sedan stopped at the curb when the sun was just showing above the rim of the Cascade Mountains to the east and the rain-washed sky was clear and newly bright. Waldo hopped from the driver's seat and trotted toward Boots' parent's row house, and was lifting his foot to mount the stoop when the door opened and Boots stepped out.

"Well, some people in my new outfit can keep a schedule anyway," Boots grinned as she stood before him, clothed like he had never seen her before.

Waldo's eyes widened as he took in her exposed shoulders and her bare legs below her skirt, and her sandals - and the parasol she carried. The tough sergeant blinked then shook his head has if he had just taken a body blow.

"What's the matter Waldo, do I look that bad?" Boots grinned.

"Hell no, Ma'am!" He gulped, "You look good... You look Girl!" he sputtered in the same confused voice as he had at Rick's the night before.

"Thank you friend you're very perceptive, and that's the plan."

"Good plan. Now let's move," Mack snapped through his window from the back seat of the sedan.

Waldo hurried to open the rear door, and averted his eyes as Boots flashed quite a lot of leg while she scrambled in. Then he rushed back to the driver's seat and powered the sedan, and waited for orders.

"I sure hope I can get the hang of this damn thing," Boots muttered as she pulled her skirt down and favoring her sore hip, settled into the seat. "I haven't worn a dress for twenty years, and it feels funny. Breezy even."

"You look just right for today even if slightly older, and somewhat fuller," Mack said dryly as he glanced at her hair and her new bust line. "Anyway, what's in the bag and the box, Ma'am? And why the umbrella?"

Boots replied in a bland tone, "The umbrella is part of my special super shielded com set for use in Olympia, General and also, my public name is Helen for this visit."

Then she acknowledged the subtle authority of his well-fitted civilian jump suit by brushing her fingers over his sleeve. "You look pretty right for today too Mack. Do you use the same tailor as my Dad?" She smiled at his sardonic nod, "Good. Now ask me what's in this box again."

"I'll bite. What?"

"You both get to bite real good guys. Mother sent us therms of excellent coffee and some butter-rolls too so we wouldn't too flat to put up a good fight later on if we have to," she announced as she opened the food container and passed an insulated mug over the front seat to Waldo.

"Ma'am, I'm startin' to like your outfit already and I've only been in it for twelve hours," he said over his shoulder as he accepted the mug. Then he opened it and simultaneously sipped the coffee while with he steered the vehicle away from the curb and on down the street, in relatively good repair for S'attl because of the status of her parent's neighborhood.

"Thank your mother for us both," Mack added as he accepted a mug and a roll, "Now let me tell you about Regina Drake."

"First, you tell me how good her eyes are."

"Better than mine, why?"

"You'll see when we get there. Now brief me please," she ordered in a crisp tone and by so doing, took command of the mission.

*

During the long, difficult drive south out of S'attl toward Olympia as the sedan lurched over the rough surface of roads that were once smooth Boots listened to Mack's briefing on Regina Drake. She focused intently on his words and asked probing questions that at first irritated him, because of her interruptions. But then with an effort he checked his instinct to control the conversation, and deferred to Boots' lead as he noted the direction of her inquiries.

When he had satisfied her as best he could about the woman's character and history -and his best was very good, Boots lapsed into silence and settled back in deep thought as Waldo drove them through what had once been the broad suburban areas around the one-time city of Seattle.

Mack respected Boots' silence and waited for any other questions she might have for several minutes. Then while he remained alert to her with part of his mind, he let himself gaze out at the landscape they were traveling through, and remembered its history with grim sadness.

*

The Chin had struck Olympia with tactical neutron warheads to western states as they had the other cities on the beginning of the war in 2244, but since they needed immediate use of Seattle and its large harbor, rare on the Pacific coast, their master war plan called for taking that city by conventional means. The Chin supreme command ordered that this be done by their assault troops swiftly over-running US forces in the area, forces they assumed would be weakened and demoralized by the massiveness and brutality of their initial attack.

*

Mack stared grimly out the window and contemplated the cleared vast expenses of ground where the suburbs of Seattle had sprawled. The ground was being hand-cultivated today by thousands of workers stooping in the soy fields that had replaced the suburbs, either by default or design.

Neither Boots nor Waldo gave the fields or the workers a second glance however, since they were too young to know of this land being used in for any other purpose.

He thought, "The damn 'clave governments are real good at handing out hoes to the people, but damn slack about giving them any hope." Then he remembered when he was a new lieutenant just out of his academy in a time when young officers received a more leisurely education before they entered the world.

His training had been longer than that of the war-children like Boots, who had not been born when the media-addicted country he had sworn to defend was attacked two months after he had been commissioned. But the compressed and focused officer training Boots and others had received as the war dragged on had proved quite effective, he reflected.

"And very damn effective, when there's natural talent in the equation," he thought as he glanced at Boots' profile.

*

As soon as all of their first strike missiles had impacted, gigantic Chin submarines surfaced at carefully chosen landing sites all up and down the coast of the area they claimed, and each off-loaded assault troops with their equipment - including those units assigned to take Seattle by a conventional frontal assault from its assumedly ineffective defenders.

However, this assumption by the Chin central command was found to be flawed when their field commanders attacked the Americans in Seattle.

The ensuing battles destroyed much of the city's suburban surrounding infrastructure, either as the attackers took it out, or as its defenders razed it to create clear-fire zones. The Chin stubbornly refused to use tactical nuclear weapons during their siege of Seattle however, because they wanted the area to be immediately useful after they took, and to save the face of their war planners.

The Americans tactical used only nukes sparingly, and only on distant Chin logistics complexes because they intended to reclaim their land, and so wanted to keep it livable. The conflict between the two forces was thus very conventional, but very deadly because of modern weapons, such as the military laser.

*

Boots finally shifted her position and cleared her throat, "Actually Mack, I've never been to Olympia. How will we get in to see her?"

"Through the front door," He said with a cold smile, "With attitude. The goons guarding her know better than to question someone dressed like me, or you and drives up in a car like this."

Boots nodded, "Good. But what about the locator bug that's always in a car like this?"

"Remember what Bobby said last night, we are riding in one that has multiple personalities, and does not repeat everything it hears."

"Good again, how does that work?"

"Tell her all of it now, Waldo or she'll keep nibbling away at us until she knows every damn detail anyway," Mack ordered with a chuckle.

"Yes, Sir!" Waldo replied as he steered the sedan over the neglected pavement of the highway, "Ma'am, we mole into the maintenance logs of all their staff cars and see which ones they take in for repair, and that list is way big anymore, OK? Then whenever we are out in this one and it is queried, the new ID unit we made for it answers with a signature from on that list. Sneaky, what?"

"Yes, and cute too. But what about its locator responder if the Governors want to know where this buggy is?"

"Gov gets his answer from back at the Academy whenever we go out to have fun, because this one has a twin squealer on duty, in a locked garage. We also got squealers for it hidden in some other interesting' places too," Waldo said with a chuckle as he maneuvered the sedan around a small crater.

"We can control the squealers from this car here if we need to, as well as from Bobby's place, or from Rick's if we want to make things really fakey. It also has a decoy vid feed so if they click on that bug, all they get is pic of an empty car sitting in a garage."

"You have had this kind of decoy feed rigged in Bobby's cars for a long time, haven't you? Even way back when I graduated from the Academy and as I recall, you used it then to feed them a pretty interesting vid you created," Boots murmured.

The back of Waldo's neck reddened as he sputtered, "I just did what Bobby said , and made it lively so's they wouldn't wonder why he wanted to park, and just talk uninterrupted with you on the way to your first post."

302

"Well you made it pretty lively all right. Bobby gave me the chip when he dropped me off at the training depot. He told me I could either look at it or chop it, so I did both, in that order," Boots said with a grin. "Friend, did you ever think about a second career, like writing X-vids for the Network?"

Waldo's only response was to gulp and hunch down in his seat. Mack stayed silent, but smiled at Boots' friendly teasing of Waldo.

"Anyway, it looks like you got our immediate survel problems covered pretty well, and that's good. Now see if you can drive smooth for a bit so I can make some notes," She said as she pulled her gray sketch box from the Mexican tote bag and flipped it open on her knee.

"Yes Ma'am!" Waldo replied with relief as he slowed the sedan and concentrated on navigating over the broken road.

Boots moved on the seat and curled one leg under her, both to favor her hip and to steady the box. She tugged at her skirt for a moment as she tried to cover her thigh then with an impatient shrug, she opened the pad. She flipped past the pages with Bila's improbable drawings and two more blank ones as well before she unclipped a pencil and began to write.

Mack noted that her sketch box was Army issue and that its surface was worn from much use. He knew that these boxes were only issued to those who had talent in doing rapid sketches, an archaic skill the Special Forces had found to be quite useful during a war in which electronically transmitted images could be intercepted, and manipulated by the other side.

Mack thought, "She's good at everything else, so if they issued her that box this could be interesting," but remained silent in respect of her concentration. He also reined in his curiosity, except for a single flick of his eyes toward the sheet upon which she was printing. He saw that she was writing short, numbered paragraphs and so creating a page of information that could be absorbed, and understood with a brief glance.

"Looks mighty like a battle plan to me," he thought as he turned his eyes away, "But it's hers, not mine." He had taught himself years ago to read copy which was upside-down. He did not watch Boots' writing now however, because he also learned to value his personal honor above all else.

*

"Thanks, Mack. I appreciate your courtesy, and tact," Boots murmured as she finished writing and closed the pad and the sketch box. "It really does look like we will be able to work together."

He turned and met her knowing gaze with a stare. Then he relaxed and said with a smile, "Ma'am, I know that you will tell me what I need to know whenever it's time for me to know it."

"Thanks again Mack, but this time for your vote of trust," Boots said in a low voice as she held his eyes for a moment longer. Then she winked at him and called out to Waldo, "Hey friend, are you looking for a place to ferkin' picnic on this damn road, or is your H-tank going empty? Anyway, how 'bout making this heap hop forward, OK?"

"Yes Ma'am!"

*

Waldo braked the sedan to a stop at the gate into the capitol complex in Olympia. It was now closed to protect its archives and library, "For the Good of the People" as the faded and peeling signs attached to the wire fence surrounding it proclaimed.

There was no other identifying signage on the high fence that surrounded the area of the government buildings, and Boots and Mack saw that all the buildings appeared to be vacant as Waldo had driven along the line of razor wire toward the entry. They also saw that all titles cut into the stone of their facades had been draped with gray canvass.

Waldo opened his window as a dull-eyed person in a rumpled black jumpsuit stepped out of a rusting metal guard shack beside the gate.

"This place is closed. Who are you and what're you doing here?" the man growled.

"This is General McAuliffe, and he is here to see Madam Drake," Waldo snapped. "Who are you?"

"Yes," Mack added as he lowered his window and stared at the guard. "Just what Is your name, and your number?"

The guard's eyes widened as he looked at the green military sedan and its tough driver in Army uniform, and then at the authority on the face of the richly-dressed civilian in the back seat.

His slow synapses finally fired, and he stepped back and nervously waved them on through with a sloppy salute, then stepped back in the shack then and absently glanced at the registration number that appeared on the vehicle ID screen after the sedan passed through the gate, but as he sat and turned back to the Network vid on his display again, he didn't notice that the number was different from the one on the car's bumper.

*

The next guard boredly waved them through a second gate in the inner fence surrounding the old executive mansion, now shuttered and vacant. Waldo parked the sedan on the crumbling pavement of the circular drive before it and Mack stepped out.

He stood with his hands clasped behind his back as he announced in a tone that made the gate functionary come awake, "We are here to visit Regina Drake, do you have any questions for us to answer?"

"N-no Sir..."

"Good," Mack growled as he turned and walked around the car to open Boot's door and gallantly hand her out.

The guard nervously gestured toward the extensive grounds of the mansion beyond a high wire fence and waved the two through its narrow personnel gate.

Mack and Boots walked into the overgrown space, then Waldo climbed out of the driver's seat and stretched. He leaned nonchalantly against the sedan's front fender and crossed his arms and stared at the guard in stony silence until the man dropped his eyes and shambled back to his guard shack.

*

Boots and Mack strolled through the overgrown grounds until she paused before a dead snag, all that was all that was left of a stately shade tree. It had sprouted sizeable saplings from its roots which had not been affected by the neutron bomb blasts however. Boots also saw that spring flowers were blooming in a few newly cultivated beds around the overgrown lawn.

"Looks like there's some life here after all," she muttered. Then she continued, "But what's that old bit about the Tree of Liberty?"

"Watering it sometimes can be painful as I recall," Mack said, then he led her toward a small cottage at back of the compound which was surrounded with tall shrubbery.

They were approaching a trellis gateway in the hedge when a "Woof" sounded, and a large yellow Labrador bounded out of the opening.

"Stand Kayak!" a voice called and a woman stepped out of the hedge and stood before them, brandishing a pair of old-style hedge clippers. She had long hair that once was auburn but was now mostly white and she wore a worn green coverall that had dirt-stained knees. She was short and sturdy and while her face had started to wrinkle with age, her clear brown eyes were lively and bright.

"Since you have been so nice to come to call and give me an excuse to put this frightful tool down for a while, General," the woman said as she looked sternly at Mack, "You may approach the throne and give me a kiss."

Mack and Regina greeted each other with a formal embrace and ritual air-kisses, then the woman turned with a smile and gestured through the gate, "Come into the garden and sit with me, I have lemonade and extra glasses."

At the woman's gesture of friendship, the dog moved forward, and after a sniff, recognized Mack with a lick and a whine. It then inspected Boots for a moment before turning back to its master.

The two followed the woman and her dog into a spacious lawn surrounded on three sides by tall hedges of boxwood that backed up to a small cottage. The space inside was filled with flowerbeds laid out in formal precision, and wooden benches stood within a grassy plot in the middle of the beds. A tray with a thermos pitcher and six tall glasses stood on a side table.

"I always set extra places, just in case company drops by," She smiled as she dropped the clippers on the grass, stripped off her gardening gloves and signaled for Kayak to sit.

"I don't loose hope easily."

"Governor Drake, it is my pleasure to present Helen Hamier to you. She is another old friend, and I think she shares some of your interests," Mack said in a quiet voice.

"I am very glad to meet you, Helen and please call me Regina. But you aren't old enough to be his old friend young lady, and I certainly am not the Lieutenant Governor any more.

"Would you like some lemonade?"

"Mack and I first met each other way back when I really was young, and according to Article III, Section 3, you still are.

"And yes, I would love a glass," Boots murmured with a crooked smile.

Regina started - then stared at Boots for second before she sat on one of the weathered redwood benches and patted the seat beside her.

"Come sit here next to me and tell me about your self. Mack, would you be so kind as to pour for us all please?"

"Delighted to, Ma'am."

"Mack told me that you liked to garden, but he really didn't tell me how beautiful it would be. Do you mind if I make a few drawings of your flowers?" Boots murmured as she brought out her sketch box.

"Dear me no, but this little place is not nearly in the shape I would like it to be, and there'll be much more in flower later in the year."

"I love your spring blooms, but perhaps Mack will bring me again to see them when they are in their full summer bloom, if you wouldn't mind."

"I love company and I don't get enough of it, so if he doesn't bring you back I'll break out of here and fetch you myself. But for now, what would you like to draw?"

"I like the colors of that lilac over there so I'll see if I can mess it up with my scribbling," Boots said as she opened her box and flipped to the first blank page on the pad.

"Mack, would you mind terribly if I asked you to hold my parasol over us? The sun is glaring on my paper and I am afraid I won't get the colors right," Boots asked in an innocent voice as she met his eye, and gave him the slightest of nods.

"Glad to Helen," he replied with a cherry nonchalance that matched hers and a quick nod of his own.

Regina saw the interplay between the two, then after a moment she nodded herself and said, "Mack, you always are the perfect gentleman."

"Thank you for the kind words Regina, but sometimes it is very easy to be one in the right company," he said as he opened the parasol, and positioned it so that Boots' lap and sketchpad were shielded from the bright sunlight.

The fact that her pad was also shielded from the spy cams mounted in the tree snags and under the eaves of the cottage, as well as from the surveillance satellites overhead was not lost on Regina.

Boots quickly sketched the lilac bush in full flower, using her colored pencils to bring it to life on the page as Regina looked on. When she finished the picture, Boots tore it from the pad and handed it to Regina.

"You are very, very talented Helen. May I keep it?"

"Of course, I did it for you. But it's not my best. Shall I do another?"

"Yes, please do. I am fascinated by how quickly you work."

Boots took a sip of lemonade and began sketching the flowerbed beside the lilac, as Regina casually placed the first sketch on the side table where it was in full view of all the watching lenses.

Boots finished capturing the flowers in the bed in an impressionistic riot of color on the page and offered the whole pad to Regina, instead of tearing out the sketch.

Regina shook her head, "Mack, this lady is a significant talent isn't she?"

"I've known that for some time, and I have been proud to watch her develop it over the years. She also worked on a piece as we were driving over. If you would care to look at it turn the page."

"It's only an outline so far and needs to be more detailed for it to have the effect I want," Boots murmured as she looked at Regina with cautious eyes.

The older woman gave Boots a second piercing glance, then carefully keeping the pad in the shade of the lacy white parasol Mack held above them, lifted the sheet with its rendering of her flower bed.

When she saw Boots' action plan for the Restoration neatly printed on the next page and recognized what she was seeing, Regina gasped then she glanced up at her old friend. At Mack's nod of approval, she read the outline, and then again more slowly while Boots and Mack waited in silence.

Regina finally tapped the paper where Boots had cited Articles III and X of the Washington State Constitution.

"You have done your background work very well and I think your overall outline looks promising. I am also beginning to recall that I have heard about your earlier works as well, "Helen".

"Correct me if I'm wrong Mack, but I believe I've been told that whatever this woman has done before was always executed with a high level of competence."

"I can confirm that her work has been quite good in the past and gives every promise of becoming brilliant now, and very soon."

"Helen", do you really think you can complete this picture?" Regina then asked in a tone that mixed authority with hope. "It's a very difficult subject and one that hasn't been attempted before to my knowledge. If I help you, I am like that legendary Kentuckian, Daniel Boone. I only have one shot in my rifle so I must use it with a very careful aim."

Boots gazed at Regina for a long moment then she answered, "Yes. I can. One good shot from you is all that it will take to complete this picture. I will need some more help to mount and display the canvass though, but I already have some very competent volunteers."

"Are you helping her, Mack?"

"Absolutely! Wouldn't miss this exhibition for the world."

"Well then, perhaps I can help as well, by providing support here," Regina said as she tapped her finger on Boots' paragraph about the legal issues.

"Thank you, Ma'am. Your help will make the picture complete.

"When we have it ready to unveil we will bring it back to you for the party.

"Would you like to keep the flower bed sketch as well?" She then asked as she held out her hand for the pad.

Regina took one last, long look at Boots' battle plan before carefully tearing the flowerbed sketch free. "Amazing how good art can enrich one's life, isn't it?" she murmured as she casually laid the sketch on the table in open view next to the first one.

"Yes it is. And thank you Mack, for your gallant duty with the parasol," Boots said. "I'm glad that none of your friends happened by to see you holding my lacey accessory."

"If one is in the Highlands of Scotland and meets a man wearing a skirt, wise ones know to leave him alone."

"Many also have, unfortunately for themselves attained that same level of wisdom about me, when I hold a parasol for ladies," Mack said with a with a dry sniff as he closed it and took his seat. "Those who haven't yet are doomed to learn..."

"But now I propose a toast with Regina's excellent lemonade, "To what comes next!"

"Hear, Hear!" the two women respond gaily and almost in unison. Then after performing their light-hearted ritual for the benefit of the hidden microphones and cams, the three lounged on the benches and chatted innocently for another half hour, until Mack and Boots excused themselves to return to S'attl.

"Thank you Ma'am, we will keep you informed of our progress on making the picture come to life," Boots murmured as she took Regina's hand and squeezed in farewell at the trellis gate in the hedge.

"Good. I will start looking in my closet for party clothes. When you come back, I hope you will give me time to dress properly."

"Absolutely Governor, this party can't start without you," Mack said in a casual tone, but with a sincere gaze, and Boots mouthed, "Soon," as she bent to scratch Kayak's ears.

Then Boots stood, and she and Mack left without another word.

*

"Thank you Mack you spoke true last night and I appreciate it," Boots said when they settled into the seat of the sedan and Waldo steered it out through the gates.

309

"I am also really impressed that Regina is a good gardener."

"Thank you Ma'am, but why so?"

"Gardeners are decision-makers, and good gardeners can be quite ruthless when they need to be."

Mack chuckled, "I had a maiden aunt who was very much the gardener, and you're right. She was a ruthless old biddy with a whim of iron when it came to her garden, and her family. Interesting that you recognize this trait though."

"That's my job, but because you did speak true about her and took me to meet her, it's now going to be show time damn soon isn't it?"

"Yes Ma'am," he responded with a straight face, almost.

"You're just about as good at covert manipulations as Marybell aren't you?"

"I have to doubt that Ma'am. She seems to be the best at many things. But what comes next?"

"Next is me wondering if I can actually do what you all need and hope for. What happens if I fail you?" Boots asked in a whisper, her face suddenly solemn.

"What happens if we don't follow you?" Mack replied in a soft voice. "Slow death for us. What happens if we do follow you? A fast death maybe - but maybe we will be free again. That's an easy choice for all of us. So don't waver, because you have an ultimate weapon you can always depend upon, and use."

"What's that?"

"Us, and our belief in you."

Boots bowed her head and breathed deeply for several seconds then she raised her face and smiled at Mack, and continued as if they hadn't had spoken.

"After the Gala this evening, we need go back and secure the communications asset I mentioned last night. Marybell and I must get to a drop point in BC without undue notice tomorrow.

"Then after we are on-site with the asset, I want a reinforced heavy weapons squad to para-motor in as soon as you can organize it. They will need extended duty rations and gear for a month, and should bring several long flyswatters with them as well.

"I also want them to bring a bunch of extra capacitors and two of the new high-efficiency chargers. There's an H source at the site, but it really could use an added splash of super bugs.

"I want Rick's best com-spert to come with them too, with whatever he needs to hook the asset up to your universal net.

"I will provide coordinates and the homing audio signal for their landing when you advise me of their deployment over a secure comset you will get for Marybell and I to take with us.

"And finally," Boots grinned, "I want the squad medic to carry a complete birthing med-kit, with both pink and blue baby blankets. Any questions?"

"What will the audio signal be?" Mack asked, not bothering to write notes as he memorized Boot's rapid-fire instructions.

"You heard it last night. Is there anything else?"

"No, Ma'am," Mack replied, grinning like a skull, again.

Boots nodded with the same battle smile. Then she said to Waldo in the front seat, "Sergeant, we got to get back in `S'attl. What are you going to do about it friend?"

"Hang on Missy - S'attl coming right up!" he answered as he accelerated to the maximum feasible speed over the almost ruined highway.

Boots grunted while bracing herself and her tender hip against the swaying and jolting of the sedan, "Just because he slammed my butt on the floor bucho times when I was young, does this mean he can still treat me like this now?"

"Yep," both men replied, almost in unison.

*

Puss yawned and stretched, and hopped from the bed to her feet in one bound. She stretched again then smiled at Helen. The woman was across the room at her easel, sitting half-perched on a tall stool while she was sketching on a canvass.

"Mornin' Mother-two. How's your bottom feel, and is there anything I can do for you?"

"My bottom is fine. Don't fret yourself about a big thing like that. But after you shower, would you mind posing for me for a little bit before you go out?"

"Glad to, but what are you doing?" Puss asked as she paused at the bathroom door and looked over Helen's shoulder at her roughly blocked sketch.

"I was fascinated by the contrast in you last night, between the soft femmey you showed at first, and then the strong way you handled yourself when you relaxed. I want to see if I can catch that." "Silly, aren't I?" Helen

311

finished with a light laugh.

"Anyone who can do Kris like you did," Puss said as she pointed to the charcoal on the wall, "Is not silly. I would be honored, and your bottom isn't big, Ma'am. It's real nice. What do you want me to do?"

"Go shower first, and I'll tell you when you come out."

*

Puss stepped out of the bathroom toweling her hair, "Ready, Ma'am."

"Thank you, dear. Could you please slip into what you had on last night and just sit for a few minutes like you were then, with your glass and cigar?"

"Sure, all though it's sorta' early in the day for whiskey - in peacetime anyway," Puss grinned as she stepped into her satin jumpsuit and pulled it up to her waist.

"Would you also do a portrait sketch of me when you finish, one I can send it to my folks?"

"Of course Dear, I would love to try but I'm not very good."

"Mother-two, don't cow flop me," Puss grinned as she sat where she had the previous evening and flourished her empty glass and a cold cigar butt. "You're way over the top good."

"Thank you, dear now hold it right as you are. Good, that's exactly what I want," Helen murmured absently, as she peered with frowning concentration at Puss for a moment then began sketching rapidly.

She stepped back after five minutes and inspected her work with critical eyes, then nodded. "You may stand down now dear, as you mil-types say."

Puss moved to Helen's side. "Hey Mother-two, you're making me way too pretty,"

"No Dear, I am just capturing what I see. Now what kind of portrait do you want for your parents?"

"Just a head, looking like this," Then Puss braced to attention and her eyes became as green ice and her whole face suddenly projected a grimness that made Helen gasp.

"You're sure? Do you want to show this part of you to your parents?"

"Yes. They will understand and appreciate it, if you show me wearing what I'll put on for it."

Helen stared at Puss for a moment then she whispered, "I learned something of your strength last night, but now I see all of it. I just hope I can capture the force or whatever it is in you that you are showing me now."

Puss relaxed and smiled, "Hey Mommy Two, I'm just a simple out-of-work Injun ex-ground grunt. That's all."

Helen replied with a dry sniff, "Marybell, you're about as simple as a sunrise, and just about as awesome. So to use your crude street expression, don't you cow flop me. Now go put on what ever you want to wear and give me that look again."

Puss stepped into the bath for a moment and returning said, "It doesn't matter what I am wearing, all I want you to get is my face."

Then she displayed the real strength of her inner self again while Helen intently absorbed her face for many heartbeats, until she set a blank sheet in place and began sketching.

Fifteen minutes later Helen sighed, "I think I have it. Good enough to start anyway. I must do this one first so I can clear your face and eyes out of my mind. Until I do that I won't be able to finish the other one. I can see why you and Kristina do so well together though. You both have the same core of steel."

"Hey Mother-two, I'm just a sneaky little injun. Kris is brilliant," Puss murmured as she stepped back into the bath for a moment to clean her face. Then she pulled her baggy `Clave coverall from her pack and changed into it. She announced as she wrapped her gray clave raincoat around her, "I'll be back in two or three hours. Are you really sure your incision is OK?"

"You're sweet to ask dear, as well as awesome. I'll be fine."

*

Puss left the row house at a brisk pace along the sidewalk until she turned a corner and approached the main road that fronted the privileged area where Boots' parents lived. She had noted the route to their place as Waldo had driven them from Rick's the previous evening, so she knew her location now, and her destination.

When she rounded the corner, Puss assumed the slouching posture and scuffing pace of the `clave-dwellers, and lowered her eyes as she pulled her hood up over her head when the late morning rain cloud drifted across `S'attl, and began spattering her with the fat drops of its half-hearted morning shower.

Any pedestrians on the crumbling sidewalks who were too distant from a transporter stop were suspect if they were in an area of privilege like the one Puss had just left, so she shambled to the nearest transport pickup point and merged into the short queue of gray-clad figures already there.

Puss again held back from the group's stumbling surge toward the rusting vehicle when the transporter finally appeared and creaked to a stop in the middle of the street. She took a place on the outside platform instead as it lurched into motion.

Puss rode the transporter to the transfer point at the blank-windowed City Building, then caught another of the lumbering vehicles that was routed toward the older city and what was once the waterfront.

Puss ignored the warnings on the vehicles did all young `clave dwellers, and stepped down from the platform while the transporter rolled down a street near the heart of `S'attl. She took several quick steps to maintain her balance then turned and slouched toward a three-story building in the middle of the block.

It was built with the institutional yellow brick of three centuries ago which proclaimed it a governmental building. It was ill maintained now, and serious cracks were apparent in the masonry of its walls. The legend cut in the stone lintel over its main entryway read, "Seattle Public Health Department".

A small plastic sign has been bolted onto one side of the stone pilasters framing the entryway. It read:

FORENSICS LABORATORY.

RESTRICTED SPACE.

GOVERNOR'S PERMIT REQUIRED FOR ENTRY.

Puss paused for a moment and frowned, then noted that the heavy glass doors into the lobby were slightly ajar, and that their locks were battered and rusting. She pushed the door open and stepped in, then halted when a hoarse female voice whined, "Help a friend, will ya'?"

Puss turned and saw a woman sitting on the stained terrazzo floor of the lobby. She was surrounded by bundles and bags.

"A dispo," Puss thought. "The Govs booted her out on to the street, and pretty far back too." She looked at the woman's weather-beaten complexion but she noted the woman's faded beauty and a certain robustness in her arms and shoulders.

"You look like you could still help yourself some if you wanted to," Puss said as she stood smiling down at the woman.

"Yeah I could, if I hadn't worked for Boss Rat…"

"You worked for the Rat?"

"Yeah, and I was pretty good too - 'till they pushed me to a place I just couldn't go. So they de-listed me," the woman muttered.

Puss' eyes widened as she realized that the woman's refusal to perform some extreme act for the Network's cams had opened her to the ultimate sanction in the 'Clave. The Network had used its influence to have her identity canceled, and so removed from all lists authorizing even basic food and shelter for the woman.

Whereas displacement merely canceled one's allocation to private quarters, the woman sitting on the floor before her did not officially exist, and so was reduced to scavenging her life from the alleys and other dark places of S'attl.

"Hey friend, will this help?" Puss smiled as she tossed the woman a small-denomination bearer chip.

The woman snatched it out of the air and inspected it, then smiled tremulously, "It sure will friend, thanks mucho!"

"Nada," Puss said as she read the faded building directory in the hall, "Glad I could help." Then she bounded up the stairs next to the inoperative elevator.

*

Puss paused at the third floor and removed her raincoat and dropped it on the floor. She assumed her usual air of authority and strode down the musty hall to the frosted glass door marked "Forensics Spectrographic Laboratory".

She took a stance before it and rapped imperiously, knowing that in all likelihood the door would be opened after she was inspected. And indeed it was a moment later by a short wide-shouldered young woman wearing a white lab coat, who stood staring at Puss.

"Yes?"

"Lulu?"

"Yes. Who're you?"

"Kris told me that you could maybe give me some info. I'm Marybell."

"So you're Captain Cook's little friend," Lulu said after staring at her for a moment longer. "I've heard about you, I think," she continued with a slight smile, and wary eyes.

"What do you want?"

"Just a little carbon 14 date on an artifact we picked up out in the woods a couple of days ago, that's all."

"That's all? Like I do them every day? Like I should drop everything?"

"Well," Puss smiled in her most winning manner, "Kris did say that you are the best mass-spec gun in the West. This sample is a surprise for her."

"And I'm supposed to still dance around on one toe any time she wants, after all these years – and what she did to me?"

"I do that now for her," Puss said quietly. "Can you do the test by tomorrow?"

The woman glared for a moment then she shrugged. "Oh, come on in dammit. Let's see what you've got. Maybe I'll suck in her bait one more time after all," Lulu said tonelessly.

Then as Puss walked past her into the lab an expression of pain, and something else flashed briefly in the woman's eyes as she closed the door. But her face was wooden again when she turned back to Puss.

"Lucky I'm not busy. What do you have that's so damn important anyway?"

Puss removed a small plastic envelop from her pocket and placed it on the surface of the white laboratory counter in the cramped room. It contained four short pieces of brown leather thong.

Lulu poked the envelope with her finger, "This looks fresh. Why do you want a test?"

"Kris has made a bet with a guy about it, and you know how competitive she can be," Puss grinned.

"Yeah, don't I? But who's the guy?" Lulu asked with a frown.

"An old friend of hers, a fellow named William. He's from Ockham."

"Never heard of him, or that place either. Anyway, lucky for you I've got an accelerator for this gun as well as a chromatograph so I can shoot it for you," Lulu muttered in a grumpy tone as she waved toward the complex instrumentation on the bench.

Then she continued as her professional interest was caught, and she involved herself in the problem, "You have enough sample here, barely. But if it has recent contamination on the surface, the isotope ratio could be thrown off. And I won't have time to decon the surface and still do a straight burn if you want results tomorrow,"

"How much off?"

Lulu peered closely at the scraps in the plastic envelope. "Well, the specimens are pretty thick so the surface area to mass ratio isn't too unfavorable. So maybe there'll be a 10% uncertainty factor to the date, if it's not too far back. Can you cope with that much slop?"

"Hey Lulu, all we need is to fire one round somewhere down range. After that Kris can zero in all the rest of her shots however she wants," Puss smiled, while at the same time considering this woman, whose aura was somehow beginning to trouble her.

"OK, you talked me into it. Come back in the morning and I'll have something waiting for you."

"Thanks."

*

"See you back here about 1600 hours?" Boots asked Waldo as he pulled to a stop before her parent's home.

"Sure will. And I'll wait outside the Rat's Nest in lurk mode until you come back out, or we have to go in to get you," he replied with ice in his voice. "But we'll be in a different buggy."

"And there will be more force with him, just in case," Mack added. "Waldo can whistle them up as appropriate, but the best short-term outcome is for you two to extricate yourselves as peacefully as possible. So be very, very careful tonight Kris."

"Don't worry Mack, this is not a frivolous mission, and it's sure as hell not a crash-and-burn! I've got too many miles to go with you guys before we reach the town-o," Boots said in a quiet tone as Waldo started to open his door and hand her out.

"Waldo, Pu-lease!" Boots grinned, "I'd rather do it myself!" as she scrambled from the rear seat.

"Now you guys get gone till tomorrow," she ordered through the open window.

Mack chuckled as Waldo abruptly closed his door while the back of his neck turned red, again.

Boots remembered to walk as Helen would toward the stoop of her parent's home while the sedan pulled away from the curb. She punched in the door combination and called, "Kris, I'm home," in her mother's light tone.

"Well, 'bout time!" Helen growled from the door of the vid room. She was still clad in Boots' baggy sleep shirt. "I figgered you'd fallen off your sketch pad and got lost out there."

Boots sounded her mother's light laugh again, "Well I must say that it is nice to see you taking a day to rest yourself for a change. Is Marybell up yet?"

"Up and out, but due back sooners. Anyway, let me show you what I've

317

been workin' on while taking it easy," Helen continued in her daughter's voice as she stepped back into the vid room. When Kris followed, her mother activated the decoy feed again, then she smiled, "I am glad you're back dear. Were you successful?"

"Biggers. But that now means that the rocket is going up damn quick and sooner than maybe we thought."

"Better now than later I'm sure," Helen said quietly as she stripped out of Boots' sleep shirt and held it out.

Boots nodded as she in turn removed her skirt and blouse and exchanged clothes with Helen. "Here, you need this way more than me," she grinned as she also removed the bra, and tossed its padding on the couch. Helen merely shook her head with an exasperated smile and was in the act of slipping it on while Boots was carefully smoothing and folding the antique scarf, when the front door monitor signaled that it was being accessed.

"Where'n hell is the duty officer 'round here?" Puss called cheerfully as she entered the foyer.

"Front and center, Trooper One!" Boots ordered, "Report to tha' ferkin quarterdeck double time!"

"Well, it looks like I found the women's dressing room anyway," Puss grinned as she stepped into the secure space of the vid room and tossed her backpack on the couch. Then she picked up the small pile of her lingerie, and addressed the garments tenderly as she cradled them to her breast, "Did you guys have fun out there on your trip, and was big old Krissie nice to mama's little snuggies, Hmmm?"

"Actually, they enjoyed the outing and making new contacts as it were, but more on that later. Did you get to Sergeant Bill's place?"

"Sure did, and he had our stuff all ready," Puss nodded toward her pack. "Who's Sergeant Bill?"

"A fellow I knew in the service Mother. He's retired now, and has a small practice for selected clients. Sergeant Bill is the best dirty trick gadget maker there is.

"That makes me worry dear. Are you sure you can trust him, because you know that things usually aren't what they seem here."

"Bobby is one of his main clients, and Rick is another."

"Oh! Enough said," Helen smiled. Then her face clouded, "When are you leaving for that terrible spectacle this evening? And are you hungry?"

"Twenty hundred hours. And yes," Boots held up a cueing finger to Puss who grinned, then the two began chanting softly in unison, "Real Food, Real Food," as they started a shuffling dance around Helen.

"I like your act girls," Helen laughed, "But you don't have to dance for your suppers. What would you like?"

"Anything that's quick. It would be a good plan for us to eat something now, and then do short kitty naps before show time. But first, let's replant my butt bug, what say?"

"Good idea Buddy. You two assume your usual positions, and I will make you sore once more. Mother-two. Do you want me to numb you up again"

"No Dear, we don't have time," Helen replied as she dropped to her knees, then lay down on the thick plush of the carpet, supporting her chest on her elbows. "As you girls say, just Do it, Dammit!"

"Mother! Such language!" Boots chuckled as she dropped to the floor beside Helen.

Puss removed the bandages from their two incisions and prepped the skin around them. Then as she began to reopen and spread Boots' incision, she whispered, "Hang on Buddy, I'll be as easy as I can."

"I know," Boots grunted.

Then, Puss whispered again after a moment, "OK, she's ready. Now it's your turn, Helen."

"Do your worse dear. I'm glad to be of service."

"We'll talk about this later mother, butt thanks for now. And that's a pun!" Boots grinned.

"I know dear. What gene pool do you think your horrible sense of humor comes from anyWAY?" Helen gasped as Puss probed for, and then removed the tiny device.

"Gulp!" Boots grunted when Puss inserted it in her incision, then her voice changed, "When you close me back up Buddy use your doctor glue. A bandage would show under what I'm going to wear tonight."

"Ja Boss."

*

Boots wakened at 6:00 PM and nudged Puss in the bed beside her. Then she stretched contentedly as she reflected on how much she felt revitalized after the late lunch Helen had made for them and her two-hour nap.

"Mmmm," Puss purred as she also stretched. "This little interlude has sure pumped me and you back up way big."

"It did, Kiddo, but how do you know what I'm feeling?"

"Hey, you're easy. It's me that's hard to figure," Puss said with a giggle. "Want to shower first, or second?"

"It's my place and my shower, so I go first!" Boots grinned as she hopped from the bed that took up most of the space in her small room and pulled off her shirt. Puss remembered that the room was not shielded, so she kept her glance casual as she inspected the incision on Boots' hip. She saw the wound was still smoothly closed with the surgical adhesive she had applied to it, and that the anti-inflammation agent was keeping the spot from reddening and thus being noted by the surveillance cams.

"She looks pretty normal for those peeking bastards," Puss thought. "But it'll sure hurt when I open her up again."

"I'll be quick 'cause I gotta' dig my party clothes out of the closet, if I can find what I want," Boots said over her shoulder as she stepped into the small bathroom.

When she emerged from it toweling her hair ten minutes later, she found Puss standing before her bookcase, slowly leafing through a tattered volume.

"We had scanned copies of this at the school back home on my reservation, but I've never held the real book before," Puss said quietly.

"You've read it? It's one of my favorites."

"Mine too," Pus replied, as she gently slid the old copy of Rudyard Kipling's "Kim" back into its place on the shelf.

*

Puss stood nude before the mirror in the bath. She had finished her hair and was carefully doing the final touches to the cosmetics on her face, drawing three very narrow vertical lines in the middle of her brow with a black eyeliner pencil. She inspected her reflection critically for a moment, then called over her shoulder, "How wild we be lookin' tonight Boss?"

"We're going to distract 'em with our dazzle Dearie, so do your dammdest!" Boots answered with a laugh.

"Ja Boss, wilcomp!" Puss giggled and her eyes suddenly gleamed with mischief as she rummaged in her small cosmetic case. She worked on her face for several more minutes then added two final exotic touches to her body before she put on her costume for the evening. She stepped back in to the bedroom where Boots was still dressing as she had when she presented herself the evening before, a time that now seemed long ago.

"Like it?"

Boots' eyes widened as she looked at her friend standing the door to the bathroom. Puss had heavily pomaded her hair and combed it straight back to resemble a stiff copper helmet. Her eyes were darkly mascaraed and she had emphasized their color using a matching green eye shadow that glittered with copper highlights. She had also enameled her lips a thick glossy white, which matched the low-slung and very narrow white breach cloth as her only garment except for a hip length high-collard cloak with of the same leather. The cloak was tied around her neck and pushed back from her shoulders.

The white of her garments and lip-gloss emphasized the gleaming copper of her skin and the sultry perfection of her body, as did the large faux emerald she had cemented in her navel, and the copper-speckled eye shadow that she had also applied to her nipples.

As her costume differed markedly from that of the previous evening, so to did her pose. She now stood with her feet spread, and her fists planted on her hips which were thrust aggressively forward. Her eyes smoldered with animal sensuality as she looked at Boots.

"Great Buda's Bunions, just who'n hell are you anyway?" Boots whispered, her eyes widening as she received Puss' full effect.

"You're repeating yourself Buddy, 'cause that's what you always ask Bila," Puss laughed as she stepped into the room and out of her pose. "And anyway Kiddo, you look pretty damn high-voltage yourself."

Boots took a deep breath then it exhaled with a whoosh, "Nothing like you do though. You're real dangerous, Missy!" she murmured as her eyes showed a brief flash of lust, "Lets get back here early tonight, OK?"

"Only if you promise to not tear my off party dress," Puss leered. "But I do get to peel you out of you outfit," she said as she gazed at her friend.

Boots wore a pair of low-waisted full-length tights of a shimmering blue that were the same color as her eyes, and which were extremely form fitting. Her only other garment was a short bolero-style vest made of linked rings of dull black metal. The rings were 25 mm in diameter and their color and rough texture emphasized the whiteness of her bare skin beneath. A linked belt of the same black metal was slung loosely around her hips with a closure that was a complex buckle with a crimson stone set in its center.

The only jewelry Boots wore was a slip-on choker collar of the same black metal as her vest that was set with a single stone matching the one in her belt. Her lips were made up with a glossy crimson that matched both stones and she had emphasized her eyes with heavy mascara and blue eye shadow. Her hair hung free as she always wore it, and she projected a disturbing image of armored sexuality that caused Puss' eyes to widen in turn, as she felt the Boots' full effect.

"Where are the accessories that friend Sergeant Bill made for us?" Boots asked after they both regained control of themselves.

"Right here dear," Puss said with a grin as she turned to her pack and pulled out a package. She opened it on the bed to reveal two pairs of women's ankle lace-up dress boots with 8-centimeter spike heels, and two pairs of short leather dress gloves. One pair of both shoes and gloves was black while the other was white. A small black pistol was the only other item in the bundle.

"Hmmm," Boots said as she picked up one of the black shoes and felt its pointed toe, and then flicked its slender heel with a forefinger, "Looks good."

"Carbon fiber reinforced ballistic plastic toe caps and heel spikes, and thin super traction soles, just like we ordered," Puss said quietly as she examined a white shoe.

"Lucky for us he got them ready in time for tonight," Boots murmured as she picked up one of the gloves.

"Lucky for us that you got great tactical ESP, to foresee a need we didn't know was coming but needed to fill anyway, Buddy," Puss said with a slight smile.

"We do sorta make our own luck, don't we?" Boots murmured as she pulled on a black glove, and felt the thin layer of woven fiber armor over her knuckles and lining the edge and inside of her hand under the thin black leather.

"He showed me what this stuff does. You can grab a Jap sword by the blade and not get a scratch, and you can punch and chop with them real hard too," Puss said as she sat on the edge of the bed and began lacing on the white boots.

Boots pulled on the other black glove, so elegant and innocent-seeming then sat beside Puss and laced on her own black footwear. "Well, he got my size right, and the finger tips on the gloves are pretty sensitive for fine work," she smiled as she knotted the last lace then stood and took several steps. "My namesakes feel good too, but where are we going to carry the pistol? It's not like we have heaps of hiding places in these outfits," Boots said with a chuckle.

"Trust me Sweetie," Puss replied as she stood and tried the feel of her own boots. Then she pulled on her gloves and held up the small pistol.

"Two shot derringer, total non-metallic, including polymer springs and inorganic ignition and propulsion system – so no magnetic pings and no propellant sniffer signature. The max kill range of the fletchettes are fifteen meters, the accurate range is seven - and now you see it, now you don't," Puss grinned as she lifted the front flap of her breechclout.

She tucked the flat little weapon into a pouch sewn onto the inner part of the garment against her lower belly, then let its front flap fall again into place again and concealing the fact that she was armed.

"As long as someone doesn't get all hot 'n grabby at me tonight, this should be OK. You think?"

"Pretty good," Boots nodded. Then she asked in an innocent little girl's tone, "But what about me, if I get all hot and grabby?"

"If you don't know where my safety catch is by now, Kid, you be in deep noodles, particularly with what Sergeant Bill loaded into the fletchettes..."

"What's that, my little Killer Kitty?"

"A genetically engineered mutation of the venom of the Malayan Krait. It kills within two seconds."

"Sergeant Bill be baaad. But that's good for us, right?"

"Right Buddy, but now another question. Do we want to wear our ears?"

"I think so. Someone might talk behind our backs, and I'd hate to miss any good gossip," Boots said with a grimace.

They both rummaged in their packs until they found the small cases containing more of Sergeant Bill's handiwork, tiny devices that were amplifier-transceivers that fitted deep in the ear canal and rested against the eardrum.

"The batteries are still pretty fresh and we haven't used them much lately," Puss said as she fitted a slender plastic probe from the case into a minute socket in her ear piece, and used it to carefully slide the device into her left ear. Once it was positioned, she twisted the probe slightly to lock it in place.

She waited until Boots had inserted hers as well, then moved her jaw from side to side slightly to activate the device.

"Amplifier is good, I can hear your folks downstairs."

"Me too. Now send."

Puss moves her jaw again, then turned away from Boots and whispered indistinctly into her hand.

"Well, they're working, and you're one too!" Boots turned away and whispered behind her hand.

"That's not humanly possible! And it would hurt anyway," Puss dead-panned as she pushed the probe into the hem of her cape. "Might want to un-plug before we get back home."

"Good idea, and let's take our stuff in the car with us. Waldo can keep it safe," Boots nodded as she loaded her pack.

Puss did so as well then she announced, "Now we check in with your folks and wait for Waldo, right?"

"Ja Boss."

*

"Well, what do you think about our party clothes? Are we good enough for the Governor's Gala?" Boots asked when they stepped into the vid room.

Hector and Helen looked up from where they sat on the sofa, and stared at the two women for several seconds.

"You are major dangers!" they gasped almost simultaneously. Then Helen whispered, "Kris, you look like the ringmaster for one of Rat's 4X kink-vids."

"Thanks Mother, Buda knows I try."

Hector shook his head as he inspected both of them, then he grinned as he patted his wife's knee, "Dammit gal, this once I really pity Rat..."

Helen's voice changed, "Please be very careful dears, I am getting a funny feeling that someone or some thing is looking at us now or probing at us somehow, and my feeling is getting more intense."

"What do you mean Mother?"

"And how can you tell?" Hector asked quietly.

"I am just feeling now and don't know what it is yet, but something hap-pened today that is very strange. While you two were napping, and before you got home dear, I checked my net messages. I don't do that very often any more. But there was a new one that someone had left anonymously."

Boots tensed, "What did the message say?"

"Something about an offer to come here and demonstrate a party."

"Were the exact words "If you want a real wild party, come over to my little place on the wild side of the world!" Boots asked.

Puss gasped, "That's a signal you left for Molly!"

"No dear," Helen shook her head. "I saved it, and it said, "If you want a real wild party, I will come over to your place on your wild town". Would you like to see it?"

Boots frowned. "Molly changed it for some reason. I think she's trying to

324

say that the trouble is here, but what does she know that we don't?"

"Who's Molly," Helen asked just as the front door chimed.

"No time to talk now, Waldo's here. I need to think about it anyway."

"We need to think about it," Puss countered as her eyes grew cold and her face became a hard mask.

"Ja Boss, but first things first, OK?" Boots grunted as she stalked into the hall and grabbed her raincoat and pack.

Puss followed her, "OK, but we take care of our friends right after this little show, you hear?"

Boots nodded, "I hear. Clear and loud!"

***

Chapter 15
The Gala

May 4, 2276 AD,
`Clave of S'attl

"Where'd you find this one?" Boots asked as the two women climbed into the rear compartment of the executive-grade taxi. "It looks like it's in better shape than most."

"It's Rick's, and it sure is," Waldo said as he powered up the large sedan.

"What kind of special tricks does it have, compared to the one you drove this morning?" Boots continued as she leaned back in the seat, wrapped in her `Clave raincoat to hide her costume.

"As many as Bobby's car does. That one is out behind us as backup, with some of the new squad he's organized for your mission. You two gave him a headache about that though."

"Explain yourself soldier," Puss growled from beneath the hood of her raincoat where she slouched back beside Boots.

"Well," Waldo chuckled, "When Bobby put out the call for some of our trusty de-mobilized vets this afternoon, it turned out that he had to whack `um back with a stick because he got way too many volunteers for your woods-walk in BC."

"Why for?" Boots asked.

"Because when he told them about the mission, and that Captain Cook and Baby Bird would have the con they all wanted to jump on board and they don't give a greasy Chin chopstick what the mission is,"

"I ask again, Why?" Boots snapped.

"They just want the chance to fight beside you two, Ma'am. So do you want two squads? A heavy company? A full battalion? You can have as many troopers as you want,"

Boots was silent for a moment, until Puss grasped her hand and tapped, *"We got good backup here!"*

"Yes. They give we honor," Boots tapped back, then she murmured to Waldo, "Thanks old friend, that's real good to know."

"But we might be in a hurry when we exit Rat's Nest tonight, and maybe come out through a different door." she continued, her tone all business again.

"How can we find you in a hurry?"

"We'll find you. We added butt bug locators to both cars when we got back from Olympia this afternoon, so now we can vector in on you quick if you need to hack out in a hurry."

"It was Mack's idea and Rick had the equipment at his place. And the sensors under the rear seat in this crate have already scanned in your perky little IDs even as you lolled on them in idle ease," Waldo chuckled.

Then he turned his attention to driving the taxi - toward the Network building in the old part of town by the waterfront.

"I'd say we really do have good support tonight, don't you think Buddy?"

"Yep," Puss muttered from the depths of her coat. "It's sorta impertinent tho."

*

Waldo rounded a corner and drove toward the building that was the Network's main production studio for its worldwide broadcasts. The studio was located in S'attl because of the security inside the 'clave under martial law and the venality of its military government, as well as Seattle's tradition of lawlessness. The Network's ability to buy official blindness to the barbaric meat grinder of their 4 and 5X vid products from the Governor was a key element in the profitability of the Network.

Top management was acutely aware of this, and also knew that maintaining the status quo in S'attl was vital, as were the Network's silent partners in the major governments of the world. Therefore martial law was still kept in force on the west coast, even after the Chin war had ended two years ago.

The Network building was the newest one in S'attl. It had been built quickly during the later tactical stages of the Chin war, after martial law had been declared and the Pentagon had installed a military governor for the enclave.

This first governor had been appointed by President Pitson, and had been given the unprecedented authority to designate his own successor.

The governor just prior to the current one had decreed that the Governor's title should always be capitalized when spoken, one of the many whimsical dictates he issued. He held the position for only a short time however, before expiring under rather strange circumstances one evening at a private entertainment hosted by the Network. He was wearing pink tights, a tutu and ballet slippers at the time...

His successor, General Benjamin Butler VI, held all of his predecessor's decrees to be sacrosanct and enforced them with vigor, along with those of his own.

*

The architecture of the four-story building was bland, and anonymous. It stood in an area of abandoned single-story warehouses, so its upper stories overlooked a large expanse of commercial and industrial space in the old part of S'attl, an area was now sparsely inhabited during the day...

Waldo halted the taxi behind a short line of vehicles unloading passengers beneath the portico to the building. The three could, if they had thought about it looked across the street at the seawall holding back the waters of the harbor, slowly rising as the polar icecaps continue to melt.

They didn't however and Waldo inched the cab forward, until it was their turn to stop under the portico. He leaped out and opening the rear door with a flourish, handed Puss out onto the pavement. Then he assisted Boots to exit last and so acknowledged her rank.

Waldo's trim gray coverall and chauffeur's cap and dark goggles, and the obvious luxury of the taxi all signaled that its occupants were of the upper levels of 'clave society and therefore were not to be hindered.

Boots slipped out of her coat and casually handed it to Waldo, as Puss did a second later.

"Wait for us," Boots ordered, as she hid her amusement at Waldo struggling to hide his reaction to their costumes.

"Good thing he's got his goggles on," Puss whispered behind her hand.

"I agree total with what you say sweetie! It do look like we'll have some funs tonight," Boots said aloud with a slight smile, as she heard Puss' voice in her ear device.

Then with a quick nod and wink of approval to Waldo, she turned and strode past two black-clad doormen into the building. Puss followed a half step behind.

The lobby was small and starkly bare with its walls and ceiling paneled in brushed stainless steel and its floor of polished black tiles. The guard in the armorglass booth facing the door wore a pink jumpsuit, and was female.

She also had a circus clown's broad smile painted on her face but her eyes were cold and hard, as she stared at the two women for a moment before glancing down at the small display screen in her booth. She looked back up at Boots and Puss after another moment then, still showing no expression waved them toward an elevator that was the only exit from the lobby.

The doors slid open with a "whisssh" as the woman keyed a switch on the consol before her and the two stepped into the elevator. Boots nodded to the woman wearing the painted smile, then winked to her as the doors closed.

*

The elevator had floor-indicator lights, but the buttons in the car were locked, so the two were forced to wait passively while the car began its ascent.

Puss took Boots' hand and tapped, *"Been here?"*

Boots casually rested her arm across Puss' shoulders and tapping on it, replied, *"Not here. Only to bottom. Cells there."*

The elevator stopped and its doors hissed open to a wide corridor where a sign on a gilded easel directed them to their right, to the "Gala".

The way to their left was blocked by a metal lattice gate, so they shrugged and walked along the plush hallway until another sign directed them to their left, into the door of a room that pulsed with noise and energy.

"Welcome," a statuesque nude woman exclaimed from the doorway.

"You are very beautiful," she hissed as she stroked the three meter-long Indian rock python coiled around her hips.

"Come in and let me introducssse you."

The serpent's scale pattern of black and gray diamonds was very attractive, and the same pattern was also beautiful on the woman where it had been applied with precision tattooing over her entire body, including her face and bare scalp.

While she was greeting them, the python flicked its forked tongue out at Boots and Puss. The woman flicked out her tongue at them as well when she finished speaking, and they saw that it had been surgically split and lengthened to complement that of the snake.

"Fowow me," she mumbled as she turned and undulated before them through the door into the noisy room. "Let me presssent you to the Director," she then hissed as she paused before a man reclining on an ornate couch.

She and the snake both flickered their tongues again then the woman turned and swayed back to the door caressing her reptile companion.

"I believe I know you," the man said as he rose from the couch. He was slender and dressed in a perfectly draped toga. He continued in a cool voice that was clear to them in spite of the noise in the crowded room.

"They call you Puss and Boots, correct? And I understand that you are very competent in your work for us" he continued, as a slight smile appeared on his patrician features but did not reach his eyes.

"Thank you Director, and unfortunately they do, sometimes," Boots murmured with a smile.

"Generally not to our faces though. At least not after the first time," Puss added serenely.

"Yes, I'm sure that is true. Anyway, welcome to our little divertissement for General Butler. Please feel free to indulge yourselves with our food and stimulants, and do amuse yourselves with the talents from our studios as you wish."

"And," he continued as he openly stared at Boots' face and body and then at Puss', "We will be staging a show later this evening that I believe you will enjoy, from what I have heard of your interests anyway," he said with a cold smile as he gestured toward a red velvet curtain covering the wall on the far side of the room.

"I am sure we will, Director, since every Network production we've seen so far has been fascinating to the extreme," Boots responded blandly, "And we thank you for your hospitality."

"Yes, we really appreciate being included tonight, much more than we can say," Puss added with an almost sincere gush.

"Ah! That reminds me," the man replied. "Puss, if I may call you that to your face without prejudice?"

"Of course you may Director."

"Thank you. I understand that you were involved in an affair of honor several days ago. If my information is correct your opponent, who somehow lived, is also here tonight as my guest. While I am sure that you are quite familiar with the Code, my duty as a host requires me to remind you that this constitutes a Subsequent Meeting..."

"We were Director and I do know the Code quite well, but I do thank you for warning me that the Colonel is here tonight," Puss replied in a serene tone.

*

The Code Duello was quite specific about any subsequent meetings in public of two duelists in the event that both survived, and it was a grave breach of the Code for either to acknowledge the existence of the other in any way. Each was also charged with making all efforts to not confront the other and thus avoid social embarrassment for any non-involved parties who were present at such a meeting.

*

"You are quite welcome," the Director smiled again, as his eyes roamed over Puss' body. "Now, please join in the pleasures we offer here, and let my people and things entertain you," he finished with a graceful wave.

"Sounds fine to me," Boots nodded and taking Puss by the hand, turned and strolled toward a crowded bar at one end of the long narrow room.

"We talk later. Now get drinks. But not drink they," She tapped.

"Right. This bunch serve bad wine."

"Big true."

The two inspected the crowd of forty or so filling the room as they slowly made their way through it. Boots noted that togas appeared to be the garb for the guests of honor while others were costumed in wildly imaginative and varying ways. She chuckled at her intuitive choice of dress, and that of Puss'. She also noted that the talents from the Network who were mingling with the guests all wore fanciful costumes as well, what there were of them.

"Think he's real?" Puss murmured as she nodded toward a muscular nude male on a platform who was striking various poses before a crowd of admirers. The man had gold leaf on his eyelids, as well as on several other parts of his body...

"Yep," Boots grinned. "But he's damn sure not what you'd call natural. He was engineered in the Petri dish, in some places..."

"Good. I was sorta' worried for a minute," Puss said with an exaggerated sigh of relief.

"What a kinky jacket and belt," a sultry voice murmured from behind Boots. "I loove them, I truly do."

The two turned to see a slender woman striking a pose, with her chest thrust out and her back arched. Her long inky black hair was cut in a page-boy and her pouting mouth was heavily crimsoned. She was clad in a set of black lace lingerie in the style of the mid-Twentieth Century, including a garter belt supporting black silk stockings.

"Ooo, I'll just bet that they're heavy, and scratch and pinch you a lot," she added with a shudder of delight.

"Actually they're titanium so they're quite light and I had them made smooth - on the inside," Boots smiled with half-closed eyes, drawing another shudder and gasp from the woman.

"Oooo! You're Soo strong," the woman moaned...

"Well, that rig you have on is major kinky too," Boots said, "And I always wondered how you keep those things on your legs up."

"Yeah, I figgered a gal had to use glue, or thumbtacks even," Puss added with a straight face, as she eyed the stockings on the woman's legs.

"Oh don't be a silly!" the woman tittered. "I'm Bettie and they are real silk! I just love the feel of real silk, do you want to feel?" she whispered as she lifted one knee.

"Nice," Boots responded as she brushed her gloved fingertips across the woman's thigh, "Where did you get them?"

"Yeah, I'd love to have some for myself," Puss added with wide eyes, "Where do you find things like this in the `clave?"

"Bennie gets them for me," Bettie answered smugly. "He knows I like them and how grateful, and innovative I can be," she finished in a husky purr as she slowly raised her leg straight over her head and pointing her toe, stroked the back of her thigh as she balanced on one foot.

A shrill whistle sounded at that moment from a group standing near a lavish food table at the other end of the room.

"Oops! Gotta' run," Bettie squealed as she dropped her leg and scampered toward the whistler.

"Looks like this Bennie's got her trained pretty well," Boots muttered with a crooked grin as she turned towards the bar.

"Yeah. And funny how she wears the same stockings we have in our locker," Puss chuckled.

*

"What's the blue stuff?" Boots asked one of the harried bartenders, who's multi-colored body paint was streaked by rivulets of perspiration while he worked to serve the crowd.

"Steroid Curaçao, it's pretty wild."

"Good. Give me a short one. I like the color."

"What's the pretty green one?" Puss asked her eyes wide and innocent.

"Crème de Cannabis, real mellow," the bartender snapped as he deftly poured a half-flute for Boots.

"I'll take some of that, but not too much. I don't want to lose control."

"Don't worry kid, I got ya' under control" Boots leered, as she placed her arm around Puss' waist, and tapped, *"This only carry for show. Understand?"*

Puss reached for a snifter from the bartender, who suddenly became aware of her sexual aura and her body. He handed the drink to her mechanically as he stared in awe. She giggled and winked at him, then turned to Boots.

"'Course I understand, you masterful savage," Puss purred. "Now give me some food, so I'll be strong later and can take everything else you're going to give me tonight..."

The stunned bartender stared with his jaw agape at the two women as they walked back into the crowd arm in arm, until a thirsty guest jabbed at his arm.

*

Boots and Puss paused before a dais in the center of the room. It supported a white sculpture of a threesome, frozen in the act of a very complicated coupling.

"I didn't think that was humanly possible," Puss muttered. "Good piece of statuary though."

"That statue just blinked," Boots grinned.

"How they do that?" Puss asked.

"Excellent muscle tone and deep hypnosis. I am their coach," A throaty voice sounded behind them. "I've posed like that myself and it's fun - for a while."

They turned to see a petite woman with short curly blond hair and ebony skin that was fully displayed under the transparent vinyl jumpsuit she wore. Beads of perspiration dotted her brow and the suit stuck wetly to her body.

"Thanks for the intel, but you look sorta' heated in that outfit. Why you wear it?" Puss asked.

"Yes, I am hot and the sensation is wonderful, all slithery on my skin," the small woman sighed as she stretched, and then wiggled briefly before them.

"I think you like to experiment," Boots said. "I'm Kris and this is Mary-

333

bell. We're a field crew for the Network."

"They call me Onyx, and I'm an artistic director for the Network, and indeed I do like to try new things," the small black woman responded with a bright smile.

"Which X levels do you direct?"

"The levels of Life! I believe in sensations, not axe murders," Onyx answered, her voice suddenly quiet as her expressive black eyes flicked momentarily toward a couple standing beyond the food table across the room.

Boots glanced in the direction Onyx indicated and saw a stoop-shouldered gray haired man wearing a stained medical coat and a wiry female wearing white body paint with harlequin makeup on her face and shaved head. The unlikely pair had their backs to Boots and Puss, but after a moment they turned and parted to reveal the third party to their conversation, a person in a body brace sitting in a wheel chair.

"Why it's Colonel Kink as I live and breathe, and it look's like she's just had some new iron screwed into her spine," Puss purred. "But who's the two that the bitch is yakking' with?"

"You don't recognize them?" Onyx hissed as she abruptly stepped to one side, and pulled their gaze away from the three.

"Thanks for your move Onyx, but the good Colonel has already spotted us," Boots smiled with ice in her eyes as she turned toward the small black woman, and placed herself so that her right ear is directed toward the trio across the room. Then she moved her jaw slightly.

Puss glanced at her friend and saw the concentration in Boots' eyes, so she turned to Onyx and asked, "How long can your statue folks hold their pose?"

"I don't believe that you don't about know Freddy and Heidi! They're the Network's top 5X draw!"

"Hey, we spend lots of time out in the woods and they got no vids in the bush," Puss smiled. Then she gestured toward the white sculpture, "I ask again, how long can your talents hold it?"

"Until I release them, which I'll do in several more minutes, so their circulation won't get hurt," Onyx said, "But you two not knowing about Freddy and Heidi," she shrugged and rolled her eyes, "Is way much over the top.

"Anyway, after I bring them out of their trance and they do the rest of their act," she waved toward the frozen threesome, "I can leave before the main 'entertainment' starts.

"Watching the sort of thing Terry has tonight is not my kind of sensation. No way not at all," she finished darkly with a grim shake of her head.

"What's that?" Boots asked as she suddenly brought her focus back to the two and their conversation.

Puss looked at her friend with a cocked eyebrow and Boots shrugged, slightly. Then Boots smiled at Onyx, "So tell me about this entertainment."

"It's a game, only there's no way to win if they make you play," Onyx muttered with a haunted look in her eyes.

"So tell me about it,"

"No. See it for yourself if you really want to know. I have told you too much already," Onyx said, and then with closed face she announced in a bland tone, "Nice talking with you ladies, and anyway, I hope you enjoy the rest of my little show tonight."

Onyx turned then and made her way through the crowd around the dais and her talents. The small black woman clapped her hands sharply once, then twice again. The three frozen forms came to life at the sound, and began to act out their coupling while the spun sugar coating sprayed on their bodies cracked and flaked away with their movements and dusted the onlookers around them.

"Wow," Pus exclaimed as she grasped Boots' hand. "That gal's got some kind of great muscle control!" while she tapped, *"Hear anything?"*

"Those guys are pretty good too," Boots chuckled, as she tapped, *"Some thing up with they. I not catch what."*

After five minutes of increasingly complex and innovative activity, the performers ended their act in a frenzied climax of energy, and collapsed in a heap on the dais. The audience applauded politely but Puss and Boots saluted the three by whistling shrilly and gesturing with raised glasses.

Then they both glanced from the corners of their eyes, and saw that Freddy and Heidi had turned again to the colonel in the wheel chair and were ignoring them and the crowd around the perspiring former statues.

When the three talents could breathe easily again, they stepped down into their audience and gracefully accepted the foundlings and other gestures of appreciation from the crowd as they followed Onyx toward the exit.

"Some act, huh Buddy?" Puss grinned.

"That was just an act? Golly Budas gal, I thought that it was True Looove they were showing us," Boots said straight-faced. "Anyway let's go see who, or what is at the food table."

As Puss and Boots turned away, the woman with the snake and the gilded man mounted the dais as a different, and larger audience gathered around.

"Looks like threesomes are big tonight," Puss commented dryly as she sidestepped a toga-clad male lurching toward the new show, who was supported by a giggling adolescent girl wearing a half-mask in the form of an owl's face, a billowing feather cloak and nothing else.

*

"The theme here appears to be somewhat acute don't you think?" Boots muttered as she gazed at the array of foods on the large tables arranged in a hollow square. The Network's buffet was lavish and opulent, but it was made up entirely of various kinds of speared foods. Kebabs and satay skewers were being grilled to order by several chefs in the center space of the tables, dressed in only the tall hats of their profession and the elaborate cold hors-d'oeuvres arrayed on the table were also speared on skewers as well...

The centerpiece of the main table was a red-colored ice sculpture of a demon holding a trident aloft upon which a cherub was impaled. As the ice melted in the warmth of the room, the cherub appeared to be shedding slow tears.

"Hmmm, you're right. It does all look sort of prickly, now that you mention it." Puss whispered.

"Oh there you are! Come meet Benny," Bettie squealed from the other side of the large table where she stood next to a bulky man draped in an untidy toga with food stains down its front and with an oversized laurel wreath askew on his head.

Boots nodded with a smile and stepped around the crowd gorging on the Network's spiky bounty. Puss followed after handing her untouched drink to a waitperson circulating with a tray for empties. The waitperson wore the standard white jacket of the profession, but her only other garment was a grass skirt that was parted fore and aft...

Bettie and the man stood amid a small circle of people whom were either wildly or barely costumed. They all watched Boots and Puss approach with wary eyes and Boots recognized their attitude, as the anxiety all syncopates feel toward new entrants into the court of the power figure who could threaten to their status as lapdogs.

"Benny, these are my new friends," Bettie trilled then she purred as she squeezed the man's arm and leg-hugged him with her thigh, "Aren't they just a couple of real hottos though?" The man had a drooping black moustache and his features were puffy with the soft flesh of indulgence, but his eyes glittered like black marbles as he peered at Boots and Puss. He stared rudely for a moment then he pointed to Boots with a thick-fingered hand that had black hairs sprouting from its knuckles.

"Who're you?" he grunted.

"Yes, just who are you? Please present yourself to General Butler," a slender man standing beside the General snapped. He also wore a toga, but it was clean and fastidiously draped, and he resembled the Director who had greeted them on their arrival.

"They call me Boots, and this is my friend Puss. We provide special services to the Network," Boots replied as she looked at the man she instinctively knew was the Network executive tasked to be the General's handler.

"Well, I might like some of yur' services later on tonight," Butler leered with a slur, which caused Bettie to pout theatrically.

"Err, I don't think so General," the executive stammered, his demeanor shaken as he realized who the two women were.

Boots nodded at his statement as she continued to hold him with her eyes, and grin at his discomfort.

The executive placed a hand on the General's outstretched arm, "This is our best field collection team Sir," he continued hurriedly. "They are very, very proficient at what they do, if you get my meaning, Sir."

Butler shrugged the man's hand away as he continued staring at Boots and Puss.

"Nah! They're too damn light-weight to collect anybody."

"Oh no Sir. They just sent us back a very valuable associate who had defected because of a troublesome attitude. We are now in the process of reprogramming this person, and he will return to service soon.

"But I believe you two have some unfinished business back out where you collected him, don't you," the executive added with a hint of malice.

"We did extend our contract," Boots murmured, still holding her crooked grin and gazing at the man, "But while we looked for several more days, we found no sign."

"Well, we had a signal today that your second mark had been collected by a group of independents. But then they defaulted on the delivery for some reason. Perhaps you can find out why - when you go back to complete your contract," the executive hissed, flushed at his lapse of control.

"What's all this damn Network shop talky-talky anyway? It's boor-ing! Get me another drink Bettie, and some caviar. Jump dammit!" Butler growled. "And when's that damn special show you guys promised me gonna' start anyway?"

"This little man don't like us biggers, but why's he talking about some independents?" Puss thought as she glanced between Boots and the executive and Bettie rushed toward a bar in the corner of the room.

Boots' face was calm and her voice cold as she whispered, "We will attend to this situation and it will be the very first thing we do tomorrow."

"Good. I will inform the Director," the executive snapped. Then he turned back to Butler and showed his teeth in an opossum-like smirk as Bettie rushed back with a glass of murky brown liquid and large can of caviar in a bowl of crushed ice. "Don't you like how well we have trained her, General?"

The executive didn't note the sudden blaze in Boots' eyes as he turned to fawn upon Butler, but Puss did...

Bettie handed the glass to Butler then scooped out a heaping spoonful of the pearl-gray roe and held it to his mouth with a tremulous smile, "Here honey, and there's lots more when you want it, Sweetheart."

Butler took a gulp of his drink, which Boots recognized as the manic-personality enhancing drug of choice among the most extreme of the `Clave sybarites. Then as his moustache dripped, he opened his mouth for Bettie's spoon.

While all eyes were focused on the strange scene taking place between the two, Puss grasped Boots' hand and tapped, *"What is?"*

"Molly say trouble here. He say trouble there," Boots signaled back.

"What us do?"

"Much not right. Max alert!"

"Yes."

"That caviar looks real good," Boots smiled to the circle around Butler and Bettie. "May I have some?"

"Oh no, I'm sorry but it's special for Benny. Just like I am," Bettie simpered as she loaded another full spoon into Butler's waiting mouth, and rubbed her thigh against his.

"Here Darlings," a porcine-faced man draped in a lavender toga lisped as he stepped into the circle, "Have one of these instead." He selected a tray from the food table and offered it to Boots and Puss. It had a mound of pea-sized orange salmon eggs on shaved ice, and a holder clipped to its side with small silver needles.

"I'm Terry, and these are my favorite! The flavor is so intense – they're divine!" the man sighed as he selected a needle with his pudgy fingers and held it daintily while he skewered six of the eggs, then he sucked them into his mouth.

"These eggs have been fertilized," he murmured after licking his lips, "So they all have embryos inside that are alive - at least until you pierce them," he finished with a cryptic smile.

"Terry has such exquisite taste don't you think, Benny?" Bettie sighed, and caused the man in the lavender toga to lower his eyes and smile depreciatingly.

"You know of course that he's the chief procurer for our studios, and he always finds the best talent out there.

"Why he even found me," she added brightly to Boots.

"Really?" Boots murmured as she took a needle from the holder, and selecting randomly, skewered several of the eggs from the tray.

She popped them into her mouth and chewed for a second as she considered their flavor while Puss watched her with feigned nonchalance.

"Very nice. What other exotic things do you have for us to enjoy this evening?"

"You will soon see, you big Danger Dolly," Terry simpered, as he began stabbing more of the salmon embryos and slurping them noisily into his mouth.

"Dumb thing you do! May be bad. Like wine!" Puss tapped as she placed her hand on Boot's hip.

Then she exclaimed, "Hey Terry, can I taste some of those fish babies too?"

"Of course you can my dear little Sex Dream. And if you roll your dice right, you can taste anything else we have too," The man in the lavender toga smirked as he offered Puss the tray and stared at her body while ignoring her face...

"Thank you Terry, you're so very kind," Puss gushed as she selected a needle and stabbed several of the orange eggs.

"Mmmm! These are way good, and I really like the slight crunch from their little developing spines. You are a true connoisseur, Sir!" she exclaimed brightly.

"You must be very intelligent to notice that my dear," Terry murmured as his eyes roamed over her body, "We need to talk later...

"But now excuse me please," he sighed as he replaced the tray on the table. "I really must see about making my show go."

Boots clasped her friend's hand as Terry walked away. She tapped, *"Why you eat that?"*

Puss stared back at Boots for a second then tapped back, *"You take chance. Eat. I eat what you eat."*

Boots' mouth twitched in a slight smile as she gave her friend's hand a squeeze. Then her smile faded and she muttered in a tone below the noise in the room, "OK Buddy, stay here now while I go to pay my dis-respects to Colonel Kink."

Boots strode around the large food table and the crowd indulging on the Network's bounty and toward the woman in the wheelchair on the table's far side. She was facing Freddy and Heidi and talking with them as Boots approached. The two paused and stared at her over the Colonel's head. The woman in the chair sensed a presence and was starting to wheel around, when Boots spoke.

"Hello, Colonel. How was the rest of the party the other night? Apparently I drifted off. Too much of some unknown stuff I had put in me somehow, I suppose..."

Boots then took a stance with her feet apart and her fists planted on her hips. She inspected Freddy and Heidi as if they were things found under a particularly dirty rock, until the woman finished turning her wheelchair, and looked up with sparks of hate in her dark eyes.

Boots smiled down and continued in a tone of only slightly exaggerated courtesy, "That's all right Ma'am, please keep your seat. You know you don't have to stand for me."

"Thank you. I will keep that in mind when we meet again, which will be soon I am very sure," the woman lisped and mumbled around her swollen tongue, while quivering with barely controlled rage.

"Now if you will leave us Captain, I wish continue my conversation, which you have interrupted. I suggest spending time instead with your little redskin friend, and enjoying her while you can."

Boots looked at the woman in the chair for a moment with a slight smile on her lips but the blue heat of welding torches blazed in her eyes.

"Spending time with Marybell is indeed a pleasure for me, and actually the two of us have all the time in the world to do so."

"We will also be happy to show you just how much time we have left, and how little you have left, whenever you are up for another demonstration, as it were," Boots whispered.

Boots' smile broadened then, as she noted that the woman wore her body brace over a black uniform with a Network emblem on its collar.

"Ah, and I see that you have new clothes and jewelry!" she finished in her mother's light social tone, "They are so quite right for you Darling, and I do hope you enjoy the party tonight. Ta Ta!"

Boots then turned without acknowledging the existence of Freddy and Heidi, and stalked back around the food table.

"Well that was pretty quickie Buddy," Puss murmured, "What did the crazy lady have to say?"

"Not too much actually. Her tongue seems sort of sore, so she didn't talk so very good," Boots chuckled as she draped her arm over Puss' shoulders. "But now she's wearing a new uniform under that brace, with an interesting rank flash on it."

"She make bad thing with they two. Not know what thing. She new force boss here," Boots tapped.

"That's nice," Puss said sweetly as she placed her hand on Boots' waist. *"I hear they say. Bad to me. That not new."*

Boots looked down at Puss and smiled as she signed, *"Bad yes. For her. Us finish job you start."*

"Thank you friend."

Boots was still holding Puss' hand and smiling to her, when Terry clapped for attention where he posed before the red velvet curtain covering the long wall of the room.

"Listen to me please," he shrilled several times.

He continued after the raucous noise diminished in the room, "Our new game is about to begin! So if you will pay attention, I will explain how it is played. Gather around, if you would be so kind."

The crowd moved slowly into a semi-circle in front of him, with General Butler and Bettie in the forefront along with the Director and the other men in togas, each accompanied by one or more of the talents.

The snake woman and the gilded man stood with the Director and Puss noted that, while much of the man's gold leaf had been rubbed away, plentiful traces of it now showed on the tattooed woman's skin, and on the python's scales...

Boots led Puss to the rear ranks of the crowd and they became even more alert as the guests rustled into silence.

"We are holding a contest tonight to benefit six recently collected undocs and to give them a chance at attaining documented status," Terry shrilled. "We are doing this to demonstrate the Network's humanity to the world."

"But, in order to enliven the boooring nobility of our purpose," he continued with a smirk, "We will also have a little sport, by wagering on their performance as they try to survive, Err, I mean win their way through a few random obstacles toward the Door to Freedom."

Terry raised a lavender-draped arm and held up his forefinger as he simpered with a knowing wink to his audience, "And to be sporting about it, the locations of any possible hindrances to our contestants are unknown, even to me."

"Now dear celebrants, you will each draw a number to find the contestant you will sponsor, and when your entry competes, you who have drawn that person will cover all wagers on his or her performance from the rest of us, devising whatever odds you wish."

"There are only two basic areas of wagering however. The first is straightforward, whether or not the contestant is successful. The second," he paused with a leer for effect, "Is how well they cope with any interruption to their progress ...

"There are forty-two of us present here by my plan, so seven of us will form the backing pool for each of our hopefuls.

"And to make things work smoothly, each group of backers will move to the center here when their entrant makes the attempt, so the rest of us know to where to slap down our credits and try to beat the odds at the same time their contestant does!"

Boots still held Puss' hand where they stood at the back of the crowd. She tapped as she glanced around at the men in togas, both the organizers of the upcoming "contest" and its patrons, *"I think this be rough. Watch how you look."*

"You be right. But these bad rats die soon. OK?"

"Way OK!"

"Now people," Terry gestured grandly, "Let the Fun Begin! Everyone step up and draw a number"

"We still don't know what this game is," Puss whispered behind her hand.

"I wonder if those poor Undocs do…" Boots murmured as her face became impenetrable, "Let's go draw."

When their turn came at the large silver bowl Terry had placed on a stand before him, Puss withdrew a folded slip of paper and opened it to find the number 6.

Boots drew and opened hers to find the number 5.

"Hey, this won't work," Puss announced gaily. "We can't bet against each other! We know way too much about how we always cheat! Anybody want to swap a 5 for a 6?" she laughed. "I'll make it worth your while."

Bettie looked at her number, and then squealed, "Benny's got a 5 and I'm a 6, so you got a deal, Sweetie. But now, let's see who's luckiest tonight," she giggled.

Terry made a grand gesture toward the red curtained wall, "You will have only three minutes to assess each contestant and make to your wagers, before they are assisted to begin their attempt, so make the most of your time," he finished as the curtain began to rattle open.

***

Chapter 16
The Game

May 4, 2276 AD
`Clave of S'attl

Bila awakened for the second time.

The first time he had slowly become aware of two long shapes coming into focus close before his eyes. He had considered them fuzzily for several moments then as his mind cleared he had recognized them as his own naked thighs. He had shaken his head and sat upright, almost. when he had attempted to rise he found that he was strapped in a cold metal chair in the middle of a harshly lighted gray room.

He also remembered that he had easily broken the plastic fetters restraining his arms, and after a struggle, regained his feet. He demolished the metal chair in the process.

Bila had prowled the 10 meter-square space with its blank walls of a smooth gray stuff that felt like stone to him, solid except for a single entry point that was closed with a panel like he had first seen in Molly's cabin. He remembered how the thing she called a door worked, so he inspected the panel closely. He first pushed against it then he lunged against it.

When it didn't move he decided that the things that made it work were on the other side, and had continued pacing, and inspecting the space that held him.

On his tenth circuit around the cold cell, he noted a hole in the floor in one corner, and from the stains around it and a lingering odor, he recognized it as a necessary place.

He shrugged, then used it.

He continued slowly pacing the space, inspecting everything in it and in so doing worked the drug out of his system. He kept up his slow pacing for several hours while lost in thought but alert to his surroundings.

Then he had seated himself on the floor across from the door, and as far away from the necessary hole as possible. To rest, and to wait.

Several minutes later a small port opened in the door, and one of the insipid food things Marybell had offered him the night he first found her and Kris fell into the room.

He had looked at it for a moment then he picked it up and tore open its wrapper. He had looked at the featureless brown mass inside, what his new friends had called a "rash bar" for a moment, then he had sniffed it. He also remembered his sudden anger as he had sensed a new odor in this thing - much like that he had smelled from the exploding things around the cabin.

With a roar of rage he had hurled the rash bar at the panel closing him in the cell and was glaring around at the small space, when the port in the panel opened again. His last memory of that time was of a black tube pushing through the small opening, and then a hisss...

*

The second time he awoke he was lying on his back. He reached up and felt a rigid surface above him that was both rough and smooth. As his mind cleared and his eyes focused, he saw that it was a mesh, woven like when his people made their baskets, but it was hard and the stuff looked like the blade of the knife he had given Molly back at the cabin after Kris and Marybell had left and on the day before the man on the horse had come up the ridge.

This mesh had the same coldness as that blade.

The space he was laying in was not small enough to cramp him and while he could draw his knees up, he could not sit upright. He rolled first to one side then the other and peered closely at the construction of the thing that held him. He saw that its back and the ends next to his head and feet were solid, and that the mesh above him was round where it arched over him.

He gazed around at the construction of the thing, and then looked closely at the place where the mesh curved down to meet the flat back panel. After a moment he saw that there was a seam, or place of joining where the edge of the mesh met the flat metal on both sides of the back. Then he noted that they were the same things along the seam that had let the door in Molly's cabin swing open or shut.

He rolled on his back again and saw that another seam ran down the

345

middle of the arch above him, and it had things on it like those that kept Molly's doors closed. Things she had called latches.

The mesh was too tightly woven for him to get any more than the tip of his little finger through, but the seam between the two pieces of mesh was poorly fitted and he saw the cross-bars that held the two halves together. The seam was wide enough to accept the blade of the big knife Molly had given him, and he was sure that he could use it to open the latches.

But he was naked, and his belt and pouch were gone as well as the knife, so he strained at the mesh several times and tried to shake the latches free. When this didn't work, he relaxed and began to wait as a caged tiger does, one that remains patient for weeks or even years - until its keeper finally makes a mistake...

*

The door to the room opened with a clank, and as Bila watched through the mesh, two men in black coveralls entered the space pushing a wheeled metal rack. He had sensed their presence a moment before they opened the door so he was not startled by their entry.

They pushed the rack to the bottom end of his cage and adjusted it, then they stepped around to his head and stooped, and he felt the cage sway as they lifted it upright, and put him on his feet inside it.

"Gadamm, this one's some way heavy meat," one of the men panted hoarsely.

"Yeah, an' they say he's some strong too. Watch him good."

"Sheet, he ain't goin nowhere, `sept out on that new fun floor. What's that thing gonna' do anyway?"

"Don't know. They're keepin' it real quiet. Anyway clamp him down and lets roll him on out. He's the last one and Mr. Terry's got us on a tight time line."

"Well, Mister Terry can just come down here and hump some of this weight his own self dammit!"

"You don't want to be around Mr. Terry when he's humpin' anything. And way damn sure not when he's putting on a show, unless you're brain dead," the second man grunted as he stenciled a large red number on the mesh front of Bila's cage, now upright on the low wheeled rack. Then he continued as the two guided it out of the cell, "`Course with you, that's sorta' hard to tell sometimes."

"Ferk you, and help me push dammit."

As the contraption rolled down the dank hallway with its steel wheels scraping on the rough concrete floor, Bila balanced on the balls of his feet in the cage - tensed for action and patiently waiting his chance.

*

The red velvet curtain slid back with a rattle to reveal a lofty space on the other side of a waist-high railing, and it became clear to Puss and Boots and the others in the group who were not totally chemically-impaired in the party was on an extensive balcony over a large open floor.

The crowd rushed to the railing, and buzzed with conversation as they looked out and raucously speculated about the entertainment to come.

Boots pushed her way to the rail and saw that the floor of the space was paved in square mirror tiles inlaid into a metal latticework, and there was an open archway from the floor to her right.

To her left, she saw a wall that had six doors in it, and as she watched, the doors opened and six cages were rolled out. The cages were vertical half cylinders and their fronts were made of a metal mesh that was too fine to show their contents clearly, just the restless shadows within them. Each cage had a large numeral stenciled on its front - 1 through 6.

Boots tapped with a stony look, *"Look much like Rome arena. Get hard."*

Puss nodded as her face became bleak, *"I hard now. And later when we kill they."*

"Yes," Boots tapped, as Terry sang out with a shrill giggle, "Now this is number one, and the fun has just begun!"

The first cage on the floor opened with a clang. A skinny naked youth stood on its base, and hesitated as he looked at the expanse of the floor, and toward the open door on its far side. He hesitated for three minutes, while Terry called for wagers to be placed with the youth's backers.

He remained in the open cage until he suddenly began to hop around, as if his feet were burning. Then with a look of distress, he stepped onto the mirrored floor and after a second, launched himself in a wild run toward the opening on the other side of the floor.

He had made six leaping strides in his attempt, then as his foot landed on one of the mirrored tiles on the floor an eight-foot long steel spike erupted from it and impaled him.

Because of his stretched-out stance as he ran, the round pointed shaft entered his body through his lower abdomen, and exited under his shoulder. It pierced his bowls, spleen, liver and a lung. His momentum caused him to spin around on the spear as he screamed. Most of the audience on the balcony cheered, and clapped in delight.

"Alright, any more bets on this one? He could last a pretty long time!" Terry called from his post in the middle of the balcony.

After several moments of gleeful wagering activity by the crowd, Terry announced, "Time for Number two," as the first contestant shuddered in shock and a pool of blood spread on the floor between his legs as he slid down the spear that impaled him.

The number two cage door clanked open to reveal a naked oriental male, a Chin army deserter caught in a routine Undoc sweep. He stood frozen as he stared at the first youth's still twitching and wheezing body for three minutes while the crowd on the balcony noisily called out their wagers, and their catcalls...

He also began hopping from one foot to the other, slowly at first. His hopping became more frantic and he began moaning pain until finally he screamed and leaped out onto the mirrored floor.

He stood rigidly for a moment then stepped cautiously onto another tile toward the door from the floor. After a moment, he cautiously stepped onto another, and paused again as the crowd jeered at him. Finally, he shrugged his shoulders and walked boldly forward.

The shaft entered his groin and emerged at his collarbone after passing through his bladder, bowels, diaphragm and heart. He died in an instant, and as his legs relaxed, his body slid slowly down the shaft to kneel awkwardly, as his head lolled forward.

"Hey!" a voice rang out from the balcony. "That weak-kneed scummo just cost me much credits! Damn his worthless butt back to China anyway!"

"Well, my Number One is still holding on anyway, get your chips ready! I bet real long," one of the toga-wearing guests of honor sneered.

"Hey Sucko, I'm not worried. He can't last that long," a crude voice slurred in reply...

*

Bila heard the cruel shouts of the crowd of people he could see through the mesh where they stood behind a railing above the level the wall to his right.

They were dressed very differently than Kris and Marybell had been when he met them, and were laughing and calling to one another as they looked out on the place where the two men were stuck on the spear things.

He did not understand most of their words, but he recognized the tone of the crowd, and knew them to be spectators of death. He had heard these voices before in a few of his people, when they had all been at the killing grounds.

He forgot that thought however as he did his instinct of pity, while he watched what was taking place on the shiny floor, until he heard a child whimper in the cage next to him.

He had felt no confusion about the world he now was in, not since the dart sunk into his chest as he was racing to attack the man that unnaturally was on the back of a zaldi.

He had been conscious but helpless when he was carried to the grassy flat and pulled up into the black `copter, and dropped on its vibrating and strangely smelling floor. Then a man in black had sprayed something in his face, and the next place he had known was the gray stone room.

When he awakened the first time and as he rode in the cage to this floor, he had focused on escape, but now as he heard the child whimper again and a mother's quiet crooning, he was suddenly filled with a bright anger.

Then he heard the clang as another cage opened to the raucous noise of the people leaning over the balcony. It was nearer to him now, but he couldn't see what was happening, until a hoarse voice shouted in a voice that stilled the crowd.

"Ferk you bloody Bastards to Hell! And may you burn there forever!"

A gray-haired man with a craggy face strode out onto the floor and into Bila's view. He squared his bony but still-broad shoulders, and shook his fist at the balcony as he started marching toward the archway.

The first shaft erupted six squares out and caught the skin of his thigh, but with a grunt of pain he jerked loose and strode forward again as blood spurted from the wound.

Three meters further on as he paced toward the archway labeled "Freedom", a second shaft erupted from the mirrored floor and killed him cleanly.

As the man slumped to the floor, Bila heard a voice shrill over the hubbub of the onlookers, "Bastard yourself! You didn't give me any time to get my bets down dammit!" He then heard the crowd erupt into mocking laughter at this outburst - mostly...

*

Boots stood with Puss at the left end of the balcony railing where they could look down on the cages next to the arena floor below them. Cage number six was the closest and almost beneath where they stood.

They had made small wagers on the first contestant without knowing the game, because Terry had coyly brushed aside all inquires from the crowd as to its nature.

The two had bet that the Undoc would not go free, because of their familiarity with the Network's general tendency to trample on truth and justice. But as the real nature of this contest was revealed when the youth was viciously skewered, Boots and Puss had snapped into combat mode and shut down all their emotions, almost...

"Shat. Shat. Shat," Boots tapped.

"Yes. Is Shat. Boss Rat die for this," Puss replied, as her hand quivered in rage where it rested on Boots waist.

"No. I am Shat to work for Boss Rat. I not know they do this at Undocs. I not see vids they make. I blind. I not think. I stupid," Boots signaled as she looked at her friend, her eyes stark with pain and her face suddenly ashen.

"No. You not stupid. You now awake. World sleeps. Now you wake up world!" Puss tapped to Boots, as she stared out at the arena floor where the first youth's form was still twitching.

With a supreme effort that Puss somehow also felt, Boots willed herself to become strong again - and hardened her face once more. She stared at the chattering crowd on the balcony as she slowly tore her betting slip into tiny pieces.

The two watched in stony silence as the Chin deserter attempted to avoid the floor while the raucous howling of the rest of the crowd echoed in the room. Then when he shrugged in contempt and marched forward to meet his fate, Boots murmured in a voice of ice, "The Chin breed real men too."

"It's good that it will be quick," Puss whispered as she noted how the shaft pierced his body a moment later and then glanced at the first youth, still twitching in a widening pool of his blood.

*

The old man cursed the crowd and marched contemptuously to his death. They gazed down at the his twitching body his face still holding its look of contempt, and Puss murmured softly, "You know, that's the same thing my father would say, and do if he was caught up in this damn mess ".

"Mine too," Boots replied, "I know, now..."

The uproar the old man had caused by his refusal to play according to the Network's rules subsided after a bit and Terry clapped his hands for attention, "I'm sorry!" he called.

"Please," he shrilled then continued as he got more of the unruly crowd's attention.

"Because of the very unsporting conduct of contestant Three, I will personally match your winnings by a like amount in the next two contests!"

Part of the crowd whooped in drunken delight, but another part still grumbled so Terry clapped his hands again.

"And," he called, "I will buy back any slips you might have made on the side on that tiresome third person."

"Anyway, Number Four is an interesting entrant, a member of that pesky bunch of Haida Indians that keeps attempting to return to the islands north of us, to begin living in squalor again as their ancestors did."

"He and some others recently sneaked out there again in an attempt to start an illegal settlement on the island. Luckily he was picked up by another one of our fine collection teams. It is unfortunate that they could not join us tonight because of recent, but unrelated difficulties in the field."

"Anyway, all you sporting guys and gals and whatevers, get ready to place your wagers!"

"Hmmm, you think he's talking about a team that might have jumped into a hot bunker?" Puss murmured to Boots.

"Watch what you say here!" she tapped on Puss' waist, and ended her signal with a pinch for emphasis.

"I will, but I'm taking names," Puss growled as she leaned forward with her elbows on the railing and stared at the floor.

The doors to cage Number Four then clanged open to reveal a man with an ample stomach but with very sturdy shoulders and legs. He wore his silver-streaked black hair long and his short beard was mostly gray. His skin was the color of old ivory and his face was bold, and his dark eyes were filled with hate as he glared up at the crowd on the balcony. He leapt to a stance before cage number five, then stepped out onto the floor as he began a deep-throated chant that filled the lofty room.

"That's his death song," Puss whispered with a wooden expression as she gripped the hand rail.

Boots heard her friend's words in spite of the storm of complaining calls and shouts from the frustrated bettors, including Terry's angry shriek, "You come back here and do it right Damn you!"

"Looks like the real people are down on that floor tonight," Boots whispered back with a slight tremor in her voice.

"But why do it in front of the next cage?"

The Haida maintained the volume of his chant as he moved boldly forward, and Puss frowned as she noted that he stepped on each mirrored tile in his path toward the door, even though it is not necessary to do so because of their spacing. Suddenly her eyes blazed and she tapped to Boots, *"He clear way for Five!"*

The man made his way an incredible half the distance across the floor, and was almost in front of the center of the balcony when a shaft erupted and took him in the center of his lower belly. Because of his stance when it struck, the shaft shattered his upper sternum as it passed out of his torso between the ends of his collarbones, then it entered his head under his jaw and erupted again almost mid-line from the top of his skull.

His mouth stayed open as the last reverberations of his chant died away in the space, and his unseeing eyes bulged in their sockets. But then as his legs collapsed and he slid down the shaft, his body and glaring face remained upright, and he resembled a gruesome version of one of his people's totem poles.

The partygoers were shrill in their disappointment, and pelted his quivering body with drink cups and other food items.

*

Bila noted the actions of the man with the long hair as he watched through the mesh of his cage, and the path the man took out on the deadly floor as he stepped over to begin his walk to death from the cage he was in him.

Bila watched the man's actions intently, and heard a sudden intake of breath followed by a moan of anguish from the shadowy figure imprisoned next to him when the man was impaled.

He listened to the confused hubbub from the balcony as he gazed at the man's body, then accompanied by a particularly angry bellow, Bila saw what he recognized as a steaming piece of grilled meat sail down from the crowd of onlookers and hit the man's body and bounce off. It landed on the floor several tiles away and a shaft erupted from the tile where the meat landed.

"People, don't waste food on that dead hunk," a voice shrilled. "There's much more fun to come!"

Bila looked up through the mesh and saw a plump man on the place above him who wore a robe the color of his favorite flower that bloomed in

the warm-time each year. He also recognized the man's voice as the leader
of those on the balcony who took pleasure from hurt. He growled deep in his
throat, then the doors of the cage next to him clanged open.

*

"Don't worry friends," Terry called, as his voice cracked. "The best is yet
to come!" Then he ordered with desperate authority in his voice, "Number
Five Maestro, if you please!"

Boots growled, "Shat. This looks bad."

Puss tapped, *"Hold it. Be hard,"* as she gripped her friend's hip.

The doors of the fifth cage opened to reveal a slender young woman with
long black hair holding a baby to her breast. Her skin was the same color
of aged ivory as the man now transfixed in front of her, and the color of her
waist-length hair matched his. The baby was a six-month old boy and very
active.

"Here we have a bitch from that pesky bunch of Haida Redskins and
as a bonus, we have a second variable, one of their whelps... Depending on
where it crawls, things could be interesting for you sporting side bets," Terry
finished with a hysterical giggle.

The young woman hesitated for only a moment, then holding her son to
her naked breast she stepped forward along the way her father had pointed
out to her.

The crowd was mostly silent as the young woman cautiously followed
the old man's path across the mirrored floor while clutching the baby with
trembling arms as she tried to sooth its fretting.

"Ha! This 'ish more like it," General Butler shouted with a slur. "Anybody wanna' bet on a twofer?"

His syncopates laughed raucously and chimed in with shouts offering
odds and accepting wagers, while Boots saw the gleam of tears that begin
coursing down the woman's cheeks as she neared her father's grotesquely
skewered body.

*

Bila watched through the mesh of his cage as the young woman stopped
behind the old man's body and saw her shoulders shake as she held the struggling baby. Then she looked at the other shaft that was triggered by the piece
of hot food thrown from the balcony, where it had erupted through the floor -
close by the man's body but without a victim.

She shrieked as she looked imploringly up at the crowd lining the rail of the balcony, "I don't know where to go next! Please don't hurt my baby!"

Bila quivered with the effort to maintain himself as he heard the anguish in the woman's voice above the hubbub from the onlookers. He glanced up as the man who led this evil thing, he who wore a robe the color of his favorite flower and was using a tiny spear to stab little bits of orange food from a tray held by a young boy with a painted face.

The man then ate what he had speared as the young woman stood in frozen fear holding the child, screamed again, "Help Me! Please!"

"Oh, all right," the man in the lavender toga shrilled. Then he scooped a handful of the crushed ice from the tray, molded it into a ball, and accurately tossed it onto a tile one meter from where the young woman was standing.

"Try there."

She looked up in gratitude and said, "Thank you," through her tears as she took a long step onto the tile where the ball of crushed ice landed.

She was struggling to regain her balance on the foot she had on the tile when a shaft erupted and entered her lower belly. It emerged above her shoulder blade and stopped her forward motion, causing her to rotate around it and face the way she had come.

Bila saw only confusion in her eyes for a moment, then she screamed and the baby she held began crying at her fear. Miraculously, she stopped her screaming and fought the shock to her body as she tried to comfort the child.

She held the baby even as her arm movements were made awkward by the shaft through her torso and as her legs collapsed, and she slid down the shaft of the spear into a squat on the floor.

Bila's eyes clouded with rage and he slammed his body against the doors of his cage with enough force to rock the heavy construct. Then with a supreme effort, he regained his icy calm, and waited...

*

"Rat die. Tonight," Puss tapped with a hand that shook so much that she had to repeat her message several times, both to make Boots understand, and to get her friend's attention.

"Yes. Tonight."

"Oops! Bad call on my part, please forgive me Dear Lady. But you get a free re-run if you want," Terry giggled to his audience as the young woman, now coughing blood, still feebly tried to comfort her baby.

"Anyway, he continued briskly, "Our last contestant is quite unique, and when he was examined when he was brought in, we first thought to use him for a number of productions in the studios. But then we ultimately decided that the risk of his intractable traits escaping to the gene pool of all the Citizens Needing Our Leadership was too great. Therefore, the Network's loss is your final entertainment tonight.

"I must say however, that this specimen is magnificent and a true primitive. Why he was even carrying these artifacts as his only weapons when he was collected yesterday." At that, Terry snapped his fingers and the young boy with a painted face dropped the bowl with its small remainder of ice and salmon eggs, and raced to retrieve a cloth wrapped bundle from beneath the drapery of the food table. Rushing back through the crowd, he breathlessly offered it to Terry.

"Would you look at these," the procurer giggled shrilly as he unwrapped two flint-tipped light spears and a throwing stick. "I think they're awfully apropos for the remainder of his evening, don't you?"

Then he trilled, "And now for contestant Number Six! Place your bets please, and you backers of Number Six please move to the center box," as the doors of the last cage clanked open to revealed Bila, glaring at the deadly floor.

***

Chapter 17
The Pursuit

May 4, 2276 AD
`Clave of S'attl

Puss gasped, and went rigid as she squeezed her friend's wrist with a grip that would have broken a `clave-dweller's bones.

Boots clinched her fist and hissed, "Dammit Buddy, slack off! We've got to trust him!" Then she took a deep breath and turning, forced their way through the crowd to the center of the balcony. She called out, "Alright you people! I think this one's gonna' make it, so I'm covering all your sucko bets!"

Terry glared at Boots with a venomous look then he turned to General Butler who stood next to him, swaying as Bettie struggled to support the man's bulky form. "Well General now I know we're going to make some big credits off this arrogant young slut, because the odds are all on our side!" Then he sneered to the crowd, "Make lots of bets with her, all you boys and girls and whatevers. It's going to be easy money time real soon!"

*

Bila ignored the strident noise of the voices on the balcony as he stepped out onto the floor. He stared at it for a moment, then he carefully paced over to the path the young woman and her father had taken across the shiny things, and followed it until he knelt next to her where she slumped on the floor, feebly struggling to hold the squirming baby as she gasped for breath and quivered in agony from the shaft piercing her body. He blocked out all of the cacophony of the audience as he gently lifted her head and looked tenderly into her eyes.

"Take baby?" he asked.

"Please," she whimpered as her life began to fade, and her grip on her child slackened.

"He name?" Bila urgently whispered as he continued to ignore the rowdy crowd and concentrated on the dying young mother's voice.

"Gwaii, after our home," she whispered as she released her grip on the baby boy.

"Gwaii!" he said as he took the child in one arm, and tenderly caressed her brow for the several more moments it took for her eyes to close peacefully in death.

Bila rose then and turned to face those who lined the balcony railing for the first time since his cage had opened. He glared at them for a moment with feral rage then he reached for the vacant spike protruding from the floor near the old man's body, the one triggered by the hot food missile - and holding it for support with his free hand, stepped over to its tile.

When nothing further happened, Bila snarled, and suddenly spit at another tile a meter beyond where he stood - and smiled as a shaft erupted from its center with a whoosh. After considering for only a second, he took a long step to it, and grasping the shaft, stood on it in safety with the baby cradled in his other arm.

He paused there for a moment as he chose another tile, one that was a meter and a half away and spat on its surface. When a spear also erupted from its center, he heard the shrill voice of the leader of the sickness on the balcony shout, "He's tripping them! Someone stop him, Dammit!"

Bila leapt to the tile he had just triggered and, as his foot landed on it, steadied himself again as he grasped the shaft. He chose another tile, and spat again. When nothing happened, he spat at another, and then another until one finally discharged a spear. He leaped to that tile, and balanced himself again with his grasp on its shaft, still carefully cradling the baby boy in his arm.

He selected the tiles for all of his next leaps in the same manner, and as he moved across the mirrored floor in this fashion, he also became aware that the shafts turned in his hand as he grasped them - and slightly rose as they turned. He considered this as he continued to make his unorthodox way toward the open portal.

*

"Do something, Dammit," Puss hissed as they stood in the center of the balcony over the floor. "He's gonna' get hurt!"

"No. We don't have to just yet, because he won't. He's already figured it out," Boots whispered in awe as the shouts of the crowd resound faintly outside of the bubble of silence the two women had willed around themselves. "Like I knew he would," she added with an admiring shake of her head. Then she frowned as a fleeting half-formed thought passed through her mind.

"How can you say that, Dammit? What do you know?" Puss hissed again, gripping the balcony railing and looking down at Bila as he moved closer to the open doorway with each studied leap.

"Him. I'm starting to know him better every time I see him go in to action," Boots whispered as she snapped out of her sudden reverie. "He figured that the spears had heat-sensitive triggers before I did! Just watch him Buddy, but damn-sure be ready to go war-mode when it's our turn!"

*

Bila crossed the remaining space in four more leaps and landed balancing on one foot, grasping the shaft he had triggered out of a tile two meters from the edge of the shiny floor in front of the open door. He willed more saliva into his mouth, now almost dry from his spitting as well as stress and was choosing his final path, when two burly men in black coveralls appeared in the opening.

Bila glared at them for a moment then, spit on the tile immediately before him. When its shaft erupted as he expected, he grasped it in his right hand and turned it, and felt it rotate and rise. He twisted the shaft until it came loose, and then pulled it from the floor with a scream of triumph that echoed in the large space and was heard on the balcony by those who could hear, and understand what it meant …

He stooped and placed the baby on the tile between his feet and then with a swift lunge from his crouching position, Bila extended one foot onto the tile before him and thrust his shaft into the belly of one of the black-clad men, as his people did when they speared the fat fish that swam in the rivers each year at the start of warm-time. Then with a motion they also used, he flipped the man out on to the mirrored tiles at the shiny floor.

Four shafts erupted with a hiss and pierced the man's body from the four tiles he landed on. The man screamed and drummed his heels on the floor as he vainly pulled at the spikes protruding from him for a moment, then wheezed and gurgled weakly for moment, until he died.

Bila ignored the pandemonium from the balcony and freeing his make-shift spear from the first man, planted one foot on his still quivering chest and lunged at the other guard.

His point pierced that unfortunate just below his sternum, and as Bila churned it in his chest the man also died, as the bear in the valley had done, except quicker.

Bila was recovering from his lunge and starting to withdraw his spear when he heard a mechanical clanking. He looked up and saw that metal gates were beginning to close from each side of the archway. He snarled, and with a heave of the shaft in his hands flipped the second man's body across the portal so that it blocked their track.

He then lifted the baby from between his feet and with a grim smile placed him to lie across the first guard's torso between two of the shafts that pierced it, and finally turned his face to those on the balcony.

*

"Somebody do something!" Terry shrilled. "He's getting away!"

"Hey, 'cept for that girl, this ain't been no fun, Dammit. You guys are runnin' this show like a bunch of Gadamm soy farmers," General Butler slurred. Then he shouted at Bila standing 30 meters from him at the edge of the deadly floor, "An' what tha' Ferk are you lookin' at? You damn Undoc Renegade?"

Boots bared her teeth at the outbursts of these two men in togas in the same death grin she always showed when the fighting began, and Puss was quivering with the intensity of her own battle mode, when Bila raised his gaze to the balcony.

They both saw anger blazing in his eyes as he stared for a moment at Terry and Butler, the obvious leaders by their position at the front of the crowd, both by their shouted commands and comments. Then he passed his glance swiftly along the rest of those standing at the rail - until he saw Boots and Puss.

His eyes paused for a second as he recognized them, then with a slight smile that they saw clearly across the distance, he turned and spat on another tile beside the dead guard's body. When that shaft erupted, he released it with a twist, and after a glance to see that the baby was still safely perched on the dead man's chest he hefted the shaft and balanced it in his hands.

It was made of tubular alloy steel, 3 cm in diameter but quite light for its size and length. The threaded fixture on its butt end was small, and Bila found that it did not adversely affect the shaft's balance. Its long smooth point was not barbed, and was extremely sharp.

"War-mode Buddy! He's in action now and it's our turn next," Boots hissed.

Bila bared his teeth in a crooked grin as he hefted the shaft for another second. Then with a scream of rage, he grasped the butt end in his right hand and momentarily balancing the shaft with his left, hurled it at the man in the flower-colored robe who had lied to the young mother...

He paused for a second to watch its effect then after a glance back at the child, he spat on another tile near his feet - and freed another shaft...

*

The spear transfixed Terry and entered his body at his navel and passed though his liver and one kidney before it erupted from his back. The momentum from Bila's throw caused the point to not only pass through Terry, but also to thrust deep into the side of the Network executive as well who had been standing close behind the procurer, whimpering in fear as he stared down at Bila over Terry's lavender-draped shoulder...

Terry screamed, and after a horrified look down at the metal shaft protruding from his toga, he screamed again as he clutched at it and then screamed again as he fell to the floor, and then again, and again - until he finally died several minutes later, much to the relief of those who were forced to stand near to him by the crush of panicked crowd.

The executive clutched at his side where the point had pulled back out of his abdomen when Terry fell, and shrieked in pain - and then again in fear when he looked down with shocked eyes to see his own blood spurting through his fingers. He coughed and collapsed onto the carpeted floor and writhed for a short time in an ever-widening pool of his blood...

*

Bila looked up at the crowd on the balcony, now milling about in fright like a herd of long-noses at killing time – all except for Kris and Marybell. The two women stood in tense silence at the rail with deep concern plain on their faces. He gazed directly at Marybell for a second longer, then he smiled, and turning, launched his other spear at the fat man wearing the bushy wreath on his head.

Without waiting to see the effect of his missile's impact, Bila wheeled and scooping up the baby boy with one hand, jerked the shaft free from the guard's body that blocked the clattering gates and squeezed between them as they still were attempting to close. He turned to the right in the dim hallway behind the portal and disappeared at a run.

*

"Damn, if our man don't give good chaos when he do crank up," Boots gritted as she squeezed her friend's arm. But Puss, who was hyper-tense and battle-ready only a moment before, was now distracted and suddenly unfocused. "Did you hear him?" she whispered with wide eyes.

"Hear what?" Boots grunted, as she grimly watched the aftermath of Bila's second spear.

General Butler was in a manic state because of the drug he had been drinking throughout the evening, so when Bila's shaft was flying directly at him, his enhanced reactions had allowed him to grab Bettie by the shoulders and jerk her in front of him as a shield, a second before the shaft impacted.

It entered her chest just below her black brassiere, and because of the impetus Bila had given it in his rage, it trust through the small woman and through Butler's left arm as well.

As the two women had watched, Bettie looked down in astonishment, then they heard her moan, "Oh, Bennie - it hurts," as she sank to the floor, staring down with shock at the shaft piercing her torso.

Boots forced herself to wait another moment while Butler kicked the little woman aside with a clatter of the long shaft transfixing her and shouted, "I'm hurt! Do something about it, Dammit!" Then he trampled unheedingly on Bettie's hips and the abdomen of the Network executive dying on the floor next to Terry's body, and kicked over the Colonel's wheel chair in his lumbering escape from the menace on the floor below.

The Colonel's body brace held when she fell to the floor and she was writhing in agony at the Director's feet as he screamed into a handset he pulled from his toga, "Alert! Alert! Escape! Medics to the balcony!" Then he looked frantically around - and found Boots standing beside him, her hands on her hips and her feet planted astride the Colonel's struggling body.

"You want him back?" she smiled, her voice clear to him through the uproar as the crowd shouted and squealed in their floundering attempts to escape the terror they perceived beyond the balcony.

"Yes dammit, I do. But there's something funny about you two, so I'll do it my way," the Director hissed over the noise of the crowd, his aplomb shattered as the grotesque Gala he had staged to appease the General's bizarre lusts disintegrated around him.

"Do you want him back?" Boots repeated, without changing her expression.

"Yes, dammit! But my men will get him dammit!"

"Like those two just tried to do down on that floor? I think not. So I ask you again - do you want us to pursue him?" Boots continued calmly, but now with a look of death in her eyes.

"Yes, dammit! Do it!" the harassed man now on the edge of hysteria, finally snapped as he looked wildly about to see what General Butler was doing in the tumultuous crowd.

"Thank you Director, we shall," Boots smiled, with an expression that the man would recall afterward.

"Grab those spears Buddy, we might need them! That big Undoc looks real dangerous," Boots called in a theatrically loud voice as she stepped over the Colonel writhing impotently on the floor. She turned and shouted, "And let's go after him like the Director says, OK?"

"Ja Boss," Puss shouted eagerly, and then she forced her way through the milling crowd and leaped across the room to collect Bila's things where Terry had dropped them. She found that his pouch and belt were also in the cloth wrapping his spears and throwing sticks and tucked them under her arm as she slammed through the milling crowd back to Boots.

"Which way to the floors below?" Boots demanded of the harried Director as Butler bellowed like a wounded bull in the background.

"To the left. Here's a key card for the stairs. And catch him for me quick dammit, or you're next," the distraught man snarled as he looked anxiously to the fat General ranting in the midst of his clamoring syncopates.

"Thank you sir, and I really will to do it to you – just as soon as I can," Boots said with a smile over her shoulder as she trotted toward the door. Puss gave the Director a cherry grin and a friendly wave as she hurried behind her friend.

*

Boots snapped in the hall, "This way," and raced to the left toward a lighted exit sign over a door. She waved the card at the lock and threw the door open to reveal a stairway and immediately began running down it, her new boot soles giving her secure traction as she precipitously descended to the next floor. Puss followed a second behind, and gained on Boots because of her superior agility.

They exited the stairwell at the next level into a drab corridor stretching both left and right. Boots paused and looked around for a second until Puss snapped, "This way," as she started racing down the corridor to their left.

"What'n ferk you doing and where'n ferk you goin'?" Boots hissed.

"This is the way we go! Get on board, dammit!"

"Ja Boss," Boots shook her head and frowned she trotted behind her friend down the crudely finished cement hallway, its status obviously less than that of the Director's level.

They reach a dead-end that forced another choice of directions and Puss turned left without hesitating and started down that dank corridor until Boots caught her arm.

"Why go this way?"

"Because this is the right way, dammit. Now let's move it!"

"How do you know that?"

Puss glared at her friend, "When we got time I'll explain. But fer' now, just follow, OK?"

"Ja Boss."

They reached a crossing at the end of that corridor and Puss turned to the right again without a pause, and suddenly began silently sprinting on her toes past the blank doors along its dim-lit length. This time Boots raced in silence behind her friend without question.

They rounded a final corner in the corridor to see Bila, standing at bay against its dead end. He stood in a pool of harsh light from a bare light in the ceiling and was feinting with his steel shaft at two black-clad guards who confronted him. He still clasped the baby boy to his chest with one arm, and was repeatedly thrusting his point with his other hand at the men to hold them off.

The man on the left was covering Bila with an assault rifle while the one on the right was cautiously aiming a tranquilizer gun.

Puss snarled, and signaled to Boots to take the man with the trank gun as she stooped and placed the flint-tipped spears silently on the floor, and jerked free of her cape.

Boots gave a quick thumbs-up, and unsnapping her linked belt, leap forward toward her man as Puss eyed the distance to the one with the rifle.

Her face hardened into a killing mask as she took three running steps, then flipped forward to land on her hands. Completing a tight front leap with a spring from her arms, she sailed over toward the man with the assault rifle, and slammed feet-first into the small of his back. Her reinforced spike heels rammed deep into his body and carried floor grit and fibers from his clothing with them as they pierced his kidneys.

The man was instantly stunned by massive shock and thrust forward
under her impact. He began to die even as Puss gracefully rode his body over
as he fell forward. The man slammed face down on the floor and his dropped
rifle was still clattering when she pulled her heels out of his back with a wet
sucking sound as she completed another flip to land in a crouch in front of
Bila.

"Hello Friend," Puss grinned as she straightened, "Nice to see you
again…"

His face brightened, and he gave her a crooked smile…

When Boots had snapped the release on her belt, multiple two centimeter-long meat hooks sprang out of its buckle. She gripped the free end of the
belt and swung its chain like a morning-star mace at the guard aiming the
trank gun at Bila as Puss leapt toward her own quarry. The buckle wrapped
around guard's head and as she jerked the belt back, the hooks slashed across
his face and eyes.

Just when Puss landed before Bila, the second guard screamed and
dropped his weapon with a clatter as he turned to escape the pulling pain
across his face, only to receive Boot's flat-footed kick to his chest. She sunk
a spiked heel into it under his sternum where it pierced the tip of his heart's
left ventricle. Then as she twisted and pirouetted to pull her heel free from
his body, the man collapsed and also begun dying as his shocked heart ceased
pumping.

"Hello Bila, welcome to S'attl'," Boots smiled as she stepped over the
guard's still-quivering body.

The man now smiled broadly and nodded to both women, "Friends."

"And I'm real glad to see you can cope with our bad people so good," Puss
added as she took his arm and squeezed it.

"So am I, but now let's move out," Boots said as she turned and motioning them to follow her, trotted between the dying guards on the floor and
back along the corridor.

Puss snatched up her cloak along with Bila's spears and pouch when
they reached where she had dropped them and called for Boots to stop.

"I think he might want these back, Buddy."

"You friends are my. Thank at you I," Bila said as he passed the baby to
Puss and dropped the steel shaft on the floor with a clatter. He tied his belt
around his waist then looping the thong of the curiously-carved stick around
his wrist he grasped his light spears and reached for the baby again as he

continued, "But S'attl' people not are."

He nodded to the child he cradled in his arm which had remained calm and passive ever since Bila had accepted him from his dying mother. He asked in a flinty voice, "Why hurt they mommy he?"

Boots looked at the big naked man in the stark hallway and saw the concern and anger on his face. He stood holding his primitive weapons in one hand while cradling a baby in his other arm and his only concern was for it and its young mother's fate. Her eyes suddenly misted as she choked, and could not give him an answer.

Puss saw Boots' reaction and said quietly, "I think we better go for now, and talk later," as she gripped her friend's arm and beckoned to Bila.

Boots took a deep and shuddering breath then she shook her head and grasped Bila's arm as she hissed, "Follow me Friends. I know the way out of this Rat-trap now - finally Dammit."

*

"There's a guard cube around this corner. It covers the door to the back street where us contractors drive in with our catch. The guard's always prickly about letting anyone go out though, and I don't know if the Director's card will work for a building exit," Boots whispered as the three paused in a passageway near the lighted area at its end.

"The guard's a he, right?" Puss grinned.

"Yes, at least almost always. Why? " Boots asked with a frown.

"Its gender actually doesn't matter, just wait here and watch, OK!" Puss said as she stepped out of the corridor.

She strolled into a drab concrete space that had a guard cubicle sitting beside a large metal door in the outside wall. Puss swayed her hips as she slowly advanced under the harsh lights toward the cubicle, staring at the man behind its armorglass window.

"Hey, Power Person, that bunch upstairs is way much too dumbo for me to stay with. They be duller than a Chin Church on Monday morning."

"So why don't you come out here, and do me Big Guy - like I know you can?" Puss moaned as she took a stance with her hips thrust forward, and began caressing her breasts with one hand while stroking her belly with the other.

"I like it hard and rough, and on a dirty floor — so come out here and give it to me Mister Man. Do me Now!"

The man in the cubical was used to controlling the entry of those brought into the complex, but was not used to dealing with any who approached him from the inside who were not Network functionaries - and he was definitely not used to receiving the blatant sexual invitation Puss was sending him.

He gasped and gulped, then flushed and became agitated as Puss continued to stare at him while she moaned with desire and stroked her breasts and belly. She leaned back and thrust out her pelvis, and began writhing with her legs wide-spread, and moving her hips in an unmistakable invitation.

The man glanced hurriedly around at the small survel screens in his booth then abruptly activated the booth door control.

Puss panted, "Yeess!" when he rose and stood in the open door with a vacuous leer on his face. She sensuously slid her right hand under the front flap of her breechclout, and thrust her hips toward him one last time as he started to step out, then with an angelic smile she jerked out the small black pistol and fired one shot.

The crack of its report was mild, but the cloud of gun-smoke was extensive because of its ammunition. The little plastic pistol was loaded with black powder, a mechanical mixture of nitrate, sulfur and charcoal that was the first propellant developed for guns a millennium ago. Additionally, the load's primer was made of potassium chlorate, red phosphorus, and phosphorus sesquisulphide, the same mixture that had been used to make strike-anywhere matches for the last three centuries.

The construction of the pistol was totally non metallic, so it did not trip metal detectors and while smoky and smelly, both the propellant and primer had the virtue of being made of only inorganic chemical and thus did not trigger most explosive sniffing devices - as Sergeant Bill had intended when he created the little pistol for his two favorite clients.

The projectile it fired from its seven millimeter bore was a flechette and it struck the guard in his throat where its glass tip shattered and released the synthetic karat venom. The man's motor nerve functions ceased in two seconds and he gasped, collapsed and began dying with his body sprawled in the booth's open doorway, as Puss had intend when she timed her shot...

"All clear gang, Let's move!"

"Hey Buddy, if you ever start doin' that damn belly dance in front of me, I'm way gone!" Boots grinned as she motioned Bila forward. He strode into the areaway carrying his spears and cradling the baby boy in his arm with thunder on his face.

"We baby make safe. Come back. Kill rats," he declared quietly. His very soft declaration once more filled the space where they stood.

"Well Buddy, looks like Bila's got the agenda pretty well figgered out, so I reckon all we got to do is to come up with a battle plan, right?" Puss grinned.

"Yep, it sure do, but that's for later. Right now you got to activate the street door control from in the booth, which probably won't work if the booth's door is open. So, go cope Sweetie," Boots said with a grin to her friend.

"If I do it good, it'll cost ya' a backrub, OK?"

"OK, dammit! Now just do it!"

Puss stepped into the booth over the dead guard's body and located the door control button, conveniently labeled "Outside Door". She jerked her flechette from his neck and hauled his body back into the booth with one arm around his chest while she held down the button labeled "Booth Door" with her other. Positioning his slack form back on his stool, she rested his forehead on the outside door button then leaped through the door from the booth just before it hissed shut.

The door to the outside began rattling open a second later and Boots gave Puss a happy hand-slap as she grinned, "Good goin' Buddy! But now it's back to the barn time so let's pound ground!"

"Ja Boss!"

"Ja Boss," Bila echoed, causing Boots to smile and Puss to laugh aloud as they ran out onto the street as with another rattle, the door began rolling down again.

*

The three trotted along the sidewalk at the rear of the Network building until they reached its corner. They stood back-to-back tensely at guard by the curb for a moment, until a sedan showing no lights came around the corner from a side street and accelerated toward them. It braked to a sliding stop and the driver's window opened.

"You folks lookin' for a ride?" Waldo asked cheerfully. "But I do charge more for extra fares," he added as he looked toward the large naked man who stood on the sidewalk with Boots and Puss. A man who cradled a naked baby in the crook of one arm and held two spears in his other hand while he starred at Waldo with a look that the sergeant really didn't want to explore at that moment...

Boots jerked the rear door open and jumped in and reaching for Bila's spears, deftly fitted them lie across the seat backs. Then she reached for Bila's hand and pulled on it while Puss pressed on his back as they both urged him into the cramped space.

Puss discarded the spent flechette in the gutter as soon as Bila was seated and jumped in to sit on his lap as she slammed the door. Then she gently took the baby from his arms and began making little crooning sounds to it as she cradled it in her breast.

"Max plan change old friend," Boots announced to Waldo. "The cat's in the wok way biggers in Rat's Nest right now, so let's move out! Raise Mack or Bobby for me, and we damn sure don't want to go back to my folk's place tonight, OK?"

"Yes Ma'am! And by the way, thanks for making my life fun again," Waldo chuckled as he powered up the sedan. "Mack's waiting for your call, and don't worry about the car behind us. It's our backup, and they carry heavy," he continued as he handed a comset back over the seat to her, "This one's secure, punch number three."

Boots clicked the instrument on and waited for a moment as all of the subtleties of its circuits and routings reacted, then she smiled as she heard the grizzled General's growl crackle in her receiver.

"Mack, you really are a jewel of perception! Yes, things are different than when we last spoke," she said with a chuckle.

"The situation has now been advanced to big and quick, and perhaps to critical with regard both to Butler and the S'attl Network apparat as well. This is for reasons I will explain when we meet. But right now we need a safe place to land tonight for our talk."

"OK, I'll tell him. Waldo, Mack says Rick's"

"I figgered he would. Tell him that's where we're headed right now."

"You heard that, OK? But I need for you to tell Hector and Helen about the plan change – and that things might get pretty stiff for both of them very soon as well. So if you would please, I would like for you to also think about some arrangements for them."

"Thank you, they will appreciate that Sir," Boots said quietly after a moment. Then she continued, "What was the cause of the advancement? Interesting is a mild term, but you will be briefed as soon as we get there."

"Let's just say that the Network has just discovered just how much it underestimated the capabilities of new asset we have, to its very great discomfort."

"Oh and Mack, please see if someone can have us a baby bottle and some formula when we get there," Boots asked with a chuckle. After she listened with a grin to the crackle in the receiver for a second, she finished, "Yes Sir, I know Sir! I'm out."

"OK, I heard that. What's the body count, and who gets the free brass job, you or Baby Bird?" Waldo asked as he steered the cab around a late-running public transport bus lumbering down the middle of the street.

*

It had been a Special Forces tradition during the war albeit a very unofficial one, for each unit to give a free kit cleanup to the trooper who came back from a penetration mission against the Chin with the highest number of confirmed kills.

At the end of each mission the whole group was allowed to rest for a day then they were paraded in full dress the next morning.

The collector of the highest body-count had his or her kit and uniform cleaned and prepped by their mates for the parade, while the honoree took an extra sleep-in. This could last for almost an hour, if the honoree was able to ignore their mates' whisperings of derogatory and salacious comments around his or her bunk while they shined the honoree's brass and boots. Boots, Puss, and Waldo had all taken a number of these naps during the war...

*

"Well old friend, you ain't gonna' believe this, but the big guy back here took the prize tonight," Boots chuckled, "I got one and my little Buddy got two in her own sweet way, but he got five known and a casualty, which was none other than our good General Butler."

"But I don't know how are we're going to shine his brass tomorrow, since he doesn't wear any. His name's Bila by the way, and he's our new friend."

"Did he do it with these things?" Waldo asked as he indicated the two flint-tipped spears that lay across the seatback next to him, while being careful to not touch their points.

"No friend, he didn't," Boots replied with a crooked grin, "Bila was forced to improvise, so he used munitions provided by the Network..."

*

Waldo turned the sedan into the dark alley behind and below the block of buildings that included Rick's Club Ancienne, and blinked his brake lights twice to the military sedan following them. He drove slowly down the littered alley until he reached a rusting corrugated metal door in the side of a decrepit brick wall. He halted the sedan and pressed a button on the dashboard.

When the door silently rolled up, Waldo dove into the dark space inside and the heavy military sedan followed, to a stop beside the taxi.

The metal door rolled back down, and when its sponge-rubber flanges had sealed the spaces around the door lights came on, and Boots and Puss, and Bila could see the large space around their car.

"Welcome back to the club," Rick said with a smile as he walked forward, still in his white mess jacket and a lit cigarette in his fingers. Mack stood beside him in his army greens, with a look of unholy joy on his face.

"Your briefing, Ma'am," he murmured, "But only if you are ready to give it to me, of course."

"You know, Mack, you get to gallop sooner than anyone else I know. I like that," Boots said with a grin as she climbed out of the sedan. "And you're right Sir, we need to talk biggers, but this is the first priority," she added as Puss climbed out of the back seat with the baby cradled to her breast. The little boy was starting to whimper and fret, and smears of green mascara were now on his lips.

"Baby feeding and tending are another of our services, Ma'am," Rick chuckled as he pulled a comset from a pocket and spoke into it, "Kinder care please - Maria, to the garage."

"Thanks Mack. I would like to introduce you to Bila now who is also known as Trooper Three now," Boots said as she reached into the back seat of the sedan and pulled on Bila's arm.

Bila ducked his head and stepped out of the rear door and stood erect. He first looked to Puss and saw that she held the baby safely. Then he inspected the two men who stood before him.

"They friends you? Or kill we them?"

"They are friends Bila! I will tell you when killing time starts, OK," Boots muttered to the man as she grasped his arm and shook it. "Be nice."

Bila glanced down at her then he turned again to the two men who stood before him, the black man in the white coat and the old man with the sharp eyes. He looked at them for another moment, then nodded and held out his hands with his palms upward as he said, "Friends!"

"Friend!" Mack immediately responded as he slapped his palms on Bila's out-stretched hand. Rick did the same a second later.

Waldo climbed out of the driver's seat of the taxi and said to Bila, "Friend."

"Friend," Bila nodded as he turned and held out his hand to Waldo as well. Then he asked the three, "Friends at Kris and Marybell you?"

Rick smiled as he watched Bila dominate the space around Mack and himself, then he answered, "Yes, we are."

"Good. Good you be," Bila announced.

Rick nodded to Bila then he turned to Waldo, "Are your troops hungry?" he asked as he gestured toward the six people who had piled out of the military sedan and were now standing in a line at parade rest, with their eyes straight ahead, while observing Puss and Boots and Bila and their costumes, or lack thereof.

"Rations are always a good idea for troops," Mack replied with a dry smile, "Feed them out here while we go talk in your den," he said as he gestured toward a door in the wall of the large garage. Rick nodded and gestured with a slight bow to Boots. She motioned to Bila and Puss to follow then glanced around at the number and types of vehicles in the large space. "Looks like there's good backup here too," she whispered she started to follow Rick.

"Hey gang, got any clothes that'll fit Bila?" Puss asked, with sudden authority.

"Good thinking young lady," Mack said, "There are some spare greens here in Fort Rick's totally unofficial supply room. I'll get him the biggest set I can find, but while I am looking for them, all of you wait for me - and don't even think about starting your brief until I get there," he said, with a stern look at Boots.

"No Sir! Understood, General, Sir!" Boots answered briskly as she hit a brace and snapped him a salute, with a twinkle in her eyes. Mack automatically returned her salute then turning, he shook his head as he walked toward a steel door set in the far wall of the garage.

"What Mack calls my den is a fully secure conference room," Rick was saying when another door opened, and a motherly little woman wearing a white smock stepped into the garage. She smiled at Puss who was still holding the baby, now beginning to squirm and whimper in earnest.

"I take you to up to nursery little man and make all better," Maria said tenderly with smiling dark eyes as she reached out her arms for the child.

"He will be fine," Rick said when Puss hesitated, and Bila frowned. "Maria is very good with children."

Puss looked at Rick then she smiled up to Bila, "It's OK," she nodded as she gave the child to Maria. "This nice woman will feed him and get some clothes on his poor little cold bottom."

"What you name little man?" Maria crooned as she cradled the baby in her arms.

"Mother he name say Gwaii. He be Gwaii he," Bila announced quietly in a voice that did not allow argument.

Rick and Waldo glanced at Bila, with respect. The two knew that while size was always a poor second to a person's projection of authority, this strange naked man had both.

"Maria, the baby's name is Gwaii, OK?" Puss said to the nurse as she patted the little woman's shoulder and Gwaii's bottom.

"Call us please when he is happy again, Maria," Rick added. "We will be in room 001."

The little woman was walking toward her door and cooing to the fretting child when Mack walked out of the supply room with a bundle in his arms.

"I heard your talk about cold bottoms. See what these can do for Bila's butt," he said with a dry smile. "These are the biggest we have."

"Rick, you got any army whiskey in this chat room of yours?" Puss asked.

"We do have a utilitarian bar and I believe we have some of that particular poison, since Bobby also uses it occasionally to kill some of his brain cells."

"Hey! Don't forget about mine," Waldo grinned.

"I can never do that Sergeant," Rick answered, "But Marybell I believe I owe you some catch-up rounds of that horrible potion, as well as of the some cigars that you did not get to appreciate last night."

"Good, I'll like that. Just give me a minute to get our packs so we can cover our own cold behinds too," Puss said happily as she turned and trotted toward the sedan.

"I'll get them for you, and then you two can change in the conference room while we dress Bila out here," Waldo said as he ran to the car and opened its trunk with a grunt.

"While we are forced to stand here and wait for all this damn non-focused activity to be done," Boots muttered impatiently, "Tell me how much armor is in your taxi's butt," as she watched Waldo strain as he lifted the trunk lid.

"Quite a bit" - Rick answered with a rumbling chuckle, "One never knows when unfriendly persons might try to make one's joy ride unhappy."

"The conference room," he continued as his face changed and he nodded toward the third door opening into the garage space, "Has a new combination.

I altered the keypad code last night. It is now 74-1776."

"I like it," Boots said with a crooked grin after she thought for a second. Then she turned as Puss and Waldo walked back with her pack.

Puss asked, "What code?" Rick gave the door code then she agreed, "Yep! It's a code that's real easy to remember, for some of us yet alive today anyway." Then she asked Waldo, "But why do you think Bila needs help in dressing?"

"Flint tipped spears aren't usually issued along with Army greens, but it sorta' looks like he really knows how to use those things. So, because he's a friend of yours I'll teach him how to use Army zippers."

"You're pretty perceptive old friend, but he's a friend of 'Ours'," Boots said quietly.

"Yep Sarge you really are, and he really is," Puss said to Waldo. Then she added as she turned back to Boots with a grimace, "But for right now, Buddy lets go change clothes too, 'cause I'm getting a little chilly."

"I can tell," Boots said with a pointed glance at Puss' nipples. "But why didn't you pull your cloak around to cover your front?"

"I didn't want to get green streaks on the lining," Puss muttered from the side of her mouth.

"Unh-hunh, I can see how that might could happen..."

*

"Please feel free to help yourselves," Rick said as he placed an antique lithographed advertising tray before them. It held several bottles and a small stack of cheap plastic glasses, and became the centerpiece of the plain plastic-topped table where they all were seating themselves. The walls of the small room were padded with corrugated foam and the space was lighted with four oil lamps.

"There are no electronics in here of any kind except for one, and all wireless transmissions are blocked with a special screen, so feel free to talk in here as you wish."

Boots, now wearing her army jumpsuit, removed her black gloves and poured a splash of vodka for herself. Taking a sip, she sighed and leaned forward with her elbows on the table.

"This is good," she said, as she sipped again. "We didn't really taste any of the stuff they were serving at the Gala for a number of reasons, so I'm real happy to get a real drink now. Thanks, Rick."

"But now troops, ready or not, it looks like the time for action is almost here. Boss Rat is going to be sore biggers after tonight. Not only did he loose some of his top talents, but General Butler took a hit as well, and so now that wart on the butt of the world is mad as hell at everyone."

"And friends, I am deeply sorry, and ashamed that it has taken me way too damn long to hear the nasty music Boss Rat has been playing all along while I've worked for him. But yesterday I started getting my brain straight as I told you last night. And this evening I finally realized what is going on here at the micro level."

"It's now clear to me that the Governors and Boss Rat are pretty much one and the same here in S'attl, and probably everywhere else in the West as well. Therefore when they hit at us, Butler's security force in some way or another will be the ones to do it for the Network."

"So what can you tell me about that bunch?"

"Years ago when the state of emergency was first declared by the Governors of Washington State, Oregon, Alaska and California," Mack answered, "This allowed martial law to be imposed by orders from Washington to those battle commands, the Army's internal security force was made up of our normal military police units."

"But when the mission directives from the Military Governors started becoming nastier, and progressively weirder vis-à-vis the civilian population in all the 'Claves, the better people began opting out of that service whenever they had a chance."

"So here in S'attl anyway, those who are left in the Governor's security force today are the lowest achievers that ever were in the services, or people who were actually discharged as undesirables."

"Interesting. Doesn't sound like a real fearsome group though," Boots said with a smile like a wolf.

"It may not sound that way, but did you ever have to jump down into a large nest of rats, all infected with rabies?"

"No. And you make your point, Sir." Boots nodded to Mack "But now to switch focus slightly, at this very moment, yours truly and hers truly," Boots continued as she motioned to Puss, now wearing her clave jumpsuit but still with her eye makeup from the Gala.

She was smiling as she held a half-empty glass of issue whiskey and a lit cigar, then she winked.

Boots snorted she then continued as if she had not been interrupted.

"We are officially in pursuit of him truly," as she pointed toward Bila who sat next to Puss at the table and now wore a green army jumpsuit that fit his frame except where it was tight across his shoulders. He was gazing at Puss' smoldering cigar.

"However, this charade will not be viable for much longer than the coming twenty-four hours, so we must consider our next actions damn quick."

"I believe we will experience an extreme response from the Governor and the Network very soon because of tonight, but also because of their loss of a four-man collection team up in BC - day before yesterday."

"Are you two guilty of this deed?" Mack asked.

"Of course," Boots answered with a bland smile. "They were trying to collect us."

"Hey dammit, it was my turn to push the button," Puss said with a sweet smile, "So I get to claim all of them for my "Life List"."

"So be it!" Boots said with a grin, "Anyway, while a violent response is what we had intended to provoke at some point from the Network and from General Butler, Bila has advanced our timetable tonight way biggers." Then she turned and smiled to Bila, "Thank you, Friend."

He nodded to her gravely, "You thank Friend too. When kill more they we? No - kill more them of?"

Waldo said with a grunt, "I like this man. He thinks like I do," as he stood and held out his hand across the table to Bila.

"Yes, friend. We will kill soon!"

Bila gazed at Waldo. Then with a crooked smile he leaned forward as he said, "You look know good kill to. I you like, friend!" and he slapped his hand on Waldo's.

"Congratulations Waldo, "Boots said, "I think you just made the Alpha Team."

"Great," Waldo replied. Then with sudden caution he asked, "But who's the team leader?"

"Well, the job sorta' rotates," Puss murmured as she blew a smoke ring, "But when it's Bila's turn you always know it somehow..."

"Are you three heroes hungry, or did you have your fill at the Rat's Gala?" Rick interrupted.

"Yes. And yes," Boots said quietly, and Puss nodded with a grimace. Bila frowned then his eyes clouded as he gazed off in to space.

"Thank you Rick, some food will be real good. But it's also time to talk," Boots continued, in a voice that still controlled the room. "And can we link

Bobby and Barbara in here with us?"

"Done, Ma'am, but why don't you people eat first, so you will be strong enough to talk afterward?" Rick chuckled as he pulled out his comset.

"Chef, make up six night-owl specials if you would please, and send them to the people in the garage, and three more for room 001." Then after a pause as he gauged Bila's size, he added, "No. Make that four for 001 if you would please."

"Thank you, Rick. We'll eat fast, because we don't have much time," Boots said quietly, "Then we'll talk."

The black man nodded to her and clicking his comset off, rose and stepped to a plain metal credenza on one wall of the stark room. He opened a drawer and removed a modern desktop trans-send unit and uncoiling its connecting wire, placed it next to the drink tray in the center of the table. He positioned the unit and punched in a code sequence on its keypad.

"This has the same security as the one we used last night, but without the early 20th century cosmetics I'm afraid. Bobby and Barbara coming right up," he continued with a smile.

"What about Bird Nose?" Puss asked.

Rick glanced at Mack with a question in his eyes, and Mack turned and looked to Boots for a second before he faced Rick again and nodded.

Rick turned to Puss and smiled, "Good idea, Ma'am. I apologize for my oversight."

"Thank you Sir, "You learn quick, I'm glad about that," Puss said, with a little smile.

"I try, Ma'am" the Rick responded with an approving nod as he punched an additional code in to the black box on the table before them, and thereby acknowledged that Puss was an equal in their war counsel.

*

"Bobby here, and Barbara is also plugged in," The colonel's voice sounded from the speaker, "Who's there?"

"Don't be so controlling Colonel," Barbara said in a dry voice, "I'll speak for myself."

Mack responded crisply, "Kris, Marybell, Rick, Waldo, Bila and I."

"Good. Now sound off," Bobby responded with equal crispness, but after a second, he grunted, "Whoa, who is this Bila?"

"Mack here,"

"Kris here,"

"Rick here,"

"Waldo here,"

"Marybell here, and don't you forget it!"

Bila's eyes suddenly sparkled, as with a crooked grin to Puss he leaned over to the trans-send unit on the table and announced in a baritone voice with authority, "Bila here, and don't you forget it too!"

"Jesu H. Ferkin Christos, who in-hell is that?" Bobby's voice sputtered from the instrument.

"Yes, I'd like that intel too, daughter," Bird Nose' voice crackled from the speaker.

"Daddy, his name is Bila and he's our new friend."

"He's new alright, but are you sure about the friend part daughter? Be honest."

"Honest, Daddy, in fact, Honest Injun' even," Puss said with a grin, caus-ing the others at the table to either look at her with a question in their eyes, or in Boots' case to groan.

"Thanks Daughter. Understood, and I admit that I deserved that," Bird Nose' voice sounded from the instrument again, "I'm sorry for the interrup-tion. Please continue."

"Security is never an interruption Colonel. Your question was entirely proper, particularly in view of our newly changed timetable, which we will discuss in a moment," Boots replied.

"But now that all intros are out of the way, I really would like to take a little time and eat something tonight - finally. And I'm quite sure Marybell and Bila would as well. So you guys tell war stories for a couple of minutes until it's time to talk about real stuff, if you would please."

A chorus of dutiful "Yes, Ma'ams" responded, from both those sitting around the table and present on the transceiver. All remained silent during the short time while the three attacked the classic full-dressed hamburgers with accompanying fries that Rick served them from a tray brought to the room's door.

"Well Rick, I sure do like your night-owl special, and I really must come back for another one sometime," Boots sighed five minutes later as she wiped her mouth.

There had been a moment when Bila looked with cautious indecision at the platter that Rick placed before him. He had paused while watching Puss from the corner of his eye. She had smiled without returning his glance, and seizing her burger with both hands taken a healthy bite. Bila had grunted then copied her action.

Mack watched Bila and Puss as this by-play unfolded, and the pleased smile that broke across the man's face when he tasted his first mouthful. The grizzled general had lifted an eyebrow, but said nothing.

Boots also had noted Mack's interest in Bila from the corner of her eye while she was attacking her own hamburger, but had said nothing as well.

When the three sighed in satisfaction after they finished wolfing down their food and were wiping their mouths, Mack also noted that Puss had to show Bila how to use a paper napkin...

*

"Now it's time to talk. We need to reach an agreement on what our next steps will be, damn quickie," Boots announced as she pushed her empty plate aside, "So first of all, where do we stand regarding our available force?"

"We already have a partial inventory of the WNG assets as well as access arrangements to them, thanks to Barbara who can respond with eager enthusiasm when pointed in the right direction," Mack replied with a straight face, and in an innocent tone, which caused a significant snort to sound from the unit on the table.

"Count yourself lucky General that I am an expert both at receiving, as well as giving direction...

"Anyway, Ma'am," Barbara continued, "I have located and secured access to two squadrons of Mark VIIs and a battalion of heavy armor, and I have also alerted all the demobilized units of the WNG to standby status by means of a communications tree of their former officers and NCOs."

"Our people sewed their patches back on their uniforms almost without exception, and are waiting for further orders. Those few who where reluctant to do so when asked are now staying in places where they're protected from any potential harm to their persons."

"Very good, you are an asset to us way sure," Boots said into the transceiver. "Now, Sergeant Waldo, what have you been able to discover about our supply of small arms?" Boots asked with an evil grin as she turned to him at the table.

"Well Ma'am If you will recall, I have also been tasked to be on the road a lot lately, so in order to carry out my main mission, I followed one of your universal dictates, Ma'am. I coped!"

"How?"

"Through delegation to Sergeant Luis, my backup buddy in the Chin tunnel details during the war. He graciously agreed to provide our group with the intel you requested Ma'am, whilst I have been occupied with various other duties, such as being a chauffeur and a coat-catching flunky, Ma'am/ Sir." Waldo said with a snap and an evil grin. "So may I bring him in to report directly?"

"Yes Sergeant, you may."

Waldo stepped to the door of the conference room and opening it, waved to one of the troopers sitting on the vehicles in the garage, and finishing their night-owl specials.

A moment later a short wiry man with a nose like a raptor's beak strode into the room.

Sergeant Luis, please tell Captain Cook what you have found."

Luis stepped forward and replied with a stern face, "I tell you once Waldo, but I now tell her an' you again so both you listen good, Dammit!" Then he reached out with the toe of his boot and kicking around Waldo's empty chair, seated himself at the table across from Boots.

"I haf' found enough small arm catches and squad weaponry for a regiment," he continued as he leaned forward with his elbows on the table.

"I also locate battle control personal `puters enough for a regiment, an' the operative command an' control systems for them."

"The location information I already send to General Barbara Shaw.

"So now Master Sergeant Waldo, do you require anytheeng else of me?" the compact man with the thousand-meter stare in his dark eyes asked, as he continued looking at Boots.

"Thank you Luis," Waldo answered.

"Would you like to go out with the group tomorrow to BC, or do you want to wait here with us for here the big one?"

"Both."

"Ma'am," Waldo asked, "If you have duties for me other than this BC operation, I would like to propose Sergeant Luis as my replacement. We call him the "Cisco Kid", by the way.

"Yes. I do have other work for you," Boots said. Then she smiled at the wiry man with the tense face across the table from her, "And yes Luis, I have good intel on you too, so welcome to the Alpha Team."

"Thank you, Ma'am, I theenk."

Boots' face changed and she glared at him, "We will do this op my way or you will be one of the first casualties, do you read me clear little sergeant?"

A smile slowly spread across Luis' face and his dark eyes sparkled as he rose to his feet, "Shat Ma'am, I am not all that little, as I can show you pretty quickie. But with tha' attitude you have Seester, we might even ferkin' come home again from this crazy detail!"

Boots looked at him for a moment then she grinned slightly as she touched her forehead, "I like you Luis, and with you on board, Sargento Grande, I am quite sure we will do just that. Thank you for your good work."

"Now please stand down until it is time to go, Sir."

Luis stared at Boots for a moment while she returned his look without blinking, then he winked, and raised his hand in the same casual half-salute she had just given him.

"Si, Mi Capitána," he whispered as he turned and sauntered from the room.

"Damn! I've never seen him salute anyone before. He's got two Silvers and three Bronzes and a whole string of Purples," Waldo said, "Congratulations Kris, err – Ma'am."

Boots smiled back at Waldo and shrugged, then her voice changed to command tone as her face hardened and she swept those at the table with her gaze.

"This morning Mack and I secured the legitimacy we need to begin the Restoration - and tonight an incident occurred that while happening earlier than I had planned, has caused much greater discomfort to the Network and the Military Governor than I could ever have hoped for."

She grinned and gestured toward the large man sitting beside Puss, "And Bila here was the agent that very effectively put Rat's Nest into panic mode tonight."

Bila looked at Boots, and a grin spread across his face, and his eyes sparkled as he nodded to her, "Si, Mi Capitána."

Boots blinked, then started to continue, "So I --" when Bobby's voice sounded from the speaker.

"Hold please! I've got a telcom coming in on my other secure circuit."

Those at the table and on the com-net waited in silence until Bobby came back on a moment later. His voice crackled from the speaker, "Washington has just scrambled an S/TFB-330-T at Boeing Field to go into Pitson National in DC! The ground crew is configuring it now for launch at dawn tomorrow!"

"How you know that?"

"The plane is USAF, but the duty pilot is WANG and she just called me."

"So who's riding in the trainer's seat?" Boots asked.

Bobby's grin somehow came through with his transmission as he responded, "The Network Director…"

"Ooo! He's been called up to the Principal's Office for a spankin'. That's gonna' burn his scrawny little butt biggers!" Puss said with an evil grin, as she took another sip of whisky and a puff on her cigar.

*

The S/TFB-330 was a movable-wing long-range fighter/bomber aircraft that was capable of astonishing speed and maneuvers when flown by a competent pilot. The Chin central command had greatly respected this aircraft, and considered it to be their worst airborne menace.

However Washington had maintained total control over the use of these superb assets, particularly during the later phases of the war and somehow, they were seldom "available" to fire support those who were fighting the Chin in the bloody quagmire on the ground…

The trainer version of the aircraft had a second seat forward of the pilot's position, but its controls could be over-ridden or locked out by the pilot.

*

"How long for them to arrive DC?" Boots asked.

"At Mach 2.5 and with no ordinance so she can carry extra fuel for a non-stop, I would say a little less than an hour." Bobby replied. Then he drawled, "However I suggested to Wanda, our pilot that she looks around for some headwinds."

"Good thinking Colonel, and I can see why you earn all the credits we pay you to be in our outfit. But now Sirs and Mesdames, what's your best guess as to when the Director or his replacement will come back? Because soon thereafter our life will become full of opportunity as it were.

"You first, Mack."

"Thank you for the honor of being first Ma'am, but it would help considerably if I knew just exactly what it was that you three did to stir up the Rat's Nest this evening that got the Director called on the carpet."

"Point well taken as usual, Sir. We first met Bila when we were up in BC on our most recent trip, and we left him there to protect the other new asset I told you about last night. But he was collected somehow for Boss Rat yesterday and turned up on the menu tonight at the Gala along, with some other unfortunates.

"Rat made Bila angry however, so when he decided to leave their party he killed two of their guards, a slime-sack named Terry who was Rat's chief talent scout, as well as the Network's designated fetch-dog for Butler on his way out and through no fault of his own, a poor little back-warmer missioned as Butler's comfort girl.

"Aside from the Terry insect getting what was way over due him though, the best part about tonight is that Bila also stuck a spear through Butler's arm with his Parthian shot.

"We saw all of this and decided to leave when Bila did, so after we linked up with him in the basement of Rat's Nest, Marybell killed two more guards, and I finally got to kill one before we left."

"When we were all out on the street, I heard a bugle-call and Waldo's cavalry came galloping over the hill just like he said he would."

Those both at the table and on the phone were silent for a moment as they absorbed the facts, and implications of Boots' story.

Then Mack spoke, "I assume that the baby, Gwaii I think you called him," he nodded to Bila and then continued quietly, "Was at the Gala as well."

"Yes. They had him on the menu along with his mother and grandfather, as well as Bila and three others. Rat brutally terrorized them one-by-one, and then murdered them all to amuse Butler and the other guests."

"Bila was scheduled to be the last victim, but he didn't play by their rules as I just pointed out, and he brought Gwaii along when he left."

"Well, now to respond to your initial question Ma'am," Mack growled, "First light is 05:00 hours here, so the Director will land at Pitson a little after 06:00 Pacific which is 09:00 there."

"He should be at the Network headquarters in the old Statler hotel building within a half hour after landing. Since this kind of meeting usually does not last long," Mack continued in a dry tone, "He, or his replacement, should be back at the airport around 10:30 DC time, and airborne soon thereafter. They should land at Boeing Field around 09:00 hours local."

"If he then 'copters to the Network Building, he should be at his desk a little before 10:00, about what I assume would be his normal start time."

"What does anyone else think?"

"Sounds good to me," Bobby and Barbara said almost in unison from the phone and EB grunted an affirmative a second later. The others at the table nodded, and Boots said, "Thank you Mack, It sounds good to me too. Now EB, do you have some way to confirm Mack's estimate of their departure time tomorrow? If you can, would you pass the intel along to Bobby."

"I'll work on it Ma'am."

Bobby chuckled, "I've heard him say that before, and whenever he did, things always got done."

"Gwaii is Haida, right?" Rick suddenly asked.

"Yes. But now he's ours now, OK?" Puss announced, "Or mine anyway!"

"Us," Bila said in a quiet voice. "Mommy he Gwaii us give."

Puss smiled at Bila's statement of fact, and nodded.

"Later on the kid, OK?" Boots snapped. "We have a bunch more ground to cover tonight."

"Now for you on the phone, I will block transmission for a moment for deep security reasons. Barbara, Mack will brief you and Bobby in person later this evening, and Bird Nose, your daughter will brief you in a moment in the unique way that only you two have."

"I am closing for several minutes, starting now," and Boots finished as she touched the off button on the transceiver. Then she rose from the table and stepped to her pack lying on the floor next to the wall. Retrieving her sketch box, she reseated herself and placed it on the table.

"Waldo, I want you to organize and take whatever assets you think necessary to secure the person of Governor Regina Drake in her residence at Olympia without being obvious about it. You will protect her until my signal, which will be soon and you will leave on this mission after we break tonight, as soon as Bobby and Barbara are briefed."

"Mack, after you brief our friends, I would like for you to accompany Waldo on the initial penetration in Olympia, to assure the Governor that we are who we say we are."

"I suggest you meet her in her garden when she walks Kayak tomorrow morning."

"Then Sir, after you have had your fun skulking around in the field once again with Waldo and his troops, and have made the introductions, I would like for you to return here, to what apparently has become our command post at Rick's," Boots paused, and looked around at the black man with a raised eyebrow.

He nodded with a grim smile as he lit another cigarette.

"Mack," Boots continued, "I would like you to also notify the WNG, and the WANG to be ready to be called out soon in coordination with Barbara -

very soon."

"Yes Ma'am," Mack replied briskly, "And thank you also, for the complement, of leaving the details to us."

"That is why you and Barbara and Waldo have the jobs I gave you, but don't worry Sir, things will get much more complicated very soon."

Then Boots opened her sketch box and tore out the page of carefully printed notes she had shown Regina Drake earlier in the day.

"This is my plan for beginning the Restoration. This is the only copy. Please read it, but do not mention its details aloud. Instead, reference your comments and crits by the item numbers, if you have any," Boots said quietly. Then she passed the page to Puss.

Puss scanned it and then re-read it intently, then passed it to Waldo without a word.

Waldo read the page quickly and as he did so, his eyes widened. Then when he finished, he passed it to Rick in silence as well. Rick read it quickly, and gave a deep sigh as he passed it to Mack.

Mack glanced at the paper, then broke the silence as he said to Boots, "I already had an idea about what your planned after this morning, Ma'am."

"I thought you did, Sir."

Mack leaned back in his chair, and smiled at Boots with pride.

Rick finally spoke, "Thank you Kris."

Waldo just shook his head in awe, his eyes still wide and Puss sighed as she turned and grinned at her friend.

"You give good plan, Ma'am!" She said as she held her arm up in a clinched-fist salute.

"Don't get Ooopy on me now Troops!" Boots growled, "The work and the risks coming up for us will make the Chin War look like it was a kiddo day care picnic! Feel-good time among us comes later. If ever, OK!"

"But now to continue, Marybell, when we go back to BC tomorrow to secure our new communications asset,"

"Asset Molly?" Bila asked.

"Ha!" Puss exclaimed. "He knows what we're saying, just like Molly said!"

"Yes. It is Molly, and we will go back to her tomorrow. And we will take friends with us to keep her safe. And you will come too," Boots said to Bila as she broke from her command mode and smiled at the large man.

Mack observed the by-play among the three but again said nothing.

Boots changed her voice again and continued, "Marybell, after we set things up in BC with Molly, I am returning to `S'attl day-after-tomorrow, but you will stay with her and command the force Bobby will send up with you."

"Your mission is to bring into operation and protect at all costs, the capability we have found there with the help of Rick's communication person. You will hold the key to our ability to make this restoration work, so don't let go Buddy, OK?"

Marybell looked at her friend for a moment, then her eyes and face became cold and hard again, as they had where she had found Bila confronting his attackers in the corridor only an hour before.

"Shat, I thought you wanted me to do some real work! This mission is an easy-do. The troops you send up will be a help, but they aren't really necessary, because I'm on the warpath now and going after Rat scalps way biggers."

Boots grinned, "I know that Baby Bird, dammit! But you having an SF heavy squad with you out there will make me a much calmer person back here, OK?"

"Ja Boss," Puss said with a tight grin. "But none of your super troopers had better get in my way when I start to party with Rat, OK!"

"I will make absolutely sure that they understand exactly how your command structure works, my little Killer Cutie, OK?"

"Good. I thought you would..."

"Good. I am glad you have faith in me," Boots muttered.

"But now, I would like for you to like to go back on the phone and tell EB and the East Coast group what you have just learned about the plan, if you would be so kind."

"Yes Ma'am," Puss responded with precision as she stood and calmly saluted her friend. Then she seated herself again and pressed the button to reactivate the transceiver on the table, and said after a moment as the circuits connected.

"Kencuttemaum, Kowse. Netapewh!"

"Kencuttemaum, Amonsens," Her father replied, "Netapewh!" After this exchange, which translated as, "Greetings Father. I stand before you," and, "Greetings Daughter. I stand before you," Puss proceeded to give Boots' action plan to her father, carefully using expressions in their language to explain its details in a manner that no eavesdropper to the transmission who was not Pamunkey could possibly understand.

When Puss finally finished speaking, there was silence on the line for a long moment then it was broken by a sound bursting from the speaker that combined the eerie keening of the Confederate battle yell with an ancient Pamunkey war-chant.

"I believe Daddy approves of your plan," Puss drawled to Boots as its echoes died away," And I feel that he is quite interested in what comes next."

"I've heard him make that that sound before and blood and thunder always happened when he did it, every damn time," Bobby's voice murmured from the speaker.

Barbara added, "I've heard about it too. You guys called his war-cry the Chin Chiller, right?"

"Bird Nose, I thank you for your approval," Boots said, with a smile in her voice so obvious that the colonel felt it back in Virginia.

"Now get ready to make any response necessary over there when my, no - Our plan is activated out here."

"Please coordinate with Bobby and you two report back to Mack or Barbara when you've got it together. Action might be in a day, a week, a month, or a year but stand ready, OK!"

"Yes Ma'am! And thank you Ma'am! East Coast assets will be activated and ready! And you may call me by my real name, since we are all now family in a manner of speaking. I am Eagle Beak," he snapped with pride and power obvious in his voice.

"And I am Calling Dove," Puss whispered to those at the table. "Be careful, Daddy," she then said softly into the speaker.

"Thank you, and the same to you, Daughter. Take care of your friends, be sure to guard your rear - and never forget that all of your ancestors walk with you."

"Thank you Daddy, Sir! And I know they walk with you too."

"They do," Eagle Beak's voice responded from the instrument with a quiet confidence that was obvious to all. Then he continued briskly with his voice all business again. "Ma'am, may I ask if you have anything else for us now?"

"You may always ask, Sir, and you will always get an answer, to the best of my abilities," then Boots continued, "Anyone have anything else? If not, we have a heavy bunch of days ahead of us starting tomorrow, so speak now or hold it till later!"

When no one spoke, Boots said crisply, "Dismissed!" and clicked off the transceiver.

Rick smiled, "The bunks in the room adjoining this one are not comfortable but they are clean, if narrow and the shower has a hot water. Please make yourselves at home." Then he nodded to Bila as he turned to leave the room, "And as much as you are able to do Sir here in our despicable `Clave..."

"Rick, do you have a secure line in there, or should I use the one here? I want to talk to my parents," Boots asked.

"There is one in the bunk room, but without the speaker function. If you punch in the entry code to this room followed by your parent's number, the secure system will be activated and you can talk to them with safety."

"What about a call to someone not on the secure lines?" Boots continued.

"Your call will be untraceable, and your voice will be disguised enough to fool the monitors. But you will have to give some kind of recognition sign to the person whom you call since they won't know you."

"Thank you Rick for all that have done, and will do," Boots murmured.

"My only reason for doing what I do, what I have done and what I will do Ma'am, is that I have a great desire to live free with my friends," he said quietly as he left the room.

*

"Alright, Trooper Three, now it's time for you to learn Army-style body sanitation. You listen to Trooper One and do what she says while I call home," Boots grinned.

Puss took Bila by the hand and led him into the large utilitarian bathroom adjoining the squad-sized bunking area off of Rick's conference room.

"This is the place where you clean yourself, and this is the toilet where you squat, and this is where you brush your teeth, and shave if you're a guy," Puss said as she pointed out the room's features. Then she unzipped her jump suit and proceeded to demonstrate how a toilet was used. Bila observed her with quiet amusement, and nodded in understanding when she stood again and flushed the commode.

"Now, let's take your jumpsuit off friend, and I'll show you how to get clean in the shower, OK?" Puss said as she nonchalantly stepped out of her suit and dropping to a bench, unlaced and removed her white boots.

"Looks like I'll have to clean the heels on these things pretty quickie," she muttered as she examined the stains on them, now drying from red to brown...

Bila fumbled with the zipper of his jumpsuit for a moment, and then grunted in approval as he pulled it down, and grunted again as it entangled and yanked out several of his chest hairs. He dropped it around his feet with a smile of triumph, and shuffled over to sit on the bench next to Puss. He raised one foot and fumbled at the latches on the army boots Mack had given him. Puss leaned over and carefully showed him how to release the boots. He pulled them off, and then standing, stepped out of his jump suit with obvious relief.

"You wear things `S'attl in not easy from get," Bila said with a grin.

"Let's go shower now, friend," Puss grinned back as she jumped to her feet and led him into the multiple-person shower stall.

"Shower what?"

"Just watch me." Puss said as she turned on one of the heads and stepped under its steaming spray with a sigh of pleasure.

"You rain make cabin in," Bila grunted. Then he felt the temperature of the spray as Puss began soaping herself. "You cook little bottom you Molly like do. No - did!"

"What?" Puss called above the sound of the spray as she scrubbed at her face with one hand and her breasts with the other.

Bila repeated himself, loudly.

"Whatever. Anyway, get wet Mister!" she ordered as she turned on the showerhead next to hers.

"Cook Bila not, OK?"

"OK tough guy, you got it cold," she said with an evil grin as she adjusted the faucet, then her eyes widened as Bila stepped under the chill spray and echoed her pleased sigh, as he stretched and turned under its tingling icy needles...

She watched him for a moment, then shook her head and squirted a handful of soap from the dispenser on the wall. She announced as she stepped clear of her spray, "Cold water won't do it Buster! Step out here where I can get to you. I don't do your kind of showers so good."

He stepped before her with a slight grin and stood as she smeared soap on his chest, "You do your front, like this," and Puss quickly lathered her own chest, belly and arms," and I'll do your back."

"Yes Ma'am!" and he began rubbing the soap on his chest and belly, but when it lathered, he paused and smelled his hand, "Bila different sniff!"

"Different is bad?"

"No. Good, I think," and he began soaping himself again, with a slight twitch at the corner of his mouth.

Puss stepped behind him and slathered soap on his back. "Don't worry friend, you smell good both ways," she murmured softly. Then with a toss of her head she reached up and began vigorously scrubbing his shoulders.

Bila tensed after a moment at the same instant her hands slowed in their stroking of his back, as a wave of familiarity swept over her once again, like the one that first night. The night when she had sat with Boots by the campfire and watched him draw his impossible animals...

Bila turned to face her and they gazed at each other for a moment, then he said so quietly that she could barely hear his voice over the hiss of the sprays, "Now you back do I."

Puss looked up into his eyes and saw something in them that was both longing and pain. She nodded, and still feeling the detached familiarity turned her back to Bila.

He began stroking and rubbing it with care in a way she instinctively knew to be non-sexual. But as she stood in the middle of the large shower stall feeling the strokes of his hands on her back, Puss felt a tingling at the base of her neck and her detachment deepened.

She suddenly seemed be drifting and she begun to sense, but not see clearly, images of strange animals and people on the periphery of her vision.

Puss gasped, and wrenched herself back to the reality of the shower stall. "OK Buster! I'm clean enough. Let's rinse!" she yelled as she stepped under his cold shower spray and after gasping several times, grabbed his hand and pulled him under it with her.

*

"Hey, you two! Any more than five minutes in the shower stall by one or more troops may constitute sexual excess by someone with someone, or someone with themselves even! And if so, ya' gotta' go see the Chaplin, and she gets real grumpy about all you soapers!" Boots yelled from the bathroom door.

"Don't listen to her friend, let's continue and ignore all such minor irritations," Puss said as she turned the shower taps off and tossed Bila a towel from a stack outside the stall.

Bila dried himself and then wrapped the towel around his waist before he stepped into the bathroom and confronted Boots. Puss noted this from the corner of her eye as she stood casually nude before one of the sinks, drying her hair and carefully removing the last traces of her makeup.

"Bila me boy, we gotta' make you look more Army if you're going to wear

389

Army greens in public, and those the only clothes here in the 'clave that will fit you for damn sure, Boots said, "So come out here and sit on this bunk while I shape you up."

Bila sat at her direction and Boots wrapped a sheet around his neck. Then she carefully trimmed his hair into the above-the-shoulder length that the Special Forces had adopted as their winter cut because of the extra insulation it gave their necks from the cold.

He sat quietly as she snipped away and Puss, after drying herself and pulling on her sleep-shirt, sat on a bunk and watched them, also quiet.

Boots finished Bila's hair and lifted his chin as she looked at him, "Shave time, OK?"

He gazed up at her, then with a twitch at the corner of his mouth nodded. Boots nodded in return and using her scissors to trim his beard and moustache short, lathered his face and began to shave him with an army razor.

When he turned his head and presented his cheeks and throat to her as she delicately scraped his whisker stubble away, Boots muttered, "Someone has done this for you before, right?" Bila nodded but remained silent, with his eyes focused far away.

Boots wiped Bila's face when she finished and handed him to his feet then turned to Puss. "What'ya think?"

Puss looked at the two handsome people standing before her. She started then gasped. Bila and Boots both had the same gleam in their eyes, the same set to their jaws and the same pride in their stance as they gazed at Puss with identical expressions on their faces.

Puss stared at them for several heartbeats before she shuddered and turned her head.

"It's been a long day folks," she whispered, "So I'm for the sack now 'cause I'm on information overload way biggers all of a sudden..."

Boots frowned at her friend for a moment then said, "Right. Good idea after a long day. Let's all flop."

Bila looked intently at the two women each in turn then announced, "Yes. Sleep now good all for is."

*

Puss lay curled in a ball in her bunk in the darkened room and was trying to will her restless thoughts to be quiet and allow sleep to come, when she began to feel a calmness growing within her and with it a warm strength touching her mind with delicate feather-like strokes.

She sighed happily as she accepted the comfort and whispered, "Thank you Bila…"

*

Boots laid on her narrow bunk, her mind churning with the complex thoughts, ideas, passions and fears that she held within herself in a mélange as complex as her Persian scarf, until also she felt a soft wave of comfort and confidence that started at the edge of her awareness, but then built slowly in her mind until she knew that she could find answers to all of her worries.

She smiled and thought as she drifted off to sleep, "So that's how you calmed Gwaii."

"Yes."

***

Chapter 18
The Carpet

May 6, 2276 AD,
Washington, DC

Wanda took the S/TFB-330-T in at a high level along the entry corridor down the Potomac River, passing over McLean and the historic home of the CIA as she headed toward Pitson National Airport in Virginia across the river from Washington DC. She was flying at a greater speed than was normally permitted but she had received special clearance when she first entered the controlled air space surrounding the District three hundred miles out. She had given her flight number and her personal reco-code to the tower then she had asked the mil-traffic controller, "OK for a drop-in?"

*

This was the informal name of a maneuver that only this particular aircraft was able to perform with survivability, and it was developed by ace pilots during the Chin War as a means of delivering ordinance accurately on unsuspecting targets.

To do it, the pilot puts the fighter-bomber in an almost vertical supersonic dive and pulling it out at the last minute, moves the back-swept wings to their forward position and reverses most of the thrust of its engines all at the same time as he or she brings it up to the horizontal. This makes the aircraft suddenly pause just above the ground and provided a wonderful platform for blasting any nearby targets, or to land quickly on its downward-directed jets.

This maneuver was only possible because of the uniquely strengthened materials used in the plane's airframe and wings and the special suits worn by the pilots. The irradiated polymers used in the aircraft's construction

were reinforced by fibers of elongated atomic clusters of carbon and titanium
grown in an orbiting space-factory that were a triumph of technology.

NASA had completed the factory just before the Chin attack and its
products were some of the key elements that caused their invasion's ultimate
failure. However this highly advanced facility had since been shut down
and declared redundant by the Pitson Whitehouse. The President did this
by secretly issuing his Executive Order Number 30,007-S in response to a
complaint from the European Union. Their Central Secretariat declared in a
private communiqué to the Whitehouse that, if production of the S/TFB-330
were continued by the United States beyond the end of the Chin War, the EU
would feel "uncomfortably less than equal".

Pitson and his wife, Belladonna Jones, had issued many secret Executive
Orders during the time they had held the Oval Office because they preferred
the populace by this mechanism, a populace that was encouraged to be more
concerned with the Network's latest programs than that "dull stuff" in Washington...

The flight suits worn by the pilots of the aircraft were smart garments
that sensed the condition of his or her body during violent maneuvers and
would instantly adjust to compensate and protect its wearer from the enormous G-forces that the aircraft could withstand. The suits were basically a
form-fitting womb for adults, and for that reason they were called "mommy
suits" by those whose lives depended on them.

Needless to say only highly competent pilots were permitted to, or even
interested in doing a drop-in.

*

"OK, Wanda. Give us a show," the voice in her headset responded to her
request, a voice that was familiar to her.

"Yes, Sir! Wil-comp!" Wanda replied with a tight grin as she fired two of
the aircraft's assist modules and sped it up to Mach 2.8, much to the distress
of the passenger in the forward seat when his helmeted head slammed back
into the headrest. She tipped the craft's nose over and dove down at the
airport on the Potomac at the same speed - until she hauled the plane up,
flipped the wings forward and firing the retros from its three engines, abruptly stopped almost all headway. She slowly descended on her down-thrusters
to the runway apron at an end of the field distant from the terminal, where a
black limousine sat.

Nothing happened for several minutes after Wanda settled the plane on the tamarack and powered the hatches open, then the Director shakily rose from the forward seat. He fumbled his facemask open, and vomit poured out of it, dripping down to stain the front of the mommy suit he wore over his regular clothing. He looked around at the space of the airport distractedly with his hair wildly rumpled and his eyes disoriented.

Two men in black climbed from the limousine, hooked a boarding ladder to the fuselage below his cockpit and waited impassively until the Director shakily climbed out of the aircraft and down on to the pavement. They efficiently removed his helmet and flight suit then and ignoring his reeking face, grasped his arms and hustled him to the waiting sedan.

Wanda looked on from the cockpit with a face of stone as the limousine drove away. While she watched the Director's departure, she pictured her youngest brother in her mind again. He was a handsome nine-year-old lad who had been recruited one day in his school two years ago by a man named Terry, who said he was from the Network's advertising agency. Terry had exclaimed that her brother was perfect to appear in a children's product commercial, to be shot and completed that day, and had arranged for the boy be excused from the rest of his classes.

Wanda and her parents had called the school when her little brother had not come home that evening, and learning that there was no record of him from a bored school functionary they had frantically called the Network. They were told that they must be mistaken since no commercials had been filmed that day. The next day and for weeks thereafter, whenever they searched the `Clave government records they could access, all they found was the notation, "Person Not In Database"...

*

The black limousine pulled to a stop in the restricted area on a street at the side of the Network building, a four hundred year old structure that still quietly dominated its area on 16th Street NW, three blocks from the White House. It had been a premier hotel in Washington for centuries and "the" lodging place for most important persons visiting the capital, until the Chin issued their ultimatum.

As the possibility of a Chin invasion became more likely, the Network's operating partners had quietly voiced their concern to President Pitson about the safety of their headquarters in Hollywood. Since Pitson had been given a silent partnership in the Network as had many other heads of state particularly those of the European Union, he ordered the Army to commandeer the hotel for use as a new Network headquarters because, as he said in his weekly address to the public, "The American people disserve a secure place where those who produce our few comforts in these trying times can to continue to do so."

Interestingly, the US Navy had attempted to commandeer the building as its construction was completed in 1942, just after the second war between the United States and Europe had begun. It was called the Statler Hotel then, but the Navy had been subtly out-maneuvered by the building's manager then, so the building had opened as a hotel in 1943. It had remained as a hotel until its owners in the 23rd Century found they were no match for the Network's maneuvering...

*

The driver sent a signal and a metal door rolled up to reveal a blank-walled space that could just accommodate the limousine. He rolled the car into it and the door closed. The Director rubbed at the skin of his chin which was becoming chapped as his vomit dried on it, and stifled a whimper.

*

The automobile elevator had been secretly built in to the hotel during its construction to allow a polio-crippled President of the United States to appear in public and make inspiring war-time speeches in the main ball room of the hotel, without the embarrassment of having to be trundled through the lobby in his wheelchair by his Secret Service agents...

*

The platform began to rise with a whine and the well-maintained machinery carried the limousine up to mezzanine level, where a personnel door in the other side of the elevator slid open. One of the men in black stepped out of the sedan and with the help of his partner in the back seat, urged the Director into an anti-room beyond the door.

"Wait," the second man told the driver who nodded without a word.

The space that had once been the Presidential Ball Room in the glory days of the hotel was now filled with office cubicles that housed the Network's accounting and administrative staff. The Network's architects had in their reconstruction also created a hallway leading from the original anti-room to a single passenger elevator at its far end. Discretely, the long hallway had a low ceiling that isolated it from the large room and there were no doors along its length.

The Director was walked down the corridor, and urged into the elevator car which had only two buttons. The first man pressed "Up". When the doors opened after a silent moment, the two marched the Director to a paneled door in an opulent foyer on the top floor of the thirteen-storied tower of the building, the area where its palatial suites had been converted into equally palatial executive offices. The first man tapped on the door.

"Please come in," a pleasant female voice sounded from a speaker, and as the door swung inward an extraordinarily beautiful blond woman rose from an ornate desk at one side of another paneled door in the sumptuously decorated room.

"Ah, Director! Welcome to Washington. Please have a seat, Mr. Jacobs will see you soon," she said with a polite smile. She had no sarcasm in her voice and only a slight hint of it in her pale blue eyes. The two men in black walked him into the office and seated the Director in the chair she indicated then stationed themselves on each side of the doorway to the hall as she signaled it closed again.

She reseated herself at the desk and turning her attention back to the computer in its surface, began interacting with the screen in silence.

The Director was still upset from his flight, his suit rumpled and he had the taste of vomit lingering in his mouth. He felt a sharp spasm in his empty stomach while he forced himself to appear at ease in the subtly-uncomfortable chair she had offered him. He realized that the woman also had not offered him coffee or the use of the executive washroom to freshen and relieve himself, and she had not come forward to greet him at the office door.

She had previously done all of these things, and with a much warmer smile each of the many times he had come east for a meeting with the Chief Executive. But this time she had not.

His stomach spasmed again, more painfully now than when the plane had landed...

*

Twenty years before, Marvin Jacobs had been a bright young aide to the Chief Executive of the Network at the time Bradney Pitson suddenly declared his candidacy for the office of President of the United States. Jacobs contrived to get himself dispatched to assess, and then to report back on the capabilities of this unknown upstart by his Chief, Rolf Olsen. Jacobs had interacted with Pitson for a week while watching the man handle himself with the public. Then he knew the Pitson would win, and saw with crystal clarity that his own future would be linked to this charismatic upstart.

During this time the two men were together they also forged a bond between themselves, one that combined wary distrust and the recognition of a mutual dependence which they knew to be necessary for each to achieve their own goals.

This wary bond of mutual mistrust was the same of link that Pitson already had with his wife, Belladonna Jones, who was the Vice-presidential candidate. Pitson recognized that mutual need coupled with arms-length distrust was the best basis for a successful relationship in power, and to him there were no other kinds of relationships...

Jacobs reported back to the Network with his assessment of Pitson, delivered first to Olsen, then soon afterward to the three Managing Partners, the supreme authority of the privately-held Network. Olsen was not a man of great foresight, and so allowed Jacobs to present a briefing to the Partners in person, and to answer all of their questions. His report as well as the sophisticated panache with which he delivered it was pivotal in their decision to bring the full weight of the Network's media power into Pitson's camp.

The rest was history, both the brilliant success of the campaign Jacobs subsequently helped organize for Pitson, and Olsen, whom the Partners quietly replaced with Jacobs six weeks after the election.

Marvin Jacobs had risen rapidly through the ranks of the Network organization to reach his position as Olsen's aide by digging his climbing spikes into the backs of others on his way up, but he had done so with his natural gift for subtlety. Therefore it had not been obvious when he began covertly lobbing the Managing Partners for a new position in briefing sessions for them on the progress of the election campaign.

Marvin had now held his position in the Network with treachery and cunning for the past eighteen years as his good friends, Brad and Bel had held the White House.

*

The beautiful blond looked up from her computer screen where she had actually been playing chess on line with her twin sister, the administrative assistant to the Network's Chief Operating Officer in Moscow. She smiled brightly at the Director as she detected his slight twitches of bladder urgency in spite of his feigned body language of nonchalance, twitches that she had been waiting for him to display.

"Mr. Jacobs will see you now, Director," she smiled brightly as she rose and stepping around her desk to the door, opened it and murmured, "Mr.

Jacobs, Sir. The Studio Director to see you, as you requested." Then, still holding her smile, she turned back to the unfortunate man and waved him in.

Marvin Jacobs was standing with his back to the large room that was the center of day-to-day operations of the entire Network. The walls were lined with small vid monitors silently displaying a changing selection of all of the Network shows being broadcast and the web versions of the print media still being produced, principally for distribution in Africa, the Indian Subcontinent and the rural parts of France and Quebec.

Jacobs stood before a large window looking down 16th street in the late morning light toward Lafayette Park and the north front of the White House.

"We have worked together for a long time, Bradney and I," Jacobs whispered to the window. "To bring order to this intractable country."

"Order which will finally allow us to also give contentment to the people here, as I have helped do in the rest of the world."

He slowly turned from the window. "You have made a significant contribution to this effort, Jason. However," he whispered as he looked at the Director for the first time, "It seems that the operative word here may be "have", as in the past tense..."

Marvin Jacobs was a short man, somewhat pear-shaped, and had bushy black eyebrows sprouting above horn-rimmed glasses with large tinted lenses that partially obscured his eyes. He picked up the single sheet of paper on the bare surface of his enormous desk with a surprisingly dainty hand. He looked down at it for a moment, then seated himself in the throne-like leather desk chair and flourished the sheet with a sigh.

"I am beginning to sense a slippage of control in your operation, which as you know is the most vital function of our organization," Jacobs continued in the same whisper as he stared at the Director standing before his desk, twitching slightly...

"First, your chief coder escaped with a strange young girl, who apparently was really your best coder. Then you couldn't find the pair for two years during which time our product did not deteriorate, but was not improved. And you couldn't find them, in spite of all of the resources that General Butler made available to you."

"Then after two years, we received a clumsy blackmail threat from this renegade coder. You dispatched what you said was your best team of collectors but they only sent back the man. The next day some very, repeat, very talented person briefly disrupted our broadcast of a simplistic cooking show, and by a method that my best people still can't fully determine."

"Then on the following day we received a signal that the young girl coder had been collected by a free-lance group, but this turned out to not be true. Interestingly, this group has not been heard from again after they delivered a large Undoc to our transporter, with promises to also deliver the girl within an hour, which they did not do."

"Then the rather innovative Gala you staged in S'attl to amuse General Butler, the one person essential you and your staff continuing to produce innovative output from our premiere studio, and the engine driving the profitability of our X sector which is the most lucrative sector we have, things seem to have taken an unfortunate turn," Jacobs' face reddened then and he jumped to his feet and screamed at the Director, "And you let Butler get wounded buy this same big Undoc when he escaped from the lax security at your really dumb event!"

Then, as his mouth sprayed spittle across the expanse of his desk, Jacobs screamed again, "And as he escaped he killed one of our best X-staff people and Butler's favorite back-warmer, and others as well!"

He glared through his tinted glasses at the Director standing at quaking attention before him and dropped his voice to a whisper again, "Jason, this kind of thing is really, repeat, really bad for business. The Managing Part-ners, the people I report to really, repeat, really do not like things that are bad for business."

"Therefore you have one month to straighten up your command area or I will be forced to seek other means of effecting a positive change. And if I am forced to do that, you will become Unavailable, and then learn at first hand about the things Heidi likes to do with, and to intelligent and sensitive male Participants.

"This is a special interest of hers, and I am told that she can get quite innovative."

"Do I make myself clear?"

"Yes, Mr. Jacobs," the Director whimpered, as he suddenly clutched at his crotch in an attempt to control his bladder.

"Good. Dismissed."

The Director turned and rushed from the room, to be met by the beauti-ful blond assistant. She closed the door to Jacobs' office and taking his hand, led him into the lavish executive washroom and pushed him toward one of its marble stalls.

When he stepped out a few moments later, she was leaning back against the sinks with her suit now open to her waist, and displaying the small strip of black lace that strained to contain her significant breasts.

"Here, let me help you," she smiled as she zipped up his suit and tenderly washed his face. Then as she dried him and lotioned his chin, she murmured in his ear while pressing her breasts against his chest, "You really do want to make Marvin happy, don't you?"

"Yes," the Director whimpered, as he stepped back into the office and toward the two men in black still standing by the door.

The blond woman, who had a doctorate in social psychology, shook her head as the outer door closed behind the three. "Not a significant player any more, in any way," she muttered as she went back to her desk and resumed her chess game with her sister in Russia.

Her doctorial thesis had been on the accelerated libido effects observed in six-year-old girls after viewing pornographic vids for two months, and had been immediate accepted with acclaim by her committee...

*

"You did that pretty well, ya' old shark, got him in squirm mode real good," President Pitson announced in a hoarse voice as he opened a hidden door in the office paneling and stepped into Marvin's office.

During the centuries preceding the Chin War, but much more so in the years wile it had dragged on, the number of subterranean access tunnels and private subway passages under the Capitol area had been greatly expanded, and now one connected the basement of the White House to the Network CEO's office.

"We will see. Jason was good once, but seems to have lost his edge lately."

"Well, if he doesn't perform and you do give him to Heidi, save a vid chip for Bel. Wife's a big fan of hers."

"Yes," Marvin smirked, "We know."

*

"Welcome back Director. Climb on board for another fun trip!" Wanda gritted as the two men in black boosted the Director, clad in his vomit-stained flight suit up the boarding ladder into the front cockpit after they had clamped his reeking helmet over his head.

The mil-traffic controller in the tower at Pitson National whose familiar voice Wanda had heard on her incoming flight, announced into his mike set,

"Clear for max takeoff - and Wanda, have a good flight home."

"Thanks. Give my regards to all the guys over here."

"Wil-comp. You do the same for me out there, OK?

"Wil-comp again, Squaw-man. We go now."

"Go War Chick," the mil-traffic controller said quietly, then clicked off his microphone. He looked around at the numerous vid screens in the control tower with other controllers sitting before them, monitoring and dealing with all of the air traffic in the eastern part of the country.

"Looks like a little slack time coming up for me. Think I'll check in with the home place," he muttered.

"You be nice to her, she be nice to you," a civilian controller chanted from her seat, as she signaled she was now covering the screens for her mil-traffic friend.

"You don't have any idea where my "nice" even starts, little one," he said with a leer as he stepped into the hallway outside of the tower's active floor and opened his personal comset,

"Honey, what's for supper tonight?"

"Oh really!" he grunted. "Well, don't tie your apron strings too tight, I'll be home sooners!"

She giggled then spoke into her comset, "Yes, Big Chief, will-comp!" Then the woman in their kitchen clicked her husband off, and the look on her face changed to the cold competence of a warrior as she punched in a long set of numbers into a different, and somewhat bulkier comset. When the connection was linked, she said quietly into the handset, "Yoowah paspeen", which was "He goes," in the language of the Pamunkey.

She clicked the larger comset off and turned back to the kitchen counter, and her expression changed again to that of a caring wife and mother as she began making supper for her family.

*

The intercom sounded, "Code black, Miss Petruschika."

"Yes Mr. Jacobs," the blond assistant replied, "Just a moment, Sir." Then she quickly typed an email message to her sister, and smiled at the reply before shutting down her computer and activating the lock on the door to the corridor.

She rose from her desk and stepping to a closet, opened its door. Standing before it, she stripped out of her clothing and carefully hung up her suit and undergarments, then opening a drawer she retrieved and stepped into a

401

sturdy black garter belt. Balancing first on one foot then the other, she next drew on and attached a pair of long black cotton lisle stockings and stepped into a pair of shining black patent leather shoes with 10-centimeter spike heels.

She opened a cosmetic cabinet in the closet and perfumed herself with the acrid essence of frankincense and heavily lipsticked her mouth to resemble an open scarlet wound. She darkened her eye makeup and hanging a long, large-beaded rosary around her neck, arranged the strand so that her breasts thrust through its loop and the crucifix hung just above her navel.

She finally fitted the starched white wimple of a traditional nun's headdress over her hair and around her face and put on a pair of gold-rimmed spectacles with plain glass lenses.

Miss Petruschika inspected her image in the full-length mirror on the closet door with an ironic smile for a moment then she stuck out her tongue at herself. She clasped her hands genteelly at her waist and assumed a serene and virtuous expression, and walked toward the door to Jacobs' office while swaying her flawless white hips in exaggerated provocation...

***

Chapter 19
The Participant

Boots opened her eyes and stretched. She thought for a minute and then realized that she felt more relaxed than she had for months. She rolled over and looked at the bunk where Puss had slept. She saw that it was empty and that Bila, already dressed in army green, sat there.

"Where's Marybell? In tha' shower?" she asked sleepily.

"Marybell go lab she. She go Lulu say she."

"Shat! How long ago?"

"Time water cook water cabin at," then his brow wrinkled. "Bad?"

"Twenty ferkin' minutes! Shat!! We gotta' go find her! Lulu can be trouble…"

*

"Wait for me, I'll be right back!" Puss yelled to the taxi driver as she jumped from the cab's rear door and ran into the door of the yellow brick municipal building. She bounded up the stairway and trotted to the door of the laboratory, hoping that Lulu was early to work. She tried the door and when it opened, she saw the woman sitting on a lab stool at the bench with the GC/ MS machine.

"Oh, hello. I didn't think you would be here this early. I'm just re-checking my results. Pull up a stool."

"How long? I'm on a pretty tight schedule."

Lulu glanced at her wrist chrono, then with a calculating look at Puss said, "About five minutes."

Puss nodded and took her seat on a second stool and watched the woman in the white lab coat as she moved her fingertip up and down a printout page of calculations and compared them with ponderous care to another printout of a graph.

After Puss watched Lulu go through the same maneuver the third time, she frowned and stood, "I really have to move it, so I can come back later if you're not finished, OK?"

Lulu glanced at her watch again and then shrugged, "All right, you can take it as it is, but I won't sign the report." Then she looked at Puss directly for the first time with an honestly quizzical expression, "The specimens seemed to be very fresh leather so that is why I was re-checking my results. Where did you find them?"

"Way back in a cave, up in British Columbia. But I really gotta' go."

"Well, here's the report. Good luck on your next trip," Lulu said, as her expression changed from of open interest to one that was closed, with hooded eyes.

"Thanks biggers! Kris was right, you're a real friend," Puss smiled as she folded the report without reading it and slid it into a breast pocket of her green jumpsuit. "Laters!"

Lulu watched the young woman trot through the door from her laboratory, and an anguished look suddenly appeared on her face as she whispered, "Sooners, I hope for your sake. I really do..."

*

"Hello friend," the bag lady smiled, as she looked up from where she was settling herself in the foyer of the building as Puss came running down the stairway, gripping its handrails in a controlled sliding fall.

"Hi. Don't have time to talk now."

"Just take a second, please. You helped me so much yesterday, I really want to repay..." the woman smiled tenderly as she offered an apple to Puss.

"Not necessary," Puss said, and then she paused and bent to take the apple. "OK, I'll have it for lunch."

The woman smiled tremulously again as she extended her arm to Puss, and released the lever of the sleepy gas canister she had clamped in her armpit.

*

Sleepy gas was the common name for the ubiquitous tranquilizing agent used by the Military Governor's security force as well as by the Network. The

404

agent was packaged several ways, including in a small instantaneous release canister like that which the sweet-smiling bag lady with the sad eyes had held under her arm-pit.

The agent was also addictive to some people, mostly women and so they were quite happy to go sleepy themselves when they gassed down a designated target for their employer...

*

Puss muttered, "Shat..." as she collapsed on top of the slumping bag lady.

"Think she's out good?" a thin-faced functionary in a black coverall asked as he peered through a doorway in the back of the stairwell.

"Sure is. Mabel in spite of bein' the doper she is, always remembers to come through on a pickup," his burley partner growled as he pushed past the thin-faced one into the foyer. "'Specially when she gets a good whiff of sleepy too! That slut will do anything for a sniff of sleepy. You ought to see her act some time when she really wants it."

"Anyway, grab this one's ankles and let's move! Freddy's wants to start on her real quick for some reason..."

*

The army sedan screeched to a stop in front of the old municipal building as Waldo skewed it across the front of the battered taxi sitting at the curb. Boots leaped out and yelled at its driver, "She was a red-head right? How long have you been waiting for her?"

"'Bout twenty minutes. She said she'd pay for me to wait. But w-who are you?" the man behind the wheel of the decrepit 'Clave taxi quavered as he looked up at the black-haired fury glaring at him.

"Her friend," Boots hissed. "What else have you seen?"

"Nothin, 'cept a black van came out from behind this place a coupla' minutes ago."

"Shat! Pay him off Waldo! Up to the lab Bila - quick!" Boots snapped as she turned and sprinted toward the doorway of the building. Bila leapt from the rear door of the sedan, and after stumbling momentarily until his feet steadied on the pavement, raced after Boots.

She paused in the lobby as she glanced at the slumped body of the bag lady for a second then wheeled toward the stairway. Bila's nostrils flared, "This place sniff Rat sniff," he growled as he stared at the woman's slumped form in the corner, and remembered the concrete cell...

405

"Later! Let's go!" Boots snapped as she bounded up the stairs.

Bila followed her, taking the steps three at a time. Boots ran down the hall to the frosted glass door labeled "Forensic Laboratory" and tried its handle. She found it locked. She tensed in frustration before turning to Bila.

"Open it, please."

Bila looked at the door for a second then delivered a flat-footed kick at its lock. The doorframe shuddered but held.

He snarled then, and launched himself toward the opal glass door shoulder first. It held under his impact, but the old building's wooden frame did not. It shattered and as the door swung away on one hinge, Bila burst into the laboratory. After taking several running steps, he regained his balance and halted beside the lab bench under which Lulu crouched... He stared down at the cowering woman as Boots strode into the room.

"Thanks friend," Boots muttered as she kicked aside broken pieces of the doorframe littering the floor.

"Hello Lulu, long time not-to-see," she said with a smile that did not reach her eyes, "How've you been? And here, let me help you up from down there.

"I'm looking for a friend of mine named Marybell. She said she was coming to see you this morning. Have you seen her?"

"No. I haven't. And who do you think you are, to break my door like that?" Lulu snarled as she glared first at Boots then craned her neck to stare up at Bila, who stood very close above her.

"That door will cost my budget way mucho to fix, and I'm real tight right now, anyway," Lulu whimpered as her voice suddenly changed. Then she continued, pleadingly, "You said one time back then that you loved me – why don't you like me now?"

Boots looked at the woman and saw the pain in her eyes, and hesitated, until Bila flared his nostrils and sniffed.

"Marybell be here. Soon. Before soon be!"

"Make her talk Bila," Boots snapped, with death in her voice.

Bila stepped behind Lulu and before the woman could react, lifted her to her feet and wrapped his arms around her chest below her breasts. Then he contracted his arms and stopped her breathing. Lulu's face turned red as she struggled to get air into her collapsed lungs while Bila held her in his intractable grip and ignored her kicks at his legs and clawing at his arms.

Boots stared at the struggling Lulu for several moments, until the color of the woman's face changed from red to a bluish shade.

"Talk now?" Boots gritted.

"Talk now?" Bila echoed as he relaxed his grip and steadied Lulu in his arms.

The woman bowed her head and panted for several moments, until Boots slapped her face, "Talk bitch - Now!"

Lulu recoiled and slumped but Bila held her under her arms, and squeezed her chest again briefly as a reminder.

Lulu gasped for air then looked at Boots, and her face became a mask of tragedy. She moaned as tears welled in her eyes, "I'm sorry, but you made me love you back then, and I still do. I helped you get what you needed, but you never came back to me..."

Boots grabbed her hand and gritted, "Facts now, or I start breaking your fingers!"

"She was so pretty and so nice, that I hated her! I heard about her duel with your Colonel and what she did to her," Lulu whimpered. "So I called yesterday after your friend left, and told the Colonel that Marybell would be back here today, alone." she finished in a broken whisper.

Boots stared at Lulu for a second while her mind raced. Then she recalled her encounter with the strange threesome of the Colonel, Freddy and Heidi at the Gala. Her face became death incarnate, "Shat! You gave her to the Rat!"

Boots turned and raced toward the door, snapping back over her shoulder, "Bring her along - however!"

Bila stared into Lulu's eyes for a second and she saw the same promise of death on his face as on Boots'. Then he took her wrist in a grip she couldn't break. She sobbed and stumbled obediently behind him as he rushed into the hallway.

*

"Rat's Nest – as fast as you can get there!" Boots growled to Waldo. Then she snapped, "You got a sleepy shooter in this crate?"

"Right here," he replied as he tossed several small cylinders over the back of the seat while accelerating the heavy sedan to a high speed and activating its siren.

"You can take it like a trooper, or I will stick it to you anyway," Boots gritted to Lulu.

The woman held out her arm as she whispered, "I'm sorry," and pas-

407

sively allowed Boots to inject her.

Boots watched Lulu as the woman drifted into slack unconsciousness. "Take her to a secure place," she ordered Waldo as she looked down at the woman lying now across her lap, and at her relaxed face with a sudden tender memory… Then Boots returned to the reality of the careening sedan. She said to Bila, "Strip," as she tugged at the zipper of his green jump suit. "You're gonna' be the bait! And I'm damn glad we brought your spears!"

*

"For a little one she's damn heavy," the thin-faced functionary grunted as they carried Puss' limp form in from the garage where they had parked the black van.

"Quit snarlin' dammit and help me get her up on the table. I don't know how much sleepy she got, and Freddy wants us to give her a full prep."

The two men in baggy black coveralls lifted Puss up onto a stainless steel gurney in a small, starkly lit room. Its blank walls were painted with white enamel that was peeling in places and the bare concrete floor had a drain in the center. Stainless steel cabinets stood against the walls and there were several pieces of medical equipment on wheeled stands.

The thin-faced man giggled, "This is gonna' be funs," as he hefted an electric scissor.

"Yeah. Wonder how long she'll last tho?" the burly man asked as he unlatched her boots and pulled them off.

"Yeah, funs," the thin-faced man leered as he began shearing off Puss' 'clave jumpsuit. He cut slowly up each sleeve and through the collar, then pulling the zipper down her chest he peeled the suit away and with a dainty snip, severed the front of her bra between her breasts. "Nice rack," he muttered as he squeezed them with harsh hands.

Puss' eyes were open and aware and very cold, but the thin-faced man did not look at her face as he continued to cut her clothing away, and fondle and probe all of her helpless body.

"Hurry up, dammit! We gotta' get her ready. Maybe Freddy will give you some of her parts to take home when he's done, but right now, quit poking her and help me get her on the pot, dammit!"

The two lifted Puss' naked body from the gurney and sat her on a stainless steel commode.

"Strap her down and hold her head back while I put the tube in her."

"Hey, I like doin' that," the thin-faced man whined.

"Yeah, like the last one I let you do. You missed his gullet, you bastard and stuck it down his windpipe instead and drowned the poor sucker. Heidi wasn't too happy about that," the burly man muttered as he used a tongue depressor to open Puss' throat and then slid a small tube down her esophagus.

"She's not too big, so two liters ought to do it," he muttered as he fitted the other end of the tube to a stainless steel hand pump and began forcing a very powerful and quick-acting purgative agent into Puss' stomach. Her eyes were still open as her head lolled back against the headrest built into the commode's structure - and they were now glacial...

Puss' belly heaved after several minutes and then she shuddered as all of her intestinal tract voided in one painful spasm. Her body was still quivering from the effect of the purge when the burly man said, "OK, you can pull the tube back out."

The thin-faced one giggled, and then removed the stomach tube from Puss' throat half way, then thrust it back down her esophagus again. Then he pulled it out half way again. "Dammit! Stop playing with the bait! That's Freddy's job, an' you'll get me in trouble if she ain't in good condition when he's ready to start the show."

"Oh, all right," the thin-faced man snickered, "But let me do the catheter, please."

"Naw' you take too long, an' we gotta get her on the stage sooners. I think she's startin' to come out now anyway," the burly man grunted as he knelt before Puss, still strapped on the commode.

He waited for several moments then muttered, "Alright, she's empty now. Let's get her back on the cart," as he released the straps around her knees and torso then got to his feet and grabbed her under the arms. The thin-faced man grabbed her behind her knees and they heaved Puss' limp form back onto the gurney.

"Roll her over, I gotta' mark her butt bugs so we can pull 'um when she's finished," the burley man said. As the thin-faced one pushed her over onto her belly, Puss' face was toward the burly man, and she saw him pick up a black box from an instrument cart.

"Would ya' just look at those dimples! Best I've seen all year," the thin-faced man leered as he pinched at Puss' bottom.

"Out of my way nut-basket! When I've marked 'um, you put the gag on her, OK?"

Then he slowly stroked one buttock with the end of the black box until a soft chime sounded. He held it steady against her flesh for several seconds, until a second chime sounded with a different note. Then he repeated the procedure on her other buttock, after he noted that the instrument had stamped the location and the depth to Puss' first bug in blue ink on her skin.

When the instrument had chimed twice again, he said, "Flip her back over and let's move her out to the stage now, and don't play around with her gag too much, dammit!"

*

"Trouble with you is that you are a pervert, and I'm only doin' this job to make a living" the burly man whispered as the two sat side by side in the back of the tiny auditorium before the stage where Freddy and Heidi performed.

"Yeah, sure. So why do you always wait 'till it's over before you go home for supper, Mister Just-a-Job Man?"

"Shaddup! They're starting."

*

Freddy and Heidi took their places at the front of the small stage before a closed curtain made of a slick semi-transparent red plastic. He slipped the loop of a tiny headset over one of his large ears and after seating the receiver in its hairy depths, adjusted the slender wire of its microphone near his mouth. Heidi did the same and then they whispered in turn, "Test, 3-2-1."

The main cameraman nodded after he listened to the earplug of his vid recorder for a second, "Real clear." The camerawoman who did the close-ups for "color" nodded as she focused her recorder on Heidi's face, "Clear here too, and you're looking real good for this early in the morning my pet."

"Thanks, Little Yummy, but this one could be quite protracted. Are you sure you're up for it?"

"Hey, fun's fun – no matter how long it takes," the short blond woman with the hard eyes and powerful thighs answered, as she re-checked the focus of her recorder by zooming in on the nail of Heidi's middle right forefinger. It was enameled red like her others, but it was five centimeters long and filed to a stiletto point.

"Alright people, hear me! This one has major profit potential for the Network and therefore for us also, as well as max entertainment value," Freddy announced with a cadaverous grin. "So lets do it right! Lights! Cams! Action!"

"Welcome the Freddy and Heidi Show Faithful Viewers!" he began, "Let's

Explore once again, Just How Far We Can Go!" the man announced gruffly as he stared into the camera and exposed his stained teeth in a feral smile.

"We have a rare treat this day, and a double one at that, my fellow examiners of the extremes of human experience! We are going to perform the ancient Chin procedure known as The Death of a Thousand Cuts. And, to make it doubly interesting, our participant is a full-blooded -"

"Please excuse Freddy's dreadful pun, Darling Fans," Heidi interrupted with a bright smile as she thrust her face in front of the main cam and struck the pose of a classic comic ballerina with one finger under her chin. "Sometimes it just bubbles out of him!"

Freddy replied in a kindly avuncular tone, "Oh Heidi! You're such a cut-up, you little rascal! Anyway to continue, our participant today is a full-blooded American Indian, a member of a people known historically to put their captives to death by means of unspeakable tortures as a test of the captive's bravery.

"The Indians, who all knew that they could themselves be subjected to these horrible cruelties if captured, were also taught from birth to be defiant in the face of pain and to actually laugh at their tormenters and taunt them, even to the extent of suggesting more painful acts to be carried out upon their own bodies.

"Over the next several hours, or even days perhaps if we are lucky, Dear Viewers we will see if this ancient and admirable spirit still exists in an Indian woman today!"

"Now Fellow Explorers, behold our Participant!" Freddy finished as he pressed a button on a control module.

Lights came on behind the shiny red plastic curtain and the whine of a hydraulic motor sounded as an indistinct shape slowly rose from the floor and hinged up to the vertical. After the machinery behind it stopped with a clank and an abrupt jerk, the curtain rattled open to reveal Puss, nude and strapped to two stainless steel columns. Her wrists and ankles were attached to them so that she is held upright in a helpless "X" position, and she had an inflated gag strapped in her mouth. Hate sparked from her eyes as she quivered with rage and strained at her bonds.

"Ahh, a magnificent specimen, don't you agree Heidi?" Freddy exulted as he stepped to Puss at the center of the small stage. He slowly ran a bony finger down Puss' chest from her neck to her belly. Then he pushed it deep into her navel as if he were testing the ripeness of a melon in the market. "Very good muscle tone too," he added with a theatrical aside to the cam, "This one might last a long time."

Heidi moved to his side and stroked the inside of Puss' thigh, then pinched it viciously. When Puss did not wince, Heidi giggled then rose à pointe and pirouetted and bent slightly from her hips. She ran the tip of her tongue lightly across Puss' armpit, "Mmmm, tough but tasty. Just the way I like 'um..."

Freddy turned to face the main cam. "This show has several unique features Dear Extremists, which I will explain now that you have met our lovely Participant."

"The original procedure in the courts of the ancient Chin emperors called for the subject to be arrayed as you see here," he gestured to Puss, "And to be prepared by thorough purging to make things a bit less messy, which our staff has done to today's participant by the way."

He smiled as Heidi pirouetted again; then again placing her finger under her chin and assuming the exaggeratedly innocent look of a comic ballerina again, squatted toward the cams.

"Additionally, all major blood vessels that are severed during the application of any particular procedure will be plugged in order to preserve the participant's good health, so to speak. The cuts we will use were originally described on a thousand folded strips of paper - which was invented in China, by the way," he interjected in a professorial tone.

"They were all written on paper that was white, except for four which were on red paper, and the strips were placed in a wide shallow basin on a stand where the subject could see them.

"The four red strips all instructed the delivery of instant death, but since each strip was drawn randomly by a deaf and color-blind scribe, only the subject and the executioner could see these tickets to freedom as it were, as they randomly appeared when the scribe stirred the strips in the bowl before making his selection.

"Legend has it that the subjects, after being subjected to a number of the instructions on the white strips of paper, always screamed as they tried to direct the scribe's hand toward those red papers, for as long as they were able to speak anyway.

"However, dear Fellow Voyagers to the Limits these are modern times and while our cuts will be authentic and will cleave true to the ancient Chin tradition --"

"Oooo! Bad pun - Down Boy!" Heidi giggled and with another pirouette, curtsied to the main cam.

Freddy assumed a look of mock exasperation with his hands on his hips. "How can our audience learn, with cut-ups like you in the classroom?"

"Oooo! You win with that one!" Heidi smirked.

"To continue," Freddy said primly as he lifted a large volume and opened it for the cams, "The descriptions of the various procedures are described in this ancient text was found abandoned in a Chinese general's quarters after their recent withdrawal. They have been faithfully scanned into a database that will be displayed on the screen you see behind our participant.

"Each procedure will be diagramed for you to enjoy and for us to follow, but its details will not become clear to the participant until we carry it out."

"Additionally as required by the text, the timing of the application of each new procedure will be always preceded by a chime. We have re-created this sound in the interest of authenticity," Freddy said as he pressed another button on the control module in his hand.

A gentle chime sounded, one that was so sweet it made one think of a mother summoning her beloved child to lunch.

"The text of the original book notes that subjects always began to scream at some point when they heard the chime. How soon this particular one will, only time will tell," Freddy murmured as he turned and ran his fingers through Puss' hair, and then across her face.

Her hate and disgust were openly apparent during all of this taunting discourse and she continued to quiver with rage while she strained at her fetters, and hissed viciously around the inflated ball gag strapped in her mouth

"However Fellow Explorers, before we depart on our ultimate investigation of the outer limits of pain, we are tasked by an important client to carry out a private consultation with this participant before we begin our main event. But worry not! When we have fulfilled the instructions of our client, you will not only be able to view the final result, but she will just be warmed up, as it were for the Big Show!"

"Cut!"

Then Freddy smiled with half-lidded eyes as he continued hoarsely, "Alright crew, change your vid chips, and let's try to make the Colonel who is our client, as well as our new Security Chief, real happy with us."

"Yes my pets," Heidi added with a smirk and an exaggerated comic ballet curtsy to the two with the cams. "A happy Boss Cop makes us all sleep with our loved ones more secure, don't you know," then with a giggle, she hungrily kissed both cam operators.

"Enough of that soft stuff you three, Dammit. Action time!"

"Now my dear Marybell, you will learn the consequences of making a Network primary functionary uncomfortable," Freddy smiled blandly to the cams as Heidi trotted offstage, to immediately return rolling an instrument cart that she placed in front of Puss' straining form. A package the size of a shoebox rested on it next to a bundle rolled in cheap plastic canvass, along with a number of stained surgical instruments and rusty industrial cutting and clamping tools.

At Freddy's identification of his client, Puss' eyes had changed, to reflect the green frozen core of a glacier. She ceased struggling, but remained as tense as the hammer spring of a cocked pistol.

"These are the instruments," Freddy leered into the cams as he opened the bundle and lifting out a large handful of stainless steel needles and displayed one first to Puss then to the cams. It was 60 centimeters long and six millimeters in diameter, with a flattened head fifteen centimeters wide on one end, and an acutely sharp point on the other.

"And this is our pattern - which we are tasked to follow precisely, by the way," Heidi smiled. Her black eyes glittered with madness as she opened the package and held up a soft plastic female doll before Puss' eyes for a moment, then turned and presented it to the cams.

The doll was nude and anatomically correct, and its face and body was an exact match of Puss'. It had been computer-generated by a 3-D imaging program that was used to laser-carve and color her image in the receptive plastic medium from archived survel cam views of the young woman.

The doll's body and limbs were pierced in many places with small versions of the long needle that Freddy held in his hands.

He fondled the full-sized needle with a dreamy expression on his cadaverous face while he gazed at the doll and the places the miniature pins were inserted in it. Places that would cause maximum pain in a real person.

He sighed and showed his stained teeth in a beatific smile, "Heidi my Dear, our contract requires us to be very precise in our placements of these beautifully made instruments in order for us to create an exact replication of this model.

"Therefore because the participant's body is so very tightly muscled, we may well have to use the mallet to get them placed correctly. Particularly those that are to go through the major joints, such as her hips and shoulders…"

Heidi giggled, then turned to the instrument cart and holding up a stained sculptor's lignum-vitae maul, pirouetted and presented it to the cams as she performed slow-motion mime of hammering.

The camera-woman doing color zoomed in on one battered face of the maul, capturing the old brown bloodstains on it and the tiny chips of bone imbedded in its striking surface.

*

"OK Bila, here we go again Buddy," Boots gritted as they piled out of the taxi when Waldo brought it to a screeching stop at the curb. The two stood before the same back street door to the Network building that they all had exited from the evening before.

The naked man said with a crooked grin, "I glad – No, I Am glad, we do this in warm time, or my bottom butt be cold."

"Alright Smarto, that's for later! For now, just do what I told you, OK?" Boots hissed as she slapped Bila on his butt, and returned his grin for a second. Then she turned to the door and wiped the Director's card over the keypad.

"Ja Boss," he whispered as the door into the Rat's Nest rattled open once again.

"Who'n hell are you?" the startled guard in the armorglass cage challenged nervously as he looked at the two improbable figures that came through the door, which had opened without his control.

"I'm Boots, and this is the mark the Director sent me out after last night. He's supposed to go to Freddy quickers, OK!"

"What studio is he in? And snap it up, function person, this is biggers from the top!" and Boots waved the director's key card before the man behind the armorglass.

The guard was dull, but he had heard about something happening the evening before. No details were available to him because the new Chief of Security had not reviewed the previous day's survel cam vids, and the Director is away for the day.

He hesitated as he eyed the competent woman standing before him holding her very large and naked prisoner by fetter straps around his wrists. When he realized that she was also carrying two primitive spears in her other hand, he sputtered, "Hey, no weapons in here! That's the rule."

Boots smiled, "These aren't weapons function-person, they're props that Freddy wants for the act." Then she snapped with glaring eyes, "Now get out here and get us to him dammit, or Freddy will be using you next!"

The man looked down at the vid screen for a moment then sputtered, "But they've already started. Nobody can go in there now."

Boots glared at the man for a second then hissed, "If you don't take us to Freddy's studio this instant, the Director will learn later today just how much of an obstruction you are. Do you really want that to happen to you, and your family?"

The man gulped then whined, "I'm not supposed to leave the door..."

"Lock it dammit! It'll take five minutes then you'll be back and the Director will be happy, which will be good for both of us," Boots suddenly grinned to the man.

He hesitated under the spell of her authority and her blue eyes that now suddenly were friendly, then he opened the door of the booth and unknowingly stepped over the spot where his predecessor had died the previous evening.

"Alright, they're in Studio X, one level down and to the right. I'll get you through the stairway doors," he muttered as he hurried into the hallway leading from the entryway.

"What about the door into the studio," Boots asked casually when they paused before the stairway door in the hallway that he had just opened.

"Oh no sister!" the guard suddenly snapped. Then he hissed, "If you ain't got that code I'm no gonna' help, 'cause you ain't got nothing I want that bad!"

"And all of a sudden something tells me that you ain't real!" the man snarled as he turned and started racing back up the hallway toward the safety of his booth.

"Bila! Stop him! We need to find Marybell sooners!" Boots gritted.

Bila dropped the fetter straps he had been only holding in place around his wrists and leaped toward the guard. After four rapid bounds along the drab corridor he grabbed one of the fleeing man's ankles and slammed him on the concrete floor.

He maintained his grip on the man's leg as he dragged him back to where Boots stood, as tigers do when taking prey to their feeding place, and as cave lions did fifteen thousand years before...

Boots looked down at the stunned guard squirming at her feet. She said without emotion, "Bila, make him take us to Marybell."

"Yes. He that do. Now," Bila said with a face of stone as he jerked the guard upright and glared at the man, who began to whimper...

*

"We will use a black spot to mark the entry point, and a red target circle to show where we want them to exit," Freddy announced in a professional tone as he took two markers from the instrument cart and offered the red one to Heidi.

"Now My Pet, please remember that the closer we come to the middle of your little circles, the bigger our bonus will be.

"Particularly when the needle that goes in here," he suddenly snarled as he viciously rammed the tip of the black marker deep into Puss navel.

"Ooo, that's gonna' be real tricky, but I know that you can come through in the end, as it were, Big Boy," Heidi simpered, and after glancing again at the plastic model, flourished her red marker at the cams before stepping around behind Puss. There she began crooning the old children's ditty, "We Go In and Out the Window," as she squatted, and probed...

Puss willed herself to remain motionless and be non-reactive to the assault on the privacy of her body by the two perverts. She thought of her ancestors instead...

"Another one goes in here," Freddy murmured as a drip of saliva flowed from the corner of his mouth. He gripped Puss' right breast and made a black spot on its skin next to her right arm, then he gripped her left breast and marked the skin of its inner side, and leered at Heidi, "Your turn."

Still crooning the ditty for the children's game, Heidi carefully marked red target circles on each of Puss' breasts, opposite from those made by Freddy. Suddenly she announced with a bright lilt in her voice, "Darling! Do you know what we are going to have here?"

"My goodness no, my little Aventurix!" Freddy paused and showed his stained teeth again as he smiled to the cams, "What will we have?"

"Why, shish ka-boobs, My Pet!" Heidi smiled brightly as she did another Commide d'la Arte curtsey to the cams, then arched her back and purred loudly, as she pushed a red-gloved fingertip into each side of her own minimal breasts.

"Oh, you Little Smarto! And I'll just bet that you can make her really smart in other places too!" Freddy leered as he reached around and squeezed Puss' left buttock. "We also have to do some action back here, in the rear echelon so to speak!" he continued as he flourished the steel needle toward

Puss' hips.

"Ooo, Shish Ka-butt!" Heidi grinned with a cold glitter in her eyes. Then she flounced around with a flourish and presented her narrow white-painted bottom to the cams - and waved back and forth while pointing a red-gloved finger at each of her hips...

Puss willed herself to remain unfeeling and calm throughout Freddy and Heidi's studied attempt to break her spirit with their taunting words and extreme actions. Her anger caused her body to be rigid in spite of being held open and helpless by the restraints on the steel posts, and violated by the marking pens in the hands of the two posturing maniacs.

She continued to try to eject the gag strapped in her mouth until she willed herself to stop staining, and to remember her people. Then Puss became icily calm and ignored Freddy and Heidi as she thought of herself, and who she was. A memory came into her mind of the time when she was 13 and her father had taken her to a place in a forest she did not know and had left her naked and blindfolded, honor bound to find her way through her trial of passage.

She also remembered him hugging her before he drove off in his little truck. He had whispered, "You are not alone, all of your ancestors walk with you."

Puss remembered opening her eyes several minutes after her father had left, and sinking to sit on the ground in the little sun-lit clearing. She had emptied her mind then in preparation for the trial ahead, and now recalled the gentle breath of a breeze that had wafted over her shoulders which had assured her that she was not alone.

*

Puss' eyes widened when she again felt a slight stirring of air on her body as she hung helplessly on the stage, and suddenly she felt again that she was not alone ...

Puss brought her focus back to her two tormentors when Freddy ordered, "Remove her gag. I want to mark her cheeks where this needle will go in through her tongue. Have the forceps ready to secure it if you would, my Dear Depraved Dolly."

Heidi smirked as she released the strap holding the cruel gag in Puss' mouth and watched with a fixed grin and glittering eyes while Puss coughed and hacked to clear her throat, then lifted her head and said with a glare, "You have ten seconds to release me or you will suffer much!"

"So do it Now!" she snapped with chilling authority.

Freddy smiled tenderly like an uncle would to his fretful niece as he leaned close to her face.

"You will be released, My Sweet, but only in due course. And only after you have screamed for a long - long time, and are finally imploring us to give you the release of death. But we won't do that until we have finished with all of the very subtle and complicated procedures we have planned for you, my dear little Participant."

"After all, we can't disappoint our viewers," Heidi added. "Your endurance is the key element in our show, my pet," Heidi smirked as she brought her face close and thrust her tongue into Puss' ear, "So stay strong for as long as you can..."

"For the record," Freddy continued in a crazed caricature of the calm tones of a scientist, "The stern look on your face and your proud pose are now being recorded, and will be replayed again and again in the final edited vid of our proceedings, in counterpoint to the changes in your demeanor and your expression that will occur over time.

"Changes that are inevitable as we explore your tolerance for pain, and you witness our destruction of your beautiful body," he finished in a tender whisper.

"Considering her muscle tone however," Freddy suddenly guffawed with a leer to the cams as he again rammed a bony forefinger deep into Puss' navel with one hand and viciously squeezed the firmness of her right breast with the other, "Your release might only come after many very long hours, or days even of the fun-filled activities we've planned for you."

Puss stared at Freddy for a second, then she spat accurately into his left eye. A second later, she turned to Heidi whose leering white-painted face was still close to hers, and spat on the bridge of the woman's nose.

"Let me go Now! Or start singing your death songs!" Puss snapped.

Freddy fastidiously wiped Puss' spittle from his eye with a tissue from a box on the instrument cart, then picking up the large needle he had flourished before her earlier, said, "You should really save your body fluids My Dear. You will soon need as much of them as you still can retain, without a doubt."

Then the man smiled beatifically to the cams again as he gripped Puss right breast and pulled at it with a squeezing grip.

"I really think that one of the most delicious moments of each new

Exploration is the look that appears in a Participant's eyes when an outside force invades their body for the first time, and they finally learn the truth of pain - and that they are helpless to prevent it," Freddy slurred with a drivel of saliva again showing at the corner of his mouth.

"And the outside force is Us," Heidi giggled as she did a ballerina's formal courtesy to the cams.

Puss spat twice again with exceptional accuracy and hit the lenses of both cams. Then there was a slight noise from the blackness beyond the brightly-lit stage where the four were standing around Puss' helpless form. They heard a rustle followed by a muffled sound from the back of the dark room, like twigs snapping...

"Cut!" Freddy snarled. "Dammit you two," he shouted. "Time is money! If you perverts can't sit quiet, leave now! And if you disrupt us one more time, you're next - understand?"

Without waiting for a reply, he turned back to the cam operators. "Clean your lenses and let's get started! We got much work to do on this little piece of bait before we can all go home." Then Freddy snapped, "Action!" as he gripped Puss' right breast again and poised the long needle in his left hand

The male cam operator focused on Puss face as Heidi moved aside slightly to clear his view and the woman operator focused her cam down on to the inner side of Puss' breast, and the red-marked circle where the large needle would emerge when Freddy completed his thrust.

"Look into my eyes Little One, and so begin your Pilgrimage of Pain," Freddy intoned as he began pressing the sharp point of the needle against her skin.

Puss held her head erect and thrust out her chest as she glared, and snarled at him, "You scummos never learn."

"Ah, but perhaps I will soon from the sound of your screams," Freddy sneered, but his momentum was chilled for a second by the confidence Puss showed, and his eyes wavered under her stare.

Then with a grimace, he recovered his control. "Enough talk! Now we begin," and he was tensing his left arm to thrust the needle into Puss' flesh when he suddenly shuddered, as the point of a spear erupted through the fabric of his stained coat with a sodden crunch slightly to the left of his sternum.

Puss was still staring at Freddy when he looked down in unbelieving eyes at the glistening flint point protruding from his chest. She watched the gray-haired man strain to raise his gaze back to her face. When he met her eyes again he saw the death in them she had foretold, and he slumped to the floor as it began...

Puss noted in the slow motion of the scene that the tip of the spear protruding from Freddy's chest scratched her right thigh as he collapsed, but the sound of another crunch a second later drew her attention to Heidi, in time to see the woman's body jerk and her eyes glaze, as a steel throwing knife sunk into her neck above the scarlet ruff.

A third crunch sounded almost immediately as another spear sank into the chest of the male cam operator and the sound was repeated a second later when another knife slammed into the female cam operator's neck.

They both staggered and their cams clattered to the floor as they collapsed to sprawl beside the still-quivering bodies of Freddy and Heidi.

"Well Buddy, you sure know how to grab center stage! But I'm glad we got here before your big opener, so to speak," Boots grinned as she and Bila stepped out of the darkness of the tiny auditorium into the lighted area in front of the platform.

Puss looked at the two for a moment, then she gasped weakly, "Thanks Friends," as her eyes rolled back in her head and she fainted, and hung limply by her wrists from the steel frame.

"Shat! Get her down!"

Bila snatched up a long-bladed knife from the array on the instrument cart and tenderly supported Puss' body as he carefully cut the fetters on her wrists, then passed the knife to Boots who stooped and freed Puss' ankles. Standing again, Boots said, "Put her here," and helped Bila seat the limp woman on the edge of the low stage.

Boots gently pushed Puss' head over to a position between her knees and held it there for several moments, until Puss recovered from her faint and took a gasping breath, and raised her head.

"Thanks guys. Got anything to eat? I'm empty."

"Couldn't wait for breakfast this morning, huh?" Boots smiled. "Field bite OK?" she continued as she pulled a large wafer from a pocket in her green jumpsuit and stripped away its protective foil.

"No – yes, but I'm really empty. They purged me so they wouldn't get their hands dirty," Puss mumbled as she chewed on the high-energy emergency combat ration.

"Bastards!" Boots snarled as she un-wrapped another wafer and offered it to Puss. "Two of these ought to hold you 'till we get back to base."

Puss chewed the second one more thoroughly before swallowing, then she held out her arms and gritted, "Help me up!"

Bila and Boots steadied her on her feet a moment as Puss took a deep breath and straightened her shoulders. "Thanks Buddies, real much..."

"Hey, no biggers. Fiends don't let friends hang around with the wrong crowd," Boots murmured with a smile on her lips, but her eyes were serious and concerned as she squeezed Puss' shoulder and then stroked her forehead.

"They hurt try you – No. Try to hurt you. They die," Bila added softly as he caressed Puss' other shoulder. Then his face hardened.

"Molly vid show. Them," he gestured at Freddy and Heidi's bodies sprawled on the stage, "Hurt girl. They want hurt you way that?"

"Yeah Kid. Just what was going on here, and why you got spots?" Boots asked, as she touched the red and black marks on Puss' breast, and then on her shoulders and hips.

"That's where Colonel Kink wanted these," Puss answered grimly as she plucked the long needle still in Freddy's slack hand and brandished it.

"To be stuck in me here and to come back out here," as she touched first a black spot on the front of her left hip, and then the red circle high on her left buttock.

"And through your hip joint, right?" Boots asked in a flat voice.

"Yep."

"What's this, the roadmap?" Boots asks in the same grim tone as she gestured toward the doll.

"Yep..."

Bila stared at the doll, bristling with miniatures of the needle Puss held and which was an exact tiny copy of her. He grunted, and grasped the long-bladed knife again. "They come not back now, ever," he announced.

Then bending over Freddy' body, he rammed two fingers into the dead man's eye-sockets and lifting his head up from the floor, cut it free with three well-placed slashes of the knife that was to have been used on Puss...

Bila sat Freddy's head upright on the edge of the stage, then turning to Heidi's body severed her head below her ruff in the same manner and set it beside Freddy's.

He was turning to the slumped bodies of the camera crew when Boots felt Puss' shoulder tense under her hand. "There're two more around here some where," she hissed.

"Yep, there were anyway. Bila found them when we came through the blackout curtain into this little slaughterhouse a couple of minutes ago," Boots chuckled grimly.

"You know, I've never seen two necks broken by one man so quick before, and at the same time even..."

Puss nodded, and then she asked, "How did you get in here?"

"Walked through the door, with Bila as my prisoner then he persuaded the guard to let us in your studio."

"How'd he do that?"

"Bit off his little finger..."

"Oh." Then she whispered, "But why does he do this?" Puss nodded at Bila, and his grim work

"It's OK, Buddy. If I've guessed right, it's just the way of his people..."

Puss watched as Bila quickly severed the heads of the two camera operators and holding the knife in his teeth carried them to the edge of the stage by gripping their slack jaws like bucket handles. He placed them with the other two, then without a word turned toward the darkness of the small theater.

Puss was still light-headed and slightly detached from of the effect of her violent purge even as she felt her energy now returning, so while she watched what Bila was doing she also reflected on his abrupt attack on the bear that had threatened her and Boots back in the little valley.

She shook her head again in wonder at the explosive force this gentle man could show when he decided to act. She blinked her eyes at the primal scene, then a sudden intuition about his intentions caused her to snap out of here reverie and call, "Don't get blood on the little Rat's suit, I need it."

"Ja Boss," Bila grunted from the darkness.

"Hurry it up Buddy, we got to get out of here damn quick! Rat's Nest is gonna' go orbital when the Director gets back in town this morning!" Boots called.

"Ja Boss," Bila grunted again, and stepped back into the lighted area around the stage a moment later carrying two more heads by their jaws with a relatively clean black jumpsuit draped over his shoulder.

"Chaos! I said he do chaos good, didn't I?" Boots whispered with her eyes wide.

"Yep. You did. And he damn sure does," Puss sighed, with her first tentative smile since being freed from her fetters. Then the young woman took a deep breath and resumed her normal self as Boots ordered, "OK, Troopers, enough play! We now focus on getting the ferk out of here, and I think we're gonna' have to fight biggers to do it"

"Don't worry Buddy, I've got our mission extract covered!" Puss said, "Along with my own goodies now," as she pulled on the black jumpsuit. "Where's the entry guard by the way?"

"Sleeping it off behind the blackout curtain - with a bandage I was nice enough to put on his hand."

Puss folded back the long cuffs and legs of the suit to fit her limbs, then she squatted and removed the recording vid chips from each of the cams that lay next to the headless bodies of their operators. She placed the chips carefully in a breast pocket, then turned and strode into the anti-chamber where she had been so callously prepared for her ordeal.

"In here, Troops!" Puss snapped.

Boots and Bila followed her into the grim room with the stained concrete floor as she began rooting through the refuse bin in a corner where Rat's thin-faced functionary had discarded the remains of her green jumpsuit. She found that her credit chips and personal items were gone, but that the report from Lulu was still intact in what remained of a breast pocket.

She retrieved her boots from the bin and balancing on first one foot then the other, latched them on. Then with a sudden insight, she searched the pockets in the Rat's suit she now wore, and smiled when found the rest of her belongings...

"Alright Troops! In a minute we go!" Puss said as she stepped to the instrument table and picked up the bug locator the older functionary had used on her. "You take this Buddy, and go to the van in there. I'll be back in a short," as she pointed toward the garage door, then turned and raced back into the studio.

Boots and Bila were sitting in the black van in the garage space when Puss bounded in through the door from the prep room five minutes later. She still wore the black jump suit but now her face was altered with grease paint to that of a circus clown, similar to the entry person's at the front door of this building the previous evening. She also wore dark glasses and was tucking one of the long needles up her sleeve.

"I figgered Heidi would have a dressing table back stage, and she did," Puss said in response to the looks her friends gave her when she jumped in beside Bila She slammed the door and asked in a cold voice, "Now, where does Colonel Kink live?"

Boos said from the driver's seat, "Close to my folks. I'll show you where."

"And let me guess, you have a mission and you don't want to be recognized, right?"

"Right."

"She lives alone, but she's probably got a nurse with her now, and the nurse is more'n likely a submissive," Boots murmured as she powered the black van. "Happy Hunting."

"Thanks Buddy, I value your intel." Then Puss turned to Bila, "I thought you might want these," she continued in the same tone as she offered him the two flint points snapped off 12 centimeters back from their heads.

"Thank you. Sticks find easy. Good sukarri more hard to," Bila responded gravely. "You good do."

Puss relaxed and smiled, "No big man, you do good..." But after that fleeting smile she gritted, "Now dammit, let's go!"

"Lucky for you I know how to drive one of these things," Boots grinned as she found the control for the garage door after a moment's search of the dashboard.

"Lucky for you I can remember stuff, like where they parked this van, while I'm under Rat's dope," Puss snarled. Then she reached over and squeezed Boots thigh, and caressed Bila's hand resting on her shoulder. "Thanks again, and way big, Troopers..."

"Nada, Buddy," Boots smiled as she accelerated the van and scraped its roof under the still-opening door.

"Friend," Bila whispered.

*

Boots swung the van to a stop next to Waldo's taxi at the curb near the back door of the Network building. She dropped her opaqued window, "It's us! Follow, OK?"

Waldo stared at the black van, then looked at Boots for a second before growling over his shoulder, "Stand down gang, she's ours!" Then with the blissful grin of an attacking wolf, he signaled an affirmative by flashing the age-old thumbs-up signal and powered up his sedan to follow, as Boots sped off through the insignificant S'attl's late-morning rush hour.

*

"Park here and you two get in with Waldo. I've got a delivery to make upstairs..." Puss said in a very quite voice as she signaled Boots to stop on the street before the entry to a luxurious apartment block.

425

"Ja Boss," Boots said," as she brought the vehicle to a stop at the curb.

"You me need kill help?" Bila asked.

"Thanks Buddy, but this one is all mine," Puss responded with a smile that was serene like the happy expression of a child riding a merry-go-round, but the light of war-joy gleamed in her eyes as she hopped out of the van...

*

"Delivery for the Colonel from the Network," Puss ordered into the speaker as she faced the vid cam beside the main door.

"Please come up," a voice responded that was softly female despite the distortion of the poorly designed communication systems' speaker, and the door latch clicked. "Number 28-B," the voice whispered.

Puss pushed the door open and strode to the elevator door in the small lobby, and punched the number of the Colonel's apartment. When the elevator stopped, its doors opened to reveal a voluptuous redhead in a caricature of a retro Twentieth Century nurse's uniform. Her skirt was very short, and the top three buttons of her starched blouse were undone. She smiled at Puss tremulously as she whispered, "What is your will with me?"

Puss thought, "This has gotta' be one of these new engineered ones like Golden Boy last night. Bet she's got built-in beat-me genes and it looks like her skin would mark real good too."

"I have a delivery for the Colonel from the Network," Puss said to the exotic and erotic creature as she waved one of the cam chips. "Please inform her of this and then report back here to me."

The redhead murmured with downcast eyes, "Yes Powerful Mistress." Then she turned and walked back down the hall, and Puss saw that many red welts crisscrossed the backs of her thighs.

"My Main Mistress will see you now," the redhead announced in a soft voice as she returned and stood before Puss with downcast eyes.

"Good. Now you will go to your room and not come out until the Colonel calls for you," Puss snapped, as she grasped the young woman's hand and squeezed it with a grip that caused pain.

"Oh Yeess," the young woman gasped as she sank to her knees before Puss. "I will do anything you ask of me." Then when Puss released her hand, she rose and swayed toward a door in the hallway. "Will you squeeze me again sometime, please," she whispered over her shoulder as she entered her small room.

"We'll see," Puss said as she strode down the hall to the main room.

"Hurry up dammit and bring it to me!" The Colonel was shouting as Puss entered the room. The woman was sitting in her wheel chair before a large vid screen showing a documentary on the finer points of punishment whipping the Chin used in their factories. Puss smiled...

"I bring the first draft to you of our performance of your commission, and we at the Network do hope that you are pleased with our show. If you wish Colonel, I will play it for you now."

"Yes, give it to me!" the woman in the chair hissed without bothering to glance at the Network messenger standing beside her chair. Her eyes gleamed...

"Yes, Colonel," Puss responded quietly as she stepped to the large vid and canceling the current show, inserted one of the chips she had brought from Freddy's reeking studio.

"Ahh," the Colonel hissed. "You people really are good!" she murmured as the screen lit up and displayed Puss' trussed form spread-eagled on the columns. "But turn up the volume, I want to hear everything!"

"Again, as you wish, Colonel," Puss hissed through clinched teeth. Then she wrapped her arm around the woman's head and immobilized it with her amazing strength. The woman began struggling with a sudden foreseeing, then Puss thrust the long needle into the Colonel's ear channel, and after churning its tip around for a second, pushed it on through the woman's medulla oblongata and forced it out of the quivering and gasping woman's other ear.

"Die slow, scum..." Puss muttered as she turned and strolled back down the hallway of the Colonel's apartment to the elevator, and took it back down to the street where her friends were waiting.

"OK Buddy, just what went on up there? You were only gone for five minutes."

"You were right about the Submissive, she was real obedient," Puss whispered as she settled between Boots and Bila in the back seat of Waldo's sedan.

"Follow us troops," Waldo muttered into his comset as he pulled away from the curb.

"That's good, but where's your souvenir needle?" Boots asked cautiously.

"Oh, I left it where I used it."

"To?"

"To pierce her ears."

"Pierce her ears?" Boots grunted, swaying with the motion of the swerving sedan as Waldo led their backup sedan in a race toward the airfield through S'attl's decaying streets.

"Yep - in one, and out the other," Puss responded in a voice that was suddenly brittle. Then she began trembling. "Shat! I'm sorry folks," I don't know what's wrong with me," she whimpered as she continued to shake.

"You've been in heavy combat Kid whether you realize it or not. It's OK to shake," Boots murmured as she grasped her friend's hand.

Bila said nothing, but he wrapped his arm around Puss' quivering shoulders and cradling her head against his chest, began softly humming a wordless tune. Puss' reaction to the stress of her experience began to fade, and when Waldo finally drove the sedan toward the gate of the National Guard post and airfield, she sighed and sat up, and whispered, "Damn, I'm sure lucky."

"I am too, Buddy," Boots murmured.

"What lucky?" Bila asked as he squeezed Puss' shoulder.

"Lucky is having friends. Like you two," Puss whispered after a pause. She paused again then said with a sigh, "That's major luck."

***

Chapter 20
The Congress

May 6, 2276 AD,
Pamunkey Indian Reservation, King William County, Virginia

"Welcome to the reservation, Congressman," Eagle Beak said in the twilight as he guided his plastic replica of a traditional Pamunkey dugout canoe alongside the sport cruiser that had just dropped anchor in the broad bight of the Pamunkey River. "How was your voyage down the Potomac?"

"Uneventful. Not like some other trips I've done back when I used to get hump-um' calls about to go pull your bongos out of the bushes," the gray-haired man standing on the foredeck of the boat grinned as he finished securing his anchor rode. "And dammit, you can still pull a sneak just as good as ever!"

"Thank you Suh' as one of my ancestors said to Mar's Robert once, back during the late unpleasantness…"

"Mine did too you damn redskin unreconstruct! I've got two ancestors who marched with Bobby Lee's boys."

"Thank you again Suh', I appreciate the compliment of including my tribe with you paleface power folks of the old south," Eagle Beak said with a grin.

"You total goat vent, get up here and drink with me!"

"Ja Boss," Eagle Beak said as he secured a painter from his canoe to a stanchion and chinned himself up onto the cruiser's foredeck. "You got limes for them Daiquiris? And rum too I hope. Us redskins be biggers on paleface rum."

"Did I say goat vent? I meant to say sheep ferker," the gray-haired man said with an evil grin.

"I save the world's wazooter time after time and again," Eagle Beak moaned theatrically, "But just one time, with one scrawny sheep and what's the only thing the world remembers about me!" he gasped as he pressed the back of his hand against his forehead.

"Hey redskin, I know how Baaad you are, but also how good. Anyway, the sheep probably loved it, so knock off you crappo. Stand down and follow me," the US Representative from a conservative district in the hill country of North Georgia ordered.

He led the way aft on the narrow walkway around the pilot house and stepped down into the cruiser's open cockpit and unlatched a cooler compartment. He set out two glasses, a bottle of white rum and several limes. Then he dropped to sit on the stern seat.

"Ice is in the cooler, and I don't do sugar with my daiquiris," Charles C. Calhoun continued with a grin as he motioned to the other fish-fighting chair bolted to the deck, "So mix us drinks Mister EB, then sit and tell me why you called me to come down here in such a hurry even though I'm in recess, and made you me to come by water too."

"Time to talk Sir!"

Eagle Beak filled two tumblers with ice, crushed the juice of a whole lime into each without bothering to cut them open, and then filled the glasses to the brim with rum.

"I talked to my daughter out west yesterday and I thought you might want to hear her news, but it'll cost you a cigar!" he said with a crooked grin.

"I thought it'd come to bribery with you redskins sooner or later, so I'm prepared and you got a deal," Charles replied as he opened another compartment under the thwart and held out an ornately labeled cigar box filled with large Havanas.

"Feel no guilt about smoking them by the way. These were a cheap attempt by someone to buy my vote on something or other, sometime back whenever," Charles added as he pulled out an aged briar pipe and a pouch of Turkish latakia for himself.

Both men sipped their drinks and puffed their tobacco in contented silence in the deepening twilight of the evening while they watched the ripples appearing on the still surface of the broad river, as the fish began to feed.

Eagle Beak broke their silence after ten minutes by asking quietly, "You still keep this sludge-scow at the marina I told you about?"

"Yep. Their dockage fee is unbelievably good, but I think you know about that somehow."

"Yep. And that's why we can talk now without fear of ears." Eagle Beak set his drink aside then and leaning forward, began telling the Congressman in detail about the extreme level of dissatisfaction and distrust the military at the field level had with their high command, and especially President Pitson, their Commander-in-Chief.

Finally he added with an apologetic smile, "And present company except-ed, the folks who wear green or blue are pretty up to their chins, to make a really bad pun with Pitson's lap-dog Congress as well because it only spends its time, and its wheels in recess."

Charles laid his pipe on the thwart beside him and carefully set his glass next to it. He rested his elbows on his knees and bowed his head. After a long pause he responded while still looking down at the deck.

"You're way damn right about a lap-dog label for the Congress friend, and I'm not sure I shouldn't have that name either. But I have quiet-talked with a lot of members on both sides of the Hill, the ones not total de-brained anyway. While none of them like it, they don't know what the hell to do about it. The Network has all of us in Congress buggered to some extent and Boss Rat is way deep into a goodly number. So Pitson gets pretty much what he wants, which is a free hand to run the country for their own benefit," Charles finished in a dead voice.

"Their?"

"He and his wife's, and the Network's. The Network just wants profits. Those two want absolute power but shat, you know that probably better than I do," Charles said, his shoulders still slumped as he still stared down at the deck.

"No. Not better anyway," Eagle Beak said as he took a sip of his drink and a puff of his cigar. "These are very good by the way," he murmured as he blew a smoke ring into the still air. Then he stared at Charles. "Dammit Congressman, get your head back up!"

"Before you came home and got elected, and back when I called you 3Cee, you and I fought together in some real good fights in some real bad situations, and we won every time. Remember?"

Charles slowly raised his head and looked at Eagle Beak with a tight smile, and nodded silently.

"So, you want to go to war one more time, for something that's worth it all the way big this time?"

"You always did make good missions Bird Nose," Charles suddenly grinned. "So what you got for me now?"

The big man said quietly, "From now on, you may call me by my tribal name of Eagle Beak," then he grinned back at Charles, in a certain way.

"Shat! I've seen you look like that before!" Charles said with a grunt. "Now I know it's going to get bad, and I'm going to hear your damn Chin Chiller yell again before it gets any better!"

Eagle Beak nodded to his friend then proceeded to outline the details of the action plan Puss had relayed to him on the phone the previous evening. When he finished his briefing, and without giving the now wide-eyed Charles time to comment, he continued to describe the clandestine organization that had begun slowly creating itself ever since the insane, meat-grinder phase of the Chin war had begun, soon after Pitson had entered his flagrantly un-constitutional third term in office.

"Unholy Shat by all the crappo that's Holy!" Charles exclaimed, "I've had a feeling ever since the war ended that there was some kind of funny electric-ity in the air, but I had no idea about this and I don't think anyone else in Washington does either. How did you guys do it?"

"Three Cee old buddy, if you will think back to during the war, those who survived did so by learning how to evade and confuse the enemy until the time was right to strike. Right?"

"Right. And you taught me enough about that to let me come home again and without too many holes in my hide either," Charles whispered.

"Well," Eagle Beak drawled, "A bunch of us, mostly Army, but some fly-guys too decided a long while ago that we better expand our definition of Enemy to include certain elements behind us as well as those Chin bastards out in front."

"The anchor-clankers decided to play it safe in their own little world however and still do, in what there is left of our Navy now. But our bunch which had no name until a couple of days ago, has been evading and confus-ing everybody in every way we can all this time ever since."

Then Eagle Beak suddenly bared his teeth in a ferial grin, "'Course, us Pamunkey been evadin' and confusin' you palefaces ever since 1609, when Powhatan hit you at Jamestown for biting the hand that was feeding you, as it were." He relaxed then just as suddenly, and showed the same smiling face to his friend as before.

Charles shook his head as he stared at his old friend for a moment, then took a large swallow of his rum, coughed several times and finally said with a sigh, "OK, two things Colonel."

"One, if you're thinking that you can suddenly call me, a duly elected member of the US Congress down here to your fever swamp on this short notice and then recruit me for this craziness that you have just described, you're crazy! But you just did. So where do I sign on?"

"Two, why now all of a sudden?"

"I respond to your comments in your order Sir. "One. Yes I do, and you just did. Thank you Charles," Eagle Beak replied in a level voice. "And two, because the catalytic factor we have been waiting to emerge for about ten years finally figured it out this week, and decided she was ready."

"She?"

"She. Her name is Kristina Hamier. She was a Special Forces captain until she was demobilized two years ago. You probably know of her by her field name though, Captain Cook."

Charles looked puzzled for a moment, then he said with an evil grin, "Oh yes, I do. I've heard some strong words about her, and she's good." He paused for a moment then as he murmured, "But I seem to recall another girl. One who long ago, also put on armor in order to lead her troops against a powerful oppressor. So tell me Eagle Beak, thanks for the honor by the way, does this Kristina Hamier wear asbestos underwear?"

"The issue has already been raised Congressman."

"And its resolution?"

"We're all gonna' wear it and we'll make damn sure she doesn't need hers! But now, let's paddle over to my yohacan. Possum Sprout has food for us, and a dinner companion for you."

"That sounds nice but who's this 'Possum Sprout'?

"And also," Charles asked in a stern voice, "What `n hell is the name of this bunch you have dragged me into, just for the record, of course!"

"Possum Sprout is my wife and though it's not official, the group will probably be called 'The Restoration'."

"Your wife must be very nice to let you get away with calling her that. But your, no - our group's name sort of sounds like a North Georgia roadhouse dance band."

"Yep Congressman, she is and she's a friend of mine too," EB whispered, "And you're right, our new name does but I think you'll like the tunes we play.

"Anyway, meihtussuc," he said as he drained his tumbler and standing, tucked his cigar behind his ear.

"What's that mean, you pesky redskin?" Charles chuckled as he finished his drink and knocked out his pipe.

"Come and eat," Eagle Beak's white teeth flashed as he smiled in the gathering darkness and lowered himself back into the dugout, "And don't forget the cigars," He ordered as he steadied the craft while Charles climbed down from the cruiser's foredeck.

Both men stepped out of the repro-dugout into the shallows after a short paddle to shore and dragged it up on to the sand of the river bank Eagle Beak led the way toward a yellow light shining from the doorway of the elongated dome structure that was his home.

"Chamah, wiowah!" a small woman called in a pleasant voice as she stood into the lighted door.

"Chamah, Wironusqua!" Eagle Beak answered as he walked into the light and embraced her.

"I keep telling you silly, I am only a Noungass, your wife. Not a Queen!" the small woman sighed as she returned his embrace. "Now introduce me to your friend."

"Charles C. Calhoun, meet Possum Sprout, my wife, mother of our daughter Marybell and my max leader for many years."

*

Marybell had been born on the small reservation of the Pamunkey tribe, all which remained of Powhatan's nation of the eastern Algonquin Indians. The reservation was established by the Royal Colony's governor in 1658 and was in the tidewater area of Virginia on a tributary of the York River.

Her father and her mother were both highly educated and of relatively pure Pamunkey blood, and they had chosen to move back to their ancestral lands and live with others of similar background in a style overtly resembling that of their forbearers, who were on-site to meet Captain John Smith when he founded Jamestown in 1607.

While they lived in homes that were very similar in appearance to the traditional woven reed-covered long houses built by their ancestors however, the group was careful to not forego the benefits of power from small fuel cells to support their modern sanitation, heating and communication devices. They also relied on the strength and permanence of modern materials in the construction of the houses, and on trail bikes and small trucks for transportation.

The members of the tribe dressed according to the tradition of their forbearers on the reservation, and they made all of those garments and footwear from deerskins they collected and tanned themselves after preserving the venison either by smoking it on racks in the old way, or storing it in their modern food freezers.

Many of the adults who lived in the village were able to perform the work of their careers electronically from their lodges, and returned to the large urban areas only when necessary. The less fortunate ones who needed to be away for their work maintained minimal lodgings in the cities, and came back to the reservation as often as they could.

The Pamunkey were quite competent in defensive and offensive tactics as well as in their professions, since almost all of the members of the tribe were also veterans of the Chin war.

Marybell's father was a geologist before he went into the Army's Special Forces. After a long and spectacularly effective career in the Chin war however, he had been finally rotated out of active duty. He then returned to the reservation and promptly organized and become the headmaster of a junior military academy for the Pamunkey tribe, in spite of strong resistance from the education bureaucrats.

Marybell's mother was also a veteran of the Special Forces, where she had been a demolition expert known as "Little Big Boom Woman". She had earned a Ph.D. in social psychology before she entered the Army, and is known for writing her insightful research papers on that subject, as well as for Network 1X romantic vids of the absolute sappiest kind. Both were also very lucrative...

Eagle Beak was tall and gracefully muscular with hair that was still black, shinning dark eyes and a face that would be ruggedly handsome except that he had taken his nose on the warpath too many times. Marybell's mother was petite and delightfully curvy, with chestnut hair and hazel eyes in a face of either calm beauty or wickedly elfin piquancy according to on her mood. Because of their ancestry, they both had scant body hair and their skins were noticeably the color of new copper.

*

"Chamah Charles," the small woman smiled, "Winggapo! And come in out of the evening damp."

435

"Huh?" Charles looked down to her as he said, "You are the prettiest Possum Sprout I have ever seen, whatever that is."

"I said, Welcome Friend. You really need to learn our language if you're going to be around here much. Anyway let me introduce you to another friend.

Doctor Sally Strider as she called herself before she found some of our strangeness in her ancestry.

"Sally, meet Charles C. Calhoun."

A slender woman with clear gray eyes and gray streaks in her dark hair stepped forward and extended her hand.

"Hello Charles, it's nice to meet you. You may call me Mud Puddle, and you can leave off the Doctor," said with a twinkle in her eye.

"Pleased to meet you Ma'am," Charles responded gravely to this woman, whose quiet elegance belied the threadbare checked shirt and the faded work pants she wore. "But I am confused. Do all you folks here have such descriptive names?"

"We traditionally keep our tribal names secret, except to those who are closest to us," Eagle Beak said. "They were given to us when we rejoined the tribe or to our children soon after their birth. Like our ancestors did, we make up fun names to use in public."

"Although some of our nearest and dearest," he then glowered at his wife with mock exasperation, "Take undignified liberties in their selection of a public name for a loved one!"

Eagle Beak's wife looked up at her husband, "Well, I think Bird Nose has a noble sound, and I could have named you after the bird's other end!"

"And what the hell is a Possum Sprout anyway?" she asked as she planted her fists on her hips and pouted, with laughing eyes.

"You keep asking that," he grinned down at the woman he loved. "One of these days I'll tell you, maybe."

"Accept us as we are Charles, or you'll get a max headache at the very least!" Mud Puddle said with a conspiratorial smile as she pulled at the man's hand she still held in a gentle grip. "Now come in and relax."

"Yes, let's go in and sit and eat and talk," Eagle Beak added as he followed Charles into his domed long house, his yohacan in the Pamunkey language.

The interior of the elongated structure was smoothly curved and its walls were lined with material that gave the appearance of woven reeds rather than the insulation-backed polymer fabric that it actually was. A low table sat in the middle of the space they entered with plump cushions arranged around it on the mat-covered floor.

"Would you two like more drinks and smokes?" Possum Sprout asked with an almost straight face.

"What you mean More, Squaw?" Eagle Beak demanded, striking a noble pose with his arms crossed as he glared at her in theatrical indignation.

"When old Army buddies greet one another, firewater and cheap cigars seem to always be part of the ritual," his wife said as she raised her wineglass in a toast to Mud Puddle, who returned the honor with a wink.

"Well, since this Bird Nosed renegade snuck up on my boat and forced a monster Daiquiri on me that obviously was a piece of some pernicious Pamunkey plot, I think food would be fine for now," Charles said in a pained voice as he held out his hands in innocence to the two women, while he thought to himself, "Hmmm, Mud Puddle's a funny name for an interesting person."

The woman who called herself "Mud Puddle" smiled as she looked at the compact Congressman with silver hair and honest eyes, "Hmmm..." she thought.

"Then shall we dress for dinner?" Possum Sprout asked innocently, with an almost straight face.

"But of course, Ma'am," Eagle Beak responded solemnly as he bowed to his wife with a graceful flourish.

She and Mud Puddle walked from the room and pushed through a gap in the hanging curtain of deerskins that partitioned the lodge.

"When I'm in Washington I wear my paleface uniform," Eagle Beak grinned as he stripped. "When I entertain guests here I dress like my people did. You can also, if you wish." He then opened a chest by the wall and pulled out a belt and a loincloth. After stripping out of his coverall he tied the belt around his waist and arranged the loincloth between his legs then he held out another to Charles.

"Might as well join you since I see I'm outnumbered," Charles grinned as he began removing his clothes.

The two women pushed their way back through the leather partition a few moments later. Possum Sprout carried a large covered earthenware bowl colored gray splotched with black and Mud Puddle balanced two smaller bowls made of the same clay. Both women were now nude except for napkin-sized aprons of decorated doeskin which they had tied around their waists. They smiled serenely as they presented the food and themselves to Charles and Eagle Beak.

*

Puss' mother still had the body she had enthusiastically offered to her husband when they first met on active duty at the Pentagon in Washington twenty-six years ago. They had seen each other for only two weeks, when their eyes had met one evening as they sat over sandwiches in an all-night deli after returning from a weekend hike in the Appalachians.

He had sighed happily and taken her hands in his, and had asked her with a slight smile, "How long can we go on meeting like this?"

She had returned his gaze directly and responded in a very quiet voice, "Forever?"

"Suits me!" he had said with a broad grin as he squeezed her hands. They slept together that night for the first time since they met, and were married the following morning as soon as the registry window opened in the musty old city building in Arlington.

They knew what they had was rare and genuine and, while they both really enjoyed other people, they meshed with and complemented each other so completely that they were really sufficient unto themselves in all aspects of their lives.

They both also felt the power of the sexual electricity that had immediately flowed between them when they first met, and they found that the longer they lived together the stronger their mutual attraction became, almost more so each day. Because of the joyful lust they shared which could be set with only a glance, or the touch of a single finger they really had no room in their thoughts for anyone else. So they remained monogamous by default as well as by choice but their monogamy was never, ever monotonous...

*

Mud Puddle was built like a dancer who was also a runner, and she appeared much younger than the almost sixty years that Charles calculated her to be. While rejuvenation drugs and procedures were quite common, Charles' instincts told him that this woman was natural rather than enhanced.

She gave him a slight smile as she and Possum Sprout knelt gracefully, and placed their dishes on the low table before the men.

"Eat now. We will talk again later," Possum Sprout said as she seated herself and opened the covered dish. She served Charles' plate with a helping of her stew of oysters and fish mixed with dried pumpkin and wild young greens spiced with black walnuts, wild garlic and sea salt.

Charles lifted his head as he inhaled the aroma from his plate, "My Gawd woman! This is fantastic, you must be from the South!"

"Sorry to say you nay Congressman, but some of what you call the Southern cooking actually comes from us redskins who were here first - including this cornbread. However, I will grant you palefaces the butter," Possum Sprout grinned as she passed both.

"No argument Ma'am until I finish eating anyway," Charles smiled, as he raised his loaded fork in a salute to her, then he winked to Mud Puddle, "You keep good company, Ma'am."

Mud Puddle silently returned his smile, as she tasted the stew on her plate.

*

"This is the room where I delivered your daughter, how's she doing now?" Mud Puddle asked after belching politely as she pushed her plate aside.

"Very well. And by the way, her navel is still the talk of her regiment," Possum Sprout grinned. "All the gals in her bunch were in major envy mode about it, and some of the guys as well."

"I just try to do my job, Buda knows, I try," Mud Puddle said with a straight face.

"Doctor Strider was noted in back Washington for making the most beautiful navels on the babies she delivered, before she decided to come down here," Possum Sprout explained in an aside to Charles.

"And If you ever decide to get into re-do's, you can work on mine first," she then giggled as she rose to her knees, pushed down the top of her apron and thrust out her belly at Mud Puddle.

"Hey there! Way no!" EB growled, "Woman, you got the cutest little starter spot in the whole world! I like it the way I married it and nobody messes with it except me, OK?"

Possum Sprout sighed theatrically, "Gasp, I am a slave to my own deformity I suppose..."

Eagle Beak growled, "Arrrr, me Proud Beauty, ye be mine now. But of course only if ye be so inclined - or reclined, as it were..."

Possum Sprout giggled and the two shared a brief but noisy kiss, and Mud Puddle turned to the gray-haired man and said, "Charles, can we talk about things for our post-diner conversation that are at least real and of today, instead of in babbling fits like these two?"

"Of course, my dear, but you do have to admit that they give real good babble when they get going," he responded gravely. Then he mopped up the last bite of his second helping of stew and drained the clay beaker of the corn beer that Possum Sprout had served them.

"Whoosh!" he gasped. "Old friend, you damn reverts sure know how to live! You taking any applications for this place?"

"I didn't know you were Indian." Eagle Beak responded as he released his wife.

"My children are an eighth Cherokee," Charles paused, then his face clouded and he finished quietly, "On their mother's side."

"Any news?" Eagle Beak asked in an equally quiet tone, his face suddenly solemn.

"Oh yes, quite a bit actually," Charles gritted. "They caught the ones who did it eighteen months ago, after they had done several more operations using the same modus."

"There were five of them, and they were charged with the murders, and tried in the court in Atlanta due to a venue change request." Charles continued in a dead voice.

"A law firm from Washington defended them and argued that they were just reflecting the mores of their culture, and while pain and suffering did regrettably occur, all the victims were also quite contributory, because of their physical attractiveness..."

"The jury found the gang guilty of serial murders anyway, but then the judge declared a mistrial because one of the jurors had not disclosed that she was an army veteran, and therefore tainted, in his words by - "An inappropriate hierarchal culture that assigned responsibility and guilt'."

"At the second trial," Charles continued in the same flat voice, "The venue was changed once again, to Athens where the jury pool contained a large number of academics from the University of Georgia. Their verdict was accidental person-slaughter, and the five were given two years in prison, less the time already in custody, and with early parole for good behavior."

"The five, three boys and two girls, still all teeners are out now, and prowling North Georgia once again..."

"Who were the lawyers who defended them?" Eagle Beak asked, very quietly...

"A team from the Network's legal staff."

"Were you surprised?"

"No."

"What was it that happened Charles, if you would like to tell us?" Possum Sprout asked in a soft voice.

"I'm sorry, Dear," Eagle Beak frowned to his wife. "I hadn't told you about this before, because I didn't think you would ever get to meet Charles." Then he nodded to his old comrade, "Your decision Congressman."

"Talking about bad things with good friends is good," Charles sighed. Then he began in a detached conversational tone.

"This gang stalked the spas and gyms in my district, looking for "perfect specimens" as they admitted, and actually boasted during their pre-trial hearings. One evening two years ago while I was in Washington, they grabbed my wife as she was leaving her health club."

"The gang was obsessed with trying to make 5X vids that were better, which means nastier than the Network's, so they used my wife for five days while they each took turns being the director of the show. The girls were worse than the boys…

"They took vids of what they did to their victims, but after the several judges viewed them, the vids weren't allowed in to the record. It didn't really matter because according to the coroner's reports, there wasn't much of the victims left anyway when the gang finally finished with them, including my wife," he finally muttered as he bowed his head…

Mud Puddle took his hand and held it gently without comment until he finally raised his face again. He returned her clasp then looked up at Eagle Beak and Bean Blossom whose faces mirrored his anguish.

"I'm OK now. But it's time to talk about how to change the things that need to be changed," he finished in a flat voice.

*

"One of the problems we have in the Congress today are the provisions of the Expanded War Powers Act of 2246, which we stupidly passed unanimously in 2246," Charles said with a sardonic twitch of a smile, after he savored at the taste of the wild strawberries dipped in honey that Mud Puddle had just fed him from where she knelt by his side, lightly brushing her breasts against his shoulder as she held them to his mouth. "So as long as a state of war exists, Congress is basically powerless because it made itself that way."

"Any chance for a change?" Eagle Beak asked from the other side of the hurdle around which the four sat.

"We might grow some backbone if there was an overt attempt to totally usurp our power." Then Charles continued darkly. "And we keep getting hints and rumors of some secret agreements that Pitson is making with the E-Union and other governments, but we have no verification, so the Congress can't challenge him with hearings."

"And since the Network owns the Speaker and the President Pro-Tem, not much is stirring on this front right now," he finished in a dull tone and bowed his head again.

"So what would happen if your Senators and Representatives got a clear signal?"

"Don't know, but I think they might wake up – sort of like the old German king who is supposed to sleep under a mountain in Germany, waiting for the call."

"You mean Barbarossa?"

"Yeah," Charles replied with a grin, and then a shrug.

"What about if instead they heard a call that was way more real, like "Boots and Saddles" played by a U.S. Cavalry trumpeter?"

"I think they would listen and way biggers," the man said as his eyes suddenly glistened.

"Stand by Congressman. Just stand by. But while you're doing that, please take a look at what it would take for Congress to reconvene both houses - and at your credential-receiving process for newly elected, or appointed members from the states now under martial law," Eagle Beak said with iron in his voice. Then he asked in a gentile voice, "Now about your children, how are they doing?"

"Pretty good," Charles gritted. "They're tough - like their mother was... Anyway, my daughter is a staffer on the Hill for a friend of mine from a Kentucky district. Since he is a gentleman she is safe. But my son, who's still a teener in a Washington school, isn't doing so good. Seems that he doesn't accept the teachings of the education establishment and he's quite vocal about it."

"Thank you for your discrete choice of words Charles," Mud Puddle murmured with an approving look at him, "Very gentlemanly of you to not call them by the name their crappo credo deserves..."

"3Cee never belabored the obvious back when we worked together, so I wouldn't expect it now," EB said quietly. Then he turned again to his friend, "You think your boy is ready to switch schools?"

"I'm sure of it, but it's no good. They're all the same."

"Up there, yes."

Charles frowned, and then he stared at EB, "Are you saying...?"

"We always have room down here to add a few good students. Particularly ones that tend to question authority, and most particularly ones who do it because of their genes."

"Well, he's double dammed for sure then poor kid," Charles said with a wry grin.

"Good! It's done. You send me a signal as soon as you get back and send him down on the next bus to Richmond. Tell him to pull the cord and get off at Doswell. Tell him also to message us when he gets on the bus. We will be there to get him."

"How will he find you?"

"Doswell is about as big as a minute, and my driver will have a feather in his hair OK!"

"What about fees?"

"Don't worry 3Cee, old buddy. You're gonna' pay with heap much in-kind service," Eagle Beak chuckled grimly.

"I was afraid of that..."

*

"Sounds like they're being real friendly," Possum Sprout murmured as she lay relaxed beside her husband, with love-sweat gleaming on her body in the faint light that filtered in through the small skylight in their bedchamber.

"Ha! I knew you weren't paying attention to business! You were listening in on them! Gotcha!"

"Hey big man, I always have to pay attention to the world even when I'm keeping up with you, otherwise it might sneak up on us and stab us in some strange place..."

"Granted, O Gracious Guardian of my big behind. So what did you hear?"

"Friendship. And interest."

"You said that she originally agreed to come to dinner only as a hospitality duty."

"Yep, but things can change you know. Like us in this next position..."

"Hmmm," he grinned, "Is this a change for the better?"

"Mmmm," Possum Sprout murmured as she nuzzled her husband's neck, and made him gasp once again with the delicate little touches of her exploring fingers,

*

"I have no preggers here to deal with right now, and Charles has asked me to float on his boat back up to DC with him. So I think I'll take a sabbatical," Mud Puddle announced in the early dawn of the next morning as she stood in front of the long house.

She wore a black ribbed turtleneck, tailored khakis and deck shoes and a duffel bag was slung over one shoulder. She had a slightly defiant expression on her face. Charles, standing at her side was again in his boat clothes and was smiling, albeit bashfully...

Eagle Beak and Possum Sprout stood in the doorway of their yohacan, nude with a robe of soft doeskins wrapped around them.

"Well, I see you've got your Sally outfit on again," Possum Sprout smiled, "But do you have a whole Washington wardrobe in that little sack? I think you'll need much more when you two hit the champagne circuit inside the Belt Way."

Mud Puddle's face brightened when she received her friend's subtle signal of approval, so she responded happily, "Enough to start. Anyway, I haven't been shopping for lacy stuff for a long time and I've got a bunch of credits that are going stale."

"I am very glad you are going with Charles," Eagle Beak said with a quiet smile. "You can be a major factor in the survival of all of us. I had already thought about asking you to go back with him, but it's better that you have taken that decision on your own."

Then he nonchalantly slipped out of the robe and leaving Possum Sprout draped in it, stepped into the lodge. He returned a moment later with a comset that was slightly larger than the usual ones and handed it to Mud Puddle.

"You know how to use this, right?"

"You taught me, Colonel."

"Wingan. Kicketen quier. Aumpswk niere," Eagle Beak smiled grimly.

"Kennehautows!" Mud Puddle snapped as she hit a brace and saluted the tall man.

"What'n Buda's Bedroll are you two saying?"

"Don't worry Charles," Mud Puddle murmured as she relaxed again. "We weren't talking about you. He just told me to speak to him in our language when I call, and I told him that I understood."

"Damn good idea, but why the salute? I thought you doctors didn't salute anyone," Charles asked.

"Army field surgeons do, and back when I was Major Strider, I spent all my time patching up bunches of wild folks who forgot to duck, unlike like you smart guys who didn't."

"Oh," Charles grunted with respect in his eyes now as well as interest, and something else.

"Your mission will make you both stay back on the Hill, even after things get interesting," the small woman said quietly as she pulled Eagle Beak to her side again and wrapped their robe around his waist.

"From now on you may call me Bean Blossom because now you are both as close as family." Then she continued crisply as Charles' eyes widened at her disclosure, "But your daughter might be better off down here."

"Yes," he replied after a moment, "I think she would. But I haven't been able to tell her what to do since she was six years old. So we'll just have to see about that when the time comes."

"Your two sound like interesting people. I think I will enjoy meeting them," Mud Puddle murmured. Then she continued, "And Charles, please call me Healing Waters whenever we go native..."

"I think that they will enjoy meeting you too, both as Sally Strider - and as my Mud Puddle," Charles grinned as he took her hand.

Then he ordered, "OK Bird Nose - put your damn pants on and paddle us back out to my boat in that damn fake canoe of yours! I need to catch the tide if we're going to make it back upriver to Crazy Town before it snows,"

"Ja big Paleface Boss. Wilcomp!"

***

Chapter 21
The Return

May 6, 2276 AD,
British Columbia, On The West Coast Military Highway

"Alright Buddy, this is a vid that shows how you go down a rope to the ground. It's called rappelling. It's a real quick way to go down and it is easy if you're good, and I know you're good, OK!" Puss grinned to Bila from where she sat beside him in the noisy hold of the VTOL aircraft. "Then there'll also be a vid that shows you how to use our `salt rifle, OK?"

She took another massive bite of the combat ration bar in her hand, then she waved its stub at Bila and mumbled, "And don't bother askin' what the words mean, just Do It Dammit! I'm turning on your suit `puter now and you watch, then we'll talk, OK?"

"Ja Boss," Bila grunted as he squirmed in his unfamiliar combat coverall and pulled at its tight fabric on his shoulders and thighs.

"Sit back Trooper Three, and get used to it. This suit can save your butt," Boots grinned at him from her seat on the other side of Puss.

"What butt is?"

"What Molly calls her bottom ya' Big Thud!" Puss said as she swallowed her mouthful and reaching under their slung canvass seats, slapped his.

"Oh. Save I Bila's butt more better this thing than," he grinned, still plucking at the heavy fabric of his suit. "Make `puter now go but."

Puss snorted and crammed the stub of the bar into her mouth and as she chewed, she adjusted the small eyepiece screen of the helmet that she and Waldo had convinced Bila wear when they had left S'attl. She positioned it in front of his left eye, then reached under a protective flap at his waist and keyed a signal into his suit's tiny computer.

"Tell me when you see clear, OK?" she mumbled.

After a pause Bila grunted, "I look clear – no, Clear see," as he concentrated on the small screen, and began absorbing the techniques of rappelling out of an aircraft hanging on its rotors above the ground.

"Baby Bird, if I can call you that, you've gulped down three of those half-bad things since we left S'attl," Waldo said to Puss from where he stood in the aisle before them, bracing himself on the overhead rails. "And one is enough to do me for at least four hours about any time."

"You can, and yes I have. Let's just say that I've got a void to fill. And before you even have that thought – NO! I am not preggo," Puss snapped, sputtering wet crumbs.

"Waldo, Marybell needs food biggers right now for reasons that tie directly to with us being late for launch. So be nice!" Boots added above the noise in the rattling compartment.

Waldo blushed to his ears, "Yes Ma'am! I'm real sorry, Miss Marybell."

"You call me that ever again and I will smush your face!" Puss grinned after she swallowed.

"To you, I am Friend or Baby Bird, or plain old Marybell - got that Waldo? And don't you "Ma'am" me ever again either!"

"'Course, you could call her Puss and me Boots, like Boss Rat and the others in our trade do..." Boots drawled with a crooked grin.

Waldo took a deep breath, then laughed, "That sounds like a major trip-wire to me. So OK, friend Marybell you make your point."

Then his face went grim, "When Boss Rat stops calling you Puss, I might start calling you that, since it fits you. But Rat won't do that until we make him stop, so for now," The tough sergeant continued, "Let me brief you on what we are doing since you were late for formation and we had to blast out of `S'attl in a blaze of horse glory without having time to talk."

"This trip is officially a training mission for these advanced cadets," Waldo continued as he nodded toward the ten competent-looking young people in battle gear sitting in the other canvass seats in the compartment.

"Bobby tasked me with finding a believable way for us to get you back to your start point in the bush without drawing undue attention. So like I told Marybell when we loaded, this squad will be practicing rappelling and quick winch retrieval for an hour in full combat suits out there in the B.C. bushes."

"When the first wave of these cadets goes down in their yoyo act, you three will go down with them, and then fade into the foliage while they mill about on the ground setting up a defensive perimeter around the drop point."

"You will then deploy your IR capes and skulk while the first wave winches back up, and the second one goes down and comes back up, then the first one again, et cetera, until we complete the exercise and head for home."

"Good plan," Boots murmured, her voice barely audible over the noise in the hold, "But what about these kids?" she asked. "Do they talk in their sleep, or brag about things they've done when they're awake?"

Waldo frowned at her, then replied in the same low voice, "Bobby and I selected these cadets for this mission because they all had relatives who had served under you, and lived to come home again. That's why this isn't a full thirteen bod squad, but these kids are some of the best friends you will ever have, Private First Class Kristina," Waldo snapped at her, with the same title he had used when he awarded Boots the thin black aiguillette eleven years ago on the day she had been graduated from Bobby's academy with the highest honors, but in a very unusual way...

Boots stared at Waldo for a second, before she blushed and nodded to him with understanding, and respect. Then she turned and looked at the young people in the compartment and saw that while they all tried to keep their eyes straight ahead and hold stern expressions on their faces, they kept glancing at her and Waldo.

The cadets were glancing fleetingly at Bila as well, as he sat engrossed in the vid eyepiece of his helmet, the biggest man any of them had ever seen.

Boots considered the youngsters for a moment, then unlatched her seatbelt and stood. She balanced on the swaying deck without using her hands to brace herself, and shouted to the young people a clear and compelling voice that rang above the clatter in the compartment.

"Cadets! Attend me!"

"Thank you for your service today! You all are a part of something that begins now, and can change your lives for the good - forever."

"No, Cadets, I re-state that! Today begins something that Will change All our lives for the good for all time. If we succeed."

"But even if we don't succeeded," Boots paused, then smiled to the youngsters with the brilliance that only she could project from within herself, "We're sure gonna' have a damn fun romp with the Rat along the way, no matter what!"

There was a shocked silence in the hold as the cadets stared at her in awe. Then their sudden shrill roar of approving shouts and whistles, and the tears on most of their faces, showed Boots once again the strength of the emotion and support she could call forth from those who were honest, and honorable.

She looked at the tough youngsters for a moment until they became quiet again. Then she blinked back a tear and called out tone that rang above the noise in the compartment, and gave them her highest complement, "Thanks for your vote Cadets. You now all are my Troopers! So tighten up Dammit and let's get to work!"

Then Boots saluted them and dropped back into her seat. She acknowledged their passionate shouts of approval with a wave for a moment, until silencing the cadets with a downward gesture of her hand.

They stopped their cheering, and turned their faces again to the front, frozen in determination but now also quivering with pride at being named Troopers by Captain Cook.

*

Boots and Puss, as well as Bila and the cadets all wore the latest version of the Army's smart war suit which protected, sensed, and responded to many of the physical needs of its wearer while in combat. The tiny computer built into the garment, through a sensor/antenna array across the shoulders could also up-link the wearer to a survel satellite or a recon drone during action, and so provide real-time information about the battle situation through his or her helmet's vid eyepiece and radio - if its wearer had time to access said intel after the shooting started...

"OK, you saw the vid, so you know to straddle the rope and wrap it around you, and slide down it, OK? And you control your slide by gripping the rope with this hand in front of you and this one, snugging the rope over your back and shoulder like this, OK?" Puss instructed as she stood in the cramped aisle before Bila, swaying to maintain her balance while demonstrating the Swiss Wrap with a short length of line around her body.

Bila looked at her as she posed draped in the plastic rope that was designed expressly for rappelling. "Is rope thing like sticker things I show Molly that she call rose hip vine?" Bila suddenly asked, as he swiveled the eyepiece screen away from his face. "They scratch what you say my butt,"

Puss stared for a moment at the big man with a questioning look on her face, then said, "No. The rope is smooth, and you wear gloves so you can grip it good, and you can have a pad on your crotch to protect you, at least us girls do."

"What crotch is?"

"Down here, Dammit!" Puss snapped, as she gave Bila a very business-like grope.

"Oh. What Protect is?"

"Keep it safe, Dammit!"

Bila looked at Puss then with a very slight smile, and asked, "You want safe it?"

Puss exploded with laughter, grabbed Bila's arms and began shaking him back and forth. "Yes Dammit! No Dammit! Yes and no - Dammit!"

"OK you two! It's clear you can't do rational thought right now so I'm taking the con," Boots announced.

"Ja Boss," the two responded- Puss with a giggle and Bila with a look that Boots couldn't quite classify.

She shook her head impatiently then continued, "Like Waldo said, we will drop down on the first exercise with a wave of five Troopers and the sat cams above shouldn't catch the fact that we don't come back up again because the second wave will start down as the first one is retrieved."

"When we are down and groveling on the ground under the bushes, our capes should cover our heat signature until this crate, and its cargo of – Troopers!" Boots suddenly shouted, "Exits the arena."

The chorus of responding yells with voice-changing squeaks, told her that the closest cadets were hanging on her words and passing them on to their mates out of her earshot, and knew they had just been caught at it.

As the youngsters all slumped back into their canvass seats, Boots grinned to Waldo, "You have a real good bunch of troops here, but then that's what I expect from you, old friend."

"We try," Waldo grunted. Then he asked, "You got the package your father couriered to the airfield this morning? I think it might be important."

"Waldo, I know you try. But funniest thing is you always succeed too. That's why you're here," Boots said as she slapped his shoulder. "And yes, I've got the box. Thanks, it is important. Now tell me the names of these Troop-ers."

Waldo quickly related the names of the cadets, and their relatives as Boots listened intently. When the sergeant finished she nodded to him, "Your cadets have real good parents too."

She glanced through one of the small windows in the hull of the plane after a moment, and turned to Puss and Bila, "We're close. Do you know what to do Bila? I really want you in on this op, and the big one that we know is coming too." Then she turned to Puss.

"But if he splats you and I go on anyway, OK?" Boots finished quietly as she stared at her two friends, her voice just audible above the noise of the aircraft.

Bila whispered back without hesitation as he met her stare, "Ja Boss."

Puss met Boots' gaze for a moment, then she whispered in a tone so low that Boots had difficulty in hearing her, "Well, if the pupil splats, it's the teacher's fault. So then teacher's probably gonna' splat too, right?"

"I'll ignore that. We're close. Get ready for go, Dammit!"

Puss nodded to Boots then turned to Bila and began showing him how to put on the leather gloves that he would need in controlling his descent.

The young troopers looked in open wonder at his fumblings with the gloves, and at Puss' patient tutoring of the large man.

*

"Drop point coming in five minutes!" Blared from the enunciator on the bulkhead, "Gear up, you yoyos!"

Boots and Puss checked all aspects of their battle suits while Waldo, acting as jump master and only wearing his Army green coverall, moved down the aisle and minutely inspected the suits of the ten cadets who were now Boots' Troopers. He made adjustments to them where necessary, and pointed out the dangerous potential of any mistakes or omissions. Then, after satisfying himself and receiving Boots' nod, Waldo shouted to the intercom, "Ready to clip!"

Several minutes later the sound of the engines roaring changed as the rotors on the aircraft's wings slowly turned toward the vertical under the control of its on-board control computer.

The aircraft steadied and hovered over the point on the Chin military road where Boots and Puss had been picked up only three days before. The enunciator in the hold blared again, "Booms extending! First wave stand up and stand ready!"

"Booms extended! Snap Up!"

"Go! Go! Go!"

All of the cadets in the first wave stood and snapped fasteners of their lines on to the suspension rails of the extended booms, wrapped the lines between their legs and over their shoulders - and went down in controlled slides toward the ground.

All except for one girl, who while an eager cadet was small and always had difficulty with stress tests. The girl lost her hold on the line somehow when she attempted her first snubbing grip and the line between her legs flipped her body backward so that she fell freely to the ground - head first. She went down without uttering a sound and died instantly on impact, her helmet containing her crushed skull and broken brain.

"Move! Move! Move!" a tall young boy with tears in his eyes shrilled as he ran past his girlfriend's still quivering body.

"Yes Dammit, Move it!" an equally tall girl, who was her sister, screamed. "We cry later!"

Boots heard them on her helmet comset as she slid down immediately after the cadets and said sadly, "Ferk! We really will win as long as we've got kids like this on our side!"

Bila stepped to the open door of the hovering aircraft, flexed his gloved hands, and snapped his line onto the boom extended above the open door. He straddled the line and flipped its loop over his shoulder, then he nodded to Puss, similarly roped up at his side, and held out one hand, palm up. "I now go."

"Good luck Buddy!" she said as she slapped his hand.

"Luck is friends – and don't you forget it!" he grinned as he stepped out into nothingness.

Bila dropped ten meters then braked his descent with a jerk. He hung for a moment, relaxed his grip and dropped another ten meters and slowed his descent again, this time smoothly. Relaxing his grip a third time, he slid the rest of the distance to the ground and landed lightly on the balls of his feet. He was disentangling the line from his body as Puss landed with a bound three meters away.

"OK Bila! Just what tha' ferk is it that you can't do?" she grunted as she stepped out of the loop of her line.

Bila looked at Puss with a sad smile for a second with a slight shake of his head, before stepping over the coils of line and striding to the small figure crumpled on the ground, her head at an unnatural angle.

He knelt beside her, and tenderly closed her bulging eyes and wiped away the trickle of blood from her nose. "You try good. You good friend to us," he whispered sadly as he caressed her face for a moment.

Her sister ran to them and stood over the girl's small body, and screamed her anguish to the sky.

Bila regained his feet, and wrapping his arms around the tall young girl quivering in distress, swayed back and forth gently while he hummed a wordless tune in her ear. After a moment, she relaxed and sighed as she sniffed back her tears, "Well, Monika was always too little but she never hung back, and I'll always love her."

"Me too," the tall young boy with the cadet corporal's stripes on his arm sobbed, as he dismissed the deployment exercise and ran to stand with them over the girl's small body.

"But you broke formation before All Clear, Becky. So I'll have to gig you," he said as his voice cracked. Bila reached out and brought the boy into his embrace with the dead girl's sister. The boy shook away his tears after a moment and whispered, "Well, I'll always have what we had anyway...

"But now Troopers, we gotta move!" he shouted as he and Becky stepped away from Bila. "Up the lines! Up the lines!" Then he whispered, "And we always bring our people home," as he shackled a line to the hoisting ring built into the back of Monika's war suit.

Boots and Puss stood watching with tragic eyes while the four young troopers snapped on and were hoisted back up to the hovering aircraft, along with the limp body of a small, but very brave girl, until Bila turned to them and calmly asked, "What IR capes is?"

"Damn if he isn't focused!" Boots whispered.

"You're right - but he's more right! We hide buddy, then we talk!" Puss snapped as she reached back and deployed the body heat-shielding cloak folded into the top of her combat pack.

Boots blushed as she realized this lapse in her leadership, and hastily deployed her own shield while Puss helped Bila with his. Then they moved into the shadow of the tree line and watched the young troopers, as they executed four more drops and up-snatches flawlessly.

The booms folded back into the aircraft after the last trooper in the last wave was up, and its doors closed as the wings rotated back to propeller mode. The three watched it bank and turn to the south after picking up speed and head toward S'attl.

"Bila, did you Talk to those two poor kids?" Puss whispered as their eyes followed the departing plane.

"Yes."

"To both of them?"

"Three they to."

"Three?"

"Yes. Say sorry I say little one at. Say happy she now..."

Puss gasped and started to speak, until Boots gripped her friend's arm and muttered, "Later Buddy, OK?"

Puss nodded, then just shook her head in wonder.

Bila added with a grunt. "Now we to Molly place go. Save little bottom butt her, Troopers all, OK!"

*

The IR shielding capes were a mechanism developed by the Army combat research center at Aberdeen, Maryland during the Chin war. They reduced the infrared heat signature of a wearer to below the normal sensing range of Chin survel satellites and battlefield drones, and they also were quite effective in avoiding the US survel satellite IR cameras that the White House still had over the western states, for its own reasons...

The shielding capes worked very well but heat is like all other physical entities, it can be can be changed or stored, but not destroyed. Thus the muted IR signature of a wearer of one is limited by the capacity its wearer to tolerate the buildup of the body heat trapped under it. The normal practice in battle was to flip the cape and dump the accumulated heat whenever an explosive round detonated nearby, or a large heat emitter such as a personnel carrier or a main battle tank passed the wearer.

Dealing with this need in a non-battlefield venue required a different procedure however...

*

"How're you doing Buddy?" Boots asked as she turned from gazing after the vanished plane and sadly thinking of Monika, the first casualty in her new campaign.

"I'm already getting hot and sweaty, what did you expect Max Leader?"

"What about you Bila?"

"I hot. Where water is?"

"There's a creek down the slope on the other side of the road," Boots replied absently as she scoped the cleared area around them with her monocular. "You can get a drink there if your canteen's empty."

"Good. We go at water. Get cold. IR cape better after."

"Shat! He's figgered it out!" Puss hissed. "Let's go swim for a bit, Kiddo and dump our heat in the creek!"

Boots stared at Bila for a second as he smiled at her and shrugged. Then she erupted in irritation, "Jesu's Jumpin' Joss Sticks! Our temp-sigs will total dissipate in the flowing water."

"Dammit, I gotta' ask again. Just who'n hell are you anyway Bila?"

"I Big Thud. That you me say, No! Me name."

"Well Mister Bila Big Thud, this way to the creek, and if I haven't said it before, I'll say it again! I'm sure glad you're on my side. Now let's hump to dump!"

The three wrapped the metallic laminate capes around themselves and emerging from the tree canopy, crossed the highway and began making their way down the wooded slope below its far side. Bila smiled as he paced behind Boots, and a grinning Puss followed on sure feet behind them. When they reached the bottom of the slope they found that a mountain creek did indeed flow there, and Boots lead them downstream along its bank until she found a quiet pool below a riffle. It was less than a meter deep but was large enough to hold the three.

"Bila, I'm jumping in the creek with you now, but don't you get any of your wet shower room ideas, OK?" Boots whispered with a grin.

"No Ma'am," Bila smiled in a way that made her pause, for a second.

The three waded in to the pool and submerged themselves up to their necks in its cold water. Boots and Bila sat cross-legged on the gravely bottom while Puss perched herself on a submerged bolder, then they relaxed and let their capes float on the surface.

Boots took Puss' hand below the surface several moments later, "Want to talk about it?"

"Sure, it's no major," Puss smiled at her friend. Then she matter-of-factly related what had happened to her in the Network studio after she was taken from Lulu's laboratory.

"Why did you go to Lulu in the first place?" Boots asked after Puss finished her story.

"That's for later Buddy," Puss said quietly. Boots' responding shrug was below the surface of the water but when she glanced at Bila, she saw that his face was like stone and his eyes blazed with fury.

Boots whispered, "Molly was right. He really does understand everything we say somehow. And Rat's gonna' damn-well wish that he didn't, real soon."

*

"How long, Buddy? I'm getting little-bittty cold," Puss gasped an hour later.

"Probably about now, since I'll bet your bod's reserves are pretty thin after this morning," Boots muttered as she rose from the shallow pool, and arranging her cape over her head and shoulders, splashed to the bank and began climbing up the slope back to the road.

"Takes more than a little fling in Rat's Nest to slow me down, dammit," Puss snorted as she jumped up and splashed out of the pool. Bila stood and arranging his cape and hood, waded out of the pool behind the two women.

Boots halted at the tree line at the edge of the highway and waited until her friends came up the slope. "Listen to me Troopers," she ordered as she shook the remaining water drops from her IR cape and folded it into her pack. "It's a two klick run to the bunker. I think we've obscured our patterns enough to escape their first level survel sat screens, but we need to move fast." Then she suddenly grinned, "So let's have a race. First one there gets a goodie!"

Puss laughed to Boots' back, "You're on Slomo!" as the tall woman sneaked a head start, abruptly leaping across the pavement and running up the indistinct trail into forest above the highway.

Bila held his hand out to Puss and said quietly, "I help you?"

"I don't need any help with this, but I'll keep your offer in mind, Big Thud," Puss smiled as she swiftly stowed her cape. Then she wiggled into her pack's shoulder straps and bounded across the pavement and up the track behind Boots.

Bila pulled impatiently again at the tight shoulders of his combat suit's fast-drying fabric, but after a shrug, he shook out his wet cape and stowing it, settled his field pack onto his shoulders.

Grasping the black plastic U.S. assault rifle Waldo had issued him, he grinned as he strode across the road and entered the forest, and began running in on the faint track behind his friends.

He caught up with the two women five minutes later, and slowed his pace to lope behind them as they raced along the faint trail. He was unnoticed until Puss had a feeling, and glanced over her shoulder.

"Shat! Buda's Boogers Bila, how long you been back there?" she panted.

He shrugged with a smile and held out his fist, again thumb up as he looked at her with an exaggerated question on his face.

Puss suppressed a laugh as she picked up her pace after Boots again, but the woman heard her approach and began swerving from side to side to block

Puss's attempt at overtaking her.

Bila watched the two women race each other for a moment then he snorted in amusement, and dashed forward until he is with in two meters of Puss where she ran close behind Boots, probing for a way to pass her friend. Bila loped behind the two until they followed the trail around a curve, then he dashed off into the undergrowth bordering the trail and took a straight line through the forest.

He leapt back onto the trail ahead of Boots and bounded forward at a pace that she could not match.

As he increased his lead along the faint track and disappeared in the gloom of the forest, Boots panted, "Shat! Now we'll have to track that dumbo down when he over-shoots the damn bunker!"

"Think so?" Puss panted as she caught up with her friend. Then she laughed as she pulled ahead of Boots as well, "Dumbo made you loose focus again, didn't he Buddy?"

"Did not!" Boots snapped. "But we got to catch him before he runs over this damn mountain and all the way to Ottawa," she gritted as she matched her pace to Puss' along the faint track.

*

Bila saw that the trail disappeared in a small glade under the canopy of old growth trees. He stopped, and prowled the space until he had assured himself that this was indeed where it ended, then stood in stillness and looked about the glade.

He did not note any strangeness, until he sniffed then his eyes gleamed and he began inspecting the ground until he paused and dropped to his knees at a particular place. He brought his face close to the ground, and was sniffing among the vines when Boots and Puss raced into the space.

"He found the door Buddy!" Puss snapped. "And in another ten minutes your Dumbo Savage would've opened it!

"So I figger' he gets two goodies, OK?"

"We'll talk about this later,' Boots snarled as she strode to the old spruce where the bunker access control was hidden. She knelt and reached into the cavity at its base and pressed the switch that opened the hidden door.

Bila watched what she did over his shoulder then faced forward again as the camouflaged portal hinged upward before him. He sat back on his heels with a startled grunt when it opened, then he faced Boots with a grin of triumph, "Ha! Rat koba!"

"Good goin' Buddy, you found it," Boots smiled, after a little struggle to control her pique at being bested by Bila, again.

"Yes Buddy, you do good," Puss smiled to Bila, then she turned and nodded to Boots with a look of knowing approval, "Both of you."

Boots glanced at her friend and blushed. Then she turned to Bila, "What's a koba, and this isn't Rat's. It used to be Chin but it's ours now."

"Koba Molly name cave is. Bullets this place?"

"Sure are, and damn good going Bila!" Puss smiled. "You smelled 'um just like I knew you would! We'll go get them and then get on the road to Molly, OK!"

"Actually as I recall Doctor, I right-brained his talented nose first and then pointed it out to you if you will recall," Boots chuckled, her humor fully restored.

"Whatever, anyway move 'um, Dammit! We're running late!" Puss snapped as she trotted down the ramp into the bunker.

"Alright Trooper One, you and Trooper Three will ride the cargo tandem, and I'll take a single. Now let's load!" Boots ordered as she followed Puss and stepped to the rack holding the bike she had ridden before.

"I figgered you would say that."

"Why?"

"Because Max Leaders don't hump cargo."

"Course not Buddy, we're too busy with the Big Picture," Boots laughed.

"Poot on your damn big picture! Help me with our junk!"

*

Bila stared around at the concrete room that was lit with glaring light strips. He saw that its floor was almost filled with military motorbikes in racks, and that the walls of the space were lined with storage cabinets. One corner of the room was filled with a large covered vat connected to humming pumps and blowers, and a pressure vessel beside the vat that was connected to an overhead array of piping leading to the bikes.

Bila's brow wrinkled at this complex scene, then he peered intently at the bikes themselves before turning to Puss who was loading the tandem.

"Here got two these, them – No, those. S'attl in four got," he announced as he pointed to a bike wheel.

"OK, you do the teaching Doctor, while I do the humping," Boots grinned evilly as she uncoupled her bike's hydrogen tank charge line and rolling the machine free of its rack, kicked down its stand. "Explain centrifugal force to

him, in ten words or less," she continued over her shoulder as she shrugged
her combat pack off and strapped it to the bike's carrier bars.

Puss glared at Boots' back, which was quivering with silent laughter
as she hung a pair of panniers over her machine's rear fender and clipped a
cargo basket to its handlebars.

*

The Chin motorized trail bikes were ruggedly simple machines, but extremely well engineered and the Chin units that were issued them had found
they were very effective - as did the US troops opposing those units...

The fuel cells that powered them were compact, lightweight and superbly
efficient. Their frames were made of an alloy steel that, while heavier than
more exotic and expensive material, was also was very tough, so rough use
rarely disabled the bikes. Skilled riders could rapidly cover very steep terrain
because both wheels were powered by small but extremely efficient electric
motors in their hubs. The U.S. troops called these bikes "wall climbers", and
tried to capture them at every opportunity.

*

Bila continued, "How this not fall down? Two got things this. S'attl
things four got."

Puss stared at Bila for a moment and found honest interest on his
face, mostly. Only the slightest twitch of a smile showed at the corner of his
mouth.

"These are wheels Bila, and this is a bike. Bikes have two. We were in
cars in S'attl and cars have four wheels, but when bikes go, they stay up like
cars OK?" Puss explained patiently.

"Why?"

Puss cleared her throat. "If a certain Professor will now pay attention, I
will explain why to you in ten words or less."

"You have tha' podium Doctor," Boots snorted as she began loading containers of 25 millimeter rocket grenades into her panniers.

Puss smiled at the big man sweetly, "Trust me Trooper Three, you'll see.
And that's an order! There Buddy, a ten word explanation!"

"Only because I'm lenient on contractions today," Boots grunted. "But
now start humpin' stuff!"

"Got you, didn't I!" Puss grinned as she twisted the valve on her tandem's recharge line to full open and topped off its hydrogen tank.

*

This machine was almost twice as long as Boots' and it had power in both wheels as well. A vertically articulated joint was also built into in the middle of its frame because of its length. The joint was controllable by the driver, and this control allowed him or her to snake the machine over rough terrain as easily as the single bikes with their shorter wheelbase.

The tandem also had a large cargo rack between its two seats as well as rear wheel panniers and a cargo basket over the front wheel. Both the front handle bar and the top of the cargo rack between the seats had been equipped with motorized mounts for Chin assault rifles, which could be slaved to the small screens on the driver's helmets for targeting.

*

Puss shut the valve off after watching the tandem's fuel gage a moment then disconnected the recharge line.

"Help me roll this pig out Bila," she grunted as she unlatched it from its rack.

"Bike pig now? What pig is?" Bila grinned as he helped her steady the machine while she rolled it free and dropped its kickstands.

"This one's more like one of your ferkin long-noses," she grunted as she shrugged out of her field pack and strapped it to the bike.

Bila shook his head and muttered, "Baby only one." He watched what she did with her pack then removed his own and asked, "Where go?"

"Right here," Puss indicated a spot on the cargo rack. "Where it will balance mine." While Bila was attaching his pack to the bike Puss began rapidly filling the cargo racks with rations, ammunition for both US and Chin weapons, bedrolls and spare clothing, and finally several more IR cloaks along with a set of tent poles.

She was checking and tightening the cargo hold-downs when Boots held up two large pistols and asked, "Do we want to take these old things? They're pretty heavy."

"Hell yes, 'cause they're heavy out the front end too," Puss said, "Gimme my Dirty Harry for sure!"

She took the large revolver from Boots and snapped its cylinder open to check it.

"How much ammo we got down here? I brought two hundred rounds from our big bunker before we turned it into a Rat cooker."

Boots peered back in the cabinet. "It looks like three hundred more."

"Let's take it all, since we're likely not coming back here for a while,

461

right?"

"Right," Boots grunted, and after passing five of the heavy boxes to Puss, placed the other five in her own bike's panniers. "Want your shoulder holster too?"

"Also, hell yes! This thing isn't much use if it's packed away."

"Right again Buddy," Boots grinned as she tossed a holster to Puss, and they both slipped their arms through the loops and tightened the straps around their torsos.

*

This type of holster was the most efficient way to carry a large pistol and these were quite large. They were three hundred year old Smith & Wesson revolvers in .44 Magnum caliber, with barrels that were over 15 centimeters long. Boots had discovered them in one of the nitrogen-filled sealed caches of civilian arms and ammunition she had found, originally hidden in anticipation of the extensive weapons seizures conducted by the US and Canadian governments in the middle of the 21st Century.

*

Puss flipped the cylinder of her pistol open, then Boots did as well and both women loaded with cartridges that were the diameter of their forefingers, and almost half as long.

They snapped their cylinders closed and holstered their weapons as Puss commented with a grim little smile, "They don't make 'um like this anymore."

"Nope, they're afraid to," Boots grinned, "By the way, I've always wondered, why do you call yours by that name?"

Puss chuckled, "When I was growing up back on the reservation, we had lots of copied old books to read, and a bunch of restored old vids that schools don't have now, because the edu-crats are afraid of them.

"Anyway, there were some vids my dad liked to watch about a policeman from 300 years ago who didn't take any cow flop from anybody that messed with his mission, baddos or cop-crats either."

"Dirty Harry was what they called him, and he carried one of these big poppers in a shoulder holster," Puss grinned as she caressed its walnut grip. "I liked watching them with my dad."

"I'm glad you explained it to me. I always thought you were referring to an armpit condition you got when you carried that thing too long," Boots responded gravely.

Then at Puss' rude noise she murmured sweetly, "But if you stick your tongue out like that much more Missy, you'll start catching flies..."

Puss snorted in a marked manner as she turned to Bila, and noted he was looking intently at the open box of cartridges on the seat of the tandem bike.

"Want to see one?" she asked as she held out a fat nickel-plated cartridge with a blunt lead-tipped bullet.

Bila took it and examined it closely, then hefted its weight in his palm.

"What name this – No! What this name?"

Puss looked at Bila for a second, "This is a .44 Magnum, why?"

"Molly rifle shoot bullets say she - no, she name .22. But .44 be more big than two Molly bullets. Why?"

Puss stared at Bila for a second then she grinned, "Wow! Molly taught you this much math in one day?"

"Actually Doctor, Bila learned this much math in one day!" Boots muttered out of the corner of her mouth to her friend, before answering Bila's question.

"The number .44 tells how wide the bullet is," she explained as she took the cartridge from him and pinched its tip between her thumb and forefinger. "Molly's .22 bullets are only that wide," Boots continued gravely as she held her thumb and forefinger close together. Then with a flash of insight, she finished, "This is the way numbers measure things."

Bila considered the gap between her fingers for a moment before nodding firmly, "Molly me teach you numbers say how many things. You teach me numbers say big is how. Numbers you smart, no - your numbers very smart!"

Boots considered the large man for a moment as he smiled broadly with the joy of learning, then she grinned as she slapped his shoulder, "Numbers aren't the only smart thing around here Buddy."

"You hit tha' ferkin' X- ring this time Professor. I can see two real smart things here right now." Puss whispered.

"I see smart things two, this place in," Bila said quietly. "Now go we Molly at, no. We go Molly to?"

*

Boots mounted her trail bike and powering it, steered slowly up the ramp into the clearing. Puss clipped two Chin assault rifles to the motorized gun mounts on the tandem and slaved both of them to her helmet eyepiece, then she climbed on the saddle and motioning Bila to follow, powered it and guided it up the ramp behind Boots.

"Climb on back here and put your helmet on," Puss ordered Bila as she balanced the machine outside of the bunker and indicated its rear seat while Boots closed the camouflaged door.

He watched Puss for a moment as she fitted on her own helmet and snapped its chinstrap then carefully copied her action before straddling the seat behind her.

Puss chuckled into her helmet's intercom mike, "Hear me Big Thud?"

"Hear I, Trooper One. We go kill Rats like do we S'attl this day now?" Bila responded with no humor in his voice.

Boots, listening to the two on her own helmet intercom heard Puss gasp then sigh, "Sorry Bila. I stopped thinking for a while. But know this! I will not ever, ever forget who you really are, and what you did for me this morning."

"Trooper One, Big Thud me. No, be Big Thud I you for times all, OK?"

"Marybell, quit bawling like a lost calf! You can do that later!" Boots snapped when she heard Puss' sudden sob in her earpiece.

"Like the man says, we got Rats to kill dammit, so let's move `um!" Boots snarled into her mike as she powered her bike and kicking dirt with both wheels and sped along the faint trail.

"Hang on Buddy with your hands here, and put your feet here," Puss whispered into her mike as she shook away her tears and reached around to show Bila the handgrips and foot pegs for the rear seat. Then she grasped the handlebar controls, "Now we go to Molly really quickie!"

"Ja, Buddy."

*

Puss brought the tandem to a sliding stop at the juncture of the faint trail and the Chin military highway where Boots sat balancing on her bike, waiting. The tall woman nodded to her friend, now obviously in control of her self again and blew her a kiss, before she pulled down her helmet visor.

Puss returned a thumbs-up to Boots as she lowered her own visor then turned to check if Bila had properly closed his, which he had.

The two women powered their bikes and rolled out onto the pavement. They accelerated to a maximum safe speed and made good time as they sped along the empty highway northward. They traveled three hundred kilometers in four hours until they pulled off at a level spot for a short rest.

The three separated and discretely relieved themselves, then they sat on the ground next to their bikes and the two women opened combat ration bars.

Puss offered one to Bila, with an encouraging nod. He accepted it and after sniffing it cautiously, wolfed it down. "More good than rash bar, some little," he grunted.

"Yep," Puss grinned. "How do you like your ride so far?"

"Good more than run, some little," he responded gravely, but the slight twitch showed at the corner of his mouth again as he rubbed his crotch. "Bike better than slide rope, some little."

"You can always walk, you know," Boots said with the same straight face as his, and the same little twitch at the corner of her mouth.

"Walk slow much too. Kill who bears next you go at cabin, lay grass again in?"

"Gotcha! And he gotcha good again Buddy, admit it!" Puss giggled.

Boots glared at the two and her face turned to stone for several seconds, long enough for her to see the faint ghost of apprehension that appeared in their eyes. Then she laughed and slapped her knees. "Alright now you two, now who got who?"

Bila stared back at her, then at Puss sputtering at his side. He broke into a wide smile, and closed the conversation. "All got friends. That why lucky we – No! Are lucky…"

*

The three mounted their two bikes five minutes later and sped northward on the straight road, and crossed the many large rivers and fjords again on the small personnel ferries guided by the tethering cables strung between their banks.

Bila watched Boots at their first crossing, as she adjusted the movable fins mounted beneath the small scow that propelled it across the stream by the force of the current. Then he peered curiously at the long, low concrete structures built into both banks of the river.

Puss noted his interest and explained how the Chin engineers had spanned the water for heavy vehicular traffic in a way that was secure from aerial attack.

Bila immediately grasped the concept of a bridge on pontoons that opened in the center, with its two parts swinging into hardened shelters along each bank when not in use.

"Chin koba cave make bridge for. Chin people smart."

"We generally found them to be so," Boots muttered.

"In some ways, anyway," Puss added with ice in her tone, as she instinctively stroked her hip.

*

The three drove 90 more kilometers and an hour later reached the point where the old logging road met the military highway. Boots turned east on to it and lead their way up its rutted surface for a hundred meters until she powered her bike down and signaled Puss to halt. Since they were above the 50th parallel, the afternoon sun was still high in the sky in the late spring.

Boots dismounted and stood her bike. She stretched her arms over her head, then bent stiff-legged with a grunt and touched her toes several times before she finally high-kicked each leg over her head.

"Dammit, I'm getting too old for these butt-busters! Next trip I want to be in Bobby's staff car."

"Well Buddy," Puss grinned as she and Bila dismounted and stood the tandem, "You will probably have one next time, if we aren't all in meat wagons heading toward the incinerators."

"Thanks for those comfort words, little Sally Sunshine! Anyway, we don't leave the pigs in the bushes this time; we go straight up the ridge and down to the cabin, OK! Then we look for a place to park 'um under shields until their cells cool down."

"You place want IR sat not bike see?"

Boots tensed then relaxed with a sigh, "Yes Bila, I do. What are you going to teach me now?"

"You've been sort of slow so far Buddy, but I think you're finally starting to see the big picture, about him anyway," Puss grinned. Then she struck a pose by propping her elbow against Bila's chest beside her, and leaning against him with her ankles crossed and a smirk on her face.

Bila ignored Puss' weight as he explained earnestly to Boots, "We go at cabin. We take not bikes there. I show where new put IR beams Molly do. I show koba cave for put bikes. Koba cave good place put Molly and she - no, her 'puter. So sats not she see. Molly me show on 'puter how IR sats people cabin in see."

As he ended his recital, he finally looked down at Puss, propped against him as if he were a tree trunk, and chuckled as he ruffled her hair.

"How's that for a sneak deploy plan, O Max Leader?" Puss asked with a grin.

Boots gazed at the man for a moment then she nodded as to an equal. "Damn fine plan Bila, Thanks."

"But as for you, my impertinent little poopsie, just remember that Big Thud and I can always turn you into giggle-jelly again anytime we want to if you push us too far." Then she mounted her bike and ordered, "Now let's roll on up the damn ridge!"

"Hang on Buddy, and you stand up on the pegs when I do, and tell us when we're close to the trip lines, OK?" Puss laughed into her helmet's intercom as she and Bila remounted.

"Ja Buddies," he grunted and gripped his handlebar as Puss powered the bike and kicking dirt with its wheels, followed Boots along the logging road toward the old burn clearing at the foot of the mountain where they had hidden their machines before climbing the ridge above the little cabin - on a day that seemed a lifetime ago...

*

"We close new IR beams place Molly put," Bila said quietly into his helmet mike.

"Power down Buddy," Boots replied as she slowed her bike and brought it to a stop halfway up the ridge. Puss halted the tandem and dropped her feet on the ground to balance the machine.

*

After they had left the old burn area at the end of the logging road, they had entered the forest proper, and the capabilities of the Chin bikes became obvious. The two women had taken the quietly humming machines at almost full speed over the forest floor swerving around the towering boles of the old growth trees and the sparse under story vegetation and their wheels scattering showers of leaf mold and sandy granites soil as they mounted the ridge.

Bila had no trouble hanging on and after Puss went over a small stone outcrop the first time and the tandem landed back on the ground with a jar that made him grunt he also learned to anticipate when it was time to rise from the seat and stand on the foot pegs with his knees flexed.

*

"Where do we go from here?" Boots asked as Bila raised his helmet visor.

"I you show. You me behind come," he said as he climbed off the tandem. "We IR beams cross."

"If you're on the ground, you'll slow us down," Boots muttered.

"Bet'cha a backrub that he won't," Puss said.

"Although it truly is a gamble, war is not a game of chance Dammit! But you're on this one time. So why don't you think Bila on foot won't slow us

467

down, Doctor?"

"To quote a certain Professor, "you know what I know", so you figger' it out Sweetie!" Puss then whispered into her helmet mike "Come on Bila, show us the way and yes, we will cross her IR beams."

"Now go we," Bila announced as he nodded to Boots with an almost straight face, before turning and trotting up toward the crest of the ridge. Boots powered her bike and followed him, first at the lowest speed at which the machine was stable then with increasing speed as Bila picked up his pace. Puss grinned as she piloted the tandem behind Boots. Then she laughed aloud as saw Bila began taking shortcuts over or through obstacles that they were forced to steer around, and so made the two women increase their speed to almost their previous rate in order to stay with him.

"OK, you win, Miss Smart Snuggs!" Boots chuckled into her mike as she negotiated her way around a large fallen spruce that Bila had leaped over with ease.

"We win Molly safe when," Bila snapped into his mike.

"Ja Boss," both women answered, with respect.

*

Bila halted his easy run up the slope a moment later and grunted into the intercom, "We place at new IR beams Molly put now."

"Good goin' Bila, and thank you again," Boots' voice crackled in his earphone.

"Why me thank?"

"Let's just say you teach me real good, but I'm sorry. I learn real slow."

"Humph," Bila snorted. "You slow, like hawk bird dive little at thing big ears with."

"That's thing's called a rabbit Buddy," Puss murmured. "And you're right, Kris is damn fast, always."

"Jesu's Scratchy Sandal Straps you two! Are we gonna' helmet yak all day, or get on with tha' ferkin mission?"

Bila chuckled at Boots' theatrical outburst, then motioning the two forward led them through Molly's outlying IR beam monitoring line and on up the slope toward the ridge crest above the little cabin.

***

Chapter 22
The Reunion

May 6, 2276 AD,
Coastal Mountains of British Columbia

"Shat! Somebody just crossed our new trip line," Molly exclaimed when she heard the warning chime sound from the panel above her computer.

"I'll go see," Jimmy said as he rushed from the back room where the two were beginning to cook supper.

"Wait, Buddy! Let's see what they do first," she called. "Like Boots said, "Act, don't React"

"OK Molly, but I want you safe," the redheaded boy said as he stepped back in the room carrying a Chin assault rifle.

"Me too and you too, but let's wait for a minute `till we know more. There's three of them that came through the line, and I think they're on vehicles, at least two of them anyway."

"OK, Molly. You tell me what to do now."

"Hang on, Jimmy, we'll work it out…"

*

"We've tripped Molly's new line, so what's next?" Boots asked as she halted and balanced her bike.

"We cross other IR line top at. Go at koba cave and cross other IR line that way. Put bikes koba cave in. Go out koba cave. Go cabin at, cross back IR line other time. Molly see come in we, then away go. Come we way this another – no, Again time. Know she we go at koba cave. Know she Bila here."

"Anytime you want take the con of this outfit, it's yours, OK!" Boots drawled, "Because it looks like you're a long damn way better than me at

469

figuring ferkin field tactics!"

"You make joke, right? Molly say joke when you say what not true, and all know not true," Bila said with a little smile.

"Interesting epiphany you're havin' once again, Buddy," Puss murmured. "As Psych-doc of this outfit, I ought to be taking notes of your progress for later review. But I don't think I'll need `um to remember it somehow."

"You joke make. You joke not know?" Bila frowned with a worried look at Boots as he ignored Puss' comments.

Puss chuckled, "Ja Boss, she make a joke, and her joke is way funny. Now let's just Do It!"

Boots nodded without a word as she powered up her bike and turned her face to the front to guide her bike, as well as to hide her sudden blush.

*

Fifteen minutes later Bila led them through Durwood's original IR trip line near the crest of the slope and turning south, led them along the crest of the ridge away from Molly's valley. He continued leading the two women on their throttled-down bikes across the third IR trip line monitoring the southern approach to the cabin and three hundred meters further up the ridge crest, until he turned down its western slope toward the old mine adit.

"Koba cave here is," Bila announced as he signaled a halt next the excavated shelf before the entry and helped Puss stand the tandem before it.

"Let's take a recon, but it looks like it might do," Boots said with a grunt as she stood her bike and reached for her flashlight.

*

The panel on the wall chimed again and Molly peered at the display on its little screen intently until it chimed a third time, with a different note. She frowned then asked, "What'n tha' Darn hell's goin' on up there anyway?"

"What?"

"They crossed the old line coming this way a couple of minutes ago, but now they've just crossed the other line across the top of the ridge and they're going away from us!"

"We still better get ready. I'll go saddle Sugar Plum, she can carry two."

"Make that three Buddy, and I'll ride with you," Molly grinned as she patted her belly, "If it turns out we need to scoot that is."

"Awwww," Jimmy blushed.

Molly turned from the computer bench and stepping to the youth, hugged him tightly.

"I warned you about my weird `Clave sense of humor already. It's not much like what you folks have out here in the clean world," she murmured into his chest.

Then she instinctively steered the conversation away from the abstract that was her forte and to the concrete where she knew him to be more comfortable.

"Sugar Plum's her name? I like it. Did you name her?"

"Naw," he grinned. "She's ten, so I was way too young. Dad told me Mom named her that when she was foaled because she was so cute."

"She sounds nice, your Mom that is. I already know Sugar Plum's nice, but I want to meet her, your Mom too, pretty quickie," Molly said earnestly as she looked up at Jimmy. Then in an unconscious attempt at Boots' gruff tones, she growled with a squeak, "Soon as we deal with the ferkin current situation!"

*

"Good place Bila, how did you find it?" Boots muttered as she flashed her light around the mica-sparkling granite walls of the chamber at the end of the entry tunnel.

"Molly me take here. This place I tell her stay go when hunt I people bad come at what Molly say west, sun go down place" Bila said he gestured toward the west. Then he spotted a tiny glint on the floor of the chamber - glittering in the beam from Boots' flashlight and suddenly stooped to retrieve an empty .22 cartridge casing.

"This Molly rifle from. I tell her inside killer here be. I outside killer be. She shoot here," he gritted.

"At what?" Puss hissed.

"Bad people west from," he muttered as he began searching the floor.

"Use this," Boots said as she handed him the bright little LED flashlight.

"Thank you. More here is," Bila grunted as he retrieved two more of the tiny brass cartridge casings. Then he started and pointed to the spot in the entry tunnel where the hound had died, "Odol here be!"

"What's odol?" Puss hissed.

"Red stuff you inside," he grunted as he squatted and peered at a small bloodstain on the uneven stone floor of the entry tunnel.

Puss jumped to kneel beside him. "That's blood! Shat! She had a firefight!"

Bila rose and paced slowly toward the mouth of the tunnel, until he sud-

471

denly squatted again.

"Say blood you here, to garun," he grunted as he touched the floor of the tunnel where Jimmy dropped the Captain's body to hide it from the Network's helicopter.

"What's garun?" Boots asked quietly.

"Stuff head in."

"Brains. Let me see," Puss hissed as she bounded to Bila and knelt beside him. "It's brain tissue alright, maybe two days old."

"OK troops, let's off-load and get down to that ferkin' cabin sooners!" Boots snapped. "I'll get what we need from mine - you get the other one in quickie," Boots grunted as she un-strapped the two packs and opened the panniers on her machine.

"Right," Puss snapped again, and sprinting back out of the chamber, and guided Boot's bike in to the chamber a moment later.

"Light combat load, OK!" Boots gritted as she removed her pack from the carrier bars and shrugged into it, "And capes. You Bila, wear your cape!"

"Right," Puss snapped over her shoulder back as she ran back out to the tandem with Bila close behind. He steadied the machine until she powered it, and followed as she guided it into the adit tunnel and stood it on the far side of the chamber.

Puss was buckling on her pack, and both women were unfolding their IR capes, when Bila said, "No."

He removed his cape from his pack, and then to the astonishment of the two women, stripped out of it, his helmet and his war suit to stand before them naked.

He groped in his pack and pulled out his leather pouch and belt, then he wrapped himself in the cape as he motioned toward his discarded suit and helmet, "Molly know me not that in."

"You and me teach she kill to shoot. Molly kill not Bila, OK?"

Boots looked at the earnest and handsome man for a moment, then she snorted with laughter, "Not to worry Big Thud, no real girl in her right mind is ever gonna' shoot you while you're undressed like that!"

"And as a favor Buddy," she continued as she bundled his suit into her pack, "I'll carry your damn laundry down the hill for ya' - but by Buda's Bunions, you have to wear your own damn boots and helmet! They're way too heavy for me to hump."

"Ja Boss," Bila grinned as he bent and latched on his footgear, then he grasped his assault rifle and his helmet by its chinstrap and led the two women out of the tunnel at a trot.

*

The alarm monitor chimed again and caused Molly to start again, "What tha' darn hell's goin' on now? They're coming back, Darn it!"

"Sugar Plum is outside the door, do we want to go now?"

"No Buddy, let me scope the scene for a minute," Molly growled with a squeak as she examined the readings on the instrument's little screen.

"Well, they came back this way after a little less than a half hour, so they didn't go up the ridge too far. And the pulse timing when they broke the beams is different, so I don't think they have the vehicles anymore."

"And they're not sneaking, or running either. The timing of their steps when they crossed the line makes it look like they're just marchin' straight to here, darn it!"

"What do we do, stay or go?" Jimmy asked, holding the Chin assault rifle in a white-knuckled grip.

"There's only three of them, and between us, we've killed that many already," Molly said quietly with her chin held high.

"So I say we stay and see who they are, but not in here. Lets get in the bushes outside and be real ready for them," she finished in a cold little voice.

"Ja Boss, Jimmy whispered. Without another word, Molly hiked up her leather dress, tied on her leggings again and changed from her moccasins into her boots. Jimmy buckled on the Captain's pistol belt, now adjusted for his waist and loaded a haversack with extra ammunition for both Molly and himself.

She smiled at him as she added a handful of jerky strips to the sack as Bila had taught her, then they both charged their weapons and stepped out into the meadow.

*

Bila motioned a halt on the northern end of the ridgeline they had just descended, above the head of Molly's valley and the little spring. They were at the point where the two ridges that protected the valley met, and where the land surface steepened down to the valley below. He had led Boots and Puss from the mine tunnel at a purposeful jog to where he knew the IR tripline to be, then he whispered for them to cross it singly, and at a slow pace.

When they resumed their jog at his lead, Puss had signed to Boots, *"You know what I know!"*

473

Boots had responded, *"Yes. He knows how signal Molly. But I told you about him first!"* Then they had grinned at each other as they trotted on down through the forest behind the big man.

"I go down. I walk cabin at. You stay water down by. You this do," he crouched and held his spread fingers before his face.

"Hide," Puss murmured, "At the spring."

"Yes, just like I told him to do when we first met – about a thousand days ago," Boots smiled to Bila.

"Do I this," Bila said as he looked at his friends sternly and he waved his right arm forward, "Come you, OK? This things you off take, Molly you see then," he said quietly as he tapped their combat helmets.

"Ja Boss," Boots whispered. "You got the con."

"Yes Bila," Puss said as she smiled to him.

He looked at them both for a second then with a crooked grin, turned and glissaded expertly down the steep slope toward where the little spring bubbled from the hillside.

"Major force in tha' ferkin bushes, Shat! Wart Face missed it by a mile! He's a Major Force in the whole ferkin World!" Puss muttered as she tightened her pack straps.

"I saw it first Buddy," Boots whispered with an unfathomable look to her friend, before she leapt down the hillside after Bila.

*

"OK Jimmy, they won't look for us here on this side, so keep your head low Buddy," Molly whispered as she wriggled awkwardly back under the brush at the edge of the tree line across from the cabin.

"Sugar Plum's safe in the trees, but you keep down Molly, 'cause they're acting' funny – like you said."

"Yeah, funny…" Molly muttered. Then she whispered in a voice so low that Jimmy could barely hear her, "Shat! I think they just went up to the cave! Bila's the only one who knows about it. Maybe it's Bila!" Then she hissed urgently, "Please don't shoot unless I do! Please Buddy?"

"Sure, but why"

"'Cause they might be my friends, coming back to us!"

"Your friends, right?" Jimmy snapped.

"Our friends, Buddy - please," Molly whispered as she squeezed his shoulder. "If it really is them coming back here, I'll know as soon as I see them."

"OK, but I'm keeping them in my sights until we know who they are!"

"You're my friend too Jimmy," Molly whispered. "So hang with me, OK? Please?"

*

Bila slid easily down the steep slope at the head of the little valley, breaking his descent by grasping the small saplings growing in the light where the old forest had retreated. He landed at its base, and impatiently crashed through the brush at the edge of the tree line, oblivious to the thorns and briar vines that impeded his way.

Boots and Puss expertly slid down the slope behind him and pushed through the dense shrubbery without a scratch, protected by their suits and helmets.

The two women paused at the head of the little valley. They watched Bila stride through the meadow in the declining light as the sun sank to the top of the ridge, toward the little cabin where Molly should be waiting.

"We stay like he say, or we do backup?" Puss asked as she removed her helmet and shook her head to loosen her hair.

"We do backup for him," Boots grunted as she stripped her own helmet off and shook her long hair free. "There was a firefight in that cave, and we don't know who won, or where the winners and losers are now. Anyway, intelligent disobedience of orders is always the attribute of a good soldier, agree Buddy?"

"Yep, and like the big man say, Now Go We," Puss snapped as she hung her helmet on her belt and charged her rifle. Then she started after Bila with her weapon at the long trail, walking at a pace that would let him gain a hundred meter start. Boots did the same and also moved away at an angle that positioned her thirty meters to the right of Puss. They picked up their pace after Bila had attained his lead, and followed silently down the meadow.

*

The sun was behind the tree line at the crest of the ridge and the light in the valley was fading rapidly when Molly spied a figure striding purposefully toward the cabin. Jimmy did as well, and a characteristic clack told her that the boy had moved his rifle's safety to off.

"Don't do anything Jimmy, Please! I think it's him."

"Who," Jimmy hissed.

"Bila, my friend. Our friend! And don't point at him, please!"

"OK," Jimmy whispered as he reluctantly shifted his aim to above the figure's head, barely.

Molly held her breath for several moments while the indistinct figure moved nearer to the cabin, then she suddenly scrambled out from under the laurel and struggled to rise. She was still on her knees when she squealed, "Bila! You're safe! I'm over here!"

"Molly!" the man called with joy in his voice as he broke into a run toward her, his cape flapping from his shoulders.

Jimmy stared in awe at the large, almost naked man running toward them for a second, and then he scrambled out from under the bush and after helping Molly to her feet, stepped in front of her and leveled his rifle. His voice cracked as he yelled at the man, "Alright, that's far enough!"

"Jimmy, you stop that right now!" Molly snapped as she stepped around him and held her arms out to Bila.

The man looked at the two young people, then stopped his run at a distance that was not threatening.

"Hello Molly. Friend," he said quietly as he dropped his rifle and helmet on the ground and stepped forward to take her hand.

"Bila, you're safe! I'm so glad! But you don't ever do that again, darn it!"

"What do I you like not?" Bila asked, his brow wrinkled in a worried frown.

"Go off and leave me like that! If we'd stayed together we could have killed 'um all without you getting collected, dammit it!"

"Are you the one who got the Chin guy and almost took Lukey out? With spears?" Jimmy whispered, his eyes suddenly wide as he lowered the muzzle of his weapon.

"'Course he is! He's my best friend in the whole world, except for you, and Kris 'n Marybell!" Molly said as she dropped her rifle in the grass and threw her thin arms around Bila's chest.

"And he's safe," she whispered while she hugged him as hard as she could.

Bila gently returned her embrace with his left arm, and held his right hand out to the boy as he smiled, "You friend Molly?"

Jimmy stared at the very large man that his newfound companion was embracing with obvious joy and his ears reddened. "Well, I thought I was, anyway," he snapped.

"Jimmy!" Molly squeaked as she stepped back from Bila and turned to the boy.

"'Scuse me Buddy," she said over her shoulder, then she whispered as she faced Jimmy with eyes suddenly large in her face, "He's my friend OK! But you're my man..."

"Awwww," Jimmy croaked as his eyes suddenly glistened and he blushed, again so strongly that his freckles almost disappeared. Then he snapped his rifle to safe and tossed it on the grass as he held his arms out to her. "You never said that before."

"I'm sorry," Molly whispered, as she stepped into his arms, "I didn't think I had to, but now I'm glad I did."

Bila looked down at the two suddenly lost in each other with a smile that was infinitely tender, but his eyes also held a distant longing...

*

"Intros look over. Move up?" Boots signed across to Puss where they stood halted a hundred meters back from the three, now barely distinguishable in the fading twilight.

"Yes. Molly look good. Bila look happy. But who other?"

"We go see. But I have idea."

"I do too," Puss signed back, with a broad grin.

"We go," Boots called aloud as she jumped forward into a double-time trot with her rifle held across her chest at high port and her cape flapping behind her. Puss did the same and the two women ran toward the small group standing across from the little cabin.

Bila heard Boots' voice and after he looked over his shoulder, he shrugged with a wry grin and waved his arm forward. "Molly. Friends now come – No, our friends are come!"

The girl quivered with joy in Jimmy's arms, then squeaked as she finished her kissing of him with a quick smack before turning back to Bila, "Is it Kris?"

"Damn right Kid! But who's your new guy?" Boots grinned as she halted her run with a stiff-legged sliding stop at Bila's side, and playfully kicked up turf by digging in her heels.

"Yeah Trooper Three, how you be?" Puss smiled as she hopped to a halt beside Boots.

"You came back, like you said you would!" Molly whispered with a catch in her voice as she held her thin arms out to Boots, "Thank you. Nobody's ever really kept their word to me about anything good before, ever!"

Boots accepted the girl's embrace, first awkwardly then on a sudden impulse, she dropped her rifle on the grass and fiercely returned Molly's hug as she whispered in the girl's ear, "We keep our word in this outfit Trooper, all of them..."

"Yeah," Puss smiled as she ruffled Molly's hair and patted her shoulder, "It makes life simpler that way."

"OK, mush time's over for now." Boots growled a moment later as she gave the girl a final squeeze. "Front and center Three, and report on your activities in our absence! Good job of reworking your alarm message to S'attl by the way. It helped us extract Bila from the Rat's Nest."

"More like it helped us let Bila extract himself, Buddy," Puss snorted.

"Whatever. Anyway, introductions first, OK?"

"Yes Ma'am!" Molly growled with a squeak. "Jimmy, this is Kris and this is Marybell, and this is Bila. They saved me from the Rat - and Bila taught me how to kill dumb birds, and Rat Catchers too..."

Molly continued shyly as she took the boy's hand, "This is Jimmy, he saved me from the Captain, and he's Trooper Four if that's OK - and he's my man now," she finished in a rush as her cheeks reddened.

"How do you do, Ladies and Sir," Jimmy said gravely as he squared his shoulders and stepped forward with his hand outstretched. "Thank you for helping Molly."

Boots stared at Jimmy for a long moment, noting that he held himself erect under her scrutiny while keeping his hand held steadily out, and that his honest blue eyes did not waver.

She nodded with a crooked grin, and accepted his hand in a firm grip. "Jimmy, you'll do. Welcome to the outfit, Trooper Four!"

"Yep, you're in the Trouble Troop biggers now Jimmy," Puss smiled as she reached to take his other hand. "You come from over the ridge to the west, right?"

"Yes Ma'am."

"Don't Ma'am me Trooper! I'm Marybell, or Buddy or Puss even, to anyone in this outfit, OK!" she glowered with a grin, "But to continue, if you're from over there, where's the rest of your bunch?"

"Jimmy," Bila interrupted in a quiet voice that dominated the space once again, "You friend Molly at?"

"Yes Sir!" the boy responded decisively as he looked up to meet the very large man's probing amber eyes.

After examining him for what seemed an eternity to the boy, Bila suddenly smiled and held his hand out to Jimmy. Then he held out his other hand to Molly. The two obediently clasped his in silence while Boots and Puss looked on quietly.

Bila held Molly and Jimmy's hands in his for many heartbeats as he looked down at them standing quietly before him and returning his gaze unflinchingly.

"Molly, you friend at Jimmy?"

"Yes Sir. Real much, Sir!"

"Good." Bila said quietly, as he joined their hands, and held them between his for a moment.

"I think we just be at wedding." Puss signed to Boots with finger taps.

"Yes. But they honeymoon no be long!"

Bila released Molly and Jimmy's hands and glanced around at Boots. "Yes," he said to her astonishment. Then he turned back to the two who still stood before him with their hands clasped and stars in their eyes as they gazed at each other.

"Marybell say." Bila continued gently, "Where is rest you bunch of?"

Jimmy shook his head, "Well," he started then paused, "Better you tell 'um Molly. They're more likely to believe you."

"OK, but can we go back to the cabin first please? Supper's only half cooked."

*

"Good food Molly, You do an excellent Real Food supper!" Boots said as she spooned the last drop of broth from her mess kit.

"Molly Yes, cook dumb bird good you!" Bila added with a tender smile.

Molly sat next to Jimmy on the edge of the bed, with her empted mess kit on her lap. She blushed at Bila's words, "Thank you Sir, but you taught me how, and Jimmy shoots 'um in the head real good too."

Then she squared her thin shoulders and announced, "But now for my report, Ma'am," And then proceeded in her small voice to give a matter-of-fact recital of all the events that took place after Puss and Boots left for S'attl.

*

When Molly finished, Boots stared up at the two young people for a long moment, before she looked to Puss and Bila who were sitting cross-legged on the cabin floor with her, all under their capes. She laughed, "Well Buddies, it sure looks like we don't need a training camp out here. These two Troopers have damn well trained themselves pretty good already!"

479

Bila and Puss both chuckled and nodded as she turned back to Jimmy, "Where did you learn about killing, Jimmy?"

"From my Dad. He led a group of resistors around here for a long time before the Chin finally quit," the boy answered with pride, then he finished somberly, "And he almost got to live long enough to see 'um go running back to China."

Boots looked up at the earnest boy for a moment as she considered him, and the color of his hair...

"Was your father's name, Michael? Like in Red Mike McFadden?"

"Yes!" Jimmy gasped with a start, "How do you know that?"

Molly gripped his hand, "It's OK Buddy, we're with friends." The boy relaxed again, slightly.

"Simple," Boots said, "Your dad bossed the most effective and disruptive partisan outfit there was up here in Canada, and us guys in the thick of it down in the middle of the map sure did love the chaos he gave the Chin!" Boots grinned. "It's nice to know you, Jimmy. You come from real good folks. And, thanks."

"You're welcome Ma'am, but for what?" the wide-eyed boy whispered.

"For what your dad and his bunch did, that saved my bongos way many times. Your bunch kept large chunks of Chin so busy up here that they were out of our theater back home.

"Red Mike sure took lots of pressure off our butts, and we major appreciated that," Boots smiled. Then she asked in a quiet voice, "Before we get to down real business though, do you happen to remember a couple of US Special Forces guys, who would sneak up here every once in a while during the war to liaison with your dad?"

"Sure. I was just a kid then but I remember there was a guy named Bobby, and another real big guy they just called by some initials, and they were really tough, according to my dad anyway. But why you ask about them?"

"Jimmy, you've just made it into our Troop way biggers," Puss sighed, "Because I know for sure now that you're talking true about your dad."

At the boy's puzzled look she continued, "You see Trooper Four, that real big guy's initials were, and still are EB. And he's my father."

Jimmy gulped and stared at Puss with his mouth open, until Boots growled, "Number One, looks like it's time for our data drop to these two, so if you'll quit your sappy family reunion stuff, we maybe can continue!"

"Ja Boss," Puss grunted as she winked to Jimmy. He blinked at her then with a grin that filled his face, the boy proudly echoed Molly and Bila's affirmatives, "Ja Boss!"

*

"Wow! You two went in the Rat's Nest, and then you all came back out again when they didn't want you to!" Molly squeaked. "Somebody's gonna' get it biggers in a baaad place! The Network don't like lapses like that..."

"We sort of figured it wouldn't Molly gal, so that's why we decided to come back here so soon," Boots said. "We also figured that Rat, and particularly the Director in S'attl, is going to be major sore for another reason, beside Bila's unorthodox exit strategy last night."

"Why's that?" Molly asked her eyes wide.

"Because Rat pulled a sneak on us, and collected Marybell this morning through a piece of real dirty treachery," Boots hissed as her expression grew cold. "They had our Buddy trussed up in a 5X studio by 09:30 hours, and the Freddy team was already dancing around her and starting their act when Bila and I dropped back in the Nest to fetch her home.

"When we walked into that slaughterhouse Rat calls a studio, Freddy was about to make Marybell get real mad, until Bila said No to him in a major way and I made sure Heidi got the point as well, as it were.

"Anyway to speak short, we extracted our buddy and left Freddy and Heidi's meats sprawled on the stage for Rat's disposal service to hump away, along with those of their sicko cam crew and slime-sack collection team."

"Their meats will be easier to haul too, because Bila pruned `um all way good," Puss added with a cold little smile.

Jimmy glanced in confusion back and fourth between the two women, but Molly remained silent and thoughtful for a moment, until her eyes widened and she suddenly whispered, "Bila cut their heads off, right?"

Jimmy turned to stare in amazement at the girl by his side.

"Yep, he sure did, but how do you know that?" Boots asked.

Molly ignored Boots as she turned to Bila where he sat on the floor in his green jumpsuit, sweating under his cape.

She said to him in wonder, "Not many folks get into the Net anymore, but I can. And while you were away Sir, I searched some of the stuff you sorta' talked about." Then she suddenly whispered, "I hope you don't mind Sir."

"Molly, you are Bila friend. What you do be good."

"What actually did you find kid?" Boots asked, this time in a voice that was suddenly very quiet.

Molly took a deep breath before she responded in a trembling tone with an earnest face, "I don't have enough data yet Ma'am, so I'd rather not talk about it until I do."

Boots looked at the quivering but determined young girl for a second, then glanced at Puss with a raised eyebrow. When her friend immediately nodded in a strong affirmative, Boots smiled back to the girl, "OK Molly, this is your project, so it's your call." Then she complemented the young girl, and inferentially accepted her as an adult by saying with a smile, "Therefore Ma'am, you can stand down on this subject until you are ready to present your findings."

Molly's eyes widened after a second when she realized the status Boots had just conferred upon her.

Boots smiled at her for a moment longer, and then she turned and snapped, "Now for the real stuff Troopers - so listen close and well!"

"Before the Gala got grim at the Rat's Nest last night, we learned that Durwood is pretty close to being restored except for his feet, which probably are gone by now.

"This happened quicker than we hoped it would when Puss shot him up with some long-term dope before we sold him to Wart Face. So since we have to assume Durwood's operational, we must assume that Rat will make him cooperative as well. Therefore I expect he'll be leading a collection team back here for Molly sooners.

"We will not let her be collected! Understood Troopers?" Boots gritted.

"Understood!" Puss and Jimmy snapped and Molly whispered, with adoration for Boots shining on her face. Bila only grunted, and nodded.

"Good!"

"We must also expect the whole damn S'attl Nest is stirred up way biggers, and not just from Bila's actions last night.

"The Director got jet-jerked over to the Big Nest in DC before dawn this morning, and then was sent back home again around 10:00 AM local with all his orifices smoking from major abuse, according to our information anyway.

"This is probably due to Boss Rat's expression of displeasure about last night's lapses and losses. So the Director's already sore when he landed back in S'attl, but then he gets to his office and finds he's lost two of his highest profit talents, well, the poor man's probably revved way over his redline by now," Boots said with a grim chuckle.

"I had already expected action from Rat up here pretty quickie anyway even before our little final act with Freddy and company this morning, so I already arranged for a heavy squad to para-prop in here as Molly's backup.

"Their task is to deal with Rat, and some others that I also figure will come poking around here pretty soon as well, when the bands begin to play, my boys, when the bands begin to play," Boots said, as she grinned like a skull...

"Trouble is though," she said a moment later, "The squad won't get here until tomorrow night, so until our guys arrive, we five will cope with any situation that occurs. You get?"

"We got!" Puss snapped, Jimmy and Molly shouted "Ja Boss!" Bila just nodded, but the killing joy gleamed in his eyes once again.

Boots noted his expression and recognized it as coming from the same bright little coal that always ignited in the base of her mind whenever the fighting started.

Then with an internal shrug, she continued as her eyes glittered and she bared her teeth in her war-grin, "So now Troopers, here's the plan..."

*

"Wow," Jimmy whispered when Boots finished speaking. "You think just like my dad, and he was the best ambusher ever!"

"Thanks Jimmy, but let's save the wows `till we win, OK."

"Yes Ma'am!"

"Troops, you know the plan now, so - " Boots began, then she paused when Puss held one hand up and fumbling under her cape for a second, pulled out one of the different comets Bobby had given her and Boots when they had boarded the plane that morning.

"Belay things group, I just got vibrated," Puss muttered as she clicked the set on and read the message on its tiny screen.

"Was it good for you?" Boots leered.

"It is now, you perpetual pervert," Puss grinned after she considered the message for a moment. "This is in Pamunkey from one of my people back home. It seems the Governor has scheduled two `copters for soonest. One is `Clave Security and the other is Network - Wart Face's to be exact, so we all know where they're headed."

"Does it also say that a mechanic doing pre-flight maintenance checks on those birds has discovered metal chips in their rotor transmission case oil?" Boots grinned. "And that safety rules require a full check-out before they are cleared to fly again."

"Yes dammit, it does. How you know that, and just who's mechanic and who's rules?" Puss snapped.

"You're damn quick for the friend of a pervert, Kiddo," Boots chuckled. "First, I right-brained, it because I'm now starting to see how Bobby and Mack operate. Second, both the rules and mechanic are Army, because the Governor never bothered to invest in a maintenance capability for his `copters, or his ground vehicles either for that matter."

"Sounds to me like that's a Fatal Flaw…"

"Does to me too, M'Dear - indeed it does…" Boots murmured as she held up her hand for Puss' happy palm-slap.

"Does that mean they won't get here now `till tomorrow?" Jimmy asked.

"Right-on, Son!" Puss smiled. "You think quick."

Jimmy blushed, but Molly asked urgently, "Who is it that who called you, and is your comset safe? I know they have all the com-sats set up so they can archive and scan most all messages! Except for mine…"

"Real good question Molly," Boots said seriously. "The maintenance guy is a part of the organization I just mentioned, and the transmissions from these comsets go in micro-bursts, which is why Puss got a screen message instead of voice, and it was written in phonetic Pamunkey for max security."

"But the best part is that our organization's signals don't go through com-sats at all, we mole in to the Network's own vid-sats instead, and use their vacant band-width."

"Wow! I like this organization Ma'am, it's major smart! What do you call it?" the girl squealed as she bounced on the edge of the bed in excitement.

"We named it "The Restoration" and I'm glad you like being in it, because you are an important part of it, and a member for good, along with all the rest of us."

Molly raised her head in pride as she gripped Jimmy's hand.

"Is what Restoration?" Bila asked.

Boots looked around at Bila and was framing her reply when Puss answered quietly, "Bring back what is good. That's what the name really means anyway."

Boots growled as she stood up, "You got that way right Trooper One again, as usual. Now let's get to work." Bila nodded in understanding, and got to his feet as well.

"We have time tonight to do this right gang, so let's just do it! Molly, you tell us where all Durwood's little surprise packages are here in the cabin, and how they're wired."

"Next, you figure what you need to take out of here with you along with your 'punter, to keep it working and up-linked if we have to move it, and finally whatever else you and Jimmy need or want to take with you, because this place might not have much of a future when the Rat bunch gets here."

"Yes Ma'am. Do you want to see the guns? Beside those in there I mean," Molly asked in a determined little voice as she stood also and gestured toward the cupboard next to the front door where her Chin weapons were racked.

"Sure Trooper. Bring 'um out."

Molly turned and grunted as she trundled the crude bed to one side, then stooped awkwardly and was reaching for the trap-door handle in the floor beneath it when Jimmy leaped to help her.

"Let me do it please, you'll hurt yourself, and our baby," he said with a catch in his voice. "I'll go down, just tell me where to look."

The boy was lifting the handle of the trapdoor when Molly suddenly squeaked, "No! Dammit, I just remembered! I left their darn comset down there!"

"What comset?" Boots asked.

Jimmy and Molly then took turns telling the story of the Captain's Network comset, and how they had listened to it after they had killed Lukey and Carlos, and what they had overheard when they were hiding in the escape tunnel.

Boots thought for a minute then announced, "It must be same kind as the one they gave us, so it's dead for sneak-listening when the battery's out. But your info about it being in on Wart Face's local net is good to know, although we had already sorta' right-brained that possibility," Boots said, with a bland smile as she nodded to Puss.

"By your very 'scrutable facial expression, I assume you now task me to deal with this issue," Puss said with a sniff.

"Smart friend! Gawd, do this prevert like havin' a smart friend."

"You're really are a pervert dammit, and don't you forget it!" Puss said with a grin as she slid down the trapdoor into the dark space below.

*

"OK, the place is clear now Buddy. What we want to do with this damn thing?" Puss asked as she pulled herself up through the trap door a few moments later and stood before her friend, with the Rat's comset stuffed in the partially un-zipped front of her combat suit.

"Well little Poopsie, the straight Rats might like to keep it where it is right now, and maybe some of the kink ones too. But I'm not sure I'm willing to share you though, with them anyway," Boots smiled at Puss before she gave a quick wink to Bila. He answered with a grave nod, and a slight twitch at the corner of his mouth.

"However, I think we have a use for this set because it might be real informative to us, as it was to these two Troopers."

"What use?" Puss asked as she tossed the comset on the bed and groped for its battery, which she dropped on the bed beside the instrument a second later after locating it deep down her front.

"Supplying inadvertent intel," Boots deadpanned as she withdrew her own version of Bobby's comset from under her cape, and after clicking it on and carefully selecting a channel, handed it to Puss. "This Rat-set might want to lie on a couch next to a friend in that safe place, and babble about all that it hears all over our warnet."

"Wow!" Molly exclaimed. "We might be able to..."

"Yes Trooper Two, we just might. But don't count on Rat being dumb two times in a row, OK!"

"Yes Ma'am, Molly sighed as Puss gathered both comsets and the disconnected battery, and stuffed them in the front of her warsuit with another grimace.

When she dropped back into the tunnel, Boots said with a chuckle, "Hey kid, looks like yur' rack's getting a little lumpy."

"At least I got one Buddy," Puss' giggle floated up from the tunnel...

*

"Now it's time to consider parking places for both our butt bugs," Boots announced. "Keep your med kit handy Buddy, we've got some whittling to do on each other before bedtime, OK?"

Puss sighed, "Damn! I keep forgetting about the fun parts of this mission. But where are we going to park our butt bugs this time? Neither your mother nor mine are here at the moment."

"That's true, Doctor, but remember the package Hector sent to me this morning? That's what we'll use."

"And you will explain it to me in "due time", as you usually do, right?"

Boots made a rude noise then turned to Molly, "Now Trooper Three, just what goodies you got tucked away down there?"

Molly caressed her belly with a sly little grin, "A real good little one down here, thanks to Jimmy." Then she turned to the blushing boy and said in a serious voice, "There's another door down there, across from where the tunnel starts that goes into the power cell room.

"That room's really a bomb shelter," she added in her serious little voice to Boots. "And its walls and roof are real thick." Molly turned back to Jimmy, who had dropped to the floor and sat with his legs dangling through the opening, "Behind the blast door is where the other guns are and a big bunch of bullets for them too. So if you'll go get them and pass them up to me, Kris can see what we've got."

Jimmy nodded then dropped down the ladder. After a moment, the four in the front room heard a screech of un-oiled hinges and a second later Jimmy's voice sounded from below, "WOW!"

"Wow hell, Trooper! Quit lookin' and start passing iron up to me! Boots ordered. "And you sweetheart," she said to Molly as she urged the girl away from the opening.

"Sit here on the bed and take care of your kid like your man said. You are missioned to only to do that, and your `puter thing from now on."

"I'll do the weapons stuff because that's what I do damn good. ¿Sabe Ustedes?"

"Si Mi Capitána," Molly giggled.

"Smart little twitto" Boots muttered over her shoulder to the girl as she reached to grasp the barrel of the first weapon Jimmy offered up trough the trapdoor. When she felt its weight however, Boots wheeled to look at what it was that she held.

"What- in-hell's that?" Puss grunted as Boots lifted the rifle the boy handed her.

Boots gasped, "Ferk!" then she grinned as she hefted the weapon with both hands, "Unholy Sheet! I've read about these things, but I didn't think there were any left..."

"Talk, Dammit," Puss snapped as she peered at the gun Boots was holding with reverence.

Boots sighed as she cradled the weapon in the crook of her arm and stroked its gray steel receiver, "This is a Browning Automatic Rifle, Model 1918, one of the best squad guns there ever was. I've never seen one before, but our old Army, back three hundred years ago had a BAR in each squad –

and the Marines used three of these bad boys in their squads."

"Waddy'ell is so good about this old thing then, and why's it so bad?" Puss snapped.

Boots turned back to Jimmy, who was looking up at her from the trap-door opening. "Pass me up a mag and some ammo Trooper Four!"

"Yes Ma'am!" Jimmy snapped, as he dropped back down and leaping halfway up the ladder a moment later, handed a loaded magazine to Boots.

She looked reverently at the finger-long brass shells with copper jacketed black-tipped bullets in the bulky magazine. "Back then they called this gun the Rock in The Hard Place, because it always worked no matter what. And from what I've read, these black tips mean this ammo is armor-piercing."

"So?" Puss snapped again as she took the weapon from Boots and hefted it. "I like my Dirty Harry, but this big thing is way too heavy, and using three hundred year-old ammo? Not for me Buddy!"

"Good point about the ammo, and we'll sure test this stuff before we depend on it."

"Durwood told me all the ammo was reloaded by the man who had the cabin before us," Molly said in a little voice.

"Thanks Kid, that's nice to know, in a way. He sounds like he was a smart guy," Boots responded in an equally quiet tone.

"But now my little Killer Kitten," she said as she turned back to Puss, "Tell me again, just what is it that you like about your Dirty Harry?"

"Simple Sweetie, it either punches all the way through body armor at close range, or at least knocks 'um down to the ground at up to fifty meters."

"You're right Buddy and that's why I like mine too," Boots said as she patted the pistol holstered under her left shoulder. "But how would you like to punch through body armor at two hundred meters, and knock 'um down at five hundred?" she asked with a grin.

"Sure would! But this damn thing's way heavy for accurate shooting"

"That's what the bipod's for," Boots muttered as she braced the butt stock against her right hip and examined the left side of the gun's massive receiver. "Hey gang, I might be wrong, but I think this is the A-2 model from the second war between us and Europe," as she clicked the small lever on the side of the receiver through its three positions.

"If it is Troopers, this thing's got two rates of fire according to the old manuals."

"That's what Durwood said they had," Molly piped eagerly from the edge of the bed.

"They? How many you got down there?"

"Five more, Ma'am, and they're all in real good shape too!"

"Hmmm… What all else you got down there kid?" Boots asked as her eyes lit and she smiled, in a certain way.

"There's a whole bunch of all different kinds of pistols, and one real pretty rifle that shoots great big bullets. Durwood said that it was special."

"OK, we'll take a look at those later, but right now let see how this thing shoots," Boots muttered as she clicked the little lever on the left side of the receiver to "F" and fitted the bulky magazine into the opening in front of the heavy weapon's trigger guard. It seated with a sharp "click". She smiled…

Striding to the front door, Boots opened it and balanced the BAR in her left hand as she pulled the cocking lever on the receiver's right side back with a clank then slid it forward again. She looked down at the weapon in her hands for a moment, then with a shrug lifted the bulky rifle to her shoulder and aimed out into the night as she braced herself against what she could only imagine.

But then when she squeezed the trigger, Boots found that she could control the weapon, as she emptied its twenty shot magazine into the hillside across from the cabin at a rate of 350 rounds per minute.

The stuttering roar of the BAR was still echoing in the room and its ejected cartridge casings were clattering on the floor when Puss yelled, "Dammit, gimmy' that ferkin' gun, and toss me up another mag Jimmy!"

Boots grinned as she stepped back from the door and passed the heavy weapon to her friend, but then leapt away in exaggerated fear. "Poopsie, please be careful how you drive this thing, you might hurt us if you don't steer it so good!"

Puss just snorted as she snapped the fresh magazine in to the gun, then after operating its charging handle she strode out of the cabin into the dark of the evening holding the heavy rifle at the ready. Seconds later those inside the cabin heard the sound of the gun's stuttering roar once again, but this time in short controlled bursts, of three to five shots each until the magazine was emptied.

After a long moment of silence, Puss stepped back into the cabin carrying the BAR at port arms with wide-eyed reverence on her face. "Molly gal," she whispered, "I gotta' have this, Shat, I Need this and I'll give you anything for it."

Molly looked up at Puss with adoration in her eyes then she looked to Boots and Bila as well.

"You guys saved me from the Rat and Durwood. So anything that I have that you want is yours for free, and forever," she said the quite voice of an adult.

***

Chapter 23
The Accomplice

May 6-7, 2276
`Clave of S'attl

"How are his stumps healing?" the Director snapped at one of the two women standing before his desk.

"According to his chart, quite well actually Sir," the voluptuous redhead-ed submissive whispered with downcast eyes. "Doctor Freddy can do excellent work, when he's not in his studio."

She still wore the abbreviated parody of a traditional nurse's uniform that she had in the Colonel's apartment earlier in the day, and assumed the same cringing attitude before the Director that she had displayed to Puss.

The woman actually was a skilled surgical nurse in a profession that made full use of her genetically engineered proclivities. She had been programmed in a Petri dish before birth to give comfort to people usually patients assigned to her care, but not always.

She also joyfully obeyed any orders given to her usually by surgeons but again, not always.

"The operative word now is "Did", as in the past tense," the Director hissed.

The nurse cringed at his tone, then she whispered as she looked up at him with melting eyes," You're upset Sir. Would it make you feel better to whip me for a while?"

"We will save that thought for later," the Director snapped. Then he turned to his new officer of Security, "How soon can you get your people out there and collect the girl?"

"You want her collected, or just removed from the equation," the blond woman in black with the hard body and even harder eyes asked in a cold voice.

The two were standing in the Director's office where he had summoned them on his way to the Network building after his return from Washington, and after he had received a report of the events that had occurred while he had been away.

He had first called in an order to have the Colonel in his office when he arrived. His aide, the woman with the body tattoo of the Rock Python had placed him on hold and left her desk, and then returned and had hissed that the Colonel was indisposed, permanently.

The Director had then ordered the nurse to his office along with Colonel's Deputy.

"I want her back here, or you need to be refreshed as to what the term "participant" means?" the Director hissed.

The blond woman with the hard eyes removed her monocle and replied crisply, "At once, Sir, as soon as I organize a team and arrange for transport."

"Make sure it is a better team than the last one your office sent up there, the ones that seem to have disappeared..."

"It will be, Sir. Both in quantity and quality, and it will be drawn from the Governors forces and I will lead it myself," she replied in heavily accented English as she smiled, reaffixed her monocle, and clicked her heels.

"Don't bore me with your details. Just perform - or you will be our next performer."

The Director turned to the submissive nurse, "How advanced is this Durwood's "adjustment", and is he mobile?"

"According to his chart again Sir," The she whispered, "He is scheduled to have his ankle adapters attached in two more days when the shock to his stumps has subsided so they will accept the electrode grafts.

"His mentation is mostly intact again under our treatment now, with the minor exception of some strange influence that our psych people have not yet been able to define."

"I Repeat dammit, is he mobile or can he be made so?"

"Yes Director if that is what you wish, but moving him before his surrogate foot grafts have fully healed will require the use of a basket chair," She whispered with a sigh that strained the last button on the front of her starched uniform.

"Do so. Prepare him to go out with our collection team since he knows about the area and the girl. And do your jobs - Now!" the Director suddenly shrieked at the two women.

*

The Network's medical group which had been headed by Dr. Freddy until that morning, had developed a unique method to ensure that critical staffers such as computer code writers and media manipulation artists who became disgruntled about working conditions and fled the Rat's Nest, did not do so again after they were re-collected.

The medical group surgically removed the feet at the ankle of these staffers and grafted plastic sensor collars on to their stumps with circuitry connected to the larger nerve endings in their legs.

When the grafts had healed under the influence of enhancement drugs, the errant staffers were fitted with what appeared to be hooves that locked on to his or her ankle collars. These were actually small explosive devices with normally closed solenoid switches controlling their detonators.

The switches were held open by a low power radio frequency that was emitted from antennae in the walls of the broadcast control center, the post-production studios and the dormitory where all of the Network's sequestered technical staff in S'attl worked and lived.

Those who were fitted with the devices attained some degree of mobility after time, aided by canes or crutches. They all knew however that at their first step away from the rooms that now were their permanent home would result in their legs being blown off above the knees.

Several of the stubborn ones sat in power chairs, because all of their legs were gone...

*

"How's the check goin' so far?" the swarthy master sergeant asked as he walked onto the helicopter maintenance pad at the S'attl Army Air Field.

"Pretty good, but as you know, I am tasked with being very thorough," the chunky female mechanic, who's skin had an ivory hue replied.

"Well, the Rat is frettin' but we gotta' be safe no matter, right?

"Right, Sir, and I'm glad you understand what I am trying to do here."

"Nawitka, klawha mitlite kloshe" he said with a nod, which in the old Chinook trade language of all the Pacific Northwest tribes translated as, "Yes, slow is good."

"Mahsie," she replied with a little smile, which meant, "thank you."

"Waki?" he asked, which meant "tomorrow?"

She nodded and agreed, "nawitka" and turned back to her very through inspection of the helicopter's dissembled drive transmission...

*

"How do you feel?" the submissive asked the pale young man strapped to the hospital bed. "Can you understand me?"

"How do you think?" he responded woodenly without opening his eyes.

"Don't be upset," she murmured as leaned over him and gently stroked his brow, even though he shook his head in an attempt to avoid her soft hand. "You know this is all for your own good. Now you don't have to think about anything else except your work, and the pleasures you can earn from it. And if you become really accepting to your new life, why you may even whip me after your procedure is completed," she sighed with a tender smile.

"But first, the Director has an important task for you."

Suddenly Durwood snapped his eyes wide open and with a shrill giggle, squealed, "The Director! There he is! He's sitting on your shoulder! Cools, but why does he have purple hair?" Then he blinked and shook his head and continued as if nothing had happened, "What task?"

"Molly must be brought back so we can help her too. The Director needs you to assist our recovery team. We will stabilize your stumps so you can go with them and give them your guidance," the submissive finished, as she turned his head to his and kissed him.

He giggled again into her soft mouth, "Do I get to watch her baby pop out?"

The submissive looked into his eyes at his comment, and saw none of his recurring strange drug aberration this time. Rather she saw something that was the true Durwood, and not nice...

*

"This delay has been inexcusable! I will inform General Butler of your slowness when we return!" the acting Security chief snapped to the master sergeant as her collection team of ten black-suited thugs climbed clumsily into the large helicopter at dawn.

"Sorry Ma'am," the master sergeant responded, "But if you want to get there and back the machines have to work, or do you want me to send you Networkers on a one-way trip?" he asked with an impassive gaze that pierced the amour of her monocle and made her uneasy for a moment.

She snapped, "Is the Network machine finally ready also?"

"Yes, Ma'am, and your "special advisor" is already on board."

"Good!" the hard woman with the dueling scar on her cheek snapped as she leaped into the squad helicopter General Butler had transferred to his security force some years ago after its Army markings and green paint were covered with black

The master sergeant watched as the two craft rose from their pads and gained altitude heading toward the northwest. He keyed the send switch on his curiously different comset and spoke one word, "howh!" which in Chinook is, "turn to!"

The duty monitor in the basement of Rick's club repeated the word in acknowledgement when he received the Sergeant's message, then he consulted a list of Pamunkey words. He picked up the handset of Rick's elegant retro early 20th Century telephone and dialed the connection. After the bulb in its base glowed green, he spoke, "Amuwoir!" twice then broke the connection.

The duty communications monitor on the Pamunkey reservation understood the man's words, "take heed!" and then relayed theses words on the safe link out to Puss in British Columbia.

***

Chapter 24
The Welcome Committee

May 7, 2276 AD
Coastal Mountains of British Columbia

Boots, Puss and Bila had all spent the previous night in the tunnel where their heat signatures were hidden from the sat cams. Once they had settled into its confined space, Boots had stripped out of her combat suit and laid face-down on Bila's IR cape on the dirt floor.

"OK, Kid, cut me free."

"As you wish Ma'am," Puss murmured. Then she had carefully reopened the incision in Boots buttock while Bila held a bright little LED flashlight to illuminate her work.

After she had sealed the glittering little pellet in one of the storage capsules that Hector had sent to the airfield that morning, she had medicated and closed Boots' wound.

"Alright Long Knife it's your turn at bat. Now your worst, but don't forget in your bloodlust that it's under Rat's blue mark on my left bun. So don't cut at any of his red or black marks, OK?"

Boots had responded tenderly as she rose to crouch under the low roof of the space as Puss flopped over on her stomach, "Ja Boss, blue on left side," as she pinched Puss right buttock.

"Dammit - you're never gonna' get past recruit with me unless you know left from right soldier!" Puss snorted.

"Oh, then this is where I stab you, right?" Boots then asked as she used a disinfectant wipe to swab around the blue mark that Freddy's prep team had stamped Puss buttock with their implant locator. Then as Bila held the light,

Boots began cutting. And she probed and Puss stoically endured the pain, Boots continued in a whisper, "These red and black marks Freddy put on you Buddy, how about if I kiss them instead?"

"And Bila kiss. Make sick Rat stuff not on you more."

"Thanks Buddies, I'll thINK about that later!" Puss had gasped as Boots pulled her implant free.

Boots closed the incision and secured the tiny device in another storage capsule. Then the three spread out Bila's Cape as a ground cloth, and laid down to sleep together under Puss' cape for warmth.

They wrapped in each other's arms because of the confining closeness of the tunnel and Puss had nestled between her friends. The two women favored their left hips, and Bila pulled them to his chest with his arm across both their shoulders.

Boots resisted at first then as Puss snuggled to the man's bare chest with a sigh, she had finally relaxed her tensions and nestled against her friend's back. She also accepted the comforting weight of Bila's arm on her shoulder.

Boots was drifting off to sleep and she sensed that Bila was as well, when somehow she felt Puss' voice in her mind, "Thanks again guys…"

*

The three awakened before dawn and climbed up into the front room. They stretched and shook themselves awake, then wrapped themselves in their IR capes and Boots opened a combat ration. Puss opened two and handed one to Bila. They stood by the cabin door and chewed their cakes while Boots and Puss quietly discussed the upcoming "visit".

Molly stepped out of the back room and piped, "The oatmeal is almost ready, and I put rose hips in it."

Puss smiled at the girl, "I'll get some in a minute," then turned back to her conversation with Boots. Bila grinned, gulped the rest of his ration and strode purposefully into the back room, patting Molly's shoulder and muttering, "Real Food," as he stepped past her.

She smiled with pride at his eagerness for her cooking, and turned to straightening her bed. Then she paused, and asked in a little voice, "Do you want to look at the pretty rifle now?"

"Don't think I have time for that, we've got a war to fight…" Boots said absently over her shoulder.

"You just might need it when the war starts, Ma'am!" Molly suddenly snapped in a tone that made Boots pause, when the girl slapped a pillow for emphasis.

"OK kid. But make it rapid, dammit!"

"Jimmy, would you please go down and get it for her," Molly called, then asked with a smile, "And the box of ammo too please. You'll know which one it is, 'cause they're the biggest bullets down there."

"Sure," the boy grinned, as came in from the back room wiping his mouth. He opened the trapdoor and dropped into the tunnel. They heard the scrape of the blast door's hinges again, and a moment later he passed a rifle up to Boots, and climbed out of the tunnel with a plastic box in his hand.

Boots perfunctorily grasped the rifle by its barrel as he handed it up, then her eyes widened when she saw what she held in her hand. She lifted the weapon and inspected it with sudden reverence, as she noted the beautifully figured wood of its carved walnut stock, the delicately chased engraving on its action, and the legend cut into the steel of its barrel, "John Rigby & Co - London - .416 Rigby Express".

Then she looked at the rifle's muzzle, and her eyes widened again at the size of the large dark hole in the end of its barrel...

"Here's the ammo ma'am," Jimmy grinned. "And I think from the weight, that these rounds are loaded with DU penetrators."

"Shat! How do you know about them?" Boots snapped. But then she crooned as she lifted the rifle to her shoulder and cradled her cheek against its stock as she sighted at the far wall, "Hello you Big, Beautiful, and waay Baaad Boy..."

"Dad told me about the Chin's depleted uranium rounds. But these look like someone turned the copper driving bands down to fit this rifle."

Molly piped. "Wow Jimmy! How did you know that? That's what Durwood told me about it! But he only shot it one time, 'caus it knocked him back flat on the ground. He said it would be a real good 'copter gun tho."

At Molly's statement Bila grunted. He set down his mess-tin and then stepped to Boots' side. He gestured toward the rifle in her hands while looking at her with a silent question. She passed it to him without hesitation, but with a sudden insight.

"Make work?" he asked her after he looked at the rifle for a moment.

Boots gazed at Bila for several heartbeats then she turned to Puss with a crooked grin. "OK Buddy, now watch me create a real major force in the bushes!"

"Hey Kiddo," Puss chuckled. "He already is one all you're doing is facilitatin' him."

"Bila, this gun can kill `copters" Boots continued to him as she caressed the rifle's action with the gleam of war in her eyes, "If you hit them in the right place."

"Kill long-nose like?" he asked with a crooked grin that Boots recognized somehow. Then shook her head and proceeded to show him how to operate and aim the Rigby rifle.

Bila listened and watched with total concentration until she finished her short instruction then he nodded to Boots and carried the rifle at port arms as he stepped out through the cabin door.

He carefully loaded one heavy, nine centimeter-long round into the Rigby, aimed at one of the boulders 200 meters away that was a part of Boots' sanctuary and fired through the morning mist.

The recoil of the weapon rocked his shoulder back but he maintained his grip on it, and was able to see the effect of the depleted uranium round as it smashed on the boulder. Both the shower of rock chips and the pyroclastic flash of fire from the slug's impact were significant...

Bila paused for a moment in thought as he looked at the rifle before he brought it back to port arms and stepped back into the cabin. He held it up and announced, "This good long-nose killer. This biggers kill Rat `copter be!"

Puss whispered to Boots at his words, "Buda's Blessed rosy beads, Buddy, you're right and Wart Face was too! But you didn't create this major force. He just came out of the bushes when we needed him..."

"Yep, and he's the best major force there ever was," Boots smiled as she stepped to the big man and slapped his arm while looking up into his eyes, "You like this rifle? You want to use it to shoot Rats?"

"Yes Buddy. Do Thud, No - Thud does!" Bila responded with a smile that was identical to hers...

Puss was still gazing at the two of them with a new emotion shining in her eyes, when she started. She reached under her cape for the comset Bobby had given her and switched it to display. She read the message on its tiny screen as the others waited in tense silence until she finished and transmitted her acknowledgement.

"OK gang," Puss snapped after she clicked the comset off. "They're in the air. We got three hours plus `till they get here. What we do now?"

"Get ready to party with them, Buddy, what else?" Boots drawled.

"Thanks Friend, I thought you'd see it my way."

"Buddy, we gonna' finally have us some funs this morning, and way biggers too," Boots grinned. Then she turned to the two young people, "Molly, I need for Puss to pull some of your blood, and Jimmy, I need for you to get Molly up to the cave pretty quickie right after!"

"Why?" Puss asked.

"Remember what my dad said about butt bugs night before last? And what Bila said when we pulled Molly's bug? Kiddo, there's ways to use them as well as to hide them, OK?"

"Oh," Puss nodded then she grinned with the same feral smile as Bila's, when he had made the sign for "decoy" three days ago. She reached under her cape and snapping the catch that released her med kit, motioned to the girl.

Molly squared her shoulders and held out her thin arm. But then as Puss swabbed the inside of her elbow she looked away, to Jimmy. The boy took her other hand in his and patted it reassuringly as Puss carefully pierced the girl's vein with her extractor.

Bila muttered to Molly, "I say strong you before. I right say."

Puss murmured as she watched the tiny vial fill with blood, "You sure do say true Buddy, our Trooper Two do be tough."

Molly only blushed as Puss removed her needle and closed the minute puncture with a small patch. Then Puss walked into the back room with the vial.

Boots continued while she ruffled the girl's white hair, "Molly, now that you have donated to the mission as it were, get your `puter ready to move with you. Then you two get to the cave quickie because this place is probably going to be the centerpiece of a firefight way big in a little while!"

"Take Marybell's comset with you too, OK?" she added as she gestured to Puss when her friend returned to the front room.

Puss nodded, "Done," to Boots then she handed her set to Molly. "You can listen in on our warnet if you click this stud here and you can read any incoming messages from our warnet on its screen by clicking here, because this set will signal you like it did me just now."

"If you don't recognize the language, read the words out as they appear anyway, and I will understand what you say."

Boots added, "But do not, repeat, Not break in for any other reason after the party starts unless it's way important OK? Because we will be pretty busy dishing it out to your visitors."

"Yes Ma'am!" Molly replied with a firm little voice and large eyes as she laid Puss' comset on the bed, then turned and trotted awkwardly into the back room and her computer.

"That's the same thing my Dad always told me too," Jimmy said quietly, "About listening in that is."

"Your Dad was a good fighter Jimmy. Now I task you with being one too and a good Molly protector as well. She is way necessary to our mission so I suggest you carry sufficient force with you to the cave, OK?"

"Yes Ma'am!" Jimmy grinned in a way that was not rat-friendly at all as he jumped to the cupboard beside the front door and snatched out two Chin assault rifles. He slung four bandoliers over his shoulder as he added, "And I'll ride Molly up there on Sugar Plumb so it'll be easy on her."

"Good thinkin' Trooper," Puss grunted when the girl rushed back into the room with a metal case. Molly also grabbed her rucksack from its hook beside the door and after thrusting the case and the comset in it, slung the sack over her shoulder.

"OK, I've put the brains out of the big box in this bag," she exclaimed to Jimmy, "So let's get gone Buddy!"

"One more thing Molly," Boots said, "Bila needs your little rifle today, OK?"

Molly grabbed her Ruger from the cupboard without a word, and all of her extra magazines, and handed them to Bila.

"Thank you Molly, it I safe keep."

"I know that Sir, you are real nice, Big Thud, Sir," Molly whispered, then she looked to Jimmy and the two clasped hands for a moment, before he stepped through the door and she followed him out into the morning mist.

"Looks like there's some hope for the world yet." Boots muttered as she watched the two leave.

"Yep," Puss said.

"Biggers yep," Bila said.

"Shat!" Puss snapped when she heard his comment and spun to stare at him. Boots just grinned...

*

The three stood in front of the cabin as they watched Jimmy lead the pony up the ridge with Molly on its saddle clinging to the horn. Bila was wearing his warsuit again, and was grimacing as he stretched his shoulders against its fabric and sweated under his cape.

"We will use helmet channel fourteen," Boots announced as she turned back to business after watching the two disappear into the forest. She punched that number in to her suit's tiny computer and then said, "Here Bila, let me do yours too."

"Hey Buddy, there's only twelve channels on these damn warsuits, and you know that, dammit!" Puss frowned.

"Bobby and Rick planned ahead, and had their guys rig some suits, including ours with two extra channels that nobody else has," Boots said with another crooked grin. "They also built our new comset specs into them. That's why Molly can monitor for you, my Randy Little Redskin!"

"Hey, I'm really getting to like this Restoration outfit," Puss said as she grinned, "Looks like there maybe is a brain somewhere up its food-chain after all, just when I was starting to wonder."

Before Boots could reply with a rude noise, Bila spread his fingers before his face, and then his ears as he muttered, "Extra channel we make – no, make us words hide Rat at?"

Both women started, then spun to stare at the big man for a moment before turning to each other and simultaneously whispering, "Shat!"

Boots turned back and looked into Bila's intent face for a second then she nodded to him with a slight smile, "Yes." She then she shook her head and gritted to them all, "Enough of this idle yakey Troops! Buddy, you check the hotplate temperature again while I redo the circuits."

"Bila, you move on out to your station. Let us know when you're there."

"Ja Boss," the two snapped as Puss ran into the cabin and Bila began trotting down the little valley toward the three boulders carrying the Rigby at high port and Molly's little rifle slung over his shoulder, while ten heavy cartridges clicked against each other in a pocket of his warsuit.

Boots ran to the small boulder near the cabin where the remote sensing and arming controls for the cabin were hidden and dropped to her knees. She groped in the cavity under it for a second before pulling out the small box as Molly had instructed, then she waited.

Puss' voice sounded in Boots' helmet's receiver, "Pot's right, and at blood heat," just before she bounded out of the cabin door.

"Good." Boots said.

"Bila?"

"Station place at," his voice sounded in both women's helmets. "IR cape on me Max leader like want, OK?"

"OK," Boots said while glancing at Puss and shaking her head, again.

Puss just shrugged and rolled her eyes.

Boots snapped into her helmet mike, "Troops, I hereby call this meeting of the "welcome committee" to order, you all know the plan so let's do it. Now!"

Puss nodded, trotted around the cabin and on up the ridge behind it. Her strength made light of the two weapons she had slung over her shoulders as she mounted the slope, and the bulky bandoleer that hung around her neck bumped against her belly with her steps.

Boots pried off the back of the little box and reset the circuits inside it as Molly had instructed, then she closed and replaced it. She bounded across the little meadow to the tree line and pushed her way into the bushes at its edge, at the same place where Puss had waited for Durwood to be flushed out of the cabin.

"On station here," Boots murmured into her helmet mike.

"On station here," Puss panted a moment later.

"Good," Bila muttered. "Now Rat kill time soon come ..."

*

"My cabin's intruder trap control box is hidden here," Durwood's voice giggled over the speaker as a red spot appeared on an enlarged sat view of the cabin's site on the holograph screen on the wall of the black squad helicopter's passenger space. His voice continued in the Acting Security Chief's comset, "You reach under this rock and there's a box. Turn all the buttons on the front of it to "off" and then it's safe to go in."

"You are sure?" the hard blond woman asked in accented English asked as she inspected the display through her monocle.

"Sure as snot's slick!" Durwood giggled again, his voice sounding shrilly over the background noise of the accompanying Network 'copter where he sat in a special chair behind Wart Face and the co-pilot, a chair that pumped medication into the stumps where his feet used to be.

"You had better be correct in what you say, otherwise I will personally cut away parts of your body, ones you deem important for recreation in your miserable life..."

"Just so I get to watch her baby come out, then saw its feet off while she watches! That's what you promised me, and that's all I want!" Durwood's voice shrilled from the speaker.

The hard blond woman sneered, then clicked her set to the intercom channel in the squad 'copter and snapped, "How much longer to the site?"

"Ten minutes, Ma'am," the pilot replied as he glanced at his nav-screen display.

"Good! Activate the locator and the IR scanners! And you call me Sir!" she snapped as she flexed her arms and cracked her knuckles...

"Yes Sir," the pilot said perfunctorily as he switched on the two surveillance systems.

*

Bila heard the faint thudding of approaching helicopters where he waited behind the three boulders, before Boots or Puss.

"Rat come," he muttered into his helmet mike as he flapped his cape to release his accumulated body heat, inserted a small curved magazine into Molly's rifle and charged a round. Then he thumbed three of the very large rounds into the magazine of the Rigby and chambered one by closing its bolt. He clicked the rifle on safe and leaned it against one of the boulders, and waited.

"Good ears Trooper," Boots said as she flapped her own cape. Then she whispered, "Wonder if Wartsy's mike will have loose lips again," as she loaded her assault weapon's lower barrel with a 25 millimeter rifle grenade and charged its cartridge barrel with a round from the clip. Then she dropped to her belly and crawled to where she had a view of the cabin and its approaches from under the brush. Once there, Boots snuggled the weapon's stock to her cheek with a little sigh of pleasure...

*

"Party time," Puss muttered into her mike as she flapped her cape. Then she got to her knees behind the same fallen tree from where Boots had ambushed Durwood only three days before. She placed her monocular and the old bandoleer with its bulky magazines close at hand then loaded her assault rifle's lower barrel with a grenade and charged its rifle barrel before leaning it against the log.

Puss laid the BAR across the log and pulled the big gray gun's charging handle back then slid it forward again as its bolt clanked and chambered one of the long brass cartridges. Puss hugged the big gun's stock against her shoulder as she aimed it down into the valley, and her eyes became as cold as the green ice in the core of a glacier...

*

"What do you read on the IR scan and the locator?" The hard blond woman snapped

"She's in there," the co-pilot grunted as he transmitted a satellite image of the cabin to her holograph projector. It showed a blinking red spot close to the structure's rear wall, and nodded toward the screen of the locator, which now displayed Molly's name and ID number.

"What about any other elements in the area?"

"None to speak of. There are a couple of small fuzzy hot spots, but they are so minor that they're probably just animals."

"Probably?" the hard blond woman snapped.

"Surely," the co-pilot said in response. As a Network employee, he had escaped service in the Chin war and thus he had no experience with the practical stratagems of those who had been in combat...

"Good. Land us and we will do the collection!" she snapped back.

*

Two black helicopters appeared from the east following the curve of the main valley, and as Bila watched from behind his boulder, they floated down toward the flat where he had first met Kris and Marybell.

The large `copter with two rotors came directly down near the place where he had killed the bear. It hovered for a moment just above the ground, then landed with a rocking hump. A door opened in its side as its vanes slowed and ten men in black coveralls stumbled out of the craft.

Bila noted that they were led by a trim black-clad figure who gave orders with strong gestures of command, and who exhibited female characteristics under her tailored coverall. The group formed up under the person's direction and began advancing toward Molly's cabin.

Bila flicked his helmet mike three times with his fingernail, then twice again as Boots had instructed. He focused his attention on the large helicopter after he sent that signal, its engine now silent. The other helicopter with the white Network symbol on its side had landed also, but he saw that its rotor continued to turn slowly as its motor whined, and it squatted like a black spider on the green grass of the meadow.

Bila smiled when he glanced back at the large `copter, and saw two men appear in its doorway. They sat down on the edge of its opening and stuck small smoking things in their mouths as he had seen Rick do in `S'attl at the club place.

He considered the men and the distance to them from where he lay, the same distance he had carried an unconscious Boots to safety among these boulders two days ago. His eyes glittered as he rose to his elbows and trained the sights of Molly's rifle on the two men, and waited.

*

"I vill disconnect the traps, then you vill go in and get her! Her signal shows she is in the back of this stupid shack,"

"Yes Ma'am," the squad leader growled.

"You will call me Sir in the future if you are wise!"

The man gulped, and nodded.

"Good. Now go and get the girl win I signal to you," the hard woman snapped over shoulder as she sprinted to the small boulder where Durwood had told her the trap controls were hidden.

She groped in the cavity under it until she found the little box, and turned the switches mounted on its front panel to the off position as Durwood had instructed. Then she imperiously waved her squad forward, and was stunned when the first two men through the cabin doorway had their feet blown off by the mines that exploded in the threshold.

The woman ignored their screams as she shrilled to the squad leader, "Go over them you stupids! Get me the girl! Now!"

The next two men who rushed to obey her order had their legs blown off by a second set of mines in the door jambs.

*

"Time to dance troops," Boots murmured into her helmet mike as she keyed another button on her suit's computer and the lilting tune of the U.S. Cavalry's "Garry Owen" began to play softly over their warnet.

The screams of the four figures thrashing in a bloody tangle in the doorway masked the "whomp" of Boots' rifle grenade.

"Ja Boss," Bila responded, as he took aim on one of the two men sitting in the doorway of the large `copter, who now were craning their necks at the sound of the mines exploding at the cabin as their smoke-things dropped from their mouths.

He fired at the one on the right first, then at the one on the left. The sound of Molly's rifle was again as the snapping of twigs.

Both of his shots were to the forehead and the two men died instantly as the little bullets splatted their brains in the same way as they had the rash bars on Molly's target frame.

Bila laid the little rifle aside then bounded to his feet and flapped his IR cape. He grasped the Rigby rifle from where it lay on the grass and took a stance behind a second boulder where he had a clear view of the Network `copter. He clicked the Rigby's safety off and waited.

"She was sitting next to the Colonel at your party, but she ran out when I called my challenge," Puss gritted into her helmet mike as she dropped her monocular. "That bitch is mine! You can have all the rest of `um!"

"Ja Boss," Boots grunted as she fired her second rifle grenade. The effect of the first one was just registering on the group in front of the cabin as Boots spoke.

It exploded in the midst of the Network squad when its proximity chip set it off at chest-height and scattered notched segments of its wire-wound warhead among them without preference...

Boots' second grenade added to the shambles, and its report told the Acting Security Chief finally that things were amiss.

She screamed into her comset, "You told me wrong! I will kill you, you stupid!" as she sprinted away from the cabin and toward the two `copters.

"Remember Buddy, she's mine!" Puss snapped.

"Ja Boss," Boots said into her helmet mike, as she opened fire with her projectile barrel on the reeling black-clad figures still standing in front of the cabin.

The Acting Security Chief's voice crackled over their warnet from Puss' comset in the tunnel and was relayed to their net, "We have been betrayed! Hold that person until I get there!"

"Don't think so Dumbo," Puss grinned as she flipped up the ladder sight on the BAR and adjusted its sight to 200 yards then targeted the woman in black sprinting toward the two helicopters. She calmly killed her with four precise bursts of five rounds each from the heavy gun.

The impact of the first slugs spun the hard woman around for a second then as the booming roar of Puss' gun sent the rest of the bullets through her body their impact bounced her around in a grotesque dance until she slammed down on her back in the meadow.

The Acting Security Chief died glaring up at the clear blue sky through her monocle, which some random muscular spasm had kept in place.

"Sheet! We're outta' here!" Wart Face's familiar snarl sounded from Boots' other comset, relayed up from its twin in the tunnel.

Boots murmured into her helmet mike, "Your turn Bila!"

"Thank you, friends," his voice sounded in their helmets in a tone that made both women pause, then Puss whispered, "Major force, right."

"Yep. Major major..."

The rotor of the helicopter with the Network device on its side began to spin faster, and then blurred as the craft started to rise. Bila watched it go up until it was fifty meters above the ground, then he dropped his cape and stepped from behind the boulder.

He trained the Rigby on the `copter and pictured in his mind what he remembered of its interior when he had been hoisted into it and dumped on its floor. He also remembered where the person who had made it go had sat, and where its noisy parts were.

Then he fired, and working the Rigby's bolt, fired again.

The first depleted uranium round penetrated the light metal in the bottom of the Network `copter, passed through Wart Face's lower body, and smashed on through the roof of the craft and hit its rotor transmission case.

The rotors had began to shudder in their spinning when Bila's second bullet smashed directly into the turbine drive casing of the craft's engine and wrecked it with a flash of pyroclastic sparks.

The stricken `copter swung first onto its side then it overturned and flew itself into the ground, and exploded with a huge fireball.

Boots listened to Durwood's shriek on her comset as the craft flipped and plunged toward the ground.

She smiled...

"Is it over yet? Are you guys OK?" Molly's voice sounded with a worried tone in their helmets.

"Sure is, Kid, and we all be good," Puss responded. "But I think we got a real mop job to do at your house now."

"Molly gal, this first little dinner-dance is done, but now we got to get ready for the big party, which is going to be a bit fancier I suspect," Boots added as she clicked "Gary Owen" off".

"Durwood not hurt Molly now more," Bila said into his helmet mike as he watched the flames roar around the burning helicopter where it lay atop the remains of the bear and her cub and Molly's first four visitors. Then he added as the rank odors and smoke from the impromptu funeral pyre wafted around him, "That pretty killsong, Kris. When we kill we more Rats?"

"Funny how quick he gets tha' big picture," Puss said.

"It's gonna' be real funny if we don't get our own big ferkin picture together dammit! So crank up your butts and let's get moving! Ooopy time comes later – if we live through our next damn party!" Boots answered with a growl.

***

Chapter 25
The Proclamation

"There's a lot of heat signature flaring up down there now. What we do `bout that?" Puss muttered into her helmet mike as she stood behind the fallen log, calmly watching Wart Face's `copter burn in the valley below.

"Good question Buddy. Jimmy, how fast can you get back down here on Sugar Plum, with that riata I saw on your saddle?"

"Way quickers. But who'll guard Molly?"

"We will," Puss snapped.

"Who's this we, Buddy?"

"Me and my new friend, the Rock! Golly-Gee guys, do I ever love this gun!" Puss responded with joy in her voice.

"Well, hump `um Honey! We have to move this meat quick while that fireball is still mostly blanking the sat cams."

"I go now. Jimmy, you do it!" Puss snapped into her helmet mike as she grabbed her big weapon and its bandoleer and began sprinting on up the crest of the ridge toward the cave.

*

"Jimmy, you and Bila put them all in the squad `copter," Boots ordered.

"Ja Boss," Bila's voice sounded on the net. "I come you at. Take Rats dead `copter to at."

"Stay put, Trooper Three. Jimmy will bring them out to you," Boots answered.

"What good's that going to do, Ma'am?" Jimmy asked as he uncoiled his

509

lasso and flipped its noose around the neck of a black-clad body crumpled on the ground in front of the cabin. "They'll still be here if someone comes and sees the `copter."

"I've got an idea, Son. No, instead make that, Trooper Four!"

"Yes Ma'am. You be boss," Jimmy grinned as he mounted, and after snubbing the rope around his saddle horn urged Sugar Plum forward with light heel touches.

Bila was standing beside the open door of the large `copter when Jimmy rode up dragging the first body. His eyes widened when he saw the boy sitting atop the same animal, and guiding it with straps attached to its mouth as the other man had done - the man who had shot him with the dart thing. Bila stared at Jimmy for a moment, then he relaxed and his expression changed to one of quizzical interest.

"Why you sit on zaldi? Food it!"

"What?" Jimmy asked with a puzzled frown as he reined in Sugar Plum.

"Zaldi is eat for, not on sit for."

"No! Horses are friends! Nobody eats horses! Not around here anyway."

Bila approached the horse and its rider with caution, and examined the saddle and tack intently. Then he noted how easily Jimmy sat on Sugar Plum and how calm and accepting the horse was of the boy's weight, and of the body it pulled behind it.

"How you zaldi horse let you on sit? Dead pull Rat?"

"You mean ride her?" The boy asked with a startled look then he thought of what Molly had told him of this strange man.

"OK, you start when they are just young foals, and you are real gentle, and you get them used to having little stuff on their back, and then heavier stuff, until you can ride them yourself. Then you can train them to stand while you rope, and to pull.

"You can pet her if you want, she's real friendly."

Bila considered this new idea for a moment then he slowly reached for the horse's head. It whickered and met his hand with its velvet nose, then rubbed its muzzle against his shoulder.

"Hey, she likes you! Now I know you're a good guy!"

Bila smiled as he stroked Sugar Plum's nose and then, reached up and scratched her ears. He looked up at Jimmy and grinned, "Zaldi horse thing smart is – no, Is smart thing." Then he startled Jimmy by announcing, "I eat zaldi-horse not now more. Friends they!"

Bila bent and released the noose, and then with an easy heave tossed the limp black-clad form up into the passenger space of the craft.

"More bad they get now you," he said with a grin to the boy, who stared at him with his eyes wide at the man's easy strength.

*

"OK, that's the last," Boots muttered into her helmet mike, "Except for her," She gritted as she paced out to the Acting Security Director's blood-stained body.

"Hey there, War Chick, what do you need to count coup from this bitch?"

Puss' voice crackled on their warnet, "Her monocle, and maybe an ear, but I'll collect it when I get back down there."

"No time. We got to stuff this meat away while Wart Face is still burnin' bright. But I can do it for you, since we're the same as one, right?" Boots replied as she knelt by the hard woman's corpse.

"Right," Puss' voice snapped over their warnet, "Do this for me and you will like my payback, I guarantee!"

Boots murmured sweetly, "Honey-chile', this is what friends are for," as she plucked the eyeglass from the woman's cooled but still grimaced face, and the comset from her clinched hand, and then sliced off the ear that was uppermost on her head.

Boots tucked the trophies in a belt pouch and slipped Jimmy's waiting noose around the dead woman's neck.

"Your turn Trooper," she said to him as she stood, then saw his sudden reluctance. Boots looked up at the boy on his horse for a moment then she said in a level tone.

"I know it's hard for real men like you to deal with this sort of thing, because she's a woman. But Jimmy, this bitch was going to take Molly back to the Rat to get her feet sawed off, OK?"

The boy's eyes suddenly blazed and without a word, urged his pony into a gallop, and dragged the Acting Security Director's body bouncing across the ground toward the large `copter as ancient warriors did with foes they had vanquished in combat.

*

"OK, Trooper Four, nice job. Now you and Bila empty out this arsenal Molly has been sitting on all these years and hump all that stuff up to the cave," Boots said into her helmet mike.

"Can they bring our mattress too? It deflates." Molly's little voice

511

sounded on the warnet.

"Of course they can Trooper," Boots smiled, "And the rest of your `puter stuff too - on their second trip. But force comes first!"

"Thanks Ma'am, and I'm real sorry I talked mean to you this morning."

"Molly Gal, I herewith order you to talk mean to me any, and every time I need it! And that goes for the rest of you troops too! Understood?"

Their responses of, "Ja Boss," were all chuckled, rather than answered in reverence or fear, as Boots had hoped that they would be...

*

"Not much chance to cook Real Food for a while troops," Boots grunted as she peeled the wrapper from an army combat ration where she sat in the cave leaning against her trail bike.

The four sat with her, all of Molly's munitions were neatly stacked along one wall and Sugar Plum stood behind them, munching the oats in her nose-bag.

"These things don't emit heat like a cook fire does," Boots chuckled, "And they sure don't cause rash bar gas at all."

"I can hang on `till we can cook Real Food again, Ma'am, and these are way good anyway," Molly mumbled with a full mouth.

"Strong words Gal," Puss said, "I like that." Then she turned to Boots as Molly blushed and Jimmy smiled.

She said with iron in her voice, "OK! Now that the "incident" you made cryptic reference to back at Rick's apparently has occurred and with a major bang as it were, what is your and our next step, O Supreme Strategist?"

"Funny you should ask, Poopsie One, and as an aside, it's obvious that my having increased your tofu ration is having some effect."

After the echoes of Puss' really really, rude noise died away in the cave, Boots continued, "As soon as our guys get here tonight and we get them oriented, I am going to be snatched up back to Olympia."

"When I get there and after you have established a new and improved link with the equipment that is coming, we will make an official proclamation from the Governor's Mansion. A super-compressed vid of that proclamation will then immediately be sent out here over our special net."

"Molly, you will receive it then you will break into the Network's regular broadcast system and re-transmit the vid throughout the world."

"You will have help from our best com-tech who is bringing our best equipment with him tonight, but Molly, you are the only one who can do the mole."

"So can you do this, and will you do this?" Boots asked the girl in a very quiet voice.

Molly gasped, and though her voice quavered she answered, "Yes Ma'am, I can do it, and I will too."

"Thanks, Molly, you are a good Trooper." Boots whispered.

Then Boots ordered as she go to her feet and flipped out the sleep pad from her pack, "Now let's all slap the mats while we can yet today since we, and especially me are going to be up most of this ferkin' night."

Boots touched the pad's tiny switch and it began to inflate on the cave floor. Puss unrolled her's as well and then showed Bila how to operate his.

"This thing smart be, Sugar Plum like," he muttered as he lay down on his mat and closed his eyes.

Puss and Molly looked at each other, and smiled at Bila's words. Then Puss glanced towards Boots and saw that her friend was gazing down at the man, and was oblivious to everyone in the chamber. As she watched, Boots shrugged after a moment then laid her pad next to Bila. She continued standing in hesitation for another moment, until she lay down beside him, and sighed as she snuggled up against his broad back...

Puss winked to Molly, then spread her pad next to Boots' and snuggled up to her friend's back. She yawned and then chuckled silently at their new sleeping arrangement. As she closed her eyes, she heard Boots' almost silent snort...

Jimmy held Molly tenderly in his arms on their mattress across the chamber. She kissed him and whispered, "I really do know I can do what I need to Buddy, now that I've got you."

"Awwww," was all he said as he returned her kiss.

Sugar Plum continued munching her oats where she stood above Jimmy and Molly's bed, content to be near the boy and the girl who was now its friend too.

*

The aircraft carrying the heavy squad Bobby and Mack had dispatched was informally called a Queen Bee, because on covert penetration missions, it laid many "eggs" - power-chuting Special Forces troopers.

This one had left Boing Air Base as the sun was setting, ostensibly on a routine night training flight without passengers in order to give its WANG crew airtime to fill their quotas for the month.

Its pilots had taxied the aircraft at the far end of their designated runway and once there, they had applied its brakes while they revved its engines and checked all its flight systems thoroughly, as regulations required.

They did this checking very thoroughly, so the aircraft remained at the end of the taxiway somewhat longer that was usual. They had stopped it next to the main runway, but slewed so that one of its side jump-doors was facing away from the control tower, and the plane's bulk hid the large army transporter that rolled up to it from the shadows moments later.

The transporter had driven into the restricted flight line through an unauthorized gate in the perimeter fence, one that somehow had been deleted from Boing's base master plan and therefore did not officially exist.

When the transporter backed up to the aircraft, the plane's navigator had opened the jump door and sprinted back to his cramped desk in the pilot's compartment as the heavy squad in the transporter scrambled their gear and themselves into the plane.

They did it in four minutes, as Luis stood at the back of the vehicle and timed them with his field watch. When their loading was complete, he nodded and gave a thumbs-up to the driver as he leaped into the plane and helped the jumpmaster slide its door shut.

The driver drove the transporter away from the plane, and on out through the gate that wasn't officially there...

*

The Queen Bee approached Kitimat at an altitude of 10,000 meters after exiting the S'attl control zone and the pilots had climbed it to that height. When the aircraft neared that area, the pilot gradually brought the plane back down to 2,500 meters. He leveled at that altitude and the co-pilot slowed the forward-thrust turbines and activated the down-thrusting ducted fans built into its wide wings. After the craft had stabilized in this new slow mode, the pilot dropped its speed further, to ejection rate and the co-pilot switched on the red ready-light in the personnel hold.

The jumpmaster got up from her canvass seat and stood in the aisle. She ordered, "Fly Guys! Stand up and snap on!"

Bobby's thirteen volunteers stood as a man or woman. They snapped the jerk-pulls of their power `chutes to the overhead line and formed up in a file before the closed jump doors, then waited.

The jumpmaster pushed her way past them and on to the compartment abaft the side doors. She re-checked the power chutes on the cargo pods and

514

then switched on the slave control receivers on each of the eleven units. After checking that the rear cargo door was clear and ready, she made her way back through the rattling belly of the aircraft to her position between the jump doors.

"We're ready whenever you can find the spot, Bird Boys," she snapped into the mike in her flight helmet.

"I hear. Stand by," Sounded from the compartment's speakers. The Troopers carried out a last check of their own equipment as well as of their buddies to the front and rear of them in the line.

Then they waited, again.

*

"Jump in one minute!" the compartment speaker crackled five minutes later as the ready light switched to bright amber.

"All right Fly Guys!" the jumpmaster shouted. "You will each launch interspersed with your own cargo pod except for Luis and Charlie! They go last!"

"As soon as your chutes deploy, you will take command of your pod and steer it and yourself clear of the jump slot!"

"You will then click on Luis when he powers toward the drop spot. There, you will circle until Charlie receives the vector and reco signal.

"At that time you will land - and just Do It! OK!"

Then the tough jumpmaster, who had made five hundred drops herself, gritted with a sudden catch in her voice, "Break-a-leg Troopers, I think this trip is the start of our best op in a way long time!"

While her words were still ringing in the compartment, the jump light changed to green for a moment, then the lights went off and both the jump doors and the cargo door whined open. All of the troopers and the jumpmaster closed their visors and activated their helmet night vision system at this signal, and switched on to their warnet.

Sergeant Luis looked at his squad lined up before him in the odd green light of his visor display for a second then he snapped into his helmet mike.

"OK mi Muchacos y Muchachas., ¡Arriba- Arriba! ¡Andale!

"Cisco say Go Go Go!"

The troopers shuffled forward one by one and stepped out into the empty dark.

Luis stood last in line, and squeezed the jumpmaster's butt as he touched his helmet to hers for privacy. They both covered their mikes with their fingertips and Luis murmured, "Save me a space beside you at thee victory parade."

"You're sure there's going to be one?"

"Why you theenk I waste my time on this crazy op otherwise, Mi Gatito Poco, eh?" he responded as he gave her butt a final squeeze, then waved as he stepped out into the night to follow his squad.

*

The troopers wore smoothly-rounded, hard plastic back packs under their `chute packages that were power units, which they activated as soon as their canopies had deployed and stabilized.

Their cargo containers were equipped with these parachute packs as well, and each trooper controlled his or her assigned pod from a remote control module strapped on their left wrist, except for the two troopers who were left-handed.

The rounded backs of the power packs opened when the chutes filled, as the hard shells of beetles do when they take flight, but these panels opened into very wide-bladed propellers which began to spin slowly and almost silently to create a powerful thrust.

The propellers were driven by small, supremely efficient electric motors powered by equally efficient fuel cells built into the packs and this mechanism made the troopers effectively individual aircrafts, capable of flying up to forty kilometers in an hour from where they had launched.

The motors and fuel cells that gave paratroopers the gift of silent flight had been developed late in the war by the US Army research unit at Aberdeen, Maryland. They were based on the Chin trail-bike motors, but the resulting design represented a major leap in technology beyond that, which the Chin had not fully grasped before their abrupt pullout.

During this late phase of the conflict, the United States combat and technical command levels in the Army and Air Force had also learned, finally, to not pass detailed information about every tactic or mechanism they developed up to the highest command levels. Particularly those that were closely connected to the White House...

Therefore this capability of airborne troops to be widely mobile with silence had only been whispered of, or mumbled about in the Pentagon. Thus the Commander-in-Chief, and therefore the Network as well were not well briefed about the power-chutes capability.

*

Charlie, as he was called was of Chinese ancestry. His father, an organic vegetable farmer in California with a farm near Bakersfield had been disgusted and then enraged by the original Chin ultimatum. When they invaded, he had immediately joined a local resistance group and had fought the Chin very effectively both as a partisan activist and as an infiltrator, until he was finally captured.

As an example to others of Chinese extraction who might be also in rebellion to the Chin occupation, Charlie's father was suspended by his ankles in a public park in Bakersfield and then slowly cutting two from his crotch down to his head with an electric chain saw wielded by a burly Chin military policeman wearing a yellow rain suit and a transparent face shield.

Charlie, who allowed his close friends to call him "Charlie Chan" after an almost-forgotten minor movie character of three centuries ago, never forgot how his father refused to scream while they were killing him...

Charlie had transferred his bright and burning hate from the now-departed Chin Army toward those in the United States who had let his father die by prolonging the senseless war. His hatred was controlled however, and its main manifestation was his unceasing effort to be the best communications engineer that he could, in the service of those whom he trusted to bring about change.

Since Charlie was brilliant as well as dedicated, his best was very, very good. When occasionally asked about his dedication by someone who did not know his history, Charlie's response was, "Consider your breakfast of ham and eggs."

When he received the inevitable blank stare, he continued, "The chicken was involved, but the pig was committed." Then he would go, "Oink" at his listener...

*

Boots awoke at the sunset as she had willed herself to do before allowing sleep to come. She thought for a second, then she remembered where she was, pressing herself against Bila's warm back and feeling Puss nestling up against her back as the trio lay in Molly's cave.

"Shat!" she snapped as she flipped their cover cape aside and bounded to her feet. "Work time dammit," she shouted.

Puss and Bila awoke as she jumped and leaped to their feet as well. They were reaching for their rifles and combat gear when Boots murmured, "Good exercise gang, but these incoming are going to be friendlies, OK?"

"OK, after I see 'um," Puss gritted as she hefted her BAR and clicked a full magazine in the big gun.

"OK, maybe," Bila grunted as he charged the magazine of the Rigby rifle and worked the bolt to chamber one of its long cartridges.

"Jesu's Jingle-bells, if I don't have a good set of Baaad Troops! You two wouldn't trust your own mothers!"

"Yes, we would, once we saw that it was her," Puss smiled grimly as she worked her weapon's charge handle with a click and chambered one of the big brass rounds.

"Alright you two hardened killers, put your safeties on and follow me out to the landing field. Our guys should be dropping in sooners." Boots said as she pulled on her IR cape and strapped her field pack to the carrier bars on her bike. Slinging her rifle, she mounted it, and after dropping her helmet's night visor, guided it out through the shaft into the rapidly gathering dusk.

Puss and Bila followed her on the tandem, with Bila' voice on their war-net muttering, "Helmet smart thing be," As he discovered the capability of his night-vision visor.

*

They rolled along the ridge and then down into the little valley beyond the cabin and stood their bikes in the shelter of the three boulders. Boots pulled the small case from her pack that Bobby had given her the previous morning. Then she led the way past the silent squad transporter and the still smoldering pile that had been Wart Face's copter.

Boots paused in the broad meadow of the larger valley and said, "Looks like a pretty good drop spot to me. What you think Buddy?" as she placed the case on the ground and knelt beside it.

Puss said, "It's OK, if Bobby's boys are any good, and if they really are Bobby's boys that drop in on us. But Buddy, I've already been collected once this week and that'll do me for a lifetime."

"So while you lay out the welcome mat, we're going to cover your big butt from the bushes," Puss gritted as she snapped the safety off of her BAR.

Bila had listened to at Boots' words until Puss readied her rifle, then he stood with the Rigby at the ready and stared into the dark around them.

Puss made the Amerindian sign for, "Beware" and indicated a direction with her chin. He nodded and disappeared into the shadows and she trotted off a right angle to his path.

Boots shook her head, then knelt and opened Bobby's case. She extended

518

its tripod legs and unfolding the instrument, spread its small umbrella antenna and clicked a button on its side.

"Now you all hush," She muttered into her helmet mike as she tuned the instrument and got to her feet again. It hummed for several moments as it came to life then its antenna dish began to swivel around as it aimed up into the night sky, and steadied then a green light began to blink slowly on the instrument's small control panel.

"Stand by Troopers, I think this is them," Boots muttered.

"Sure-sure, Buddy! Bila, watch the sky and get ready."

"Ja Boss," he grunted.

"Buda's Brass betel box!" Boots muttered, "Why does it have to be me that has all these tough smartos around?"

"Because you've grabbed our attention when you started this op, you poor sucko!" Puss snapped into her helmet mike. "So you stay here and be bait, dammit. But me and Bila will wait to see who they really are when they get here!"

"Ja Boss," Boots replied with a sigh. Then she turned to the instrument and clicked its respond button.

Boots watched as the little box swiveled with a tiny hum and aligned its lens with the direction its dish antenna was pointing. Several seconds later the instrument paused, then locked on to a vector almost straight up into the night sky. The green light began to blink very rapidly.

Boots unclipped the small microphone from the instrument and held it to her lips. She paused for a long moment as she thought about many things, then she took a deep breath and began to sing,

"Mine eyes have seen the Glory of the Coming of the Lord..."

Puss' alto sounded softly in their helmets, affirming their new mission and her own hope, "He is trampling out the vintage where the Grapes of Wrath are stored..."

"This good killsong. Like song other this day..." Bila whispered into his mike after the two finished the first verse of the hymn.

*

Charlie's chute was rigged with a transceiver set in the middle of its canopy which let it act as a large dish antenna. The instrument caught a query signal and after sounding a soft note in Charlie's helmet, automatically responded with an acknowledging burst transmission. As soon as he heard the second tone noting that an answering signal he had locked on to his receiver, Charlie responded with another signal of his own for identification. Then he adjusted the opacity of his face shield, and steered his power-chute in a circle as he waited.

A moment later the tightly modulated ultraviolet laser beam of the almost undetectable communicator Bobby had given Boots homed in on the chute's transceiver from below. Since Charlie had been at Rick's Club when Boots had made her announcement, he recognized her voice as she sang the opening line of the hymn.

"Signal's good. ID is good. I say we go!"

"I hear her too. And I like her warsong, so now we go in for good - no matter what!" Luis growled over their warnet as he banked his chute toward Charlie's. The two spiraled down following the invisible laser beam, now steadily tracking Charlie's chute as it descended, along with the twenty-two other chutes puttering along behind.

The rest of the squad formed into a long line after they descended to an altitude of 100 meters and wheeled in a wide circle, as they peered down at the shadowy ground.

"Take us in Charlie," Luis ordered into his mike.

"Going down," Charlie chuckled as he cut his motor. After he felt the click of the propeller folding shut, he began a controlled spill of air from his chute until he pulled it up at the last minute and made a soft landing 20 meters from where Boots stood. Luis landed at Charlie's side a moment later and after the two collapsed their canopies and shed their harnesses, Luis strode to the tall woman.

"¡Hola! Seester!" he said with a smile after he raised his visor. Then he snapped Boots a very formal salute, "Special Squad on duty Ma'am. Permission to bring `um down?" He continued, with a twinkle in his dark eyes.

"Si, Sargento Grande!" Boots murmured as she returned his salute with equal precision.

"Captain Cook say yes! So come on in to roost, mi pollos pocos," he growled over his squad warnet as he winked at Boots.

"Hi Luis, glad you could drop in," Puss announced as she walked out of the shadows, cradling the BAR in her arms.

"Baby Bird got herself a beeg gun now," he grunted as he held out his hand.

"And I'm not the only one," she grinned as she took his hand in a firm grasp, and nodded over Luis' shoulder to Bila who had silently moved to stand behind the man.

Luis turned slowly until he saw Bila, and looked up at him, and at the Rigby the man held casually under one arm.

"You do pretty good sneak Señor. That good for me to know."

"Luis, you'll find that Bila can do lots of things pretty good - including think," Boots murmured as she gazed up at the dim shapes circling overhead.

The troopers began steering their slaved cargo pods down to the meadow into the slight evening breeze. Each trooper slowed the ground speed of the pod he or she controlled to almost a walk after guiding it down to an altitude of three meters, then killed its motor and blew the small explosive bolts holding the shroud lines to the leading edge of the canopy.

The canopies collapsed as the bolts detonated and all the pods thumped on the grass without damage.

When the troopers began to drop in and land themselves, Boots nodded to Puss, "Pretty good drop-in, right Buddy?"

"Not as wide as a church door, nor deep as a well, but `twill do - `twill suffice,"

"Right Luis?"

"You talk funny words Baby Bird," he snapped. "You boss us funny too?"

Puss' eyes froze at Luis' sudden confrontation. She bent and laid her BAR on the grass, and straightening again stared at him through the gloom.

"I have two ways of bossing Sergeant," she snapped. "Both of them are pretty funny but one of my ways won't make you laugh at all. So, which one do you want me to use?"

Luis stared back at the young woman for several heartbeats - long enough for him to realize from her stance and the glare in her eyes that he had finally met his match, or perhaps even a superior.

Bila observed Luis' education silently, except for a slight twitch at the corner of his mouth. Boots did the same.

When he finally realized his moment of truth, Luis gave Puss a slow and casual salute, "I like to laugh Seester, so let's try and stay happy."

Puss smiled at him as brightly as a spring day as she held out her hand instead of returning his salute, "I think we're going to laugh a lot together on this op, Cisco!"

"Si," the proud descendant of Conquistadors smiled as he took Puss' hand and gave it a formal shake, "I think so too, Mi Capitána."

Boots nodded in approval of Puss' handling of Luis' test of her will and authority, and turned to watch the troopers drop down into the shadowed meadow.

She happened to glance at Bila as she did so, and was taken aback when she noted that he was also smiling, and nodding in approval at Puss' response.

"Shat!" Boots whispered to herself. "He really does understand what we say."

Then she dropped that thought and turned back to Puss, "Go take charge, Honey chile", they be all yours," as she gestured toward the troopers, now all on the ground and dealing with their chutes and shedding their harnesses.

Puss nodded, turned and paced ten steps forward and snapped in a parade-ground voice, "Troopers! Hear Me Here!" She waited silently until they had all moved into a loose line before her.

"First, if you have Bobby's new warsuits on, switch to channel fourteen."

After all the troopers grunted their affirmatives, Boots continued, "The IR sat cams are a problem here, so get covered and stay that way.

"Next, deploy your fly-swatters to cover this area and the small valley to the south. We do not know who will come at us, but they won't be happy when they do, and they probably won't be a bunch of dumbo Rats either.

"The H source here is in the basement of the cabin in the south valley. Full charge your capacitors."

"Finally, deploy your personal positions up on the ridges to cover this landing site as well as all of the south valley."

"Beware of foot poppers."

"We have some monitor lines up the main ridge at the head of the south valley and on the other side of its western ridge, so put your monitors along the crest of the one to the east, then select and prepare your positions and fields of fire. This valley will be the kill zone if we are lucky and they take the bait."

"Then after you are finished with these minor duties, you will all rotate down here, where your med person and I will carry out a simple procedure on your butts. You will thank us for many times over in the days to come," Puss ended with a chuckle.

"What this procedure, Mi Capitána," Luis asked.

"We have just found that the ID bugs we all got about five years ago not only tell who you are Cisco, they also tell where you are. Not a good thing in our line of work…"

When the answering chorus of grunted approval died down, Luis asked, "How long this take? We got preety much stuff to do…"

"About five minutes per, unless we gotta' plow through a lot of hair," Puss chuckled to the squad. "And don't worry, we will use med glue on your incisions and you won't feel a thing, almost."

"Any more questions anybody? Cisco?"

"Good plan Ma'am, no questions!" Luis growled from behind her.

"You wait here Sergeant, I have a mission for you," Puss ordered over her shoulder. Then she continued crisply, "Rick's com-spert, front and center, and the rest of go do your jobs."

As the troopers began trotting back into the shadows toward their cargo pods, Charlie strolled to Puss and drawled, "Hi."

She said with a chuckle, "OK, tech-type, what happens if someday the whole world's net crashes in on you key-clackers?"

"Then I'm out of a job. But until that happens, you need me biggers!" he said with a smug grin.

"I'll ignore that for now son. Did you get a bug stuck in you the same time we all did?"

"Yes Ma'am," Charlie responded as he straightened, and changed his attitude.

"You will be in a shielded duty post for the time being, so I will attend to yours after the immediate fun dies down."

"Talk to Kris about your task now while I stand back," Puss paused, then growled into her helmet mike, "And watch these good troopers Just go on, and Do It!"

The squad members all stopped unpacking their gear, and gave the traditional Special Forces' cheer, "Do It!"

When their, "Do It!" sounded in her helmet. it heartened Puss, as well as Boots. Luis merely nodded, and Bila remained silent while he watched the troopers in the green glow of his night visor.

Boots strode to where Charlie stood with Puss after a moment, "Hello, I'm Kris. You're Rick's main com-spert right?"

"I know you," he gasped. "I saw you dance at the Club the other night – and make a toast. I'm Charlie. When do I start?"

Boots held her hand out, "Go get your stuff then hump it to those boulders and load it on the tandem bike that's parked there. After that, I'll take you on a little ride up the hill to Molly's place."

Charlie grasped her hand as he whispered fervently, "Thank you, for what you do," then he turned and trotted back into the night.

Boots shook her head, and blinked for a moment before turning back to where Luis stood, staring at Bila through half-closed eyes. Bila was returning the man's inspection with one of his own - and both were wary.

"Luis!"

"Si, mi Capitána," he replied as he turned to her.

"I'm Kris to my friends, or Seester to you even, OK?" Boots chuckled.

"Theen you call me Cisco if you my friend, dammit!"

"Si Cisco, mi Compañero. But Bila is my friend as well, so you two shake hands dammit!"

At Boots' words, Bila smiled and shifting the Rigby, held out his right hand. Luis glowered for a second then he grunted, "You back me up - I back you up, OK big man?" as he slapped Bila's hand.

"OK friend!" Bila responded in a calm voice then he added earnestly, "When me fly you like teach?"

Luis showed a frown at this strange request, until Boots snapped, "Later on that issue Cisco, and enough of this lover-dover crappo anyway! Can you fly a MULL-25?"

This was the standard "Multiple Use Load Lifter" helicopter used by the Army, one of which stood near them filled with the remains of the Network's latest collection team.

"You mean the one over there? Like a ferkin' bird!" he smiled.

"Good. Repack your chute, then lets go cut your bug, and here's what I would like for you to do while we take care of the rest of your gang."

"It's our gang now, Seester," Luis muttered...

*

"Hang on Charlie, we go now!" Boots ordered as she powered the tandem bike and steered it from the boulders toward Molly's cabin and the ridge above it.

"Oink," he replied.

"Oink?" Boots grunted as she guided the tandem in to Molly's valley.

"I'll explain later Ma'am."

"You do that. I'm the only one who gets to be cryptic in this outfit."

"Yes Ma'am," he gulped as he gripped his handles when Boots took the humming, dirt-kicking machine up the ridge faster than Charlie thought was possible.

*

Luis climbed into the MULL copter and settled himself into the pilot's seat after giving a disdainful glance at the black-clad bodies piled in its cargo compartment. He started the turbines and when the craft came alive, powered its doors closed. When all the indicators showed ready, he engaged its two rotors and as the turbines whined up to operating speed, he moved the joy-stick to begin lift.

The craft lurched slightly, then rose from the ground in a cloud of dust from its prop wash and rapidly gained altitude, as Bila watched up through his night visor with envy.

Luis took the craft up to three thousand meters and turned it to the west toward the Pacific. A moment later he adjusted the copter's autopilot to follow the azimuth he had selected and switched the fuel jettison valve open. Finally, he armed the two incendiary grenades he had taped in the co-pilot's seat beside him, setting them for "impact" before rising from the pilot's seat and entering the cargo compartment.

Luis buckled on his power-chute and opened the side door, "Happy landing, Rat meat!" he sneered as he gave the pile of bodies an ironic salute and stepped into the night.

The MULL 25 continued chopping onward as Luis' chute opened below it and he began flying back toward the valley, guided by the ultraviolet laser that Boots had left running.

"Preety good outfit so far," Luis grunted when his transceiver chimed to acknowledge a link-up with the beam.

The MULL-25 flew steadily toward the west for another fifteen minutes as its fuel drained away. Its turbines stopped then, and their drag through the gear trains prevented the rotors from freely spinning as autogiros, so the craft immediately nosed down and crashed in to on a mountainside near the sea. The two incendiary grenades exploded at the impact and created a significant fireball and heat signature.

The disappearance of the MULL's signal confounded the Network technicals back in S'attl, who had tracked its ID locator all day via the communications satellites. They were already puzzled about what had become of Wart Faces' copter when it had stopped transmitting a signal earlier in the day, for some reason they had not been able to determine.

The technicals had not reported his 'copter as being missing since the squad 'copter had continued to transmit while it remained stationary and apparently on the ground throughout the day.

Now they were forced to face the unpleasant task of reporting the loss of the two signals up their chain of command, as well as the oddly short and aberrant final flight path of the MULL-25. However they ignored the time lapse between the disappearances of the two signals in their report. They also did not report that they had failed to check the day's archived photo images from the survel satellites monitoring the area, and they had forgotten to check the infra-red band altogether...

*

"Governor," Mack said as he rapped on the open door of the Executive Office in the Capitol Building.

"Yes Mack, come in please," Regina replied as she stood from where she had been kneeling and polishing the front of the ornate desk in the center of the room.

"We just intercepted a signal from the Network building to their headquarters in Washington. Looks like Kris has made it happen already. And let me get someone to do that for you, Ma'am."

"Thank you for the thought Mack, but I want to contribute something to our little show tonight, and anyway, I like the smell of furniture polish. It's so clean and new," she smiled as she seated herself behind the desk.

Her expression sobered then as she put on her reading glasses, and chose several sheets of heavy bond paper on the desktop. She selected a stylus and signed one of them and passed it to Mack. As he was reading it, Regina signed the second and slid it across the desk to where he stood and placing a third sheet before her, waited.

Mack scanned the first sheet then after glancing at the second, he looked up. "Congratulations Governor," he said quietly.

"Thank you Mack. I have already commissioned Barbara, and told her these would be forthcoming."

"Now, what about this?" she asked as she slid him the third, unsigned sheet.

He looked down at it on the desktop before him and read it for a long moment.

"Thank you for the honor Ma'am, and I will be proud to serve," he announced in the same quiet tone as he looked up and met her eyes.

"Both I, and the State of Washington appreciate your help Sir," Regina responded with a slight smile as retrieved the third sheet and signed it with a flourish. Then after opening a desk drawer and removing a small velvet case, she rose and stepped around the desk. "Raise your right hand please." When he had done so, she continued.

"Do you, Anthony McAuliffe, solemnly swear or affirm that you will carry out the duties under the Constitution of the State of Washington of the office that you are about to assume, and that as Attorney General, you will faithfully uphold and carry out the statutes promulgated there under?"

"Governor Drake, I do so swear and affirm."

"Thank you Mack," she said with a smile, "But keep your hand up."

"Do you, Anthony McAuliffe, solemnly swear or affirm that as Chief of the Washington State Patrol, you will enforce the constitutionally promulgated statutes of the State of Washington and defend and protect the public order and safety?"

"I do so swear and affirm, Ma'am."

"Thank you again Mack," Regina murmured, as opening the little velvet case, she pinned a heavy gold badge on the left breast of his gray civilian suit.

"But now Chief, it sounds like there's some public order and safety that needs attending to, don't you think?" Regina said with a twinkle in her eye.

"Indeed it does Ma'am, indeed it does. So if you will excuse me, I will attend to my duty."

"This might help you in doing that Mack," Regina muttered, as handed him the last sheet on her desk. It was folded in three, and had "Warrant to Conduct Search" printed across its back panel in bold letters.

"Leroy Bean, an old friend who had retired from the bench just as the war began, has agreed to be our Acting Chief Justice. He told me that he would do it for as long as his ninety-five year-old hand could sign a writ."

"You have many good friends, Governor." Mack said as he accepted the warrant.

"I know Mack," Regina whispered, with a sudden catch in her voice. Then she strode back around the Governor's desk and resumed her seat. Taking a deep breath, she ordered, "Mister Attorney General Sir, now just go on and Do It!" as her eyes sparkled.

"And pass the word to Barbara about my proclamations, if you would please."

"Yes Madam Governor, I will!" he replied as he left the office with a spring in his step.

*

"General Barbara, I am given to understand that you have some assets which you can make available to me," Mack grinned to the wiry woman with the brush-cut hair in Army green, who sat at a field desk under an IR - proof awning erected on the terrace of the Capitol. "And I have some intel from the Governor for you, Ma'am."

"Thank you, Mister AJ, I do to. And if the intel is what we have been waiting for, we are ready to roll!"

"Then roll on War Chick! Regina say Go," Mack whispered as he gripped her thigh under the desk.

Barbara snapped, "About Face!" and all of the aides standing around her field office turned their faces away from her desk...

Mack sighed after several moments, "More later, OK? We have work to do now."

Barbara gasped, "Alright dammit, but not too much later, OK!"

"Yes General, as you command." Mack grinned as he straightened up.

"Don't look smug in front of my troops you old goat! You just got an intro..."

"Yes General, and I promise that I will remember your words later - but for now, I want troops, Dammit!" Mack growled as he strode out through the encircling line of military aides, all facing outward from the command tent, as they tried to hide their smiles of approval of their two leaders.

*

"You have all taken the oath that deputizes you as members of the Washington State Patrol" Mack announced through his bull-horn to the four hundred members of the Washington National Guard battalion standing in ranks before him in the parking lot behind the Capitol building.

Many Mark VIIs, transporters, and military sedans were aligned behind their ranks and all of the vehicles had "WSP" freshly stenciled in large letters on their sides, and the sedans were equipped with blue lights on their roofs as well.

"You will all remember that it is your duty to act as sworn peace officers of the State of Washington, and to respect the rights of any persons you take into lawful custody under a lawful warrant of arrest."

Then Mack grinned like a skull, which caused a thrill throughout the front ranks arrayed before him and roared, "Troopers! Form Up and Move Out! Go to your missions! First Company, follow me!"

*

Two mark VIIs rumbled down the streets of the old part of S'attl and wheeling their machines with sparking screeches from their treads, the drivers took up positions before both the front and rear doors of the Network building. They swiveled their turrets to cover the entrances.

Mack stepped from a military sedan with blue lights flashing from the new rack on its roof and strode to the speaker on the wall beside the rear door of the building.

"Washington State Patrol here," he growled into its grille, "We have a Warrant to Search! Open this door. Now!"

Mack looked at his watch and after thirty seconds had passed without a reply, then waved to the driver of the Mark VII and stepped back.

The driver rammed her Mark VII into the overhead door and collapsed it. Then she backed up and rammed the front of her tank all the way through the opening a second time and swept away all remaining parts of the doorframe. With its front still in the entryway, she swiveled her forward turret toward the guard booth to the right of what had been the door.

The functionary in the booth was scrambling to escape when she depressed her gun as much as possible, selected a round, and fired. The blast from the round which was only a blank salute, was directed over the top of the booth because of her gun's mechanical limitations, but the effect of its force in the confined space of the entryway ended all opposition the Patrol's access to the building…

The driver put her Mark VII into reverse and centering her front turret, backed the machine out onto the street again. She swiveled it about its own axis with more screeching and sparks from the pavement, and parked along the street's centerline. She loaded both her turret's guns with anti-personnel rounds and swiveled them to cover each direction along the street.

Mack waved toward the doorway, and two squads of deputized MPs hit the street, loosened their pistols and formed in a line before him.

"Everyone this building is considered to be a material witness," he growled, "And will be held only as such, until and if other charges may be warranted. Now let's go! Armor suits first at each entry!" He waved his squads forward through the space that used to be a door and the armor-suited troopers lead the way, with large WSP brassards prominent on their shoulders.

"We're going in the back now, what's the word out front?" Mack growled into his comset.

"We're in the lobby but the elevator is inoperative and the lobby door is too small to get a VII in to open the booth."

"Anyone in the booth?"

"No Sir."

"Well use a sticky, but place it so you don't break the controls."

"Yes Sir! That's what I was waiting to hear Sir!"

"Well son, don't wait next time, use your initiative," Mack growled to the section leader.

"I will Sir!" Then Mack heard the "whomp" of an exploding limpet grenade over his comset. "It's just that I'm used to fighting Chin," the section leader continued calmly, "Not our own people, Sir."

"Good point son. It's hard to know what's right in a civil situation, but I hope you can learn fast."

"Thank you Sir, and we've got the elevator working now."

"Good, go catch some Rats, and remember, armor-suits first at each entry, OK!" Mack snapped.

"Yes Sir, and thanks."

"For what son?" Mack chuckled, "You're just learning on the job."

*

The Military Police teams raced through the Network building and the officers arrested every person they encountered who was not in a holding cell in the basement. Those unfortunates were taken into very gentle protective custody and carried immediately to a military hospital. The others were loaded into the transporters the police had brought with them, and when they needed more transporters, Mack requested them from Barbara, when he realized the large number of "witnesses" they were taking into custody.

The team that opened the computer and broadcast control center on the fourth floor had been told to handle any persons they encountered without feet with care for those persons, and for themselves. Therefore the electronics expert with team was able to disconnect the bombs attached to the ankle-stumps of five young people who had been imprisoned in the building.

The tears of relief from the three young men and two girls who were now released from a bondage that they had thought unbreakable wetted the uniforms of the troopers who carried them down for transport to the hospital...

As all of the initial entry teams discovered and removed the persons they found still in the Network building, Mack's computer forensic team followed behind and removed computer memory units and sequestered all other items that might prove to be evidentiary. This team was not particularly skilled at investigating their own countrymen but they had been very effective when Chin command centers had been taken, therefore they used their same tactic in the Network building, "If it don't look important, it probably is. So take it all!"

The team was tireless in their work and took vast quantities of data based on this dictum, including witnessed pics and vids of everything they found in the Network building. They didn't finish their work until noon of the next day.

*

Mack had received an organization chart of the S'attl Network office, which one of Rick's experts had moled from their net and used the information to direct a second unit to arrest those Network personnel who did not live in the main building.

The sergeant in charge had gulped when she had noted the locations of the addresses she was tasked to raid after Mack handed her the list, then she had said, "If you say so, Sir!"

"Sergeant, these people are wanted for questioning in our courts by your Governor! I don't say so, Regina Drake does!"

"Yes Sir!" the woman snapped, then marched to one of the military sedans, and waiving her two squads to follow her, climbed in and ordered its driver to the addresses Mack had given her. The blue lights began blinking on its roof as they drove away.

*

Luis cut his power and drifted down to land easily in the large meadow again. He had unlatched his harness and was folding his chute when Puss walked to him.

"Good job Cisco, glad you're on this op. How's your butt?" she grinned as she switched off the UV laser beacon and folded it back into its small case.

"Me too Lettle Bird, and it still got lotsa' hair on eet, OK!" he replied with a slight grin. "But sure look like someone around here know how to kill good."

"I figgered you would have hair on your butt, Cisco, but thanks. These Rats were easy. They always are, but now comes the stiff part. Kris is going back to Olympia tonight and real soon, she will transmit a file to Molly from there. Molly with Charlie's help, will then mole into the Network and broadcast the file over all their channels, whether they like it or not. Super soon after that broadcast, we figure the Network and their government buddies will come looking to shut down our direct-to-the-people info channel.

"Luis, that must not happen, OK," Puss finished quietly.

"I might be dumb ground grunt, but I can smell some light now at the end of thees ferkin' tunnel we all been in so long, and it smell like roses to me. So I will not let that light go out. But what force you theenk come at us?"

"Thanks Luis, I am suddenly smelling roses too, but remember we're in Canada, or whatever passes for it these days. That's why your warsuits are sanitized."

"I know that," he replied patiently. "I double check my squad before we leave S'attl."

"Do you also know about Ottawa's Blue Gang?"

"Some barracks cow flop only. But they government gave up out here long time ago."

"When I was a kid in school, I was taught that governments never give up, and don't like anyone who talks back at them either. I believed my teachers then, and I sure as hell know that they spoke true now," she said with steel in her voice. "So my friend, get your guys ready for a major attempt to shut Molly down, which will be coming at us from Ottawa major soon."

*

"It's damp in here," Molly announced after she finished demonstrating her computer's capabilities to Charlie, "Good thing these Chin field 'puters are just about everything-proof." What about yours?"

"Oh, it's good too, so it can live in this cave with yours. I've brought a folding bench and seat too, so now you don't have to squat on the floor and hold your keypad on your knees either," Charlie smiled to the serious young girl, whom he had immediately liked when Boots had introduced them, and now was beginning to respect as well.

"That's nice, 'cause I don't squat so good these days anyway," Molly giggled.

"OK you two technoids, quit showing your thingies to each other, and get on with figuring how we'll do our mission from in here," Boots announced in a friendly growl. "And Jimmy, let's step outside and talk security for a short bit, before I have to go let a plane catch me,"

"Ja Boss!" both youngsters responded immediately.

"Ja Boss?" Charlie wrinkled his eyebrows.

"That acknowledgement of an order is an old tradition in our outfit," Molly proudly replied. "But let's talk linkages and transmissions now, OK?"

"Good, I brought a bunch of different linkers, and I had guessed that you had one of these `puters." His eyes grew cold before he continued after a second, "Because the Chin left a bunch of them behind when they finally ran."

Boots watched the two begin their serious collaboration then nodded Jimmy toward the adit passageway.

"Son. No make that Trooper Four, I will stay on guard here for now. You grab one of the extra IR capes in the rear panniers of the tandem and then trot down the hill and find Marybell. Tell her that I want two of her troopers with a fly-swatter to dig in up here as protection for Molly. Say I want them to be her best and meanest, OK! And I want her to do their bug extractions first. Also, be sure to give my message to her only so you don't mess with her span of control."

"Ja Boss! Jimmy snapped, "And don't worry, my dad taught me all about unity of command, Ma'am"

"Like I said before, you had a good dad, and he was a good teacher but for now, just Do It!"

"Ja Boss," the boy snapped again over his shoulder as he dashed back into the chamber in the hillside. He emerged a moment later wrapped in a cape, and began running down toward the little valley without another word.

"This whole op is one way damn long shot," Boots muttered as she turned and walked back to join Molly and Charlie, "But kids like him do make our odds some better."

Molly announced with a smile over her shoulder, "We've figured out how to link these suckers Ma'am, and we'll have giga-power at least!" then she squealed, "You won't believe what I can do, it's going to be way off the scale!"

Charlie had unfolded and positioned the battlefield computer stand and so it now had both their computers and displays set up on it.

"Yep, and the dishes I brought are way more discrete compared to the ones the Durwood person used," Charlie added. "We'll put them up in the trees around this place and they don't have to be wired in. They use UV laser from this linker," he smiled with pride as he held up a dull-colored, multiple-lensed ball the size of a grapefruit.

"So, how do your dishes see through the trees and hit the sats with their signal?" Boots asked with a cocked eyebrow.

Charlie's chest swelled with pride, "I designed them so that each dish has a nano-`puter with a program that continually runs up and down the frequencies, to avoid leaf and needle interference from trees as the wind moves the branches. Then whenever there's a gap in the foliage, the dish does a burst transmission to the sat."

"Good," Boots nodded with respect. Then she added with a wicked smile, "But what if the wind don't blow?"

Charlie grinned, "Each dish also has an IR pulse laser, so it can blast a hole through the bushes if it needs to."

"Good again," Boots smiled. "Sounds like you two are going to do the job right, so get on with it, while I grab a few nods until Jimmy gets back with the bulldogs to guard your door."

"By the way, I am loaded and locked and the slightest funny footstep will set me off biggers. So while you do your task, be assured that I'm on guard, even if my eyes are closed."

*

Boots bounded to her feet an hour later with her pistol in a combat grip as she covered the entry to their rock chamber.

"It's me, er us," Jimmy gulped, as he looked down the large bore of Boots' ancient .44 Magnum.

"OK, Son. You and your guys come on in." Then she smiled evilly over shoulder to Molly and Charlie, huddled at their computers.

"Didn't think I could do it, did you?"

"No Ma'am," Molly gulped, as she leaned her little rifle back against the rock wall. "But I sure do now…"

Boots smiled, as she nodded toward the girl's rifle, "You did correct, Trooper Two. Always have a backup!"

Then she turned to the two large troopers who had walked into the chamber behind Jimmy.

"Guys, meet Molly. You have already met Jimmy and you know Charlie already."

"What you will be doing here is protecting a most vital asset to the Restoration. If you believe in the Restoration, you will guard these three and this site well."

Their growl of affirmation caused Boots to nod, and Molly's eyes to shine.

"The Rat's a minor force in what we are doing, except for their top people. Those are a part of the big apparat that the military Governor works for covertly, and that apparat has a lot of tentacles into places that aren't widely known. So expect heavy hits from different forces that may come from strange places, but there won't be any of ours that come at you."

"Why?" the burley corporal asked.

"Because."

"Because why Ma'am?"

"Because I think there is a consensus all across our force Trooper."

"I know that Ma'am, I just wanted to see if you knew that too."

"I do now, Sir," Boots smiled as she tapped her brow in a friendly salute to him, "And I hope your butts aren't too sore."

"We'll live Ma'am," the corporal replied as he gave her a very formal salute, and turned to the trooper standing at his side, "Let's deploy now, and make this place safe like the Captain said!"

When the two had trotted out through the adit, Boots turned to Molly, "Come here Trooper Two, and gimme' a hug."

Boots held the girl in a strong embrace for a moment, then ruffled her hair, "You're gonna' be OK, Right?"

"Right, Ma'am! "Real right!" the girl whispered up to Boots, with pride and love on her face.

"I knew it Kid," Boots murmured as she gave Molly a final squeeze. "You guys are good too, right?" she smiled to Charlie and Jimmy.

"Ja Boss," they both snapped.

"Then I'm gone," she grinned as she saluted the three and wrapped her cape around her shoulders as she turned to leave. "But don't worry, I'll write if I find work," she yelled over her shoulder as she trotted out through the adit.

"Good troops. Damn if I don't have good troops," she whispered as she trotted on down toward the little valley,

*

Boots walked to where Luis stood within the three boulders, now the temporary command post for his squad's deployment as well as its de-bugging station. They were all under a canopy of IR capes. He held a flashlight trained on the bare bottom of a female trooper lying on her stomach between Puss and a woman with a small red cross on her shoulder. The two were kneeling on either side of her and Puss was just closing her incision as the medic placed the device in one of the small containers.

"How much faster are the smooth ones compared to the hairy ones?" Boots asked with a chuckle.

"'Bout a minute less," Puss grunted, "Except for Cisco here. He's got 'lotsa' hair on his butt so it took us twice as long with him!" she replied a wink to the sergeant.

The medic and their patient giggled.

"Any more sass at you leader," Luis grunted, "An' I make eet real hairy for you two troops anyway. I gotta' take these sheet from mi' good frien' Baby Bird, but you war chickies work for me!" Then his teeth flashed in a smile.

"Are we dead now Cybill?" the woman on the ground asked in a theatrical whisper.

"Not yet - at least I don't think," the medic deadpanned as she winked at Luis.

"Enough pad time! Pull you pants back up and go do you job dammit!" Luis ordered.

"Ferk, and I was having so much fun!" the trooper snorted as she bounded to her feet and nonchalantly pulled her black lace panties back up and zipped her warsuit.

"Golly Gee Gal, they didn't issuing snuggs like that when I used to be a trooper," Boots murmured. Then she continued as the tough woman blushed, sort of, and Luis laughed, "How many more to go?"

"We got them all now, except for Charlie," Puss said as she mock-glared at Luis, "And just because you picked on my patient, you get to strike the tent!"

"Si, mi Capitána," Luis smiled.

"Good. Now to switch subjects to the task at hand, anybody got a chute with a lot of power left?" Boots asked.

"I had these guys full charge one for you while you were up there in the hole in the hill," Puss grinned as she got to her feet and Cybill began cleaning the instruments and repacking her med kit for her next use.

"Damn! Extra tofu in the rations really is a good thing!"

"Hey, I go with Bila every time, because he really knows about food!"

"So, what do I know about?"

"Winning, I hope. Now strap this thing on and get the hell on with your job Buddy." Puss snapped, with tears suddenly glistening in her eyes.

"Ja Boss," Boots murmured as she hefted on the chute pack and fitted its straps around her shoulders and thighs. When she had the harness and controls adjusted to her satisfaction, she grinned, "Permission to get gone Ma'am?"

"Only if you come back again, dammit," Puss whispered. Then she pulled Boots' head down for a long and deep kiss, before reaching around to give her a very authoritative slap on her bottom.

Luis just shook his head, and followed Boots and Puss as they walked in silence out into the main meadow.

Luis and Puss opened Boots' chute and spread its canopy out on the grass behind her, then Boots closed her visor, took ten running steps to inflate her chute as she gave her motor full power - and lifted up into the night sky.

*

She banked her power-chute it to a turn once she was above the tree line, and then began soaring upward in a lazy spiral.

As her hum of her motor thrust her upward at a rate of 130 meters per minute, she could only make out the landform below through her night-vision visor, until the edge of the waning moon appeared over a ridge and added its light to the night.

Boots drank in the beauty of the monochrome landscape below as she continued to rise until she checked the instrument cluster strapped on her wrist.

"Five hundred more to go before pickup level," Boots muttered as she clicked on the transponder in the top of her chute, "Then we head straight east like the man said, while hoping like hell that someone knows what tha' ferk they're doing up here…"

*

"Signal, Sir."

"Anybody we know?" the pilot asked.

The copilot grunted, "The box says it's her anyway."

"Let's go then", the pilot said as he banked the Queen Bee into a turn toward the east and descended to an altitude slightly below 2,500 meters.

*

Boots heard the chime of the transponder in her helmet. It indicated a contact, and that it had received a recognition signal.

"I'm really getting too old for this physical stuff! When do I get to sit around and just make policy, dammit?" she whispered to the sky as readied the catch line coiled at her waist, and steered her power-chute steadily eastward at a precise altitude of 2,500 meters.

*

"Contact on radar, and it's one of our chutes."

"Good," the pilot muttered. He ordered into his intercom, "Jumpmaster, get ready to welcome visitors aboard!"

"Sir!" the compact woman responded as she buckled into a safety harness and clipped to the hook-up cable, then keyed the switch that slid the large port in the roof of the cargo hold open. The navigator stepped in to the compartment a moment later and after harnessing up himself and also clipping on, made his way back to join her in the billowing wind-stream from the open hatch above them.

The copilot slowed the speed of the twin-tailed aircraft again while increasing the thrust of the ducted fans in its wings as the pilot steered it on a steady course to pass under the power-chute they both could now see hanging in the air in front of them.

"Well, well. Lookey here! Someone is trying to pick this old chickie up, wonder who?" Boots muttered into her helmet mike.

"Only people who have been told to use channel fourteen, Captain Cook," sounded in her helmet.

"Bobby really does his job well," Boots thought as the large aircraft slowly moved from her rear and stabilized below her and then matched her airspeed.

Boots maneuvered her power-chute until she was hanging just above the open hatch in the roof of the almost hovering aircraft, then she released her catch line.

Its weighted tip dropped into the open hatch five meters below her and the jumpmaster grabbed it. She cleated it to a stanchion and then changed the compartment lights from night-vision red to white.

Boots killed her motor at this signal. It folded its propeller as she triggered the explosive bolts holding the front shrouds to her chute. The fabric collapsed and she dropped through the open hatch as the jumpmaster hauled in the catch line. As soon as Boots thumped on to the mat on the compartment deck, the jumpmaster began pulling in Boots' streaming chute while the navigator un-clipped her harness from her shroud lines and un-snapped the motor's straps on her back.

"Nice of you to drop in, Captain Cook," the man grinned, "And glad we could catch your act!"

"You're glad? I'm ferkin' ecstatic!" Boots gasped...

*

The Queen Bee landed at Boing AFB, bucking a slight crosswind on the runway its pilot selected. Ordinarily he would have taken it down on the main strip and landed directly into the wind. When he had given his selection to the tower however and had been questioned by the duty civilian controller, he had replied, "WANG flight A34476/T, training for adverse conditions. "You clear us for runway 02. Now!"

The civilian controller had gulped, and responded, "Yes Sir!" in a shaky voice.

"Thank you Controller. You guys do a much good job," rumbled in her headset, and caused her to blush with pride as she watched the Queen Bee's pilot bring the craft down at a slight angle into the crosswind.

He taxied the craft to the end of the landing strip and then wheeled it around on to the taxiway where he had first loaded Bobby's troopers. Once again, a side door was out of the view of the tower...

The gate that wasn't officially there slid back again, and a heavy military truck drove up behind the aircraft. It stopped and doors immediately opened, and five troopers in warsuits scrambled out to form a defensive ring in the shadows around and under the aircraft.

When they were positioned, the unit leader tapped his helmet mike three times, then three times again. A moment later a luxury taxi drove through the gate and pulled up beside the plane.

The jumpmaster opened the side door of the aircraft. Boots stepped to the edge of the darkened compartment and was tensing to jump down to the tarmac when Waldo and Bobby leaped from the taxi and braced themselves below the doorway.

Bobby looked up to her, "Now you can jump without breaking something, dammit!"

Boots leaped in to space and held her legs straight out as she fell in a sitting position. Bobby and Waldo caught her easily in their arms and after a bounce, flipped her to her feet.

"Thanks guys."

"You're welcome, but now get your Restoration butt in motion, Ma'am!"

"Yassa' Massa' Bobby!" she smiled again, but only for a second before she asked, "Is Regina secure and is the Capitol? And did you bring my bag?"

"Yes to your last, and also yes to your first two questions."

"The Governor was actually covered within two hours after you went back north yesterday Ma'am. Waldo did such a good sneak that the guards did not have a whiff, until about another two hours ago, Ma'am."

"What happened then?"

"That's when a column of Mark VIIs rolled up and took their gate and gate house down. Seems Governor Drake got busy today after she had a com-chat with Mack about a force that flew north this morning."

"Among other things after that discussion, she commissioned Barbara as Adjutant General of the Washington National Guard. General Barbara then immediately passed on a hot Stand-by to a big bunch of former Guardsmen. They slapped their patches back on and moved to assembly points she and Mack had selected."

"Why did this happen two hours ago?"

"Rick's number two com-spert got an intercept of a signal going to Boss Rat that one of their `copters, as well as one of General Butler's had gone missing up in B.C."

"Since this message also indicated the probable loss of a number Network security personnel who had no business in that area," Bobby continued with a straight face while Waldo grinned like a skull, "Governor Drake had no choice but to order the Guard to active duty to "quell" lawless behavior that the current local authority could not control."

Bobby finally relaxed his expression, and drawled, "When you decide to do Incident, Ma'am, you sure do it fast - and big."

"Why thank you, Suh. So kind of you to notice," Boots smiled for a second. "Now we go, OK!"

"Yes Ma'am!" he replied as he saluted her, and motioned her toward the taxi.

"Troopers, you lead," Waldo ordered the five guards, who immediately piled back in their truck. He flashed a red LED flashlight twice at the perimeter fence as he jumped in the driver's seat of the taxi, and followed the military truck back through the unofficial gate.

Both vehicles paused outside of it until the other five members of Waldo's security squad scrambled from their cross-fire positions along the fence, then closed the gate and piled into a second military truck and followed the taxi as the small convoy drove toward Olympia.

*

"Where are her guards now?" Boots asked quietly as their convoy passed along the fence that sealed off the Capitol complex.

"Being questioned about their crime, of impersonating peace officers,"

Waldo chuckled.

"When you guys do take charge you do it way fast, and biggers too," Boots laughed, with a snort. Their convoy drove through the shattered remains of the wire gates a moment later and halted before the columned façade of the stately old Capitol building. Boots stepped out of the taxi, and gasped.

Every window in the imposing building was now un-curtained, and glowed with warm light. The canvass that had obscured the proud title on its pediment had been torn away and high atop the building, the Stars and Stripes fluttered beside the vivid green Washington State flag on poles before its floodlit dome.

"Congratulations Bobby," Boots said quietly as she gazed around at the Mark VII fighting vehicles with WNG newly painted on their armored sides. They were parked in strategic locations around the building with their turrets trained to cover all approaches, "This operation is starting to look very competent." She also sensed, rather than saw the dim shapes of many ground troops deployed in the shadows around the grounds.

"We had to blow a small back door for initial entry, but the front door is now open for you Ma'am, and Governor Drake is waiting in the Executive office," Bobby said in a formal voice as he saluted Boots.

"Thank you Commander," she replied with equal formality. She turned, and was picking up her bag when Bobby said, "Allow me, Ma'am," as he reached for it. "It's more appropriate this way."

"Thank you again Commander, you pay me a very high honor," Boots said as they walked toward the main stairs of the building and began climbing its forty-two steps. Bobby just smiled and followed one pace behind Boots. Waldo remained behind and deployed his squad around their three vehicles.

Boots muttered under her breath as they neared the top of the flight, "Ilea ferkin jacta est way biggers now,"

"In hic ista viratas, Ma'am..."

When Boots and Bobby finally stood before the imposing double doors of the building the two guardsmen in crisp Army green guarding the entry snapped from parade rest to attention and presented arms.

Boots returned their honor with a grave salute while Bobby stood at attention slightly behind her, as military courtesy dictated. The two guardsmen slammed the butts of their rifles to the ground and snapped back to attention then resumed their position of parade rest while staring ahead with faces of stone.

Boots noted that the woman wore as many campaign ribbons on her chest as the man in the second before the doors opened, and the Chief Sergeant Major of the Washington National Guard in full-dress uniform welcomed her into the building.

"Permission to return to my command, Ma'am?" Bobby asked as he handed Boots' bag to the Chief Sergeant Major.

"Permission granted Commander. Keep up the good work."

"Thank you Ma'am, I intend to," Bobby replied as he saluted and doing an about-face, marched back down the steps.

The grizzled Chief Sergeant Major, his sleeves stiff with service marks and his chest glittering with decorations, announced, "Governor Drake will see you now Ma'am," as he gestured toward the ornately marbled main hallway.

*

"I've got a bleep!" Molly whispered from where she sat at the field bench, staring intently at the screen of Charlie's computer. He had linked it to her Chin computer, and thus multiplied their combined capabilities by five orders of magnitude.

Charlie leaped up from where he was sitting cross-legged on his cape to escape the damp of the cavern floor. He leaned over her shoulder.

Jimmy grabbed his assault rifle and trotted out of the chamber to where the burly corporal stood in the shadows on guard in front of the chamber's opening.

"Party time coming up, like my dad used to say," Jimmy hissed.

"Thanks," the corporal, a Hokkaido Indian responded. Then he grinned, "I got to fight with Big Mike on some ops a while back. Looks like history might repeat, no?" he murmured as he lifted his visor and tapped his helmet mike six times in rapid succession.

Jimmy gulped, "I sure hope so Sir," as he turned and dashed back into the chamber. He heard Molly squeal as he entered, "Charlie, you did it! It's coming through!"

"That part was easy," Charlie replied calmly. "Sending is more tasky – after you have finished the real work of doing the mole."

"Un-huh," Molly nodded absently as she concentrating on the hyper-compressed file going through its numerous stages of unfolding. When the process was finally complete the question "OPEN?" appeared on Molly's display.

"Guys, I'm sorry, but I've got to view this first and then do the mole without distraction. So if you don't mind, step outside – Please," she announced in a little voice that Jimmy and Charlie obeyed without question.

*

Molly called from the mouth of the adit a half hour later, "I'm ready now," with a catch in her voice.

Jimmy rushed to her, "What's wrong?"

"Nothing - nothing ever again," she whispered. "Come back in and see why."

Molly turned and seated herself with a grunt at the computer again as Jimmy and Charlie gathered behind her. "Can you hook this feed to your warnet channel 14?" she asked Charlie.

"Just you watch Ma'am," he smiled as he leaned over her shoulder and entered a short series of code lines on her display with rapid keystrokes. After a second the word "link" appeared.

"Hit that and you will have a hook-up to our warnet here for both voice and vid, which will be secure from back-feed to your main transmission."

"Thanks, Charlie. And I'm sorry I made you guys go outside but,"

"Big nada Molly," Charlie interrupted. "You gotta' do it your way, OK!"

"Yep," Jimmy added, "'Specially when your way is way good."

"Thanks guys," Molly sighed, then unconsciously mimicked Puss as she growled, "But let's Do It Dammit!" as she cued "link" and switched on the computer's microphone.

"Hello all you soldiers on this net, I'm Molly. Please excuse me if I don't talk your mil talk right, but set your helmet vid screens to this channel," then she continued with sudden passion, "And watch the start of something new when it comes up!"

She switched the mike off, and after splitting the screen, brought up the hundreds of lines of code she had just entered, and the thousands of lines that the linked computers had generated in response to her initiating commands.

Molly tensely scanned them as they scrolled on the display, and occasionally stopped to enter final corrections muttering, "Shat" under her breath at each one.

Charlie and Jimmy stood at her back and almost without breathing watched her do what only she could do, capture total control of the Network's world-wide broadcasting system.

Finally Molly slumped against the flimsy backrest of the field bench and flexed her fingers for a moment, before muttering, "It's main view time out here, and it will hit them right at late-night back east." A moment later she sighed, as she slowly raised her right hand and keyed "Execute" with a delicate finger-stroke.

"What about the rest of the world?" Charlie whispered.

"It will repeat it every three hours until I stop it."

*

Boots watched her own image appear on the vid screen in the Governor's office after an inane 1-X Network show was suddenly blanked out. "Is that the impression I give?" she muttered as she saw herself, strongly commanding in her black silk suit with her hair up and standing before a blue backdrop. The image zoomed in to her head and shoulders as she began the opening announcement while looking solemnly out from the screen.

"Good evening ladies and gentlemen, and citizens of the State of Washington. Your program has been interrupted for an announcement of critical importance to us all.

"My name is Kristina Hamier, and I now direct you to the Executive Office in our Capitol Building in Olympia where our Governor, Regina Drake will address you."

The scene changed from Boots to a brief exterior shot of the Capitol Building, blazing with lights and its flags proudly flying high, then it changed to the Executive Office, and the Governor.

Regina was seated behind an ornately carved mahogany desk inlaid with redwood, and the great Seal of Washington State was displayed on the wall behind her flanked by the American and the State flags.

"Good evening my fellow citizens. My name is Regina Drake," she announced crisply, "And I am Governor of the State of Washington under Sections 3 and 10 of Article III of our State Constitution.

"My predecessor, Governor Rayburn Smith was elected to this office in 2240 by the voters of Washington State at the same time I was elected to the office of Lieutenant Governor.

"Unfortunately Governor Smith was a casualty in the recent war, therefore I became acting Governor upon his death under the provisions of Section 10 of our Constitution. Additionally since no state elections have been held subsequent to his death, I am still your acting Governor under the provisions of Section 3," she concluded briskly.

She leaned forward then and clasping her hands on the desk, continued with a solemn voice as her eyes projected an electric authority from the screen.

"It has come to my attention that many crimes, incursions and other activities which are forbidden by the statutes and regulations of Washington State have recently occurred, despite any efforts by present authorities to prevent them.

"Therefore I have, and only with great reluctance," which caused both Boots, and Puss watching on her helmet eye-screen up in Molly's valley, to snort, "Taken the following actions," Regina said with a sadness that was only slightly theatrical...

"My predecessor, Governor Smith was forced to declare a state of emergency for our State in 2244 with Proclamation WS-143002 when we were suddenly attacked and invaded by the enemy.

"Today, May 8th, 2276, I have signed Proclamation WS-143003 which ends that declaration of emergency and returns civil rule to our State and communities under the laws of Washington State and our various local ordinances.

"Also today under the provisions of section 2 of our State Constitution, I have raised the militia by activating our National Guard and Air National Guard to enforce our laws and to assist local jurisdictions in enforcing their ordinances.

"In addition, I have used my powers under Sections 10 and 42 of our Constitution to appoint an Acting State Attorney General, an Acting U.S Representative and two Acting U.S. Senators to represent Washington State in the Congress of the United States.

"I have also, under the provisions of Section 15 of Article II, appointed an acting Mayor of the City of Seattle."

Regina paused then and smiled as a mother would to her child, "Finally, I have scheduled general state-wide elections for six months from today, and I am eager to advise and assist our communities and counties in scheduling elections for their local officials."

Then Regina closed by saying, "Citizens of Washington State, thank you for your interest. You may rest assured that your safety and, and independence are my only concerns."

"Good evening."

As Boots and Regina watched, the vid screen then flicked back to a shot of the Capitol building and stayed that way. Five minutes later, when the vid screen still showed only the building with its flags flying proudly, Boots laughed to Regina, "Damn! Our Molly-gal is very, very good, don't you think? She's making them take time to think – all over the world!"

"Kristina, when Mack brought you into my garden I first liked you instinctively. Then I was impressed with your art - and your concept of effecting change. Both gave me some glimmer of hope after the years of dull grayness that I have endured. But in the last few days you have given me back my youth, and my fire. Thank you…"

Boots gazed at the almost white-haired little woman whose dark eyes now sparkled with power as well as life, then she grinned crookedly, "Like they say, "chewing the string doesn't prove the pudding", and "wait 'till the credit clears the bank.

"We've got a long bumpy road ahead."

"I know that dammit," Regina said, "I'm not innocent about your world, even though I have been sealed away from it for too many years. But, don't forget that I am also a politician and as such, I have an exceptional ability to calibrate people when I first meet them," Regina continued in a severe tone, "Therefore, I know of what I speak. We will win!"

"Thank you Ma'am," Boots sighed as she bowed her head.

*

"Damn if this Restoration group ain't some kind of strong medicine," Puss' father grunted as their vid screen continued showing the Capitol in Olympia. This was after the vid that his wife had scripted – replete with heaving bosoms but not much else really prurient, had been pre-empted and Regina Drake had tossed out her stun grenade.

"You think that 3Cee saw it?" Puss' mother asked, just as the thicker comset beside their bed chimed…

"Bird Nose!" she heard the Congressman yell, "What the hell is your bunch trying to do? Start a revolution?"

"No, 3Cee, a Restoration…"

"Good! These same noises have just started showing up on my private intel-net from Cali and Alaska all of a sudden as well. Looks like your bunch has started a trend," Charles chuckled. His voice then changed, "One that I'm sure has been noted in that House down the Hill from us…"

"I'd expected that," Puss' father grunted as his wife listened on the auxiliary earplug. "Nice to have been proven right once again."

"If you're talking about that time we had leave in Yakima, remember that it was a female truck-loader after all!"

"Sure-sure, that's what all those robots morph into whenever they want a quick fix..."

"Curse you Bird Nose. You haven't seen the last of me!" Charles chuckled again.

"Certainly hope not. Now, just go do your job and keep me informed about the degree of Bradney's frazzlement."

"Do It," Charles growled as he clicked off.

"Another good trooper is on our side. That's nice to know, M'Dear," Puss' father muttered as he wrapped his long arm around his wife's small waist.

*

"This is good, right?" Mud Puddle whispered as she caressed Charles' shoulders and back where they lay on the large bed in his house in the power-elite area of Georgetown, until she dug her fingers into his muscles and grunted in response to the sudden violent urgency of his need.

"Yes. Is GOOD – Good – good," he finally sighed.

Then he whispered into her ear, "And you will learn how good you can be in other things in the days to come soon my love - perhaps even in killing rather than healing..."

***

Chapter 26
The Reaction

May 8, 2276 AD,
Washington, D.C. And British Columbia

"What-is-going-on?" Marvin Jacobs hissed as he stabbed the all-stations button on his desk intercom. He was glairing at the many vid screens that lined the walls of his office in the Network's Washington headquarters. All of them were showing the same picture, a view of the Washington State Capitol building in Olympia, where they should have been showing the many different shows the Network had scheduled for broadcast in prime evening time.

Marvin wore a hastily-tied dressing gown and his hair was tousled. He had rushed to his office in from his suite in the building moments before when he received an emergency call. He quivered with rage and shock at the confused babble crackling from the desk speaker. He screamed, "One-at-a-time!" Then he whispered in a voice of palatable menace, "What is going on here? Sat feed - what happened?"

"We don't know Sir," the answering voice gulped. "We lost all of our uplinks just before that broadcast and even now that it's over, we still can't get them back."

"It will be best for you if you do so soon." Marvin screamed again, showering the intercom with salvia.

"Engineering!"

"Yes Sir?"

"Did all the links go at once?"

"No Sir."

"Well then, where did this start first?" he hissed. "And if I must do your job for you, I don't need you do I?"

"N-no Sir," the voice from Engineering gulped. "As far as we can tell someone grabbed a couple of our sats in the Northern Hemisphere first, but the grab spread almost immediately to all of others and they are still not responding to our control signals."

"Find out which ones were the first to be grabbed, Now!"

"Yes Sir!"

At that moment Miss Petruschika stepped into his office without knocking and silently passed him a note. He glanced at it, and slapped his forehead before waiving her out and screaming into his speaker, "Ten Minutes! I want answers in ten minutes. And normal feed restored dammit!"

The echoes of his voice were still ringing in the room when all of the vid screens blinked, and began showing the usual miscellany of Network shows being aired once again.

"Hey! Good work, whoever..."

"I'm sorry Sir" the voice from Engineering interrupted, "We didn't do that. Someone just gave us back control."

"Dammit!" Marvin screamed as he jabbed the intercom off and struggled to bring himself back under control. He took a number of deep breaths then pausing after he counted his pulse, he lifted a hard-wired comset from a desk drawer, "Yes Bradney?"

"No, I didn't pay too much attention, I was busy trying to get our feed restored dammit!"

"Now Sir," he whined after a moment, "We're all on the same team, right?"

After another moment of listening, Marvin's face paled and he gasped, "NO! They can't do that! You must stop them!"

Miss Petruschika stepped back into his office at that moment and said with cold eyes, "I just received an emergency call Sir. Our S'attl studio building has been entered and is now being searched."

Marvin gasped, "How? Who?" as he covered the mouthpiece of the comset with a hand that suddenly was shaking.

"I was told that the authority is a search warrant issued by the new Acting Chief Justice of the Washington State Supreme Court. It is being carried out by elements of the Washington National Guard that have been activated by Governor Regina Drake, who still holds office under their Constitution. The Acting Attorney General has just deputized them as Washington State

Patrolmen," she recited coldly.

"Additionally some personnel in the building have already been taken into custody and bussed away in fetters." She smiled, "You really should have listened to Governor Drake's announcement, Sir!"

The comset in Marvin's hand suddenly squawked, and he put it slowly it back to his ear. "Yes Bradney. I'll be there right away, Sir."

Marvin carefully replaced the comset in its drawer and gently pushed it closed – then he suddenly retched and vomited on the polished surface of his desk.

"Towel, Miss Petruschika," he gasped after a moment.

Her face was expressionless as she stepped into his personal wash-room and returned a moment later with a hand towel. She handed it to him without a word and stared at Marvin as he cleaned his chin, and wiped at the front of his dressing gown.

He dropped the towel on the desk and with a sigh, opened the hidden panel and stepped into the small elevator that took him down to the tunnel leading to the White House.

Miss Petruschika watched the panel silently close then stalked back to her desk in the outer office. She seated herself and after linking to her sister's private computer Moscow, transmitted a brief message in an unbreakable code the two had developed based on their shared childhood memories and experiences.

A moment later she got a one-word acknowledgement that her sister had received her message. "Да!" it agreed in Cyrillic.

Miss Petruschika smiled as she shut down her computer and rising, stepped to the costume closet. She retrieved a small tool from her cosmetic case and returning to her desk, opened her computer's case and removed its memory unit.

After placing that unit carefully in her handbag, she shunted the computer's secondary memory into active mode and re-closed its case. She powered the machine again, and smiled as she scrolled through the innocu-ous trivia she had pre-loaded into the secondary. She shut the machine down again and after placing the little tool in her handbag, began checking all the drawers in her desk. Finding nothing of consequence to remove, as she had always had intended, Miss Petruschika closed and locked her desk and rose again from her seat.

She strode back to the costume closet and dropping the silk kimono she wore, dressed herself in an elegant suit and heels and grasped the slender ebony walking stick she kept in it. She thumbed her nose at her reflection in the mirror and lifting her short skirt, slammed its door shut with an expert fighting kick.

She walked through the outer door of Marvin's office suite and as it automatically swung shut with a soft click, Miss Petruschika strolled down the opulent hallway. Her small purse hung by a slender strap from one shoulder and she swung the walking stick jauntily in her left hand. She carried the stick as a chic fashion statement, but she never mentioned her expertise in fencing with the seventy centimeter-long epee blade sheathed within it.

She left the building and strolled down 16th street in the warm night, an obvious member of Washington's power elite, at once confidently beautiful and beautifully confident. But there was also some subtle thing about her poise that silenced the catcalls which the homeless grate-dwellers usually showered on attractive pedestrians. Her persona also made the night-stalkers look for other prey so Miss Petruschika was not hindered as she walked to the corner, and waited for a cruising taxi.

The driver of the first empty one she hailed immediately braked to a stop and ignored the angry honking of the sedan forced to halt behind him as he keyed the door open for her. She stepped into the passenger compartment and flashed her diplomatic passport to the man, as she directed him to Pitson National Airport and its restricted international terminal.

She showed her passport again to the sharp-eyed person at the door of the discreet building at the south end of the airport complex, along with her unrestricted travel permit. Upon receiving his silent nod of approval, she entered its small but opulent waiting room and took a seat on a couch. She reclined on it with her long legs attractively displayed and snapped her fingers at the sharp-eyed person. When he rushed to her side, she motioned him to kneel on the floor beside her sofa. Overwhelmed by her cool blond beauty, he dropped to his knees and panted, "Yeess?" as he ran his eyes up and down her body.

Miss Petruschika placed a forefinger under his chin and delicately turned his gaze from her thighs back to her eyes. "Cold vodka," she murmured with a smile, "Now!" in a tone that compelled obedience.

Miss Petruschika boarded a supersonic jet reserved for those of her status thirty minutes later and began a series of flights that would take her ultimately to Sri Lanka, where she would meet her sister.

The two had long planned to take an extended tour of the shrines there, which they understood had recently reinstated the practice of temple prostitution. She and her twin had been sexually adventurous since puberty and they enjoyed occasional field trips together, to conduct what they smilingly called, "in-depth" studies of group social interactions...

*

Pitson and Jones were standing in an auxiliary command room deep under the White House which had interactive vid screens lining its walls. The screens all showed different mouthing faces, but they were muted except for the one displaying a wild-eyed General Butler clad in a rumpled pink dressing gown, with one sleeve cut off to accommodate his bandaged arm.

He was sputtering, "And then they opened up the City Building, and just took it over!" when Marvin Jacobs was frog-walked into the room by two Secret Service agents.

"Who?" Jones snapped to Butler's image with venom in her voice, "Took over your building?"

"This new national guard police force, along with some man who claimed to be the acting mayor of Seattle!"

"What are you doing about it?" Pitson hissed.

"Nothing," Butler whined, "I can't do anything. They've put all of my security force in to barracks, and I'm confined to quarters with a guard on my door!"

"How many of these guards were there, you idiot? And where did they come from?" And who-in-hell is this Hamier woman anyway?" Pitson rasped.

"Five hundred at least. They just rolled up in transports with some Mark VIIs and took over the whole `Clave. I don't know anything about her, but you've got to Dooo something!"

"Idiot!" Jones snapped as she muted Butler and clicked to the screen that showed the Studio Director, his strained face staring from an opulent room that was his apartment in the up-scale area of S'attl.

"Who is this Kristina Hamier, Director," Jones asked with a purr.

"One of our collectors Madam," he gulped.

"She doesn't appear to be very loyal to you, or our Network tonight, does she?" Jones purred again.

"She was our best, until she went rogue," the Director whimpered.

"Where the ferk did this damn moose come from before you made the mistake of hiring the bitch?" Pitson shouted hoarsely.

"She was Army, that's all I know..."

The pudgy four-star general, who had been studiously effacing himself in the back of the room, suddenly snapped his fingers, "Dammit, I thought I recognized her. She's Captain Cook!"

"Captain who?" Pitson rasped.

"That was her nickname. She was one of the best tactical commanders in Special Forces, and she always completed her missions," the General mumbled, "No matter how tough we made them..."

"You ferkin Idiot!" Pitson roared at the Director's face on the screen. "You picked one of those damn Army ultra-survivors to be a collector, and then you let her get in and learn all about our deal!"

The Director cringed, then suddenly glanced off-camera and froze with a look of shock on his face was obvious on the screen, until his vid transmission was cut off a second later.

Jacobs' comset chimed inside the pocket of his stained robe at almost the same instant.

"What?" he hissed into it where he stood in a corner of the room, trying to efface himself as well as to suppress his memory of Miss Petruschika's last comment.

He listened for a moment, then announced to the room with a false brightness, "My engineers tell me that the very first sat that was invaded tonight was over Western Canada!"

"Get me Ottawa, and wake up you know who!" Pitson rasped.

*

Pierre Bohica was born in Quebec, but he always resented the fact that he was not fully French because of the Italian ancestor who had given him his surname. He had been brilliant in his secondary school in the écoles of Quebec Cité and thus was awarded one of the few scholarships made available to French-speaking foreigners by the École Polytechnique in Paris, which its administration did occasionally, in the interest of diversité.

The Revolutionary Committee in 1794 during the Terror had established the École Polytechnique to be the premier institution in the new school system they had decreed for France, so it had been an exclusive school from its inception.

The École had maintained this exclusivity over the centuries by accepting only the top one tenth of one percent of all secondary school graduates in France each year, thus it was indeed an honor for a foreigner like Bohica to be admitted.

When he arrived at he campus for his first term in the fall of 2246 however, he had found that his Canadian version of the French language was amusing to his French-born classmates, and because of this as well as his origin, he immediately became the target of many wickedly subtle japes at his pronunciation and provincialism.

Therefore, as converts often do, Pierre struggled to erase his Quebecois patois and to become more French than the French. He also fiercely immersed himself in his studies, so much so that he generally shunned the diverse social life in the many student clubs on the campus.

Ultimately, Pierre graduated with high honors from this institution, born in the Revolution, enshrined in French culture by Napoleon and still dedicated to producing an educated elite to govern the masses, that the founder knew could not be trusted to do themselves.

Thus, L' École Polytechnique produced a steady stream of graduates who devoutly believed they were destined to guide the ordinary people and so they almost always entered government service.

Pierre was forced to return to Canada soon after receiving his elaborate diploma however, because he found that he was frozen out of the French civil service, and that of the EU as well due to his origin, and his lingering Quebecois accent which he could not control.

This bland rejection by Paris and Brussels greatly embittered him, but toward his fellow Canadians rather than the Europeans because of his self-perceived flaw of being born Canadian, rather than truly French. He was careful to keep this feeling hidden however, so he was quickly accepted into government service by Ottawa.

Pierre began applying his new skills in economics, technology and French logic once he was there and advanced rapidly. He discovered that he was able to anticipate the needs of his superiors and fill them, whether a need was official or not. His covert ruthlessness toward any who were possible rivals was also instrumental in his climb to power.

Therefore when Buffington "Buffo" Smythe, a determinedly ignorant populist from Alberta was elected as Premier, Pierre was easily able to get himself appointed to the staff of the Privy Council.

Pierre's portfolio for his chair, Deputy Minister to the Deputy Prime Minister, included the position of Coordinator of National Security and Intelligence among his acknowledged powers. It also made him the commander of the covert national para-military force that was not acknowledged in any public document. This force had been originally created from secretly retained elite units when Canada officially disbanded its armed forces in 2200, as a gesture of good will to the world.

The funding for this force had never been acknowledged, and the Government always hid it among the budgets of other Ministries. The existence of the force was heavily veiled because its only mission was to suppress any dissent in the Canadian populace, dissent that might cause "discomfort" in Ottawa.

The force did not even have an official name, but despite all of the Government's secrecy measures most ordinary Canadians knew of its existence and its purpose. When they whispered about it among themselves, they called it "the blue bunch"...

Pierre had met Pitson after he and Jones had been elected to their second terms when Pitson came to Ottawa on a state visit. Pierre had sensed an opportunity, so he took personal charge of the security for the visit. Therefore while the universally-loved Mounties from the Solicitor General's Ministry were obvious in their traditional red coats and shining brown boots all along the parade routes and at the various functions, people from Pierre's force in drab civilian clothing were stationed in the crowds, with silenced pistols and sleepy injectors in their pockets.

Pierre also had the good sense to import a team of highly innovative and athletic prostitutes from Quebec Cité and station them discreetly in Pitson's guest quarters in the Prime Minister's Mansion. Pitson was quite pleased by this hospitable gesture, and the relationship between the two men had grown over the years, into one of mutual wary respect for each other's guile and ruthlessness.

Pitson had also ensured that Pierre was rewarded each time he provided certain confidential information over the succeeding years, as well as for occasional "special services" by his covert force. These rewards had been so generous that at the present time, Pierre's silent partnership share in the profits of the Network was larger than his Prime Minister's. This fact was unknown to Buffo, of course...

*

"Pierre dammit!" Pitson roared at the interactive vid screen showing Bohica's patrician features, "There's been some kind of satellite takeover from out west in your cleared lands dammit! That's where this interruption came

555

from! You do something about it all right, while I tend to this damn run-away Governor in Olympia!"

"Oui, mon Ami, but you do not have to shout."

"I'll ferkin' well shout until this whole cluster clutch is ferkin fixed again!" Pitson rasped as he glared at the screen.

"Calm yourself my Pet," Belladonna Jones murmured with hard eyes as she glared around at the others in the room, "You and I will fix things first, then blame will be assigned..."

"We will attend to our end," Pierre sniffed haughtily from the vid screen as he clicked off with an imperious gesture.

Jones abruptly waved toward the door after Pierre's response, and the plump four-star general and Marvin immediately slunk from the room along with all the other aides.

"Don't worry Pretty Boy," Belladonna whispered as she squeezed Bradney in the one place that was still private to the two of them, "We know what we are doing."

"Yeah, sure Bell-bottom, but now I'm starting to think that someone else out there does too..."

"Sir!" Pitson's cadaverous-faced Secret Service Chief announced from the doorway, "The Network building in S'attl is now being searched by this new Washington State Patrol, and its employees, and participants are being taken into custody."

"We know that already, Dammit!"

"I'm sorry Sir," the man whispered, "But I've also been told that records and memory units are being seized as well, under a search warrant issued by the new Acting Chief Justice for the State of Washington."

"Shat! Shat! Shat!" Pitson groaned as he tore at his hair, and Jones began to hyperventilate...

*

"Chaos! Kris and Molly give way good chaos don't you think?" Puss murmured into her helmet mike as she and all of the squad guarding the little valley watched the end of the Governor Drake's announcement, and then the image of the Washington State House that returned to their helmet eye-screens for five long minutes.

"Si, Mi Captaine," Luis whispered. "But now I know what you and Kris are up to for real, so I got to say something to you, for the honor of me and my troopers, dammit!"

Puss took a deep breath and tensed herself for whatever she was going to hear next, "And?"

"And about ferkin time Seester! Now we just go on and Do It, Dammit!" he roared. The rest of the troopers echoed over the net, "Do It, Do It!"

Puss was silent for several moments, then after getting her voice back under control almost, she replied in a tight whisper, "Thanks, and biggers guys." She collected herself after another moment, took a deep breath and announced, "But you all get ready to be much shot at soon, because we have just broke their mold for the whole world!"

"Ferk their mold! We don't need no stinking mold! And anyway, we shoot way better than they will ever know, until it's too late for all those ferkers anyway," Luis snarled.

"Do It! Do It!" the troopers chanted to re-enforce his words.

"That good fightsong. That three be good fightsong day this," Bila muttered when the others on the warnet were quiet again.

"Yep Buddy, you got way right, all these tunes are good for fighting. But now we're going to see fight-time for real!" Puss said on the warnet, as she nodded to Bila standing by her side. Then she snapped, "Jimmy!"

"Yes Ma'am!"

"Go and fetch your folks over here quickers! The coming reaction is not going to be soft and fluffy, OK!"

"What do you mean Ma'am?" the boy gasped.

"If the bunch that they send after us is what I think it will be, they just shoot at everything they see. There's no way they can find the source of Molly's transmission, but they will destroy everything they find that is human culture out here because they are a blunt instrument. Take a trooper with you Jimmy and move as fast as you can!"

"Can Joseph Whalekiller come with me Ma'am? He knew my dad."

"Sure Trooper Four. Luis, can you cover Joseph's job for a while?"

"Si Boss Chickie, and I want to meet the person who did thees mole anyway, he is way good!"

"I think you will be surprised Cisco," Puss chuckled. Then she ordered, "Get gone Jimmy. Now!"

Molly asked in her little voice after a moment, "What about the militia guys over to the East?"

"What about them?"

"Well, whoever is coming will see them too, and they are pretty much unco."

"What's "unco"?" Puss snapped, "And be quick Molly, we don't have much chat time left."

"Unco means uncoordinated, Ma'am! Are you going to just stand by and let these poor drunk folk in cammy get all shot up by the bunch you say is coming?"

Puss growled in the back of her throat, then she asked, "OK, Molly, can you contact them?"

"Yes Ma'am, through a link Durwood set up that can't be followed back to here."

"Good. Tell them to take to the woods, OK!"

"Ja Boss!" the girl replied. "And thank you Ma'am..."

"You're welcome. And Molly, you're really are nice to dumb animals, OK!" Puss chuckled, then she paused.

"Hold up. Ask if any of the cammy guys want to actually be warlike instead of just talking about it. If they do, tell them to come to our party, if they can find their way here in the dark."

"What party?" Molly asked with suspicion.

"The one we are going to have here as soon as all Rat's buddies in high places get their ferkin hymn books open to the same page!"

Molly giggled, "Maybe Charlie and I can close their book while what you call a "party" happens."

"Talk fast," Puss ordered. Then she listened, and began to smile as Molly explained what she and Charlie proposed. When Molly finished Puss asked, "You think you two can really do that?"

"Yes, Ma'am, I know we can," Molly answered with pride.

"Do it, Troopers," Puss ordered, "And tell the cammy guys that decide to join us to head for the mouth of your valley instead of over the ridge, and that the password through our line is "restoration", OK?"

"Yes Ma'am!" Molly whispered, "And you're really nice too."

Puss shook her head in silent negation, as she considered how she planned to use any of the militiamen that did show up.

*

"General McAuliffe, I know you are a bit occupied right now, but do you or General Shaw have a fiscal audit team you can send me?" Hector Hamier spoke into his comset from where he stood in the center of Benjamin Butler's office in the S'attl City Building.

"Thank you for the thought Sir, but let's see what kind of Mayor job I do before you waste any more good words. And yes Sir, I said auditors. Financial operations have always been pretty much compartmentalized in the `Clave administration, but now that I've had a chance to open some boxes as it were," Hector said as he glared around at the opulence of Butler's office, "I have found some tracks that need to be followed."

"What tracks?" Hector responded, "Sir, tracks like the discrepancy in a rough mass balance I just calculated between the amount of soy grown each year compared to the amount fed the people in the `Clave. There's a big difference Sir, and no answer as to where the rest of each year's crop went. That's the kind of track I'm talking about Sir!"

After a pause, Hector continued with a smile, "Thank you Sir, I appreciate your help, and I will make good use of their time."

He clicked his comset off and turned to the two people who stood in cringing attitudes in the doorway of Butler's office.

"First of all, Don't' cringe!" Hector ordered, with a smile that took the sting out of his words. "And thank you for coming out in the middle of the night to be a part of something that may be dangerous. You both have worked in my office for many years and I know you are honest people in a world that is usually not so. That is why I asked you to join me tonight. You saw the vid. The state of emergency is over along with the military Governorship, and I have been appointed the Acting Mayor of Seattle.

"I very much need your help to track down what looks like a major theft of public money," Hector finished as he looked at the two, Richard, who was small but had intelligent eyes and Sheila, a pudgy girl with an honest face.

"So, will you help me in this?"

The two glanced at each other for a second then they both answered almost in unison, "Yes Sir!"

"I thank you, and the City of Seattle thanks you as well," Hector said with a slight catch in his voice. He cleared his throat then continued. "Start with trying to find all of the records of soy production over the years and then look for any shipping records you can find. I don't know if you can get into Butler's `puter or not, but see what you can do."

"I've got some ideas Sir, and Sheila does too. So let's see if we can track what that damn beast has been doing," Richard snarled. "Butler had my sister taken when she asked for better food for her work gang. She never came back home..."

*

"Alright Luis, I gotta' grab some pad time if I'm going to be able to dance good when the party starts. Can you take the con for a while?" Puss asked the man standing with her and Bila inside the boulders with his IR cape draped over his shoulders.

"Not only will I take it Seester, but I will give it back to you un-broke when you wake up again!"

"Thanks Luis. I figgered' you would be pretty good, because Bobby sent you out to us."

"Hey Baby Bird! Bobby didn't send me dammit! I come here because I want to, OK! He say you two war-chickies be good so I come to see for myself. That's all."

"And?"

"He be right," Luis responded with a rare smile. "Now go flop on you pad, OK!" he growled as he flicked a casual salute to her and trotted out from the circle of boulders back toward Molly's rock chamber.

"Soon bad people more come?" Bila asked quietly as he placed his hand on Puss' shoulder.

She felt the unspoken need in his question even as she felt the same need surge within herself. She gazed at him for a moment then clicked off the warnet in her helmet and pulled it from her head.

" We've got some time, so spread your cape on the ground," she whispered as she tuned her private comset to the command channel.

Bila spread out his cape on the ground and she unlatched and kicked off her boots then opened the front of her warsuit and slipped out of it, and watched Bila do the same.

She wrapped her cape around her bare shoulders and reached for him, "Get under this with me. I think there's going to be a lot of heat that we will have to hide real soon," she whispered as she drew him down with her and urged him onto his back.

Puss placed her comset next to Bila's shoulder then she raised her leg and straddled him as she spread her cape over her shoulders. She gave a shuddering sigh as she lowered herself and when she had fully joined them, she quivered deep within as she leaned forward and kissed him. She looked down at him with wide eyes and whispered, "Now, take me with you, where we went before..."

Bila stared up at Puss with a solemn face and shining eyes as he caressed her head with both of his hands, then her shoulders and finally her breasts. He breathed deeply then gently gripping her hips began moving her in a slow rhythm.

She rested her forearms on his shoulders and curled her fingers in his hair as she stared unblinkingly into his eyes and allowed him move her as his hands directed. She felt her tension begin to rise and moaned instinctively, then sighed and relaxed as Bila kept manipulating her body to meet her needs. Each time she was ready for a higher level of tension he guided her to it while he looked into her eyes, and then slowed again until finally she exploded with wild lungings in a wave of bright passion.

He groaned and exploded as well, and she sensed the door open between them once again... But this time she felt the vast gray cathedral of Bila's being merge with a clear golden light that she recognized was the essence of herself – and then their two entities soared far above the ground. That which was her spun with the soul of him in a stately waltz and she experienced the pleasure and comfort of a belonging as she had never known before even as she somehow saw the world beneath her in a dim monochrome.

She then felt Bila direct her sensing to the south where a richly complex blue sphere glowed small in the distance.

She felt him direct her again, but this time far to the east, where dim shapes flickered indistinctly at the edge of her vision. She did not know the flickering shapes, but they were somehow familiar and she felt a need to examine them, until that which was Bila gently guided their merged beings back to earth where their bodies lay entwined.

She felt their mutual wave of sadness and reluctance on parting to re-enter their bodies, then Puss blinked her eyes and gazed down at Bila.

She caressed his broad brow as she kissed him softly, then sighed, "Who are we Bila?"

He smiled up to her and gently stroked her back and hips and slowly shook his head, "I know not. You we like? I we like."

"I we like," she said tenderly as she kissed him again, then she sighed again, "And I suppose that's good enough for now."

"The blue was Kris, right?"

"Yes."

"Can she feel us like this?"

"Not know. Maybe little some."

"I think so too. But what were those other things?"

"Bad. You not place that go. Place that Bad!" Bila whispered as he gripped her shoulders and gently shook her.

"Ja Boss. It's sleepy time anyway," Puss sighed as she lowered herself to his chest and pillowed her cheek on his shoulder. "I'm not too heavy am I?"

"Not heavy. You good sleep larru."

"Wass' larru?" Puss mumbled.

"Thing sleep under. Take off orkatz deer." Then he chuckled, "You little. You make larru little,"

"Jus' `member buster, you got enough hide to cover me n' Kris both," Puss mumbled sleepily as she nipped at the skin of his neck.

"Ja Boss. You little do sleep now, OK?" he whispered as he embraced her under the cape.

"OK Big Man, only thirty minutes tho'. Then it's time to get `n go..."

He thought about many things as he felt the woman sprawled atop him relax and drift off to sleep while he held her in his arms. Bila felt her soft breath on his shoulder as she slept and his thoughts were pleasant, mostly.

*

"Good op so far, Madam Governor," Boots announced with a crooked grin to the group sitting around the ornately carved conference table in the Governor's office. "But now we must remember the prayer offered on our ships when we fought British navy in 1812."

Barbara and Regina looked puzzled, but Mack and Bobby smiled grimly and nodded. Waldo wrinkled his forehead, then muttered, "OK, I'll be goat, what prayer?"

Boots returned Mack and Bobby's nods, then the three chanted in unison.

"Lord, Make Us Thankful for That Which We Are About to Receive,"

"And Mindful of the Needs of Others!"

"What's that mean?" Waldo asked then his eyes widened, "OK, I get it! Incoming and then outgoing, right?"

"Like I said, Smart Troops are good to have," Boots said with a nod to Waldo before continuing, "We are going to experience some incoming very soon and it will be major compared to what Rat tried to do, but it will be nothing at this stage that Marybell's squad can't handle. The problem comes after Marybell and her gang of efficient killers totally smush the wave of enforcers who will attempt to shut Molly down."

Mack looked at Boots for a moment then he growled, "Ma'am, I suggest that it might not work. Get Molly out now and extract your troops and their friends as well. Leave their minor equipment as a throw-away to whoever comes in."

Boots gazed at the grizzled general while she considered her options, and him. "No Mack, you are talking tactics. I am doing strategy," she said. "We will show our real power here because we can - not just our war skills like we did to the Chin. We couldn't control our ferkin strategy during that war, but we can Damn well do so now!" Boots finished with a snarl.

Then she abruptly turned to Regina at the head of the table. "Please excuse my language Madam Governor. That was very unprofessional of me."

"Kristina, it is never unprofessional to say what we all know to be true."

"Thank you." Boots said with a nod and a grim smile, which Regina returned.

"Now to continue Ma'am, what Marybell and her squad will it to whoever comes at them, and I pity those poor suckos, will be of major importance to the Restoration."

Boots took a deep breath then continued, "There was a flag flown in the early part of our Revolution in 1776 if you will recall. "It was a simple device. Its field had only thirteen red and white horizontal stripes overlaid by a realistic American rattlesnake. It also had a motto along its lower edge, "Don't Tread On Me".

This is the challenge we are sounding to the world once again, and the forces that want to keep us in the `claves.

"None of them will be real happy about what we've done today," Boots continued, "To say nothing about what Marybell will do to them next and the shock Governor Drake will give the White House when she sends two acting Senators and a Representative to Washington with their credentials.

"Their unhappiness is what we want however, because then we will then see who strikes back at us and we will know now who it is that 'would be king'.

"When we find who that is, we will know who we have to take down to finish the Restoration."

Mack gazed at the tall woman with blue fire in her eyes for a second then he nodded. "I withdraw my suggestion Ma'am. Your plan is best," he said quietly. "What do you want us to do now?"

"Thanks, Mack," Boots said with a smile. "I can't predict what will happen next but I can predict that something will. So everyone, activate whatever ears and eyes we have, and Rick."

"Yes Ma'am,"

"Be sure the direct link between Marybell and her father is as secure as can be. This is very important to us."

"Consider it done, Ma'am"

"Good. Now let's all make our survel and intel as good as it can be while we wait for their next boot to drop," Boots said.

Then she gasped, as a flow of warmth suddenly flooded through her mind. She stood and lifted her face toward the ceiling, and stayed rigid with clinched fists and closed eyes for several seconds - then with a sigh, she relaxed and opened her eyes again and continued, "So are we now ready to party?"

"What happened to you just now, Kris?" Mack interrupted in a serious tone as the others looked at her with concern, and confusion, "You aren't hearing the bells too, are you?"

"You mean like Jean's petite mals before battle? No Mack, you don't have an epileptic at the con here," Kris replied with equal seriousness.

"I do believe I felt some friends as they saw stars though," Then she said, "Now that I have reassured you that I'm not crazy, at least not any more than the rest of you," Boots said with a grin, "Tell me how can we monitor the air traffic into Marybell's theater from down here?"

There was a moment of silence, until Barbara spoke, "How about another training flight, but with an Argus this time? We can have it practice linkups with the USAF war sats, with permission per the request of the Governor to their base at Tacoma. At least until they get new orders from Washington," she continued with a tight smile.

*

The Argus was a long-winged aircraft designed to fly high above battle-fields for days if necessary. It carried no offensive weaponry but its defenses were very advanced, and it had wide-ranging radar and optical capabilities that were extraordinary, as well as the capability to link with USAF survel satellites. It could gather battlefield intelligence in several ways and make this intel available on the unit warnet of the grunts fighting on the ground. The aircraft was named "Argus" because its many eyes could see everything.

This asset had been controlled by the Pentagon during most of the war and thus by the White House as well, so the planes had been deployed only occasionally, when particular US units were receiving excessive stress from the Chin.

The USAF had finally transferred a flight of Argus to the Washington Air National Guard during the last years of the war because their own maintenance personnel's skills had much degraded compared to those of the WANG mechanics...

*

"Good idea Ma'am," Bobby said to Barbara. He turned to Regina Drake and explained, "WANG was assigned a flight of Argus several years ago Governor."

Regina nodded then asked, "Would you like for me to talk to the WANG Commander about this training mission."

"Yes Governor, I think it would be very appropriate, particularly after tonight's broadcast," Mack answered. Then he nodded to Boots, "That is, if you concur, Ma'am."

"Mack, I will always trust you when you do your General Officer thing, because I am really just a ground grunt after all."

All at the table, including the Governor answered her statement with snorts of disbelief. "I know people, and flowers." Regina said, "But you know war as well as people and flowers. So no false modesty Kristina, it ill-becomes you."

"Yes Ma'am," Boots said with a crooked smile, "And thank you Ma'am."

"To continue however, we had a need to provide intel on unfriendlies approaching Molly's site to give them early warning. It looks like you have addressed that need now, Sirs and Mesdames but how soon can we get Argus up in the sky and when can we link Molly directly into it? And finally, when can we link EB directly to both the Argus and Marybell?"

"Those links will be done as soon as I contact my communications people, who are on standby tonight, Ma'am," Rick answered.

Regina nodded, then rose from her place at the head of the table and stepped to her desk. She took her seat and reached for her desk comset, "Chief Sergeant Major, please get me General Wells at WANG-COM. I am sure he is available tonight."

*

Puss wakened a half hour later. "Your still here, tha's nice," she sighed into Bila's neck.

"You here be. That nice big, "Bila whispered into the hair on the top of her head.

"Thanks Bila, you're sweet too. But it's work time now. I gotta' check the trooper's positions. I liked ours tho," Puss whispered as she crunched him with a pelvis thrust, then slowly left him and got to her feet. She began dressing rapidly while still wrapped in her cape.

"Do It!" he grunted as he bounded to his feet and climbed into his jumpsuit and latched on his boots.

"You go to Molly for now, OK?" she told him in another whisper as she slipped on her helmet and clicked into the war net again.

He nodded to her and she smiled to him, then she asked, "Luis, Molly. Any word?"

"Welcome back to the world, Seester! All quiet now - too quiet for me. "Molly 'es into survel sat transmissions, but visuals no good 'till morning and the IR bands don't see anything moving."

"OK, tell her to keep looking and Bila is on his way to the cave now. And Luis,"

"Si Mi Capitána!"

"I'll meet you at the top of the ridge above the cabin. Let's do a walk-around and see how well our guys have set the table for our party."

A muted chorus of groans, chuckles and mock snores sounded on the warnet for a moment, until Puss growled, "And the notes I take will go in your permanent records..."

*

Puss and Luis checked each trooper's position and their fields of fire, and his or her alternate positions and fallback routes. The two made minor suggestions in a few cases but the troopers had positioned themselves well. Most were aiming down into the valley from the sides of both ridges with overlapping fire zones and they had laid out alarm lines well up the slopes behind their positions.

They had also set two heavy lasers, called Fly-swatters in hidden emplacements near the base of each ridge near the mouth of the valley and had slaved them to Luis' third laser on the ridge above the spring at the head of the valley. These powerful pulse lasers could be remotely controlled through their operator's eye screen and their firings were not interrupted by foliage. When the three were linked together under the control of a single operator, they could converge on heavy targets with deadly effect. When they were released to be aimed individually, there were multiple hells to pay...

All of Puss' troopers had made firing points that were invisible to more than a casual glance and they had made maximum use of ledges and fallen timber to hide the signs of their work.

*

Luis and Puss stood at the mouth of the valley beyond the boulders near the charred wreck of the Network `copter.

"You give our people good kill ground for when they come in this valley, but what if they not do that?" Luis asked.

"We've got the ridges covered too, and I have a couple of more tricks in my pocket, some Erakas, as Bila calls them," Then Puss suddenly dropped into a crouch and hissed, "There's somebody out there," As she grabbed her big pistol.

"You pretty damn good, Seester!" Luis whispered as he armed his assault rifle and flopped on the ground in a firing position.

The moon had set and sky was showing just a hint of the pre-dawn pearly glow. In this indistinct light, Puss sensed rather than saw three figures step out of the willow scrub lining the little stream in the main valley. Then they waved their arms, and one called hoarsely, "Restoration!"

"Hmmm, lookin' better and better," Puss murmured.

"If you are armed, drop your weapons and advance with your hands up!" she called, "And stand apart when you come!"

"Stop there!" she ordered a moment later when the figures were close enough for her to get them in her sights. "Who are you? Talk quick!"

"We got a message. It said that they was coming for us. The rest of our bunch cut and ran to the woods but the message said you might want some help over here..."

"Good, but how can you help? And come to where we can see you clear. Now!" Puss snapped.

The three men walked hesitantly toward the sound of her voice with their hands still in the air. They were dressed in bits and pieces of old Chin and American army clothing and wore an eclectic mixture of field gear. One was heavy-set with bushy black hair covering his head, most of his face and whatever else of his skin that showed. The other two were smaller, blondish, and their beards were skimpy. The aura of body odor from the three was so strong that it was almost visible. The black-haired one grunted, "Well, we can shoot pretty good, if you're not gonna' run and hide from them too."

"We don't run, and we only hide until they're in range," Puss said softly in a voice that somehow was not soft.

"We will let you help if you follow my and Luis' orders exactly, otherwise get gone!" The heavy-set man looked at Puss and Luis for a moment as they stood before him in casual confidence and control, then he grunted, "Yes Ma'am."

"Good. Now retrieve your weapons and then I will tell you what to do."

"What the sheet we need these losers for Seester?" Luis hissed as the three turned and lumbered back to get their weapons. "You say we got thees whole op covered already!"

"There is no such thing as having too many credits or too much sex, or too many sneaky tricks Cisco! These guys are going to be our Forlorn Hope."

"What'n ferk ees that?"

"How much military history do you have Luis? Ever read about the 30 Year's War back in 17th Century in Europe?"

"Only that it went on for thirty years and those stupid ferkers only fought thirty-three battles in all those ferkin' thirty years, and nothing was changed when it was over! Way dumb op! Sort of like what we just did with the Chin."

"Congrats Sargento, you got the essence of it real good and your thought-ful comparison shows you have major insight as well," Puss smiled to him in the growing light of the dawn. "That war was actually the beginning of modern warfare as well as the arms industry, if you can believe that."

"But I cut to the bottom fast since these militia guys are coming back quickers. A Forlorn Hope was a force of expendables which were sent out in most of those battles back then as advanced skirmishers to lure the opposing force into a selected battleground."

Luis touched his brow to Puss as the three men panted back with old Chin weapons in their hands, "You be way, way hard Seester! I like that."

"Thanks friend, I try." Puss said with a cold smile.

Then she turned to the three militiamen. "OK, first off, do your people know about IR shielding from the survel sats?" When they stared blankly at her question, Puss gritted, "Do you have any way to talk to them now?"

The heavy-set man mumbled, "Well I got a comset, but I don't know if they will be listening, or if their batteries are even charged..."

"Try anyway, Dammit and tell them to all get underground! Their infra-red heat signatures can show their positions to the force that's coming! They need to dig in real much!"

The heavy-set man's eyes grew large and he fumbled a Chin comset from his pack. He punched in a code and began calling a reco-signal.

Puss nodded to Luis and motioned him out of earshot of the worried man. "Send them to the head of the valley up past the cabin. Give them capes and helmets and some of our comsets but make sure they can only get channel 12, and give them reco numbers like Camo 1 and Camo 2, OK?"

"Tell them to stay under their capes and only show themselves and fire once or twice on your or my command - then to run away and into the bushes. Check their weapons to see if they are any good. Replace as necessary and then send them to their posts."

"I am going to rig the lures, that Bila called "erakas" in the cabin. They will bring this new bunch to it like buzzards to a battlefield, but I want these cammy guys to pull much of them past the cabin and on up the valley where the rest of our guns are..."

Luis stared at Puss for several seconds then he snapped a very formal salute.

"Thank you Ma'am, for just showing me why nobody ever wants to fight you - ever. Baby Bird, you really are a killer."

"Aw shuckey Cisco, I do this kinda' stuff just for funs," she smiled to him serenely as she holstered her big pistol and began trotting back toward Molly's cabin.

*

Puss stalked into the adit after being challenged by a guard outside, and congratulating him on his challenge. She found the chamber filled with people, and a horse.

Jimmy turned to her with a smile, "Thank you Ma'am for letting us come here. This is my mother Donna," he gestured to a small woman with a motherly bosom, a sweet smile and sad eyes.

"That's my sister Sharon over there," he grinned, "And this is my kid brother Little Mike," he said as he held up a three year-old boy with bright red hair.

Puss looked at the group standing between her and Molly at her computer. She smiled perfunctorily...

"Glad you all could come, and we'll talk more later. But for now, keep tha' ferk out of my way until this party is over!" she ordered as she pushed through the group that included Joseph Whalekiller, who stood very close to Sharon.

"You Corporal – to your post! Now!"

"Yes Ma'am!" Joseph sputtered as he dropped the girl's hand and raced from the cavern with cheeks that were bright pink on his ivory face.

"Fun time comes later," Puss gritted to the slender black-haired girl in buckskins, "It's war time now sister!"

Sharon blushed deeply but met Puss' gaze, as the woman inspected her with eyes that were penetrating.

"It was your first time, right," Puss whispered after a moment.

"Yes," Sharon sighed.

"Was it his idea, or yours?"

"Mine. I felt that I had waited long enough - and he is so big and strong. And I liked his chest..."

"Good! I need him for this op and I'm glad I won't have to shoot him now since it was your idea to go bouncy in the bushes!" Puss hissed.

"But keep your hands off his big strong chest, and everything else he has until this is op over and he's off duty, OK!"

"Yes Ma'am! I know how to follow orders Ma'am," Sharon responded fervently as she hit a brace with her shoulders thrown back. "And can I have a rifle Ma'am, and go with your troopers? I know how to shoot, and I can fight too!"

"I knew your dad, so I believe he would have taught you well. I say yes, Trooper Five, and welcome to this crazy outfit," Puss said.

"Yaaay!" Jimmy shouted in approval and Sharon grinned to him, but his voice echoing in the rock chamber made Sugar Plum toss her head and scrape at its floor with a fore-hoof.

Bila stepped to the horse and grasping its bridle, soothed it quickly with a caress to its ears. He smiled and said over his shoulder to Sharon, "This outfit good be you in. I show Real Food you soon."

Sharon gazed at the really big man who was handling their horse so easily until Jimmy gulped, "Bila! You said you wouldn't eat Sugar Plum!"

"Trooper Four! This horse trooper be we like! Trooper eat not trooper - OK!" Bila chuckled, as he stroked Sugar Plum's neck.

"Well, it's pretty clear she likes you, so I'll show you how to groom her," Jimmy announced, with a voice of hesitant adolescent authority as he stepped up to Bila.

"Me show," Bila smiled.

"Sharon, forget those two and listen to me," Puss snapped.

"Yes Ma'am!" the girl replied as she braced to attention and faced Puss.

"Now that you are Trooper Five, I assign you to Sergeant Luis. He will use you dispassionately, because Joseph would not be able to do so after you two romping around."

"You will find that I, your Max-leader can ignore a lot of stuff my troopers do in the bushes. You made a good choice in Joseph by the way, so be nice to him."

"But," Puss continued in a tone of compelling authority, "I live for the completion of the mission and for the safety of my troops."

"That is why I won't let you fight beside Joseph because personal relationships can give me un-professional results. You will fight for Luis instead."

"But Sharon...

"Yes Ma'am?" the girl gulped with wide eyes as she now realized the full force of the woman's persona...

"I note in passing Kid," Puss muttered, "that you've got a pretty good chest yourself..."

***

Chapter 27
The Mobilization

May 9, 2276 AD
Cold Lake Weapons Range in Alberta, Canada
and
The Coastal Mountains of British Columbia

"Form up a full platoon!

"We are ordered to minimize a serious threat to public tranquility here," Captain Campbell growled after he clicked his comset off. He brought up a large-scale map of British Columbia on the wall screen and pointed to a spot near Kitimat.

His finger was stubby, freckled and sprouted red hairs. He wore the dark blue fatigue uniform of the Special Unit, the one that Ottawa did not acknowledge existed.

"I suggest First Platoon, A Company, Sir!" the Master Sergeant snapped, "They are very good at minimizing, Sir!"

"See to it. Tell off a gun-ship as well and arm it for anti-personnel. We leave at first light, and I will join you."

"Sir!" the Master Sergeant barked as he stamped one hobnailed boot and braced at attention. He swept the Captain a salute in the style of the old British Army, then turned about with another foot-stamp and marched out of the Captain's office to the barracks ready room. He did not wait for the Captain's casual return of his salute.

"Orders Boyos! We've got work! First Platoon A Company, fall in on the grinder with full field gear in ten minutes!" the Master Sergeant growled into the intercom on the wall. He also wore the blue fatigue uniform that gave his unit its bitter nickname among the people of Canada of "The Blue Bunch."

*

The Blue Bunch were barracked on an air base in the vast area that had once been the Canadian Air Force's live fire practice site at the Cold Lake Weapons Range in northern Alberta until the Government abolished their military in 2200. The base had been reported as closed then, and the range officially designated a wildlife research area.

The Canadian government had seized almost 1,200,000 hectares of ancestral lands from the indigenous Cree and Déné tribes in 1952 when the range was first established. The tribes had been shut out of their hunting grounds for two and a half centuries by the time Ottawa returned the range to "nature".

The Indians soon found that they were still not welcome there. Their hunters learned this when they were confronted the first time they tried to enter their lands again after the "Ultimate Demobilization" as Ottawa termed it.

The men who stopped the hunting parties wore the uniforms of the Ministry of the Environment, and were heavily armed. They gruffly insisted that the pristine nature of the reserve must be protected from human interference - to keep "important research" from being disturbed. The Dénés and Cree hunters shrugged and walked away. They finally stopped trying to hunt there after several more such confrontations...

The whites living in the town of Cold Lake to the south of the range also learned about this new order of things, after several determined hunters failed to return home.

The population of Cold Lake was much smaller now anyway, because Ottawa had declared it expendable when the Chin invaded, so most of its citizens left there for the safety of Eastern Canada.

*

The Master Sergeant considered how his group operated as he stood in the predawn in front of the barracks, listening to familiar sound of helicopter engines warming up while he waited for the platoon to assemble.

"The Campbell himself is coming today," he thought. "That means somebody in Ottawa is real mad about somebody out in BC," He smiled to himself, "And that means we're going to make it real bad for everybody out there."

The Lieutenant and the Platoon Sergeant trotted up two minutes later as the last blue-clad figure raced to join the unit. The men lined up into a parade formation of four squads of ten men each.

The Platoon Sergeant ordered them to attention and called the roll, then did an about face with a foot-stamp as the echo of the last shouted "Here!" died away.

"First Platoon, A Company, all present, and ready for inspection Sir!" The Sergeant barked as he turned to the Lieutenant who stood behind him.

"Thank you, Sergeant," the young man with the old eyes drawled. He turned to the Master Sergeant standing at his side.

"Please inform the Captain that my platoon is ready for inspection."

"Yes Sir!" the Master Sergeant barked with a foot stamp and a sweeping salute. He turned with another foot stamp and marched back into the barracks.

He knocked on the frame of Captain Campbell's open office door stamped his foot, swept a salute, and barked, "First Platoon ready for inspection, Sir!"

"Very good. But now forget the parade ground crappo, all right! You're making way too damn much noise this early in the morning!"

"Right, Sir," the Master Sergeant replied, in a conversational tone as he leaned against the doorframe and lit a cigarette. "What's next?"

"Check their gear and get 'um loaded, and then wait."

"Right, but how long?"

"Until our liaison lands here from Washington. He's in the air now."

"Olympia?" the Master Sergeant asked with a puzzled look. "I saw the vid last night."

"No." The Captain replied with a cold smile, "Washington D.C."

"Oh..."

*

The comset in Rick's secure basement room chimed. Mack was sitting at the conference table with his portable computer and the two WNG first lieutenants he had picked as his aides sat across the table from him with theirs. He called them his "dog robbers" according to old military usage, and the two accepted their new titles with pride.

Mack paused in the rapid-fire string of orders he was giving and showed a brief smile as they typed furiously to catch up on their notes before he clicked the instrument on.

"General," Bobby's voice sounded.

"Yes Bobby?"

"Our Argus is up and now linked to the survel sats."

"What is the level of your message to me?"

"For now, Sir, secret."

Mack nodded to the two aides. They had abruptly pushed their chairs back and started to leave when they first heard Bobby's voice, but now seated themselves again at his gesture.

"Continue."

"The IR bands are picking up unusual activity at Cold Lake."

"Their Cold Lake base, the one they said was closed years ago and would not let us use during the war?"

"Yes Sir, same one."

"Interesting," Mack murmured in a neutral voice. "Keep me informed on developments, and keep EB plugged in as well. He will copy Marybell until she is linked directly to Argus."

"Yassa' Boss! I go now," Bobby said with a drawl as he clicked off.

"Damn all those unreconstructed Southurns anyway!" Mack said with a grin to the man and woman across the table from him.

They returned his smile tentatively then they asked almost as one, "Next item, Sir?"

"Next item is a major one. We must see to the provisioning of the all the people who are soy workers. I have found that they are on a short supply string, so you two have my authority to do what ever it takes to feed these people, and feed them well."

"Anyone who gets in your way will not be happy when I finish with them, I guarantee!"

"Yes Sir!" the two aides gulped in unison.

"Good. You now have my agenda for this morning, so do it!"

"Yes, Sir!"

*

The AS/TFB-330-T landed at Cold Lake at dawn on the airstrip that wasn't officially there and taxied over to where five mist-gray helicopters sat idling. Bradney Pitson's Secret Service Chief was the single passenger in the forward cockpit of the fighter. He waited until the ground crew attached a boarding ladder, then he climbed down. He directed them to open a cargo pod attached to the plane's bomb rack and to remove a bulky instrument case, then motioned a crewman to follow and walked to where Captain Campbell stood waiting.

"Hello. You don't need to know my name. I am here to see that the job is done right this time."

Captain Campbell's eyes blazed for a second then he snapped to the gray-faced American, "Get aboard Yank! You're making us run late." He did not salute as he turned and stalked toward one of the four transport helicopters. These were the E-union's version of the U.S. Army MULL, and carried the four squads of First Platoon, A Company of the Blue Bunch. The fifth helicopter was a fast and maneuverable gun-ship that could mount a variety of weapons.

As Captain Campbell had ordered, it was armed with anti-personnel capabilities this morning...

*

Puss was resting on her pad in the crowded cavern when the comset Rick had given her tingled softly. She sat up and read "Kencuttemaum Amonsens" on its small screen. She returned her father's greeting by typing in "Kencuttemaum Kowse" and pressing the send button.

"You're got a message?" Molly asked from where she lay on the air mattress next to Jimmy.

"Sure did."

"Is it secure?" the girl said with a frown as Jimmy helped her sit up.

Puss watched the screen for a moment before replying with a slight smile, "I'll read the signal to you and then you tell me how secure it is, OK?"

"Ja Boss, I think," Molly answered, suddenly suspicious.

"Amuwoir! Yowgh cunnaivwh tshehip weyak ireh. Necut pokosack tshehip.

"Vdasemeodaan arrokoth muskiedues nepawwshowghs. Comotinch. Necut. Ningh. Nus-necuttweunquaough."

"What the darn ferk does all that mean?" Molly squawked.

"Is this message secure enough for you?" Puss asked, with an almost straight face.

"Sure is," Charlie grinned. "What did your folks have to say?"

"Quick thinking son," Puss smiled as she punched in another message and sent, "Kenah Kowse!"

She read aloud a moment later, "Paskeaw kensekit Amosens! Noumais." She smiled as she blinked away a tear, and typed in, "Nowmais Kowse."

Puss closed the comset and keyed her warnet.

"Hear me troopers!"

"I just received a message from my father, whom I suspect some of you know. He said "Take Heed! Four long ships and one gun-ship come to you.""

"My own guess is they will be here sometime late morning. I also think that the four long ships are squad carriers and will land while the gun-ship stays in the air as backup."

"We're about to have us a full platoon of the Blue Bunch for brunch boys and girls, so let's get ready! But only fire on my command."

"You know we all be ready now, Baby Bird," Luis snapped over the warnet. "But what you father's name?"

"Good for you, Sargento Grande. I figured that you'd be ready, and I figured you would correct me too," Puss chuckled. "As for my father, he only went by his initials when he was in the service, EB..."

"Holy Sheet Seester! He's one of the great ones! You his daughter! No wonder you boss this op!"

"Nada Luis, I just learned what little I know from guys like you. But enough yakey, I've got more work to do." Puss clicked off the warnet in the middle of a chorus of agreement and approval and turned, "Molly."

"Yes Ma'am?"

"My father also said, "To sneak into the Eyes in the Sky and the Moons. 6-1-2-3,000". The eyes in the sky are our Argus observation planes, and the moons are our war sats, but do you know what these numbers mean?"

Molly frowned and was shaking her head slowly, when Charlie jumped to his feet.

"Wow! You really do have friends in high places! That's the reco code that links all our war sats to Argus. Nobody has it unless they are real special!"

"Well, I think we're all pretty special, but that code sounds way too simple. Do you know how to use it?"

"Sure do Ma'am, and it's not simple at all. That's really a key to a code, and it's no good to anyone who doesn't have the code memorized. I do, and I'll show Molly how to use it too."

"Do that. And anything you two see, or do when you get in," she said with a cold smile, "Tell me on channel 13, OK?" That way I can assess your intel first, alone."

"Yes Ma'am!" they both answered, as Jimmy helped Molly to her feet and Charlie took his seat at the computer bench.

"You more words say with father you," Bila stated quietly from where he stood beside Sugar Plum holding a grooming brush.

"Yes, we did. I thanked him and he said, "Kick butt Daughter." Then he said, "I love you", and I told him that I loved him too. That's all." Puss answered with a little smile.

"You daughter good," Bila nodded as he abruptly turned back to the horse and began brushing its flank.

"Thank you Bila," Puss whispered as she stepped to him and squeezed his arm.

"Thank at father you. He good say. He father good," Bila grunted while keeping his gaze on the horse's flank and continuing his methodical brushing...

"I do," Puss whispered as she patted Bila's shoulder, "Every day..."

*

"We're in!" Molly squealed, "And I can see them coming now – straight in from the east!"

"How far?" Puss snapped.

"About five hundred klicks out."

"Speed?"

"Wait a minute, let me check. Got it! About two-twenty klicks per hour!"

"Hell, we've got enough time for a couple of drinks, and a good cigar even," Puss chuckled. Her statement caused everyone's eyes in the cavern widen except Sugar Plum's.

"Well shat, if all you folks are this hot to party we might as well go on and get ready for them now," Puss muttered as she keyed the warnet.

"Here me Troopers! Incoming in about two hours!"

"Molly and Charley, I want the tactical war sat overheads fed into our channel 14 optics when this bunch gets into our area. Be sure and include the IR bands, because even if these guys have IR scanners, It's credits to chopsticks they don't have personnel capes.

"Finally, let me know if you two moles are successful with your "idea" OK?"

"I will be at my station on the ridge above the cabin where I will help Luis give fire control."

"Your station Luis?"

"You already know that, Baby Bird, I be at Molly's fly-swatter."

"Good. I have a new trooper for you. Sharon's green, but she knows the basics and she's game. Where do you want her?"

"I will send her to do back-up for my gunner-medic, Cybill, that good place."

"Si, Luis."

"Now hear me troops, Luis has the con up the valley from the cabin and we let him have any of this bunch that get past us, OK! They'll belong to him and his guys...

"And this outfit does brass jobs too," Puss chuckled.

A chant of, "Do It!" over the warnet was her answer...

*

"Why are we turning to 280 degrees? My information shows the site is a straight 270 from where we are now?" Pitson's Secret Service Chief snapped as he looked up from his hand positioner.

"My orders are to minimize all anomalies in this area. We are aware of three such out here and I am going to deal with each of them in turn," Captain Campbell responded with a cold voice and a very cold stare. "I suggest that you do not interfere with me when I am carrying out my orders..."

"Well then, Captain, carry out your minimizing fast," the gray-faced man snapped. "Also, do your anomalies have ID implants like ours and if so, what frequency do your people use?"

"The older ones will have them, and my locator technician is prepared to scan as soon as we are in range."

"Have him link to my unit then Captain - but only as a suggestion of course," the man smiled blandly as he gestured to his open case on the floor before his canvass seat, "Ours has a much greater range..."

"Corporal, do so!"

"Yes Sir!" the technician responded. He opened his tool kit and began making connections as the five helicopters cruised westward at an altitude of 6,000 meters through the passes in the Canadian Rockies, and the rising sun began lighting the peaks around them.

*

"Sir! We've got us a mole, and a damn good one too!" the electronics officer in the WANG Argus muttered over the intercom. "He got one of our code keys somehow and it looks like he knows what to do with it!"

"Which key, Sparky?" the pilot snapped. Then he ordered, "Take over First while I deal with this."

"Yes Sir," the first officer replied as she took control of the plane and kept it steady on its long oval course 18,000 meters above the US-Canadian border.

The crew of the Argus was tracking the five craft from Cold Lake with their instruments at this altitude as well as with the visuals from the USAF

579

war sats.

"This is turning into a sort of funny training mission though," the first officer added under her breath with a frown.

"The key he is using is "Six–one-two-three thousand", Sir," the electronics officer answered in a puzzled tone.

"Well good! Way damn good!" the pilot sighed as he relaxed and grinned, "Can you send a signal back down our mole's path?"

"Sure I can, but it'll warn him off before we can catch him..."

"This is a good mole, guys. He's a she, and she's ours," the pilot replied. "Trust me - and First!"

"Sir!"

"You don't know just how funny this mission is going to get, beginning now and please note that I have stopped using the term "training.""

"Yes, Sir!" she said as war-joy lit her face...

"Sparky!"

"Sir!"

"Feed these two signals back down to the mole."

"First, send "Restoration" then follow it with, "Welcome aboard, Molly!"

"Yes, Sir!"

"Sir, Molly is replying," then he added after a pause, "And you ain't gonna' believe what she has done!"

*

"Captain Campbell, I'm picking up signals with our locator, Sir!" the technician announced as he watched his consol in the command squad helicopter. "And I've got some buildings on our visual too."

"Good! Run the signals through our archive, and see if we can get a read on who these grub-butts are!"

"Have him search my files as well Captain. We have very good data on our own anomalies, and some of them might have joined up with yours," the gray-faced man said with another unctuous smile.

Captain Campbell watched the screen of their on-board infrared scanner over his technician's shoulder as it began to show the glowing red dots of heat signatures. They were in the woods around the compound of ramshackle buildings that huddled in a mountain valley. He keyed his mike.

"All squads, land and deploy to those huts!" he ordered.

"Gun, herd those in dispersed in the woods back out so we can relate with them."

The gun-ship increased speed and sailed on past the squad 'copters as they angled down toward the valley.

The gun-ship hovered like a dragonfly above the treetops, and the people cowering below in the forest for several moments. Then its pilot began firing short bursts from his small-caliber guns at two of the glowing dots he saw on his helmet eye screen. He ceased firing after a moment and buzzed his craft back and forth above the other red dots...

"We see you all!" the copilot's voice boomed over their loudhailer. "The rest of you, go to back your place! Do it now, or we will give you all what your friends just got."

"I said do it, Now!" and the pilot fired another burst at the hillside toward a third red dot. The pilot watched then, as all the glowing dots on his eyepiece begin moving back toward their compound, all except for his first two targets, whose heat signatures had faded from red to pink...

The lieutenant formed two of his squads into ranks in the open space of the compound after the platoon landed. He aligned them as the adjacent sides of a hollow square...

Captain Campbell stood at the apex of the angle the ranks formed, and glanced again at the printout the locator tech had given him. He waited while the platoon sergeant led the other two squads in a search of the compound.

*

"Miss Marybell, Ma'am," Molly's little voice sounded in Puss' ear on the overriding channel 13, "The Argus sent us a signal a little while ago. It said Welcome, and I told them how to use the code patch I sent them."

"I thought they would," Puss whispered where she stood on the ridge above the cabin.

"Did they like it?"

"Yes, they thought it was pretty neato too, but,"

"But what?"

"I can see from their sat images that some 'copters have landed at the cammy-guy's place!"

"Shat! Go to high resolution and let me know what happens next, as soon as it does, OK!"

"Yes Ma'am," Molly replied, her voice now somber as well as small...

Puss keyed channel 14 of their warnet, "Troopers! The incoming bunch is now just over the hill. They are apparently involved in some op there for the moment, but they will be here soon. Stand by!"

Puss switched back to channel 13. "Molly, you better stay only on this channel with me for now, OK! It always overrides in my helmet. "

"Yes Ma'am," Molly responded in an abstract tone, then she moaned, "OMYGOD! What are they doing?"

*

Captain Campbell watched as the Corporals of the first two platoons pushed and shoved the people to stand before him within the angle formed by the two squads. They were a motley collection of decrepit men, slatternly women and dull-eyed children. They numbered fifteen in all.

"Welcome back," he said in a cold voice.

"We know that some of you are sought for inquiries by the RCMP, and that one of you is a fugitive wanted by the United States."

"We have also found evidence that contraband activities have taken place in your dwellings in defiance of regulations issued by the Government to protect your wellness."

"Finally, we have determined that the rest of you are guilty of knowingly aiding and abetting these violators, and condoning their breaking of the King's Peace as well as that of the E Union."

"Lieutenant!"

"Sir!" the young man with the old eyes responded, with a foot-stamp and a sweeping salute.

"Carry on," Captain Campbell murmured as he turned and strolled back toward the command helicopter with his hands clasped behind his back...

*

"They've killed them! All the cammy people," Molly sobbed on channel 13.

"How?"

"They just made them stand in front of some lines of soldiers, and then shot them – all of them! I can see the dead children's faces..." Molly choked in a tearful whisper.

"Be tough Trooper Two! We Will get that bunch of cowards sooners, but now you've seen the big picture and know who Kris is really fighting so I repeat, be tough Trooper Two!"

"Yes Ma'am - I can do it!" Molly whispered after a moment. "But please make it way bad for this bunch if you can please. I thought Canadians were nice, but these aren't..."

"Wilcomp Molly, and thanks for holding on when I need you," Puss murmured before she clicked to channel 12.

"Camos, hear me! They will be here soon. Do you understand your jobs?"

"Yes Ma'am," a voice she recognized as the hairy one's rasped, "We're supposed to lead 'um up on past the cabin so you can shoot 'um."

"Good. Just remember, stay under your capes until we tell you to do something. They won't see you that way," Puss ordered as she switched to channel 14. She took a deep breath then said in the tone of a condemning judge, "Troopers, hear me! A new order! I have just hoisted the red flag to the incoming bunch based on the latest intel..."

"Red flag! That mean No Quarter," Luis grunted, "You sure?"

"Yes Sergeant, I am sure! We will take no prisoners now, after what they have just done."

"Si, Mi Capitána. I think from you voice this bunch be way bad."

"These are not soldiers. They are hired killers of women and children and have no honor."

"No Quarter!" her troopers roared over the warnet.

"You think true, Cisco!" Puss gritted. "And gang, you are smart troops, and by Buda's butt boils, I do like Smart Troops!"

*

"Fly a slow low pass over this valley," the Secret Service Chief said. "I am picking up a signal!"

The pilot of the lead squad helicopter glanced over his shoulder at Captain Campbell, and after receiving a nod of approval, reduced speed and dropped to an altitude of 300 meters. He led the flight of five 'copters along the length of Molly's valley before pulling up at its head, and circling back over the eastern ridge.

"She's here! And the Hamier woman is too by God!"

"They're both in that cabin down there. We have to take them now dammit, and none of your "minimizing" here, Captain! Washington wants them alive, and you will make that so, if you want to keep Washington happy as well as your Ottawa," he hissed.

Captain Campbell keyed his mike and snapped, "Normal squad approach with standard tactics. Third and Fourth, put down at the mouth of this valley and take the two ridges! First and Second, when they are in place we will land and secure the anomalies in that cabin, alive!"

"Sir!" the squad leader of the First nodded from his seat, and the other squad leader's voices echoed from the receiver.

"Gun ship, stay up and on watch. You may minimize any additional anomalies you see!"

"Sir!" the receiver crackled.

"What is your "normal approach", Captain?" the Secret Service Chief gritted.

"We surround our objective with two squads, then enter it with the other two," Captain Campbell explained patiently as if he were talking to a child, or a Member of Parliament. "By so doing, we thereby constrain the premature departure of any with whom we wish to speak, without undue danger to my men," the Captain finished with a cold smile.

"Don't waste my time! They know we're here now but they will escape while you play safe soldier! You will go straight in and get them - if you want to keep your rank!"

Veins bulged in the Captain's neck and his face flushed in fury as he stared at the Secret Service Chief for a moment, while the flight crew and the squad in his 'copter looked away.

"I am in command here, and responsible! We will do it my way! Do you understand?" Campbell snarled, "All squads, re-confirm!" When he heard his sergeant's replies again, he turned to the Secret Service Chief again and smiled, "All of my transmissions are recorded for Ottawa, and all of what we say in this craft is as well. If your attempt to countermand my orders causes undue causalities to my men, you will answer for it! Do you understand?"

"Humph! What you say means nothing to me, Captain!" the Chief said with a snort. "Just go on and get your people to do their work as best you can dammit! Washington listens to us as well," he glowered, as he touched one of the large buttons on his black trench coat.

"But if your way does not produce the results I want, it is you who will answer for your failure!"

The Captain sneered, "What you say really, really means nothing to me. I hope you can understand that!"

Two of the twin-rotored squad helicopters landed below the mouth of Molly's valley while the lead helicopter and the other squad ships circled above. Their doors opened as soon as they touched down and the two squads leaped to the ground. The men formed into skirmish lines and trotted toward the ridges and began climbing up toward their crests.

*

"Troopers, this bunch is acting way smarto and they are using good

584

tactics too," Puss muttered on channel 14. She watched the sat link for a moment longer on her helmet screen, before continuing, "So cover your backs good guys! Looks like they're coming at us both fore and aft!"

"Luis!"

"Si Mi Capitána!"

"Don't swat that gun ship until my call, which I will give when some of them move on past the cabin. Un-slave the other swatters after you take it out and use yours on any meat on the ground at your end."

"Troopers, you fire at will at all meat in the open when the gun-ship goes down, then use your sat IR feed from Argus to spot and snipe the ones on the ridge behind you."

"Have yourselves a real party in the woods guys and gals, and you can drop your capes because Molly fixed it so they can't see you after they land!"

"You two slave swatter folks! Use them on the ones in the open after the gun ship goes down. But do not burn their squad `copters, we need those to go home! Whoever is closet, shoot dance-gas grenades through their doors instead and take out the pilots while we party with their ground-grubs!"

"You order dance-gas Seester! You real mad at that bunch, right?"

"Yep Cisco. Biggers..."

*

"Third is in position to the east, Sir," the squad sergeant's voice rattled from the lead helicopter's speaker.

"Good. Fourth?" Captain Campbell asked.

"Two more minutes, Sir!" the sergeant of the Fourth squad panted over the intercom link.

"Make it so!" the Captain ordered. "First and Second, we will go in now,"

"Sir!" the lead `copter pilot, and the sergeants of the First and Second squads responded. The two ships banked and headed toward the little valley.

They set down moments later in front of the cabin as their prop-wash flattened the grass. The Lieutenant led the First squad as it scrambled to the ground with weapons ready while the Second squad leaped out of the other craft.

The men trotted toward the cabin and formed into a semi-circle before the little building. Captain Campbell then jumped from the lead `copter followed by the Secret Service chief, who stumbled when he hit the ground.

"Lieutenant, send a detail into that building and bring me those two inside – alive!" the Captain called.

"Sir!" the young officer with the old eyes snapped and pointed to the sergeant of the First squad. The man saluted with a confident grin, then waved to three of his men and led them in a rush through the cabin's splintered and blood-spattered doorway.

"Lieutenant," the sergeant called from the doorway two minutes later, "There's nobody in here!"

"They Are in there! The locator does not make mistakes!" the Secret Service Chief shouted.

"There's nothing in here but a pot of warm water on the cooker, with two little pill bottles in it..." The sergeant called back.

*

Puss watched the figures in front of the cabin through her monocular. She noted the two in blue who were obviously in command, along with the one in the black coat. She keyed channel 12, "Camo 1, what's your position?"

The bushy-haired one rasped, "About half way up the valley, Ma'am, down in the grass."

"Camo 2 and 3, where are you?"

"Luis put us together, up here by a spring."

"Good. Camo 1 on my command, jump up and take a shot at them, then run like hell's behind you straight for the eastern ridge."

"Camo 2 and 3, when he goes in the woods, you hop up and take a couple of shots at the bunch chasing him, then run up the south ridge behind you."

"It's pretty steep," a voice whined, "And the brush is real thick. They'll catch us!"

"Don't worry son, we won't let them get that far."

Puss waited a moment for the three to ready themselves then she whispered, "Camo 1, you go, now!"

She had watched the blue figures bunched before the cabin while she gave her orders to the cammys. Now she zoomed up the power of her monocular and trained it on the faces of the command figures. She watched the one in the black coat wave his arms at the other two until she heard the crack of a rifle.

She zoomed back to wide-view, and saw one of the figures in front of the cabin fall.

"One cammy guy can shoot anyway," Puss thought. Then she switched to 14 and keyed her mike.

"Lock and load gang," she whispered. "If you're not already!"

"Shat, Baby Bird!" a female voice announced on their net with a chuckle, "All of us know to be that way all the time whenever you run the op!"

"I know your voice Fancy Pants. You will report to me later, about your serious breach of com-dis rules as well as the underwear regs in my outfit!" Puss murmured as she zoomed back on the leaders before the cabin."

One of the command figures abruptly waved a squad after the sniper running to cover. The squad double-timed toward Camo 1, and Puss smiled when he made the tree line well in front of the blue-clad men. She switched back to channel 12.

"OK, Camo 2 and 3! Do your bit, now!" Puss whispered as she turned her gaze to the head of the valley.

Two figures rose from the grass in front of the spring after a moment, and stood for another moment. Then they both fired short bursts toward the running men. Puss glanced back at the squad just in time to see one of them stumble and drop to his knees.

"Well I'll be bonged! Looks like there's two cammy guys that can shoot," she muttered as she watched the squad leader halt his men, then wave to-ward the cammy men by the spring.

They were still struggling through the dense brush at the tree line when the blue-clad men began firing. One cammy gave a high-pitched scream and collapsed onto a tangle of thorn vines. She could see his body jerking as the blue-clad figures kept firing, but the other dropped to his belly and snaked out of sight.

"Their bunch can shoot too," she whispered as she watched the squad leader wave five of his men toward the spring and the other five on toward the place where the first sniper had run into the woods.

Puss switched to channel 14, and waited...

The gun-ship's pilot then made a major mistake by flying an intimidat-ing low-level pass above the valley moments later rather than patrolling the ridges above as the Captain had ordered.

Luis' grin was obvious in his voice, "Target Seester! We swat that fly now?"

"Go Cisco! Go Troopers! Go, Go!" Puss growled into her helmet mike as she trained her big gray BAR toward the figures standing before Molly's cabin and worked its charging handle...Luis tapped the button on the control module in his hand and activated the three lasers. The two slaves hidden at the base of each ridge rose into firing position as their tripods extended under the control of their linked computers, then swiveled to follow Luis' master as it tracked the gun-ship rising above the head of the valley. When it circled back over the eastern ridge, Luis clicked his firing key and all three lasers flashed. Their red pulses burned bright holes through the gun-ship's rotor transmission casing and its two pilots. The craft somersaulted when its rotor snapped away and plunged upside-down on the slope across from Molly's cabin. It began to break up as it crashed through the trees, then it exploded when it hit the forest floor. The fireball that rose above the treetops was significant...

"Lasers un-linked! Time for you cook you own meat!" Luis snapped on the warnet as he depressed his laser down toward the valley. The two gunnery troopers took control of their lasers and slaved them to their own helmet screens, then grunted affirmatives as they began blasting into the bunched figures in the valley along with Luis.

All three targeted the men in blue they could see and their lasers swiveled to follow their gaze. They fired short pulses in order to save power because while their targets were soft, the beams had to burn through tree branches to hit them.

*

Captain Campbell watched Second squad as they charged after the sniper, and then toward the other two that suddenly appeared at the head of the valley. He wheeled to his Lieutenant and the Secret Service Chief. "These look like part of that group to the east!" he said. "What is going on here? And what's this funny cooker business?"

"I don't like our situation, Sir." the Lieutenant said as he glared at the Secret Service Chief. "It's going sour!"

"I told you they knew we were coming! I told you to go in fast – but no! You did it your way and you let them get away!" the man in the black coat screamed.

Captain Campbell's face flushed and he was opening his mouth to speak when the gun-ship roared over their heads. He glanced up at it as it climbed and begin to circle over the head of the valley - and then watched it go down after the laser beams flashed.

"What tha..." he muttered then he shouted, "Incoming! Take cover!" as laser hits on some of his men his men in the meadow and made puffs of black smoke spout from their bodies while others began to fall from the gunfire suddenly erupting from the forest.

*

Puss watched the blue-clad figures mill about after the crash of the gun ship while the three in authority waived their arms. She brought her helmet screen to her left eye and focused on the satellite view of the area, and the glowing dots of the invaders on the ridges. None of them were near her position above the cabin, so she laid the BAR across the tree trunk once again. She clicked its change lever from S, to the A of rapid fire and aimed at the three figures as they finally scrambled for cover. She hit the one in the black coat with a three-round burst and fired another burst at the two in blue as they both sprinted into the cabin.

"Shat! I missed," Puss gritted.

"I heard your big gun all the way up here," Molly's little voice suddenly piped over the private channel 13. "Has it started?"

"Bet your straps it has! You got intel for me?"

"The Argus says our code is working Ma'am and I needed to know that you were safe, and I don't have any straps."

"I'll get you some when we finish this. Thanks for your good work and the thought, but stay off this channel for now unless it's way important, you hear?" Puss hissed.

"Yes Ma'am," Molly gulped as she clicked off channel 13 and ceased overriding Puss' warnet connection.

"Repeat Seester! Where you be?" Luis' voice sounded on channel 14.

"Right here Cisco, I've just been talking with Molly. Looks like you guys are doing a bang-up job so far," Puss whispered into her helmet mike as she looked down at all the blue figures lying in the grass.

"You make funny joke, but what about they ferkers in the cabin? I blow eet away?"

"Not yet! Hold them in it until my command. I'm going hunting after the others now. "Whalekiller!""

"Ma'am!"

"Go hunting on your side too! All you guys on both ridges - get ready for a game drive and you can drop your capes. Argus can still see us and them, but they can't see us with their gun ship down and Washington can't see anything, thanks to Molly!"

She smiled at their whispered affirmatives as she laid the BAR under the fallen tree and covered it with leaves. "Don't worry Rocky Baby I'll come back for you real soon." Puss whispered as she dropped IR cape, grabbed her assault rifle and began stalking the blue dots that showed on her eye screen.

*

"Will she be all right?" Molly asked as she looked up from her computer screen to Bila.

"Marybell OK be," then he added in a whisper as his eyes seemed to look far beyond the wall of the cave, "Good hunter she..."

"I'm glad you know about her Sir," Molly said with a little smile. Then in an unconscious echo of Boots' growl she continued, "Because she's important to our mission." She squeezed Jimmy's hand as she sighed, "And mine too."

Bila nodded to the girl with affection in his eyes then he announced, "Stuff ready get," as he waved his arm around the chamber, "Go time sooners come!"

***

Chapter 28
The Party

May 7, 2276 AD
Coastal Mountains of British Columbia,

Puss slaved her assault rifle's sight to her helmet computer and switched her screen display from overhead to horizontal. This changed the image feed from the Argus circling above to show all the blue dots from overhead to ground view.

"Brightest Dot, Bestest Shot," she grinned as she mouthed the mantra from basic training referring to the helmet computer's capability to receive signals from an Argus, gauge the density of the vegetation between its wearer and a target, calculate the chance of a successful hit and then show it by degrees of brightness.

Puss watched the progress of the dots for a moment, then swung her eye screen aside and used her wilderness skills as she stalked to meet the line of blue dots climbing toward to her. She went silently along the crest of the western ridge toward them and lurked behind the bole of an old-growth pine. She checked her helmet screen again and saw the blue dots were still moving along the crest of the ridge toward her, then she expanded her view and saw another cluster of blue dots moving up the crest of the eastern ridge. She noted that the dots in both groups were staying close together and moving rapidly over the rough the terrain.

*

The rattle of firing in the valley had slowed now to occasional bursts from her troopers in the upper end of the valley. Puss knew Luis had ordered it directed toward Molly's cabin to pin the two leaders inside.

"Heads up troops, Puss whispered into her mike, "Looks like the rest of them are trying to get you from the rear, and we all know that can be painful unless we take precautions... I will let them move past me toward the cabin over here then I'll snipe them from above while you guys turn around and say "howdy" from where you are. Please remember me though - and so aim low."

"Who's in high position on the east ridge?"

"Whalekiller here, and I like your fight plan, Ma'am,"

"Good. Now you do like I do. You downhill troopers on the east ridge, turn and meet them when Joseph pushes them to you. Then we'll see who gets the brass job, OK!"

"Do It!" the troopers all muttered in her earphone. Puss showed a fleeting grin as she dropped to crouch in the shadow under the massive root cluster of an ancient pine tree that had been downed in a storm. She waited now, and watched the ten blue dots on her eye screen move toward her. She heard the noise they made then, and she saw figures in blue jump suits trotting through the trees a moment later. Puss grimaced at the noise they made as they crashed through the understory bush then tensed as the first man in the line waved toward the valley below. The group changed direction at his command and picking up their pace, began double-timing down the ridge toward Molly's cabin.

Puss flipped her eye screen back down and bounding to her feet, followed behind the last blue dot until it became bright before her left eye. She paused and holding her rifle at her hip, moved its muzzle until the thin black crosshair covered the dot. She fired a three-shot burst, and the dot stopped...

She loped down the slope until she paused again, and trained her sight on the next blue dot, and then the next that was clear on her screen. She killed them both with short bursts but the only reaction from the squad was to increase their pace down the ridge and ignore the ones who had fallen. Puss shook her head with another grimace and began running after them again with eyes that were very cold.

*

"Troopers! They come down the western ridge now, about face and present arms!" Puss whispered into her helmet mike as she paused behind a tree for a moment.

"East ridge, you OK?" she then asked.

"We OK. We track and attack," Joseph Whalekiller's voice sounded in her helmet.

"Good. Remember, no quarter!"

"No quarter is no problem for me. Rat collected my father and my sister along with her baby last month," Joseph replied in a very flat voice. "This bunch works with Rat, right?"

"Right," Puss whispered as she thought back to the Gala, and remembered the bravery of the two Hokkaido Indians, and the baby boy Bila had rescued.

*

Sharon had saluted back in the cave when Puss had offered her a Chin assault rifle and a bandoleer, then the young woman had clipped a magazine on its side and charged a round with practiced motions.

"Looks like you know what you're doing," Puss had said with a nod. "Let's go outside and I'll show you how to use a helmet and a cape."

"The Gov's survel sats can't see us when we wear these capes," Puss had said when they stood in the flat outside of the adit. "But Argus can because our helmets tell it where we are."

"Don't worry though, our Argus doesn't tell everything it knows and it doesn't talk to the bad guys either, OK!" she had finished with a crooked grin when she placed a helmet on Sharon's head. The young woman had listened and looked, then her eyes had widened as Puss showed her the full capabilities of the combat helmet, including its visual link to the Argus flying above them.

"This blinking red dot is you, OK? This always shows you where you are."

Sharon had looked at a view in the tiny helmet screen Puss positioned in front of her left eye and saw an overhead of the ridge where they stood, but without vegetation. It also had shown fifteen red dots, two of which were very close on a small flat in the side of the ridge. One was blinking...

"Wow!" Sharon had whispered. This is great!" Then she had sighed, "I wish my dad could have had these..."

"Me too," Puss had replied as she patted Sharon's shoulder. Then she had snapped, "But now it's time you go to war Missy!"

"Yes Ma'am," Sharon had gulped.

"Luis, give Sharon a beacon. Sharon, go to Luis and do what he says."

A second red dot then had begun to blink on her helmet screen.

"Go now, Trooper Five!" Puss ordered.

"Yes Ma'am, and thanks!" Sharon had grinned as she turned and loped with long strides up through the forest.

*

Sharon trotted to a position near the base of the eastern ridge. Her buckskins blended into the colors of the thicket where Cybill was hiding and she panted as she dropped down beside the woman, "Luis sent me to back you up. Is this OK with you?"

"I heard that you were coming Missy. You're young but Luis just told me you might do", Cybill whispered as she covered her mike with a fingertip.

"My dad taught me pretty good," Sharon whispered back. "I'll try."

"Do you know how to kill?" the woman hissed.

"Yes, if I have to..."

"You'll have to do today. This is a bad bunch coming at us, and our job is to make them not!"

"Not, like in not alive?"

"You catch the ball quick, but can you handle that?"

"Yep," Sharon said as she half-opened the bolt on her assault rifle and displayed the round in its chamber.

"Looks like you might be capable kid," Cybill muttered." So I will trust you with my butt when the party starts..."

The two then heard the crackle of assault rifle fire from up the valley a moment later, then the stuttering thunder of Puss' big rifle.

"And it sounds like that's about now!" Cybill grunted. "You know battle first aid?"

"Mom taught me about that real good."

"Good. Now watch our backs. I'll cover our front."

"Yes Ma'am!"

"You'll do kid," Cybill muttered. Then they both heard the sound of a crash and an explosion in the distance, and a quiet ding from her weapon signaling Luis had un-slaved it.

"It's party time for real now!" Cybill whispered as leaped from the thicket to her laser and plugged a slender cable into the control unit mounted on its tripod. She placed her eye screen on targets in the meadow and as she focused on them, the hot end of her heavy projector swiveled toward the blue dots in her cross hairs and she began to pulse it.

Sharon was fascinated and watching her eye screen where the blue dots were showing a red halo as their heat signature suddenly increased when Cybill and the other laser gunners hit them, until she heard footsteps crunching on the leaves.

She didn't react in time...

A blue-clad figure stormed down the ridge behind Cybill and fired a burst at her where she stood next to her laser and concentrating on the figures the meadow.

Cybill slumped and Sharon screamed in rage. She spun about and empted her magazine at the man, then snapped another stick onto her rifle and leaped to where he writhed on ground in the pine needles. "Die you bastard," she yelled as she emptied the second magazine into his face. Then she ran to where Cybill lay. She knelt and cradled the woman's head on her lap.

"I'm so sorry," Sharon said with a sob, "I let you down..."

Cybill's lips twitched and she forced from her throat, "You do goo... Thank fo--" then her eyes glazed and her head lolled back across Sharon's arm.

"She's dead!" Sharon screamed after a moment of silent shock as she held Cybill's body in her arms and rocked it in her grief.

"SHUT YOU UP, Silly slut!!" Luis snarled on the warnet. "You get out my op if you can't handle a hit on us! You disgrace you father! You go back to cave, Now!"

Sharon shuttered at Luis' voice. She took a deep breath and stood, letting Cybill's body slide from her lap. "Sir," she whispered into her mike after a moment, "Trooper Sharon ready for duty, Sir."

Luis kept her waiting for a minute before he grunted, "You get second chance now because of you father. But no third chance ever again from me, ¿Sabe Ustedides?"

"Yes sir, and Ja Boss!"

"OK. We see..." Luis grunted. Then he snapped, "Now go here and do some good fight G'dammit!" as he showed her another beacon that was at the base of the eastern ridge.

"Yes Sir," Sharon gulped. Then she sobbed, "Thank you, Sir," and bounded down the slope to her new post. "And thanks for what we had Joseph," Sharon whispered to herself as she ran toward the beacon Luis had had given her, "Now I can be happy if it's time for me to die."

*

Sharon paused every two hundred meters to check her bearings and eye screen for a moment as she panted, then began running again. She was at the base of the ridge when she checked her screen for the last time and saw two blue dots also closing toward her beacon.

"Look out! They're behind you," Sharon panted into her helmet mike.

"Behind who Little Buddy?" Joseph growled over the war net.

"The who I'm supposed to back up down here!"

"Fancy Pants," a female voice broke in, "And I've already picked those two up but get your bongos on down here anyway, "little buddy". It's party time!"

"I'm Sharon and here I come," the girl panted while she trotted northward inside the tree line.

"I see you, Sharon. I'm taking us exclusive."

The U.S. warnet allowed those on the general unit channel to create an exclusive link for local tactics with any others that a fighter designated. This feature was developed early in the Chin war and greatly reduced chatter and traffic confusion on the American warnets. The Chin never used this logical concept however because their battlefield communications were all one-way, from the top down...

"Sharon, suggest you move fifty meters up-slope and take them from the flank while I take their front. They can't see our heat now that their `copters are down, and they only know where I am if someone saw my muzzle flashes when I asked their `copter pilots for a dance," the woman chuckled.

"Good plan," Sharon whispered as she slowed from a run to a silent stalk and dropped her cape. She began angling back up the slope and moved silently from tree to tree, pausing at every tenth step to check her screen. She had been able to elude the Captain for the two years he held her mother and brothers hostage because of the skills her father had taught her. The times that the Captain had lurched out of her mother's cabin and thrashed around the ridges searching for her were the only amusing memories she had of that terrible period in her life...

"Thanks Jimmy," she whispered as she slipped through the forest, "Molly told me you paid him back - real good."

*

Sharon paused for a last check of her screen and saw the two blue dots a hundred meters to her front and Fancy Pants' beacon fifty meters to her left, just inside the tree line.

"Face time now," she whispered as she flipped the screen away from her eye and leaped forward. She heard the two before she saw them, "Not too good in the woods," she panted, then she saw a flash of blue through the shadowy gloom of the forest. Sharon began a silent run, dodging around the tree trunks until she had a clear view of the two men. She sighted on one and was squeezing her trigger when she heard a short rattle of gunfire from her left. Her target crumpled and fell, but the other blue-clad figure dodged behind a tree and returned fire.

She heard a grunt in her earphone, then Fancy Pants gasped, "I'm hit."

"Not again!" Sharon sobbed. She emptied her magazine at the man in blue behind the tree and he spun and fell. She bounded down to the trooper's position and leaping over a log found Fancy Pants tightening her rifle sling around her thigh.

"I'm too damn dumb!" the woman grunted when Sharon dropped to her knees beside her. "I stood up for a good shot at them and took the one but I let the other bastard take me Dammit!"

"I can help," Sharon whispered. "How do I get to your leg?"

"Combat suits are wound-friendly and there's a med kit on my belt," the woman grunted. "Un-zip it at my waist then un-zip it around my leg. I'll need a bullet patch, and two if it went through." Then she forced a smile, "Thanks for the backup."

"You're welcome, Ma'am," Sharon replied as she opened the woman's suit and examined her wound. "It went through and looks clean, and there's not too much blood so it missed your artery." She groped in the woman's med pouch and found two compresses, and snapping their med pods, applied them over the entry and exit wounds.

"You can take the tourniquet off now I think," Sharon said as she sat back on her heels and inspected her bandages wrapped around the woman's smooth black thigh.

"I can see where you get your nickname tho," Sharon grinned as she nodded toward the woman's underpants, a riot of scarlet and gold lamé brocade. "They really are fancy! Wish I had some like that."

"Thanks again for the backup," the woman sighed as the drugs in the compresses took effect, "And you will have some like mine when we get out of here I promise," she said as she removed her helmet.

Sharon gasped as she saw the woman's face and head. "You're beautiful!" she whispered to the exquisite ebony Nefertiti before her. "What's your real name?"

"Thanks much again Sharon, but for your nice words this time. You couldn't pronounce my name though. I'm Ethiopian and we love bright colors, but my name in the language of my tribe has sounds you can't make. So just call me Fancy Pants, or Panty for short. Then the woman became serious, "I'm stable now so if you want to help some more, go check those `copters to make sure all their crews are deaders. Stay upwind though, and do Not breath deeply. Dance gas dissipates in a half hour, but never take chances!"

"Yes Ma'am, will do!" Sharon said as she clipped a fresh magazine on her rifle.

"And Sharon, trust me," Pants grinned, "You don't have to use a full stick every time. Three pops will do."

"Yes Ma'am, my dad taught me all about that too, but I've been hunted ever since the Chin pulled out and war ended, until your bunch came anyway. Now I'm the hunter, and besides it feels good when I do it..." Sharon grinned and was turning to go to the helicopters when Joseph's voice sounded in her earphone.

"You've been quite for along time Little Buddy. You OK?"

"We're OK Big Man, I've been on exclusive with Panty. She took a hit in the leg, but how did you break in on us?"

"Thanks for your help, Little Buddy," Fancy Pants said with a grin after placing the tip of her finger over her mike.

"She's stable, right?" Joseph's voice insisted in Sharon's ear.

Sharon gave Fancy Pants a friendly wave then made a rude gesture toward the top of the ridge, "Yes, but she will need a litter," she replied. "I'm going to check out their copter pilots now like she told me," Sharon added. "But I want to know how you broke in on us?"

"Rank hath its privileges as well as its obligations Trooper Six," Puss' whisper sounded in her earpiece. "Looks like you're doing a pretty good job so far though."

"I knew there was another reason to like you, Leather Gal" Joseph chuckled. Then he growled, "But it's still party time,"

"Yes! Now you go do some more good hits for us Missy," Luis' voice snapped as he broke in as well.

"Yes Ma'am! And Yes Sir! And Yes Sir! But my name is Sharon dammit and don't you ever forget it! Damn all your hairy butts anyway!"

"You'll do, Sharon," Luis said with a chuckle.

"Ja Sharon," Joseph replied next, "But don't forget to come back, OK!"

"Your dad taught you much good stuff Sharon," Puss added, "Now go on use it! As for all you others," she hissed, "Quit doin' your personal yacky on my damn warnet, Dammit!"

Puss was obeyed immediately.

"I pity any poor ferkers who make either Puss, or you real mad!" Fancy Pants said with a chuckle as she blocked her mike and waved Sharon toward the meadow where the helicopters sat.

*

Joseph spoke on the command channel several moments later, "Sorry for breaking com-discipline Ma'am, but I was sort of interested in how she was doing."

"Understand Joseph and accepted. Look's like she's good for a keeper too, so congratulations. But now what's doing on your side? Be quick!" Puss whispered into her mike as she stepped behind another tree and watched the remaining men in blue lumber on down the ridge.

"The rest of my bunch except for the outriders that Sharon and Pants took out have just turned down-hill and are moving in a line abreast. So all I have to do is go from left to right. Right? " he said with a grin that Puss could hear.

"Good plan Whalekiller. I have been going from back to front over here and taken three out already, but my bunch won't stand and fight. Ten to nada yours won't either."

"Think you and me can take them all before they get to the valley, Ma'am?"

"I think we should we let our troopers have some fun. I go to the general net now Joseph, just listen."

"Yes Ma'am!"

"All right gang, I've got seven bad guys in a file in front of me and Whale-killer is chasing seven in a rank down his side. Suggest you all turn and take them from the front while he and I, your max leader snipe their butts. Is this workable?"

"Do It!" her troopers all growled.

"Make it happen!" she whispered as she started running silently after the squad, following them by the noise they made as they crashed down the slope. As soon as she came close enough to see the blue of their uniforms again she halted beside a tree and watched them. Puss shrugged when she saw they were still moving at an urgent trot and forcing they way through the under-story growth. She flipped her eye screen aside and used her open sights to kill the two rear-most blue figures with two short bursts. The rest of the group ignored their fallen members again, and continued their rush toward Molly's cabin. Puss shook her head as she remembered this same blind obedience in the Chin troops when they were ordered forward during the war.

"Damn, I hope that crappo attitude isn't showing up in the rest of the world now," she whispered, before she said over the warnet, "Only five coming down the west ridge now troopers, think you can take them out?" She got her answer a moment later when a rattle of gunfire erupted from the valley. Puss dodged behind a tree and grimaced as bullets whizzed past, or thwacked into its trunk.

"G'dammit I don't like wild shooters! We will have a Major lecture about wasting ammo when this op is over!" she said with a snarl.

*

"You and yours safe Joseph?" Puss asked on the general net from where she stood just inside the tree line at the base of the ridge, after the firing had stopped. "We be good over here and we got all of ours. Any left on your side?"

"We OK," Joseph's voice sounded in her earpiece, then she heard a single shot ring out followed after a second by a long burst of fire. A voice sounded on the warnet a moment later, "Shat! The sneak bastard got Fred, dammit. But there's none left over here either, now..."

"Their commanders are still down here though," Puss answered with an iron voice as she touched her suit's tiny keypad and highlighted the two glowing blue dots in Molly's cabin on all their helmet screens. "All of you assemble at the edge of the meadow sooners and you troopers who are good with grenades, prepare to fire two volleys on my command. Load first with HEAT and then Hot." "Yes Ma'am, but we're all good with grenades," a laconic voice drawled in her earpiece.

"So prove it."

Puss then switched to channel fourteen and asked in a very gentle voice, "Molly, are you ready for us to blast your home?"

"Yes, Ma'am," Molly sighed, "I've got all the stuff out of it I really want and Jimmy has too - and it wasn't a good home anyway."

Puss switched back to the warnet, "Troopers! Report when you are in position. Then she switched to the command net, "Luis, Molly's safe now. Put Bila on our command net then you two move forward quickie and help keep those two pinned in the cabin. I can't see the front door from my station but I will cover their hidey hole."

"Si, Seester," Luis responded after a moment and Bila grunted, "Ja Boss.

Ready at go now we!"

"You get picture pretty quickie Beeg Man," Luis' voice sounded in her helmet, "But how you know it time to go?"

Puss listened as Bila answered, "Hear die they. Come we now. `Copters down. All Go troopers!"

"How you know that?" Luis asked, with an unusual uncertainty in his voice.

"You no hear die they?"

"No."

"Hear all I. They bad die. Much hurt with. You more listen kill time next do we"

"OK." Luis paused for a moment, then Puss heard him answer, "Ja Boss." and she heard Bila order, "Go we now, Troopers out move time!

Molly Sugar Plum ride. Charlie, Jimmy help she."

Puss shook her head then whispered, "I'll think about this tomorrow..."

*

Puss heard the boom of Bila's Rigby five minutes later followed by a burst of assault rifle-fire after another minute. "Congratulations Luis, you almost kept up with him," Puss said into over the command net.

"Where thees man come from?" Luis' voice panted in her ear, "And why we not have heem to kill Chin with us in thee war?"

"Two good questions Sargento. I have some thoughts on the first but nada on your second," she answered as she heard Luis fire another burst and the Rigby boom again.

Her troopers began announcing, "In place," after another few minutes. She waited until they had all reported.

"Ready?" Puss asked.

"Ready!"

"Execute!"

Eleven rifle grenades exploded against the front and sides of Molly's cabin seconds later, then eleven more arced in and exploded with the white heat of incendiary warheads. Six of these hit where the first wave of high explosive had smashed holes in the walls, three landed on the roof and two sailed precisely through the shattered doorway.

"Dammit troopers, you ferkin do speak true," Puss muttered as the building burst into a ball of flames.

A figure that looked more like a torch than a human leaped through the doorway a moment later. Joseph Whalekiller stepped from the edge of the forest and killed the old-eyed young lieutenant with a single shot. Captain Campbell stayed inside the roaring inferno of Molly's cabin however, and they all heard his hoarse screams until he died.

"All troopers! Attend me!" Puss ordered after several minutes. "Assemble at their 'copters with all your gear. When we are loaded, torch any we don't need."

"Luis, see if the two cammys want to go with us, then have some of your guys go back with Bila to get Molly and Jimmy's stuff while I run up the ridge to collect my new old friend."

"Si, Mi Capitána."

"Go get Fancy Pants, and bring Cybill and Fred home too. When we go, no one and nothing is left behind!"

Jimmy's voice rang clear over the general sounds of agreement on the warnet, "What about mom and Mike, and Sugar Plumb?" he gulped.

"I said All Troopers son," Puss answered. "Donna was married to Big Mike and Little Mike is his son so they are troopers by blood. Sugar Plum is different though."

"W-what do you mean?" Jimmy stammered on the warnet, now suddenly quiet.

"She earned the honor all on her own, just like you and Molly have done," Puss answered in a quiet voice.

Puss let them all cheer on the warnet for several minutes before she asked, "We do have two other 'copter drivers beside Luis, don't we?"

"At my count Ma'am we have six including me," Joseph answered with a chuckle, "After all, General McAuliffe said you wanted talent for this mission."

"Sure looks to me like he found some too, but now, move out! Yacky time comes later, OK!"

"Ja Boss!"

*

"Action appears to be over, Sir," the battle observer announced on the intercom from his station at the main display in the U.S. Air Force Argus flying far above Molly's valley. He could see not only the sat feed he was giving Puss' troopers but also the position of every aircraft in the air all across western North America, and his screen highlighted those that were military.

"What's the score, Lieutenant?" the Pilot asked.

"I have two helmets not responding, so I think we lost them. I can also see two non-troopers on visual with the rest of our guys, and something that looks mighty like a horse. They're all loading their gear and themselves into three MULL 'copters. I see another MULL starting to burn close to a second 'copter already burned out. There is a third downed in the woods and the cabin is burning - and damn if they didn't just load the horse too!"

"What about the attack force?" the Pilot snapped.

"There are no vitals showing from them at all, Sir."

"Good. Sparkey, link me to their warnet."

"Yes, Sir!" the communications technician, always called that in the service, said as she set the frequency and opened the link. "You're on, Sir."

"Argus to Ground Grunts," the Pilot said. "How was your party?"

"Ground Grunts to Argus. It was short but sweet," Puss' voice sounded on their intercom. "Thanks for the backup friends."

"You're welcome. We think we know the score down there but you say for sure, and identify please."

"We got what we came for and more," Puss replied, "But two good troopers and a local friendly lost it all, dammit. Anyway, this bunch was major bad so we made sure they lost it all too."

"Red flag?" the Pilot asked.

"Real red."

"Good decision, Ma'am. We watched when those bastards outted that bunch close to you. What's next?"

"We're taking our folks in these 'copters back to the barn," Puss replied, "So tell your folks at home base who we are, OK!"

"Yes Ma'am, wilcomp - but is that a real horse we saw you loading?"

"Yep. We salvaged some of the bunch's jumpsuits that were not too burned and used them to make a footing for her in the cargo bay of our third 'copter. Jimmy jumped her in and she took it like a trooper. She's fine. Her name is Sugar Plum by the way and she's a real sweetie," Puss chuckled.

"Ooo-kaay, if you say so Ma'am," the Argus pilot drawled, "But I repeat, who are you who is boss of this op?"

"Oh, I'm sorry. I forgot. They call me Baby Bird."

"Jesu-Buda Ma'am!" the Pilot gasped, "You boss this op?" then gaining control of himself he continued, "We'll watch over you as you go home and let certain folks know you are on your way!"

"Thank you, but I've already had a private chat with one of them so he and his friends know we are coming home, and I'm just ground grunt, so don't you Ma'am me, OK!"

"You're The Baby Bird," the Pilot said answered, "So that makes you a real "Ma'am" to me no matter what you say."

"Thank you, Sir. You are a true gentleman," Puss murmured.

The Pilot was a very experienced war flyer with many missions to his credit, but he blushed at Puss' words.

Sparky saw the Pilot's blush and after Puss clicked off, giggled. The Pilot glared at her for a moment then he grinned like a teen-aged boy after his first kiss.

***

Chapter 29
The Intervention

Captain Campbell's screams were recorded by the automatic monitoring function in Ottawa, until his microphone melted. The staff there had taken a lengthy afternoon tea break however because the satellite feed showing his mission to the Kitimat area was mysteriously blanked out so did they not listen to the recording until the U.S. survel satellite feed was restored later, just as abruptly as it had been lost.

When they returned to their screens they saw nothing they recognized in the real image bands, but they immediately spotted three large heat signatures when they switched to infrared. The technician at the screen hissed between his teeth, switched back to the real image band and zoomed in to a little valley. He saw the smoking remains of a small cabin, the smoldering wrecks of two helicopters and many figures laying in the meadow. None of the figures moved, and most were naked.

The technician also realized that he had not seen heat signatures from the figures when he scanned the valley on the infrared band several minutes before, and he recognized the two wrecked helicopters as part of Captain Campbell's force, so he clicked to the Captain's voice monitor. He saw that it had stopped recording, and backed it up and played the last three minutes on the chip. The staff all listened to the sounds of gunfire followed by explosions and Captain Campbell's hoarse shouts and then his screams until the recording stopped...

The staff looked at the clock and then at each other. It was now 19:00

hours in Ottawa and they knew that Pierre Bohica retired to his quarters at 18:00 hours. The staff also knew that disturbing the Under Secretary with bad news was always a major career shorting error therefore they decided to wait until the morning to report Captain Campbell's apparent death, and the obvious failure of his mission.

*

The WANG Argus monitoring Puss' mission had blanked the USAF survel sat images from the valley with the code patch Molly had written, therefore the Secret Service monitoring room in Washington did not get visual coverage restored until 17:00 hours. These technicians were not on break however so they quickly located the little valley by the heat signatures of the cabin's ashes and the downed helicopters.

They also saw figures in the grass that did not show heat signatures, including one in a black trench coat. They checked the recording of the Secret Service Chief's voice monitor next. It was still playing, but there was no sound.

A technician fast-backed the chip until he heard noise, then he played on the speaker. They all first heard their Chief's voice and others in shouting argument, then there was a rattle of small arms fire and then screams.

The last coherent sounds on the recording were the splat of bullet impacts followed by a grunt in the Chief's voice, then a thump. Sounds were muffled and unrecognizable after that until the technician fast-forwarded as he watched the intensity screen and time meter. When he saw a small cluster of peaks in the almost flat intensity line at an elapsed time of 52 minutes from the last coherent sound, he stopped and backed the chip again.

The sound was still muffled when he played it, but they all recognized a number of explosions, followed for several minutes by what appeared to be screams. There was only a hiss of white noise after that...

"Get the Deputy Chief," the senior technician finally said. "After we give him this intel we let him take it on up to the Oval." The monitoring staff all agreed this was a good plan, and safe.

*

"Madam Governor," Boots announced as she rapped her knuckles on the carved frame of the open door to Regina's office.

"Don't you Madam me young lady!" the white-haired woman with lively eyes ordered in a mock stern voice from behind her ornate desk. "I answer to best to Regina, or even better, Ginny!"

"OK, Ginny," Boots answered with a grin, "I have just learned that our troopers have hoisted the Rattlesnake flag way biggers, so it's time for the next step. But only if you concur, Governor Ginny, Ma'am."

"I heard that the Chin placed a very large price on your head during the late war, and now I can see why," Regina said with a sparkle in her eyes. "Kris, you have the ability to make the things happen that you want to happen, whenever you want them to happen. This is a very powerful talent."

"It's not me. My friends do it for me," Boots whispered as she bowed her head for an instant, then braced to attention again. "Governor Drake," she announced in a strong voice, "The enticement and subsequent destruction of a foreign force, as well as the extraction of our own force all have been carried out successfully. Our troopers are now returning to base and will land at the WNG field in approximately two hours."

"Would you consider meeting them when they land?" Boots then asked with a look that was innocent, somewhat.

"Yes Kristina, I will meet them when they land, but one of these days I might put a price on your head myself!" Regina said with a slight smile.

"Thanks Ginny, you've just told me I'm still going in the right direction," Boots answered with a crooked grin.

*

"Washington Air National Guard tower here, Incoming helicopter flight identify yourselves, Now!" the duty person in the Seattle tower ordered. Then the thick comset he had placed on the dusty top of his consol when he came on duty dinged...

"Yes," he said after he clicked it on and listened for a moment. "Yes, Sir!" he said again, before clicking it off.

"Incoming helicopter flight! You are cleared to land at WNG airfield pads 041, 042 and 043. You will be met upon landing." Then the duty person in the tower heard another chime on the thick comset. He listened for a moment again, then clicked the set off a second time and went back to the 'copter pilots.

"OK incoming friends I have also been informed that you will be welcomed major, so I suggest you be wearing wear dress blues, tennis shoes and a light coat of oil when you de-plane," the tower controller said with a chuckle.

"Thanks WNG Tower," Puss' voice crackled in his ear. "I will attend to this intel now but then I can always attend to you later, right?"

"Yes, Ma'am," Tower gulped, "I didn't mean..."

"Son, I'm coming home after a short but real hard party so I'll let you live to learn. But don't you ever ferk with me or Hoppy again, OK!"

"Yes Ma'am, I sure won't," Tower gulped again, "But who's Hoppy?"

"Old joke son. Ask me about Hop Along Cassidy, and what he did to all those Indians later when I have time for you."

*

The three black helicopters paused and hung on their rotors above the pads at the Washington National Guard airfield, then slowly let down. Their rotors were still spinning when their doors opened and Boots and Regina walked forward to meet them from where they had been standing beside an Army sedan.

Puss jumped down on to the tarmac from the first helicopter and took ten paces forward. "Troopers, Fall In!" she shouted as she turned to face the three craft. Their rotors slowed to a stop and Luis and the troopers jumped out of the first and second helicopters. They formed up in a precise rank before her still wearing their stained fighting suits and combat packs, and carrying their weapons.

Puss ordered, "Render Honors!" The troopers braced to attention and presented arms.

Puss turned on her heel to face Boots and gave a very formal salute. "Field Force Alpha reporting back, Ma'am. Mission carried out."

"Thank you, Sergeant" Boots said as she returned Puss' salute. "I understand that you were successful, in several ways."

"I lost two troopers and a friendly Ma'am so I do not consider my mission successful Ma'am," Puss answered with bleak eyes.

"Marybell, if I may call you that," Regina said as she stepped forward. "You and all your troopers have served the cause of freedom and of our safety very well. Therefore as Governor of the State of Washington, I am awarding all of you Medals of Gratitude which I will present to each of you at the Capitol after they have been struck."

Jimmy mounted Sugar Plum in the bay of the third helicopter when he heard Regina's statement and urging the pony with his knees jumped her out on to the to the tarmac.

"Hey Governor Ma'am!" he shouted, "What about Molly and Mom and Sharon and Little Mike and Sugar Plum, and him?" Jimmy asked in a voice that started strong, but ended with an adolescent squeak.

Regina was startled when the horse leaped from the third helicopter, then she looked up at the red-headed boy astride it and shook her head.

"Ginny," Boots whispered, "Marybell told us that she was bringing some new troopers back with her too."

Regina then watched as a very pregnant young girl and a young woman, both clad in buckskin, an older woman carrying a red-headed child and a hairy man in cast-off camouflage clothing all climbed down from the third helicopter and cautiously moved to stand behind the line of troopers. She smiled and nodded, but her eyes widened when Bila stepped to the door of the first helicopter.

He paused for a second them jumped down to the tarmac and walked to Puss' side.

"Be here Trooper Three," he announced. He added with a glare in his eyes, "Be troopers them good. All. Every!"

"I agree with that!" Puss said as she waved toward the people standing behind her squad. "Governor, these people are troopers too, Dammit!"

Regina looked at the large man and the tense woman beside him in their muddy combat gear who now dominated the scene. She saw something in their faces that made her whisper aside to Boots while still holding Puss' and the big man's gaze, "I see what you mean when you say that your friends do it for you. These two are very strong friends."

"Yes, and I am very lucky," Boots whispered.

Regina looked past the mud-smeared man and woman to the proud troopers, and the motley group behind them. She looked then at the boy sitting calmly on his horse for a heartbeat, then turned her gaze back to Puss and the big man and muttered, "This crazy thing just might work after all."

Then she took a deep breath and ordered in a strong voice, "Give me all of your names and you all will receive our Medal of Gratitude in Olympia!"

"I will attend to that Ma'am!" Puss said as she saluted again. "But what about Sugar Plum?" she then asked with a little smirk.

"If that boy can ride his pony up the steps of the Capitol, she will receive her medal too! Son, you have a real good horse so take care of her!" Regina said as she looked at Jimmy. "I used to be a rodeo clown for fun in my spare time so I know something about good horses, as well as how to dodge bad bulls."

Jimmy's eyes widened, and he was opening his mouth to ask a question, when Puss asked, "Madam Governor, are we dismissed now? We really would like to stand down because we're all major hungry for real food, and I really do want a shower."

"Well Done Troopers! All of you! Dismissed! All my troopers are dismissed," Regina called as she waved her hand.

The squad gave a cheer of "Do it" and began trotting toward the trucks that had pulled up on the tarmac. Jimmy dismounted and after dropping the pony's reins to ground-tie it, helped Charlie load his and Molly's equipment into one of the trucks. Then the troopers helped Charlie into the truck up and Joseph boosted Sharon up as well, with a very friendly butt squeeze.

Sharon smiled…

Luis escorted Molly and Jimmy's mother and little Mike to a personnel bus and Jimmy leaped into his saddle again, and trotted Sugar Plum behind the bus as it drove away from the apron.

The hairy cammy guy scowled at first, then began running after the troopers in the trucks. "Hey! Wait for me," he shouted.

Puss took Bila's hand and strolled over to Boots and Regina. "Madam Governor," Boots murmured, "I would like to present my friends to you. Marybell Bowling has been important to me for a very long time, and Bila had recently proved himself to be equally so in the recent past."

Regina looked at the two, first at Puss standing with easy confidence and meeting her gaze with hard eyes that also seemed to smile, then up to Bila whose eyes showed great strength but did not threaten.

"Kristine, you told me that you had good friends, and I now see that you spoke the truth," Regina said to Boots then she turned back to Marybell and Bila, "I hope you two will become my friends as well because your friendship would be important to me,"

"Ma'am, we already are, and have been ever since your announcement the other night," Puss said as she held out her hand.

"Friend!" Bila announced and held his hand out palm up.

"Ginny," Boots whispered sotto voce, "As I have learned, you're stuck with them now. You can't back out of this, ever."

Regina took both of their hands, Puss' small strong one and Bila's massive one, and said as she looked at the two, "Thanks for the warning Kris, but I wouldn't even if I could."

"Now lets get you back to what passes for civilization around here," She continued, "Marybell, you and Bila get in the car with us and my driver will drop you off wherever you want. I need to borrow Kris for a while but I will send her back when I have finished with the lady."

"I suggest Rick's, it has facilities for smelly troopers and I have a staff meeting there in about two hours anyway," Boots said as she climbed into the sedan and seated herself on a forward seat.

"Since Mack followed your suggestion and furnished me with a helicopter for my office because of the deplorable condition of the roads, you will have no trouble in meeting your commitment," Regina said as she hopped in to sit beside Boots. The driver drove the sedan three hundred meters over to a small army helicopter with "Washington State" newly stenciled on its side. After she and Regina climbed out of the sedan, Boots stuck her head back in the sedan's rear seat and ordered, "Save me one of Rick's Midnight Specials and a drink too, OK!"

"Vodka is not an issue but don't be too long, because Bila and I are gonna' eat all the damn cow in sight!" Puss drawled as she slapped his thigh.

"Real food, real food, real food," Bila chanted. Then he said with compelling eyes, "Come you us soon us at or..."

"You're repeating yourself, ya' Big Thud," Boots interrupted with a laugh. "Let's go Ginny before it gets over our ankles."

***

Chapter 30
The Reaction, II

"Sir," the Deputy Chief of the Secret Service, an organization known with gallows humor in Washington as the "SS", announced when he was ushered into the oval office, "We have a situation!"

"What the hell is going on now, and where's my Chief?" Bradney snapped.

"Your Chief is part of the situation, unfortunately," the functionary answered in a bland voice.

"Talk straight!" Bradney ordered as he jumped to his feet and stormed around Queen Victoria's desk.

"The Canadian operation to plug the Network mole-hole apparently failed, Sir."

"Sat intel went dead while their force was in route. When we got the feed back,"

"Or someone gave it back to us," he thought,

"We located the site of the interference, but all the Canadians were dead, and most of their uniforms had been stripped off. Our Chief was also on the ground, and we couldn't get a signal from his transmitter."

"Get me René," Bradney yelled!" His aide's voice sounded moments later on Bradney's desk speaker.

"Secretary Bohica is on line, Sir."

"René, what tha' hell is going out there? You said your bunch could handle this little thing!"

"Unfortunately, Monsieur Le Président," Pierré responded in a very frosty tone, "My best intelligence on the situation is that some of our esteemed tranquility associates were assaulted while performing their assigned task by elements that apparently came from the country you currently are attempting to rule. This is unacceptable!"

"Ferk your attitude thugs, Bohica! They failed and don't try to blame it on us. Just tell me what you are going to do about this mess next!"

"Nothing - since an important group of my Assurers of National Comity is dead on the ground at this site and will be gnawed on by wolves before we can retrieve them, my gunship and one of my helicopters are destroyed and three more have been seized by these obviously capable persons from the place you used to call Seattle.

"Instead, Monsieur Le Président you just tell me what you are going to do about "your" mess next," Pierré replied with a dry sniff, before clicking off.

Bradney abruptly left the Oval Office, and paced to the West Wing, and the privacy of his Presidential suite.

*

Charles C. Calhoun listened for a moment when his thick comset buzzed, then jumped from their bed. He called for his car, and then showered and dressed in five minutes. He was walking toward the bedroom door of his town-house in Georgetown when Sally Strider flipped their bedcovers covers aside and arched her back in a very attractive stretch.

"Don't stir my mind right now darlin' Mud Puddle," Charles said with a grin as he left their bedroom, "You stay here. I have a restoration to kick off!"

"Ha, I get it! Fire fight for you before fun-fight with me," she shouted after him. "Thanks for the thought Congressman, but I don't do Georgetown nearly as well as I do war!" Charles turned back and said, "If we're lucky, we'll do both fights in that order, then we'll see about taking on Georgetown after this is over."

"Yes," Sally murmured. "And we will do it to them all in due time."

Charles C. Calhoun shook his head and murmured, "Uppity woman you are baaad! You'll be this man's burden forever," as he walked toward the door again.

"I heard that Lover, and I'm really impressed by your vast and deep understanding of me," Sally answered as she bounded from their bed and ran in to the shower, "But you better just damn well wait for me!"

She emerged four minutes later and after hastily toweling herself, ran to her closet and pulled out a dress Army jump-suit. She slipped into it and balancing on one foot then the other, latched on a pair of well-shined combat boots.

"Strider, S." she snapped as she braced to attention and saluted," Major, United States Army Medical Corps, reporting for duty, Sir!"

"Because," she continued in a drawl, "You'll need someone beside you to bandage your big butt when you forget to go low."

"You want to do war with me? Then get yourself hard because it's almost war-time now and we're going to do the restoration with force, if it's necessary," Charles said with stony eyes.

"Good, it's about time that you and I grew some backbone," Sally answered, "And now Lover Boy, you'll find that I can kill as well as cure."

"That's good to know. I'll cope with the deeper implications of this later, but we go now!"

"Yes Sir!" Sally answered.

*

Helen Hamier walked into one of the soy worker's barracks and looked around at the people sitting or lolling on their bunks in the long drab room. She saw that most of them were as dull-eyed as beasts of burden, but some showed confusion on their faces at not being called out to the fields that morning.

"Who is your gang leader?" Helen asked of the room.

A small woman wearing a tattered coverall in the uniform gray of a soy-field worker stepped forward. She was slender and did not have the usual bloat that the 'Clave ration bars gave those forced to subsist on them. She also had a certain look in her dark eyes that showed Helen she was a survivor, and thus a possible asset.

Helen looked at the woman's small face for a moment then whispered, "I think you might be able to help me, what is your name?"

"Why you want to know? And why don't you just wave your wand at my butt anyway?" the woman snapped.

"I don't have a wand and those things are never going to be used in Seattle again, so you will just have to tell me," Helen smiled. "Now, your name please"

"Jackie," the woman whispered dully. Then she raised her head and shouted, "Jacqueline!" with hope suddenly on her face.

"Good, I need you to take over the food distribution for this barrack now, and to oversee the cooking of meals. The city will provide the groceries but you must see that it is cooked properly and served equitably. Will you do this?"

The woman who called herself Jackie stared at Helen for a long moment, then she whispered, "You'll trust me to do this for these people? To help them?"

"Yes, of course."

The grey-clad woman's eyed showed sudden tears, then she knelt and reaching for Helen's hand whimpered, "Thank you..."

Helen grabbed Jackie's wrists and pulled the small woman back to her feet. "There will be no hand-kissing ever again in Seattle! If you work for me you will stand tall," Helen said with a snap in her voice.

"Who are you?" Jackie asked with wide eyes.

"My name is Helen Hamier and I have just been appointed the Acting City Manager of Seattle by Governor Regina Drake."

"Who's she?"

"Did you see the vid the other night?"

"Yes, but I didn't understand it," Jackie replied with a frown.

"She governs our state now. Martial law is over and we will be ruling ourselves again very soon," Helen said. "I think you will like the change."

Jackie stared at her for a moment then took a deep breath, and Helen sensed that the woman was dealing with all of the indoctrination the `Clave had given her over the years and comparing it to what Helen had just told her.

Jackie straightened her shoulders after several moments, and Helen saw a change in her face.

Helen asked, "Will you work for me?"

"Yes," Jackie answered, in a cautious voice, I will."

Helen looked Jackie for a moment longer and then asked with a smile, "Do you have any children?"

"No. I can't, because of something they did to me when I was just a kid. It hurt my stomach a lot and they didn't tell me why they did it."

Helen stroked the slender woman's brow, then she asked, "Would you like to be a foster mother for a nine year-old girl we have just rescued? She's an orphan and the Rat amputated her feet."

Jackie gasped, then shook her head vehemently, "No I couldn't. I wouldn't know how, and I'm afraid..."

"What are you afraid of? You just said you wanted to help these people here and you thanked me for the chance," Helen asked in a soft voice while her eyes bored into Jackie's.

"That's different. Here, I'll just be helping them eat better. But being a mother? Me? No! Never!" Jackie snapped.

"Why not?" Helen pressed.

Jackie glared for several seconds at the tall woman who was calmly dominating her, then her eyes faltered and she looked at the floor. "I don't know how. I never knew my mother and I'm afraid I wouldn't do it right for the girl."

Helen smiled and raised Jackie's head with a gentle hand, "This girl doesn't know how to be a daughter either but she needs to learn. Maybe the two of you could teach each other?"

Jackie hesitated, her mixed emotions plain on her face.

"She's quite bright and isn't afraid to speak her mind, and her eyes are the same color as yours," Helen said with a smile. "Why don't you wait until you meet her before you decide?"

"Oh, all right," Jackie sighed in resignation, "But I haven't promised you anything..."

"Of course you haven't. I'll bring her over her over for supper this evening, but now you have work to do. There's a food truck coming by soon. I know all these dorms have kitchens even though no one has used them in years. Organize your gang here and get it cleaned up and ready to roll as the mil-types say," Helen continued with a light laugh.

"OK, but I don't know how to cook much, and what about the fields?"

"Most folks don't know cooking any more," Helen responded, as a memory of her daughter and Marybell's enjoyment of the meal she had made for them floated across her mind, "And field work has been canceled for now until it has been reorganized. Can you read?"

"Of course!"

"I thought so. Instructions, called recipes will come with the food and the driver will check out your kitchen to see what extra stuff you'll need," Helen finished briskly then she squeezed Jackie's hand, "Thank you for joining our team, very much."

Then Helen said over her shoulder as she walked toward the door, "I'll see you again tonight, and I will be major hungry!"

"Thanks, I think," Jackie muttered to Helen's back before turning to the others in the room. "Alright gang," she shouted, "Off our butts and on our feet! We've got work after all!"

*

Helen walked back into the dormitory just as the last worker had been served at the window of its newly re-opened kitchen. They were all sitting at the communal tables and muttering their appreciation as they wolfed down Jackie's food.

Helen carried a young girl astride her back and asked cheerfully of the room, "Got room for two more hungry folks?" She then walked to the serving window and squatted to let the girl stand. The girl's legs ended just above where her ankles would have been, and their stumps had small hoof-like plastic pads grafted on them.

The girl braced herself on the crutches she had slung across her back then clumped to the serving window. Helen watched her with a slight smile but did not offer to help.

"May I have some food please?" the girl asked Jackie, who was still behind the serving counter.

Jackie looked at the intense dark haired young girl on the other side of the steaming food pans. She was pale but not sickly and she showed an extraordinarily force of will for her age.

"Well?" the girl asked, causing Jackie to start and then sputter, "Of course! Tell me what you want and I'll carry your tray for you."

"I want some of everything, and I will carry my own damn tray if you don't mind,"

Jackie looked at the proud young girl for a second and saw something of herself, then she filled a compartmented tray with the foods she had prepared all that afternoon after several false starts.

"Thank you and now I will do it for myself," the girl said as she took the loaded tray in both hands and manipulating the crutches clamped in her armpits with only her shoulder muscles, clumped her way to a vacant space at the nearest table.

Jackie watched the girl, ignored by the others at the tables, except Helen, as she made her way across the floor and was struck with an unfamiliar feeling.

It made her choke while she filled a tray for Helen and one for herself. Her eyes blurred for a moment when she left the kitchen and walked cautiously to the table where Helen sat beside the girl who was beginning to eat.

617

"Room for one more," Jackie asked after she shook her head and her tears away, as she stood at a vacant place across from them.

Helen remained silent as she accepted a tray from Jackie and remained so until the girl finally replied with a smile, "Sure. You make way good food too."

"Thanks," Jackie sighed as she placed her own tray on the stained table and took her seat. "You really think it's good?"

"Sure is!" the girl mumbled as she took another greedy bite of the small hamburger she held in both hands.

"I'm glad you like it," Jackie said as she tasted what she had struggled to prepare all afternoon.

"Like it? Your stuff is way good," Helen smiled as she dipped a strip of her fried potato in the coleslaw on her tray and slurped it sensuously. Then she looked at Jackie in a certain way.

"My name is Jacquline. What's yours, and how old are you?" the slender woman asked, with a tentative smile.

The girl choked down her mouthful and sputtered, "Dammit, why do you want to know that?"

Helen placed her hand on the girl's shoulder as she murmured, "Jackie has just fed you the best food you've probably ever had, so try nice - please."

"OK, but why do you want to know my name Dammit? Rat knew my name and you see what he did with my feet!" the girl snapped with blazing eyes while Helen looked on without expression.

"Why? Dammit you answer me!"

"I don't really know," Jackie sighed, "Maybe it's just because maybe there's some way I can help you, sometime, maybe."

"Why-in-ferk would you want to do something that dumb?" the girl squawked in a tone that caused a few of the work crew to look up from their trays, for a moment.

"Maybe because someone has helped me all of a sudden, and I want to pass it on."

The girl looked around to Helen sitting at her side and snapped in her little voice, "You're in on this aren't you?"

"Yes, Dear," Helen answered with a smile. "Actually I started it, but now you two have to finish it, don't you," she continued with a light laugh as she got to her feet and carried her tray to the bus window, and walked out of the long room without looking back.

"OK," the girl muttered as she watched Helen leave, "My name is Jacquline too, and I'm nine I think."

*

"We need to confer when you have time" the message said that was blinking on Helen's wall screen when she returned to her home at the end of her first long day of serving the public.

The message was signed by the Governor's office in Olympia and it gave a number. Helen punched it up on her wall comset, and was answered with, "Regina Drake here."

"Yes Madam," Helen said, then she listened as Regina asked in a very formal voice, "Helen Hamier, would you agree to serve as an acting Representative for the State of Washington in the United States Congress?"

"I am very flattered Ma'am, but why me?"

"I trust you to do what's good for all of us. That is why I call on you now."

"Thank you, Ma'am. I will be honored to serve."

"I and all of our citizens thank you Helen. I will have the necessary credentials prepared for submission the Clerk of the House, but in view of the current non-traditional situation today I will also prepare a package for you to present to the Clerk personally."

"I will be back to you as soon as this is done. Thank you again. Transmission is over."

Then Helen listened as Regina's voice continued on the thick comset Hector had given her, "We're off the open line now and we are secure. I'm sorry for my deception but it was Mack's idea on how to carry out Kris' thoughts about showing the flag as it were, in case certain people are still listening."

"Thank you for playing your part Helen, and for accepting a lightening quick promotion from city to federal government. We need all the help we can get in these fast moving times."

Then Helen heard her say, "I also understand that Kris, the woman who woke me up and kicked me out of my garden beds only days ago is your daughter."

Helen smiled as she spoke into the comset, "Yes Governor, Kristina is my daughter, and if I could be as strong as she is, I would be very happy."

"Apple and tree, just remember the apple and the tree," She heard Regina say with a chuckle.

"Mack and Bobby are arranging transport and will give you the schedule." Then Helen heard Regina finish in a serious tone before she clicked off,

"Take care over there, and pack an armor vest among with your ball gowns."

*

"Your mother is an impressive woman in a very modest way," Regina said after she clicked off from Helen. "I have learned that in her first day as City Manager she organized the feeding of all the soy workers in the C'lave well as finding homes for the Network's slave computer people, and just now she didn't blink at my throwing her into the Beltway."

"I'm learning a lot about her also, and damn quick too," Boots said with a little smile. "But who do you want for our Senators?"

Regina got up from her desk and strode around it to the ornate conference table in her office. She leaned back against it and crossed her arms.

Boots spun in her chair to face Regina. "My my, but you're real spry!" she said with a grin.

"Thanks to you and your bunch of crazies yes, I am getting that way again. Also thanks to you, I have also remembered the value of good friends in bad times."

"So I consulted with my good friend Mack in my selection process. Then I had to make some quick changes in the government of Seattle in order to acquire Helen, and to appoint Rick Blaine as Acting Mayor.'"

Boots cocked an eyebrow, and Regina said with a smile, "Yes Kris, your father is now an acting Senator, along with one Demetri Kostanis whom Mack recommended, and whose wife finally agreed to allow him to serve."

"I didn't tell your mother about Hector because that's his job, but now she will have someone to dance with at the embassy balls, won't she!"

"No wonder they kept you locked away all these years Ma'am, you could have manipulated Washington as easily as Mack did the `Gon if they had turned you lose," Boots said with a shake of her head as she got to her feet. "But I have to run now. It's staff meeting time."

*

Boots climbed out of the sedan driven by a WNG trooper. "Thanks for the ride, how long can you wait?"

"Until you're ready to go Ma'am, and Waldo told me to give you whatever you need as backup. Here's my call buzzer," he said as he lowered the passenger window and passed a small black box out to her.

Boots looked at the size of the hand that offered the box and then at the arm behind it. "Thanks Trooper," she said, as she thought, "This guy is big enough to make even Bila sweat, a little." She turned and walked through the door into Rick's Café.

"Welcome Ma'am," the hat-check person said with her bright-painted smile.

"Do you really like that outfit Rick has you in?"

"Oh yes! This was my idea total, and I love doing retro," the woman said. "Rick even found me some real silk," she continued as she lifted her skirt and with a dancer's sweeping high kick, showed her shiny silk stockings.

"Wow, that's impressive," Boots said, as she thought, "Things can move way quickie in S'attl."

"I'm sorry but we are full this evening," the Maître d'Hotel announced with a sniff as he steeped into the paneled foyer, then he recognized Boots. "Except for your party of course," and snapped his fingers to summon a young waiter.

The boy gulped after he ran into the foyer and recognized her, and said, "I'll go tell Rick that you're here " Then ran back across the dance floor once again.

"It's nice to be remembered, I suppose," Boots murmured while she waited. When the panting young waiter returned, the Maître d'Hotel nodded to her and motioned. The young man opened a covert door in the paneling of the foyer and led her along a short passage to a steep, ship's companionway-like staircase.

"This goes down to Rick's secret basement place," he whispered with wide eyes.

Boots smiled, "Thanks again, son," as she grasped the handrails and slid down to the basement Navy-style without using the steps.

***

Chapter 31
The Reaction, III

May 8 and 9, 2276 AD
Seattle

"Thank you for coming Sirs and Mesdames but please don't stand for me," Boots said when she opened the heavy door from the stairwell and walked into the harsh light of Rick's safe room. "Sorry to be late, but when I finished the vid of tonight's broadcast," she continued as she slid a metal chair back with a scrape on the concrete floor and took her seat at the plastic-topped table, "I got involved in Regina's latest re-organization.

"Thank you Rick, for agreeing to be the new mayor of Seattle. I also thank you father, for agreeing to jump from City Hall to our Congress after only one day in politics."

Rick nodded and touched his brow to her. Hector smiled, then shrugged.

"I also understand that you'll have an acceptable escort for the swank parties in D.C. as well," Boots continued with an almost straight face. Helen snorted, then blushed as she others around the table looked at Boots.

Puss and Bila were in fresh uniforms with their hair still damp from the shower and were grinning with their mouths full of Midnight Specials. Rick nodded with dignity while Bobby, Waldo and Barbara kept their faces straight and settled back in their chairs.

Mack said with a frown, "Dammit Kris, why do you always start your meetings with bomb-shells! Try being conventional for once!"

"Mack, my specialty is being unconventional in almost everything I do, so just cope with me, General Sir!"

The General who wore no insignia frowned for another moment, then said with a wry grin, "OK, you're right again dammit. Not trying to fix a thing that ain't broke fits you real good.

"But now turning to operations, with your permission Ma'am," he continued, "Barbara and I have some updates for you since Marybell is back from what I understand was a successful walk in the woods."

"It was very much so, but before you and Barbara report, tell me where our new troopers are now," Boots asked.

"Molly is an impressive young lady," Mack answered. "She and her friend Jimmy, as well as Charlie are set up here in here in Rick's com center. We are in the process of hard-connecting them to the com center at the Network Headquarters since it has the best transmission capabilities in the world. Rick has arranged private quarters for her and Jimmy, and Charlie will bunk on premises for the time being.

"Jimmy's mother Donna and her daughter Sharon are helping run food distribution for the city and the hairy cammy person is doing odd jobs for them. Sugar Plum is pastured in the outfield of the WNG baseball diamond, and Little Mike is helping Guwaii keep Maria on her toes. End of report, Ma'am."

"That sounds good Mack. Now, since we are out to restore the rule of law, how long can we legally keep Rat out of his Nest?"

Mack answered in a solemn tone with a twinkle in his eye, "This is a crime scene Ma'am, and the rule of law requires that we keep it sequestered for as long as we, the Washington State Patrol are doing our very, very thorough investigation."

"Chief, I am impressed by your professionalism in matters of criminal investigator," Boots responded with an equally solemn voice, and a wink. "Now give us your updates if you would please."

Barbara opened a small notepad on the table before her then answered without referring to it, "There are four hundred main battle tanks parked at what is left of Fort Lewis down by Olympia, enough to make up an armor brigade."

"As to California, we think there are four hundred mains parked with the Marines at Twenty Nine Palms and another six hundred in at Ft. Irwin out in the Mojave, but none of these have been maintained since the Chin pulled out," she finished with a grimace.

Mack took up the report, "We have five hundred Mark VIIs at various locations in Washington State, including the twenty on loan to the WSP here in Seattle," he said with a slight smile, "And another thousand in California, split between Twenty-Nine and Irwin. Most of those are also in a poor state of readiness as well."

"What rail armor movers do we have?" Boot asked.

"Not many. All most of all of our heavy rail carriers have been modified to carry soy from here to back to the East, so our armor doesn't fit on them as it did during the war. Why do you ask?"

"No reason yet, just a feeling."

Mack leaned forward in his chair, "Kris, I'm learning to listen real good whenever you have feelings, so talk!"

"I don't really know," Boots said as she got to her feet and began pacing back and forth on the gritty floor of the room, "But my gut says that back east is the next arena. That's where our new Congress-persons are going with their credential stun grenades, and things could get "interesting" in a hurry after they arrive, particularly if the Cali and Alaska interim delegations show up as well."

"What do you mean?" Bobby asked.

"Congress has been in recess for twenty years," Mack answered, "While our country has been ruled by Executive Orders. What do you think the White House will do if Congress re-convenes?"

"Ruled is the correct term, Mack," Boots drawled as she sat down, leaned forward in her chair, and took several French fries from Puss' platter.

"Big Picture stuff always makes her hungry," Puss said sotto-voce to Bila. He nodded while he continued eating, and watching Boots intently. Boots wolfed down the fries, then licked her fingers with a sensuous grin.

"So Barbara," she continued, "You and Mack now connect with your NG counterparts in Cali' and Alaska and see if they are willing to join our party, and then get them to talk about it to the Regulars and the Marines in their states as well. Then find out how many armor assets we can all get back into working order."

"Why are you interested in armor all of a sudden," Bobby asked.

Mack leaned forward and answered with a cold smile, "Because almost all of ours is parked out here in the West and rusting away, while that of others is in good shape across the Pond and much closer to our East Coast, and it is ready to load."

Boots said, "You are very good Sir, as I have noted before."

"Who do you think they are?" Bobby asked as his eyes gleamed.

"I don't know for sure but I feel them out there," Boots said as she paused and gestured toward the east. "I was taught a long time ago that power lust is very strong in some people," she said as she remembered her old art professor's words. "And when their power is threatened, they attack the threat. That is why we could need a major force back east very soon because some of them aren't going to like what we are restoring here, and it's not just about Washington State."

"Bobby, you will need about twenty five hundred people to make our armor brigades work, so you better start looking."

"I've got a pretty good list already Ma'am, both of WNG types and de-mobbed regulars," Bobby said, "But I'll jump on it now."

"I sort of expected you would Suh', now that the drums have begun to play," Boots said with a crooked grin -which Bobby returned.

"Barbara and I will attend to the armor and road issues," Mack announced as his eyes gleamed, "What's next?"

"When you make informal signals to your best contacts at Fort Lewis and the other regular Army posts here and in Cali, sniff them out about their understanding of the term, Lawful Orders."

"Wilcomp Ma'am, and I see the pattern in your thinking," Mack said, "We will prepare a force to move to the east at your call."

"That's good to know General," Puss suddenly said as she wiped her chin and reaching for her cigar in the ashtray. "But now it's time to move part of our Command and Control function the east," she continued, after she puffed it alight.

"Bobby, how soon can you and WNG get a forward CNC set up on my reservation in Virginia?"

Bobby and Mack stared at Puss, and Barbara raised an eyebrow at the woman who was suddenly intruding in their planning. Rick and Hector just smiled however, and Waldo grinned when Boots said, "Don't worry folks, whenever Marybell decides to take the con I've learned to listen real good, and then do what she says without question.

"So now if you would please, set up our forward communication and command center where she says over there, with safe links to Molly and her new crew back here.

"Mack, would you and Barbara also see about chatting up the Virginia National Guard and getting them to station a MULL unit at the Pamunkey reservation from their field at Richmond. This action would only be for cadet training purposes of course."

Puss looked around at the people sitting at the table. After a moment she said with a tight little smile, "You heard the lady. Do It!"

Boots watched as all of those at the conference table obeyed Puss without question, and began talking with each other and making notes on the nitrate paper sheets which they would then flash-burn after memorizing. Bila ignored the others and watched the two women.

"How 'n hell can you do this, and be right every damn ferkin` time?" Boots hissed to Puss.

"Because I'm the best the tactician there ever was outside of you, Poopsie One," Puss whispered with a grin.

"You're doing major strategy here you pesky Redskin!" Boots whispered back with a grin of her own, then she murmured, "Don't overplay your hand Pussycat, we need these folks to keep feeling good."

"I know that," Puss replied. "But it is nice to see that I still have some few lingering wisps of recognition in my old age."

"Shat, you are just are back from directing the killing of more than fifty bad guys in the last two days and taking out seven of them yourself! You don't cause wisps of recognition, Buddy. You cause major fear and respect, except in the case of Mack. He has no fear, but he does respect you."

"Now I think I know why you want us at the reservation, but you tell me so I'll know for sure."

"Simple," Puss answered, "It's the most secure place in the east for us to wait and watch while you and Molly chill their blood with your vid interrupts."

"They are going to make something happen way quick and it will be centered in DC, so my reservation is the best launch point when that big party starts, right?"

"Right, and funny how you always pick up on the important stuff," Boots said.

"I know, and I also know that you and Mack will handle the details. But now it's question time," Puss replied as she clasped Boots' wrist. *"Why me collected to Rat Nest?"* she asked with finger taps.

Boots looked at Puss with an unfathomable expression, then she clasped Puss' forearm and tapped, *"Because thing I do with Lulu way back."*

"Why she do this me now?" Puss tapped as the others around the plastic-topped table continued their discussions. Mack divided his attention between

the logistics of the CNC expansion and the two women, and watched Bila watch their silent conversation. "He's hearing what they say," Mack thought to himself, "But how?"

"Because you me be two now." Puss tapped *"Lulu hear `Clave talk on us."*

"Where Lulu?"

"Waldo," Boots asked, "Where did you park Lulu yesterday?"

"The detention barracks at Camp Murray is only 30 klicks away but that takes too much time with the shape of the roads now, so Rick offered me a facility," Waldo answered.

"Where?"

"Here, in room 1776."

"That's where we stayed with Bila last night," Puss muttered.

"Yep," Boots answered.

"I think I'll go in there now," Puss announced as she scraped her chair back and clinched her cigar in her teeth as she stalked toward the door of the room.

"I don't think it's going to take very long, or to be real pretty in there," Waldo muttered.

"You may be surprised Sergeant," Boots said as she leaned forward in her chair and reached for the drink tray in the middle of the table.

She smiled as she poured a small vodka for herself and watched the others, as they watched Puss enter room 1776, and Bobby and Barbara winced when Puss slammed the door behind her.

*

"Hello Lulu. Why did you do that to me?" Puss asked in a level tone as she stood before the compact woman sitting on the edge of a bunk with her head in her hands.

"Do what?" Lulu asked in weak defiance without looking up.

"Sell me to Rat, Bitch!" Puss snarled around her cigar as she grabbed the woman's short hair and jerked her to her feet.

"This is for what Freddy did to my belly," Boots said as she slammed her fist into Lulu's stomach,

"And this is for what Heidi wanted to do to my boobers!" Puss said as she slapped Lulu's breasts, first with one hard hand and then the other.

Lulu gasped in agony, then bent double and dropped to the bunk. She buried her face in her hands and moaned when she got her breath back, "I'm sorry. I'm so sorry, but I loved her and then I heard she loved you, and you

627

are so beautiful..."

"So you sold me to Rat to chop in to little pieces. Thanks for the kind thought," Puss snarled as she gave Lulu a round-house punch on her shoulder and knocked the woman to the floor between the bunks.

"Go on and do it, but please make it quick - please," Lulu whimpered.

"Do what?"

"Kill me..."

"Don't be a silly, it's going to be much worse than that," Puss said with a sudden grin as she removed her cigar from her teeth and held it between her thumb and forefinger.

"You're working for me now, so get back on your feet, woman."

Lulu braced herself against the bunks and slowly stood. She gasped when Puss hugged her and slapped her on the shoulder, "We need talented people and I don't hold a grudge. First time's forgiven."

Then she whispered as she stared at Lulu, "Second time you die real bad, OK?"

Lulu shuttered at the truth she saw in Puss cold green eyes, "Yes Ma'am, I understand."

"Good, I thought you would. Now come out into the new world with me," Puss said as she gestured with her cigar toward the door.

*

"I'm pleased to say that we have another science asset," Puss announced as she led Lulu into the conference room and wrapped her arm around the woman's wide shoulders. "Lulu has decided to join the Restoration."

Boots looked at Lulu and noted how she held herself stiffly, as if she was hurting in various places.

"Thank you all," Lulu said quietly as she looked at the floor, "It's nice to be back now and maybe I can help you, again," she continued with a catch in her voice. Then she raised her eyes, first to Boots' hands resting on the plastic table top and finally to her face.

"Welcome aboard Lulu," Boots said with a slight smile, "It's nice to be working with you again too. Now go with Marybell and she will put you back in greens, where you belong."

Boots waited until Puss led Lulu out the door into the garage and closed the door. "As to the rest of you," she continued in her normal tone, "I hope you now have learned that Marybell uses a different play book than we do, and so you can never prejudge her. Buda knows I can't."

"Moving on though, Mack, I want Charlie to come with us to our Virginia CNC so he can interact with Molly back here, as we declare our cyber-war."

"Done, Ma'am," Mack said with an approving nod.

"Done, Ma'am," Rick echoed.

"Good. We also need a bunch of good engineer teams to start converting all the soy rail stock back into armor movers, and another bunch to patch up some of the roads around here. Bobby and Barbara, can two handle this?"

"Of course," Barbara answered, "How many carriers do you want, and which roads?"

"If I know Kris," Bobby drawled, "As many as we can convert, and the roads are the ones that lead to the rail yards. Captain Cook always liked to take massive force for her parties."

"Bobby's right, although not very respectful," Boots said with a little smile as she took another sip of her vodka.

Hector cleared his throat after remaining silent all during their meeting, "Thanks for letting me sit in on this. I've learned a lot and I'm glad to be a part of what you have started, so tell me what I can do next."

Mack replied, "Just keep on do what you are doing, Senator because I know you will be very good at it, Sir."

Rick and Barbara nodded approvingly, and Bobby and Waldo gave a thumbs-up. Boots grimaced, then whispered in sotto voce as she looked at Hector, "Buda's bunions gang, looks like we got another smart one on deck! How'n hell us get so lucky so quick?"

Hector just touched his brow to his daughter, again. Then Bila asked in a voice that was quiet but commanding, "Killsong time more soon come?"

"Soon Bila, soon," Puss said as she patted his hand in the silence that followed his question, that was also a statement.

Boots tossed off her vodka and stood, "And sooner rather than later. Adjourn?" she then asked of the table and found them in agreement.

***

Chapter 32
The Homecoming, II

May 8 and 9, 2276 AD
Seattle and Virginia

"OK, can I slap the pad now? It's been a real long day," Puss asked where she stood with Boots on the pavement in front of the Café beside Hector and Bila. A second sedan pulled up to the curb a moment later just as the very large trooper jumped out of Boots' sedan and opened its passenger door.

"Bila, you go with dad and he'll take care of you. We'll see you in the morning at the airport."

"Ja Boss," Bila answered as he followed Hector to the second vehicle, and climbed into the rear compartment without hesitation.

"He's starting to get smart about cars," Boots murmured to Puss as they settled into their passenger seat. She gave the driver the address of her apartment then and after he powered the sedan and pulled out into the street, she turned to Puss and said "A pad slap is a good idea Kid, but we have to pack too. I know what to take to wear inside the Beltway but what do I take to wear on your reservation?"

"You'll learn that we be simple folk down there, and live real natural," Puss said, "I think you'll like how I dress you, after you get used to it any-way."

"Lay on McDuff, and we'll see if I survive in this place you call, "down there."

"You almost-literate twit," Puss snapped, "I'm tired and grumpy right now Gadammit, but I'll always tell you when I'm going to kill you OK! 'Till then be nice to me Dammit!"

"Ja Boss," Boots whispered contritely, as she remembered that Macbeth's last speech really invited McDuff to attack him, and that McDuff was the better swordsman, and killed him...

*

Boots paused in the hallway before the door of her apartment and looked through the hidden peep hole. "I know Dad has shut down most of the Gov's survel system, but old habits die hard," she whispered.

"Old habits can be good things. See anything?"

"Nope," Boots answered as she took another look through the lens set in the drab wall of the corridor, then re-hung the drab picture to hide it again and keyed her door. The two stepped into the small comfortable space.

"Nothing's changed since we were here last time, but how long ago was that?" Puss asked in a low voice.

Boots looked around then replied with a shake of her head, "Days, years - a century? It's hard to remember."

"You got that right," Puss said with a sigh. "What time do we go tomorrow?"

"Dawn patrol," Boots answered with a grimace as she stepped to the kitchenette and opened the wine cabinet. "Think we can find anything that's safe to drink in here?"

"Probably not," Puss sighed again as she plopped down on the edge of the bed. "But what I really need Buddy, is a big slug from our bottle of soldier whiskey. Then I need a real hot soak and some oblivion time. I brought back a big bunch of bad images from this op that I really need to dump."

Boots walked into the tiled bathroom without a word and started the large tub filling from the hot tap. She waited until steam was wafting up from the rising water, then she went back to the kitchenette and keyed her secure cupboard open. She selected a bottle of the harsh liquor and cracking its seal, poured a large measure into a vessel that was also in the cupboard. She turned and still without a word, offered it to Puss.

Puss took a sip, "This is nice - and it's in a real gold julep cup too," she said in a tight voice. "Where did you get it?"

"Bobby gave me this cup years ago, for my times like you're having right now."

Puss took a long swallow without holding her nose or shuddering, "Gold makes it better somehow," she gasped when she could talk again.

"That's what Bobby told me too, but now it's time to tend to you," Boots said as she pulled Puss to her feet and half led, half carried her into the bathroom. She helped her strip and climb into the tub, and refilling the cup, placed it near her hand.

"Gurgle when you're ready to come out Buddy," Boots said as Puss sank into the steaming water, "I'll go pack us."

Puss opened her eyes and murmured as she sat up in the tub, "Pack all my stuff except for a spare pair, and let's take all our jewelry too."

"Sergeant Bill's jewelry?"

"Of course silly," Puss whispered. Then she drained the cup and closing her eyes, sank back into the hot water with a long sigh.

*

Boots awoke in the dark room at 04:00 hours as she had willed herself to do after she had pulled Puss from the tub, dried her relaxed body and guided her to their bed.

Then Boots had opened her secure cupboard again and poured herself a double shot of Polish vodka, drained it in one long swallow and waited several moments to feel its effect.

She had dropped into the bed beside Puss then and had gone to sleep next to her friend.

Boots now asked, "You OK?" to Puss curled beside her.

"Yep, and good to get!" Puss said as she stretched and yawned.

"Do It!" Boots said as she slapped at the light sensor on the headboard and flipped their cover off.

Puss leaped from their bed and made it to the bathroom in three long strides.

"Ha! Beat you Buddy! First in, first out!"

Boots smiled at Puss' renewed vigor then she bounced into the bathroom and began prancing before her enthroned friend. She whined while clutching herself, "Gotta' go Mommy, gotta go!"

Puss answered with a relieved, "Ahhhah," as she hit the button and let the mechanical marvel administer to her with a whoosh and a splash. She then vacated the throne and said with a bright smile, "Next Please!"

"I'll Next Please you biggers when this op is over Missy! But now you get dressed Dammit, we got a plane to catch," Boots said as she plopped onto the throne and relaxed with her own sigh of, "Ahhaaa".

"I'm all better now, but let's take that gold cup with us, because I think we're going to need it again," Puss said in a voice that was suddenly grim, again.

"I've already got it packed, my little Danger Dolly," Boots answered.

"Good. You learn quick as I have noted before," Puss said as she pulled on her army coverall and combat boots.

"I'll learn you with a big stick if you aren't out on the pavement in full gear in five minutes!" Boots yelled from the throne.

"Be there before you Sluggo," Puss said as she grabbed her back pack and ran to the door. She keyed in Boots' combination and stepped through it as it opened.

"You're not supposed to know that code!" Boots yelled as she hopped up and ran out of the bathroom door, and jumped into her army jump-suit and boots.

"Must be that your gettin' sloppy in your old age, Buddy. I've watched you open it mucho times and I learn quick," Puss yelled from the hallway.

"I have actually noted that ability in you, Doctor," Boots answered as she zipped up her suit and grabbing her own pack, leaped into the hall and slammed the door behind her.

"But we go now."

"Ja Boss."

*

A large army sedan drove onto the tarmac at the WNG airfield and met Mack who was the first to arrive. Hector climbed from the sedan and handed Helen out, and they waited until Mr. Kostanis and Bila stood beside them. Bila was in army greens that were now tailored to fit his shoulders, but Hector wore a civilian suite as did Helen and Mr. Kostanis. The men's suits were cut in the mode of Washington and they wore the classic red neckties of inside the Beltway. Helen was dressed in a pants suit and had a lacy white bow at her neck.

The three new delegates began chatting to cover their excitement, but Mack and Bila remained silent, pleased at the prospect of action. Then the transporter trucks rumbled to the apron and Luis and his squad jumped out along with Charlie. They were loading their equipment and gear in the cargo compartment of the Mother Hen when Waldo drove up with Boots and Puss in their sedan. Mack walked to meet them and handed the two out with calm dignity.

He saluted Boots than asked of them all, "Are you good to load?"

"We be good," Luis shouted from where he stood, with his squad at at-

633

tention behind him and Charlie slouching at one side with his hands in his pockets.

"Mack, I didn't order this much force Dammit!" Boots said as waved toward the thirteen troopers after returning his salute.

"Ma'am our forward CNCs are always backed up. You know that," Mack replied.

"And I really wanted this one to be too, "Puss said in a quiet voice. "My own folks are very good, but more is always better. Mack, thank you for anticipating."

"You're welcome Ma'am."

Boots looked at Mack then Puss. Then she looked at all the rest of those on the tarmac who were watching her as the gray Mother Hen's turbines whined and its rotors slowly spun. She shrugged after a moment and nodded. "You win. We go now," she said as she slapped Mack's shoulder and then ruffled Puss' hair, "On to Richmond, right?"

"Don't push your luck you big Damyankee," Puss hissed with a mock glare, "We're going to my reservation, not to that still sad town!"

"OK, let's load," Puss ordered, and smiled to Hector and Helen and Mr. Kostanis as she slapped Boot's shoulder. "We go now, like the lady said!"

"Do It!" Luis' squad shouted as they began scrambling up the landing ladder into the Mother Hen, and the last two of them grabbed Charlie hustled him up with them.

Boots turned to Helen as Puss went to urge Bila and the other two delegates up the ramp, "Mother, I hope you aren't disturbed by being around this bunch of soldiers. They might look rough, but they really are our friends."

"Dear, I am excited by being around this bunch of rough soldiers." Helen said with a lady-like purr.

"Well then take it out on Dad, OK!" Boots hissed.

"Oh I fully intend to darling daughter, as soon as I get him alone again," Helen answered with a lady-like leer.

"Mother, Plueese!"

*

The pilots of the Mother Hen leveled it off at an altitude of 3,000 meters and set its cruising speed at 350 kilometers per hour in order to minimize the discomfort of their passengers in the jump-bay of the craft, notorious for noise.

Boots looked at Hector and Helen across the aisle from her. "Alright

634

gang," she yelled above the rattling in the compartment, "We have a rough ride of about twelve hours in this crate, but you seem to be taking it pretty well. We'll stop for fuel at Minot AFB in South Dakota and then at the IANG Hulman field at Terre Haute in Indiana. You will be much more comfortable after we land in Richmond, however because Congressman Charles C. Calhoun, an old army buddy of Marybell's dad, is sending ground transport to VNG Byrd field. They will take you to Washington and from what I have been told the Capital Police do it pretty well."

"That will be nice if they do, but we'll just have to wait and see, won't we," Helen answered with a lady-like yell as she nodded to first to Hector then to Mr. Kostanis, sitting on either side of her in the hard canvass seats.

Hector added in a voice that carried across the noise in the compartment, "Darlin' Daughter we old furts have very tough butts, otherwise how do you think we could have survived in Seattle all these years?" He grinned when Boots just shook her head, again.

*

The Mother Hen approached Minot AFB for a hot refuel after four and a half hours of flight time. Tower had received a signal from WANG earlier in the day. "I didn't think you guys still existed," The USAF controller had replied to WANG headquarters in Olympia. Then he repeated his message to the pilot of the Hen when the plane entered Minot's airspace.

"We be alive and well and we be on a training mission to Virginia. If you will check our fuel credits, you will see that we have some left."

"You do WANG 2276001, but from over five years ago!" the controller answered, after hesitating a second.

"So?" the Mother Hen's pilot said as he circled the field.

"So land on runway 2 and taxi to the fuel pad. Glad to have you guys back."

"Glad to be back friend, but you don't know the full story just yet. Hunker down and wait for the word."

"If you say so friend," the controller replied, as his dour face suddenly lit with a little smile.

*

The Mother Hen got a similar reception from the IANG tower at Hulman International in Terre Haute when it needed to refuel after another four plus hours in the air. IWANG tower directed them to the National Guard fuel pad without question. This time Boots allowed quick personal pit stops for those in need, while their craft was being serviced. They were airborne again in ten minutes.

*

The Mother Hen approached Richmond International in Virginia. "We see your approach WANG Flight 2276001, "Welcome and you are cleared to land on pad 2." VANG Tower messaged.

Their flight had been uneventful due to good weather and because both Bobby in the west and EB in the east had messaged their clandestine network of Army and Air Force veterans about its flight and the importance thereof. This informal network had created itself perforce in the last stages of the Chin War as a means of survival for those in it, and it had many members.

"I say again, welcome to Virginia, WANG flight 2276001. There is ground transport on its way for your important folks. After they de-plane, one of our VNG birds will then take you to King George County and stay with you while you are there."

Boots had unlatched her seat belt when the Mother Hen was tilting its rotors and made her way forward to stand behind the pilots as they landed the craft in a cloud of dust blasted up by its down-thrusting exhausts on the Virginia National Guard pad at the south side of Byrd Field.

She had motioned for a spare headset to the co-pilot and the woman had passed it to her in time for her to hear Tower's second transmission.

"That's good to know Tower," Boots said with a growl, "But all the folks on WANG flight 2276001 are important!

"Some will exit here for a really unfriendly duty assignment then the rest of us will go to another other place in Virginia, which is a friendly place."

"Yes Ma'am," Tower responded meekly.

"Thanks Tower, glad you understand me, and keep up your good work!" Boots said with a smile in her voice. Then she then turned and motioned to the jumpmaster.

The woman leaped from her seat ran to the rear of the compartment and keyed open the side and rear doors, and extended their ramps to the tarmac. Boots waved toward the open door to Helen and Hector and to Mr. Kostanis.

Helen offered one of the paper tubes which she had carried in her lap all during the flight to Puss.

"Here, Dear, this is sketch you asked me to do," Helen said as she stood. "I'm afraid that it's not very good but I tried my best."

"The other you carry is the one of Kris, right?"

"Of course, Dear! We all need to be reminded of just what this Restoration is all about, don't we? Particularly in Washington," Helen answered with a bright smile as Boots led the way down the steps of the ramp and away from the prop-wash of the still spinning rotors.

The jump master began pushing their baggage down its ramp, and Luis went to the rear to help, after giving her another butt squeeze.

"Quit that Dammit - for now!" the jump master hissed.

*

A black limousine followed by a black personnel carrier sped across the field and pulled to a stop where the Mother Hen stood on the tarmac. Both vehicles had obscured windows and sprouted many antennae.

"Those ferkin' cars look like ferkin' spiders laying on their ferkin' backs," Puss snorted as she looked at the scene through the Mother Hen's open door.

A large man climbed out of the limousine. "Is Kristina Hamier here?" he asked.

"I'm Kristina Hamier," Boots said as she stepped forward.

"Nice to meet you, Ma'am, I am Lieutenant O'Connor of the Capitol Police and I have orders from the Sergeant at Arms of The House of Representatives to convey some Congresspersons to Washington."

Boots looked at the man so obviously Celtic with his red hair and red face as he stood at attention, then she smiled. "Congratulations Lieutenant, you are right on time and the persons you seek are here with me. Their luggage is at the stern of this plane."

"Thank you, Ma'am! We will get right on it!"

"I am sure you will, and you will get my folks safely to Washington as well, or I will hunt you down and eat your liver!"

"Yes Ma'am, wilcomp!" Lieutenant O'Connor replied with a slight smile, "The Capitol Police are tasked to keep all Congresspersons safe as well as all our buildings. That's our only job, so I think my liver may be safe, in the short term anyway."

Boots nodded to him then turned to her parents and kissing both of them, whispered, "Now just go Do It, OK." Hector and Helen returned her kisses in tender silence then they and Mr. Kostanis climbed into the limousine as three men in combat coveralls jumped from the escort van and loaded their luggage into its rear compartment.

Lieutenant O'Conner said in a low voice, "Don't worry Captain Cook, your friends are in good hands - now that the word has been heard."

"What do you know about that?" Boots hissed.

"Just enough to know to lay low and wait for the next word." The man answered with a twitch of a smile.

Boots said, "Lieutenant, I see that the Capitol Police are staffed with intelligent officers who know what the Word means."

The red-haired sergeant gave a very formal salute to Boots, "Yes Ma'am. The force has been expanded recently to include a big bunch of old SF furts, like me."

"That is a good thing," Boots said as the man climbed into the limousine beside the driver, "Us old SF furts are still the best ones, right Lieutenant?"

"Yes Ma'am, and Do It!" he answered with a grin, then motioned to the driver as he closed his window and the limousine powered up and sped silently away with the escort van close behind.

"One more good guy for our side," Boots whispered, then she ran back to her aircraft and leaped up the ramp. "We go now!" she yelled.

The Mother Hen's jumpmaster pulled in its ramps and closed its doors, and after a VNG MULL lifted off from the pad next to theirs and started on a course to the southeast, the Hen's pilots revved up their rotors and lifted off to follow, as Boots flopped into the seat beside Puss and buckled up.

Puss groped in her pack and pulled out her bulky comset. She punched its signal button and turned its volume to high, "We're close enough to go direct now," she yelled to Boots. The set chimed a moment later and Puss spoke into its mouthpiece, "Kencuttemaum, Kowse. Nouwmais. Near husque kear yohacan."

"Ough! Wingapo, Amosens. Nowmais," crackled from the set.

"What did you two yack about this time?" Boots yelled with a crooked grin.

"I said, "Hi Daddy, I'll be home soon, so they will have time to get ready for us."

"What did he say?"

"Good. Welcome, Daughter."

"OK, so what's Nowmais mean? You both said it."

"You really ought to learn Pamunkey, Buddy," Puss whispered in Boots' ear. "It means "I love you"...

*

The two aircraft landed forty-five minutes later at dusk on the parade ground at the Pamunkey reservation. Puss leaped from the door of the Mother Hen as soon as it opened, pulled her helmet off and ran to where her mother and father stood waiting. She embraced them both with her arms and a body slam, "Hugs, and thanks for being!" she whispered.

"Hugs back!" they both murmured as they squeezed her in their arms and kissed her forehead.

"Now, Darlin' Daughter, what and who the hell have you dragged home with you this time?" her father asked with mock severity after their silent moment of love. Her mother just smiled and reached to straighten Puss' helmet-rumpled hair.

"The Restoration, with some folks who will make it go and some more who will guard our butts while we do it," Puss answered her father proudly, before hissing to her mother,

"Thanks, but I really can do that for myself now!"

Her mother just smiled...

"Humph," EB grunted, "I hope you will fully brief me very soon, Daughter," Then he gestured to the Mother Hen and the MULL with the Amerind sign for *"Welcome"*.

"Yes Sir! Wilcomp. Now I would like to introduce my friends to you and Mommy." Puss turned and whistled shrilly, then waved the army sign of "forward" to the aircraft.

Both pilots cut their still-idling engines and as their rotors slowed to a stop, the Mother Hen's side ramp slid out when its door opened and Boots appeared, with Bila beside her. She walked down the ramp, but he paused in the doorway for a moment and gave the sign for "friend" before he followed Boots.,

"Who in the hell are these people?" Eagle Beak asked as he looked at the big man, then signed *"friend"* to him in return.

"She is Kristina Hamier. You have talked to on the phone, and have known about for years. He is our friend Bila, and Kris and I ask ourselves that same ferkin' question every ferkin day," Puss answered with a grin.

Boots and Bila walked to meet Puss' parents as Luis led his squad came from the Mother Hen and ranked them along side the plane. The four man crew of the Virginia MULL did the same and stood in front of their craft. The troopers and pilots all assumed the posture of at ease, and waited.

"Kristina Hamier, let me introduce you to my father, Eagle Beak and to my mother, Bean Blossom," Puss said in a formal tone.

"I am very pleased to meet you Bird Nose, and you too, Possum Sprout. Baby Bird has told me many things about you, as have many others. Those things have all been good I might add," Boots said with a grin as she held both hands out to the tall rugged man with the crooked nose and the small woman who looked exactly like Puss except for her black hair. Both wore Army greens without insignia.

"I am glad to finally meet you too, you blazing Restoration idiot, Ma'am," Eagle Beak said with a wide smile as he took her hand. "Welcome to the last sane place in the US, and I assume that we will talk more about this crazy idea of yours soon."

"Don't take his pronouncements too seriously," Bean Blossom interrupted, "His nose is crooked, but he usually thinks straight."

Boots nodded and smiled politely, then looked to Puss with a cocked eyebrow.

"Look Kid," Puss said, "You're just meeting them. I grew up with 'um and I still don't know waddy' ferk they're ever going to say, or do next..."

"Who is your other friend?" Eagle Beak interrupted as he looked at Bila. The man was bigger than he and he sensed an aura of great strength in him. Eagle Beak signed, *"Who are you?"*

Bila signed in reply with a motion that Eagle Beak almost understood.

"Do you know what he is saying, Daughter?" he asked.

"Daddy, his name is Bila and you can talk to him. You just have to listen to what he says and then think. We do it all the time!" Puss answered with a sniff.

"But beware that he can understand most all of what we say, and seems to know what we think too."

"Bila, welcome friend," Eagle Beak announced as he held his hand out again. Bila grabbed it and said, "Daddy you Marybell? You daughter good do!" Then he smiled at Bean Blossom and reached to take her hand, "Marybell good be. You mommy her like!"

"I see what you mean Daughter, but now that the intros are over, let's move it!"

"Sir!" Puss replied with a snappy salute and took his hand as she led him to where Luis stood with his heavy squad. The troopers and the Virginia NG crew were all at ease and Luis gave Eagle Beak a casual Special Forces salute, then held out his hand.

"You have a most remarkable daughter," Boots murmured to Bean

Blossom while they watched Puss and her father interact with Luis and the troopers.

"I know, and she always picks very remarkable people to be her friends. Congratulations on being one of them," the small woman said.

"I have been honored by her choice, Ma'am, and I am also impressed by your choice in husbands, he is a famous man," Boots said, "But it is time to think about our work now."

"Of course it is, so let's Do It! And when you need blasting I'm your gal. They used to call me "Little Big Boom Woman," Puss' petite mother said with a sweet little smile.

"Shat! You're her! I know about you. You blasted the Chin into chop-sticks mucho times," Boots' eyes widened. "If you're her mother and EB is her father, no wonder Marybell is as good as she is."

"Thanks for your kind words Kris, but Marybell is even better than you, or she knows," Bean Blossom replied.

"She is bred of me and of him, but she hasn't been pressed enough yet to show just how good she can be. When the time comes, Marybell will do whatever is needed," Bean Blossom said. Her voice was serene but it had an undertone of iron.

"I'm have learned that too," Boots said as she smiled to Bean Blossom, then turned and walked to Puss and Eagle Beak standing with the squad.

*

"We have made a number of hidden fire points in the woods around the reservation both for ground and air defense," Eagle Beak said, "And we're real good as to squad arms, but we are light in the heavy stuff except for the kindness of some friendly armorers at an Army post we will not name. They condemned a couple of perfectly good Fly Swatters while on maneuvers, and then told us where they had dumped them."

"We bring three of theem things weeth us, Sir," Luis replied. "You got H source to charge our capacitors?"

"We have a large bioreactor, and those same friends also scrapped an extra bunch of perfectly good capacitors," Eagle Beak replied, "So we have plenty power. "Do yours have incoming acquisition radar?"

"Yes Sir!" Luis said. Then he smiled, "Up to two klicks out, Sir."

"Good. Ours don't, so we will slave them to yours. And it looks like we now are pretty set for air defense now." Eagle Beak pulled a comset from a pocket then and clicked its send button, "Red Feather, Thunder Cloud, Carole. Report!"

Puss spun around when she heard those names and then to her amazement, the three best friends from her academy days burst from the building at the edge of the parade ground and sprinted toward her father. The two muscular men and the tall wiry woman in army greens slid to a halt before Eagle Beak and reported almost in unison, "Yes Sir!"

"Sergeants," he said to the men, "You two cope with the needs of Sergeant Luis' squad. Show them our firing points then see that their gear is either emplaced or humped to their bivouac in our machacammac, and tell them the word means Longhouse after they can pronounce it."

"Sergeant Carole, you show the Virginia helicopter crew our ave-fuel tank and machine shop, then you take them and their gear to the machacammac as well."

"Yes Sir," the three said almost in unison and were turning to leave when Puss yelled, "Just a firkin minute Bird Nose! I would like to say "Hi" to my old buddies, If you don't mind!"

Puss' father looked at his daughter, then surrendered his authority for the moment. "She's been able to take charge ever since she was six," he muttered to Luis.

"Tell me bout it Colonel! She do that to me two days ago like nobody ever do before!"

Puss ignored the two men as she opened her arms to her friends, and companions in the wilderness trial they had all undergone when they were only thirteen years old.

*

The four children had been left by their parents in different places, naked in an unfamiliar forest. They each had been given a small knife, a belt and a length of cord and had been instructed to find food and to equip themselves for battle as they made their way to an unknown place. They also had to locate this place by clues their parents had left for them.

Each of the four had found the subtle markers their parents had left for them, and all had arrived at their goal in their allotted three days. They had done so with varying degrees of style, but they all earned the forehead paint streaks that signified they were now Pamunkey warriors, even at their young age.

Puss had completed her test in a spectacular manner however, so she was awarded three streaks of black. Her had eyes widened as the elder of the tribe marked her forehead to show that she was now a Werowance, a Pamunkey war chief.

Eagle Beak was the only other Werowance in the tribe, so he and his daughter had spoken to each other as equals ever since that day.

*

"How'n hell are you jerkoids" Puss yelled as she spread her arms. "I haven't seen you since the Chin laid ancient eggs!"

The two men and the slender woman wrapped their arms around Puss and squeezed her, then they grabbed her waist and heaved her in the air as they shouted, "Fly Baby Bird, fly!"

"Cute, real cute," Puss said with a grunt as she landed on her feet. "Now go do your jobs you bastards and we'll talk biggers later, and maybe I'll teach you some new stuff.!"

The three looked at Puss, then grinned to each other. "Present Arms!" Carole yelled and they turned and bending, pointed their bottoms at Puss' face and waggled them for a moment before double-timing off to carry out her father's orders.

Puss was bent over howling in laughter at the antics of her friends when Eagle Beak placed a gentle hand on his daughter's shoulder.

"Calling Dove," he said, "You were a leader even in school and I am still proud of that trick, when you organized your fellow cadets into "presenting arms" to me on the parade ground.

"You then turned into an exceptional field asset for us during the war and made me even more proud of you, but you are working at the highest level of this Restoration now and you're not a ground grunt any more daughter. You are a major player.

"You have been naturally moving toward command all your life, so don't be afraid to take it now, and to do what you feel is necessary. When you have the nerve to take the con, you can win battles - and the war."

Puss stopped laughing and her eyes became wide and solemn. She wrapped her arms around her father's chest and murmured, "Thanks Daddy, I hear you and I'll do my best."

"I know you will my daughter, and I know that your best will be good enough." He said as he caressed her head.

"Our daughter, dammit," Bean Blossom added as she straightened Puss' hair, again.

Puss released her father with a squeeze and patted her mother's shoulder, then she turned to Boots.

"Grab your stuff and I'll show you where we'll slap the pads here, and what to wear when we go tribal tonight."

Boots noted the slight twitch of a smile on Bean Blossom's face, and thought to herself, "Little Krissie better watch her butt around this bunch of pesky redskins!"

*

Thunder Cloud and Red Feather lead Luis and his squad through the second-growth pine woods surrounding the reservation. This forest was on land the tribe had purchased when the neighboring farms had either been abandoned or sold because of their owner's fear of the rising sea level. The tribe had bought this additional acreage as it became available because the Pamunkeys knew that the rhythms of the Earth always fluxuated, and they were content to live with those rhythms as their ancestors had done for eons.

"You guys make pretty good war places in these woods," Luis said to Red Feather after he had seen how the Pamunkey had placed their firing positions and laid out their kill zones. "Thanks for showing me theem."

"You're welcome, Sergento Grande! Now let me show you and your gang where to slap the pad."

"How you know that name Kris an' Marybell call me?"

"Sir, we're all pretty connected around here."

"Shat, maybe I be attached to a unit wit' some class after all..."

"Class! You want to see class Sargento? Here's some Pamunkey class!" Thunder Cloud snarled as he hooked his foot behind Luis' leg and dropped the man to the ground.

"Good move Sergeant," Luis grunted. "Now let me show you mine," as he leaped to his feet and feinted with a left kick, then changed to a right kick and caught Thunder Cloud as the young man was dodging. Thunder Cloud noted Luis' shift however, so he was able to partially roll with the blow.

"You preety good Sergeant," Luis whispered, "So maybe I'll let you live."

"Thanks, and welcome to the Reservation," Thunder Cloud gasped as he jumped to his feet, feinted and then kicked at Luis' belly, "But don't ferk with us Pamunkey!"

Luis grunted as he partially blocked the young man's kick, then he got his breath back and said with a little smile, "I say you preety good Sergeant, an' you show me that now. But don' make me get mad..."

*

The Pamunkey long house was built with modern materials that appeared primitive. It was domed and covered with what looked like woven reed mats, and inside the long walls were lined with low frames which could be used either for eating tables or sleeping places.

The troopers clattered into the building and Carole was assigning bed spaces to them as well as to the Mother Hen and VNG MULL's crew when she glanced around and saw Charlie leaning against the door frame.

"You in this bunch too?" Carole asked the compact young man.

"Yep, I'm their boss `puter person," He declared as he stopped lounging and walked to meet her. "Nice to meet another Pamunkey woman," he said as he looked into her dark eyes, "Are you as good as Marybell?"

"We're all pretty good, you audacious Paleface butt vent," Carole answered with a sweet smile. "Now shut up and listen!"

Carole turned and announced in a clear voice, "Here me Troopers! You are all invited to the welcome feast we will put on tonight in your honor."

"We will make a supper of our foods, and there will be some paleface beverages as well. Or you can remain in here and eat rash bars if you prefer. Your choice."

"If you do come to our meeting this evening however, I suggest that you wear our traditional Pamunkey summer dress. We will be doing so and you might feel out of place if you don't. Red Feather and I will show you about our dress, to those of you who want to."

Luis stepped forward. "What dress you give me tonight, tall chickie?" he asked - then grunted as Thunder Cloud threw a deerskin belt and breach clout at his stomach.

"Want me to show you how to put it on," the compact jumpmaster asked Luis, as she squeezed his butt with an almost straight face.

"Hey war chickie, you see almost all of me this evening if I dress local, right? What you wear?"

"You think you be pretty good Cisco, and maybe you be. I'll watch for you around the fire tonight. Then you'll see," the jumpmaster answered with a slight twitch of her lips, and then of her hips.

"Maybe you all will see us all around the fire tonight troopers if you dress right, to make a real bad pun," Carole continued with a laugh. "Meet with us on the parade ground in an hour. Now all stand down!"

Charlie watched Carole allow Luis and the jumpmaster to interrupt her announcement, then smoothly take charge again, "Hmmm, strong woman here," he thought. "Wonder what she looks like in whatever these women wear when they go native?"

He smiled at Carole.

Carole saw the smile on Charlie's face and thought, "Hmmm, he looks sort of smooth, but tough..."

*

"Here's your Pamunkey outfit Buddy," Puss said as she handed Boots a 30 cm. square doeskin apron decorated with sewn-on beads and patterns of colored porcupine quills after leading her into her parent's house.

"This is it?"

"Yep, and all of it. It's called a pagwantawun and it is what all us gals wear around here in the summer. It's a very cool way to dress in hot weather." Puss said with a laugh. "You can also wear mocs like I do, but you really do have to watch where you sit."

"So I see, you pesky redskin," Boots laughed as she began stripping out of her Army jumpsuit, "Butt, to make a really baad pun, O' Pesky One, what did you learn from Lulu's report, which you so carefully rescued from the trash bin at Rat's nest?"

Puss' face changed and she stopped laughing. "Lulu said that the specimens were barely enough for a test but they were pretty thick so the surface area-to-mass ratio wasn't too unfavorable, but there could be a 10% uncertainty factor in the result if it wasn't too far back."

"Then she asked me, and I'll ask you, can we cope with that much slop?"

Boots saw that Puss was totally serious about what she was saying, so her tone was respectful when she asked, "What kind of test did you ask Lulu to run?"

"Carbon 14 dating."

"Where did you get your specimens?"

"I snipped them from the ends of Bila's boot-laces."

"And?" Boots asked in a very quiet voice.

"Bila's boot-laces are, plus or minus Lulu's uncertainty factor, between thirteen thousand and sixteen thousand years old," Puss whispered.

Boots felt the same sudden tingling in the back of her neck as before when she confronted the mysterious aspect of Bila, but she could not suppress it this time.

Puss said with a slight smile, "You're getting the feeling aren't you. I

646

know you are because I am too, but we have to go now," She added as she grasped Boots hand and guided her to the door.

Boots walked with her friend, but her eyes were wide, and focused far away...

*

Mack had watched the Mother Hen lift off, and the general who wore no insignia had whispered as his eyes followed the departing plane, "This one aircraft is carrying all of our hope for our whole future."

"God of Us All, please watch over them."

Mack had sent Eagle Beak a message in the clear when he arrived back at Rick's communications center but he used the informal Special Forces code to give the Mother Hen's real ETA in Virginia.

Eagle Beak heard the numbers that Mack sent in clear, and then his cough, which signaled him to subtract six and a half hours from the numbers Mack had spoken. This was the SF code they had all developed to confound the Chin back then, and now he knew the Mother Hen's ETA-Virginia.

Mack had sent another number in clear, followed by a sneeze. Eagle Beak heard that number as well, deciphered it and told Bean Blossom, "Looks like we have twenty-four new friends coming to visit." She had smiled then, and called the women of the tribe together to prepare a traditional Pamunkey feast of welcome.

*

The tribal council place was centered on a large stone-ringed fire pit at the edge of their academy parade ground. It was lit with a bonfire of native pine that would burn hot and quick and native oak which would make glowing coals that would smolder for a long time. The members of the tribe gathered without ceremony in the circle in their native dress as the chatted with each other. When their guests appeared at the edge of the firelight, also hesitantly wearing the same, the Pamunkey walked to meet them with open arms and led them to seats around the fire.

"Like it?" Puss asked with a wicked little smirk.

"You pesky redskins have a life here that I might want to live, after we do this restore thing. You taking applications for your tribe?" Boots murmured.

"We'll see," Puss said, "But let's do the restore thing first."

"Ja Boss..."

A proud Pamunkey woman walked into the circle of firelight then and

647

said, "Come and eat," as she waved her arm toward the black iron pots and pans suspended over a cooking fire at one side of the circle.

Puss walked to the woman, "Thank you Ancagwins Crenapo, your food smells very good," She said in a formal tone, using the woman's Pamunkey title for the evening.

"I am glad you like its smell Calling Dove, would you like to eat of it?" The woman replied in the same formal tone.

"Yes, I and my friends would like to eat of your food."

"I welcome you and your friends to eat, and I hope you enjoy the food I have made."

Puss bowed her head to the woman who had accepted the title of Pot Woman for the evening, and then made a graceful gesture to all those sitting around the fire.

The members of the tribe urged the visitord to rise, and ushered them to a hollowed-out log filled with ice and various bottled beverages. The Pamunkey and their guests all helped themselves with grunts or giggles depending on what they wore and then formed themselves into a food line. They got to know each other while they chatted and sipped their beverages as they waited to be served by the Pot Woman and her smiling helpers, one of whom was Marybell's mother.

*

"I know way much about good food dammit, but what-n' hell is this?" Boots sighed as she leaned back against a log, "I ate two bowls of it, and a bunch of that over-top bread stuff too."

"We didn't give you real Pamunkey food because we didn't think you guys would like our fish and acorn stew or our boiled terrapin, and I don't like it much either. This was called Burgoo by the old Caribbean pirates, and then the Scots immigrants in 1735. We make it with our own stuff now and this bread is made from corn. We use venison and the veggies we grow and dry for winter, and whatever else our hunting guys and gals bring home," Puss said as she leaned back against the log at the edge of the fire circle, and belched in a very lady-like way.

Boots belched impressively herself, then asked, "So what's next, now that you have a bunch of our almost naked troopers eating and drinking amongst your almost naked folks?"

"Funny you should ask, O' Person with a Truly Naughty Mind," Puss answered in a voice that lilted at first then ended in a whisper.

"You can stay here and observe or even interact with them if you wish, but I am going to a place where I have always found peace, and time to re-build my soul. I'm taking a sleep pad with me and that's all."

Boots turned to Puss and looked at her, as she stood with an expression that was now serene. Boots asked in a soft voice, "May I come with you?"

"Yes, I would like that," Puss said. Then she whispered, "Bila?"

Bila was sitting on the far side of the fire from them among the squad members who welcomed him as one of their own. He placed his dish on the ground and nodded to his new friends, then got to his feet and strode around the fire pit. He reached for Puss' hand, "We now happy place go at river you?" he asked.

"How-in-hell did he hear you from over there?" Boots hissed as she leaped to her feet, "And know what tha' hell you said?"

"Wait and see," Puss answered as she clasped Bila's hand and led him out of the circle of firelight.

. "Ferk any wait-and-see crappo Buddy, I'm right behind you two!" Boots growled.

"Good. That's were I want you to be," Puss answered over her shoulder.

*

"This is where I have come to ever since I was a kid. It's always been my peaceful place," Puss said as she sat down and leaned back against the trunk of an old cottonwood tree on the bank of the Pamunkey River. The light of the rising moon was beginning to glisten on the broad expanse of its water and highlight the ripples made by the fish as they began feeding. "Welcome to my place, friends."

"This is a beautiful place and thank you for bringing me here," Boots said in a whisper.

"Place good be this," Bila announced in a quite voice as he sat down at Puss' side and leaned back against her tree.

"I'm glad you like it," Puss said. "Sit down Buddy," she continued as she patted the sandy ground, "We need to talk about war in my peaceful place. I don't like to do it, dammit, but we must. So talk."

Boots dropped to sit cross-legged by her friend. "I feel that war will come to us soon," She said in a quiet voice, "From the White House fiirst, but mostly from the EU in Brussels.

"Our White House and the Chin really don't like independent peons. That's why the Chin war went on for so long, because both of those forces tried to use it to chop us stubborn bastards up.

"The EU also really doesn't like us ether because we are citizens and own our government, in theory anyway. They prefer subjects which they own as they do in Europe, so I expect them to be Pitson's next partners in trying to put us down," Boots said.

"But we will resist again, and will win finally as we did before, but it's going to be a major fight and will take a major effort for us to finish the Restoration," she finished quietly.

"We will win Buddy," Puss answered, "Because we know way much more about how to do major war than that dumb Euro bunch. But if even if we don't win, we're going on one hell of a trip because our Restoration is worth it!"

"Win us!" Bila said in a sudden growl, "We three are. One be we. We us more them strong than! We it do!"

"What'n hell is he saying now?" Boots asked with a frown.

"He always speaks true, Dammit," Puss snapped, "So I think we need to listen good!"

Bila wrapped one arm around Puss' shoulder and clasped her to his breast, then he reached across her and pulled Boots to his chest as well. She resisted, until she felt the man's steady strength surround her then she relaxed and twisted to sit across both their laps.

"Ferk, why not?" she whispered.

The three sat with their arms around each other as the moon rose higher and brightened their view of the river, then Bila said as he looked up at the sky, "One three we be."

"You're repeating yourself. What'n hell are you saying?" Boots muttered with her face pressed against his chest.

"Stop your talking and just listen, and feel what he says, Dammit" Puss said with a snap in her voice.

"We see now us be," Bila said as he gently lifted Puss' face to his.

She smiled and her mouth was reaching for his lips when he whispered, "Kris too. Time now is."

Boots stiffened when she felt Puss' arm urging her toward their faces, then she placed her trust in Puss, and let herself be guided into a three-way kiss.

Boots felt a sudden surge of warmth when they joined their lips and then she felt Bila and Puss' persons merge and leave their bodies, and soar into the sky above as she watched in her mind, until she felt herself being drawn up with them. They carried her far above the earth and she felt her being merge into a spinning globe that she knew somehow was them all.

As it whirled there was a pure golden light in it she knew was Puss and a cool grey vastness that she recognized as Bila, and infinitely complex and ever-changing thing with the multiple swirling colors of a Persian scarf appeared - that she finally recognized as herself.

The three soared above the land and hovered for a moment until Bila directed their eyes to the east where black clouds were forming near the ocean. Then he led Puss and Boots up above that scene and then somehow into a place she knew was long ago.

He showed them a brief flicker of large shapes and shadowy human forms, and then took them back to where they sat on the bank of the Pamunkey River.

The three slowly ended their kiss and Puss murmured, "Whoosh! Is this all it takes for us to go there now?" Then she sighed, "I sorta' liked it the other way too though, Ya' Big Thud."

Boots gasped and was silent, until she said after many heartbeats, "Interesting trip, but I think we all need to talk about what comes next."

"Yes we do Buddy, but we will talk first about now," Puss answered as her voice changed.

"You felt Bila our first time didn't you? That's why you got mad at me for being with him.

"And you've been feeling what I've felt whenever we were with Bila all along haven't you? I know you have, but you've been ducking it because you don't know what it is.

"And you know as well as I do that what we have with Bila is real even if we don't know what it is.

"But not knowing doesn't matter anyway, because Bila is real, we are real, and whatever there is between the three of us is real – and it is good, dammit!"

Boots sighed then she kissed Puss softly on her lips. Then she turned to Bila and pulling his head to hers, gave him the same gentle kiss.

"You're right, Doctor, as usual.

"I did feel something the first time I saw him," she said as she squeezed Bila's hand, "And my feelings got stronger almost hour by hour. They're as strong as yours now and you're also right that it doesn't matter what it is, we three are all that matter,"

Then Boots said in a low voice, "And maybe we three are all that matter in our whole ferkin' world now. Anyway Bila, what does your name mean in our language?" she asked as she looked up into his eyes, that were somehow bright in the moonlight.

"Bila hunter be. Bila seeker be. Bila me be."

Boots thought about Lulu's improbable finding, then gasped as she had a sudden insight about the dim flickering shapes he had shown them,

"I am glad you found us," she finally whispered as she kissed his hand, then hugged him.

The two women had felt a strong empathy with each other ever since they first met, but Puss gasped now when she felt the depth and clarity of Boots' new insight.

"Welcome home Bila," Puss finally whispered after she could speak again and hugged him then with her arms and her leg.

"You're right dammit, we three really are one..."

"You're right too, Doctor, as usual. Thanks for setting me straight, again," Boots murmured with a sigh where she lay across them with her face pressed against Bila's chest.

Bila stroked Boots' forehead and Puss' back. "Bila home happy at now. Kris and Marybell home be Bila for," he said in a whisper.

Then his voice changed, "Bad them come here. Kill we how they?"

"Don't worry big guy, kill time is coming soon," Puss answered as she sat up, "And our Kris has a plan. Don't you Buddy?"

"Ja Boss. That's my job, while you and Bila take care of our really important stuff," Boots answered. She squeezed them both, then she sat up and they saw her eyes blaze with blue flames as she announced in a voice that rang in the canopy of the cottonwood trees lining the river.

"Friends, you first saved me from being one of them and then you gave me back my soul. Now you have given me my strength! Thank you.

"No, you Are my strength!"

Bila and Puss said nothing. They just gathered Boots back into the circle of their arms and held her until she sighed, and was calm again.

***

Chapter 33
The Treaty

May 9, 2276 AD
Brussels

Belladonna Jones looked from the display screen on the wall when Bradney lurched through the door of her private office. The display was split, with
the document she was reviewing and annotating on one side with her hand
keypad while the other showed an archived vid of Freddy and Heidi at their
most innovative.

Belladonna had muted it however in order to concentrate on her work,
mostly.

"Bel, those bastards on the West Coast are out of hand!" Bradney rasped.
"Our sats show all of Pierré's force down and dead out where that dammed
interruption came from in Canada!"

"Our SS Chief is dead too, we gotta' do something!"

Belladonna shut down her display and got to her feet. "First, get in here
and close that damn door!" she ordered.

When Bradney did as he was told, she continued, "Now that we are
totally secure tell me what happened, and do get control of yourself!"

He told her then and she listened, and answered probing questions as
best he could with the information the Deputy Chief had given him.

Belladonna considered all that Bradney said as she sat again, and leaned
back in her chair. She stared at her husband for a long moment, then smiled
in a certain way as she steepled her fingers.

"Perhaps it's time to invoke the Treaty we have with the E-Union doesn't
it, my Pet. Agree?"

"Hell yes!" Bradney answered, as his face, and whole attitude changed from petulance back to command.

Belladonna just smiled at him over her fingers while her eyes grew hooded, and began to glitter...

***

Appendix

Final Lecture and Research Assignment,
Graduate Level Course 603
"History of The 23rd Century, Part 2"
Historical Sociology Department,
New University of Oregon at New Eugene,
Spring Semester,
2452 A.D.

LECTURE – SECTION 1:

In the year 2244 of the Western calendar, and a lucky date according to their traditional numerology and therefore a propitious time, the government of China in Beijing declared to the world that it needed more room in which its peoples could thrive. They therefore laid claim to a part of North America - specifically the states of California, Oregon, Washington and Alaska in the United States, and the Canadian province of British Columbia.

Beijing justified this claim by asserting that because of the superiority of Chinese culture, the rest of the world owed them more room in which it could flourish. The Chinese also demanded that the two governments of those places evacuate all inhabitants in the claimed area who were not of Chinese ancestry.

Beijing delivered their assertion of claim, along with threats of swift and forceful punishment for any attempts to oppose it for one week directly to the American and Canadian citizens via pirate vid broadcasts interrupting the regular programming at prime viewing times in those countries.

Stern warnings were also delivered by the same method to the people of the European Union and South America that promised severe action in the event either attempted intervention on the side of the United States.

Beijing ignored the Indian subcontinent and Africa and the hereditary tribal chaos of the Middle East however, and in turn those places gratefully sidestepped the whole issue.

Canada had disbanded its military establishment as a gesture of good will to the world at the end of the previous century except for several elite units. These were reformed and secretly re-trained to be an alternate national police force. This force was separate from the Mounties, who were revered by all Canadians. The government never publicly acknowledged the existence of this new force, however after it was established they used it to quietly, but vigorously control the Canadian subjects. Whenever the ministers deemed it necessary, they used this force to restore, or instill Public Decorum. The citizens of Canada learned about this force by whispered word-of-mouth soon after Ottawa established it however, and began calling it the "Blue Bunch", with stoic Canadian understatement.

Therefore, Ottawa did nothing in response to Beijing's announcement, except to mobilize the Blue Bunch to arrest the large number of Canadians who expressed open outrage at the demands by the Chinese. About 300,000 such protesters were rounded up in all, and the Blue Bunch transported them to "re-orientation" facilities above the Arctic Circle in the Northern Territories. Ottawa began a massive campaign of public education at the same time, on the "Dangerous Effects of Patriotism", in order to preserve in the words of the Prime Minister, "International Hegemony".

Since the Chinese issued their ultimatums in the spring of the year, the death rate of the Canadian detainees from exposure in the camps up on the tundra did not become significant until the following winter...

The situation was different in the United States in that the nation still maintained a strong military establishment, with a bureaucracy extremely skilled in defending its existence against budgetary and policy raids by other cabinets in the Federal government. Therefore, the Chinese ultimatum was rejected and the war began soon thereafter.

Beijing suddenly became silent after seven days of their shrill rhetoric and remained silent for the next four weeks, during which time the government leaders in Washington and the other Western governments did nothing except pose, and utter nonsense for the press cams. While this regrettable lapse in leadership was taking place, a thousand giant Chinese troop submarines crossed the Pacific and positioned themselves in the near-shore waters along the western coast of North America.

These vessels were slow moving, thin-skinned and shallow running but each carried 500 Chin (as the invaders came to be called) assault troops with their equipment. Rather cleverly, the design of their hulls and nuclear propulsion systems gave them the sonar profile of blue and sperm whales, and their underwater speakers emitted accurate renditions of whale songs.

This was an effective cover for the Chin approach because the population of real cetaceans in the Pacific had grown quite large and very noisy under the protection of various international treaties.

The U.S. Navy's underwater sensing equipment immediately picked up all of this sudden increase in activity however, and its observation satellites easily tracked the paths of the near-surface subs. Naval Intelligence thus had enough evidence to support their recommendation of preemptive missile strikes because of the obvious threat posed by the Chin submarine fleet.

Environmental and animal protection groups and a number of Congresspersons objected though, and deemed that the due diligence clauses in the numerous marine animal protection treaties that the United States had signed over the years were binding. These groups sued for performance in a federal court and were awarded a decision from a three-judge panel that no "warlike action" could be initiated without a public consultation as long as there was a possibility that some of the designated targets might be protected creatures...

Since there is always some doubt in war, a review of the Navy's evidence by a panel of outside stakeholders in the well-being of whales was required by the implementing regulations of the treaties. A six-week public notice of intent to create the panel was also required, before the first such meeting could take place...

LECTURE - SECTION 2:

The Chin high command launched an ICBM strike against most of the cities in the western North American area they claimed when they received a signal from their submarine fleet that it was in position. These multiple-warhead missiles carried neutron bombs since the goal of the attack was to eliminate soft targets while avoiding major property and infrastructure damage.

The original capability for developing and delivering such warheads had been obtained covertly from sources in the United States over two centuries before the attack, but the Chin scientists and engineers had made considerable advances since and advanced far beyond those first crude designs. These ICBMs used were their latest design, the existence of which the Chin military high command had hidden from their own government as well as from the numerous ineffectual international arms control groups still junketing about the world under the aegis of the United Nations.

The Chin military had found that deceiving the UN inspectors was not particularly difficult because those bodies tended to focus on intramural spats over funding, rather than maintaining any effective surveillance.

Each Chin missile carried three hundred of their newest and most efficient warheads, all MIRV'd to blanket the cities they targeted. As an example, ten of the missiles hit Los Angeles and arrived at midnight, and mainly in the suburban bedroom areas. Each of their three thousand warheads was a one-kiloton neutron bomb, and their total effect was to instantly kill or severely harm the Angelinos in a 125 square mile area of the city.

The effect on the surviving residents was also as planned, a mass panic evacuation after the impacts during which over a quarter of the survivors, mostly the old, the young and the weak, died during that chaotic night.

Those that did survive the crush to flee Los Angeles mainly headed east or northeast, into the Mojave Desert past Palm Springs or toward Barstow. A sizable number went to the northwest however, into the San Joaquin Valley toward Bakersfield.

Those escaping from San Jose and to a much lesser extent those from the confines of the Bay Area mostly headed east toward Stockton, because the few remaining local radio news broadcasts were reporting that Sacramento was also severely damaged.

China had launched numerous civilian satellites during the preceding decade that all conformed to international communications traffic requirements. Thus the United Nations deemed them innocuous and the US State Department did so as well, in spite of extremely strong-worded classified internal dissents from the CIA and the National Security Council.

The Chin high command activated the powerful surveillance cameras in these satellites when they launched their attack and so their targeting specialists were easily able to pinpoint the masses of fleeing Californians.

They launched multiple flights of missiles toward the areas where the refugees huddled in the broad farmlands of the Central Valley and fired another blanketing wave of missiles toward the desert flats. Both of these barrages arrived just before dawn on the second morning after the initial Chin attack, but they now carried an extremely virulent and quick-acting nerve agent. The multiple warheads were proximity-fused to burst at altitudes of two to three hundred meters.

The moisture in the air, which was condensing into the morning dew that was usual in these areas, greatly facilitated the delivery the agent to its intended targets. Coverage was almost universal...

The minerals and nutrients released from the decaying bodies of over twenty million humans and uncounted numbers of their pets during the next several years were very beneficial to the soils in the areas where the refugees had huddled. When the wet seasons began, particularly in the Mojave, the native vegetation flourished with an unprecedented lushness. However, the litter of the slowly rusting hulks of millions of vehicles as well as ongoing military operations prevented much in the way of coherent viniculture or other crops in the Central Valley, despite the benefits from the nutrients so released...

LECTURE - SECTION 3:

China launched a second series of missiles toward the U.S - México border at the same time as the initial wave of neutron warheads was landing on the cities of the West Coast. These missiles also carried 300 MIRV'd warheads apiece, but they were conventional nuclear bombs that had been designed to be extremely dirty. When they impacted precisely in a 20 kilometer-wide zone along the boundary between the two nations all the way from the Sea of Cortez to the mouth of the Rio Grande, they effectively created a radioactive death strip that sealed the border.

The skeletons of all of the towns and cities in that strip, and those of their inhabitants became very radioactive and thus the strip was undisturbed throughout the course of the war, and continues to be so today several centuries later.

The Chin scientists and strategists were also correct in their calculation that the radioactive poisoning potential would stay at deadly levels for a significantly longer time than usual because rainfall was rare in this desert region and so would not wash away the fallout dust from the blasts.

México however, had turned itself into a strong industrial and export-manufacturing powerhouse over the previous two centuries before the Chin attack and had so raised the relative living standard for its population to a level unprecedented since the height of the Aztec Empire. Therefore, their economy could now absorb the energies of the Mexican people and access to the United States was not nearly as important to them as it had been in earlier centuries.

The Mexican government did nothing in response to the Chinese strike except to ritually protest and deplore the deaths of its citizens in the border area, and to step up their exports to Europe and Africa to compensate for their lost markets to the North.

The Chin submarines surfaced after the missile barrages from China, and off-loaded their troops and equipment at carefully chosen landing sites all up and down the coast of the area Beijing claimed.

LECTURE - SECTION 4:

After the sudden Chin invasion of the West Coast and after a short period of surgically-targeted nuclear and non-nuclear strikes at each other's capitals, the two nations continued fighting, but at a lower level of intensity. Then after another short time in this second phase in which both sides only employed small tactical nuclear weapons, Washington and Beijing tacitly and cynically agreed to lower the intensity of the warfare again to a non-nuclear scale, but to let it continue to grind on as a conventional conflict. They secretly reached this agreement because both powers had realized that the war was actually an efficient means of population reduction as well providing a necessary external threat that allowed each government to rule by decree and ignore or suppress dissent.

Population reduction as well as population control was a pervasive issue with most governments in the world at that time because of the expected loss of low-lying coastal lands to rising sea levels due to the slow melting of the polar icecaps.

The rate of rise was still gradual but could not be ignored by governments any longer, so plans were being drawn up for the construction of dykes and sea walls to protect the cores of most of the major coastal cities in the United States and Europe. However the expected loss of unprotected lands would ultimately force large population displacements if the melting continued, which would in turn create resentment in all the affected coastal nations as migrants began moving inland seeking new homes at the expense of those already living there.

General resentment toward the nations that had the resources to protect their coastal cities and space to accommodate their people from those countries without such resources was also probable. Feelings of envy were already being encouraged and channeled by self-appointed 'Spokes-persons for the People' in those unfortunate countries.

In all their harangues however, the Spokes-persons ignored the fact that the earth's climate changes had been finally determined to be naturally cyclic and not effected by human activities to any great extent. And that this was particularly true after fuel cell technology for all stationary power generation and much of the world's mobile transportation had matured and become practical by the end of the previous century.

The general problem caused by this internal and international unrest was determined, by those who determine such things, to be best addressed in the long term by population reduction, however it could achieved. The near-term fix for the problem was also identified by the same group as the establishment of rigid controls over their peoples by the various governments. Those governments all agreed with alacrity and efficiently began to apply tighter strictures on the activities of their citizens, with the partial exception of the United States where centralizing power in the hands of the "Best People" was still met with some lingering resistance...

LECTURE - SECTION 5:

The office of President of the United States had already come effectively under the control of the Washington Bureaucrats even before the war began, due to the intricate complexities of the huge body of federal statutes and regulations created willy-nilly by Congress and various Administrations over the preceding two centuries.

These `Crats presented themselves as the only people who knew know how things actually worked in the government. The Congresspersons believed them.  They also believed that they could only obtain the goodies they wanted for their constituents with the help of these same smug functionaries.  Thus the `Crats maintained and increased their power and since they were unequaled in their ability to either obfuscate or expedite the flow of what the members of Congress wanted most – funds for their home districts. Thus the `Crat's tacitly assumed the ultimate authority in governance, and were rarely challenged by the Representatives of the People.

The emergence of an imperial Executive Branch in the United States during the Chin War happened when Bradney Pitson was elected President in 2256. His wife, Belladonna Jones was elected to the vice presidency at the same time.

These two were extremely friendly to, and supported by the international

entertainment conglomerate, an organization that flourished in this protracted third stage of the Chin War. It did so because of Special relationships
its top executives had developed with the central governments of most major
countries, relationships that gave the conglomerate monopolistic power for
the delivery of entertainment to all their diversion-seeking populaces - mostly
bored with war news now, and other information about the real world.

The conglomerate executives supported Pitson and Jones in turn because of the attitudes they shared with the two about power and control and
because what they knew about the proclivities of the couple, that were not
widely known. This aspect of the private life of Pitson and Jones was not
markedly different from the lives of the conglomerate executives themselves
as well as others in the national power elite, but those proclivities were extreme when compared to the lives of most American voters.

So while publicly supporting Pitson and Jones with all their media
power, the executives privately provided "entertainments" for the couple's
diversion during the campaign, and archived secret vids thereof for use as
bargaining chips vis-à-vis future government matters important to the conglomerate.

The conglomerate was able to sweep the photogenic pair into office with
a massive wave of favorable coverage in a saturation campaign that ignored,
and virtually denied the existence of any opposition.

Once in power, Pitson determined that he could rule best by issuing
Executive Orders rather than wrangling with a Congress that still occasionally balked at his more extreme ideas. He found these EOs to be his most
efficient tools and with Jones' eager assistance, he became quite skilled in
their use.

The couple, with the continuing support of the entertainment conglomerate also became skilled at manipulating their public image with an eye
toward remaining in office, thus they easily won the next election and kept all
of the power they had accumulated in their first term.

Four years later, Pitson declared for the office of Vice President and
Jones declared for Presidency, and again there was virtually no contest when
the conglomerate once more deftly manipulated the electorate and overwhelmed all opposition to the couple.

Pitson and Jones did not have problems sharing the Oval Office during this third term and the fourth that naturally ensued as well, because of
the large number of little secrets they had collected about each other that

were unknown even to the media executives. However, they also remained together because they each genuinely admired the other's amorality and non-traditional tastes, as well as the panache they each displayed while indulging themselves in jointly perverting the public trust.

In 2272 at the end of the couple's second terms in each office, Pitson declared for the Presidency again and Jones did so for the Vice Presidency. When a foreign journalist timidly asked about the prohibition in the 22nd Amendment against a person serving more than two terms as President, Pitson earnestly explained that the natural biological process of cellular growth continually occurring in his body had made him a completely different man from when he had last held the office eight years ago.

Twenty-four assorted scientists and other experts, all quietly funded by the conglomerate, publicly supported his position and the very friendly Supreme Court that Pitson and Jones had been able to appoint during their first sixteen years in power promptly agreed after only one day of oral presentations.

Pitson and Jones easily won the next election and thus were able to continue their long-standing tacit pact with Beijing with regard to the conduct of the war for population reduction purposes. The continuation of military operations on this low level also used up many of the more able and aggressive young men in each country, as well as women in the United States. This in turn lowered the genetic tendencies independent thought and action in both populations was considered to be an extra long-term benefit by the two governments.

LECTURE - SECTION 6:

The continuing low-level war had a negative effect on the original goal of the Chin in launching their invasion however, in that only a small number of their people settled in the newly won territories.

This was principally due to the disruptive nature of attacks by the U.S. regular forces but by the many residents of both the United States and Canada who had survived the initial Chin attack as well and chose to not evacuate when the ground war began, but to fight on as partisans.

Another, less obvious reason was that the Chin also found their people reluctant to take up homes in the unsettled regions unless they had arms to defend themselves. Beijing balked at this however, because the distribution of weapons would create an armed peasantry in the newly seized lands

that Beijing could not closely control as they did the peasants at home. This
unforeseen impasse proved to be the fatal flaw in the otherwise meticulously
planned Chin grand strategy and by preventing successful colonization of
their new territory, caused its failure and their ultimate withdrawal.

LECTURE - SECTION 7:

When Beijing's abrupt extraction of their forces effectively ended the war
Washington and Ottawa embraced the same position as China had regarding
their own people in the once-contested areas, so both governments restricted
the resettlement of the vacant western areas by US and Canadian citizens.

This was because the two governments realized that the people returning to their own or their parent's lands would also assert their right to arm
themselves even though the Chin were gone - and to vote. The overt reason
for the restriction that was publicly announced by Washington and Ottawa
through the entertainment conglomerate however was:

"Studies have proven that pioneers always suffer depression and malad-
justment due to the lonely life they are forced to lead. Therefore by keeping
you safe in your Enclaves, your Government is performing its obligation and
duty to preserve your personal wellness."

*

Enclaves, (`Claves in the usage of the time) in the parts of the urban
areas the Chin could not capture during the war that were still intact, and
not radioactively contaminated, contained most of the remaining populace
in the western United States and Alaska after the war. This population was
much reduced in number however, and existed mainly as a client peasantry
of the military government bureaucracies that still ruled under the terms of
martial law imposed on each of these `Claves after the civilian governments
had relinquished power with declarations of emergency made by the elected
Governors of the various states when the Chin began their occupation.

No `Claves or other population centers even existed in what used to be
the western provinces of Canada however because Ottawa, by the time of the
Chin withdrawal had become a signatory to the E-Union's treaty restricting
the domination of Gaia by mere humans...

Basic food was manufactured and rationed out to the Americans living
in each of the `Claves, who were in turn required to perform work as directed
by its military government. Travel from one `Clave to another or between
the `Claves and the remaining area to the east still known as the United

States by those who were not of the government or military was also tightly controlled with a pass system, and was generally discouraged.

The relatively few persons still living outside of the various `Claves, both in the United States and Canada were classified as Un-documented, or "Undocs", and while largely ignored by the military Governors during the long conflict, after the war they began to be scrutinized as potential disruptive elements to the new national order.

Many of the technologies and basic industries existing in the West before the war such as highway and building construction and machine tool fabrication, had been allowed to atrophy or disappear altogether. But the mechanisms for population surveillance and control had been highly developed in the previous thirty years and therefore were now ubiquitous in all `Claves. The Undocs on the outside had not been generally subject to those mechanisms however, and this was another reason they were deemed to be a potentially significant disruptive irritant by the military governments of the `Claves.

Higher education had also been de-emphasized for the general `Clave populations, as being unnecessary for their role as workers but the military academies had been allowed to remain open after the war despite misgivings from some quarters of both the `Clave and federal education bureaucracies, because the military Governors believed their graduates were needed to provide personnel for the `Clave police and security services.

And finally after being subjected to three hundred years of sociological tinkering the U.S. Army which had not yet been demobilized at the time of which we speak, had adopted the unit separation model of the British Indian army of four centuries ago, prior to the outbreak of the Chin invasion. Except that this separation was by the sexual orientation of the troops rather than their religion. Therefore all land forces fell into three types of units designated by small colored patches under the regular military insignia on the uniforms - black, pink or plaid as the case and inclination were.

Once the Army had been so reorganized, the Pentagon found that unit cohesiveness was greatly improved, and that the disparate units also functioned beside each other in combat very effectively.

The Navy contented itself with only marking some submarines and surface vessels with an extra Rainbow patch or pennant because of budgetary constraints and the Air Force successfully ducked the issue entirely, because of its smaller number of personnel.

The Chin army had ignored the whole question of the sexual orientation of its army except to maintain brothels for use by the troops, which they
staffed with captured American civilian women and female POWs. Their
policy was to shot, and then harvest the organs of any enlisted men who
caused problems by their overt alternate behavior.

LECTURE - SECTION 8:

The decline in something called the "Moral Fiber" of the country by various reactionary pundits, video talking heads and other pronouncers of doom,
as they either decried or dolefully predicted its occurrence in the earlier part
of the 21st Century, did in fact take place during the subsequent two hundred
years, although the rate of change, like the rising sea level was gradual at
first.

The various entertainment and communication providers in North America, pandering to the increasingly jaded tastes of a generally affluent and
consuming population there and in the E-Union, grew enormously wealthy
and powerful. Finally their executives decided to admit that this morals
thing was basically bad for business, after giving lip service to hollow codes
of content for a number of years. They knew that the capacity in a person or
populace for enlightened self-denial was not good for them, So, articulating
openly what their predecessor CEOs had known but had left unspoken as
recently as the previous decade, the media conglomerates began to use their
vast resources to defame and minimize all such tendencies in the populations
outside of their already addicted audience segments. Because they were
multi-national in their operations and ubiquitous in all nations except China
as well as being very, very liberal campaign contributors, the conglomerates
were able to influence the various governments to a much greater extent than
any of the few citizens who objected to their new stance.

Interestingly, the bureaucracies of those governments also recognized
the same threat as did the media conglomerates - that a citizen's ability to
exercise self-denial arose from a capacity for independent thought. Therefore
the `Crats found common cause with the networks -since both these traits
in the populace are poisonous to the lifeblood of any government agency or
bureau. This lifeblood is an ever-growing constituency of clients dependent
on the bureau's services, which it must have for the continued expansion of
its power, and budget.

So the functionaries in the agencies of the various national governments

welcomed the campaign by the conglomerates with bland smiles, knowing
that it would tend to further suppress maverick tendencies in the peoples
they regulated.

LECTURE - SECTION 9:

Finally, the demands for ever increasing short-term profitability trends
by the investment fund managers trading in the shares of these media giants,
as well as the ego needs of restless young management specialists within the
various companies created strong pressures for them to merge into ever-
larger organizations.

Responding to the scent of even greater earnings, the companies all finally joined themselves into a single, ultimate communications-entertainment
entity called 'The Network'. This organization also quickly became known
informally as 'Boss Rat' or simply, 'Rat'.

LECTURE - SECTION 10:

Access to what the Internet evolved into was also severely restricted at
this time as well, and generally reserved for only those in certain circles of
the government or the military. The mass of the people were instead isolated, and entertained by the single video-communications service provided
by the Network under government contracts which offered free vid shows at
basic levels, beamed via satellite to the `Clave populations in the West, as
well as to that of the remaining United States and those in most of the rest of
the world.

In addition to the vids, the Network also provided viewable texts of
various forms of fiction for those who preferred to read, as well as puff pieces
purporting to be news on current events and history. None of the texts were
downloadable however, because printing devices were tightly licensed and
paper supplies were strictly rationed, even to the relative few who were permitted to download and print.

By this simple means, information that might annoy the military Governors in the `Claves and the various governments in the future was prevented
from being archived by their citizens for reference – making history effectively become the official fiction of the moment.

LECTURE - SECTION 11:

The Network needed a continuous supply of talent at this time for many of their vid productions, since much of their programming was pay-per-view, and was 3 to 5-X rated, and the violent parts in their 4 and 5-X offerings were guaranteed to not be faked, nor done with theatrical effects or electronic image manipulation.

This is the reason, Boss Rat maintained its production studios out in the `Claves, and most particularly in the one then known as S'attl - who's military Governor, General Benjamin Butler, understood the special needs of the Network. Rat also employed contract bounty hunters to fill their continual need for fresh talent, collected from generally but not exclusively, the Undocs still stubbornly living outside the `Claves in the unclaimed lands of the western North America.

Knowingly or by accident, the Governors of the `Claves, the Pitson administration and the Network had effectively recreated the model of bread and circuses first developed for the governance of the masses by Imperial Rome...

RESEARCH ASSIGNMENT:

1) You are to carefully study the societal conditions prevalent in Western Lands at the close of the Chin War and report on them as a base line; then,

2) You are to research, and factually report on any societal changes to these conditions that occurred subsequent to the close of the conflict; and finally,

3) You are to assess the impact of any such subsequent changes that you so identify, on the culture in our 25th Century, with full substantiation from your sources and footnotes where appropriate.

ADDITIONAL NOTE:

The quality and completeness of your paper will constitute 85% of your grade for this course.